Fiona Walker lives in rural Worcestershire with her partner
and two children, plus an assortment of horses and dogs.
Visit Fiona's website at www.fionawalker.com

Also by this author

THE COUNTRY
ESCAPE

Fiona Walker

SPHERE

First published in Great Britain in 2014 by Sphere

A CIP catalogue record for this book
is available from the British Library.

ISBN 978-0-7515-4799-3

Typeset in Plantin by M Rules
Printed and bound in Great Britain by
Clays Ltd, St Ives plc

Papers used by Sphere are from well-managed forests
and other responsible sources.

MIX
Paper from
responsible sources
FSC® C104740

Sphere
An imprint of
Little, Brown Book Group
100 Victoria Embankment
London EC4Y 0DY

An Hachette UK Company
www.hachette.co.uk

www.littlebrown.co.uk

For my wise owl, hacking buddy,
fast-Googling iPhone researcher and buddha
in a Dalai Lama, with love and thanks.

'Is this thing working? . . . I think it is. The red light's on. Blast . . . get *off* the recorder, Daphne. Lie over there. No, not on the *Telegraph* – I haven't finished the crossword. That's better. Good girl. Where was I? Ah, yes, Katherine. Hello, Katherine. This is Constance Mytton-Gough.

'I was intending to compose a letter to you "to be opened in the event of my death" – such a wonderful, self-indulgent sentence to write because it affirms one is still alive – but as you know my wretched fingers are too arthritic to hold a pen for long nowadays and I don't trust that girl from the solicitor's to take this down verbatim – she's always adding whereforeins and whenceforths. I've borrowed this recording apparatus from dear Miriam, whom I trust to be utterly discreet in passing my message on to you. You must listen very carefully – I've always wanted to say that too, what fun! Where was I? No, Daphne, leave the cushion alone. Ah, yes, my death. We won't dwell on it, but when one reaches one's ninety-fifth year it is rather closer than it is in one's ninety-fourth, and I need to get my ducks in a line before I go. Where was I? I have a list somewhere.

'Ah, yes. As you know, the animals will all need looking after when I'm gone – yes, that's you, Daphne, and you two, my darlings, along with your disreputable lurcher chums wherever they are, plus the horses, of course, and all the other stock here, which is why I have made provisions. It's all legal and signed and, of course, you and I have spoken about it often, Katherine, but this letter . . . recording, whatever it is, will help verify my wishes should anybody contest the will, and I rather fear they might. The solicitors are clearly convinced I've lost my marbles. You are totally over-qualified to take on this role, but you were also over-qualified to come here and look after me, and we both know why you did that. Ignore the doubters who say a nurse from the suburbs cannot be a Herefordshire small-holder. You are young and strong and quick to learn. You love animals and are frightfully practical. Gosh, this is exhausting. I must take a breather.'

'. . . must be this one, eh, Daphne? There we go. Red light.

'Katherine, I do have several additional wishes that I want to— Hello? Oh, you're here. How awkward. Is it the yardarm already, Katherine? What joy! Set it down over there, will you? . . . What? This thing? It's a Dictaphone. Now, take these dogs out for a run, there's a good girl.

'Good. You've gone. That rather interrupted the flow, but while I remember please do something about your appearance. It's easier for you to hear this when I'm dead. One hates to criticize so take this as a back-handed compliment. You're a very pretty girl, but you give out a rather wanton message, not to mention a frightful colour clash with all that ridiculous cherry red hair and whatever it is you use to make your skin orange. Scrub up, have a bob and knuckle down to country life. Male suitors will distract you, especially at first. They'll all be circling once I'm gone and you've got Lake Farm, but I've thought of a way of protecting you on that front. Marry and you lose the lot. Tough but fair, I feel.

'Where's that blasted piece of paper? Ah, here! This must be to do with it . . .

'*Unlike the rest of my estate, which will pass to my heirs . . . Lake Farm to be held in trust after my death . . .* blah . . . *managed by the*

Constance Mytton-Gough Memorial Animal Sanctuary charity . . .
for the purpose of caring for the family pets and other domestic ani-
mals that survive me so they may live out their lives in peace amid
familiar surroundings . . . blah *. . . looked after by my former nurse*
Miss Katherine Mason, who has the right to live in the property
known as Lake Farm until such time— This isn't my Letter of
Wishes. This is the change in the will. You know about that.
The Wishes are just as important. Ah, yes. Here they are.

'First, and forgive an old bat a frightful romantic indulgence
here, you must promise me that you will only marry for love.
You may think me quite unreasonable insisting upon it, but it's
such a simple thing and I regret not doing it. The clause about
losing the farm in the event of your marriage is rather counter-
intuitive – but it's a forfeit you must be prepared to pay, and is
only there for your own protection.

'My second wish is rather more eccentric and requires a
great deal of dedication on your part, but I think it will be the
making of you. Blast. I do wish we had a bit more time to train
you up, Katherine. Think I'll enjoy my snifter now.'

' . . . think I'd remember how to turn on the wretched thing by –
ah, light!

'The Bolt. Katherine, you must ride the Bolt! It's in the
Letter of Wishes. I know you said you want to do it before I die,
which is terribly sweet of you, but it's jolly hard and quite dangerous and you have to learn to ride first. I want you to do it for
a greater reason than my entertainment, or for the Eardisford
Purse, which naturally is a part of the reward. I want you to do
it because it will set you free. You will understand what I'm talking about when it happens.'

Chapter 1

Kat dodged Daphne the dachshund's cold wet nose as she tried to change as close to the halogen heater as humanly possible, its glow making her pale skin appear curiously orange. It made her think of the weekly Fake Bake ritual she'd once endured, her freckled body smelling faintly of burning tyres while it transformed to Mediterranean bronze. When her friend Dawn had left nursing to retrain as a beauty therapist, she'd used Kat as a guinea pig and taken over the task of copper-plating her with professional zeal, first at a boutique spa, and later at her own salon above a Nascot Village florist, where Kat had also enjoyed cut-price manicures, pedicures, facials and waxing. For a long time, she'd been the glossiest, smoothest, most unfeasibly conker-skinned redhead in Watford.

Today she would be seeing Dawn for the first time in two years and worried she was now the palest, scruffiest yokel in Herefordshire, although at least she had clean jeans and a new fuchsia pink fleece, courtesy of a local promotional printing company that donated overstock and seconds to the sanctuary. Kat's new hoodie had Fresh'n'Up Thrush Relief emblazoned on the back, but its warmth was all she really cared about. On windswept and bitter February days, Lake Farm felt as though it was held together with ice. She hoped Dawn had brought plenty of layers.

A quick check in the mirror confirmed that pink definitely didn't go with cherry red hair, a trademark she refused to surrender amid the russets and olives of country life, although her natural copper would have been perfect camouflage. Kat had inherited it from her father. She sometimes wondered if that was why her mother had treated her so diffidently through childhood, this visual reminder of a failed marriage. Kat also shared her father's rebellious, daredevil streak, and entirely lacked her mother's flirtatious glamour. The many boyfriends coming and going through the Mason household during tomboy Kat's teenage years had been her mother's. It wasn't until she'd met Nick that she'd briefly become a swan.

A loud splash immediately outside the front windows made the terriers shrill with alarm, joined by enraged door-snarling from the lurchers. The splashing grew louder. Kat hurried to her gumboots: no Canada goose could generate such noise unless it weighed six hundred kilos. There was only one creature around here capable of making a splash of that magnitude. 'Please tell me I shut the gate to the spinney!'

She rushed outside, dogs at her heels, pulling on her hood against the chill wind.

It was blowing a gale, branches groaning and the roar from the millstream weir as loud as busy traffic. Black rainclouds were muscling around overhead, the lake already pitted with the first drops of a downpour as Kat scanned its choppy grey surface, seeking a familiar face.

There she was, limpid eyes glazing ecstatically as she wallowed in the shallows. Usha the water buffalo – 'the lady of the lake', as the locals called her – had been in residence on the Eardisford Estate for almost twenty years. Dating back to an experiment in farm diversification in the nineties, Usha had declined to leave Eardisford when the rest of the mozzarella-making herd were deemed unprofitable and sold on. Instead she'd waded into the deep oxbow lake and refused to budge. Admiring her tenacity, landowner Constance Mytton-Gough had decided to keep her as a parkland curiosity and estate mascot. The old buffalo still spent a great many of the summer months in the lake, wallowing contentedly, but in winter she sheltered in a wooded enclosure with two cheery alpacas, a cantankerous llama and a few determined pygmy goats that guarded the hay feeder jealously. This meant that she spent a long time staring over the post and rails to the lake, plotting her escape back into the water she loved.

'It's far too cold for you in there!' Kat shouted, remembering with horror that the last time Usha had done this she'd ended up with colic.

When rattling a bucket of pony nuts from the bank did nothing to coax the old buffalo on to dry land, Kat realized she'd have to take more drastic measures. The sanctuary's self-appointed animal expert, Russ, would no doubt suggest a patient approach. He was very hot on mimicking species' natural behaviour to try to befriend the animal kingdom – the only monarchy he acknowledged – but Kat knew there was no time for that. It had recently taken him ten hours to catch the Shetland ponies using his intelligent horsemanship techniques when they'd escaped into a field of winter wheat, and Usha was a lot more stubborn. Kat was already running late to meet Dawn's train.

'I'll use the rowing boat.' She was already running towards the jetty.

The terriers crowded around her feet on the slippery boards, tripping her, as she untied the boat and tugged it alongside the wooden walkway. The wind was now so high and bitter the boat was slamming against the jetty.

Kat looked into the boat and across the lake, the familiar panic rising. Last time she'd taken the boat to shoo Usha out – many weeks ago when the water had been much warmer – she'd only made it to the first island, where she'd been forced to wait until rescue arrived.

Legs like jelly, she clambered in, shooed the terriers away and pushed herself from the jetty with an oar. Usha was only a few metres away and she drifted alongside her easily.

'Get out!' Kat pleaded, splashing the surface with the oars.

Watching her with interest, raindrops bouncing off her head, the water buffalo was already looking uncomfortably cold.

'Scram!'

The dogs barked furiously from the jetty. The rain was hammering down now and Kat could hardly see.

Usha's thermostat finally kicked in. With a bad-tempered bellow, she flailed towards the bank, sending up such a rip tide that the boat shot backwards, prow rising out of the lake like a giant shark's fin.

'Shit!' To Kat's horror, she was capsizing. Heart pounding, she lunged towards the front, dropping the oars. At the same moment, half a ton of alarmed water buffalo reared overhead as Usha charged back to her wooded harbour, knocking the boat neatly up the bank and tipping Kat out on to dry land.

Drenched and muddy, she lay deeply stamped into the soft bank like a cake decoration in chocolate icing, winded and disoriented. Then she heard laughter and realized Russ was watching her from his bicycle.

''Mazing! How 'mazing was that?' He was pedalling towards her. 'You can take that back about not being an animal communicator. Kat Mason, you're a natural!'

'You're late,' she grumbled, squelching her way upright to shoo Usha back to her enclosure, embarrassed that he'd seen her, yet again, struggling to cope alone.

'Are you okay?' He abandoned his bike and loped alongside. 'I know you're scared shitless of water.'

'I'm fine.' Russ's dark eyes were anxious so she raised her smile to its brightest setting, reluctant to admit just how terrified she'd been. Kat's smile was a lethal weapon, a thousand watts of positivity and kindness that hypnotized all-comers. By contrast, Russ never smiled unless he found something genuinely funny or moving. When they'd first met the previous summer his hair had been dyed white with a black cross on it – something to do with a protest he'd staged with some friends outside an embassy – and she had found it absurdly funny. Russ didn't find it easy to laugh at himself, but her irrepressible giggles had captivated him and the two had shared hours of mirth over pints in the Eardisford Arms.

Officially Russ was a sanctuary volunteer. Unofficially he was much more. Theirs was still a fledgling relationship, from the laughter-laced high summer five months earlier, through an autumn of burgeoning friendship to a winter of mounting flirtation. The two had been crowned Eardisford's Wassail King and Queen in the apple orchards on Twelfth Night, sharing their first kiss after drinking a cup of spiked punch procured by Russ's uncle Bill, who was eager to see his nephew settle down at last. Russ was the black sheep of the cider-making Hedges dynasty, a free-spirited music lover, conservationist and sometime animal activist who lived in a caravan amid the fruit trees he lovingly tended.

'It's dangerous here on your own. I'll stay over.'

'I have Dawn coming.'

'You'll hardly know I'm here.'

'Is the caravan leaking again?'

'Like a sieve. Don't worry – I'll kip on Uncle Bill's sofa.' He dipped his head, smiling up at her. 'You need your space.'

The dye had almost grown out now, leaving amazing white tips at the end of his dark brown mop, rather like a pint of Guinness. It should have looked ridiculous, but the effect was edgy fashion shoot, setting off the unique square beauty of his jaw and the fierce ursid eyes. Russ was full of visual contradictions: the neatly trimmed beard was theatrically cosmopolitan, the wild mane urban jungle, the clothes rural vigilante and the dark eyes martyred. Some locals found him frightening, and his face certainly had a devilish quality, but he stood out as much as Kat did.

'No, stay. You'll like Dawn. We'll all go out later. God, I'm running so late.' She looked down at her mud-caked torso and legs. 'I thought you'd forgotten about helping this afternoon.' Russ wasn't the most reliable sanctuary volunteer, often going AWOL for days on end. By the same token, he wasn't a standard-issue boyfriend, but that suited Kat, who was wary of being tied down. He called himself a 'free-range lover'. When he was *in situ,* which was increasingly often now the weather was colder, he was a hard-working ally and an aficionado of sensual shoulder rubs and long, breathless kisses, as he demonstrated now.

He was an extraordinarily skilful kisser: tall, sweet-tongued and tactile, with a way of putting both hands to her face when his mouth sealed softly with hers, thumbs beneath her jaw, that drew down her insides with desire. She'd once thought beards off-putting, but Russ's was so soft and the long hair that framed his face so heroic that it was like being kissed by a medieval hero, her own Robin of Sherwood. She just wished she wasn't going to be quite so late.

'I've been here ages,' he pointed out, as they surfaced for air. 'I was putting feed in the woods for wildlife. Mags gave me a load of bar snacks that were past their sell-by date – the badgers love them.'

Kat eyed him suspiciously. 'Was it you who left the gate to the spinney open?'

He looked shifty. 'I know better than that.'

But Kat had no time to cross-examine him as she raced inside to change again, diving into a broken-zipped bomber jacket with Official Event Farrier on it and her only remaining clean trousers, the ageing green velvet joggers she wore to run her fitness and Pilates classes in the village hall.

Kat could no longer drive up through the parkland as she once had: the vast wrought-iron gates at the end of the lime walk on her side of the lake were now kept padlocked by order of the Big Five, denying her access to the tracks that ran around Herne Covert to the old stableyards, coach houses and kennels and on to the Hereford road gatehouses. Instead, she was forced to off-road through the woods that ran alongside the millstream.

The Big Five were the main beneficiaries of the late Constance Mytton-Gough's estate, her four daughters and only son. The quintet were all well beyond sixty and based across several time-zones with children and grandchildren of their own. None had shown any desire to take up their late mother's mantle by returning to run Eardisford, instead rushing with near-indecent post-funeral haste to have the estate catalogued and discreetly marketed to the few of the world's super-rich able to afford the eight-figure asking price.

Selling the historic Herefordshire house and its ten thousand acres was a monumental challenge, even setting aside the endless legal clauses protecting the integrity of the estate and its many tenants. Too far from London to appeal to Arabs, too expensive for pop-stars and too decrepit for corporate use, sceptical locals predicted that Eardisford would languish on the market for years. The great house's contents had been stripped out and sold to cover inheritance tax and feed the Big Five's appetite for a return from their mother's long life. In the year since her death, interested parties had come and gone, but it was clear that one thing more than any other was putting them off. Among the minefield of codicils in Constance's will that prevented Eardisford being broken up was one that had bequeathed a farm in the middle of its magnificent parkland to the Constance Mytton-Gough Animal Sanctuary, now in the care of her former nurse and occupied by the elderly animals that had survived her.

The sanctuary – known locally as the Hon Con's Zoo – had an elected committee, a constitution, audited accounts and charitable status, but the Big Five knew that this was just a legal force-field to protect it from their attempts to fight Lake Farm's exclusion from their mother's estate. The ancient steading – part parkland folly, part historic monument – was in direct view of the main house. Purchasers clearly had no desire to look out at a cherry-haired figure feeding pensionable pot-bellied pigs and decrepit horses.

The legacy might have been disastrous, were Kat not so hard-working, adaptable and uncomplaining. She genuinely loved the unique peace of Lake Farm and its elderly, demanding occupants. For the past year, she had learned on the job, sought help where it was needed and weathered real and virtual storms.

The Big Five had made it clear from the start that they wanted Kat out, so when attempts to take their battle to court failed and Kat refused to be paid off, they'd resorted to bullying. Isolated and prone to flooding, the farm was reliant upon the Eardisford Estate for services, utilities and access, all of which were denied to Kat during one of the wettest autumns on record. For weeks, she had survived on borrowed generators and bowsers, forced to access her home via public footpaths, the villagers rallying to her aid while the committee fought to get her rights reinstated. When her erstwhile ally, estate manager Dair Armitage, had turned traitor, paid by the Big Five to launch a campaign of intimidation, she'd confronted him in the Eardisford Arms and demanded it stopped.

Fearless in her determination to protect the animals, Kat had never contemplated giving up on Lake Farm. She believed that the sanctuary could eventually take in old and abandoned animals in need of care locally, but she still had a lot to prove. Keeping it running was about day to day survival, and this winter had been harsh. She was aware that the jury remained out on her suitability as a farmer – her sheep-handling skills had reduced James Stevens, the debonair vet, to tears of laughter – but nobody could fault her tenacity.

Driving out through the woods that divided the estate's old hunting grounds from its farmland, she got tantalizing glimpses of the big house she had grown so familiar with during her time there as Constance's nurse.

The stately pile had never been given a precise title – hall, manor, house or castle; it was simply Eardisford, which often caused confusion because the village that abutted its park shared the name. The sub-division to Upper and Lower distinguished the local community from the main house, and many of its cottages were still tied to the estate.

The Tudor origins of Eardisford remained on show in its half-timbered courtyard, but its east-facing front was a serious Jacobean makeover, which had added vast wings and an extra floor topped with a lantern tower, along with Dutch gables, corner turrets and an elaborate quoined, strapworked porch. The Georgians had tarted it up more, the Victorians had twiddled with Gothic touches, and a party-loving Edwardian had almost burned the lot down, wiping out one wing along with the original fifteenth-century chapel. The house remained, though, a splendid showcase of the best of British building artistry, framed by thousands of acres of parkland, gardens, farms, woodland and the erstwhile feudal village.

The Eardisford Estate had been owned by the Mytton family for several centuries. Its last chatelaine, Constance, had remained there until her death, having outlived her husband, Ronnie, who had added 'Gough' to the family name.

Kat's enduring image of Constance was at the first wassail she'd attended in the Eardisford orchards. Constance had not witnessed the ceremony in more than a decade but had insisted that her nurse must enjoy the show and that she would accompany her. Wrapped up against the frost in an ancient fur coat, several checked blankets and three dogs warming her knees, she'd arrived in grand fashion in the old golf buggy, which she complained that Kat drove far too slowly.

Now a lump rose in her throat as she remembered the nonagenarian joyfully spiking the wassailing cider with fifty-year-old calvados fetched up from the hall cellars, the golf cart weighed down with bags of mince pies and sausage rolls to hand around, as well as her ubiquitous oxygen cylinders. Constance had enjoyed the evening tremendously, telling everyone she was looking forward to coming again next year.

Instead, the toughest and funniest patient Kat had ever worked with had contracted a chest infection the following autumn and died quietly while the village gathered around the giant Bonfire Night pyre on the Green. Her five children had been at her bedside, drawn back from all corners of the world, and, as deaths went, it had been magnificently dignified and peaceful.

You're not thinking about my death again, are you? a voice demanded in her head. *How jolly morbid. And how many times have I told you what a bad lot that Hedges boy is? Frightful leftie. Brake!*

Kat grinned as the car slid to a halt amid the leaf mulch and she jumped out to open a gate. She had known Constance for little more than a year, yet she'd been more inspired by her than anyone else she'd ever met; she still missed her terribly and often heard her voice in her head. Right now it was demanding to know what on earth she thought she was wearing: *You're such a pretty girl, Katherine* (never 'Kat' – Constance had thought abbreviating names the height of ill manners), *but you have absolutely no idea how to make the best of your looks. I was exactly the same before I met Ronnie. I would have lived in jodhpurs if I could. Thank goodness he had exquisite taste, and would take me to London at the start of each season to pick out some new pieces. Every girl needs a Ronnie. We must find you a real man, not a beardy weirdo with a vegetarian dog.*

She wondered whether to risk the flooded ford track or the top one, which was on the private estate and Dair's gamekeepers had been patrolling with border-guard vigilance all winter.

Dogs make far more reliable bed-warmers than men, and are much easier to kick off, Constance lectured. *In fact, they're absolutely essential for preventing guests freezing to death in English country houses. You must lend your guest Maddie. Border terriers have terrifically warm coats.*

The elderly canine companions that had outlived Constance were now in Kat's care. Of them all, her closest allies were the pair that their late mistress had stubbornly referred to as 'the terriers' although dachshund Daphne was technically more hound ('She behaves like a terrier and so I call her one, in the same way I called Edwina Mountbatten a boho leftie. It's not just about breeding,' Constance would say); there was also a contented old Labrador who divided his time between impersonating a hearth rug and a doormat, and a brace of over-bright lurchers who specialised in theft and escapology and preferred outdoor life. Kat had banished all of them from the spare bedroom this week.

'Dawn's not a big dog fan.'

Why on earth did you invite her? Send her back. Better still, lend her the beardy weirdo. Kat imagined she could hear the delighted barks of laughter now, so genuine and unstoppable, like naughty sneezes of amusement, particularly if she was feeling confessional after her six o'clock Glenfiddich. *In India, we girls dreamed of marrying a charming army officer and returning to England to run a large country house and have families. As soon as we did, we longed to be back in the heat. Making a match is such a terribly difficult thing, isn't it?*

'I'm not making a match, Constance. I'm free-ranging.'

As she pulled out of the narrow farm track on to the village lane, she waved at ageing glamour-puss and sanctuary-committee stalwart Miriam, who was walking with local *roué* and hunting fanatic Frank Bingham-Ince, both carrying guns as casually as Sunday newspapers, dogs at their heels.

'Pretty little thing. Still talks to herself non-stop, I see.' Frank watched the car speed away. An inveterate flirt, the pepper-haired Lothario of the mounted field had a particular weakness for redheads. 'Heard she's learning to ride. We must get her out with the Brom before the end of the season.' He and Miriam were joint masters of the Brombury and Lemlow foxhound pack, known to all as 'the Brom and Lem'.

Miriam, who had been successfully hunting hounds and husbands for at least thirty years and had plans to share more than just the mastership with Frank, wasn't about to let him jink on to another scent. 'The girl's not really a natural in the saddle, Frank. Would've packed it in months ago if it wasn't for Constance insisting she had to learn as a part of the legacy. Besides, I can hardly see young Russ approving of her following hounds, can you?'

'Ah, you'd be surprised.' He gave a sardonic laugh. 'He's been following our hounds through Wednesday country all season. Hadn't you noticed? Of course, he calls it monitoring. Tell me, what is it about Russ Hedges that women find attractive?' Frank's teenage daughter's highly inconvenient conversion to vegetarianism was down to a crush on the village renegade.

Miriam flicked back her silver blond mane, kept in a rigid Duchess of Cornwall pith helmet of flick-ups. 'He's terribly sexy for an anti. And being with Kat lends him credibility. She's far too good for him, of course.' She sighed. 'My godmother would have disapproved enormously, especially all that nonsense he spouts about hugging wildlife.'

'Hope to God whoever buys Eardisford still lets the Brom and Lem hunt it,' Frank said. 'Oldest recorded coverts in Herefordshire – terrific fox country.'

'To lay trails through,' Miriam reminded him, with a wise look.

Frank lowered his voice. 'Is it really true there's a buyer lined up?'

'So I gather.' Miriam batted her eyelashes at him as she stage-whispered, '*Cash*. The Big Five are ready to sign on the dotted, but naturally there's still a lot of fuss about the Lake Farm covenant.'

There was a roar of diesel engine as Eardisford Estate manager Dair Armitage blasted out of the track in his Range Rover, pulling up beside the dog walkers and buzzing down the nearside window. 'Did you see Kat Mason drive past here?' The upper

17

part of his face was concealed as usual by a flat cap. A short, broad-shouldered Scot with a chin almost as wide as his neck, he was carrying a walkie-talkie in one hand from which a voice with a strong Herefordshire accent was shouting, 'Lost visual on Red Kitten. I repeat, I have lost visual on Red Kitten, over!'

'We've seen nothing,' Miriam said innocently.

'If I catch her crossing estate land in a vehicle without permission again, she's—'

'Ah, Dair, just the man.' Frank stepped forward with an ingratiating smile. 'What are these rumours about a buyer for Eardisford?'

'I've been told nothing.' Dair was typically brusque as he tilted back his head so that he could glare at them from beneath his cap. Then he spotted the guns.

'I hope you're not rough shooting on estate land?'

'You know my godmother was always happy for me to take something for the pot occasionally.' Miriam was indignant.

'You won't be able to do that now.'

'So they've signed already?' she gasped. 'Who is it? An oligarch?'

The cap was swiftly lowered. 'A Seth. Into big game. But you didn't hear it from me.'

'Isn't a Seth some sort of Egyptian god?' asked Frank. 'Is he Middle Eastern?'

'Yorkshireman.'

The two-way radio crackled into life. 'I now have visual on Brown Bear. Repeat, visual on Brown Bear. He is hanging round the pheasant hoppers. Looks like he's throwing Scampi Fries around.'

Dair bellowed like a furious Highland bull. He loathed Russ Hedges more than most, the smooth running of Eardisford's commercial shooting and fishing interests being regularly undermined by the man's vigilante activities. He buzzed up the window and drove off.

'How thrilling.' Miriam shivered. 'Do you suppose the new owner's single?'

Chapter 2

'You look fabulous! Your hair's so long! And you've lost weight!' Dawn managed three compliments as she burst off the train to gather Kat into a hug, then added the kindly backlash, 'A bit too thin maybe,' as she leaned back to study her friend's face. 'Where's the makeup? You're so pale. Man, look at your hands! You *need* me!'

Kat laughed. 'You look amazing too.'

'Twelve months on the high seas, babe.' Tall, curvaceous and currently bombshell blonde, Dawn was knock-out. She'd been back in England for a fortnight and the glowing Caribbean tan was not out of a bottle, the ultra-toned body shapelier than ever. With the whitest of bleached teeth and longest of French manicures, she radiated bootyliciousness, although there was something odd about her usually grey eyes.

'Are those coloured contact lenses?' Kat asked.

'Purple-tinted. Aren't they great? They're back on trend. Remember when we wore them first time round and blinked all night like we had conjunctivitis? These are much better – you can even sleep in them. You wait till you see the turquoise ones. I brought them with me in case we go clubbing. I've got *the* most sensational new dress from Topshop. Man, this weather is biblical.' She peered at the sheets of rain cascading down. 'Hurricanes might hardly ever happen in Hertfordshire and Hampshire. As for Herefordshire, well ... I still can't believe you came out here because of a typo.'

When Kat had first come to Eardisford she'd been so desperate to get out of Watford that she'd taken the first job she was offered, even though a form-filling blunder meant it was a hundred and fifty miles from her chosen area: Herefordshire had appeared instead of Hertfordshire on the nursing agency's books. Before coming here, she'd never believed real villages filled with ancient half-timbered houses existed beyond fairy tales, or night skies uninterrupted by light pollution. Rain, however, was a universal British staple.

'You did bring boots and waterproofs, like I suggested?' Kat asked anxiously. Turquoise lenses and Topshop dresses would offer scant protection against Lake Farm's damp chill.

'I'll borrow something off you. I packed my old riding gear, though. I can't believe you've taken it up – you always said you preferred the gym. Remember that place I used to go to every week out near Chesham because I fancied the instructor? He was *lush*. Turned out to be gay. There's a retail park there now. I miss my dressage.'

Kat wasn't sure what Dawn would make of the sanctuary's unrideable pensioners, blind Sid and his lame companion, or Sri, with her curling ears and evil moods.

'It's mad I've not been to see you until now,' she was saying, as they headed along the platform, dodging puddles, 'but of course your boss had just died when I was on leave last year, and then there was all that fuss about the will and where you were going to live. All sorted now, though?'

'Pretty much. The farm's beautiful. I can't wait for you to see it.'

'Shame you're not in the big house any more – I was dying to have a butcher's. Don't suppose we can sneak in?'

'It's all closed up.'

'I bet you know a way in. We'll stick on a couple of hard hats, pretend we're from the Endangered Bats Trust and no one'll notice.'

'I bet you'd be noticed.' Kat laughed. 'You really do look fantastic.'

'I'll show you the pictures of the ship when we're back at yours – I've got literally hundreds on iCloud.'

'We'd better grab a coffee then.' She steered away from the station car park. 'There's no phone signal or internet in the house, or anywhere in the village, really. Everyone on the estate uses walkie-talkies.' Russ used his to listen to the gamekeepers in case they were tracking the wild boar or planning an illegal badger cull, but they mostly seemed to discuss the contents of their sandwiches.

'That's bloody medieval.' Dawn extended the handle of her shiny pink wheelie case and followed her across the road to a new café that had recently opened boasting fair-trade coffee and free WiFi. 'On the cruise ship, I couldn't see land for miles but still had crystal clear reception and five megs connection.'

'We're too far from the exchange apparently.' Kat ordered a flat white. 'The villagers are clubbing together to get a transmitter on the church spire.'

Dawn eyed the waitress, purple eyes glittering. 'Double half-caff, half-decaff skinny soy latte, and no foam.'

'Sure.' The waitress nodded, reaching for the soya milk.

'All us spa girls drank them on the liner,' she told Kat, who knew it had been a test of yokelness: Dawn thought anything west of Heathrow was Wales.

'We're closer to London than you were in your floating

21

five-star, you know.' She affected a West Country accent as they found an empty table by the window.

'Could have fooled me. If I'm still sitting on a moving train when I reach the last page of *OK!* I've travelled beyond civilization. I could have flown to the Med faster.' She looked out at the traffic whooshing by in the rain. 'I miss having a car. I'll get a new one when I'm sorted, but everything's up in the air until we've sold the house.'

'So you're definitely selling?'

'Prices are up again. Dave's keen to get his cash out.'

When Dawn's marriage had ended amicably but painfully in formal separation, she and plumber Dave had rented out their little Victorian terrace in Watford's town centre, unable to face the trauma of selling it.

Dawn was always determinedly upbeat about the break-up, claiming everybody had seen it coming for years – a direct contrast to Kat's split from fiancé Nick, which had been as sudden as a car crash – but Kat still felt bad that her friend had gone through it without her there as support, particularly when her Nascot Village beauty salon had gone bust after a huge hike in the rent not long afterwards.

Ever the optimist, Dawn had formed a plan to save money by working for a year on cruise ships so that she could buy out Dave's share of the house, then set up as a mobile beauty therapist in an area where she already had many contacts and old clients. The house was Dawn's pride and joy, lavishly decorated to her colourful taste, with bright pink feature walls and statement furniture.

Beneath the glossy veneer, Dawn looked drained and sad. 'Dave's fed up of waiting, and I can't afford to take on his share, even with the amount I've saved. The house is worth a lot more than we paid for it – trust us to live in a recession-proof area. I need all my savings to buy equipment and set up the mobile business. I can't face another cruise contract, Kat.' She leaned forward and whispered, 'It's like working in a floating old people's home. You know I joked I'd meet a rich husband? Well, I met hundreds, and their wives, average age seventy.'

'You don't want another husband yet!' Kat feigned horror. 'You're the party girl, Dawn. Live a little. Play the field. Get divorced.'

'Fair point.' Dawn laughed. 'It's been two years since Dave and I split, but it feels like a lifetime. We're going to get an internet divorce – it's as easy as shopping on Ocado.' The purple eyes glittered. Together for almost a decade, she and Dave were a long-term double act, but they'd grown so far apart in the final years of their marriage that they'd been in separate orbits. Now she wanted to explore whole new galaxies. 'I've moved back in now the tenants have gone so I can smarten it up a bit for viewings. Mum's helping after a fashion. She's bought a steam cleaner off QVC. It's like a sauna in there most days. The sofa's dripping wet and the wallpaper's all falling off. She sends her love and asks when you're coming back to visit.'

'Soon enough,' Kat deflected, grateful to be spared an interrogation: Dawn had caught sight of her reflection in the window and let out a shriek before heading off to the loo to repair her rain-flattened hair.

Dawn had always been pernickety about her appearance. She'd also always asked a lot of questions; she joked she was Davina McCall in another life. The two friends had met at sixteen when Dawn was part of an influx from local Watford schools that had joined a bigger comprehensive's sixth form to study A levels. Totally lost in a labyrinth of corridors between lessons on her first day, she had fallen gratefully on Kat's help when the small, smiling redhead had bounced around a corner and said brightly, 'Follow my lead,' before taking her straight through the maze to their biology class. There, they'd bonded over a cow's eyeball they'd had to dissect together. To Dawn's awed admiration, Kat had plunged her knife straight in, before winking one green eye and admitting, 'We did this at my old school last term. Half the class fainted.'

'You mean this is your first day here too? How d'you know where to go?'

'I just guessed.' Kat had shrugged. It was true: finding the right classroom had been a combination of deduction and pot luck.

The two girls had gone on to train as nurses together and were part of the same close set of friends. Dawn was no shrinking violet, but she'd frequently followed Kat's lead – everybody did. Brave, generous and not at all self-conscious, Kat was often first to volunteer to try a procedure or be the guinea pig in training, first on the dance floor or to the bar, first to try the water sports or eat local food on holiday, and the first to get her heart broken. Her early romances were legendary lessons in dis-appointment.

But it was Dawn who had been the first to get a serious boyfriend – jovial, football-mad Dave. She had dragged Kat along on endless double dates to try to match her up with Dave's jolly, football-loving mates before admitting defeat. Kat preferred her men edgy and challenging.

She checked her Gmail account on her phone while she waited for Dawn to come back from the loo. It was packed as usual, mostly rubbish, but an official-looking communication from the estate's solicitor made her heart lurch. She read the first few lines and snorted with irritation at the pompous tone.

'Bad news?' Dawn sat down, hair four inches higher, purple eyes repainted with mascara and liner.

'The solicitor's in a tizz. It's a letter about the estate's sale that I have to show to the charity committee. The one they sent in the post must have got lost, and they've been trying to ring me but our landline's not working.'

'And to think I get jumpy on my own even with a 4G signal on my iPhone in central Watford!' Dawn looked horrified. 'You mean you have no phone *or* internet *or* post and you're living alone in the middle of nowhere?'

'It's only temporary.' Kat smiled as the waitress brought over their order. 'The overhead cable was running too close to a listed horse chestnut so—'

'Hang on, trees are listed?'

'Really old ones are. There's a yew on the estate that's at least four hundred. Anyway, someone official took the telegraph pole down and nobody's put it back up yet. They've promised the line will be working again next week, and if there's an emergency, I can usually get mobile reception in the treehouse.'

'Is that in the listed tree or is it ex-directory?'

'Ha-ha.' Kat grinned. Not having the internet beyond a glacially slow dial-up connection didn't bother her much, except when it came to keeping in touch with old friends, like Dawn, who weren't easy to call by old-fashioned means. In the past year, their once-regular catch-ups had become frustratingly occasional and often second hand. Under cross-examination now, she remembered why it was sometimes a relief not to have hours of FaceTime with a friend who specialized in awkward questions.

'What exactly *is* the deal with the farm?' Dawn demanded, studying the bags beneath Kat's dark green eyes. 'I thought your old boss left it to you.'

'It's in trust. I'm just the tenant.'

'But you're safe to stay there as long as you want?'

'Technically, yes, although it depends who buys the estate. Russ thinks they'll try to find a legal loophole to get me out.'

'Is he the hippie guy? The one who rescues badgers and foxes?'

She nodded, taking a sip of coffee.

'You thought he might be a bit of a Communist freeloader.'

'Not at all! Did I really say that?'

'Didn't he hijack the village cricket match to make some sort of revolutionary speech on your first date? Then he turned over the tea tables and made you pay for his supper later.'

Kat had forgotten the long email she'd written to Dawn about it. 'That was the villagers versus estate workers match, and he thought the umpire was bent.' It was the day Russ had swept Kat off her feet (almost literally as she'd been helping serve teas when he staged his Jesus-in-the-temple act with the trestles). 'He still scored a hundred. Then he asked me out, but he left his wallet in the pavilion so I ended up paying. I really didn't mind – he only ate the soup,' she remembered fondly. 'He told me cricket was invented by shepherds who played in front of tree stumps, so it's a working-class farm labourer's game.'

'And does the working-class farm labourer still bowl you over?'

'He's a qualified arboriculturalist, actually.' She knew she sounded chippy and defensive. 'You'll meet him later. He's staying in the house.'

'You're *living* together?' Dawn looked at her sharply. 'Are you sure you're ready?'

'It's been two years since Nick too.'

'That's not what I asked.'

'It's only a temporary thing. Russ respects my need for space.

We have separate rooms and he only stays over occasionally. He's a free spirit – and he's good company,' she insisted, reluctant to admit that Russ – whose caravan was far from watertight – had stayed often in recent weeks, along with his dog Ché. He had also moved in a lot of musical equipment and amplifiers that blew the fuse-box on a regular basis. For a man who insisted he travelled light, he had a lot of stuff and liked to be surrounded by beautiful things. Unearthing a chest full of saris, floor cushions, tassels and decorative *bandhanwar* door hangings that dated back to when Constance had used Lake Farm as a retreat, he'd converted a corner of the sitting room into a Hindu love temple.

'He's into Tantric sex,' she whispered to Dawn, whose eyebrows shot up.

'Is that like *Fifty Shades of Grey*?'

Kat giggled. 'No, that's BM.'

'Tantric sounds like copulating in a spray-tan booth – hang on, I think I've read about it somewhere, some shamanic foreplay thing that Sting did between saving rainforests.'

'It's a spiritual process that leads to the most mind-blowing sex of your life, apparently,' Kat assured her in an undertone, not wanting other coffee drinkers falling from their chairs in shock. 'He says it's a way of retraining the mind so that the body can let go and reach the highest plateaux of pleasure.'

'How are your spiritual pleasure plateaux?'

'It's early days. He doesn't want to rush me.' So far the Tantric sex experiment had seemed to involve a lot of meditation and listening to one another's breathing while fully clothed, and no physical contact beyond holding hands.

'You're not feeling crowded?'

'Quite the opposite, except perhaps when Mags and the band come round.'

'Who is Mags?'

'An old mate of Russ's. They've played music together for years.'

'Is he fit?' Dawn asked hopefully.

'He's a she,' Kat laughed. 'And she's scary but cool. She's found me lots of volunteer helpers, so it's a fair trade letting them rehearse in the house when the pub's skittle alley's busy. The sanctuary can be pretty all-consuming, especially in winter. Russ is helping teach me about animal behaviour and stuff, as well as how to live as self-sufficiently as possible. He believes at least eighty per cent of the food we eat should be home grown or foraged. I'm even learning some vegan recipes – you can cook pulses, but nothing with a pulse.'

'He's clearly nothing like Nick, I'll hand you that.'

'He is nothing like Nick,' she agreed flatly.

Dawn was wise enough not to push the point. 'What *would* Constance Mytton-Gough have made of an animal-rights vigilante in her sanctuary?'

'You sound like Miriam.'

'Who's Miriam?'

'Constance's goddaughter – she's one of the trustees of the charity. She's a bit of a do-gooding bossy boots, but means well, and is a total expert on anything with feathers. She's really helped me out – they all have. There's Tina, who's been teaching me to ride and is brilliant with the horses – everyone calls her "Tireless Tina" because she has three kids under five, a layabout husband, God knows how many horses at home and still manages to fund-raise for the hunt, the school and now the sanctuary. There's scary Pru, who's ancient but used to farm Hereford cattle and knows lots about the livestock, and her sister Cyn, who's much gentler – imagine Judi Dench in a Husky – and has a real knack with the feral cats. The queens wouldn't come near Lake Farm at first and hung about the main house, but Cyn lured them over with a trail of home-cured ham. Ché kept eating it, which drove Russ mad.'

'Ché?'

'Russ's dog. He's vegetarian.'

'That's cruel.'

'Depends how you look at it. Russ says pet food doesn't have the same labelling requirements as human stuff and that "meat and animal derivatives" is basically anything scraped up off the slaughterhouse floor, and that "EC permitted additives" covers four thousand chemicals banned for human consumption.'

'Remind me to pass on the Chappie next time.'

'Apparently greenhouse gases coming from meat stock now outweigh the emissions of the entire global transport system.'

'And what about the bullshit vegan arboriculturalist cricketers give out?'

Despite trying to look offended on Russ's behalf, Kat cracked and confessed, 'I give Ché tripe sticks when Russ isn't looking.'

Dawn was unimpressed by the scale of the rebellion, eyeing her old friend worriedly. She'd not forgotten how Kat had changed during her relationship with Nick, the gradual decline from extrovert to introvert, the Stepford Wife transformation during which her bright, opinionated friend had become subjugated by fear and misery, regurgitating Nick's opinions as though she had none of her own. When she'd finally plucked up the courage to leave him, Dawn had prayed that the old Kat would come bouncing back, but she was worried that the damage was still much too deep for her to surface, her need for attachment still too great. When she had been the old lady's carer, Kat had become a mouthpiece for antediluvian opinions dating back to the Indian Raj – her emails and Facebook messages had been peppered with 'frightfully', 'jolly' and even 'bang on'. Now she sounded like a member of the Animal Liberation Front.

Like most of Kat's friends, Dawn had been utterly bowled over by Nick at first, not to mention wildly jealous: he was incredibly good-looking, confident and poised, an old-fashioned hero whose character came through action as much as talk, from his gallant firefighting career to adventurous free running and arduous marathons. He raised money for charities, had loyal friends of bromance proportions, loved his mum and dad and worshipped Kat. He could even cook and actually *liked* hanging around outside changing rooms taking his girlfriend shopping. Kat grumbled about his penchant for impractical tailored dresses and high heels, but when a man so sexy was flashing the plastic why complain? her friends had countered. Besides, they'd thought she looked fantastic.

Always the laughing daredevil of her crowd, Kat had never been a very girly girl, but with Nick she became ultra-feminine, never losing the kindness or that reckless streak, yet blossoming into an irresistibly sexy, sassy woman. She'd radiated good living and loving. The couple ran together, worked out together and clearly pleasured together non-stop. Her friends, including Dawn, were green with envy.

Kat and Nick, Dawn and Dave would often go out in a group – the boys became great golf friends – and Dawn realized that the effect loved-up Kat had on people was mesmerizing. Men had started to notice her in a way they never had before she was with Nick, hitting on her all the time. In turn, Nick noticed them, and occasionally hit them back, which horrified Kat, who was happy to shrug off the advances good-naturedly and get on with life. Dawn now suspected that was where the relationship had started to show its first signs of stress fractures, although she hadn't noticed back then. Nick had a jealous streak, and was very controlling. Kat's easy-going, happy-go-lucky kindness made her vulnerable. She grew quieter, more withdrawn, letting Nick take over, both physically and emotionally. She was increasingly obsessive about exercise and lost a lot of weight, and while she still looked fantastic, she was on the borderline between ripped and skinny. Nick said she'd never looked more beautiful, but men stopped chatting her up in bars. When Dawn suggested she might be overdoing the workouts, Kat admitted Nick wanted to get her up the aisle to start making babies. 'He says he can't wait to see me eating for two.'

Dawn's own biological clock had been ringing so loudly by then that she hadn't questioned why this revelation had made Kat look so miserable.

Kat had always been very protective about her private life, then as now; her friendship with Dawn was incredibly close, and Dawn had cried on her shoulders too many times to count, but she'd kept her own unhappiness with Nick hidden behind the big Mason smile. Everybody liked Nick. Everybody liked Kat: the hospital patients and staff adored her; they put her increasing lethargy and quietness down to working too hard. Dawn upped the fake tan and recommended cucumber patches, then wept endlessly about how unhappy she was with Dave and how she wished she had the guts to walk out. Now she was ashamed that her own self-absorption had been so total that she'd not realized how desperately bad things had got between Kat and Nick. She still had no idea what had really gone wrong inside the relationship. She remembered Kat leaving him once, giving him some sort of ultimatum, but they were a volatile couple and it had seemed to be one of those rows over nothing. Dave had gone round to calm Nick down and later reported that the row had been about Nick watching too many late-night movies.

Three months later, when Kat had been admitted to hospital having almost drowned, Dawn and the couple's other friends had believed the story about her dropping her engagement ring in the river and diving in after it. Nick had swallowed a lot of water too. There could have been a terrible tragedy.

A month later, Kat had gone home on her afternoon off, packed a suitcase and left Watford and Nick with just the briefest note telling him it was over.

Nick was heartbroken. Friends rallied round. Nobody could understand why kind, joyful Kat had forsaken her hero and how she could be so cruel. Many still refused to forgive her, including Kat's own mother. One of the few friends Kat had written to after she'd left, reassuring them that she was okay, was Dawn. The message hadn't said much, just that she was sorry to do this to her but that she had been incredibly unhappy for a very long time and this was her liberation. At the end, there had been a line Dawn would never forget: *Follow my lead*.

And here she was, in rain-sodden Herefordshire, listening to a monologue about veganism and sustainability. She wanted to party like a single woman, not listen to a field guide on hedge foraging or the listed contents of a can of budget dog food.

Dawn knew she'd been fooling herself to hope for the sixteen-year-old Kat back, the burst of smiling energy that made anything seem possible. But she had hoped for more positive signs of recovery. The Kat she loved was sassy, plucky and crazy enough to take on a farm in the middle of nowhere, and the big smile was as knock-out as ever, but she had dark rings under her eyes and the fingernails on her weather-worn hands were bitten right down as she reached across the table and tapped the jewelled iPhone between them.

'Now, show me all these lovely cruise-ship pictures.'

Chapter 3

Dollar flicked through the movies stored on her tablet to watch during the flight from Mumbai to Jaipur and settled on a swash-buckling medieval fantasy starring a little-known British actor called Dougie Everett.

'*Again?*' Seth asked, amused, from the adjacent seat, his own tablet screen striped with emails.

'I like this movie,' she dead-panned.

'That is abundantly clear.' He grinned across at her, eagle brows aloft, mimicking her monotone enunciation with its perfect diction. His assistant had faultless Received Pronunciation while his own Bradford accent remained defiantly strong, peppered with 'man' and the Mumbai equivalent '*yaar*'.

She kept her face expressionless, turning slowly to look at him. 'Is that a problem for you, sir?'

The more Seth teased Dollar, the more impassive and obsequious she could be in return. It was a trick she'd developed as a form of anger management, but which was just as effective in handling the man who liked to make fun of her and himself in equal measure. Over their years of working together, Dollar's reaction to Seth's many attempts to wind her up had become increasingly poker-faced. It entertained and infuriated him. Seth took very little in life seriously, apart from his unassailable Russian business associates and his elderly mother. He loved playing games – it was what his IT corporation had grown from. Riddle-solving and gambling were specialities.

'No, I don't have a problem with it,' he said smoothly,

watching the opening credits come up. 'Perhaps you would like me to arrange for you to meet Mr Everett.'

'That won't be necessary.' She slotted in her earphones.

'The offer's there, *yaar*.' He returned to his screen, swiping the emails aside and studying a spreadsheet as the plane thundered along the tarmac.

As they climbed through the night sky out of Mumbai, Dollar watched the start of the movie, aware that she was sitting too close to Seth to risk skipping through dull dialogue as she usually liked to do to get to the fight sequences. Travelling in the smallest of his planes was always uncomfortably intimate and she preferred it when he was at the controls, but today he had work to catch up on, so Deepak, the pilot, was up front, a man with a moustache so thick and bristling that Seth was convinced it spent Deepak's nights running around a wheel in a cage.

Studying his spreadsheet, Seth let out a loud, martyred sigh designed to penetrate earphones. Dollar ignored it, but the movie wasn't holding her attention as it usually did. The love interest's unfeasibly bee-stung lips always annoyed her, along with her habit of flicking her chin up during the more emotional scenes as though she were swallowing paracetamol tablets. At least she died quite soon.

While the chin-flicking scene was playing through, she glanced at the spreadsheet on Seth's tablet and looked quickly away when she saw what it contained, but not quickly enough to stop him catching her glance and pouncing on it.

'Brides.' He sighed with mock horror.

She pretended not to hear. Then she pulled out one earphone as a thought struck her. 'Your mother put them on a spreadsheet?'

'No, I did. I still can't work out a short list. I wish you'd look at them for me.'

With effort, Dollar forced her face to remain rigid, her voice level. 'It's my day off,' she reminded him, plugging her earphone back in.

He lifted a finger in acknowledgement, chuckling to himself. Dollar loathed time off and would work all week and all year round if she could – Seth had to force her to take holidays by booking them for her or bringing her along on his. Her compromise on a designated day off was to take on only those tasks she chose to do, or which were totally essential for the smooth running of his life. Helping choose his wife was not among them.

'My mother is really putting the pressure on.' He raised his voice over the plane engine and movie soundtrack. 'She wants to arrange a match this year. She says she can't wait for grandchildren any longer. "A man needs a wife, Arjan," she keeps saying.' He mimicked his mother's strong Punjabi accent.

'That much is true,' Dollar shouted back. She was finding it even harder to concentrate on the swashbuckling action on screen despite Dougie Everett now seducing his pouting co-star in masterly fashion. His magnificent cobblestone abs would appear in close up on screen at any moment. She wanted Seth to shut up.

'So help me out, *yaar*.'

'You know my thoughts.' She turned up the volume. The seduction scene was in full throttle now and she was almost deafened by lascivious pants and an orgasmic wail so loud that even Seth jumped. They both looked politely away.

For the past four years, Seth's mother had been trying to match her successful, globe-trotting son with a bride. Many candidates had been lined up during that time – what family would not want their daughter married to such a handsome young man descended from noble warriors who just happened to be a dotcom billionaire? Seth's eligibility had been hailed in print from *The Times of India* to *Tatler*, and from *Forbes* to the *Bradford Telegraph and Argus*.

The lists of suitable girls from good families came and went, but Seth had yet to commit to a wife. It wasn't that he refused to take a bride of his parents' choosing on principle. He'd always accepted an arranged marriage would happen, much to Dollar's fury – he had, after all, asked her to be his wife once, in the very early days when they had been lovers. As far as she was aware it was the only proposal he'd ever made, but before she'd drawn breath to answer he'd listed clauses that ruled out both a ceremony and her legal status changing, effectively making her a mistress with a contract. She'd refused and removed him permanently from her bed at such speed it had almost cost her her job. She was far too good a PA to lose, though, so he'd sent her on the anger-management course and hidden his hurt and rejection behind an ever-changing bride list on which Dollar's name would never feature. Not that she had ever been in the running for the gold and red sari: Mrs Singh was old-fashioned and intractable, insisting that her son's bride must be well-born and a virgin. Dollar was neither. Seth was a good son who wanted to do the right thing by the family and to make his mother happy, but he would do it in his own time. Right now he was too wrapped up in his business interests to focus on the task.

He cancelled the spreadsheet and brought up a pdf. 'What do you think of this? Good buy or goodbye money?' It was a catchphrase he'd caught from an American transport magnate with whom he played a lot of golf. Seth loathed golf, but he saw the strategic benefits of a sport that could place a Russian oligarch, a Chinese manufacturing dragon and an Indian IT mogul in one small electric buggy through eighteen holes. The transport magnate signed a lot of deals on the fairway, and Seth had been assiduously practising his swing and muttering darkly that there had to be a better sport with which to seduce the world's biggest business players.

Taking the tablet in her free hand, Dollar saw a picture of an English country house with the single word *Eardisford*. Deducing it was from an estate agent's brochure, she studied it in surprise, although her face betrayed nothing. He hadn't talked about expanding his property portfolio recently. She could guess why.

Both earphones came out this time. 'This would be for your wife to live in?'

'I doubt it. Who'd want to actually live there?'

'It's very beautiful.'

'Glad you approve. I bought it this morning.'

Her grip tightened on the two tablets she was now holding, inadvertently sending their touch screens into action. In one hand, a picture of a magnificent ornamental lake zoomed in so a pair of swans became Loch Ness monsters; in the other Dougie Everett's six-pack was paused mid-frame like an egg box in close-up. Dollar noticed neither as her monotone deepened tellingly. 'Why didn't you mention this?'

'It's a surprise.'

'When did you go to see it?' she asked suspiciously, knowing that his professional and personal diaries had been full for the past few weeks, every appointment committed to her memory.

'I haven't yet.' He took back his tablet and adjusted the zoom to admire his new purchase, leafing through pages of high-definition pictures and florid descriptions of the magnificent historic house and its land, farms, cottages, subsidies and way leaves. 'I'm getting a bit of refurb work done before I check it out. It's one leaky old crib, man.' He made it sound as though

37

he was having a damp-proof course put into a Bradford two-up-two-down, not a major overhaul on a Grade I listed stately home.

Now Dollar's voice started climb, her eyes stretched wide: 'You bought this – this palace without even visiting it?'

'It's an investment, *yaar*. I had people view it for me.'

Jogged by Dollar's tight grip on the tablet, Dougie Everett's stomach muscles had moved on a few frames. She switched off the movie. 'Why did you say nothing to me?'

'It was a spur-of-the-moment thing.'

Dollar couldn't believe that he would make such a monumental commitment without her knowledge. She knew everything that he did professionally: she co-ordinated his entire schedule; she organized his life for him; she even had access to the wife list.

'I have a family connection with Eardisford,' he said proudly, admiring a picture of vast gateposts topped with stone pineapples. 'My great-grandfather Ram served in the 16th Infantry under Lieutenant Colonel "Hock" Mytton. The Mytton family have lived in the same home since it was built. So have my parents, come to that, but the Sycamores was only built five years ago.' He chuckled. He'd bought the big executive house on the outskirts of Bradford off plan for his elderly parents when he insisted they could no longer stay in their beloved suburban semi and that they needed more security. Mrs Singh now complained of being lonely and needing to take taxis everywhere, but her husband thought the enormous home cinema was marvellous and watched cricket on it round the clock. 'I wish Ram could have lived to see his great-grandson buy Hock Mytton's house,' Seth mused.

'That's the reason you bought it?' Dollar was even more astounded. Seth was not by nature vengeful. The only chips on his shoulder were the minuscule ones from his high-tech gadgetry.

'I bought it for this.' He flicked to the page marked Sporting Rights. It detailed a long list of Eardisford's vast hectares of native wildlife habitat and their availability for slaughter. 'Wild boar – imagine that, man. That's like the middle ages.'

His face was animated, his dark eyes blinking a lot, as they always did when he got excited by a big new investment. Last year it was Bollywood. Now, to Dollar's ongoing amazement, it was field sports. 'Hunting, shooting and fishing, Dollar. Eardisford's among the best sporting estates in England. The parkland and forestry contain every native breed of deer – it's the only place outside the New Forest to boast that. There are more game birds than there are pigeons in all the lofts in Lancashire combined. The place has been hunted for centuries – there are records of kings of England visiting for the chase and being entertained with great banquets in the house.'

'I had no idea you wanted to hunt.' She kept her tone deliberately sardonic and flat, but she found the idea of Seth in tweed strangely exciting.

'I don't. I want to make deals, and this sure as hell beats Hank's private golf course.' He had mimicked the Texan's drawl. 'Just imagine – eighty square kilometres of England's most beautiful and ancient private hunting grounds in which to entertain connections, plus "miles of double-bank coarse fishing and some of the most abundant wild game drives in Europe".' He had read the last bit from the screen and smirked. 'Igor will be eating out of my hand, man.'

At the mention of the name, Dollar let out a low snarl. The bloodthirsty Muscovite was the power behind some of the biggest military manufacturers in the world. Seth's Mumbai-based IT company was currently competing with American rivals to develop software for the flight simulators Igor manufactured. Notoriously corrupt, Igor possessed an almost obsessive passion for slaughtering living creatures. He was also a renowned Anglophile. If Eardisford's fur, fin and feathers helped secure the development deal, it could prove to be a very valuable asset indeed, although the timing would be tight, given that the race for the contract was well under way and Seth was already at a disadvantage. The first deal-sweetener the Russian had demanded had been impossible for him to deliver: Igor, whose sexual appetite matched his other cave-man urges, had made it clear he considered Seth's PA to be a corporate perk he could enjoy alongside his sugared espressos. After an awkward moment, when Dollar had made it clear she would hurt Igor very badly if he touched her up again, Seth had kept them as far apart as possible.

Dollar disapproved enormously of procuring a lavish inducement like Eardisford for a man like Igor, as Seth knew she would, but securing his share of the multi-billion-dollar contract would bring huge investment into Indian technology.

'It's a piece of history, man.' Seth was looking through the pictures again. 'My parents used to take me round places like this on day trips when I was a kid. Now I own one. There's just a small problem I need to iron out. That's what I want to pick your brains about.'

'I will have it put right immediately.' Dollar, still quietly seething about being excluded from the deal until now, was determined to prove her indispensability.

She listened as Seth described a complicated bequest in the previous owner's will that had kept a strategic farm out of the sale. 'If the sanctuary closes for any reason, the estate will have first option on the property. But Constance Mytton-Gough wrapped it up tighter than a row of Eardisford's poachers' snares, according to our legal team. There's not a lot we can do to get it without hanging ourselves, man.'

Dollar could see the inconvenience of having the old lady's ageing pets on the doorstep, particularly if the sanctuary expanded or, worse, got a public licence: then donkey-hugging children would witness Seth's shooting party return from having bagged all six breeds of native deer. Dollar was not an animal lover, and saw just as little benefit in patting and kissing them as she did in shooting them, but at least the latter provided food as well as facilitating big business deals.

'It is simple,' she said calmly. 'You must arrange to have all the old animals euthanized.'

Seth looked appalled. 'I can't do that!'

'Why not? We can make it look like natural causes and stage it over several weeks.'

'Absolutely not.' He was regarding her with such horror that Dollar realized she might have let her dislike of animals cloud her judgement, along with her eagerness to solve the problem. Now he thought she was a dog assassin. He was strangely fond of dogs – cartoon ones at least.

'I think paying off the charity is the only option,' Seth said decisively. 'The legal route could take years. The only other way to get vacant possession would be if the woman living there marries.' He returned to the Brides List spreadsheet with a heavy sigh and enlarged a photograph of a very pretty girl who looked no older than eighteen, tilting his head thoughtfully as he admired it.

He was about to consult her opinion on Shivani, a medical student from Uttar Pradesh, Dollar realised. She turned her tablet back on and resumed play, admiring the definition in Dougie Everett's upper body.

The blond actor was from one of those blue-blooded British

families who lived in houses like Eardisford, she remembered. She'd recently read an interview with him in *Vanity Fair* in which they'd quoted him saying all sorts of politically incorrect things about politics, women and hunting. It was also the interview in which the news of his engagement to Kiki Nelson had broken and Dougie Everett had gone from unknown to the name on everybody's lips.

In sharp contrast to Seth, Dougie seemed eager to marry. He'd been engaged twice in as many years, and clearly had a thing for leading ladies, his previous fiancée having been British actress Iris Devonshire, whom he'd met on set when he was still a humble stuntman working on the *Ptolemy Finch* fantasy series. That engagement had been broken when bad-boy Dougie failed to change his ways, and Dollar suspected the same would happen with Kiki, an earnest, preppy actress from old Hollywood stock, notoriously intense and a fervid social networker. His engagement to Kiki had undoubtedly helped his burgeoning acting career. The two had recently sizzled off the screen in a big-budget remake of *High Noon*. By the time it was previewing, though, rumours were already circulating that Dougie was behaving badly again. He'd recently been quoted as saying Hollywood bored him and that he missed 'British mud, girls, good manners and fox-hunting'. Most of all, he said, he missed the team of stunt horses he'd left behind in England.

Seth was taking a long time to look through Shivani's details, studying more photographs of her with her family. She listed her hobbies as dancing and cooking, Dollar noticed, gritting her teeth. He would tire of her just as quickly as Dougie Everett would tire of Kiki Nelson. Perhaps she should advise him on the Brides List after all. But if she did, there would only be one name on it: her own, with the right to take his name too. Denied

42

that, she would have nothing to do with it. She looked away quickly. On screen, Dougie was vowing to avenge his chin-flicking lover's murder by taking on the seven quests set by the evil king.

'Perhaps I should set all the girls on this Brides List a quest,' Seth shouted, so she could hear. He was familiar with the film because she watched it so often when they travelled.

'I can't see Shivani riding the seven peaks of the Mohevthrian Mountains while being chased by a two-headed dragon and a green dwarf.'

'I was thinking of something more cerebral, more feminine.'

'Candy Crush?' She felt her anger boil beneath the surface, certain this was a deliberate humiliation. Anything those women could do, Dollar could do better. She had a degree from Harvard and a body desired by the world's richest arms dealer. She could cook beautiful North Indian cuisine and arrange conferences in four time zones without blinking an eye. She could solve the problem of the covenanted farm on his new estate in no time if he'd only let her dispatch a few furry friends to the big paddock in the sky.

From the cockpit, Deepak announced that there was some turbulence ahead. Moments later, Dollar and Seth were thrown back in their seats through a series of stomach-dropping jolts, the Brides List and medieval movie crashing together as one tablet cannoned into another. Dougie's head was freeze-framed on screen mid-yell. Looking at it, Dollar had another idea to solve Seth's problem.

As the little plane bucked over the Gujarat, she hurriedly outlined her idea. 'It involves a quest and an arranged marriage,' she explained, in her most laconic monotone, 'of which I am sure you will approve, although we must first recruit somebody who is neither cerebral nor feminine.'

'Do you promise there'll be no dead animals?' He looked wary.

'Only the ones that Igor and his friends wish to kill.'

The plane finally levelled out and they resumed a calm cruising altitude. 'Excellent. What do you need me to do?'

She picked up her tablet and admired the very blue eyes and very white teeth. 'I think I would like to meet Dougie Everett after all.'

Chapter 4

'Jesus, it's like Downton Abbey!'

Having envisaged a quaint country manor in front of a duck pond, Dawn hadn't anticipated the sheer scale of Eardisford lording over its miles of parkland, woodland, farmland and lakes. Nor had she grasped quite how remote Lake Farm was. Having assumed Kat's farmhouse would share party walls with the main house, given the furore the family had kicked up about it being annexed in the old lady's will, she was amazed when they drove a good half-mile past the stately pile along a sunken lane, passing several sets of grand entrance gates, then entered woods that ran alongside a river. They crossed a grand red-brick bridge and Kat pulled up. To one side of the car lay the vast rain-pocked surface of a lake; the other side dropped steeply away to the fast-flowing water. 'This is it,' she said proudly, jumping out to open yet another gate.

Dawn could see a lot of trees and water, but no house.

Several pheasants were strutting around. 'Are they part of the sanctuary?' she asked, as Kat climbed back in.

'No, they come across from the shoots – Russ is like the Pied Piper of pheasants. Trevor's one of ours, though.' She nodded at a peacock that was watching them suspiciously from a tree stump. 'He's a much better guard dog than this lot.' She glanced back to the two terriers and Labrador sleeping on the old blanket on the back seat.

Dawn had already been introduced to the dogs in the car, sharing her seat with deaf Maddie and incontinent Daphne – they'd stopped twice on the way home for comfort breaks. She'd also met a stiff-hipped Labrador which needed a ramp to get in and out of the boot. She'd thought him gorgeously kissable until he'd panted close up and his halitosis had almost floored her.

Kat explained that she'd left the two lurchers in the house because they always tried to eat the car if shut in it.

'Jesus, what are they?' Dawn was gaping at two huge hippolike beasts wallowing in a muddy enclosure in the woods alongside the track.

'Well, they were supposed to be micro-pigs. I think.' Kat steered around pheasants and potholes. 'Constance's nephew gave them to her for her eightieth birthday, but they turned out to be a lot more maxi than expected. They're full-blown Vietnamese pot-bellies and now weigh in at about fourteen stone each – and that's after a get-fit diet.'

They drove along the edge of the lake, the far side of the track opening out into pastureland with railed paddocks to one end, where several horses were grazing, with a few sheep and a muddy duo which looked to be halfway between the two.

'Shetland ponies – they've terrorized several generations of Mytton-Gough children. They're both at least thirty,' Kat

45

explained. 'There was a little Welsh pony too, but she died just before Christmas.'

'What happened?'

'Old age – she went to canter across the field when I put hay out and keeled over of a heart attack. She didn't suffer, so it was a good way to go. She'd have been in her thirties.'

'Spice Girls, watch out.' Dawn whistled, turning to look at Kat. 'It must really hurt that they're all old and dying.'

'They're all old and *alive*.' Kat laughed, always a glass-half-full girl. 'They're having a great old age. That's why I'm here. I'm seeing them through their dotage with dignity, as Constance would have.' She turned to point at two rugged horses pulling hay from a big metal feeder in the corner of another paddock. 'That old grey hunter is "lame but game", Constance used to say – if the hunt comes past he tries to join them. He even managed to swim across the lake once, and naturally Sid followed.' She pointed at a scrawny-necked, balding bay with mad, milky cataract-blind eyes. 'He was once a racehorse and is about thirty with raging sweet-itch, bless him. Can't see a thing, but happy to follow his grey friend everywhere. And that's Sri.' Her voice changed from humour to reverence as she looked across at the chestnut and white horse standing alone at the far end of the field, proud and aloof. 'Now she *does* rule the roost. She's a Marwari. Constance brought them over from India before the war and used to breed them. See the ears? The tips meet like an arch.'

'Poor thing.' Dawn looked at the horse, which had a pretty dished face, with a big white blaze and unusual wall eyes, brighter blue than any tinted contact lens. 'Can't she get them pinned or something?'

The track turned back towards the woods, dropping sharply towards a gully, at the base of which a fast-moving stream was bridged by a stone-based ford, the car wheels sending up great waves as they crossed it.

'Thinking about it, I might not bring a car here,' Dawn muttered, as they bounced up the rutted track and into open pasture again. No wonder Kat's sporty coupé – which Dawn remembered Nick cleaning every weekend – was looking like it had just taken part in the Dakar Rally. 'Is there an easier way in?'

'They're all kept locked apart from the causeway at the other end of the lake, but that's flooded and wouldn't take a car anyway.'

Dawn looked across at Kat's determined profile. 'Don't you find it frightening, being close to all this water?'

'When I first came to Eardisford, I refused to go near the lake,' she admitted, slaloming around the ridge above a deep ravine through which the brook fell in great silvery white ribbons. 'It was Constance's favourite place – she was always asking me to row her across to the farmhouse, but I couldn't even walk over the bridge.

'She'd used Lake Farm as a retreat when she was first married, and filled it with memories of India. She got quite angry when I kept refusing to take her there, and threatened to go it alone. She could barely walk by then, but I knew she meant it. That prospect was more frightening than the water, so I . . . well, I dared myself, I guess. As soon as I found out what was here, I knew I could cope. It's a magical spot.'

A dwelling had been recorded on the site of Lake Farm in the Doomsday Book, at a time when the biggest meander in this stretch of the river Arrow still flowed freely along a half-mile arc that wrapped itself around fifty acres of spring-filled pasture and woodland. In those days, there was no lake, but over the intervening centuries, the river had found a short-cut across the open side of the arc, and the oxbow lake had started to smile on its own.

The farmhouse stood in roughly the same spot as its predecessors. With thick woods behind it, the fish-filled lake in front and fertile red Herefordshire soil beneath, it was a rich source of food and had been a ripe spot to settle, long before the lords of the manor had arrived to lay claim to the higher ground from which the main house now looked down on its humble predecessor. Parts of the main Lake Farm building were five-hundred-year-old oak lath and lime plaster, and in its time it had served as farm, fishery, battle outpost and artist's retreat. The same Edwardian who had burned down a great deal of the main house had been a rare champion, fashioning the farm as a bolthole in which to seduce his mistresses, landscaping the lake and securing its banks, creating divisions for the duck-flight ponds to either side with bridges. To the east he had commissioned the grand causeway leading across it from the parkland, with magnificent lime avenues mirroring one another on each bank. Complete with water cascades and stone statuary, the causeway bridge was now too dangerous to use except in the driest months, and only then by foot, the planking too rotten to take the weight of cars. The only practicable way to get to Lake Farm without a 4x4 or boat, these days, was via the ford leading in from the west where the brook that fed the oxbow gurgled off through the woods to join the millstream, then raced on to the river. The Edwardian had even planted an arboretum for privacy, beefing up the old woods and the lake's banks with rare specimens and flowering shrubs, although many of the trees had blown down in the gales of 1987. Now the little farmhouse could be seen in winter from the upper floors of the main house.

But unlike the magnificent exterior to the main house, which

48

an admirer could walk around to find beauty, balance and architectural gems at every turn, Lake Farm was only attractive from the front: its intricately half-timbered façade had been carefully preserved so it would not offend the grandees looking out across the parkland, the ancient farmstead peeping from the woodland behind the lake, lattice windows twinkling and smoke curling from chimneys. The water had crept ever closer over the years, now almost covering the small jetty and turning what had once been a pretty front garden into a bog meadow of wild irises, bulrushes and watercress. The farm's fenced paddocks and hedged pasture meadows stretched to the river behind it, like a green Inverness cape, and woodland bristled to each side, from the weeping willows at the water's edge through the Edwardian arboretum to the vast-trunked oaks, one of which Constance had claimed to be the oldest in Herefordshire.

Dawn, who arrived via the back tracks at the farmyard, thought the place looked thoroughly depressing. To the rear, Lake Farm was flat-faced and mean-windowed, covered with pipework and loose wires, and shadowed by red-brick out-buildings that sagged lopsidedly around a muddy yard. This was where Kat parked her car and let the dogs pile out before squelching off to fetch Dawn some wellingtons so that she could cross the twenty yards of stagnant water and sludge to the house.

Constance had stopped using it as a retreat and occasional guest cottage in the mid-eighties when husband Ronnie died. Since then, it had housed several long-term tenants, falling into increasing disrepair. In the years leading up to her death, it had been uninhabited and storms had battered it yet more, breaking down the Edwardian's landscaped defences. The lake had seeped into the cellars and even the ground floor when it rained hard.

Nothing could have prepared Dawn for the inside of the house, which reeked of damp dog and charred wood. There wasn't a straight line in the building, from the bowed, smooth-worn quarry stones underfoot, to the bulging, misshapen walls and gnarled beams and the sagging ceilings. Despite the work that had gone into drying it out, it was far from watertight, and this week had been the wettest of the year so far. Drips ran down the walls, through the light fittings and plopped in through the rattling windows. Compared to Dawn's cosy little terrace, it felt glacial. The logs and kindling in the big inglenook were damp and refused to take when Kat waved a match at them; the night-storage heaters were stone cold, as was the hot-water boiler; there was minimal furniture and no curtains, apart from an incongruous collection of throws and wall hangings in one corner that looked as if it had been stolen from an Indian restaurant after a particularly drunken night out.

It reminded Dawn so vividly of *Withnail & I* that she expected Uncle Monty to shimmy through a door in a silk dressing-gown at any moment.

Giving up on the fire, Kat stood up, threw out her arms and beamed at her. 'This is home. Now can you understand why I never want to leave?'

Dawn shuddered and pulled her coat tighter, stepping towards the latticed windows overlooking the lake, which acted like a kaleidoscope, fragmenting the huge expanse of water, trees, parkland and the grand house in the distance into an impressionist's painting of leaf, lake and light. Even rain-lashed and grey-skied, it was breathtaking.

'I can understand why you lived there.' She gazed up at the grand Jacobean façade.

'We had to duck the falling plaster every time we passed through the main hall. Constance lived in two rooms on the third floor with four oil heaters, and a tennis racquet to hit mice. It is seriously falling apart.'

'And this place isn't?' Dawn looked around the chilly room. 'Shall I call *DIY SOS* or will you?'

'It's had lots of work done,' Kat said defensively. 'Constance sold a William Hodges to pay for it.'

'Surely you can't sell people in this day and age. That's slavery.'

'It was a landscape of an Indian palace,' she said witheringly, aware that Dawn was winding her up. 'It was supposed to pay for the repairs here, but she died before it was complete and work stopped when the legal wrangle started about the ownership of the farm.'

Dawn eyed the many pans and bowls strategically positioned around her to catch drips. 'So who pays for the roof to be mended now?'

'That's my responsibility,' Kat explained, as she boiled an ancient enamel kettle on an even more historic range. 'The family won't have anything to do with it now, which I guess is understandable if a bit depressing. At least they seem to have stopped trying to bully me out. The charity trustees are local do-gooders who are all very sweet but they're more obsessed by whose turn it is to bake biscuits for committee meetings than getting things done, and they won't let me take in other old animals or seek proper funding until we know who is buying Eardisford. Constance's will ensured the house is so tightly tied to its land and farms it can't be split up, which limits the market.'

Dawn had a certain sympathy for the Mytton-Gough children, hamstrung by their mother's many clauses while their inheritance mouldered as a depreciating asset. 'If the old biddy knew it would have to be sold after her death, who *did* she think would buy it?'

Fetching down mugs, Kat confessed, 'Royalty.' She laughed at Dawn's cynical expression. 'It's true! She thought it would suit one of the princes to raise a family. The most recent rumour I heard is a Beijing manufacturing magnate buying a quiet weekend retreat for his son at LSE, but the village is full of rubbish. Last week it was a Hong Kong property tycoon.'

'Lots of Chinese whispers, then?'

She grinned. 'Whoever it is, you can bet Dair knows something.'

'Dair?'

'The estate manager – he runs the fishery and the shoots.'

'You know a man called Dair?' Dawn whooped. 'You are *kidding* me?'

Kat laughed, pulling the whistling kettle from the hob. 'I think it's short for "Alasdair". He's Scottish.'

'Even better! Please tell me he's rich and handsome. Is he single?'

'He's very tweedy and looks like Elmer Fudd,' she said, as she slopped boiling water over teabags. 'But he's definitely single.' Dair Armitage still had a bit of a tongue-tied crush on Kat, despite the dirty-tricks campaign he'd been tasked with when the Big Five had wanted her out of the farm. As her closest neighbour – he lived in one of the estate's lodge cottages – he popped in once in a while with gifts of freshly caught brown trout, but their glazed eyes had seemed to look straight through her and she had no idea how to gut and cook them so she'd secretly fed them to the cats or Ché. Shy, stuttering, yet curiously pompous, Dair seemed equally frightened of Kat's eyes and never looked into them, although he had no such qualms about staring lustfully at her chest. She'd not seen him since Russ moved in and was glad. Constance, who had been fond of

Dair, would no doubt have encouraged the match vociferously, but it was never going to happen.

But Dawn was entranced by the idea of his name. 'You *must* have a Dair in your life, Kat. What could be more perfect for the girl who'll do anything for a dare?'

'I'm not quite as brave as I used to be.'

'Trust me, living here is *well* brave.' Dawn shuddered, taking a slurp of her tea.

When they'd been student nurses, Kat had been notorious for her pluck. No challenge too great, no risk too frightening. Always the first to volunteer and the last to give up, she'd had a lust for life that left others breathless. At a mock awards ceremony the college put on, friends hailed Kat the ultimate mate they wanted onside in a crisis. At the time, her heart had been set on a career in humanitarian aid work, but then she'd met Nick and her plans had changed. As Kat's life contracted into the self-protective, imprisoned minutiae of a destructive relationship, she'd lost her natural confidence. It had started to resurface here, in her safe harbour, but it still needed a lot of buoyancy aids.

'If we knew which of the rumours to believe, life would be a lot easier.' She sighed.

'What about the solicitor's letter on your phone?'

'They emailed it because the postman won't deliver anything beyond the first gate. There are owls nesting in the box there right now, so he leaves all our post at the pub for Russ to collect, and he keeps forgetting.'

'What was *in* it, Kat?'

'Owls, I told you.'

'I meant the letter!'

'Oh, I haven't read it. It'll just be the usual guff about access rights, or another offer to relocate the sanctuary so the farm can be sold with the estate.'

Dawn groaned. Kat had an aversion to formal paperwork, which was probably why she was living in a damp grace-and-favour fleapit while ex fiancé Nick was sitting on mounting equity in the house they'd bought together. 'So why can't the sanctuary be moved somewhere else?'

'Constance was emphatic that it had to be here at Lake Farm.'

'What do the animals care as long as they're looked after?' asked Dawn, who now suspected Constance had been certifiable. The place was barely habitable. 'Why not relocate somewhere warm and dry with a functioning letterbox, somewhere a bit nearer to a road?'

'I'll show you.' Kat whistled for the dogs.

Dawn wished she hadn't asked as she was forced to abandon her mug of tea and climb back into the whiffy oversized wellies – she suspected they were Russ's – to squelch outside into the rain again.

It was still coming down in sheets but Kat seemed hardly to notice as she led her out of the farmyard and across a gnarled, skeletal orchard to the oldest oak at the edge of the woods, its girth as fat as a cooling tower's.

Beneath its vast canopy there was a cluster of tiny headstones.

Dawn's eyes filled with tears as she read the names – Toby, Alice, Mungo, Hetty, all with such short lives. 'Oh, the poor little things.'

'I know, it's impossibly sad.' Kat wrapped a comforting arm around her. 'The family buried all their favourite pets here.'

'*Pets?*'

'Yes. What did you think they were? Children?'

That was exactly what Dawn had imagined lying under their feet, a tragic illustration of infant mortality statistics from another era. Instead she was looking at the graves of some of the Mytton family's favourite dogs, whose names and dates were etched in the pocked, mossy little slabs. In some cases their likeness had been carved in limestone and marble – Benji, 1892–1904, had been a particularly roguish-looking bull terrier, while Catkin, 1907–23, was a kind-eyed whippet.

Kat patted the tiny domed head. 'This was one of Constance's favourite places. She'd talk about her childhood and the pets she remembered, like Catkin here. "Exquisite little thing – always looked like she'd faint if you so much as clapped your hands, but she was as brave as a lion, rather like you, Katherine."'

Listening to her, Dawn felt the hairs stand up on the back of her neck. Kat had always been good at impersonations – her Björk was a legend, Janet Street-Porter less so – but this was something else. The voice seemed to come from someone totally different: rich, warm and killingly upper class. It wasn't mockery: someone real was speaking. Any minute now Kat's head would spin around and ectoplasm jet out. 'I think you need a holiday,' she said kindly, wondering how best to get her on a spa break and then back to Watford.

But Kat was gazing at Gretel, 1990–2006. 'This little dachshund was Constance's closest ally after she was widowed and left here alone.' An exquisite miniature dog had been immortalized in pure white marble. 'Daphne is Gretel's last surviving daughter, now almost twenty – the last of her line. She refused to get off the bed in the final hours Constance lived. She even bit the doctor. Her head was under Constance's hand when she died.'

Dawn was unmoved. 'Exactly how many animals do you look after here? I'm talking the ones that have a pulse.'

'Twenty-nine if you include chickens, geese and Trevor the peacock.'

'Christ.' As far as Dawn was aware Kat had only ever owned one pet (Sooty, 1986–9: a guinea pig that had met an undignified end under the lawnmower). 'I knew you always wanted a dog, but I had no idea you'd become Watford's answer to Brigitte Bardot,' she muttered, looking at the little headstones. 'It's like *Whistle Down the* bloody *Wind* here.'

Kat's eyes sparkled, the same vivid green as the moss on the wet tree trunks around them. 'This is my dream gig, Dawn. I mean, how beautiful is this place? Like you say, I've always longed to have a dog and now I have five.'

Dawn prepared to step on a conversational landmine. 'Didn't Nick offer to take you to Battersea Dogs and Cats Home and get a dog once?'

The eyes went dull. 'That was only when things got really bad between us, and he said it had to live outside the house in a kennel. I couldn't bear that. I didn't think it was fair.'

Dawn wondered if there was a huge difference between that and a man who forced his dog to be vegetarian, but she said nothing. Instead, she forged on through the minefield: 'I never knew how bad things had got with Nick, Kat. I'm so sorry. If I'd known I'd have—'

'It's forgotten,' she said firmly, turning to look at the rain-pocked lake, her wet hair deepest scarlet, lashes starred with drops. She put an arm around her friend. 'I'm just grateful you've forgiven me for running off like that.'

'What's to bloody forgive? I followed my leader. And I can't tell you how good it feels to be free.'

They shared a tight hug, hammered by raindrops.

There was a loud splash from the lake. Kat groaned. 'Oh, shit. Not again.' She belted off, leaving Dawn none the wiser.

Trailing behind, Dawn saw a huge black beast silhouetted in the lake, with devil's horns and glinting eyes. She screamed.

56

With a bellow, the beast tossed its head and sent up arcs of spray.

'Ssh! Try not to frighten her,' whispered Kat, creeping towards the bulrushes with a bucket. 'She's very sensitive to noise.'

'So am I,' Dawn squeaked, hiding behind a tree as the beast bellowed again.

Rattling a soggy bucket of nuts at Usha, Kat edged towards the rowing boat that was lying on its side nearby. She was white with fear, Dawn noticed, her teeth gritted determinedly.

'I had to row out to get her back earlier,' she explained in a high voice, betraying how great her terror of open water still was.

Dawn wasn't sure Kat should float to the rescue again, especially now that their conversation had brought so many memories into high relief; nor was she keen to take the oars herself. But this time, for reasons only an ageing and increasingly forgetful water buffalo could understand, Usha waded out of the lake of her own accord, following Kat with docile good manners back to her enclosure.

'OMG, you're amazing!' Dawn followed at a safe distance, incredibly impressed. 'That is like something out of *Crocodile Dundee*. You should star in your own reality-show documentary.'

'Hardly. It's basic bribery.'

'So if I bribe you to come back to Watford, will you?'

'No chance. If I bribe you, will you come and live here?'

'Only if the buffalo goes, you get under-floor heating and Dair Armitage turns out to be the man of my dreams.'

'We'd better make the most of this weekend then.' Kat hooked her arm through Dawn's and headed back towards the house.

Chapter 5

As soon as she met Russ, the vegan vigilante, Dawn sensed something potentially unpleasant cooking at Lake Farm, and it wasn't the lentil dahl that had been left on the range too long and burned dry. It was obvious from the way he and Kat looked at one another that they were more than part-time house-mates with a casually kinky Tantric acquaintance, and equally clear that Russ, despite his meat-free diet, was full of cock and bull.

'The public misconception that shooting game birds isn't animal cruelty because we can eat them is just wrong.' Russ clearly loved the sound of his own voice, which was admittedly deep and honeyed with West Country sweetness, but nonetheless monotonous after the third tirade on the monstrous waste of raising game to shoot, then bulldozing the carcasses into the ground. 'Dair Armitage runs a pheasant concentration camp here. No more than that.'

'He sounds a great character from what Kat's told me,' Dawn said cheerfully. 'No disrespect, but I could murder some roast pheasant right now.' Her stomach gave a supportive rumble.

Kat shot her a pained look from the kitchen, where she was scraping smouldering dahl off the range, and Dawn felt a stab of guilt. She knew she should make more effort with Russ, however annoyed she was that their girls-only get-together had been hijacked by someone who looked like a Led Zeppelin throwback, lectured her non-stop, refilled his own glass without offering the bottle around and didn't lift a finger to help Kat.

Having finally got the fire going by applying a blowtorch, then feeding it and the range constant logs, Kat had succeeded in warming the Lake Farm kitchen-cum-sitting-room from damp sub-zero to moist single figures, occasionally dashing outside to collect more logs and check animals, cheerfully dipping in and out of the conversation and trying to steer Russ away from his more extreme monologues on animal cruelty. It was no wonder she'd burned supper. Dawn's ineffectual attempts to help had thus far put out the fire once, flattened two dogs underfoot and spilled rice all over the kitchen floor. Kat had banished her friend to a damp chair, where she was now weighed down by snoring terriers and listening to Russ, thrusting her empty glass at him hopefully.

'The pheasant murdering finished a fortnight ago,' he was saying. 'But they're still massacring deer, if you're a fan of wild venison, Dawn. They pick off the females because they're the population drivers, always aiming behind a front leg to get the major organs, although it usually takes two or more bullets to get the fatal shot. Even then they can take an hour to die.'

'That is really awful.' Dawn was genuinely appalled and wished he hadn't told her that.

'All meat is murder, Dawn. There's an animal's death in every mouthful you eat.'

He was obviously very intelligent, occasionally surprisingly funny, vaguely sexy in a grubby, hippie Russell Brand sort of a way, but Dawn didn't understand what Kat saw in him. It wasn't that Russ was ugly – far from it – but he possessed a face in which what should have been handsome features appeared in the wrong places. It was as though a child had taken a Mr Potato Head and crammed on Brad Pitt and Pierce Brosnan's best bits in random order – the dark eyes were too close together, the vulpine nose too high and the full-lipped mouth off to one side. The white-tipped hair was weird. She thought he was opinionated and not a patch on Nick, the hard-working charmer with the heroic job and perfect manners.

Since he'd arrived, he'd done nothing but expound his strong political beliefs from the confines of the one dry, comfortable armchair in the house, which he'd cranked as close as he could to warm his feet at the fire, now blocking the heat from the rest of the room while a noxious odour infused it.

In turn, it was clear that Russ thought Dawn was shallow and whingeing, believing that her obsession with the body beautiful was a sign of self-absorption. She also suspected that he saw her role as silent witness to Kat's history as a threat. After all, Dawn had known Nick. She'd stood by and let things get so bad that Kat had been forced to run here. For Kat's sake, Dawn decided to make an effort and include Russ in the warm spill of her friendship. 'As the curry's a bit burned, why don't I treat us all to an Indian takeaway? There'll be veggie options for you, Russ, and I know Kat loves a hot one – remember the Phall-lick from Balti Towers on the high street, hon? You still hold the Watford Pussy Posse record.'

'Tania's hen night,' Kat remembered. 'I was on the loo for a week.'

'Worth it to fit in that size eight dress from the Karen Millen sale.' Dawn got up, spilling elderly terriers, and wandered into the corner that was draped with saris. 'Have you got any take-away menus?'

'If you can find one that'll deliver around here I'll eat my foot,' Russ muttered.

'Surely, as a vegan, you don't eat cheese,' Dawn said brightly, then realized her humour was getting too sharp, picked up a feather fan and started an Indian dance.

Now holding the kitchen door open for Daphne, who was

taking her third rain-sodden pee break in an hour, Kat was uncomfortably aware that her two closest allies loathed each other on sight. Russ wore the calculating look he adopted when lined up in the pub with the village 'earthmen', the Brom and Lem Hunt foot followers who enjoyed baiting him, just as he relished outwitting them in return. Dawn's face bore the cheery, professional I-take-no-shit expression she'd reserved for dealing with quarrelsome elderly patients when she was still nursing. It was her own fault for suggesting Russ join them for supper, Kat thought. He'd offered to give her some space, but she'd really wanted them to meet, never imagining there'd be such instant antipathy.

'Tell you what, let's call a cab and I'll treat us to a night out in Hereford,' Dawn suggested, eager to find bright lights and busy bars full of strangers.

'We have no phone,' he reminded her, his voice developing a devilish edge. 'There's no way to contact the outside world in this little backwater.'

'Can't you use your walkie-talkie in the tree-house?'

'I have a better idea.' His dark eyes flashed as he looked at Kat. 'Why don't we take Dawn into our arms tonight?'

Dawn let out an amused snort, but her eyes darted nervously towards her friend for reassurance. It was obvious Kat found Russ seriously sexy, but this was way beyond their friendship boundaries. 'This is a joke, right?'

Kat laughed. 'He's talking about the Eardisford Arms, our local pub,' she explained to Dawn, grateful for the suggestion. She was sure they would get on in a more relaxed atmosphere with a roaring fire and some rocket fuel in their bellies. 'It serves a mean T-bone, and the scrumpy's fantastic. We don't have to worry about drinking and driving because the roads are private all the way there. Let's get rat-arsed.'

Dawn cheered. 'I'll just get changed. Give me five.'

'It's not really a dress-up sort of a ...' Kat's words trailed away as her friend shot up the stairs two at a time, heading joyfully for the Topshop dress, ' ... place.'

For all his boring lectures, Russ was very generous at buying rounds, Dawn conceded, as she lifted her third pint of scrumpy to her lips. In fact, her opinion of him was rapidly changing in the light of his behaviour in the busy little pub. He'd been keeping the friends regularly supplied with drinks and bar snacks in their quiet corner of the snug, crouching at the table for a quick chat each time he returned to them, then drifting back to talk to his cronies at the bar where he'd left his drink. It was clearly a position he took up regularly – Dawn suspected that Russ's orchard arboriculture work involved a lot of testing the end product – but with an end product this magical, she could hardly blame him.

'Dave would bloody love it here.' Dawn gazed around mistily, largely because the turquoise lenses made her eyes smart.

'Do you miss him?'

'I miss what we had at the very beginning. I want that with somebody else.'

The scrumpy was filling Dawn with the glow of goodwill and Cupid's arrows. It was Valentine's Day tomorrow and she suddenly longed for new love. Kat had warned her to go easy on the local brew, which had a lethal reputation, but it held no fears for Dawn, who had won bets based on being able to drink her way through the cruise ship's entire cocktail menu before performing '*Non, Je Ne Regrette Rien*'.

The Eardisford Arms was tiny and old-fashioned, perched on the bank of the river by the bridge that divided Upper from Lower, its half-timbered walls decked with hunting prints and horse brasses. The small public bar was packed with locals, all agog to know who Dawn was, and satisfyingly appreciative of her Topshop dress and turquoise eyes. One of the better-looking men had been staring at her in open-mouthed admiration from the moment she arrived.

'Calum the Talon,' Kat told her, in an undertone. 'He's a falconer. He handles the hunt's eagle owl for them.'

'Should I swing a piece of meat around on a string to beckon him over?'

'His girlfriend's the one with the pink hair serving behind the bar, so don't encourage him. The last time there was a fight in here, she knocked someone unconscious.'

Dawn studied the small, stocky Tank Girl lookalike, who was laughing with Russ as she loaded the dishwasher, reaching out a tattooed hand to ruffle his white-tipped hair affectionately. Her square face was so heavily disguised with piercings and eyeliner it was hard to tell her age, but she guessed she was about forty.

'She a relative?' She knew Russ had family in the village.

'No, but they've known each other since they were kids – she used to babysit for the Hedges family,' Kat explained. 'That's Mags.'

'*That's* Mags?' Dawn remembered the mention of the old friend who hung around at Lake Farm. 'The one with the band?' She'd somehow imagined a cross between Courtney Love and Gwen Stefani, not Peppa Pig with piercings. On closer inspection, Dawn realized she was the sort of earthy, buxomly extrovert woman who probably looked fantastic in full rock chick regalia rasping out ballads in a smoky spotlight.

'They've just formed a new line-up,' Kat said proudly. 'It was called Dirty Mags, but they've decided to change it to broaden its appeal. Russ wants them to call it Animal Magnetism to help raise money for the sanctuary. Mags is onside – she helped organize an open day for us last year, although it was mostly hairy bikers and music fans who turned up and there was a bit of a fight there too.'

'Don't tell me she broke that up as well?'

'She started it, actually.'

They watched as Mags pretended to swing a punch at Russ, cackling loudly. Heavily tattooed and wearing more chunky jewellery than Mr T, she possessed a dirtier laugh than Sid James. 'I know she looks scary, but she's soppy about animals,' Kat insisted. 'She cried so much when we watched *War Horse* on DVD that her one of nose piercings blew out. Calum's birds of prey are her babies. Nobody messes with Mags, so it's great she looks out for Russ and me. She's like a big sister to him.

'Bill Hedges, Russ's uncle, almost gave up on him as a teenager – he was always in trouble when he came here for summer holidays – but Mags helped smooth things over.'

'I thought he grew up in the village.'

Kat shook her head. 'His mum did – Bill's younger sister Gloria – but she ran off with one of the fruit pickers. They're all from Eastern Europe now, but back then they were mostly university students on summer vacation.'

At sixteen Gloria, a day-dreaming good-time girl, had fallen for wild-haired, cricket-mad politics student Paul. At the end of the summer break, they had moved into his student digs in Bristol together, and six months later she'd discovered she was pregnant. Paul was determined to do the right thing, which delighted Gloria, who found herself marrying into his wealthy Hereford brewing family, only to have her dreams shattered when he turned his back on the family fortune to become a maths teacher and lay preacher in one of Bristol's toughest suburbs, devoting himself to God and the Labour movement. To her family's surprise, Gloria embraced city life and trained as a teaching assistant, supporting her husband in all he did. The couple became key members of their teaching union, church and human rights campaigns.

'Have you met them?' asked Dawn, thinking they sounded incredibly heavy-going. No wonder Russ was such a moral crusader.

She shook her head. 'They run a mission school in Africa now and have adopted several children out there. They don't get back to England often.'

'Tough on Russ.'

'He thinks it's great now – he always had this place. It's been his second home. I think he had a lot of issues with his parents when he was young – that's why he took the name Hedges – but he's dealt with them now.'

As a child, Russ had sometimes joined his parents at religious retreats, trade-union conferences and on third-world volunteer work, but he'd always preferred spending the school breaks with the Hedges family in rural Herefordshire, where he could enjoy the space, freedom and wildlife, and was treated as the son they'd never had. Although Russ shared his father's passionate dislike of blood sports and outspoken opinions on redistribution of wealth, clashing regularly with his intransigent, terrier-loving uncle on the subject, he adored Bill's positive outlook and the country wisdom he passed on.

'His political beliefs drove him to try to take on the hunt single-handed – that was when he got into trouble as a teenager, spraying ALF slogans everywhere and sabbing, although he was nothing to do with the official antis then. They always focused on hunts closer to the cities, so the Brom and Lem had never had much trouble until Russ arrived with his aniseed spray. You can imagine how embarrassing it was for Bill, who's been a lifelong hunt supporter. So Mags helped out – she got Russ interested in Compassion in World Farming, plus the music. She taught him to play the guitar. And Bill gave him more work to do round the farm, which he loved. Russ always wants to learn about new things.' His greatest love remained the cider orchards, which the Hedges family had tended for two centuries, where he had set up camps as a boy and dreamed of a simpler life away from cityscapes. Hence his interest in arboriculture, which he had studied at university.

'He stayed on to take his master's in conservation and woodland management,' Kat added. 'Then he took a placement in Tower Hamlets to study urban forestry, where he got interested in animal communication.'

'Ah, yes, the wild, roaming herds of east London,' Dawn mused.

'He was attacked by a pitbull,' Kat explained. 'Several, actually. It got him thinking about the way we domesticate animals – or don't. He went to Thailand to rehabilitate wild dogs, and the year after that he spent the summer at a bear-rescue centre in Cambodia.' He'd remained a familiar figure in Eardisford, returning most summers and Christmases, although he was banned for a few years after the notorious Boxing Day meet when he took his anti-hunting stance too far by hijacking the hound lorry with thirteen couple on board. Nevertheless, the villagers remained fond of 'Rebel Russ', largely because of his two champions: the popular and kindly uncle who doted on him, and Mags, who mothered him mercilessly.

That's where all the free drinks were coming from, Dawn realized. It's like one big happy family in here, she thought, in a glow of scrumpy. She'd met red-faced Bill Hedges and his jolly, laughing wife, with several characters Kat had referred to as the 'earthmen', who appeared to have only one full set of teeth between them, but made up for it with half a dozen terriers straining on leads tied to their barstools. There were also young couples and old ladies, a posh toff and a bunch of girl grooms drinking in hay-scattered riding gear, all on friendly terms with Kat and welcoming to Dawn. Kat was liked and accepted, Dawn realized.

Although Dawn had lived in and around Watford all her life, there wasn't a pub she could go into these days and guarantee that she'd know anybody. Even the gym she'd belonged to for the best part of a decade had no real social side, the same faces she'd seen on the same evenings every week plugged into iPods, staring at MTV and lost in their own worlds. Being in here reminded her of life on the Caribbean liner, where the crew had become like family, the spa staff, cabaret stars and dancers always partying together late into the night. Out at sea, she'd been in suspended animation, always travelling and never arriving, until she'd grown weary of the tiresome customers, the repetitive work and the cramped accommodation. Here, there was a sense of permanence. Nobody wanted to leave. Even the lady in the great house had hung on into her ninety-fifth year.

She was starting to understand why Kat loved Eardisford so much that she'd stayed on to take up the new challenge after Constance had died, and even why she now shared her dilapidated home with Russ, the dark-eyed rebel. Kat had always been attracted to alpha men. This key player was a sexy maverick, unbothered whether he was accepted or not.

Almost everybody in the pub seemed connected with the hunt in some way, conversation at the bar revolving around that day's sport. Russ came in for a lot of goading, yet they all seemed to accept it as a part of a ritual.

'How does he cope?' she asked Kat. 'Is he working deep under cover for the League Against Cruel Sports?'

Kat laughed. 'They all know he hates hunting, and that he'll kick up a fuss and take the rise if they want a debate, but they've had every argument over the years, and they know that's the way it is. Besides, they're all united in a new cause at the moment, so there's an armistice.' She raised her eyebrows. 'Attendance at my self-defence class has trebled since the oligarch rumour started. The villagers think Eardisford's going to be awash with Kalashnikov-wielding heavies leaping from cars with blacked-out windows if the rents aren't paid on time.'

'You run a self-defence class?' Dawn was impressed.

'It's more boxercise, with a few gym kicks and throws. Monday evenings in the village hall, winter and summer, Pilates in spring and autumn. I also do Bums and Tums on alternate Thursdays. Then I have riding lessons on Wednesdays and Saturdays and meditation sessions Fridays and Tuesdays.'

'Packed schedule, then. What's with the meditation?'

'Tantric,' she mouthed, and they collapsed into giggles. 'It's just something I'm trying out.' Kat wiped her eyes. 'It's all about breathing so far – more like casual omming than casual sex. We keep all our clothes on.'

'Probably wise in a house as cold as yours. So it's not serious between you and Russ?'

Dawn sensed the relationship was perhaps not as destructive as she'd feared. Kat was going steady on the scrumpy, she noticed, but the glow was blossoming in her cheeks, and the lingering looks she was exchanging with Russ were getting hotter. With her gleaming hair falling over her shoulders like red liquorice and her deep green eyes drinking in the affection surrounding her, she looked a million miles from the wreck who'd left her nursing career, her fiancé and home on one fateful day two years earlier.

Dawn felt she should mention Nick again, but Russ had appeared at the table clutching two shot glasses brimming with something so lime green it was almost luminous. 'Hopflasks by way of apology from the kitchen. The food's delayed. Jed the chef's just heard a rumour that Eardisford's buyer's from Yorkshire and called Seth. He's run up to the church tower with Mags's Nexus to Google it.'

Dawn knocked back a slug of the shot and almost gagged. It seemed to be pure alcohol.

'Seth, you say?' Kat was peering up at Russ anxiously.

Dawn was battling to make her eyes focus. 'Not a golligarch by the shound of it. A Brit donchathink? I'll drink to that!' She drained the shot glass.

Russ looked at her levelly. 'Nobody's celebrating yet.'

'The whole future of this place hangs on who's bought the estate,' Kat reminded her, chewing her lip. 'The houses in Lower Eardisford are all estate property, tied to jobs or pensions. The same goes for the farms, this pub, the lot. Even the church and the cricket pitch are part of the estate. Whoever Seth is, he's just taken on a lot of livelihoods around here.'

She's terrified she's going to lose all this, Dawn thought drunkenly. She's just finding happiness and she might forfeit it.

'The earthmen all reckon Dair's in on it,' Russ said, in an undertone. 'He's such a sly little sod, he looks after himself first. His father's a baronet, after all. They're all fucking corrupt. He's let his game-keeping boys know their jobs are safe, which means he knows something.'

Dawn was longing to meet Dair Armitage, who was sounding more exciting by the minute. She only wished the pub wasn't spinning so fast. 'Isn't it a good thing if Dair's jobshafe?' she asked. 'Surely that means everybody's jobshafe?' She shook her head sharply. 'What was that drink?'

'Hopflask. Absinthe and apple brandy flavoured with hops – a local speciality,' Kat told her. 'The Brom and Lem hunt staff put it in their flasks. Being offered it is to be invited into the inner circle. The first time I drank it, I lost two days. Welcome. You are officially one of us.'

Dawn felt as though fireworks were going off overhead as she crossed an invisible line to acceptance. 'I knew this was a great dress. Hooray to the innershircle!' She stood up, toasted the pub at large and drained the second glass.

As she did so, in Wild West saloon tradition, the bar fell silent, a new arrival silhouetted in the door, a flat cap low over his nose, gun under one arm, shoulders as wide as barn doors. Dawn's heart skipped a beat as she took in the antiquated, earthy manliness of it all. 'Hellooo, big boy,' she said, the Mae West aside coming out far louder than she'd intended, given the bar's silence and the drunken thrumming muffling her ears.

The man reached up to pull off his hat in amazement. 'Well, hello there,' he said, in a nasal Scottish voice.

Dawn's eyes crossed and recrossed. Even through the untrustworthy goggles of scrumpy and Hopflask, Dair Armitage was a lot more attractive than Kat had made out, and nothing like Elmer Fudd. He was Bruce Willis meets Sean Connery, with a hint of Freddie Ljungberg. His dogs were pretty cool too – two pale-eyed German pointers with coats like blanket-spot Appaloosa ponies that sat at each side of him and stared up adoringly. Dawn saw no difference between Dair and the testosterone-pumped Watford hard men who walked around with Staffies in armoured collars and gave her hard, sexy looks that made her feel weak at the knees. After years of Dave lifting nothing heavier than his remote control, she had a secret soft spot for a real man. This one might be wearing well-cut wool breeches and waistcoat instead of trackies and a hoodie, but he was five foot ten of bald, hard-eyed sex appeal.

Better still, Dawn saw, she had his full attention.

Before anybody else could get to him, Dawn lurched across the little public bar. 'Just who in hell is Seth?'

'Who are you?'

'A new Dawn. Shit!' She fell over one of his dogs and pitched outside through the still-open door.

As Kat scrabbled out from the corner table to help her, she realized Russ hadn't moved. 'Quick! She might be hurt!'

'Nonsense. Fresh air will do her good,' he said coolly, eyeing the gun Dair had abandoned to rush outside and fish Dawn out of a planter filled with spring bulbs.

He carried her inside now, buckling under the weight and turning pink with excitement as her push-up bra pushed everything out of her turquoise dress.

'I'm not hurt!' she giggled, gazing up at him in drunken awe. 'You have an amazing chin.'

Settling her in a chair by the big open fire, Dair insisted on getting her a brandy.

'I'm not sure that's such a good idea.' Kat looked at Dawn who was lolling in the firelight and making coochy-coo noises at Dair's dogs. Hearing the familiar click of a barrel cocking, their ears pricked. But Russ was holding the shotgun, not their master.

'Put that down, Hedges!' Dair barked from the bar.

'Nice stock work.' Russ looked through the sights and swung round. All the earthmen at the bar ducked, terriers yapping. Only Dair remained upright, along with Mags, who was tutting at Russ from the brandy optic.

'So, who is Seth?' demanded Russ.

Dair stonewalled him. 'I'm not at liberty to say.'

'Nobody around here's at liberty when their futures are dependent upon one landowner. Not even you, Dair. We deserve to know the truth.'

Kat had seen enough: Russ would get himself into serious

trouble if he carried on like that. Stepping in front of the gun, she put her hands on her hips and tilted her head to one side to show she wasn't remotely afraid. 'Stop this now, Russ.'

'Yes, stop showing off,' Dair said drily, and picked up the brandy to carry it to Dawn. 'That gun's not loaded.'

'Unlike your new boss.' Dawn took the drink and swigged. Then she noticed Dair's blank expression. 'Loaded, as in filthy rich. Minted. Flush. Bling bling.' Her eyes were starting to cross again.

Dair took the gun from Russ and broke it across his knee, then rested it back against the fire surround.

'I love thishplace.' Dawn watched him woozily. 'Bring that gun into a boozer in Watford and you'd have a SWAT team and Shky News camped outside before you could say "Mine'sapint." I bet you have lockinshtill dawn, doncha?'

'I'll wait all night for Dawn if I have to.' Dair settled opposite her. 'Has anybody told you that you have the most amazing eyes?'

'Oh, hell,' muttered Kat, as Dawn drunkenly began on her life story and Russ stalked angrily to the bar to refill drinks and get the latest on the church tower Googling. It was going to be a long night. She hoped Daphne had enough pages of the *Observer* to keep her going.

Chapter 6

In the Carpathian Mountains, a lone rider was galloping along a snow-covered forest track at full pelt, drawing arrows from his hip quiver in swift succession to be fired from a small curling bow, each one sailing into its target with a satisfying thwack.

Horse master Valentine Lupei watched grudgingly on the monitor as the camera tracked back, its dolly racing on its rails to stay ahead of the horse. The young actor was a natural in the saddle, he acknowledged. He knew the boy had ridden many stunts in the past – indeed, Dougie Everett's transition from stuntman to actor was well documented – but his behaviour before they'd started filming had been so obstreperous and spoilt that Valentine had imagined the boasts were exaggerated.

Furious that he'd not been allowed to bring his own horses with him to Romania, Dougie had refused the training sessions on offer with the team before filming began. If Valentine's horses were top-quality stunt-trained animals who knew their jobs, Dougie claimed, he had no need to practise. Instead he had flown to England to go to a party. Today was their first morning's filming in the mountains and Dougie had left it to the last minute to arrive, transferring straight from the airport to the set, by which time Valentine was dressed in medieval leather livery, ready to double for him in the action scenes. This was among the biggest-budget movies Valentine had been involved with, and he wanted to be in front of camera as much as possible.

Now denied his chance to shine, Valentine was sulking, especially as he could see the sheer, effortless talent on display. That was why the magazines all claimed that new Hollywood Britpacker Dougie Everett was making horse-riding sexy. The number of men taking it up had reportedly shot up after the release of the *High Noon* remake in which Dougie had swaggered in and out of the saddle and seduced hottest starlet Kiki Nelson. Before that, he'd made jousting sexy in *Dark Knight*, an edgy medieval bloodbath combining beautifully framed violence with a grinding modern soundtrack and no perceptible plot. Now, starring in this fairytale fantasy adventure of horny hobgoblins and hot-lipped fairies, Dougie was making mounted archery sexy, Valentine thought bitterly. No wonder the makeup girls were all wearing their lowest-cut tops.

Valentine had deliberately mounted him on a hot-headed dark chestnut Hispano Arab, which director Bradley agreed would look terrific on film contrasted against the snow. The horse was such a handful that usually only Valentine rode him, but his plan to embarrass the actor had backfired as Dougie Everett now charged along the wide tree avenues as though he and the horse were on parallel tracks with the camera, arrows flying as straight as laser beams. Later, in a post-production edit suite, the small padded blue target would be CGIed into a giant, man-eating boar. The duo looked spectacular as they sliced past the black trunks like a moving, sparking flame.

'Great horse!' Dougie complimented Valentine, as they took a break to set up the next scene. 'He's a credit to you.'

'Where you learn to shoot arrow like Hungarian?' Valentine demanded.

'Pony Club.'

The only person sulking more than Valentine was Dougie himself, and today the boar target was his nemesis: he was deriving a manifest pleasure from peppering it with arrows.

Not only had the costume department dressed him from head to toe in leather, laces and buckles, so that he looked like a cross between Dick Whittington and a gimp, but his recent trip to England had not been a success. Caving into pressure, Dougie had agreed to attend his father Vaughan's sixtieth birthday party. Having already drained the generous trust fund he'd inherited at twenty-one, he was under family orders to step back into the Everett fold and marry, at which point – due to the archaic nature of the family fortune – he'd automatically acquire a huge stake in the London businesses and Northamptonshire farms. His father, who saw his son's engagement to Kiki Nelson as a smokescreen and firmly believed this 'acting lark' was a passing fad, had lined him up with a buck-toothed event-rider daughter of another local landowner, hoping to make a match. The girl had been hell, although Dougie had to admit the horse she'd lent him for a day out in the local hunt's legendary Friday country had been a high-grade fix for any adrenalin junkie. When Vaughan, who was field-mastering, had invited his son up front to tackle a row of six freshly laid hedges, known as the Orthopaedics because they claimed so many broken bones, Dougie had found himself smiling wider than he had in months. Keen for his country-loving son to manage the estate's farming interests, Vaughan was forever dangling the carrots of horses and hunting in front of him, but Dougie felt no draw to the flat, wet corner of Northamptonshire where he'd spent his childhood listening to his parents argue drunkenly during the interminable school holidays.

The trouble was he no longer craved the heat and buzz of Hollywood as he once had, and Kiki's devotion to acting, the body beautiful and round-the-clock networking irritated him. Her need to talk, text, tweet and Instagram non-stop drove him mad, and the novelty of his A-list fiancée telling him how 'instinctively and amazingly' talented he was had started to wear off when she'd tried to get him to accompany her to acting classes. Dougie had attended just one, at which track-suited participants 'explored Stanislavski' by wailing, groaning and crying like babies. His own cries – based largely upon a cow giving birth – had been praised for 'profound emotionality', but the experience had nonetheless left Dougie perplexed. Recognizing some big names, he'd asked Kiki afterwards why successful actors would need lessons when they had agents turning film scripts away. She'd looked at him in amazement. 'We're refining our art, of course. You are a raw *diamond* of talent, a big stud with no angles to catch the light. We gotta cut you to train you, baby.' That had made him think uncomfortably of his Friesian stunt horses being gelded as three-year-old colts, a process known in the horse world as cutting.

Two weeks on location in a Romanian ski lodge had seemed an appealing escape from Kiki and the intensity of LA, although it had lost some if its appeal when he hadn't been able to persuade the director to let him bring his own bow horse from England.

Dougie missed the team of horses he'd trained up from scratch when he'd earned his living from stunt riding alone. On the drive back from his father's weekend party to London, he'd stopped off in Buckinghamshire, where they were stabled. To his dismay, the yard was a total mess, the horses dirty, bored and under-exercised, and the work diary almost empty. His business partner, an affable ex-polo pro called Rupe, had been too busy partying to chase the public displays and corporate work that paid the winter feed bills. When he'd left him in charge, Dougie had told him that the business couldn't survive solely upon the more glamorous but infrequent commercial film and television work. Now there wasn't enough in the bank to pay February's wages and Rupe was trying to sell horses to raise cash.

Dougie had written him a cheque to buy time, but he knew it couldn't carry on like that. The reputation he'd spent years building for the team was in rapid decline. Worse, Dougie's greatest equine ally, Harvey, the big Irish grey that had first accompanied him from the hunting field into stunt displays, was a bag of bones under his layers of winter rugs, wasting away because nobody had noticed that his old yellow teeth were in desperate need of attention. The food was literally falling out of his mouth when he tried to chew it.

Instead of driving on to Stansted to catch his flight to Bratislava and meet the cast and crew at the location briefing, Dougie had spent his last day in the UK rattling around the M25 in a horsebox, taking Harvey to a veterinary hospital to have emergency dental treatment. Seeing his horses so neglected, Dougie felt as if he'd abandoned his family. He was determined to sort the situation out.

He was also determined to do something about Kiki.

Now, taking a break in his trailer while the film team set up the next scene, Dougie pulled off the Dick Whittington boots and leather waistcoat in favour of sheepskin clogs and a thick fleece sweater, cranked up the fan heater and contemplated his next move. The signal on his smart-phone was non-existent this high in the mountains so he didn't have to wade through the barrage of messages from Kiki just yet. There was WiFi at the ski centre that cast and crew had commandeered as location HQ, and he'd have no excuse to ignore her when he got back there after the day's shooting.

He knew he would have to break off the engagement soon. He deeply regretted his rash marriage proposal, made after several lines of cocaine at the *High Noon* wrap party, followed by three hours of mind-blowing sex (Kiki didn't do drugs, but she talked so much and screwed so dedicatedly that that hadn't mattered). At the time, Dougie had believed that Kiki would be good for him, and in truth she probably was. She was an incredibly talented actress, passionate about healthy living and humanitarian causes; her drive and zeal inspired him as much as her hard body thrilled him. Since they'd got together, she'd kept him in shape, helped fast-track him through the Holly-wood social scene and kicked his lazy arse to make him take his natural gift for acting as seriously as he took his talent for horsemanship. Having grown up with a series of disapproving stepmothers and disciplinarian nannies, Dougie was a dab hand at dealing with single-minded task-masters.

In turn, the man Kiki called her 'easy-going English rogue' charmed, calmed and challenged her. But he no longer wanted to be her dapper British husband, the latest must-have Hollywood accessory, like a piece of hand-made arm luggage. Travelling with her was great, but living with her was hell. She wanted to unpack him, using psychotherapy, acting lessons and detox fasting, then rearrange him to get an Oscar winner. Dougie didn't want to change: he was happy to travel light with somebody at his side and the distant horizon in his sights.

Unlike many of his commitment-phobic mates, Dougie couldn't wait to marry, seeing a wife as a much-needed anchor and marriage as something he could do better than his parents. In his teenage years he had been scandalized by his father's many well-publicized affairs and his mother's departure. Since then Vaughan had married a succession of beautiful but unchallenging blondes, several of whom had borne him more children, while Dougie's embittered mother pickled herself in martinis and wizened away, a tummy tuck at a time, in the South of France with a new husband.

Starved of affection and missing a strong role model, their son had rapidly turned into a hell-raising menace. He'd been expelled from school and later dropped out of the army, yet his birthright had propelled him through Society, where everyone knew a good marriage could be orchestrated and the future safeguarded. Dougie's great charm and many friends meant he had no shortage of takers. Thus he'd entered his first brief engagement at just twenty-four with sweet, country-loving Cressida, whose father had offered him a job in his merchant bank. This seemed to involve turning up in the City about once a month, but still proved too much for Dougie, as did staying faithful to poor Cressida. She had grown so obsessed with weddings that she'd put him off marriage for several years. Dougie had never much wanted a wedding: he wanted a wife, a strong-willed, passionate one, to share his life with.

He'd found his career in stunt riding by chance, helping out a friend at a charity jousting tournament and discovering something for which he had an exceptional talent that suited his fearless, extrovert nature. On a whim, he'd decided to set up his own team and, largely self-taught, had entertained audiences at country fairs and stately homes, at first using well-heeled connections, but soon earning a reputation as a breathtaking act to watch. It came so naturally to Dougie, combining his love of horses with high risk and showing off, that he wasn't aware of exactly how good he was until television and advertising bookings began filling his diary. Soon the film work was rolling in too. That was how he'd met Iris Devonshire, the child star of the *Ptolemy Finch* series, who was undeniably all woman by the time she shared a saddle, then a bed with Dougie in film five, and the crush she'd had on him had turned into a compelling, all-absorbing love affair. Dougie knew he wanted to marry Iris from their first night together in a London hotel room. He'd adored her beauty, her innocence and her intelligence. She'd encouraged him to read and broaden his mind until the tabloids had reported his misdemeanours just before their wedding day. Dougie hadn't been entirely innocent, but he'd been more faithful to Iris than he had to any other woman. Engagement broken, she'd fallen for another man, taken a break from acting and was now in her final year at university, existing in a parallel universe. And he was engaged to Kiki.

In his more self-effacing moments, Dougie was big enough to admit that it was as much his talent for seducing leading ladies as for acting that had given him his biggest acting breaks – first Iris and now Kiki – although directors certainly seemed to love what he did on screen. The phenomenon baffled him and had even been given its own nickname, the 'Everett Effect'. To him, it was just learning lines and speaking them over and over again. And, having burned with the desire to be a big star since his first day on a movie set, he thought now that he preferred the adrenalin kick of riding stunts. His broken engagement had made him grow up and focus on what he really wanted from life. He was thirty, and still very much wanted a wife. Losing Iris had hurt him deeply and made him question his behaviour, although not enough to change it.

He tried to concentrate on his script, running through the next scene. In this sequence he said just six words, all in made-up elf language that sounded like bringing up phlegm.

'Fireauchi blanhunt muir bechan fin nathrot!' He gave it an enthusiastic shot, like a student ordering two beers in Stockholm.

'Mr Ever After?' One of the Romanian runners came in with the sandwiches and water he'd asked for.

'Everett.' He glanced up from the script as her cleavage came level with his nose. She had a tiny tattoo of a heart on one breast.

Catching him looking at it, she dropped a big smile and two dark blue eyes into his line of vision. 'You like? Is where my heart, he lives.' Her accent was rich and deliciously vampirish.

'Actually it should be on the left.'

'Uh?

'Your heart's on the wrong axis.'

Her lips parted and a pink tongue brushed along her very white teeth. Her pupils were huge, he noticed. 'You want axes to chop wood?'

Dougie grinned. Access-all-areas come-ons were increasingly common, but 'axes' was a new one. He couldn't wait to tell Abe, his agent. He'd love that. Abe was always telling him not to mistake his on-screen persona for off-screen invincibility. When Dougie had first made the transition from stuntman to film actor, his roles had inevitably been high on violent action and low on lines, with no love interest whatsoever. His biggest fans then were teenage boys obsessed with medieval warfare. Then he'd been cast alongside a pretty Hispanic actress in *Dark Knight*. There was minimal romantic action – she'd died in his arms in the first ten minutes, after which he cut a lot of people to shreds – but the fan-mail had poured in, and the press had got excited about the 'Everett Effect'. Off camera, Dougie was a good-looking man with a certain British charm. On camera, however, something magical happened when he was in close-up with a female co-star, the long-lashed blue eyes mesmerizing, the handsome face simmering with unspoken sexual promise and fight-to-the-death-for-love loyalty. It was the Everett Effect.

Dougie Everett's celluloid sex appeal was a revelation. As a result, he was working his way to the top of many casting directors' wish lists right now and Abe was cherry-picking the roles, the latest being a huge network series that he guaranteed would propel Dougie right up there with the very biggest names. Behind the scenes, Dougie was also being offered a lot of other cherries.

'I give you anything you want, Mr Ever After,' the girl said now, the message in her eyes unmistakable, slim thumbs hooking through the belt loops of her skinny jeans, which lowered to reveal the smooth hollow above her pubic bone.

Dougie knew he should force himself to look away. Sex was easy currency in the movie business. Loyalty was harder won. He owed it to Kiki to break it off before he screwed around. But his blood was already pumping south, pulling logic from his mind as it fast-tracked instinct instead. The engagement was as good as over and he deserved cheering up.

He flashed his charming smile. 'Well I don't want axes,' he said, remembering an old *Two Ronnies* sketch his father loved. 'Do you have fork handles?'

Her dark eyes looked questioning, then a slow smile spread across her face as she took in his expression.

'I have four tattoos.' Her nails were the same shade of scarlet as the tiny heart. She unzipped her woollen hoodie. The little red heart was now riding high over a frilly bra. 'You move my heart, Mr Ever After.'

'Your heart is exquisite exactly where it is.' Dougie stood up and walked towards her. 'Please don't waste it on me.' The kick of tasting another mouth against his was just as intense as he remembered, with the sharp punch of guilty pleasure. Kissing his way down her throat, he peeled her top sideways to reveal more froths of lingerie and another tattoo, a purple star this time. He closed his mouth around a dark nipple, her breasts deliciously small, soft and natural compared to Kiki's peach-perfect, enhanced orbs. They even had an endearing scattering of freckles that reminded Dougie painfully of Iris. She looked no older than eighteen. As she slipped down on to her knees, her mouth eager to take him, he felt his cock strain against the leather breeches.

She looked up questioningly. 'Where is zip?'

'Fuck.' Going for a pee earlier had involved two costume assistants and an unpicking device. 'How good are you at knots?'

Chapter 7

Snow had started to fall once more by the time Dougie made it back on set, ten minutes late, his breeches knotted at a very odd angle. Fired up by the same wayward recklessness that had just taken him on a tour of the pretty runner's tattoos, his riding was breathtaking in its speed and daring.

The flakes fattened as the wild-eyed chestnut slalomed through the trees, kicking up ever-deeper snow before breaking out across open country to join mounted comrades, pursued by an imaginary giant boar. The crew were calling for a weather check, but the director knew this was too good to stop. After each take, Dougie patted his chestnut horse and reached forward to rub its snow-topped mane and ears, grateful for its stamina, aware that his unfit Friesians could never have taken the pace or cold. It was a tedious stop-start process. The camera trolley kept getting stuck and the scene had to be reset and repeated. By the fifth take Dougie was even feeling sorry for the imaginary eight-tusked boar. He rested the heavy sword on his shoulder and wriggled his fingers, which had gone totally numb in the thick gauntlets.

At that moment, a giant black shadow seemed to explode from the snowfall overhead.

'What the—?' The director's voice was drowned by the roar of rotor blades and the screams of cast and crew.

Now firm friends and united by exhaustion, Dougie and his chestnut were the only ones not to bat an eyelid when the helicopter loomed above the black firs in the middle of the scene, making an apocalyptic entrance. Lights flashing, it swooped down, sending snow over everything, terrifying the horses and wrecking continuity.

Trotting out of the snow cloud to safety, Dougie looked back at the carnage. While horses bolted and riders flew in every direction amid the white-out, the flashy gold Eurocopter landed on the flattest piece of land, almost vanishing in a haze of snow.

The director swore furiously through the loudspeaker for order, calling a halt to that day's shoot. The light was fading, they'd never have time to reset the scene and the fucking helicopter was in the way. It had better be the fucking Academy Awards telling him he was nominated after all.

The blades were still sending up a white-out. Head ducked against the bitter updraught, one of the grooms came to take the chestnut from Dougie, closely followed by the tattooed runner with a big squashy coat.

Having been in the saddle for almost two hours wielding a broadsword, Dougie was grateful for the early finish. His arm and shoulders ached as he clambered out of the saddle and put on the old Puffa over his costume. The unremitting cold was starting to take its toll on his body. He needed a hot shower, a painkiller and a stiff drink before he checked his phone messages.

The helicopter's rotors had reduced to half-speed. A door was opening.

'Think the talent's arrived early?' suggested the larky character actor who was playing Dougie's accident-prone goblin sidekick.

Although Dougie was the arrow-shooting hero of most action scenes, the movie's headline act was a far more established star, a former Bond actor who was being paid five times as much to deliver half a dozen lines and save the fairies.

Dougie was looking forward to meeting him – he was a lifelong 007 fan and the man was a total hero.

'Wouldn't he go straight to the ski lodge?'

'Likes to make an entrance.'

They watched as a figure leaped out of the helicopter – athletic, tall, sophisticated and possibly licensed to kill, but definitely not a lightly grizzled Welshman with a supermodel wife and a carefully concealed drinking problem. Battling through the blizzard was a very beautiful Indian girl in a wolf-fur coat and hat.

She headed straight for Dougie, her voice exquisitely deep. 'Mr Everett?'

If there was one thing more exciting to Dougie than meeting a retired Bond hero, it was being cast in the role himself. And this was the closest he'd ever come. For an embarrassing moment he was completely tongue-tied.

'Seth has sent me to collect you, Mr Everett,' she told him, pocketing the tablet she was carrying and reaching out to shake his hand.

'Who's Seth?'

'You have not received a call today?'

He laughed. 'The only calls we receive out here are set calls.'

'No matter.' She held up her arm to the pilot. A moment later, the engine pitch changed from idling to high rev. 'We have a restaurant table booked. Come.'

He looked down at his gimp waistcoat and boots. 'I'll just scrub up and change in my trailer. I must reek.'

Tutting, she walked back towards him, pressed her nose into his neck and breathed deeply. 'You smell good. You have no time to change.' Beckoning him, she disappeared into the white-out as the blades whined towards full speed.

For a moment, Dougie was glued to the spot, nonplussed.

Then, zipping up his Puffa and hoping the restaurant had a relaxed dress code, he followed her.

When Dougie had climbed into a plush leather seat in the helicopter beside the woman and strapped on the safety harness, she handed him a set of headphones, which he put on, then waited for her to explain what the hell was going on. But she said nothing, pulling out her iPad and typing into its screen instead.

'What's your name?' he shouted, over the little microphone by his mouth.

'Deepak,' came a walrus-voiced reply from the pilot as they took off. 'You have been filming a movie, yes? What is the story?'

While Dougie shared the fantasy action plot, the woman showed no sign of listening in.

Dougie studied her thoughtfully. Whoever this 'Seth' was, he went for the glamorous-assistant cliché big-time. Chital-deer-eyed, glossy-haired and pouting, she was exquisitely put together, albeit chillier than the glacial landscape outside. When he glanced at her iPad, expecting an encoded memo with Top Secret at the top, he saw she was solving a Sudoku puzzle.

Instead of flying along the river valley towards civilization, as he'd imagined, they were travelling higher into the mountains, a journey of less than twenty minutes that took them to a frozen lake. As they came down to land, Dougie half imagined that its surface would break open to reveal an amazing high-tech headquarters. Instead, he saw a huge dome of snow carved beside it, against the mountainside, too symmetrical to have been shaped by nature. It resembled a giant sculpture of a beetle, the size of an aircraft hangar, with one long central backbone from which arched limbs protruded.

'Ice hotel,' the pilot explained, as they came down to land. 'The best in Europe.'

Inside, the building was a cathedral formed in snow, the light extraordinary, filtering through the walls from outside in a curious subterranean glow and enhanced with the coloured artificial beams that gleamed from the ice walls and ceilings. Dougie felt as if he was walking inside the aurora borealis.

The glamorous fur-clad girl led him along the domed spine to a curtained archway marking the opening to a private suite of ice rooms, bathed in yet more exquisite light.

Dougie looked around for Bond baddies but there was just a luminous purple table spread with black slates topped with smoked-fish appetizers and two huge fur-lined ice chairs, one of which the girl indicated he should sit in. He imagined that the mysterious Seth was probably watching from behind a double-sided ice-wall mirror. He had to be Indian, turbanned and mystical, with dark glasses and a tame eagle on a gauntlet.

'Would you like a beer, Mr Everett?' She walked to an ice wall carved with little indentations, each containing bottles of premium lagers. 'What would you like? Vintage 3? Something Belgian?'

'Budvar's fine, and please call me Dougie.'

She uncapped it and held it out. 'Seth became a great admirer of your work when he saw *High Noon*. He believes you have serious talent. I also thought it was excellent and you are most talented.' Her voice was perfectly modulated but strangely unemotional, like a satnav. 'I recommended it to him.' Just for a moment the dark eyes flashed with something close to warmth, then shuttered back to professional cool.

'Thank you. I'm sorry, I don't know your name?'

'My name is Dollar.' Her face remained unsmiling. 'Indeed, I also enjoyed *Dark Knight*, in which the stunts were very accomplished.'

'Thank you.' Dougie's head swelled happily, as she settled on the reindeer pelt in the adjacent chair. Her face was so still and beautiful. 'When is Seth joining us?'

'He's not.'

Having been anticipating the arrival of a megalomaniac in full kurta pajama, Dougie was disappointed. The girl was ravishing, but not very enlightening company: she had yet to crack a facial expression. Right now her eyes gave him that strange, split-second warm glow, or was he imagining it?

'Seth is in Moscow this evening,' she was saying in her deep monotone, 'but we are in constant communication, and he has entrusted this meeting to me. First I must ask you to sign this.' She produced her tablet, on which was loaded a page of close-typed legalese. Scrolling down to a blank box, she held out a touch pen. 'It is a straightforward confidentiality agreement that states nothing we discuss in this room this evening will be shared with a third party.'

'Hang on, I have no idea what any of this is about.'

'You'll find out if you sign it, Mr Everett.' She waggled the stylus impatiently.

Dougie scribbled on the screen.

'Thank you.' She took back the pen, unsmiling. 'Please eat. I will get straight to the point. We would like to offer you a job.'

Dougie had his mouth full of raw tuna exploding with pink peppercorns, vanilla and grapefruit. 'Tell me more,' he mumbled, longing for beer-battered cod and chips.

'Seth would like you to be his professional huntsman. For one year initially.'

Peppercorns popping, eyes watering, Dougie stared at her in astonishment. There was no warm glow in the dark eyes now. Her beautiful face was unblinking, like that of a form-filling bureaucrat anticipating a yes or no answer.

'Is this a movie role?' Dougie had a sudden image of himself taking part in a big Bollywood dance scene, wearing gold *dhoti* and chiffon shirt, possibly matched with a bearskin hat and hussar jacket. As far as he was aware very few non-Indian actors starred in the industry's films, and those who did played baddies. He wasn't convinced it would be his greatest career move.

'This is not an acting part, Mr Everett. This is what you English call "sport".'

He took a moment to run this around in his head, now seeing himself in safari suit and pith helmet, which was no less ridiculous than the Dick Whittington boots, leather leggings and an S&M waistcoat he was already wearing when he came to think about it.

'And what exactly would this sport involve?' he humoured her. It was sounding James Bond again, although he doubted anything could come close to the twelve big-budget, prime-time, sixty-minute episodes of lush cinematography that his agent was lining up, and for which he would share the screen with several Oscar-winners.

'Seth is in the process of purchasing one of the best sporting estates in England. "Blood sports", I believe you call them: hunting, shooting and fishing.' The eyes flashed again, not so warmly this time.

'Field sports,' he corrected lightly. 'Blood sports, like bull-fighting and bear-baiting, are quite different.' Dougie's limited knowledge of Indian culture told him that Sikhs and Hindus were against killing things on religious grounds, but perhaps that was just cows.

'I apologize, *field sports*.' She spoke the words like a news-reader pronouncing the particularly difficult name of a Middle Eastern country. 'Seth has many business associates who enjoy these sporting activities, and he wishes to entertain them at his new residence. There is much work to be done, but we believe that the sport will be possible to arrange very swiftly.' She consulted her electronic pad, swiping the screen to find the relevant notes. 'The bank and lake fishing and game shoots are already professionally run, but there has not been a hound pack there for many years, we believe.'

'Well, British Parliament banned hunting with dogs.' He tried a scallop, which was so light and delicious it seemed to disappear on his tongue, leaving tiny sweet fireworks of flavour partying in his mouth.

'We are aware of the law.' She smiled coolly. 'There are kennels and stabling that were once used by a local hunt.' Her long fingers swiped again as she consulted her notes. 'That pack amalgamated with another and moved out at the time of the ban, although they still hold meetings and hunt fox on the estate.'

'They follow pre-laid scent trails, these days,' Dougie corrected kindly. 'And they're "meets", not meetings.'

'This is, of course, your field of expertise. You were quoted saying recently that you would like to hunt your own pack.'

He thought back to the drunken lunch during which his publicist had spent the entire dessert course frantically making throat-cutting gestures at him from behind the interviewer's back. The British tabloids had predictably had a field day after the feature had come out, digging up a photo of Dougie on Harvey at a Boxing Day meet years ago with the usual background about his father's love of field sports. He'd taken a battering from social media trolls and anti-hunting activists afterwards, and from Kiki, who told him to wise up on his PR, although she fell silent when one of Hollywood's biggest producers sent a personal invitation for Dougie to join him in fielding his exclusive private pack in pursuit of coyote.

'I grew up around hunting,' he told Dollar now. 'It's a great family passion.' The memory of his day spent alongside his father jumping the Orthopaedics made him smile afresh.

'You would have a team working for you, and you will have total autonomy. There will be excellent accommodation, a generous budget and a great deal of free time.' Her eyes did their warm, hypnotic speed-glow. 'This would be a *very* well-paid job.'

Dougie opened his mouth to decline regretfully but found he wanted to savour for a little longer the parallel life he was being offered amid James Bond subterfuge. This was a job he could do blindfold, and had always longed to fulfil – not a field master like his father, which any good horseman with a bit of free time and experience could manage, charming landowners and hollering at small children on bolting ponies as he led the mounted field around headlands and over jumps while the hounds ran the direct line of the scent. A huntsman ran with the hounds far ahead of the field; he trained and worked the pack himself; he was a breed apart. It was a role Dougie had idolized as a pony-kicking child, thundering through mud and birch, and understood far better than any swashbuckling Lothario he played on screen today. It had been among his many boyhood dream jobs that had been thwarted when his father insisted he go to officer training, Vaughan Everett curtly pointing out that hunt staff are paid a pittance and are technically 'servants'. In fairness, his son's other dream jobs had also included astronaut, lion tamer and, of course, British Secret Service agent with a licence to kill. This job almost ticked two of the four ambitions.

'Would Seth be hunt master?' He decided to enjoy the idle daydream just a little longer, monitoring that ravishing face for signs of life.

'No, you would.'

Master huntsman was a rare and revered role, working with

pack and field. He was the perfect fusion of upstairs downstairs, both master and servant, with the authority of one and the guile of the other.

'Could I bring my own horses?'

'As many as you like.'

He tried to imagine his Friesian stunt team galloping through plough and wet turf, high-stepping trick-trained horses that would be a laughing stock if he ever took them out with his father's pack, yet he knew they'd have the best of fun, as Harvey once had. If Dougie took this on, his horses would be safe. Rupe wouldn't sell them. He would also be a very long way from Kiki and her fervent diamond-polishing. It was almost tempting.

'Where exactly is the estate?'

'It is called . . . ' she checked her pad again ' . . . Urds-ford. It is in Herefordshire.' She rhymed 'Here' with 'beer'.

Dougie's smile widened. He'd vaguely heard of the estate, although Herefordshire was unknown territory: his forays in that direction tended to stop in the Cotswolds with friends. He tilted his head, switching on the flirtatious charm to see if he could get a reaction. 'Will you be based there, Dollar?'

The eyes glowed briefly. 'Part of my time will be spent there, yes. There is much to organize. Seth will not use the house as a residence. He does not like the English countryside.'

'So why buy an estate in Herefordshire?'

'It is a business acquisition. He has a large portfolio. The privacy and hunting it offers are unique, and the history of the house is of special interest to Seth's family. I have autonomy over the project, but I will expect to work very closely alongside you.'

'How closely?' He weighted the question with an overload of throaty flirtation.

'Very closely, Mr Everett.' The voice was utterly deadpan, but the eyes glowed again. 'I take it your answer is yes?'

Dougie had started to look for the hidden cameras. This had to be a set-up. She'd be offering him an Aston Martin, a personal harem and an inexhaustible supply of Krug next.

'I'm not a professional huntsman.' He toyed with a tiny beetroot jelly loaded with sour cream and caviar. 'I'm an actor.'

'You will most certainly be required to act.'

'I hardly think the annual hunt panto compensates for a year out of movie making.'

The room was filled with Desi music and Dollar turned away to answer her phone, her pretty face darkening. She nodded to him over her shoulder, then hurried along the corridor to take the call, although whatever language she was speaking was far beyond Dougie's schoolboy French.

A brace of waiters appeared to clear the starter and put down two steaming bowls of deep brown soup, swirled with crescents of cream and pluming with peppery promise. But Dougie had only got as far as admiring his reflection in the spoon when Dollar reappeared and started to gather up her things. 'I must go to Moscow. I will leave straight away. This suite is booked all night. You can stay here and I will arrange the transport for your return, or if you prefer we will take you now.'

'You can drop me off.' Dougie threw down the spoon, having no desire to linger in an oversized igloo wearing gimp leather and kinky boots with no mobile phone or toothbrush. 'I'm called at first light tomorrow.'

She marched towards the corridor. 'Seth will be delighted that you want to do it.'

'I'm afraid I'm not available.' Dougie finished his beer and zipped up his Puffa. 'I have work commitments lined up later this year.' And an engagement to break off, he added silently.

'I believe you are referring to the television series set during the American civil war and based upon a famous book?' She stood by the curtain to the main ice hall, waiting for him. 'We understand that the producers have yet to confirm that you are cast.'

Dougie looked at her sharply. Abe had insisted it remain totally confidential until contracts were signed. A twelve episode epic retelling of *Gone With the Wind* from the battlefield, filled with fast-galloping action, trick-riding heroics and epic love scenes, it was tailor-made for Dougie's talent and Abe was confident he had the deal in the bag, despite his client's relative inexperience. The money was sensational, less so the shooting schedule, which involved working on location in Georgia, South Carolina and back in Eastern Europe for almost a year, but that didn't bother Dougie, who saw it as a painless cauterization from Kiki. If he got the gig, Dougie was also determined to take his own horses with him.

'You know about that?' he asked Dollar in surprise.

'I know a great deal about you, Mr Everett.' The beautiful mask gave nothing away.

'Then you'll know I much prefer being called Dougie.'

Again, the eyes glowed all too briefly. 'We would like you to take this job offer very seriously, Dougie. There is an extremely generous bonus I have not yet told you about.'

They were standing together in the narrow chute leading through to the main hall, her arm barring his path where she was holding the curtain ready to draw back. The smell of her perfume was overpowering – peppery nasturtiums, sharp lemon balm and the sweetest lily-of-the-valley top note, reminding him of window boxes in Chelsea. He felt a sharp pinch of homesickness.

But he smiled easily. 'If the television series falls through, I'll get back to you.'

'Do that.' Her neat, dark eyebrows lifted and a set of perfect white teeth outshone the walls as she smiled for the first time, infinitely more beautiful and chilly. 'I will find out more about the girl in case of that eventuality.'

'What girl?'

'I have not yet told you about the girl.' Dollar led him at speed through the icy, domed hall with its Northern Lights glow. It had filled up with drinkers now, all dressed like Arctic explorers as they perched on fur-topped stools around ice tables swilling schnapps, trying not to gape at Dougie's lederhosen and New Romantic boots poking from beneath the Puffa. Many stared openly at Dollar as she passed in her furs, her rare beauty making jaws drop. The helicopter's thrum could be heard outside as its blades got up to speed.

Dougie felt his James Bond fantasy sliding away and experienced a pang of regret. Tomorrow he'd be back to makeup, kinky boots and broadswords, dabbling with his axes-all-areas girl to cheer himself up while he stewed over his disengagement from Kiki, his neglected horses at home and the pampered boredom of film work. A part of him longed to gallop through a forest shooting at more than just padded blue targets.

'What girl?' he asked again, as they went outside, but the helicopter drowned his voice. Darkness had fallen, the ice hotel glowing like a child's night light plugged into the side of the mountain.

Once they were airborne, Dollar pulled her microphone close to her mouth: 'The estate that Seth is buying – Urds-ford – has a lot of tenants. He does not see this as a problem because he just wants the main house and some accommodation for his staff with the hunting grounds, but there is a farm excluded from the purchase that he would like to acquire. Its vacant possession will ensure total privacy for Seth's house guests. The current occupant cares for animals there and claims it's a sanctuary, but really it is just a memorial to the lady who lived in the big house. This girl was her nurse, and the only circumstances in which that farm will become vacant are her marriage or her death. It is my job to ensure the farm *will* be vacant. That is why we need you.'

James Bond was back, tugging his cuffs from his dinner jacket and arching an eyebrow. 'Are you saying you want me to kill her?'

'We want you to marry her, Dougie.'

Chapter 8

'*Breathe!* Feel the force of your chakras, Kat. Feel the *kundalini* rising. Isn't it 'mazing?'

Eyes closed, Kat breathed, then paused to listen, head cocked. 'I'm sure I heard her.'

'It's a false Dawn,' Russ assured her. 'She's still totally sparko. Let's hold hands. And *breathe*.'

Kat was finding it hard to focus. The candle beside them was guttering noisily, like a blocked drain, drowning out the sitar music. 'I can't believe we poisoned my friend with Hopflasks, then let Dair bore her half to death.'

'She's having a terrific sleep. Think about your body. Breathe out negative thoughts.'

'I'm breathing in a hell of a lot of patchouli – can you move that joss stick?'

Like the incense, Tantric sex was a slow burner, but for all

96

her complaints Kat could tell something strange was happening as she matched her breathing to Russ's and let the tensions slip away. Her body no longer stayed coiled like a tight spring, but seemed to glow and liquefy, infused with a sensuality that felt no pressure or panic. As foreplay went, holding hands and humming in pyjamas for weeks on end might seem ludicrous, but she was sure she was starting to feel the benefits.

'This will take as long as it takes. Maybe weeks, maybe months,' his soft voice rolled over her reassuringly, 'you can't hurry it. If you want to reach the next plateau, Kat, you'll have to trust me to let you know when we're ready to progress.'

'You sound like Tina talking to me about learning to ride,' she joked, aware that her progress on both fronts was inhibited by an urge for small-talk to cover big tension.

'In many ways it shares the same processes, training the body to work in a new realm without thinking, taking acquired skills into unconscious thought on a spiritual level that manifests in physical reaction.' Russ didn't do small-talk. He did big breathing and long lectures. 'We're all just animals, after all – humans have the fight or flight response, like all species, and we want to fuck each other instinctively. That's what makes animal behaviour so fascinating. Tantra uses animal magnetism at its core, but raises our instinct to a spiritual level. The idea is that by holding back from orgasm, the pleasure is far deeper and greater. Look me in the eyes.'

Kat smiled at full force as she did so, hiding any doubts. Looking at him, so hirsute, academic and carnal, she was disconcertingly reminded of the day aged thirteen that she and her then best friend from school had sneaked *The Joy of Sex* off her mother's bedroom bookshelf and leafed through it. The contents had been a million miles from Nick's love of internet porn with its aggressive, priapic men, and women with hairless privates. In the smuggled book, the beards, pubic hair and smiles had mingled like Fuzzy Felt, helping the teenagers piece together the basics that would take their Justin Timberlake fantasies to a whole new level. The idea of Russ helping her discover Fuzzy Felt pleasure plateaux in a darkened room far from WiFi started to excite her again.

'When do we get to the orgasm bit?' she asked.

'When we're ready. Let's meditate now. Close your eyes again and empty your mind of all thoughts, concentrating purely on your breathing.'

With Russ's warm hands encircling hers, Kat tried to get into the zone, but was soon aware of one terrier rejoining them on the rug, another scratching to be let out and the lurchers whining at the bottom of the stairs. And while her breathing seemed calm and rhythmic enough, Russ's was very laboured: she thought he sounded as if he was coming down with a cold.

Just as she was contemplating offering him some Sinex, he released her hands so that she could place them on her chest. 'Now we'll do the chakra massage. Nine times table,' he reminded her.

Russ had explained that the chakras worked in multiples of nine, so the Tantric massage, which they must begin by performing on themselves while fully clothed, moved from chest to groin using the nine times table. Being hopeless at maths, she was always aware that she had to count out loud, which she knew put Russ off but if she didn't she lost her place long before the seventy-two rotations around the genitals and the eighty-one panting breaths that followed. They'd only moved on to this stage a week ago, and she wasn't sure it was really working for her yet. The stroking and rubbing was really quite pleasant, but the mathematics stressed her out. Russ was being incredibly patient, but she sensed he was starting to despair that she'd ever awake her *kundalini*, the sacred sexual energy force that would lift her to the ultimate plateau.

Kat counted down eighteen rotations on her breastbone before slipping her hands lower to run her fingertips around her nipples twenty-seven times, feeling them harden through the soft cotton of her top. But she was distracted by the worry that Dawn would wake up at any moment and she lost count between forty-five caresses to the lower belly and fifty-four light touches to the pubic bone.

'Look at me again.'

As she did so, a tiny money spider dropped between them on a long thread, thought the better of it and shot back up again. Kat stifled a laugh, forced back to the beginning of fifty-four touches.

Russ, who had been trying to hurry her along and had himself already reached seventy-two, was staring intently into her eyes and rocking rhythmically in the candlelight, *kundalini* clearly up and at 'em. In the candlelight, he looked both potent and poetic, his dark hair wild, unbuttoned shirt slipping off one shoulder to reveal the Celtic band tattoo on his upper arm. The Ravi Shankar CD he'd put on was jumping in the ancient player, catching on a refrain and repeating it like a nightclub DJ sampling it before releasing it to play again. It was weirdly discordant, but not unpleasant. Russ had called Tantra the LSD of mind-sex, so it seemed fitting.

'Three, two, one, *breathe* ... seventy-two, seventy-one, seventy ...' Cheating, Kat skipped a couple of chakras and went straight for the *swadishthani*, the second chakra which was right in with the action below the bikini wax. Even through loose cotton, she could feel the heat of excitement greet her, and flinched with surprise as it scorched up inside her almost instantly, like a flare going off. An equally hot blush stole across her cheeks as she gazed into Russ's dark eyes and felt her nipples buzzing.

His eyes intensified, and he nodded, rocking alongside her, matching her breaths. It was amazing.

There was a whine from the door as Daphne scraped to be let out, weak bladder at its limit.

'Ignore her,' Russ ordered.

Daphne whined again, scrabbling and spinning, rousing her deaf friend Maddie and triggering one of her barking frenzies.

'I'll have to let her out.' Kat stood up. 'She'll bark non-stop if I don't, and poor Dawn's still asleep. Shall I take her another cup of tea, do you think?'

'You've already brought three cold cups down after taking hot ones up. Be grateful she hasn't drunk them or she'd be scraping at the door like Daphne. Leave her be.'

Chapter 9

When Dawn woke up late in the morning, she was thankful at least that the rain had stopped hammering on the roof – and indeed dripping through it to ping and plop into the many bowls and buckets that had been placed around her room.

It took her several minutes to get her bearings, her head pounding. Had she been concussed?

She had no idea how she'd got into bed or where she'd been before that. She was still wearing her Topshop dress, along with a threadbare dressing-gown and bed-socks, none of which were hers.

Someone had placed a halogen heater close to the bed, although they'd clearly crept in to switch it off at some point, either to save on electricity or prevent an explosive watery short-circuit, or both. But the room was still warm enough for Dawn to slip out of bed without getting goose-bumps, stand still for a few moments to ensure her pounding head was with her, then pad across to draw back the sagging crocheted blanket that was acting as a curtain at the tiny, deep-set dormer window. She was surprised to find the sun gleaming through the trees, casting the lake and parkland in gold.

Then she gasped. The big house had disappeared beneath white sheets. It looked as though somebody had gift-wrapped it in gauze. It was covered with scaffolding. How could they have done that in one morning?

She groped for her smart-phone, which predictably had no reception but could tell her the time and day. Dawn sat down heavily on the bed. Somehow, she'd lost an entire day. What was more, the missing twenty-four hours had been St Valentine's Day.

She closed her eyes, trying to piece together the time-lapse jigsaw: her arrival, catching up with Kat, coming to the farm, meeting horrid Russ, then heading off for a meal in the pub. Had there been a meal? There was something to do with a dare, she was certain. And a bubbling green drink, although maybe she was thinking of a movie.

She couldn't remember the details of her evening in the pub at all. Dawn had clubbed her way around London in a haze of alcopops and ecstasy for years and never suffered a blackout like this one. This place had a very weird and wonderful vibe, she decided nervously, like Oz meets Salem.

The cry that came from outside her window made her jump so high she cracked her head on the low dormer ceiling. It was unearthly, agonized and urgent. Head and heart pounding, she tied the dressing-gown cord tighter and belted outside.

In the farmyard, Trevor the peacock regarded her beadily from the roof of Kat's muddy car and let out another agonized cry.

Dawn sagged against the door, wondering if she was going to pass out.

'You're awake!' Kat appeared from one of the lopsided out-buildings, wheeling an overloaded barrow, scarlet hair escaping from a beanie. 'I was about to check on you again. I tried waking you up with a cup of tea about an hour ago, but you were still totally dead.'

'I lost Valentine's Day! What the fuck happened?'

Laughing, Kat abandoned the barrow and splashed across the yard. 'You tried the scrumpy. Then Hopflask. Then brandy. Then – acting very much against advice – more Hopflask.'

'And?'

'Nobody survives Hopflask.'

'Did I sing?'

'Yup. Mostly Rihanna, but a smattering of Britney. But that was in the car on the way home, and you were only semi-conscious.'

'Oh, fuck, I was that wasted?'

'Do you remember meeting Dair Armitage? You talked to him for hours.'

'I remember absolutely nothing.'

'Oh, shit. I only let Russ convince me to leave you two chatting so long because he thought you'd find out something about Eardisford's new owner. We're pretty certain Dair knows more than he's letting on.'

'What are you talking about?'

Kat's big green eyes looked both guilty and frustrated. 'Jed the chef heard a rumour that the estate had been bought by someone called Seth from Yorkshire. When he Googled, all he came up with was an eighteenth-century cricketer and an old character from *Emmerdale Farm*. The story's probably a totally false trail, but the estate is definitely under new ownership and Dair knows who's bought it.'

Dawn rubbed her aching temples and eyed her friend apologetically. 'Even if Dair told me everything, I wouldn't have a clue.' She closed one eye as a brief, unpleasant flashback hit her. 'Was he carrying a gun?'

'Yup. Small, bald, yellow teeth, voice like Frankie Boyle.'

Dawn screwed up her face. 'No – I only remember the gun. And nice dogs. And a chin.'

'That's the one. I should warn you, he is now totally in love with you – look.' She pointed above Dawn's head.

Dawn glanced up and let out a scream as she saw two dead birds swinging from a hook.

'I *never* get a brace of pheasant,' Kat told her. 'You are something special. He's called in twice already this morning. I've told him you were meditating.'

'How quickly can you get me to the station? And you're packing too. I'm taking you out of this place, Kat. You've changed. You used to be so ...'

'Suicidally unhappy?'

'Before that. You were cocky, full of life ... you'd do anything for a dare.'

'What am I now?'

Striking a pose by the wheelbarrow, Kat had mud on one cheek and so much straw and dust in her beanie it looked like a termite mound on her head. The hair that was escaping, red as a rose petal, highlighted her winter paleness. Her wellies were patched up with electrical tape and she was wearing a sweatshirt promoting sheep wormers. She looked curiously, eccentrically beautiful.

Dawn gazed at her for a long time, hangover pinching, and saw that the big smile was no longer just a self-defence move. She had an incredible glow about her today. It was different from the old glow – gentler, more slow-burning, curiously serene – but it was undeniably there. She was genuinely relaxed. 'You're very rural,' she said lamely.

Kat took her hand. 'Let's check there's enough hot water for a shower and get you some breakfast. Then we can go riding with my friend Tina, if you're up to it.'

Dawn wasn't sure she was capable of putting a spoon into her mouth, let alone her foot into a stirrup, but it was amazing what a hot shower, a three-egg omelette and mountains of toast could achieve.

By the time they were walking through the dappled sunlight of the woods, trailed by the snuffling, panting pack of aged Lake Farm dogs, she had a real spring in her step, which turned into a nervous jog when Kat pointed out all the disturbed earth where the wild boar had been rooting. 'There's a seriously big male round here – the females are mostly at the other end of the estate; they live in groups called sounders, but the males winter out in this wood. You can hear them fighting at night sometimes. That and the stag bellowing – that's his handiwork.' She pointed at a tree stripped of bark. 'I've not seen him this year, but Russ has. He's as big as an ox with antlers like a dozen bayonets.'

Tina's little stableyard was at the far end of the village, and they stopped off at the tiny Eardisford church graveyard en route so that Kat could put fresh flowers in the little vase on Constance's grave. Eardisford's last chatelaine had been buried in the Mytton family plot in a private ceremony to which Kat had not been invited. Yet she was now the only one who visited the grave regularly. Today she had brought a spray of snow-drops.

'Constance loved them. They're late this year.' She cleared away the dead leaves from the plinth and read the lettering. 'We had the same birthday. She thought that was wonderful.' She looked up at Dawn, eyes bright. 'I told her what happened with Nick, stuff I haven't told anybody.'

Dawn was dying to ask what that was, but it seemed disre-spectful when they were standing over the grave of the dear departed confidante, and Kat was talking again now.

'She might have been old, but she was seriously sussed. Nothing shocked her. She said a lot worse went on among the army officers in India. She offered me sanctuary here as well as her animals. She left the farm in my care on the understanding that I look after them – they're all ancient, so it's not a job with long-term prospects, but I can stay for as long as I live or until I marry. Constance talked me through it very carefully. She didn't expect me to stay long, but she asked me to promise her that I would do two things before my tenure was up.'

'And they were?'

'To ride the Bolt.'

Dawn struck a pose, eyebrows shooting up.

'Not *that* Bolt. It's a horse-race thing. That's why I'm learn-ing to ride.'

'And the other?'

'To marry for love.'

'But I thought that invalidated her legacy, the sanctuary, Lake Farm . . . '

'She knew exactly what she was saying, Dawn. That's the whole point. When I'm ready to get married, I won't need a sanctuary any more.'

'What about the animals? Won't they need you?'

'I'm not about to marry anybody, Dawn. They have nothing to worry about.'

'So is Russ . . . ?'

'We're taking it *very* slowly.' The big, easy smile was back and she hugged herself happily before leading the way back through the churchyard.

Dawn wasn't sure about the 'Tireless' nickname for Tina, the riding instructor, who had a thin, tangled blond bob that looked like the mane of a toy lion, very dark bags under her eyes and seemed even sleepier than the baby strapped into the car seat on the far side of the arena rails, but she was certainly multi-tasking. As well as teaching her regular pupil and visiting friend, she was constantly on the phone or texting, checking on her kids – there was a small boy on a pedal tractor and a brat on a pony to contend with too. When she wasn't shouting at them, she was shouting at the girl groom to turn out or bring in horses, berating the two dogs that seemed intent on eating the muck heap or baiting Kat's oldies, yelling instructions to a farrier who was hot-shoeing under an archway and – most of all – shouting encouragement at Kat.

'Brilliant!' Her voice had the valley-crossing shrillness of a hunting horn, softened by a slight Herefordshire accent. 'Feel that bum coming under you and the strength in your thighs! Inside leg to outside hand, remember? Don't forget to breathe!'

'I won't.' Kat moved into a ragged canter on Tina's small, very speedy pony. 'I'm finally getting the hang of breathing.'

Dawn noted that while her friend might be breathing okay, she was riding appallingly. She knew Kat had been learning for months, but she was totally uncoordinated, losing all her natural grace and clinging on like a kid on a banana raft being towed through big waves. She got maximum points for enthusiasm and effort, but none for balance or rhythm, and Tina was clearly struggling to make headway despite heaping on praise.

'You're doing brilliantly! We'll have you in the Ladies' Race at the point-to-point at this rate. Keep your leg on and go large.' She took a call on her phone and started squawking at somebody about a hunt meet.

Dawn, who had hoped to go for a gentle hack alongside the river, let her cobby little horse walk around the sand school while she took advantage of the phone signal to check her messages, which conveniently got her out of flying around at full tilt as Kat was doing.

'You'll have to go a lot faster than this to ride the Bolt!' Tina called. 'That's barely working canter.'

Dawn took a discreet photo of Kat flying past with her arms around the pony's neck, about to text it to the Watford posse, then stopped herself. Kat didn't deserve to be made a fool of. She was determined to do this and she needed loyalty and support. She also needed a better riding instructor. Having wandered out of the sand school to sniff her baby's nappy, Tina had left the gate open and the pony Kat was riding charged straight through it and headed back to its stable. To her credit, Kat found this incredibly funny and promised to work hard on her brakes next time.

'So what exactly is the Bolt?' Dawn asked Kat, after the lesson had come to its premature halt and they walked along the sunken lane that led back to the village.

'It's Mytton family tradition, although nobody's tried it for years, not since Constance, I think. The idea is to gallop from one end of the estate at Duke's Wood to the Hereford road at the other between the quarter chimes of the church clock. It's about three miles, so fifteen minutes should be easy at a good hunting pace, but the horse and rider have to swim across a three-acre lake, which makes it almost impossible. Generations of Mytton men have tried and failed to make the time and win the Eardisford Purse, including Constance's father, Charles. Only a handful succeeded.'

'What's the Eardisford Purse?'

'I never asked.'

'Sounds bloody dangerous. Why would she dare you to do that, especially if she knew about your fear of water, and what happened with Nick? The accident . . . the river . . . ' She trailed off.

'She wanted me to start living again, especially so because she was dying. I'm sure she thought she'd live to see it, but I started learning to ride and just wasn't good enough. I'm still not.'

'You'll get the hang of it soon,' Dawn said encouragingly.

'Not for the Bolt. Especially not on Sri.'

'The horse with the funny ears?'

'Sri hasn't been ridden for years, but it's what Constance wanted. She rode a Marwari horse when she did it. She set a new record. I don't think I'll ever do it. Even supposing I can get the hang of riding, I'm too scared to swim the lake. I can't even row on it without having a panic attack.'

'Was what happened in the river with Nick really an accident?' Dawn asked quietly.

Kat threw a stick for one of the dogs. 'Do you mind if we don't talk about it?'

Trying to hide how hurt she was that Kat would rather confide in a nonagenarian nutcase with a penchant for impossible challenges than herself, Dawn went into an over-reactive flurry of 'No worry, of course, sure! Not a problem!'

Kat quickly changed the subject to Marwari horses, the rare Indian breed that Constance had been instrumental in introducing to Great Britain to help guarantee its future. 'They were almost driven into extinction during British occupation – the army preferred Thoroughbreds, and thought the Marwari a common native that was only suited for hard labour. But they're a brilliant ridden horse, with the endurance of an Arab and the fearlessness of an Iberian. They're proud too – they'd go into battle without looking back if you asked them to, but that loyalty has to be earned. Sri totally ignored me for six months.'

'I worked with a beauty therapist like that once,' Dawn sympathized. She loved horses, but she preferred them waiting clean and tacked up a short drive from the M25.

The walk back to Lake Farm was even more circuitous than the one via the graveyard as Kat needed to divert to a grand black and white timbered farmhouse with a lot of decorative, fluffy-legged bantams strutting around between its saddle stones.

'Miriam's place,' she explained. 'I promised I'd drop off that solicitor's letter.'

Then she took a big box of eggs she'd been hawking around with her to Russ's uncle and aunt (no sign of Russ in the apple orchards, Dawn noted), and finally she stopped at the village hall to write 'Fully Subscribed' across the poster on the noticeboard advertising her boxercise self-defence classes.

Now bow-legged and aching, her hangover back with a vengeance, Dawn almost crawled the mile back to Lake Farm, not caring if a wild boar charged her – in fact, she could have done with a helpful shove to keep moving. 'I don't know how you can take the pace here. I'm going to need to lie down for a week to recover when I get back to Watford.'

'You'll visit again, won't you?'

'Definitely.' Dawn held open a gate, leaning heavily on it as she got her puff back. 'Sign me up for that class when you get an opening. I'm right onside if this new landowner needs fighting. You can't let this place go.'

'You really mean that?'

'It's amazing, Kat. You're amazing. It needs decent central heating and a bloody good make-over, but it's got something magical about it. It's a healing place.'

'Come and open a health spa here,' Kat said excitedly, distracted by a large cardboard box left on the old milk churn stand at the yard entrance, from which small squeaks were emitting. 'Oh, bugger. Not more.'

'Kittens!' Dawn laughed delightedly when they opened the top to find a squirming mass of ginger fluff, white paws and pink pads and noses.

'People keep abandoning unwanted litters with us.'

'Well, you *are* an animal sanctuary.'

'We're not really set up as a rescue centre. It's bad enough that Russ keeps luring in pheasants and finding broken-winged ducks and myxy rabbits to try to bring back to life. We don't have the facilities or any way of rehoming them. I'll take these to the local RSPCA centre. We'll drop them off when I drive you to catch your train later.'

'I'll have one!'

'You don't even know where you'll be living.'

But Dawn had already picked the smallest, squirmiest kitten from the box, so tiny it fitted into the palm of one hand as she dropped kisses on its pink nose.

Kat looked at her anxiously. 'Are really sure you want a cat?'

'I promised the old Watford gang that I'd bring our lovely Kat back.' She grinned, pressing the soft orange bundle to her chin. 'I can't let them down.'

*

Miriam was so astonished by the contents of the solicitor's letter, which Kat still hadn't read, that she called an emergency meeting of the sanctuary committee and hurriedly baked lemon shortcake to offer with the coffee.

Convinced that the call to arms had come, the elderly farming sisters, Pru and Cyn, arrived at Lake Farm in their Land Rover, towing a trailer loaded with rolls of barbed wire and electric fencing to strengthen the farm's defences, along with sandbags and a generator in case Dair's dirty tricks resumed. The older and bossier Pru was a tall, thin stick of no-nonsense discipline topped with a glossy iron-grey pudding basin, like a German *Stahlhelm*, while Cyn was a small, excitable ball of romantically wild ideas with a mousy, white-rimmed bun like an iced doughnut and watery blue eyes – they were rumoured to have had different fathers. Today the spinster sisters were dressed in matching country khaki and tweed camouflage fatigues, ready for action and united in a fierce determination to protect the sanctuary.

Following hard on their heels, Frank Bingham-Ince had brought with him an ancient klaxon that could raise the alarm to the village and, indeed, most of Herefordshire, while Tireless Tina had home-made mustard spray and spare lead ropes to walk the animals to safety. Russ and Mags, who weren't officially invited because they weren't on the committee, had muscled in to offer support, talking loudly of protests and direct action.

Miriam silenced them: the spirit of the letter, she told them, couldn't have been more co-operative. Standing at one end of the long kitchen table, like a big-busted ship's figurehead in a Hermès scarf with bright coral lipstick, worn in Frank's honour, she précised the letter: 'The new owners of Eardisford would like to apologize for any inconvenience during the restoration

111

work on the house and parkland,' she informed them. 'As a gesture of goodwill, they have made a donation of ten thousand pounds to the sanctuary.'

Kat's jaw dropped. 'Does it say who they are?'

She shook her head. 'The payment is being made through solicitors.'

Kat was opening the door to let out Daphne. She jumped as she found a box of venison waiting on the step and Dair backing away, the peak of his flat cap down to the tip of his nose.

'I can see you've got company,' he said gruffly.

'I heard he's a businessman called Stefan,' Cyn was saying, the village whispers having mutated wildly between the pub and the sisters' remote farm in the last forty-eight hours. 'Or was it a Welshman called Gareth?'

'One of the ladies at the tennis club told me it's a film star called Ethan.' Miriam sounded excited. 'What have you heard, Kat?'

'A Yorkshireman called Seth.' She raised her eyebrows at Dair.

'His real name is Arjan Singh,' Dair breathed, so that only Kat could hear him, the others still unaware of his presence. 'But I didn't tell you that.' With a nod, he hurried away.

Chapter 10

'You didn't get the television series, Dougie.' Abe sounded poleaxed when he called his client. 'Another dude will carry the

Confederate flag into three million homes coast to coast.' The role had gone to a far more experienced actor, he explained. 'I just came off the phone to the casting agent and, man, am I pissed. This morning that part was yours. Now the producers have stepped in and cast someone else over her head.'

Hearing the name, Dougie was far from consoled. 'He's about a hundred, Abe, and gay as fuck!'

'He's A-list. You're not,' Abe concluded philosophically. 'But I have something else cooking, something with Kiki. You two are dynamite on screen.'

Dougie held the phone close to his head as he stalked out of the crowded bar at the ski lodge to get some air. The entrance foyer was a forest of heavy wooden folk-art sculptures that their host had been trying to flog to the cast and crew all fortnight. He leaned against a cross-eyed snarling bear, willing it to come to life and swallow him up. The civil war series had been his get-out-of-jail-free card.

He narrowed his eyes suspiciously, remembering who else had known about the project. 'Have you heard of somebody called Seth?'

'Seth McFarlane?'

'Just Seth. One name. Like Sting or Bono.'

'Yeah, sure. Dotcom billionaire worth more zeroes than the binary for my fucking IQ. He owns half of Bollywood nowadays. He's on board a few projects over here too. We're talking *major* investment.'

'Does that include television?'

'I can find out, but it won't get you the part.'

Hanging up, Dougie listened to the raucous partying in the bar. It was their last day on location. Tomorrow he would head back to LA. His little tattooed runner had been shadowing him all day, her eyes full of tears. Kiki was bombarding his phone with messages, saying how much she was looking forward to seeing him.

His phone rang again.

'Okay, what's going on, Dougie?' Abe was riled. 'Seth's just bought the production company that's making the series. It's a shit-hot investment and this civil war thing is tipped to be huge – but you probably don't want to hear that. So what's he got against you?'

'I've never even met him. His assistant turned up here and offered me a job.'

'What is it?' Abe smelt his ten per cent. 'Why don't I know about this? What's the role?'

'I'm not taking it,' Dougie said emphatically.

His agent let out a worried sigh. 'I have to warn you that if you turn this guy down I don't think you'll be working for the rest of the year.'

But when Dougie explained that taking the job would mean Abe getting ten per cent of the return from a hunt master's guarantee, an old-fashioned upfront payment that must last a year and pay for horses, hounds and hunt staff as well as his own living, his agent laughed incredulously, and told him to hang tough. 'I'll find out what the hell's going on. And I'll get back on the case with the Kiki project. Her people are super-keen. The backers are all family so nobody will buy them out of it. If it's as big as *High Noon*, it'll pay for the wedding and one fuck-off palace of a house in the hills. You'll even have space for all those horses of yours, kid.'

Dougie's heart sank. 'What if I say I don't want to work with Kiki again?'

'I'd say why let this Seth guy try to screw your career when you can do it yourself?'

*

The following morning, as the cast and crew packed their bags into taxis and coaches ready to head to the airport, a helicopter swept down towards them and Dougie groaned, bracing himself for an argument with Seth's emissary – right now he wanted to hurl snowballs at her and push her off a mountain. But it turned out it was just the transport booked to take the Welsh lead actor to the airport in style.

The little tattooed runner clung to Dougie as he left. He'd spent the previous night with her after drowning his sorrows in the bar and had been so drunk that he couldn't remember any of it.

Tired, pale and unshaven, with big blue smudges under his big blue eyes, he knew he looked a wreck, yet she gazed up at him as though she was worshipping a god. This is an industry full of false idols who abuse their position, he thought savagely.

'Is this goodbye, Mr Happy Ever After?' She used her nickname for him, lower lip trembling.

'It's never Happy Ever After, darling.' He sighed and gave her a final kiss before clambering into the car. He still didn't know her name.

On the way to the airport his phone rang, the voice newsreader cool. 'I gather you are now available for work, Dougie.'

Dougie had planned to play it super-cool if Seth's assistant made contact, to match her monotone with a faint sprinkling of 007 irony, to have charm on his tongue but murder in his eyes as he told her, categorically, to stuff her job. But he'd never been good at controlling his anger when his blood was up. Neither was he very articulate once his heart rate hit three figures, preferring a physical vent like overturning tables or running up mountains. Kiki, who was fond of stoking him to melting point, said Dougie argued like a Daniel Day-Lewis with Tourette's.

'You bitch! You fucking bloody bitch! And your boss is a fucking bastard. You're both bloody evil. Go fuck yourselves.' He hung up.

'Spot of trouble?' asked the actor he was sharing a taxi with.

'Job offer.' He cleared his throat, glaring out of the window. 'Not for me. Type casting.'

The phone rang again. The monotone was warmer, almost seductive. 'What would your fiancée think if she knew you'd been sleeping with one of the crew on location for the past fortnight?'

'Why not tell her and we'll find out? Now fuck off.'

When Dougie arrived back in LA, the city felt more alien to him than ever. Warm as a British summer day even in February, only the fake smiles were cold and glacier white. He wanted to keep Europe's chill in his bones. He longed for his team of horses close by, and he priced up flying them over and stabling them in Burbank not far from the condo he shared with Kiki, but it was totally beyond his pocket. Perhaps that was no bad thing, he reflected, after his first week back in the city. He had no idea how long he'd be hanging around. It wasn't fair to shunt them here only to move on again, and the Burbank barn was probably too close for comfort. If the wind was in the right direction, they could have pricked their black ears and heard the recently engaged couple hurling abuse at one another.

This was nothing new for Kiki and Dougie: it was a highly charged form of foreplay. They were always white hot together in bed, their passion involving ferocious arguments and intimate making up. It was exhausting at times, but they had both become addicted to it, like a never-ending game. Having determined to break the habit when he was away filming, Dougie now found he couldn't. He was angry at losing out on a big role, at being blackmailed, being ordered by Abe to put up and shut up, and at Kiki's constant lectures about the need to polish his 'talent diamond'. The petty argument that had erupted because he'd arrived home hung-over with just a bunch of thirty-dollar roses raged on long after the petals had dropped off.

It was always worse when they were kept captive in close proximity, particularly when Kiki was rehearsing for a new role and needed to let off steam. Although technically they had cohabited for more than a year, filming commitments meant they had lived under the same roof for barely a tenth of that time, and the apartment Kiki's parents had bought her when she was first breaking into the big time was far too small for a relationship that thrived on big scenes. They'd rented the Glendale condo as a temporary stop-gap, but the glass-walled box at the top of an apartment block now made Dougie felt like a toy top-shelved for safe keeping.

It suited Kiki, who didn't drink anything but twice-boiled water, barely ate more than clear soup and had a liking for see-through clothes; she was transparently needy emotionally and just as demanding domestically. Her mind and body always whirred at warp speed, needing constant activity to fuel them. Here, there was a gym and a pool in the basement, a macrobiotic café and therapy suite on the first floor, and lightning-fast WiFi throughout the building.

Dougie, who preferred to roar in a cave during times of crisis, felt like a zoo animal in a glass enclosure. For the first time since they had been together, he was out of work. He'd learned the day after returning that the hobgoblin and fairy fantasy action movie had hit serious financial difficulties during its location shoot, and the five weeks' studio work he'd thought he was coming back to had now been postponed until a new backer could be found; rumour had it the predicted cost of CGI made it impossible to see a profit and the film would never be finished.

The new project Abe had been talking up, spearheaded by Kiki's film-producing uncle and funded by the family coffers, was months away – they hadn't even chosen a script. Kiki eagerly piled up classic plays on his side of the bed and urged him back to acting class, promising they were going to be bigger than Brangelina when he'd polished that diamond. Dougie suspected the project was largely leverage to make him behave himself as he went on a trail of readings, meetings and screen tests, but even though he chased every action-movie bit part Abe put him forward for, his tetchiness won him few recalls. The Everett Effect was hard to sell when his charm was in short supply. Mostly, he paced around at home going increasingly stir-crazy, planning his exit strategy.

He heard no more from Dollar, which surprised him, given her boss's efforts to clear Dougie's diary, although he would have turned her down flat had she repeated the bizarre job offer. He refused to be coerced, which Kiki still struggled to grasp. Now that Dougie had time on his hands, the differences between them had never been more apparent. She expected him to be butler-cum-personal-trainer and sparring partner, roles for which he was ill-equipped. Home was Kiki's refuge and had to be perfectly ordered; Dougie treated it like a temporary stop-off. She considered her body a temple, requiring daily worship; he only worked out if a role demanded it. She thrived on arguments; his increasing lack of patience with them – and her – just fired her up more. The more detached he became, the more engaged she seemed to want to be.

'Why haven't I got a ring yet?' she complained petulantly.

'The diamond's not cut and polished,' he snapped.

In truth, he didn't have enough money left to buy a ring, let alone the heart to want to. Nobody working on the goblins film had been paid anything yet. His last few thousand dollars had gone to Rupe to pay the yard rent in Buckinghamshire. He suggested taking on some stunt work to help pay his way, secretly longing to be back in the saddle, but Kiki said it looked bad on his résumé and she didn't want the apartment smelling of horse.

'It's already like living with an untrained hound, baby!' she joked shrilly.

'I'd rather go to dog-training classes than acting ones – at least I might get a sausage and learn how to sit still.'

Dougie's natural instinct to sleep late, ride all day and play all night brought him under direct fire as Kiki's insatiable thirst for high drama, stoked up by starring in back-to-back gun-toting thrillers, required intense action at home as well as on set. She found the undomesticated hound easy to goad into a snarling, hackles-drawn frenzy. The couple's constant arguments meant they made up with ever-more rapacious sex, but the intimacy became increasingly aggressive. Starved of affection, with little to do, the legendary Everett waggy-tailed wit was quick to wear away.

After one particularly vicious argument, in which she told him that his inability to act truthfully was down to his mother's rejection, he'd finally had enough. He threw some clothes into a bag, ready to fly home, but Kiki locked herself into the bathroom and threatened to cut her wrists if he left so he was forced to unpack. He didn't think for a moment that she was seriously suicidal, but Kiki in full cry had to win an argument at all costs, and he didn't know how far she'd go to achieve that.

The next day, by way of apology, she bought him a horse, a

magnificent Friesian stallion called Zephyr, whose curly mane reached down to his knees from a thick arched neck as glossy black as a raven's wing. Dougie was amazed and humbled by such beauty but he longed to do something about the eight horses he'd left in England, not play with a new toy here, bought to keep him in check.

'*Now* you can buy me a ring,' Kiki insisted brightly.

Dougie had grown up around horses: he knew all about Trojan ones and looking in the mouths of gift ones. He told Kiki he couldn't accept Zephyr. She refused to listen. They had another furious row. She insisted he'd feel better when he got another acting role. 'We all go through this, baby. Actors live with rejection like physicians live with death. You have to work through it.'

Dougie knew it wasn't the rejection he was struggling to live with: it was Kiki. But later that day, Abe called and said, in his darkest tone, 'Do *not* break this up before the Oscars, kid. Trust me, you are *seriously* hot property right now.'

'So that's why I feel like I'm living in a blast furnace.'

While feathers flew in private, the press were feeding ever more ravenously off the celebrity lovebird fusion. Kiki's uncle had released just enough early rumours of the couple sharing the big screen again to get all cameras focused upon them. Their appearance at the Oscars similarly secured front pages across the globe as Kiki wowed in nude Christian Dior, flashing a rare public smile with the huge yellow-diamond Neil Lane engagement ring that Dougie had no idea how he was going to pay for. The couple scorched along the red carpet sizzling with sexual chemistry, commentators loving the way their eyes and bodies slid constantly together, the beauty and glamour, and the smudges beneath their eyes that hinted at hot, sleepless nights spent pleasuring one another.

He and Kiki might be white hot in publicity terms, but Dougie knew that his horses wouldn't eat if he didn't land a decent part soon, and his debts were racking up big-time. Despite Abe's confidence, the work offers had really dried up. Being passed over at the last minute for the big network series seemed to have sent a nervous tremor through the casting grapevine about Dougie, with the notion that he was better known for his off-screen romances than any on-screen one. Rumours of the Nelson family 'buying' their beloved Kiki's fiancé a role in an upcoming project didn't help.

The post-Oscars publicity was the wrong sort: Dougie was seen as an opportunist and a chancer. Like all rumours with a seed of truth in them, it took root as thorns grew up in his path. After weeks of recalls and meetings, there was still nothing new on the horizon beyond the vague promise of the joint project. All he currently had to keep the wolf from the door was an aftershave modelling contract, and a trendy French film company had optioned him early for a sexy cavalier role, which didn't start filming until next year. He didn't relish having to learn his part in French.

'We needed something in the diary in to make you look good,' Abe had explained. 'You know how fickle this town is. The Frenchies love you and they always secure talent early, which is great.' He'd also been doing his research into Seth, he said.

'I burned that bridge, and I had no intention of crossing it anyway.'

'It's the fucking Golden Gate, kid. It won't burn so easy. You know how much money they're offering? It's big.'

Dougie groaned. 'So they've approached you?'

'I approached them.' When Dougie howled in outrage, Abe bulldozed on, 'I figure we can use this to our advantage, kid. You could do this thing while we're waiting for Kiki's project to come together. I think there's a book in it, maybe a documentary, and a stack of publicity. It'll take the heat off you and Kiki, too. You don't want to lose her, Dougie.'

Dougie's eyes narrowed. 'I told you I'm not interested in what Seth has to offer, so whatever you've said to them, forget it.'

'They won't discuss it with me.' Abe sounded affronted. 'I told them, "I'm the kid's agent, it's my *job* to know everything," but they say it's a restricted negotiation.'

Dougie remembered the electronic document he'd signed at the ice hotel guaranteeing confidentiality. He'd certainly said nothing to Abe about the 'marry her' challenge. It all seemed too fantastical. His usual day job was much more down to earth. 'Get me a role where I'm galloping around in full armour killing peasants,' he told his agent, 'and preferably *not* speaking French.'

'Okay. I'll see what I can do. If we get a better offer from one of the big players, we'll lose the cavalier.'

Dougie, who was being very cavalier right now, longed to do just that. He remained with Kiki largely on his agent's advice, like a fading star struggling on in a bad soap opera that refuses to write him out. Such duplicity wasn't his style – he would normally bring the pain to a swift end, either by walking out or, more likely, by behaving so badly that she would make a dramatic slammed-door exit. Their relationship seemed constantly to be one hurled insult away from the end, and although the sex was still strangely, edgily sensational, it chipped away at his sense of fair play. But nobody played very fair in LA, as Dougie was learning. In his darker moments, he'd started wondering again if acting was really for him.

The confidence-knock of not finding work was not helped by Kiki starting filming the studio scenes of a very racy thriller in which she was starring opposite a hotly tipped Glaswegian actor whose cachet was rising as fast as Dougie's was falling. The edgy, craggy, working-class young Scot, beloved of critics and art-house directors, was the polar opposite of charming, blue-eyed, silver-spoon Dougie. He and Kiki bonded from the start, both devoted to their art, talking about their characters for hours.

'It's okay, I'm not attracted to Finlay physically,' Kiki assured Dougie, who secretly wished she was, giving him an excuse to walk.

Dougie knew his relationship was a time bomb and its detonation would kill his career if he didn't do something to defuse it, but his default was to seek distraction rather than a solution. In the old days, he'd have got drunk and got laid. His friends in Hollywood were expat Brits who loved to party, but Kiki disapproved of them, thinking they led him astray and lowered his ambitions, so they'd been pushed out of his life months ago. Now that his agent had Dougie under strict instructions to behave himself and keep his nose clean, rather than call up his drinking cronies, he called his old stunt contacts instead. Soon he was back on a horse every day, training youngsters for a friend who ran one of the biggest teams in Hollywood. Having languished in idle luxury since Dougie had tried unsuccessfully to give him back, Zephyr moved to the stunt team's yard too, and Dougie marvelled at his talent. He was among the most exciting horses he'd ever sat on, a big brave show-off of explosive power who lived to learn.

Riding was Dougie's solace. He relished his hours in the saddle in the dusty cool of the indoor arena or out in the sun. He had no desire to act Hamlet on Broadway, he reminded himself, as he sharpened his old skills. He just wanted to be a great performer, and if that meant jumping through hoops, he'd far rather do it on a horse. Unsuccessful auditions were demoralizing, but he had only to put his foot in a stirrup to lift his heart. And it was great to have a few dollars in his pocket from work riding, however tiny a drop they were in his sea of debt.

Kiki was not impressed. Despite grudgingly admitting that a tanned, sober and driven Dougie was better than having him loaf around the condo waiting for the phone to ring, she insisted that he'd never get another movie role if he stopped auditioning. He must also take those acting classes, she urged. She talked about co-star Finlay's amazing talent, which took her breath away. '*He*'s Stanislavski-trained, baby.'

'I'm Klosters ski-trained,' Dougie said idly. 'Do you want to fuck him?'

'Of course not!' Her blue eyes were huge and hurt. 'What makes you say that?'

He knew he was getting nastier, but her constant digs about his acting stripped him of his *joie de vivre*.

After a depressing second reading for a sci-fi thriller in which he would say three lines before being disembowelled by something that looked like a sink plunger, Dougie finally received a call from Dollar asking if he would like to reconsider the job in England in the light of his agent's interest, which 'incidentally breaks a legally binding confidentiality contract forbidding you to discuss our meeting with anybody'.

Stalking towards his cab, he snarled, 'I will not be bullied. I will not be blackmailed. I will not be bribed. I will not be b –' he struggled to think of a fourth B word '– bloody bollocking badgered, okay?' He clambered in.

'Is that one of the new restaurants off Wilshire, buddy?' asked his driver.

'Spoken like a true huntsman,' Dollar purred in his ear, but there was a slight edge to her monotone now. 'I apologize if you feel my methods are too forthright. Seth has also suggested that perhaps I was a little over-zealous, but this is my pet project and I believe that you are uniquely positioned to take it on. You will not regret it. The offer remains open.'

Dougie watched the city slide by as he headed out towards Burbank, a haze of stark lines, glittering windows and grey asphalt veins, a few dusty trees lining the sidewalks, like pall-bearers to the polluted skies. The irony was, he would love nothing more than to escape to the British countryside right now.

When Dougie's father called him to bark questions about work, wealth and health – a monthly check-up he always peppered with enticing hunting reports – Dougie was scorched with homesickness. Vaughan wanted a favour: a successful expatriate sitcom star with whom he'd been at Oxford wanted a medieval-themed dragon-slaying display for his teenage daughter's birthday. Having known Dougie since he was a boy, he'd asked for him to perform personally. 'Knows you're an amazing talent in the saddle.'

Abe advised against it: 'We don't want you to be seen as a pantomime artist, kid.'

But Dougie, who had never been a snob about what work he took – when he'd run the stunt team in England he'd been as happy to perform at the county shows as the high-budget advertising shoots – was looking forward to riding into battle in full armour again, albeit on a perfectly striped Bel Air lawn. He would take Zephyr, he decided, eschewing his friend's offer of more experienced stunt horses, although he accepted the help of two of the team's Mexican stunt riders to take some of the youngsters he'd been training that would benefit from the day out. His decision to ignore Abe's advice predictably caused another flaming row with Kiki, who was setting aside the entire day to beautify herself for a big industry celebration that same evening: 'You promised you'd come to the Du Ponts' party with me!'

'I'll be through in plenty of time for that.'

'It's beneath you doing trick-riding gigs like this!'

'Why? It's fun, and it's just a teenager's birthday party, for God's sake. I'm hardly going to bump into Spielberg.'

'How do you think it makes me look? My fiancé's a children's party entertainer now!'

The row raged on, finally ending up in bed where he did things no children's party entertainer should know and which thrilled Kiki but left him exhausted the following day, as he loaded horses into the float to drive to Beverly Hills.

Even tired and bloody-minded, the fast-riding knight in shining armour was a knock-out. Dougie might have no ambition to perform the Bard onstage, but in an open field he had just as much charisma as any Shakespearean hero. With Zephyr as his charger, near-mythical in his beauty, he delighted the crowd with his jousting skills, knocking one of his Mexican assistants unceremoniously out of the saddle many times before slaying the other who was Roman-riding the two Iberian horses in a vast tent-like dragon's costume. Their host gave him a hefty tip so that Dougie could afford to bung his co-riders fat bonuses afterwards, apologizing for the bruises. In return, when they got back to the barn, the Mexicans offered to wash and bed down the horses then clean the tack so that he could rush off for his date with Kiki.

'She breathe fire if you late, huh?' laughed one.

'Always handy for lighting a cigar.' He gave them a James Bond quip, knowing they'd love it and fall about.

Before leaving, he gave Zephyr a pat and blew softly on his

muzzle. 'I take it back about gift horses.' He kissed the animal's nose. 'You are God-given, mate.'

Kiki was waiting at the condo, already dressed and styled, tissues flapping from her neckline like an exotic insect's wings. 'You're late! The car will be here in five minutes! Go change!'

'You look beautiful, darling.' Grinning, still high from the day, Dougie sauntered to the shower, knowing this was a challenge for which he was more than a match.

By the time the car rolled up outside, he was in full tux, coolly tugging his white cuffs in line with the black ones. Floppy-haired, clean-shaven and only mildly damp beneath the starched dress shirt, he was scented with Safari rather than the awful aftershave he was supposed to be promoting, although he would hint that that was what it was if anybody asked. He looked every inch the immaculate, if rather naughty, English gent. 'Ready, darling?'

Kiki's pale eyes darkened as she looked him over, blinking in surprise, partly that he had performed the transformation too fast for her to criticize, and partly because he looked so good. 'You'll do. Let's go.'

They were attending the fortieth wedding anniversary of her current movie's elderly executive producer, Harry Du Pont, an Oscar-winning Hollywood giant who had one of the longest-serving industry marriages. All who knew him were well aware that his sexual taste was under eighteen, dark-skinned and male, but tonight was all about red, sparkling glamour.

'Oh, look, Finlay's already here!' Kiki said, with carefully modulated surprise as soon as they'd made it pass the press pack.

'Let's go and say hi.' Dougie took her arm, surprised to find her dragging her feet.

The Glaswegian actor was a dark, kilted shadow at the main

bar, radiating closed set desires. He clearly hadn't brought a date, and his eyes tracked Kiki from the moment she walked in. She couldn't look at him at all.

He's in love with her, Dougie realized hollowly. That's more than I am.

As the party wore on, Kiki and her co-star moved in different groups but Finlay watched her like a hawk. Dougie supposed he could charitably assume it was a method-actor research thing, given the script demanded that his character was obsessed with hers, as well as demanding they spent most of the movie naked, gasping, beautifully backlit and connected at the groin with modesty pouches artfully hidden. Dougie's skin had always been a lot thicker than his head, and he guessed that ignoring the dagger looks Finlay was now shooting at him was the most gentlemanly strategy. As he escorted Kiki around Hollywood royalty, his smile and charm stayed on show in a repeating loop while his mind wandered. He was in play as bodyguard fiancé tonight: Kiki needed a show of strength to back Finlay off. That made him tetchier than ever.

'Hey, you're Kiki's English lord.' A delighted crew member bounded up. 'We're all dying to meet you! I'm Erin. Do you *really* have a title?'

Kiki had boasted about something he always underplayed. 'I was born an Honourable, but given my father will almost certainly cut me out of his will, that probably makes me a dishonourable.' He trotted out the stock line with a modest smile and held out his hand. 'Dougie Everett.'

'OHMYGOD, you sound like Hugh Grant. Is that put on?'

'Trust me, he sounds like that twenty-four/seven.' Kiki smirked, her pet bounder performing as she wanted. 'Excuse me, I must just ask Beano about tomorrow's call times.'

'She is *so* amazing.' Erin watched her go. 'And she talks about you *all* the time. Wait until you meet Delphine. Her grandfather was English.' The introductions were soon coming thick and fast as the cast and crew of Kiki's movie clamoured to meet the honourable Dougie.

Their hostess, Mimi Du Pont, weighed in like a Chinese Budei in a fright wig, her cosmetically lifted smile turning her face into a mask. She was towing a lean whip of Mumbai sex appeal behind her, no doubt one of her husband's *inamorati* who would be passed off as a PA. 'We are *so* excited to welcome you, Dougie. My friend here is a *huge* fan of your acting.'

Before Mimi could introduce them, there was a loud shriek nearby, followed by the sound of a sharp slap being administered to a square-jawed, stubbled face. 'Take that back, Finlay, you fucking bastard!'

Dougie glanced wearily over his shoulder to see Kiki doing her hyperventilating-breathing-and-wobbling-lipped number as she and the Scot glared at one another, both overacting like mad. He let out a deep sigh and turned back to his companions. 'Will you excuse me?'

Before he stepped away, a business card landed in his palm and a dark hand closed over it to administer a shoulder-dislocating shake. 'Another time.'

'Absolutely.' Dougie nodded, noticing distractedly that the Indian man with his hostess had unusual grey eyes. He pocketed the card and went to deal with Kiki.

Whether she intended to make him or Finlay jealous was uncertain, but Dougie could tell it was engineered – he could almost see the Meccano bolts holding the scene together as he stepped into it. 'Is everything okay, darling?' he asked, uncomfortably aware that he sounded even more like Hugh Grant. He'd be doing the twinkle-eyed grimace at any moment.

'Fine!' she said loudly, for public consumption, before drawing him to one side and stage-whispering, 'Finlay's just asked me to go to bed with him.' When she looked up at him, her expression was innocent outrage, but her eyes flashed wickedly.

Registering her need for some chest-beating action, Dougie glanced over his shoulder at Finlay. The Glaswegian was poised for his cue, still standing his ground, dark eyes turbulent, clearly very deeply in role, but wary enough of Dougie's prior claim and superior muscle tone not to make the first aggressive move.

Still in Hugh mode, reluctant to take a head-butt, he turned back to Kiki and muttered, 'I thought you'd already spent this week in bed together, or doesn't it count when it's being filmed?'

'Why do you *never* taking anything seriously?' she hissed. 'Not even our relationship. I need your help here. You're my fiancé. Finlay's all over me like a rash.'

'What do you want me to do? Apply Sudocrem to you both?'

His phone began to ring in his pocket. He reached for it, relieved to have a temporary respite.

'Don't answer that!' demanded Kiki, furious to have her scene interrupted. 'Answer that and we're through, Dougie!'

There it was: his get-out-of-jail-free card was back in play. She had been threatening to say something like this in so many late-night fights, her anger always such a red mist of illogical threats, yet he'd never imagined the first golden ticket would come tonight. Weeks of tactical play and she'd thrown away the best line. In sudden recognition, she stepped back, a hand to her mouth, knowing she'd just offered Russian roulette to a compulsive gambler.

He held the receiver to his ear, guessing his life was about to change. But when the emotional bullet went off, it wasn't Kiki holding the gun.

The voice at the other end of the line was choked with tears and fear. 'The barn's on fire! You've gotta come! Zephyr's still in there ...'

Chapter 11

Breaking every speed limit in his borrowed car and running every red light, Dougie headed west towards Burbank like a get-away driver, taking the sharp bend at the top of the hill that dropped down to the equestrian centre so fast his car almost went up on to two wheels.

Then he saw it, a great fireball ahead of him, lighting up the night sky and casting an eerie orange sunset over the oaks.

In the hour since it had been first spotted, the fire had completely taken hold, the roof close to collapse. The LA fire department had two engines on site, the chief fire officer refusing to let his men go back inside because it was too dangerous. The heat from the blazing building was like an erupting volcano, the roar deafening. The officers had been forced to hold back the grooms and volunteers from surrounding barns to stop them running to try to rescue the last horses still trapped inside. Many were in tears.

'He can't be saved, buddy,' the officer told Dougie, grabbing his shoulders as he tried to push past. 'He won't be feeling anything now.'

He refused to listen. He would no more stand back and leave

one of his own horses in there than not try to save a brother. Dougie was certain he could hear the screams of terror and pain. It was a sound he'd never forget.

When the fire officer barred his way, refusing to let go, he rugby-tackled him out of the way. Then, pulling his shirt over his lower face, he ran inside.

He was hit by a wall of smoke so thick it seemed visceral. The only clear air was in the few inches close to the floor and he dropped into it like a commando, crawling along the aisle between the stalls, listening for sounds of life. It was strangely quiet inside, noise muffled by the smoke despite the fire raging in the timbers around him. He had no flashlight and could see almost nothing as he scrabbled hurriedly past empty stalls, the occupants now safe while his pearl was left to die.

Adrenalin spiked to maximum, he made the crouching sprint to the furthest end of the barn where Zephyr was stalled. As he did so, he heard a horse coughing and spluttering.

The black stallion was standing in the corner of his stall, strangely calm, his raven coat dull grey with smoke and welted with burns. He cast Dougie a long-suffering look through the smoke: it was as though he'd been waiting.

Sobbing with relief, Dougie hauled open the door, the metal fittings so hot they seared his palms. Zephyr refused to budge. No matter how hard Dougie pulled and pushed, he was planted.

Roof timbers were starting to come down just metres away.

'Come out, you bastard!' he screamed, hitting him in desperation. The stallion jerked up his head, eyes rolling as he backed further towards the side of the stall with its running bars that separated him from the neighbouring stable which the yard owner had stopped using because the roof leaked. And then Dougie saw the flash of white eye through the bars and a curve of blood red nostril matching the reddened welts on the ash-covered grey skin. It was one of the young Spanish stunt horses put there by the Mexicans who hadn't realized they'd changed the order. The horse let out a terrified squeal, and Zephyr gave a low, rumbling whicker in reply.

Hauling the second door open, Dougie pushed him into the aisle. He clattered out with a shriek of panic, cannoning against doors, almost buckling over.

'It's all right,' he reassured him, his voice choked with smoke. 'It's all going to be all right. You're safe with me.'

Zephyr followed him out now, still eerily calm, shadowing Dougie's stumbling footsteps as though making sure he, too, was safe. The young Iberian by contrast shook all over as he barged and stumbled towards freedom. He seemed close to collapse.

As soon as they were outside, Dougie let the veterinarian and her team of helpers take over, getting oxygen into the horses and giving the burns emergency treatment while he dropped to his knees and coughed his guts out.

'Thirty more seconds and that horse would have never made it out alive,' the vet told him later. 'I have to warn you I'm not sure he'll survive the next twenty-four hours.'

'And the black stallion?'

'I'm talking about the black stallion.'

The vets and fire officers insisted Dougie must go to the emergency room to have his lungs checked out while the horses were moved to an equine hospital. He tried to protest, but he was coughing too much. 'Give me your cell-phone number,' the vet said. 'We'll text you updates every hour.'

Dougie groped in his pocket for a card to write it on and pulled out a clutch he'd been handed that night. One word caught his eye.

Seth.

Chapter 12

One word was now on everybody's lips in Eardisford: *Seth*.

A philanthropist, entrepreneur, cricket fan and notorious technology wizard, who would almost certainly connect the village to broadband and phone signals at last, he was seen as a Very Good Thing.

Nobody had yet spotted the mysterious Seth, but his presence was felt everywhere as an army of workmen swarmed around the main house, and the lanes were choked with white vans and lorries delivering building materials and interior fittings. The Eardisford Arms did a roaring trade at lunchtime, serving builders, plumbers, electricians, architects, designers and local planners, all politely interrogated about progress.

Still hidden beneath its scaffold and sheeting canopy, the old house was having a complete face-lift to bring it up to date, with specialist teams from all over England to ensure its historical preservation, while modern delights such as underfloor heating, a basement cinema and en suites to every bedroom were cleverly incorporated without incurring the wrath of the listed-buildings officer.

News of the donation Seth had made to the animal sanctuary compounded the general belief that his custody of the estate heralded a bright future. Constance's dying wishes also seemed to have been honoured: Kat and the animals were surely safe.

The Constance Mytton-Gough Animal Sanctuary committee had voted to use the large donation to replace long stretches of broken fencing and remove rotten trees, repair the sieve-like stable roofs and reseed and fertilize the grazing paddocks for new spring growth, which pleased everybody except Russ, who had wanted it spent on a specialist wildlife recovery unit.

'That would cost five times the amount, and it's not really what the sanctuary's about,' Kat had pointed out. But as February's wet chill gave way to March's windswept bursting buds, then froths of white and pink blossom, it had become increasingly obvious that this was exactly what Russ wanted it to be about, regardless of the cost.

The open-fronted barn at Lake Farm was now lined with hutches filled with bandaged rabbits, hares and badgers that he had rescued from snares or nets, most of which died from shock within their first twenty-four hours of captivity. The burial mounds in Herne Covert were fast taking on long-barrow proportions. The sanctuary was also caring for several mal-nourished post-hibernation hedgehogs that had fallen into cattle grids, and a pair of Canada geese injured after becoming entangled in fishing line.

'He's so passionate about them all, Dawn,' Kat told her friend, during one of the long, weekly phone chats that had become their norm, slotted between the classes she ran in the village hall, nights out in the pub, Russ's band practice and their lovely, horny nights in together.

'As long as that's not his only passion,' Dawn said, her mind increasingly carnal since she'd started internet dating.

Kat thought about the Tantric sessions, her chakras revving, and grinned into the phone. 'That's definitely not the only thing he's passionate about ... ' She left a teasing pause. 'He loves his music. Animal Magnetism has its first gig soon. It's the week-end of the point-to-point.'

'Is that the horse-racing thing? You're not still seriously plan-ning to take part?' Dawn sounded genuinely worried.

'I'm definitely not good enough for the Ladies' Race this year, but the charity race is just a straight-line gallop with no jumps, and it's all in aid of the sanctuary, so I'm entered in that. Tina's lending me a horse. I'm having a lesson on him tomorrow.'

'What about the one with the funny ears?'

'I'm not riding Sri,' she admitted. 'Russ is helping me do some horse-whispering stuff, but we're not totally "joined up" yet.' She didn't confess that the mare refused point blank to let her get on. 'There's no way we'll be ready for the race, even a charity one. It's supposed to be really good fun, though. You should come. Russ's band is playing a benefit gig in the pub that night.'

'If it's that awful din I can hear now, it doesn't sound like they're ready either.'

Kat tilted her head as guitar riffs wailed through the walls from the old dairy. 'There's a band rehearsal later. Russ is running through his favourite solos. That's the Cure, I think.'

'I'd hate to see the symptoms. Isn't secular music illegal on a Good Friday in the countryside? Or is it just sex?'

'Ha-ha. It's wild here, you know. It's movie night at the village hall tomorrow, then the best ever Sunday roast with the Hedges and the village egg-rolling and bonnet competitions on Monday.'

'I can't believe I'm missing out on such debauchery.' Dawn's plans to visit Eardisford over Easter had been thwarted by house-selling stress. 'I'll be stripping all my lovely pink feature walls and toning down the main bedroom.' The little Watford house with its garish interior had been on the market for six weeks and was struggling to attract interest; the agent had tactfully suggested the colours might be putting buyers off. 'People are so dull round here. I think I might move to your village, after all. Your locals have pink hair. I can't get away with a pink wall.'

Kat laughed, although she was in a bad mood with pink-haired Mags, who had recently shown her support for Russ's wildlife emergency wing by bringing in three badly injured pheasants she'd knocked down while speeding on the back road to Hereford in her battered Citroën. She'd said boyfriend Calum always dispatched them with a shovel, so it was lovely to have somewhere to bring them for a second chance at life.

Mags delivered a fourth casualty that evening when she arrived late to Lake Farm for the rehearsal, her car packed with band members. 'Hit the bleeder as I was coming through the woods. What you do here is magical, Kat.' Mags enclosed her in a car-crusher hug before handing her a warm, limp pheasant and joining Russ in the old dairy to run through the band's eighties punk repertoire, leaving Kat to go in search of spare water drinkers and bird seed, hoping James Stevens, the dashing vet, wouldn't charge her to take a look at this one with all of the others when he came to do routine vaccinations next week. His kindness was bound to run out soon.

All the rescue cases needed veterinary care, warmth and feed, which cost money they didn't have. The income from the trust that Constance had left barely covered the costs of the original veterans, and the collection jar that Mags had put by the bar of the Eardisford Arms was nothing compared to the fund-raising needed to take on wildlife rescue. They were now just a hedge-hog or two away from the overdraft limit. Russ's plans to stage foraging workshops, vegan cooking days and a pub-quiz night had not yet got into gear. The band was admittedly donating all profits from its first gig to the sanctuary, but they had only sold three tickets so far.

In a bid to raise much-needed funds, spear-headed by MFH

Miriam, the committee had arranged for a special Constance Mytton-Gough Sanctuary charity race to be included in the local point-to-point, and Kat had agreed to ride in it. The annual race meeting was organized by the Brom and Lem Hunt and its primary purpose was to bring income for the next season, which went totally against Russ's principles. He was predictably enraged, thinking it totally hypocritical for hunt followers to help raise money to rescue wildlife: 'That's like tuna fishermen organizing a sponsored swim to save the dolphins!'

The outburst had led to their first full-blown row a week earlier.

Given that half of the sanctuary committee were also on the hunt committee and they badly needed the money, Kat had insisted they should take their support with good grace: 'Last year they raised thousands for the air ambulance, and Riding for the Disabled before that. It's incredibly generous of them to select our cause.'

'I'd rather beg on the streets than raise funds alongside that bunch of murderers!' Russ had stormed off to the pub, where Mags had finally persuaded him to co-operate in her gruff, no-nonsense way, pointing out that the sanctuary was named after a great local hunt supporter and relied upon her trust for its income: he could hardly be precious about rattling a collecting tin at a hunt event.

Kat was grateful for her support, although she now regretted offering the band the farm to rehearse in whenever they liked.

She covered her ears and shot an apologetic look at the dogs – they were all cowering under the kitchen table, apart from deaf Maddie who was sprawled, oblivious, on an armchair. Dawn was right, they sounded awful – even worse now that a drummer and two more guitarists were murdering 'Boys

Don't Cry' beneath Mags's rasping twenty-a-day singing voice. It was no wonder the group needed a gimmick. In a recent bid to secure gigs – their only guaranteed venue so far being the Eardisford Arms' skittle alley – they had not only changed their name to Animal Magnetism but also taken to wearing dramatic Gothic wildlife costumes.

It was the idea that he could wear his stage outfit to the point-to-point that finally persuaded Russ to come onside with the fund-raiser. His badger look was intimidating, a world away from anything Kenneth Grahame might have imagined sharing a boat with Toad, Ratty and Co.; the huge-shouldered, leather and fur outfit was part biker, part skunk. Mags, who had made all the costumes, was eager to don her sexy fox-orange second-skin velour to rattle collecting tins. She'd been pushing Kat to borrow a deer outfit, but she was resisting, worried that the fancy-dress theme was misleading.

Instead, she was determined to get in as much riding as she could in the build-up to the charity fun race, in which she was now entered on Tireless Tina's old event horse, Donald. If she could ride in that, she was certain the Bolt was within her grasp.

Chapter 13

'Oh, God.' Tina clamped her hands over her dark-rimmed eyes as her best horse lolloped past with Kat hanging around his neck. 'How many *times*? Sit UP when you ask for the transition.' She turned away to answer the phone as Donald came to a steady halt by the rails and lowered his neck helpfully, like a crane, for Kat to get off.

After the lesson, she consoled herself that she had to be improving slightly. She no longer ached so much afterwards, and Tina got the giggles less, although she had started to get quite short-tempered, shouting and swearing more. She'd even suggested Kat might want to try another instructor, just for variety and a fresh pair of eyes, but Kat liked Tina, who was kind, friendly and hard-working, and Constance had suggested her. She loved the walk to and from her stableyard, sometimes stopping off en route to catch up with the Hedges family or Miriam, take Russ some lunch in the orchards or visit Constance's grave, then divert home through Herne Covert and the paddocks to see Sri, an important part of their new bonding routine.

Spring had arrived with all-out fecundity. As rocket-fuel grass shot up through the drying mud, the horses were shedding their woolly-mammoth winter coats at last. It was the first time Kat had turned Sri out without her rug and her coat was a splash of Titian and white against emerald. The mare threw up her head and whinnied with recognition, making her laugh. The acknowledgement had been hard won.

Russ had been helping Kat get closer to Sri using his natural horsemanship, although the herd's wall-eyed alpha mare, who disliked men intensely, had refused to make an exception for soft-spoken giant Russ, so irritated by his slow and ponderous approach that she kicked out and nipped when he came close. Instead, he'd resorted to demonstrating his techniques with one of the Shetlands. Kat was trying to replicate them faithfully each day, although Sri often lost interest and wandered away. She'd been having more luck with the tip Tina had passed on about something called 'long lining', which involved walking behind the horse with two long ropes attached to the bit instead of reins, as though they had forgotten to couple up a carriage. It was silly but good fun, and they now went on regular blustery, sun-dappled walks around the fields with the dogs. Tina insisted it was 'essential ground work', which made it sound like they were digging ditches.

Today, she tried Russ's 'join-up' technique of approaching the mare from the side, rubbing her forehead, speaking a few soft words, then turning away. At this point Sri was supposed to follow her like a dog, a result of a lot of chasing her around that Kat had done over the previous fortnight. She set off purposefully for a few paces. When she looked back, the mare had turned away and was eating grass, but Kat had a Shetland super-glued to each leg, sniffing her pocket for mints.

She turned back to Sri and clicked. The mare let out a long-suffering sigh and wandered across, flattening her ears to see off the Shetlands before dropping her muzzle into Kat's hands and blowing noisily on them to warm them. Kat pressed her forehead against Sri's, humbled and honoured by the developing friendship.

She was grateful for the increasingly long daylight hours that kept her outside with the animals, especially Sri, who she loved more each day. There were also newborns to be tended – the pygmy goats had been randy, as well as the sheep – and the vegetable patch to plant out, along with the usual mountains of muck to shift, feeds to mix, stock to move around and repairs to make or oversee, including the ones funded by the big donation.

These were desperately needed. Two days ago, she'd returned from running her Bums and Tums class to find that two of the oldest Jacob ewes had fallen down a twenty-foot cutting and drowned in the millstream, side by side in a fluffy suicide pact.

Russ had been her saviour, rallying help from the village to remove the bodies, mending the broken fencing to prevent more escapes, making endless tea. 'Sheep have an extraordinary talent for dying,' he'd told her. 'Nothing you can do will stop them. Like twenty-seven-year-old rock stars.'

She hadn't got the reference, then felt stupid when he explained in reverent terms that Jim Morrison, Kurt Cobain and Amy Winehouse had all died at that age, 'not to mention Janis Joplin, Jimi Hendrix, Brian Jones'.

About to say twenty-seven was a pretty amazing age for a sheep, Kat had stopped herself. Russ could be tetchy about things like that. She was indebted to him for her survival at Lake Farm – he put in long hours helping around the farm and was incredibly gentle and knowledgeable with the animals – and he could be great company who never crowded her, his encyclopaedia mind was extraordinary and his kindness boundless. Yet she felt bulldozed by his good intentions sometimes, irritated that he pitched his tent on such moral high ground although he had lived rent-free at Lake Farm for most of the winter. Now that spring had arrived, it was something of a relief that he'd started spending more nights in his caravan in the Hedges' blossoming orchard. In fact, he'd become increasingly aloof lately, free-ranging of old, wrapped up with his fruit trees, wildlife and music.

Their Tantric sessions, however, had moved on to exciting new territory. Russ now permitted touching, massaging each other's chakras, albeit modestly through their pyjamas. There had been one amazing night when Kat's *swadishthani* had reached a fever pitch of bubbling excitement. But he'd got annoyed that she again lost count during her nine times table, and insisted they mustn't rush it, so they were now back to breathing exercises, asphyxiated by joss sticks and accompanied by the track-jumping Ravi Shankar CD.

Tonight was circled in the kitchen calendar as another meditation session, and Russ had been quite put out when Kat had written 'Movie Night' across the date too, but she had seen no reason not to do both.

'That rather depends on the film,' Russ had grumbled.

Kat had assured him it was a classic old Western.

The village hall's monthly film screening was always packed, and tonight's showing of *High Noon* was no exception, although the blue-rinse brigade lined up in the front row let out a chorus of disapproval to discover it wasn't the original they'd been led to believe, but a remake with unknown stars who looked about fifteen in their eyes.

Kat arrived late and bristled irritably to find that Russ, crammed into the back row with his band members, all drinking cider, had not saved her a place. The only free seat was between elderly farming sisters Pru and Cyn, and Dair Armitage. She plonked herself into it just as the opening credits rolled.

'Isn't this exciting?' Cyn whispered, as the name Dougie Everett flashed up. 'I used to hunt with his father. Terrific thruster.' She pulled out a pair of ancient opera glasses, although they were sitting barely twenty feet from the screen.

The director wasted no time in getting down to business with the two leads, who had clearly just got married, ripping one another's clothes off before the movie's title had even appeared.

Kat stared wide-eyed at the incredibly good-looking actor playing misunderstood marshal Will Kane, who was disrobing a nubile blonde in a wedding dress with great urgency.

'Gosh, he's a very smart specimen,' muttered Pru, sounding as though she was assessing a young Hereford bull calf. 'Who is he?'

143

'*That's* Dougie Everett,' said Cyn, adjusting the opera glasses. 'Looks just like his father from the neck down.'

The occupants of the village hall were now red-faced, although it was hard to tell whether this was because the radiators were at full blast or as a result of the steamy scene currently being enacted before them. Crammed between Dair and Cyn, who were both breathing very heavily, Kat was obliged to watch as handsome Dougie kissed his beautiful co-star, now hiking up her skirts while simultaneously unbuckling his belt. Watching a sex scene with an entire village was very similar on the awkwardness scale to watching a sex scene with one's parents. She fought an urge to talk rapidly and loudly about a random subject – the dead sheep at Lake Farm or the huge lorry weighed down with marble that had got stuck in a cattle grid en route to the main house – but she managed to keep her mouth buttoned. She could imagine Russ's eyes boring into the back of her head: he alone knew why this would be harder for her than most of them.

'Oh, a nipple!' Pru observed eagerly, as though they were witnessing a live vole birth on *Springwatch*.

The bride's creamy breasts spilled from her bodice and Dougie Everett's mouth moved from one to the other, drawing their buds into his lips, artfully shot to maximize the revving in groins both male and female. The urgency between the couple was real, the sexual attraction undeniable.

A familiar scythe of fear was swinging towards Kat, her pulses racing and sweat rising. She knew a big-action Hollywood bed scene was as far removed from Nick's taste for internet porn as gourmet cooking from junk food, but her response to the images on screen was Pavlovian, her heartbeat now so fast it hurt.

Beside her, Dair was breathing even more heavily. Intensely uncomfortable, she glanced across at him and saw, amazed, that he still had his flat cap pressed down over his eyes and appeared to be asleep.

'Poor chap was out all night with his keepers trying to catch lampers,' Cyn whispered, before her watery blue eyes returned to the screen and her jaw dropped. 'Would you look at that? She is completely naked. Why has she got practically no public hair?'

Someone shushed as the *High Noon* remake's seminal 'muff' scene played out on screen.

Kat's mouth went dry, a hundred far more explicit muff scenes playing through her mind, examined in minute detail by Nick as he'd coaxed her into re-enacting them with him. The memory made her feel faint. She'd just have to close her eyes and wait it out. But then the camera closed in on Dougie Everett's face and she stayed watching, unable to stop herself, as his extraordinary eyes seemed to drink in the girl with him; something about the way he kissed made for totally compulsive viewing.

Dair had snorted awake and was blinking at the screen in wonder.

'I don't remember the first *High Noon* being like this.' He admired the pair of pert buttocks on screen. 'Very attractive derrière.'

'That's Dougie Everett's bum.' Cyn giggled, earning another 'Ssh' from behind. She lifted her opera glasses again, angling them past the wisps of white hair escaping from her bun.

'Amazing the director got away with that straight after the credits,' Dair muttered.

'That boy's far too young to play that part,' complained Pru, in a disapproving undertone. 'Gary Cooper was in his fifties. And *she*'s no Grace Kelly.'

They all tilted their heads as Kiki Nelson was laid back expertly on the lacy bed.

'Dougie Everett is *buff*,' a girl behind Kat said, with a deep sigh, and her friends tittered.

'Shouldn't this be on after the watershed?' Pru's mouth turned down disapprovingly, her long, thin turkey neck wobbling as Will Kane stripped to his waist, revealing taut abs and a heavenly six-pack. 'Movie night should be family viewing, especially at Easter.'

'I read in the *Telegraph* that the co-stars are practically married,' Cyn assured her. 'It's all very respectable.'

'Dougie Everett and Kiki Nelson are engaged in real life,' Dair explained, earning a surprised look from Kat and the elderly sisters, who had no idea he was so clued up on popular culture. Having been buried in Herefordshire for more than two years without a television, and far from Dawn's regular supplies of *OK!* and *Hello!*, Kat had missed Dougie Everett's mercurial rise to fame and had no idea who he was, or Kiki Nelson of the gravity-defying breasts and feather-thin Brazilian.

'She's a lucky girl.' Cyn sighed. 'Not only is he frightfully handsome, but he's going to inherit half of Northamptonshire one day. And he hunts.'

'Good hedge country.' Pru looked more approving, her face relaxing as the scene cut to Dougie slotting a dusty boot into a leather stirrup, squinty-eyed and handsome in bright sunlight as he mounted a palomino horse and galloped off through some dust balls. '*Now* we're talking.'

Dougie Everett – who took his clothes off several more times and killed a lot of baddies at the end with gruesome, drawn-out violence – was something of a revelation. While the general consensus was that Gary Cooper was the definitive Will Kane, nobody could dispute this young man's charisma.

'Kiki's the big box-office star,' Dair told Kat, who looked around for Russ as the lights went up, only to find he and the band had already sloped out, rushing to be first at the pub bar. 'Everett was paid peanuts.'

'How come you know so much?'

'I'm a movie-trivia buff. Can I buy you a drink?' he asked hopefully, flat cap back over his nose to hide his blushes.

She shook her head, disappointed by Russ's neglect, unwilling to fight her way to his side in the crowded pub or occupy an opposite corner watching him cackling with his band, Mags and the earthmen, if he was in one of his free-range moods.

'Lift?'

'I brought my car, thanks. I was running late.' Cooking a vegan bean casserole for Russ to apologize for double-dating his Tantric night, she added silently. She'd probably end up feeding it to the pigs.

Dair stayed at her shoulder as they filed out into a cool spring night. 'How is your lovely friend Dawn?'

'Great! Got a lovely new boyfriend.' Kat was keen to deflect him, although Dawn's latest internet dating relationship had only lasted a fortnight before she found out he had a wife and two kids. 'He's a fitness instructor. Huge pecs. More tattoos than Mags, but not quite as butch.'

'Be careful when you're handling that one, Kat.' Dair cleared his throat awkwardly.

'Are you talking about Dawn's date or Mags?' she joked, trying to think up a funny one-liner about the barmaid's new vixen stage costume, but stopping when she noticed the deepening glow of the uncomfortable blush beneath the flat cap, his chin quilted with that awkward, clenched lockjaw of a man who thinks he might have said too much. 'Why should I be careful of Mags?' she whispered, stepping away from the crowd milling around the village hall porch, loudly praising Dougie Everett's talent.

Following, arms crossed, he tipped his head down so she could only see a circle of hounds-tooth tweed. His nasal Scots voice softened: 'You have a lot to learn about animal husbandry, Kat.'

'I'm trying.' She bristled, thinking he was referring to her limited smallholding skills.

'That band goes back a long way.'

She checked herself. 'Do you mean Animal Magnetism?'

'Aye. It's what I said.' The flat cap was almost combusting from the awkward blush raging beneath now, which she could see streaking into his neck. 'Although it was Dirty Mags before that, and when I arrived they called themselves the Babysitters. Things round here take a long time to figure out. They're never as simple as they first seem.'

Driving back through the woods, Kat mulled this over, but she wasn't sure what Dair had been trying to tell her, other than that the pub band had been through several dodgy names.

'Shit!' She slammed on the brakes as a figure in a hoodie stepped out straight in front of her. It was Russ, eyes white in the headlights.

'I thought you'd gone to the pub,' she said, her heart roaring from the near miss as he got in beside her.

He pulled off his hood, the white-tipped lion's mane tumbling out. 'We have a meditation date.'

As they drove on in silence, Kat found herself wondering whether, in his roundabout way, Dair had been trying to tell her that Russ and Mags had once been more than just friends.

'What did you think of the film?' he was asking.

'A bit violent. You?'

'So-so. Hollywood movies are pretty much all Republican didactic propaganda.' He glanced across at her, the bear eyes

148

worried and protective. 'We don't have to meditate tonight if you'd rather not.'

'I want to.'

'Is it hard for you? Watching such explicit stuff?'

'It's a lot tamer than the stuff Nick liked.'

'Sorry – I know you prefer not to talk about it.'

She swallowed awkwardly. They lapsed into silence again.

There was something highly charged about the atmosphere when they got back to Lake Farm, despite the dogs sniffing around as usual, the cat flap rattling, the range burbling back into life and the wet logs spitting on the grate.

For once the Ravi CD didn't jump; Kat remembered her nine times table; their eyes didn't leave one another's.

They were not allowed physically to touch, but the sensations rolling through Kat's body as she lay back after their face to face breathing and centring were like warm fingers all over her, circling, dabbing, thrumming, stroking, delving. Russ's hands moved just above her body now, from chakra to chakra, so close she could feel their warmth, the intimacy both exquisite and pure torture. His shadow was over her, huge-shouldered, dark-eyed and so masculine. She wanted to feel his weight on her. Her *kundalini* was a positive tidal wave of eagerness. She was the new bride at the start of *High Noon*. She wanted his skin on hers right now. No more chakra wafting or holding back for the ultimate pleasure. She was *ready* for the ultimate pleasure.

Bursting upwards like a body from beneath water, she found his lips with hers and tasted them eagerly, drawing his tongue against hers, gratified by its leap of response. It was a long time since they'd kissed like this. She'd forgotten how fantastically he did it, the thrum of desire whirring faster than ever.

'We shouldn't be doing this,' he said, as their mouths still

149

explored one another's lips, tongues, taste, with ever-quickening breaths. 'It's against the rules.'

'Sod the rules. Let's break them.'

He laughed and she tried to pull him down towards her, but he was an immovable rock, his hands slipping behind her back. She wriggled upright until she was kneeling again, wrapping her arms around him, climbing into his lap and pushing him back instead. Caught off balance, he tipped on to the furled saris and rugs in the glow of the fire, gazing up at her, huge and wild-maned. Kat couldn't remember ever desiring anything as much as this man, right this minute, right inside her. It was primal.

She scrabbled at his flies.

'Kat – no—'

'I said let's break the rules!'

'Please don't, Kat. Please stop.'

Nothing was stirring beneath her fingers. She froze, clenching her eyes shut, remembering her awful performance the first night they'd gone to bed together, after being crowned King and Queen at the wassail, when she had launched into her full porn repertoire and terrified the life out of Russ. Nothing had stirred that night either, not for either of them. The embarrassment had been mortifying after such anticipation, such kissing, flirting, skin-tingling certainty that they were going to screw all night in a cider haze of Twelfth Night debauchery. Then the cold splash of sitting up in a bed, admitting defeat. She'd thought she'd put him off. She didn't know what normal was any more, she'd explained. Nick had wanted her to do these things, say these things, had become more and more reliant upon it as time went on. No, she hadn't enjoyed it, not after the first few times, years ago when it had been a novelty, before it had become his addiction. She hated it now. She felt nothing. Her body froze her out.

He'd suggested Tantric sex, and it was friendly, funny, weird and sometimes frustrating, but now it had worked for her. Perhaps it had worked too well.

She looked away, her face burning. 'I'm sorry. I ruined everything.'

He cleared his throat. 'It's me, Kat. It's me, not you.'

Shaking her head, she scrambled off his lap and curled up against a chair, arms tight around her knees.

'I get too uptight,' he muttered. 'It's not you. I'm so attracted to you, but I have this hang-up from my past, a girl I loved and lost, the usual crap. It damaged me. The ignition button gets stuck.' He crossed his legs back into guru position and took a deep breath, peered across at her through his thick lashes. 'I want to find a way through it.'

'That makes two of us.'

He nodded, dark eyes glowing in the firelight as he looked up, raking his hair from his brows, the hand staying pressed to the back of his head. He reminded her of a Rodin sculpture, so magnificently honed yet rough-edged.

'I can't talk about it,' he said, his Bristol accent pronounced as it always was when he was upset. 'It's best buried.'

She understood. She couldn't talk about Nick without it hurting too much either. Like Russ, she'd only ever revealed an abbreviated minimum.

'I want you to know you're amazing, Kat. I fucking adore you.'

'I fucking adore you too.'

For the first time since he'd been using Lake Farm as an overnight base, Russ and Kat slept together. They were still fully clothed, curled up in front of the fire's embers, surrounded by snoring dogs. She felt safer than she had in months.

Chapter 14

Easter was early: the clocks had yet to go back and the last of the snowdrops were still drifting beneath the apple trees in the orchards, just starting to melt away under the sunburst yellow of daffodils and small licking flames of crocus. Hunting had only just finished, the traditional balls, suppers and horse-trading keeping the Hedges family occupied and dominating conversation when Russ and Kat joined them to share a roast at the family's little farmhouse on Easter Sunday, a nut cutlet presented to Russ with all the trimmings.

'Terrible season – wettest I can remember,' complained Russ's uncle Bill, his round, weathered cheeks already stained port red from a late-morning pint in the pub and two pre-lunch sherries at home. 'Not many farmers wanted us on the land, and all that road pounding's murder on an old arse like mine. Think I'll follow on foot next year.'

His twin daughters also declared the season a disappointment, having spent most of it squabbling over the Brom and Lem's good-looking young huntsman, only to find out he'd been having a wild affair with a local solicitor's wife and was now changing hunts to sow his wild oats elsewhere.

'Let's hope for better sport next year,' Babs Hedges said encouragingly, all her chins curved upwards in harmony with her smiling mouth as she served them all vast helpings of home-made trifle. 'Maybe a new face at Eardisford will bring us luck. Seth.' The name was now a village mantra.

'He'll ban the lot of you,' growled Russ. 'Wait and see.'

By the time the trifle was circulating a second time, Kat could see he was itching to escape, his eyes stormy as Bob complained about the number of Eastern Europeans employed by a local vegetable-packing plant, the plethora of 'coffee-coloured' babies he'd seen at Leominster market and the hunt's decision to bring in another female master the following season. 'They called Diana mistress of the hunt, not master. A woman shouldn't be a master in my opinion.'

'Goddess,' snapped Russ. 'Diana was a goddess. And she'd be obliged to hunt under the law too.' As soon as he'd wolfed his trifle, he took collie Ché and the two lurchers out for a walk.

Kat knew Russ had enormous affection for Bill and his clan, who had taken him in many times and forgiven him his excesses, but at family gatherings it was always obvious how difficult he found it to bite his tongue and not rise to their prejudices. She debated going after him, but she knew Russ was impenetrable in this mood, and she didn't want to offend the others or shirk her responsibilities with the mountain of washing-up. Russ had been uptight all morning, what had happened last night making the ground shift silently and seismically beneath them. They needed to regroup.

Kat helped clear away and tackle the dishes. By the time the last cooking pot was draining, there was still no sign of Russ, who was notorious for making himself scarce during household chores – he refused to wash anything used to cook or eat meat, which limited his usefulness after a Hedges Sunday roast. He was still missing when Babs brewed tea and fetched out the Simnel cake; the family had a very sweet tooth, which, having been denied any indulgences over Lent, was currently insatiable. Unable to face another sugary mouthful, Kat decided to go in search of the family black sheep, hugging them all farewell and thanking Babs for lunch.

'He's a lucky bugger having you, Kat.' Babs placed her worn, plump and sweet-smelling fingers on Kat's cheeks. 'There's not many who understand him, but he's got a good heart, especially with animals. He just acts before he thinks and suffers no fools. Typical Hedges man.' She nodded at Bill, who was now asleep on the recliner chair, open-mouthed.

Thinking it was a safe bet that Russ would be in the pub, Kat ambled through the orchards and across the footbridge by the ford to the Eardisford Arms, but in the public bar the earthmen were lined up on their stools like coconuts in a shy without their tall, argumentative mutineer taking shots at them. Realizing Dair Armitage was with them, Kat tried to duck out unseen, but he let out a bellow and came stalking over, flat cap peak so low over his nose that he had to tilt his head back to see her. 'Kat, would you care to join us for a drink?'

'No – you're fine, thanks. In a bit of a hurry. Just looking for Russ. Have you seen him?'

'Better ask his wife,' called one of the earthmen, with a chuckle.

'He means Mags.' Dair shot the men a warning look and hurried on, 'Russ came in here about an hour ago carrying a very mangy dog fox, spouting off about poachers. Apparently somebody's been setting snares in the spinneys around the orchards again. I'll get one of the keepers to look into it.'

The earthmen coughed and turned back to their pints.

'We offered to put Charlie Fox out of its misery, but Russ insisted on using the phone to call the emergency vet, then Mags drove him to the surgery.'

Kat envisaged another poor creature pegging out in his arms. Russ couldn't bear to see suffering and, having seen snared animals first hand, she understood why he'd done it, but it never got any easier. 'Mags is with him, you say?'

'Is that a problem?' Dair eyed her.

'No! I'm grateful he has transport this time. I haven't forgotten his last three-mile cycle ride to the vet with a dying stoat zipped in his coat. Those scars still look like multiple nipple piercings!'

'They are nipple piercings, duck,' rasped one of the earthmen. 'Afore your time, Russ was known as the Pin Cushion cos he has more perforations than a gypsy's doily. When he wore all them body ornaments, he looked like something from Bongo Bon—'

'That's enough, Dick!' Dair snapped, turning to Kat and clearing his throat. He seemed tongue-tied with embarrassment. Then she saw his gaze was locked on her cleavage.

'Take your eyes off my boobs, you leery git!' she snapped, furious that she knew so little about Russ. They'd stared into one another's eyes and massaged ninth chakras for weeks now, yet she had no idea he'd had multiple piercings.

Dair had puffed himself up, yellow cashmere sweater bulging from his tweed waistcoat, like a blue tit defending his fat-ball. 'Please remind Russ not to feed the pheasants. We're trying to round up the wild breeding stock and half of them are living it up on your farm. They're estate property.'

'I thought you just said they were wild, so surely they're nobody's property.' She'd heard Russ complaining about breeding methods many times. 'Do you really de-beak them and make them wear gags and blinkers to stop them pecking each other?'

'Of course not,' Dair huffed. 'We follow strict Defra guidelines. You mustn't listen to Russ – he reads far too much nonsense. Come and see for yourself. I'll happily give you a guided tour of the brooder huts when the poults arrive – and your friend Dawn can come along too next time she visits.' He lifted his chin again so that she could see his small eyes glittering eagerly beneath the cap peak.

'She's pretty busy right now,' Kat said vaguely. She doubted that dangling the opportunity to take a threesome tour of the pheasant-rearing pens would bring Dawn rushing back to Herefordshire, although she seemed surprisingly keen to take in the pub again and even reacquaint herself with Dair, about whom she said she'd had 'disturbing flashbacks'. Kat guessed they had to be bad, so was anxious to limit Dair's expectations. 'Big boyfriend, abs, pecs, Rottweiler, Porsche, tattoos like Mags, remember?'

One bloodshot eye fixing her from beneath his hounds-tooth peak, Dair looked as if he'd brooded over little else. 'Have you thought about what I told you last night?' he asked peevishly.

Recalling his insinuation that Animal Magnetism should be named and shamed, Kat was starting to get seriously annoyed. 'If there's something on your mind you think I should know, Dair, just spit it out. Something about Mags and Russ?'

'I couldn't possibly say.'

Kat was about to cram his wretched flat cap right over his chin when one of the earthmen called, 'You never forget your first love.'

'Be quiet, Bernie,' Dair hissed, glancing at his watch awkwardly. 'Is that the time? I really must go, I have a meet—'

'Little Kat deserves to know the truth,' came a call from the bar. 'They was the talk of this village for years, them two.'

Kat turned from the bar back to Dair disbelievingly. 'Is this true?'

'Russ and Mags were once an "item", I think it's called,' he said awkwardly. 'On and off for years. Mostly off,' he added encouragingly. 'I'm sure you know all this.'

Kat tried to hide her shock. Mags was so much older than

him, it had never occurred to her that they might have been lovers. But now she was deluged with images of twenty-something Mags seducing the child Russ over guitar lessons, Mrs Robinson-style. It all made horrible sense. Mags's band had once been called the Babysitters. Young, floppy-haired Russ, barely able to stretch his fingers around a fretboard, had been seduced by its lead singer. His tuning fork responded only to her pitch. Kat had walked into a cougar's lair.

In her mind's eye, she was currently reacting with total poise. Russ always said he was a free-range romantic, she reminded herself. He doesn't do conventional relationships. Ours is more of a house-mates thing. Mags is an old friend. So what if she's an old girlfriend and occasional lover too? Nevertheless, as she prepared herself to laugh all this off, she heard her own voice squawking, 'They went *out* together?'

'Never officially as I understand it.' Dair was redder than ever.

'There was a big falling out,' Bernie the earthman called across, 'when he went to university.'

'She took up with Calum while Russ was away studying, did Mags,' another piped up. 'Broke young Russ's heart.'

'He stayed away for years.'

'Now he's back.'

'I said no good would come of it.'

Kat closed her eyes. The earthmen were like a toothless Greek chorus. Meanwhile, her Colossus of strength was crumbling. Russ had been her protector all year and now it seemed he and Mags were Orpheus and Eurydice.

'It's all very amicable now,' Dair said, clearly concerned. 'There's no need to worry. Just be alert. I really must go. Are you going to be okay, Kat? Do you need a lift home?'

Kat could feel her heart misfiring, the machine-gun hurt of

157

being denied the truth and the mortification of being the last to know. She kept her eyes tight closed, determined not to give away how much this frightened her. It wasn't as though she'd caught the two rolling around naked behind the bar: this was just a group of drunken pub regulars winding her up. She'd always known that Mags and Russ were childhood friends, this was no biggie. But it reminded her yet again that she was the outsider, and that running away in nothing more than the clothes you stand up in doesn't mean you won't fall over other people's baggage. Trust was long haul. Taking deep, calming breaths, she started muttering under her breath.

'What?' Dair leaned closer to listen.

'I'm counting to ten.'

'By reciting the nine times table?'

'I'm fantasizing I'm kicking chakras,' she muttered, eyes opening again as the smile blazed.

The chin smiled back, looking relieved. 'Always liked a spot of polo.'

Kat whistled for Maddie and Daphne, who were flirting with the earthmen's barstool-tethered terriers, like two old ladies on the razzle. 'Thank you, Dair. You lived up to your name. It was brave to tell me that.'

'Entirely selfish, I assure you.' He was leering at her chest again, a nervous habit he appeared entirely unaware of.

'This is your last warning. Stop. Looking. At. My. Tits.'

The flat cap flipped up like a bin lid and she nodded in brief acknowledgement. Turning swiftly for the door, she tried for a dignified exit, but it took her some time to extricate the flirty old bitches from the bar, and when she finally succeeded, Dair was on her heels on the way out, breathing hotly down her neck.

She held up a hand. 'I'm fine, Dair, really. I don't need that lift.'

'I'm late for a meeting,' he muttered, in his dourest Scots drone, as he brushed past her, walkie-talkie to his ear and his own dogs at his heels, making Kat feel silly. Then he turned back as he hurried to his car. 'Your future is riding on this.'

Chapter 15

Kat trailed back towards Lake Farm through the beech woods and then into Herne Covert, indigestion staging a comeback in her churning chest, reminding her that lunch with the Hedges family had been just a couple of hours earlier. Then Russ had been her best friend in the village, her renegade, who was unswervingly honest about everything and infuriatingly opinionated about most things too. She was trying not to let panic take hold. He was still Russ, she reminded herself. He and Mags would never let the sanctuary down. She had a sudden image of them cradling an injured fox, like two indulgent parents, sharing a kiss as they chose a name.

Stop it, she chastised herself. He's on your side. He was free-range Russ, who hated red tape, acted first and justified afterwards, just as his aunt Babs had said. He believed he had right on his side, like Will Kane in *High Noon*, standing up on his own against the bullying and repression of a lawless gang and a kowtowing community. Mags was his Helen Ramirez, an old lover who had forsaken him for too many others since, whereas Kat was his Amy. She wished they could enjoy the heartfelt, intimate passion of Dougie Everett and his co-star. Instead they were hamstrung by inhibitions, needing to recite their nine times tables in pyjamas to feel safe with sex.

Kat splashed through the ford, kicking up rainbow arcs, her dark, wet enemy reduced to teardrops. It seemed ridiculous that she tackled so many gutsy tasks without a second thought – she could handle agricultural equipment, mend fencing, coppice trees, manage large animals, start a generator, ride a horse – yet her two greatest fears remained: sex and deep water. She dared herself to approach one of them now, walking along the riverbank, dropping down to the gravel edge and stooping to collect a stone to bounce ducks and drakes along the water.

Cross it! She heard Constance's voice in her head and smiled with relief at its deep, heartening familiarity.

You can do it, Katherine! Feel the adrenalin, for goodness' sake. I didn't put you in Lake Farm to rub your stomach while patting your head or whatever this Tantric nonsense is about. Your riding is frightful and you must swim in the lake soon. It's warming up.

Still deep in thought, Kat followed the river to the edge of the lake and stared across its smooth black surface, trying to imagine Constance swimming it on horseback more than seventy years ago in a desperate bid to save the estate. When war broke out in Europe, her father, Charles 'Hock' Mytton, had wanted Eardisford to pass into the hands of his brother in the absence of male heirs, his intention being to stay on in India indefinitely, but his only daughter Constance had been determined that she should take the reins. The estate was not subject to primogeniture so she had every right to inherit. To prove her worth, she'd agreed to take on the Bolt, the three-mile gallop from Duke's Wood to the Hereford road, crossing all obstacles in between, which must be completed within the two strikes of the church clock quarter to win the Eardisford Purse and, in Constance's case, the right to run the estate.

I was frankly terrified, but it was such fun! One has never lived until one has risen to a challenge like that, Katherine, racing because one's very future depends upon it. You will feel it, and nobody will betray your trust as they did mine.

Riding side-saddle, Constance had been the first Mytton to make the time in over a century and take the Purse. Nevertheless her father had stoutly refused to sign over the estate to her care until she married, which at nineteen Constance worried she was too young to do. Her heart was already lost to a young RAF officer she'd met a year earlier at a shooting party and with whom she was wildly infatuated, exchanging passionate letters, but marriage seemed a long way off. She wrote to him explaining the situation and telling him that she loved him, only to learn shortly afterwards that he had been killed in one of the first Allied raids.

I have no idea if he read my letter before he died. I prefer to think not. I loved him so very much and it felt such a frightful thing to ask; easier to treat it as a business deal, like Daddy did.

Not long afterwards, a heartbroken Constance was summoned to India to find her father gravely ill, the cancer he had kept secret ripping the life from him. In an extraordinary deathbed deal, he told her that a young officer in his regiment was willing to become her husband. Major Gough's family owned a modest country house in the Borders, he explained, but he 'knows his hunting better than any man'. Constance and Ronnie were married just two days before Hock Mytton died. Their marriage had lasted six decades and borne five children, and she'd told Kat how love had grown slowly within it. *I adored my darling, gentle Ronnie, but I confess I always wondered what it would have been like to marry for love and not duty. I think it must be such a frightful gamble. Yet if one gets it right, the jackpot is simply magnificent: a lifetime of love. You are a gambler like me, Katherine. One of us should get it right.*

Kat watched a pair of swans gliding towards her across the water and remembered Russ telling her that they mate for life, along with wolves and barn owls. He had then spent a long time explaining why this was bad for genetic diversity and species survival. He preferred the harem-band model, where family groups were ruled by a matriarchy with one alpha breeding male protecting them and mating with multiple females.

Snarling under her breath at the thought of being part of Mags's matriarchal Eardisford group, Kat looked up as a helicopter swooped low over the woods, coming in to land by the main house. There were no builders on site over the bank holiday, and she couldn't imagine any of the new owner's many advisers, lawyers and architects working through Easter weekend. Her curiosity intensified when she guessed it had to be Seth himself.

She was dying for a closer look. The boat mooring was just a short walk away, but there was still no way she had the nerve to take the short-cut across the water to the parkland, particularly with several ancient dogs in tow, so she hurried along the path that cut through the woods to the west of the lake. The water in the ford was near her welly tops as she waded through, carrying the old terriers under each arm, then dropping them on the far bank and racing on. Snuffling Maddie bounded ahead, low-slung Daphne falling behind.

Kat climbed up on to the ridge that ran around the oxbow's end. From here, she had a good view through the trees to the main terraces and could see a figure wrapped in squashy furs stalking across them, pausing occasionally to look up and hold out a tablet computer on which they were taking photographs of the scaffolding-covered house. Russ would go mental if he saw that fur coat, thought Kat, then stopped midway over a stile in surprise. It was definitely a woman. Did Seth have a wife?

'That's as far as you go, young lady!'

It was one of Dair's gamekeepers, a trio Russ had nicknamed Meat and Two Veg. While Spud and Turnip were well-meaning, if slow-witted, local lads, Meathead, the senior keeper, was a particularly nasty ex-squaddie whose main brief was to keep out trespassers, a task he took very seriously.

'You and your dogs better turn round right now, Kat.'

'This is a public footpath,' she reminded him smugly.

He pointed at the sign that read, *All dogs must be kept on leads.* 'Can't be too careful with new lambs, and there's game birds loose.'

Kat felt in her pockets for a lead, but she didn't even have a loop of baler twine. She could have pointed out that the nearest Eardisford flock was at least half a mile away, and that most of the estate's game birds were hanging around Lake Farm right now, hoping for Russ's brown rice leftovers, but she couldn't be bothered to argue with Meathead. 'I was just trying to get a closer look at your new boss and my new neighbour.'

'Nothing to see here,' he replied, spreading his arms wide as though controlling a large crowd eager to witness a grisly crime scene, not a small redhead with two elderly dogs.

But before she turned to walk home, Kat did see something. Another figure had appeared in front of the house and was walking towards the woman in the furs, tweed-sleeved arm thrust out in welcome, his flat cap pressed down low over his nose.

'Dair knows *exactly* what's going on round here.' He'd told her that her future was riding on it.

What was it he had said yesterday? *Things round here take*

a long time to figure out. They are never as simple as they first seem.

Kat thought it looked completely straightforward from where she stood: Russ was bonking Mags. Dair was double-crossing everybody. And Seth's wife had arrived.

Chapter 16

There was no sign of Russ at Lake Farm, although one of Mags's most recent road-kill pheasants had given up the fight, stiff with rigor mortis in its pen, and Usha had escaped into the lake again. Anger still cooking, Kat got on with the late-afternoon yard tasks, bringing in the three horses that were still being stabled at nights, feeding and haying them before checking over the field stock and finally coaxing Usha out with a bucket of nuts. Then she gathered the chickens, geese and ducks into their respective fox-proof homes. Trevor the peacock, who was feeling lovelorn, followed her about, calling anxiously. Finally, she checked on Russ's hutched wildlife casualties in the barn, thankful that they were all still alive, staring back at her with black-eyed fear and confusion.

The range needed relighting, and there was no kindling in the house, so Kat went to raid the wood store and groaned when she saw only huge uncut sections. Russ had come outside to chop some last night, but he seemed to have sliced no more than a few toothpicks of kindling. Her anger bubbled hotter as she reflected on the number of hours he spent outside star-gazing with no practical purpose. If he could identify the smaller constellations, predict the weather or give her some horoscope guidance, it might at least seem worthwhile, but she sometimes suspected it was his way of avoiding hard work. Whenever he did knuckle down and cut some wood, he insisted on doing it the old-fashioned way, with an axe, which took for ever and meant they were always running out. Kat checked that there was some fuel in the chain saw and, donning ear protectors and goggles, set about splitting the wood to size in a small-scale timber massacre. It was the perfect vent for her burgeoning fury.

Which was why she didn't hear the Range Rover roaring into the yard, or realize that Dair was standing beside her until he pulled the emergency cord and cut the fuel, making the saw putter to silence.

'What the bloody hell d'you do that for?' She swung round furiously and saw that the woman in the fur coat was with him. Close-to she looked no older than Kat herself, with extraordinary dark, melting eyes and the most expressionless face Kat had ever encountered.

'You are Miss Katherine Mason?' the woman asked, in a deep, modulated voice.

Kat knew that Russ would recommend muttering, 'Who wants to know?' but there was no point in denying her identity with Dair there.

'Yes – hi!' She flashed the big smile and thrust out a hand, noticing too late that it was covered with chainsaw oil and log moss. 'Call me Kat.'

The woman shook it by the fingertips, her face deadpan. 'I prefer to keep this formal, Miss Mason.'

'Of course.' Kat adopted her most formal face. 'May I call you Mrs Seth?'

For a nanosecond, the dark eyes sparked. 'I would prefer it

if you do not. I must apologize for this intrusion on a sacred holiday, but my decision to come was made at short notice. This has been my first opportunity to visit Eardisford, and my priority was to meet you in person.'

'I'm honoured.' Kat shifted uncomfortably. The woman was staring at her, unblinking. It was very disconcerting. She stooped to pick up the log basket. 'Come in and I'll make a cup of tea.'

'That will not be necessary.' Her eyes lingered Kat's face, forensic in their detailed examination of each freckle and laughter line, followed by a lengthy assessment of her body, which felt even more intrusive than Dair's habitual boob-leers. 'I have been advised that you cannot be financially motivated to leave Lake Farm. Is this right?'

Kat glanced at Dair, who still had his flat cap pulled right down over his nose, his expression impossible to read. 'Yes.'

The woman let out an irritated tut. 'Then you have not been offered the right price, Miss Mason.'

'I was told the new owners of the Eardisford Estate have no legal objection to the sanctuary.'

'That is correct, although there is an open offer to relocate it somewhere more practical. There would also be significant remuneration for you personally.'

'The Mytton-Gough family already offered that, but this really isn't about money. I'm sorry you've had a wasted trip.'

She was examining Kat's face again. 'Everybody has their price, Miss Mason.'

'Sure.' Kat smiled. 'Mine's a billion.'

Beside her, Kat heard Dair's sharp intake of breath.

The dark eyes regarded her for a long time, unblinking in that oh-so-still face. 'You have a child-like quality.'

Kat snorted with laughter.

'It is not unappealing. Thank you for your time.'

Kat gaped at her. 'Is that it?'

'Goodbye, Miss Mason,' she said, turning to walk back to the car. There were no threats or counter-offers. The conversation had taken less than a minute.

To Kat's surprise, Dair reached out and gave her elbow a squeeze before hurrying to open the passenger door for his companion.

'Turncoat,' Kat hissed, under her breath.

Watching as the Range Rover bounced away, she caught the reproachful eyes of Dair's two ultra-obedient pointers through its rear windscreen.

When Mags's elderly Citroën finally bounced along the track belting out the Buzzcocks, Kat marched out to meet it, noticing how the pink-haired one reached across to play-cuff Russ's ears and fake-punch his chest before pulling up the handbrake, the big-sisterly affection taking on a whole new perspective in the light of Dair's revelations. Tattooed, pierced and fierce, Mags's reputation for fighting might be formidable, but she had a soft side that men found irresistible. She was an earthy, ever-laughing flirt, absolutely doted on animals and, now Kat thought about it, Russ.

'You missed such a drama, Kat!' her rasping, laughing voice called, as she spilled from the car. 'We almost lost him twice. He's one tough little bastard. We called him Heythrop.' She went round to the boot and pulled out a cross-eyed, stunned pheasant.

'That's Heythrop?'

'No. I hit this poor sod coming back. Think it'll be okay after a night's kip. That,' she pointed to the back seat where Russ was stooping over a battered cardboard box, 'is Heythrop.'

'He's still a bit groggy from sedation.' Russ drew out the box with great reverence and held it under Kat's nose. The smell of rank old dog fox and antiseptic was not a winning combination. 'Lucky I caught him when I did because the snare was already deep in his throat and he was struggling like stink – a couple more minutes and his windpipe would have been cut open. This skin condition's sarcoptic mange.'

Kat regarded the scabby old fox unenthusiastically. It looked positively leprous. 'Isn't that highly contagious?'

'We'll have to be vigilant and quarantine him.'

'The vet gave him a dose of Stronghold,' Mags said reassuringly, 'so it should clear up by the time he's back on the road.' She pushed away the dogs, all snuffling round the box with interest.

'He can go in the old dairy so he's close to the house,' Russ announced. 'Fetch some bowls and bedding, Mags, and I'll get a hutch – here.' He thrust the fox box at Kat. 'Don't worry, he's not going anywhere. The dope he's just had is even stronger than Mags's home-grown happy herbs.'

She could feel the anger bubbling again, indignant at the insouciant way he acted as though he owned the place. I'm the custodian here, she wanted to rage, and why the hell didn't you tell me you and Mags were once an item? But she bit her tongue, biding her time as she watched them bustle about, arranging Heythrop's new quarters, suspicion and jealousy creating an uneasy bass chord to her heartbeat. Looking down at the manky, sedated new patient, she saw the box was lined with an old Sunday newspaper business section and in one corner, beside one of Heythrop's back paws, there was a shot of a man in dark glasses playing polo, captioned Arjan Singh. She set the box down hurriedly and reached inside. But the accompanying story was too shredded and covered in fox pee to make out.

She was so distracted, she didn't spot the fox's vulpine eyes widen as he struggled to gather his wits for a moment before springing out and legging it across the yard, hotly pursued by the lurchers.

'Shit!' Paper flying everywhere, Kat rushed after him, but by the time she'd squelched through the barn arch, he'd vanished into Usha's wood.

Russ was livid. 'He'll never survive in that state!'

Before Kat could get a word out, Mags had sprung to her defence. 'You told her he wasn't going anywhere.'

'I didn't mean "Put the box down."'

Kat bit her lip guiltily. 'I'm sure he'll be—'

'Foxes are hard-core, Russ,' Mags intervened again. 'He'll be fine. Leave the girl alone.'

'The wound will almost certainly get infected. Kat's just sentenced him to a slow and lingering death.'

'You shouldn't have given her the box to hold, Russ. Don't shift the blame.'

'And you'd know all about shifting blame, I suppose?' His fury was redirected to his pink-haired partner in crime, ursine eyes blazing.

'You can fucking talk!' Mags lunged forward with a balled fist, which Russ made to grab.

Without thinking, Kat stepped between them and found herself body-slammed from both sides, which at least silenced them both, although it left her own ears ringing and the yard spinning as she spluttered, 'Just what in hell is going on?'

'Ask *him*!' Mags spat, leaping into her car to try for a wheel-spinning exit, spattering them with mud. Unfortunately she had to stop to let Trevor the peacock strut past before finally roaring away.

'Well?' Kat turned to face Russ furiously.

'I'm going in search of the fox you've condemned to death.'
He stormed into the dark, his anger so far eclipsing hers that
Kat felt any brooding resentment vanish.

She sensed the time had now come to suggest he stop free-
ranging on Lake Farm. But even as she thought it, she chewed
her lip, not wanting to cast him out into the wilderness, like one
of his broken-legged hares.

When she emerged from scrubbing off the mud in the bathroom, Russ was already back and had lit a fire with her freshly
cut wood. He turned to look at her, huge and bear-like, silhouetted in the fire light.

'Forgive me.' He hung his head. 'I was hot-headed and judge-
mental as usual.'

'I'm sorry about the fox.'

'Maybe he does want to be back out in the wild,' he conceded, reaching for a peace offering of foraged hawthorn leaves,
hedge mustard and wild sorrel for a salad. He thrust them at her
like a bouquet. 'I shouldn't have blown up like that.'

'Shouldn't you be apologizing to Mags?' she asked spikily.
'That was quite some fight.'

'We've had worse.' His eyes fixed on hers.

'Yes. I gather you two go back a *long* way.'

'You know we do.'

'I didn't know you were an item once.'

He gave her a wary look. 'Has someone said something?'

'You know this place – rumours everywhere. Why didn't *you*
say something?'

'It was centuries ago. We were kids.'

'You were a *lot* more of a kid than she was. She was practically cradle-snatching.'

'Hardly – she's nine years older than me, and I was a pretty
grown-up teenager. I admit I was besotted with her from the

170

age of thirteen, but she just thought that was funny. Then, when I was on holiday here after my GCSEs, she'd just split up with a boyfriend she'd been seeing and was really down. We got together and it lasted on and off till I went to uni, but then she started going out with Calum and . . . I moved on.'

'I heard she broke your heart.' Kat's own was rattling dysfunctionally in her chest, unbroken but badly dented and bruised, like her ego. Then the truth struck her. 'Oh, God, she's the one who means you keep your love free-range and can never commit, isn't she?' She'd always imagined some wild Charlotte Rampling type in the animal-liberation movement, not dumpy, pierced Mags. But it all made sense. Was it really Mags who had hurt him so deeply he needed the nine times table to get a hard-on, just as Nick had left her with a body that was harder to defrost than the Christmas turkey?

His dark eyes looked at her levelly. 'It took a while to get over, but it's great we're friends again. It's you I'm with now, Kat. If you want my fidelity, I'm proud to be able to offer it.'

Kat thought he sounded as though he was presenting her with an expensive new sound system. 'You prefer free-range relationships.'

'My focus is on us right now. What we've both been through takes a lot of healing. We must learn to trust.' His dimples deepened, the dark eyes filled with compassion, the Tantric urge clearly upon him. 'Mags is history. You're the one I'm with right here, right now, Kat.'

Kat fought an urge to point out that this was pretty obvious, given they were standing alone in the house together. She could hear Daphne whining to be let out, nose rattling the cat flap. 'So what was the argument about between you?' she asked, still prickly with suspicion.

'Vin,' Russ said. 'He's the band's drummer – the one with

the beaded goatee. He and Mags *do* have recent history. He got beaten up last night and has now quit. She thinks I'm the one who told Calum she'd been shagging him behind his back.'

'Did you? Has she?' She was amazed. Russ's band always seemed so staid, their biggest fall-outs involving arguments about the definitive Clash track and who got the dodgy amp on stage. Suddenly they were Fleetwood Mac meets Abba.

'What do you take me for?' He looked offended. 'There are rumours everywhere, as you say. We're all so jumpy about the future here, it's making us turn in on ourselves. Let's find karma.' He was already lighting a joss stick and reaching for the Ravi Shankar CD.

Kat went to let Daphne out, extracting her from the cat flap where she'd got stuck and posting her through the door, breathing in fresh air and weighing up her Tantric desires. A small flame was definitely flickering, fuelled by the day's unexpected twists. She craved the sensual peace of its familiar routine and the reassurance of Russ's eyes gazing into hers, although the realization that his *kundalini* was way behind hers had knocked her back. She wasn't sure her nine times table would hold up this time.

Russ was looking like a seductive bearded guru in the firelight, cross-legged on one of the jewelled floor cushions.

'I quite like it that you're jealous.' He reached back for another cushion, placing it in front of him and patting it. 'It shows how much you care.'

She hesitated. 'I met Arjan Singh's wife today.'

Russ had closed his eyes and was already breathing deeply and rhythmically. 'Is he another sitar player?'

She knelt down on the cushion. 'Seth's wife. At least, I think she was his wife. She might be a lawyer or something. Or an assassin.' She remembered the strange way the woman had looked at her, as though examining a porcelain vase at an auction for cracks. 'She arrived by helicopter, then Dair drove her here. She more or less asked me to name my price so they can buy me out of this place.'

'They don't know you at all, do they?' He chuckled, placing her hand on his groin. 'Relax and breathe slowly. Feel the energy of your *kundalini* draw strength from mine. Today you are going to massage my chakras.'

Humming and omming, Kat tried to get into the swing, but for once she found she was counting very slowly and deliberately, delaying the progress from Russ's chest downwards as she tried to remember whether he'd taken a shower that morning. He smelt of cigarette-infused car and dog fox. She'd offer to run him a bath and carry on with the massage there, but the water needed to heat up.

Having broken off twice to let Daphne in and out again, then reminding Kat several times to keep quiet and think about her breathing, Russ's eyes suddenly went from glazed to hard focus. 'What did you say to Seth's wife when she asked you to name your price?'

'A billion,' she told him proudly.

'No, what did you *really* say?'

'A billion.' She sat back, abandoning the massage with relief. 'You know I won't be bought – the Big Five already tried that.'

'Yes, but they're as mean as weasels. They were trying to palm you off with twenty grand and three acres of waterlogged rough pasture by the main road. This man's a billionaire philanthropist. Think what we could take him for!'

'It's not about the money.' She stared at him, appalled.

'C'mon, Kat. Don't be naïve. We're probably talking about the sort of money that could turn a small private sanctuary into a huge wildlife-rescue operation.'

'The animals here are old and happy. Constance wanted them to die here. Seth will just have to wait it out until they do,' she huffed, standing up and throwing her floor cushion into the corner.

'What are you doing?'

She was snatching jewel-coloured throws and saris from the sofas and walls. 'Calling time on charlatan trick sex.' She folded up the saris and stacked them on the floor cushions, wishing they'd managed to hang on to the revving passion of wassail night. 'Face it, Russ, we're not setting the world alight here. We need to rethink this arrangement.'

Russ was watching her, dark eyes tortured. 'We were breaking through. You can't do this to me.'

'I'm not throwing you out.' She sighed, rubbing her forehead. 'I'm just cooling things. Didn't you tell me the secret of great Tantric pleasure is withholding? Well, let's withhold from each other for a bit.'

'Fine.' He forced himself to sound calm. 'Of course. That's totally your decision.'

He even helped her unhook the tasselled hanging lanterns and put them away.

'I'm here to look after you, Kat,' he promised. 'You have nothing to fear. The animals are safe. If Seth is Sikh, he's not going to allow field sports. Hunting is against their sacred code.'

'I'm sure that's a relief for Heythrop, if not the rest of the village.'

He scowled. 'Let's go to the pub. We need a drink.'

'No, thanks.' She couldn't face the earthmen lined up knowingly by the bar, let alone the cradle-snatching, pheasant-murdering, drummer-shagging cougar behind it.

'Is it because of the Mags thing?'

'Absolutely not.' She flashed the mega-watt smile. 'I'm bigger than that.'

After he'd rattled off on his mountain bike, Kat went outside with the dogs and looked across the lake to the house, all wrapped up, waiting for its new life. She should probably have gone with Russ. Nights in the Eardisford Arms always cheered her up and made her feel less threatened by the shifting political sands that came with every rumour about the estate. They were a protective bunch with many she counted as friends, far more outspoken and reassuring than the sanctuary committee, who talked endlessly about trust, both financial and moral, and thought that justice could be done with a politely worded letter and freshly baked biscuits.

Kat might need the rallying cry of the village and the uplifting back-pat of raucous bar-talk, but she had too much to stew over about Russ. If you take in the black sheep, she reasoned, you're not going to knit a white cowboy hat. He suited Lake Farm so well, the oddball animal-lover with his boundless energy and integrity. He'd made her feel safe here. But lately she'd found herself worrying that she'd yet again chosen the toughest path by sharing the sanctuary with him. Dawn certainly seemed to think so, suggesting he made Kat retreat into her hermit's shell, overwhelmed by the force of his personality and opinions when her own seemed childish and ill-informed. But she was still striving to understand a world she had so much to learn about, the country landscape Russ knew so well.

A movement in the park caught her eye. All she saw was the briefest glint of moonlight against branched antlers. It was the big stag, she realized in delight, her first sighting since last autumn when he'd been rutting. Russ would be thrilled.

She couldn't push him away, she decided. She owed it to

both of them not to rush anything or rely upon the self-protective reflex action that had brought her here in the first place.

Heading back inside, she threw more logs on to the fire, then arranged the saris and *bandhanwar* again, settling on a cushion and staring into the flames as she laid her fingertips on her first chakra. This was much easier alone at her own pace, especially if she could think about Dougie Everett's bottom from yesterday's movie night. By her fifth chakra, she was feeling decidedly hot and randy, laughing under her breath as her body fizzed and bubbled with anticipation, under no pressure to perform for once or to stir another into action, simply find its selfish pleasure.

'Oh, boy!' she gasped, astonished that she'd almost forgotten the painful sweetness of quick-fix desire, of needing to grasp the ultimate weightless freefall and hang from it.

Tantric guru Russ would tell her to stop at this point, take a break, not allow herself to go any further towards orgasm, but Kat, who hadn't felt anything as guilt-free as this since the early Nick years, wasn't about to lose the roll.

'Ohboyohboyohboy.' She laughed, rocking forwards. Perhaps there was something in all this omming after all.

'Door was open, so we let ourselves in!' called a cheery voice, and the dogs rattled up from the fireside in greeting, apart from deaf Maddie who was fast asleep.

Kat sat up, crossed her arms and mustered her brightest smile just in time to greet Pru and Cyn, fresh from the pub where they'd stopped off for the usual nightcap, faces red with Hopflask and gossip.

'Oh, how lovely, you're getting into the Indian spirit, Kat.'

'We had to come straight round when we heard the news,' Cyn panted, her watery blue eyes huge.

'Isn't it *shocking*?' Pru thundered, gunmetal helmet of hair on end. 'It's even brought some colour to your cheeks, dear child. She looks positively flushed, doesn't she, Cyn?'

'In the pink, Pru.'

'What news?' Kat asked, flustered.

'The Indian chappy who's bought the house has banned the Brom and Lem Hunt from the entire estate. Miriam's apoplectic!'

Chapter 17

Dougie could barely sleep at night, constantly reliving the struggle through the choking smoke, the fierce heat that had left his hair an inch shorter and his hands striped with welts, the terror of the little grey horse and the unflinching bravery of his young stallion.

When Zephyr's carbon monoxide levels had been tested the day after the fire, the veterinarians at the equine hospital said he should technically have been dead. The damage to his respiratory system was so severe that they had doubted he'd make it past the first week. But the lion-hearted Friesian refused to give in to medical statistics. The air in the barn had become so hot that his throat was burned inside to a blistered shred and he was unable to breathe without the nostril tubes feeding his lungs with constant oxygen while he was pumped intravenously with fluids and painkillers. Yet his dark eyes still lit up when he saw Dougie each day and he tried to whicker with painful gasps. It was all Dougie could do not to break down and cry on his thick black neck, the magnificent long mane now burned away.

'He's one seriously brave horse,' the vets told him.

In fact Zephyr looked remarkably unscathed physically, the burns and welts on his coat only superficial but, like his master, he was in deep shock, the weight dropping off him as he colicked repeatedly, his guts cramping so badly on the third day that they thought they might have to operate, which was almost too dangerous to risk in his current state. But he kept fighting to live, and that gave Dougie the strength to tough out each tortuous, sleepless night.

The fire investigators reported that it was almost certainly an electrical fault that had started the blaze. The little grey had suffered less damage to his lungs and was doing well, as were all the horses that had been rescued that night. Some, like Zephyr, would take many months to rehabilitate. Without veterinary insurance, Dougie faced astronomical bills, but he didn't care what it cost. That was not what kept him awake at night.

He'd become obsessed with the idea that his team of horses in England was in danger, but he couldn't get hold of Rupe, the mobile always going through to voice-mail, the increasingly impatient messages to call back unheeded.

The fire team had urged Dougie to go for trauma counselling, but Dougie had a deep mistrust of therapy. He knew it would pass. Meanwhile Xanax and bourbon were proving much more effective than the sympathetic eyes of a shrink.

Normally big-hearted Abe would have been his life support, but the agent was on a rare vacation with his family and out of contact. Dougie made no effort to track him down: Abe had never approved of the horses, and had no understanding of their significance. It wasn't as if any had died, yet

Dougie's world had shifted on its axis. Nothing felt safe any more.

Kiki didn't really understand either, but the incident had certainly stopped her goading him about co-star Finlay's desire for her. For the first twenty-four hours after the fire, she rang throughout the day to check he was okay and insisted that he must eat, wash and dress. After that, she clearly expected him to bounce back to normal. She was filming long hours, and when she was at home, her constant chatter washed over him. The tranquillizers and booze immunized him against her neediness and self-obsession. The stage-set politics, demanding directors and dysfunctional costumes didn't register, and he no longer responded by obediently raising his hackles when she tried to fight.

'You're not listening to a fucking word I'm saying, are you?' was her banshee scream after a week. When Dougie didn't respond, she narrowed her eyes suspiciously and demanded, 'Are you mixing meds and alcohol?'

He smiled lazily. 'Would you like me to mix you one too, darling?'

Very little penetrated. The fact that the vet was unable to continue treating Zephyr without Dougie's credit-card number was one of the few things that galvanized him into action as he went to track down his wallet, which had been missing for several days.

Kiki had taken his ash-stained, charred tux out on to the veranda to hang on the washing line because she couldn't stand the smell of smoke on it. Dougie found his wallet in an inside pocket, along with his apartment keys and a clutch of business cards. He looked at the top one.

Seth.

He must have been at the party on the night of the fire,

Dougie realized. The businessman who had bought a production company to stop Dougie getting a big role had attended the Du Ponts' ruby wedding anniversary. Had he been there by design too?

He thought back to the extraordinary meeting with Dollar at the ice hotel and her increasingly coercive calls. What was it Abe had said? *If you turn this guy down I don't think you'll be working for the rest of the year.*

Dougie felt a sudden chill go through him. On impulse, he called the number and found it picked up in just one ring. 'Seth.'

'It's Dougie Everett. I want to talk to you.'

'Good. I'll send a car.' He rang off.

Dougie's eyebrows shot up. His James Bond fantasies were reignited, but they gave him no pleasure. With them came a spark of anger he'd not experienced since the fire. How did this guy know where he was? Did the business card have a secret tracking device? Dougie could have been jogging round Glendale for all the man knew. He poured himself a large drink, remembered he was still wearing yesterday's clothes and decided to take a shower.

When it arrived, the car was an upmarket private-hire limo with a driver in grey livery. Dougie stared out at the landscape sliding by. It was several minutes before he grasped that they were heading for the airport.

'Hang on, I'm not flying anywhere.' He had to meet the vet at three o'clock, and he'd promised some expat friends who shared a house in the hills that he'd call by afterwards, knowing they wanted to cheer him up.

A smart blonde airport official met him at the car and escorted him swiftly through security and up in a lift to a VIP lounge high above the concourse, infused with the smell of wealth, leather seats and rich coffee. Several men in suits were gazing at screens small and large as they awaited flights. A woman in tailored pin-stripes gave Dougie a lingering look, taking in the dishevelled blond sex appeal amid so much monochrome.

'Seth's plane has just landed,' the airport official told him, leading the way through to a small private meeting room with walls more glacially white than those of the ice hotel. 'It's getting accelerated clearance. He will be with you in twenty minutes.'

'Lucky I caught him flying in.'

'He turned his plane around, Mr Everett.' She left him with a nod, and Dougie fought a James Bond urge to scan the room for bugs and escape routes. He had a nasty feeling that he'd just walked into a trap. Lacking sleep, still more than a little pissed, he had conspiracy theories rattling around in his head like ricocheting bullets, wondering if Seth could possibly have been behind the fire. As he waited, the man became a monster in his mind, set on destruction. At least being airside in one of the highest security airports in the world meant there was little likelihood that Seth would be armed, he thought wildly, as the door opened and he swung around – he could take the man down with one quick combat strike before he knew what was happening.

But Seth's smile packed more ammunition than a cargo hold filled with gun shells. Dressed in a suit sharper than a Kasumi blade, he shook Dougie's hand and beamed at him. 'That call was perfect timing, man – any later and I'd have been too far on my way to London to swing a U-turn. I'm Seth. Great to meet you again.' The voice was smooth and unhurried, almost lazy, the accent hard to place, with traces of Yorkshire, India and the States.

Before Dougie could say anything, Seth held up his hand apologetically as his phone burst into life with strains of a recent rap hit. 'I must take this – *Igor, kak d'ela podruga?*' He turned away, instantly talking in the quiet, lethally effective tones of a man whose business fortune earned more interest in a day than Dougie earned in a year.

Looking at the back of his head, Dougie contemplated another combat move, a blow to that neatly clipped neck bringing instant knock-down before he stood over him and hissed, 'Bully me all you like, but never, ever hurt one of my animals!' Even as he thought it, he knew he wouldn't do it. Last night's Xanax was lifting, along with his conspiracy theories.

Seth was talking in a mixture of Russian and English on the phone, and Dougie could see a predator beneath the hand-stitched wool. This was no cheery techno-geek made lucky. The face immediately imprinted itself in the mind, high-cheekboned, long-nosed and watchful, with hypnotically clever eyes. The coat, suit and shoes were all hand-made, Italian and beautifully designed in the understated way that screamed class. Seth was not much older than Dougie, but was what his City friends would call a seriously high-baller.

He turned back to Dougie as soon as he was off the phone, grey eyes serious. 'I heard about the fire. I'm so sorry.'

'Is that why you turned your plane around?' Dougie eyed him warily. 'To offer your sympathy?'

'I want you to work for me.'

'So I gathered. You're more of a no-other-opportunities employer than equal opportunities.'

'Forgive me. My assistant has been a little over-zealous.'

For a brief moment Dougie had an image of Dollar and a can of petrol stalking along the stables aisle before he dismissed it as fantasy. 'My career prospects have hardly improved in the past week.'

'You're a great performer.' Seth's pitch was as positive as Abe's. 'I loved you in *Dark Knight*, man. It was worth watching for the stunts alone. How you can ride so fast carrying a lethal

weapon is mind-blowing, then nailing it exactly on target – pow!'
He settled in one of the squashy leather chairs and indicated for
Dougie to do likewise, but he remained standing, the anger
spark flicking in his pulse. He knew he must stay calm – it was
ludicrous to imagine Seth had had anything to do with the fire,
yet he couldn't shake the notion that a man capable of plucking
him off a mountain in Romania to take him to a hotel made of
ice or turning around a private jet over LA was capable of pretty
much anything.

'Tell me, if you think I'm such a great actor, why do you want
me to put that career on hold for a year to hunt hounds for
you?'

'I don't want you to stop acting. This will be a high-profile role
for you and better paid than any movies you'll make in the time.'

Dougie laughed disbelievingly. 'I can't see the Bafta jury
agreeing.'

'You're the strongest candidate by far. You've hunted all your
life. You're a skilled archer, an experienced marksman and
horseman. I'm mad for history, and you have what it takes to
show off ancient techniques of English hunting using dogs,
employing horseback archery, along with spears, lance and
crossbow, and working with hawks. My Russian and American
colleagues would love to see all that, man.'

'I've never worked with a hawk, unless you count doubling
for Ethan Hawke in a cavalry charge when I was first starting
out in movies. And if you want someone to perform medieval
stunt displays, there are plenty of good trick riders I can recommend. I'm through with that.'

'You need a year out working for me.' Seth ignored his neg-
ativity. 'Your movie career won't go away. You currently have
more Google searches on your name by UK women than any
other British actor.'

'How do you know that?'

'I have a team of researchers. According to them, you were also once the youngest master of foxhounds in England.'

'That's only because my father had to retire from the mastership when he got banged up.' He looked down, uncomfortable with the memory. 'I took over for the rest of the season. Chip off the old block, me – just as good across trappy country, but equally unreliable and easily bought. You won't find many referees on my CV.'

'I don't need a reference, just your agreement.'

'You'd be better off with a good professional from one of the established hunts. Offer them decent accommodation and a bonus and they might even marry your unwanted sitting tenant for you.'

'I'm sorry?' Seth looked baffled.

Dougie smirked, suddenly guessing that Dollar's over-enthusiasm might have led her to omit a few key details to her boss about the job description she'd given him. 'I heard something about a girl who was left a farm on the estate.'

It was Seth's turn to duck his head and look up through a guarded forest of brows and lashes. 'Dollar has that in hand. It's of no consequence. I need you to entertain *very* exclusive clients. They will have the best sport with the most charming of huntsmen.'

'In which case, you'd be better off calling Otis Ferry.'

Seth sucked his lower lip, dark grey eyes amused, a smile showing very straight white teeth. 'I appreciate you may not be capable of providing this level of sport, and I do have other options ...'

Dougie, who would normally insist he was capable of anything, had too many shadows across his life right now to rise to the bait.

'I will pay you half a million pounds for the year. From this, you will need to cover all the expenses of the hunt, including staff and horses. Your accommodation is free, and you'll receive a generous weekly living allowance and your own transport. Anything left over at the end of the year is yours to keep, as are all tips, which I'm sure my house guests will offer. They're very wealthy men, so the tips will be generous, trust me.'

Dougie knew this was a huge amount of money and security by any huntsman's standards – most were paid less than a farm labourer and the accommodation was lousy, often damp and unheated, with no job security. The thrill was in the work. By the same token, it was a hell of a lot more than he'd ever have stood to earn as a stuntman. As an actor, only a big break would come close to matching it. This was easy money. It was an old-fashioned master's guarantee; he was paid it all up front and if he kept control of the purse-strings, he pocketed the leftovers. If he boxed clever, he could easily pay off his current debts and cover all Zephyr's vet bills.

'The position starts on the first of May, so I must have your decision this week. This is a very important position, Dougie. There's a lot riding on it.'

'Including you when the season starts.'

'I will not be taking part in field sports. My faith forbids it. Riding was my great-grandfather's passion – he was a quite brilliant cavalryman.' His eyes darkened and he looked away, watching through the window as a plane came in to land. 'I prefer flying.'

Dougie laughed incredulously. 'So why buy the best sporting estate in England and fill it with huntsmen, game and quarry?'

'It's business.' He stood up and held out his arm to administer another shoulder-loosening handshake. 'I believe in personal contact, which might seem weird for a shy kid who earned his first million sitting in his teenage bedroom creating social gaming networks. But that was why I did it. There's nothing like floating your first company on the stock market before you've lost your virginity to get you out socializing.'

'You're probably not too old to join the Young Farmers.'

That big smile stretched horizon wide, glowing like a city in a night sky. 'Dollar's right. You're "exceptionally well suited".' He mimicked his assistant's deep monotone. 'I want you onside, Dougie, man.'

'You'll have my answer by the end of the week.'

Dougie drove to the equine clinic where the vet still hummed depressingly over a dull-eyed, wheezing Zephyr and upped his painkillers, recommending a specialist hyperbaric oxygen therapy chamber in Kentucky.

'How do I get him there?' Dougie was almost snapped out of his lethargy by the idea of a long road-trip, a mission to rehabilitate Zephyr, an escape from LA and Kiki, which didn't involve poncing around a glorified stately theme park teaching Chinese manufacturing magnates how to shoot arrows.

'We'll fly him,' the vet insisted. 'Least invasive, as long as we keep the oxygen and fluids pumped in. He'll need a specialist travelling veterinary nurse, and our sister practice in Lexington will co-ordinate.' The cost made Dougie's jaw drop; the oxygen treatment alone was a thousand dollars a day.

'For that money, I'd rather fly him to England to chill out at grass with Dad's hunters,' he said flatly. That was where he was planning to send his old horse Harvey, if he could ever get through to Rupe.

'It's way too dangerous to fly him long haul yet,' the vet insisted.

Filled with self-reproach, Dougie tried calling Rupe as he

took the cab to his friends' house in the hills, but it went to voice mail as usual.

There were six missed calls from Kiki and a lot of messages he didn't bother to read as he rang her at the studio to see if he could catch her between scenes. Her PA answered.

'Like, doh? She's not filming today, Dougs. I know you've had a shit week, honey – Kiki said it was like something outta *Black Beauty* – but surely you haven't forgotten her birthday? I heard you guys had something really romantic planned this evening.'

Dougie thanked her politely, mood blackening. He *had* forgotten and would now have to throw air kisses at his friends before turning straight around to kiss arse. His birthday surprise wasn't going to go down too well either. Breaking the news that he'd been offered a year's acting work on location minus the camera and crew might be a bit left-field, but meeting Seth had finally kicked a little of the old, cocky Dougie back into touch and he was certain he could work things out. They needed some time apart. He could salvage this situation.

The party was in full swing in the little house. It was always in full swing here, and the neighbours, who had given up complaining long ago, were partying too. The place was packed. The friends fell on Dougie as if he were a long lost soldier back from the wars.

'Where have you been? Heard about the fire, you poor darling – have a drink. Have you met Charlie? Of course you have. You're old buddies.'

'I can't stay long,' he insisted, but he was soon flying on Wild Turkey, several lines of Colombia's finest and the last nullifying traces of the Xanax to stop him spiking. He didn't bother checking his watch. He felt valued and wanted here, something badly lacking at home. He was a huge success by the standards of many friends, some struggling to get breaks in scriptwriting and production, their lavish LA lifestyle propped up by trust funds. He was a star turn. 'Dougie was *amazing* in *High Noon* – did you see it? He is *so* talented.'

'We worked together on *Ptolemy Finch and the Emerald Falcon*, d'you remember?' He had been cornered by a very pretty blonde outside by the pool.

'Sure! Of *course*. How the devil are you?' Dougie kissed her cheeks, not remembering her at all. She smelt lovely and was fresh-faced, reminding him of a Swedish au pair he'd had briefly as a child who had read him Roald Dahl in a sing-song voice. 'I'll never forget our date.' She giggled. 'You were *so* funny and so hot.'

'Wasn't I just?' He was pretty wasted now, so it was hard to keep just one of her in his line of vision. She kept splitting into two, but he kind of liked that. He'd always had a fantasy about identical twins. He woozily hoped he'd been funny and hot on their date in the witty and sexy sense, rather than in the wearing-too-many-layers-and-sweating-a-lot one.

'I remember I told you I never sleep with a man on a first date so you called the waiter over and booked a table for two hours' time so you could take me straight back out to dinner.' She laughed. 'I said it didn't work like that. But then you fell for Iris and we never went out again.'

'Silly of me.' He was trying hard to stop his eyes crossing and not slur his words. 'We must make that second date some time.'

'I'm free tonight.'

He had a vague feeling he had to be somewhere, but he couldn't grasp the details. When he phoned ahead to reserve his favourite restaurant table, there was some confusion.

'You already have a table booked with us tonight, Mr Everett, sir.'

'Well, that's handy! What time?'

They had over an hour to kill. He told the cab driver to go to a club he knew where they served the best whisky sours in Hollywood, but he was so wasted he kept getting the name wrong. He also started to feel seriously nauseous as the cab crawled towards West Hollywood in heavy traffic. The cough he'd had since the fire made him sound like a tuberculosis victim. He put his spinning head in his hands.

'Are you okay?'

A warm arm reached around his shoulders, fingers tentatively stroking his hair. She was so soft, sweet-smelling and motherly. He remembered back to that yurdy-gurdy voice reading about golden tickets and Oompa Loompas. He wanted to curl up in her lap. 'I think I need to lie down.'

'My apartment's just off the next block.'

The identical twins in the small, pretty apartment went from fully clothed to naked in less time than it took Dougie to inhale the fresh white lines laid out in the bathroom. He suddenly no longer wanted to curl up in her lap, or in their lap, although her lap was still very much where he wanted to be. As she split in two and re-formed again, like a reflection in a hall of mirrors, he blinked hard to keep those delicious, creamy curves in one place, then walked towards them, unbuttoning his shirt and smiling widely.

It wasn't the greatest sexual performance of Dougie's life. The coke in the apartment had been far purer than the stuff at the party and he thought he was never going to come, the minutes rocking by as he moved her into every conceivable position to try to get his rocks off. Yet the blonde was acting as though this was the most amazing sex of her life, groaning and moaning ecstatically from the back of the sofa, the tabletop, all fours, up against the wall and on her knees.

'Are you an actress?' he asked, guessing she'd seen a few closed sets.

'Wardrobe assistant,' she panted, as he flipped her over on the bed and plunged in from behind. 'I was responsible for Purple's armour.'

That was enough. The thought of that gleaming breastplate wrapped around Iris's fragile torso, her tiny waist and small upturned breasts enclosed in sculpted silver brought a rush of heat to his groin.

The girl screamed something sounding suspiciously like 'Scrumdiddlyumptious!', which rather put him off, but he was thankfully too far through to lose momentum.

Afterwards, he was ravenous and still extremely pissed, raiding her fridge and finding only a vitamin drink and some shrivelled salad.

'Hey, I'm not about to let you welsh on a date.' She laughed, rushing towards the shower. 'I've always wanted to eat in that place.'

He'd forgotten about the table in the restaurant, which was a legendary celebrity haunt. At least they were close enough to walk, and Dougie badly needed the fresh air. As he tripped along the sidewalk, he spotted paparazzi hovering near the entrance.

'We'd better enter separately,' he muttered, hanging back. 'You go in first.'

When Dougie sauntered into the restaurant five minutes later, Kiki was sitting at his favourite table with a pretty blonde whose body Dougie had been penetrating from every known angle just half an hour earlier. Having been shown there by the maître d' when she gave Dougie's name at the door, the blonde wardrobe assistant was puce with embarrassment, too terrified to run.

'Thank you for my birthday present,' Kiki said, with carefully modulated calm, her pale eyes murderous.

For once, the smooth James Bond one-liner eluded him as he muttered, 'Oh, fuck.'

Kiki coolly removed her engagement ring and hurled it at him.

Several camera phones captured Dougie at his most ignoble as the ring hit him in the eye. The fact that he was too proud to scrabble around for it meant he'd just quadrupled his debts as he turned to leave, yet his heart felt lighter than it had in weeks. He had made up his mind. He was going hunting.

Chapter 18

Holed up in his friends' house in the hills, Dougie didn't sober up during the week that he had to prepare to leave for the UK. Nor did he pack or talk to Abe about what he was doing. And he made no attempt to contact Kiki, despite the furious missed calls queuing up on his phone. The only thing he did was organize for Zephyr to be transferred to Kentucky for his specialist rehabilitation treatment, borrowing the money to do so from one of the few long-suffering friends he hadn't fingered for cash in recent weeks.

He also called Rupe's number incessantly before giving up and ringing around mutual friends to try to track him down.

'He's playing polo in Argentina, I think,' an ex-girlfriend told him. 'It's a shame about the team.'

'What about it?' His waking nightmares of the past week seemed about to be proven real. 'Are the horses okay?'

'He sold them all, Dougie. Some big stunt trainer near Windsor bought the lot.'

Apoplectic, Dougie phoned every animal trainer in Berkshire. He still owned a fifty per cent share of the team horses and a hundred per cent of Harvey. And it was the grey he really cared about. Harvey was family. It was like a child being sold without his permission. The other horses were well trained, needed jobs and would work hard for anybody who knew what they were doing. Harvey was old, crabby and eccentric with a mind of his own.

At last, he found the new owner of the six stunt-trained Friesians and three Iberians.

'Was there a big grey?' Dougie demanded. 'An old hunter.'

'Never saw him.'

Just as Dougie was preparing to go to Argentina and wring Rupe's neck until he coughed up Harvey's whereabouts, a message came through from Buenos Aires. *Harv on his way to you! Used some of the money from selling others to buy his passage to LA. Hope okay. Know you said you wanted him there. Look forward to catching your next movie. When's the wedding? Rupe.*

To the surprise of the international transporters who had just flown an ugly grey hunter from Heathrow to LAX, they were asked to fly him straight back.

'I'm afraid there's no availability for at least two weeks,' they explained.

Dougie was not in a mood to hang around. 'I'll take him hand luggage if I have to,' he raged. 'He's trained to sit and his arse is smaller than most Americans'.' He sent a message to Dollar that he would be travelling alongside his horse as soon as the transporter found him an available slot.

Such bloody-mindedness was a deliberate form of self-destruct enacted many times before in Dougie's life, leading him to be thrown out of school and officer-training corps, his ability to access authority thwarted by an over-controlling father. He fully expected Seth's assistant to call to tell him the job offer was off. Instead, super-cool Dollar arrived at his bolthole in person the following day to escort the unshaven drunken hooligan to LAX.

'I'm travelling with my horse!' he ranted incoherently, as she picked her way around the hung-over, post-orgy mess in the Hollywood Hills house to gather what few possessions he had.

'Your horse's transport is all in hand,' she told him, in her deep, enunciated voice. 'I have made alternative arrangements.'

'What are you talking about?'

'A professional groom is travelling with him. He will touch down in England in about eight hours' time.' She glanced at her watch. 'And you will arrive shortly afterwards, if we can get you on to an aeroplane without the crew smelling that you are drunk. I told Seth he should have sent Deepak with the private jet.'

'Why didn't he?' he asked belligerently, swaying dramatically as he tried to put on a pair of shoes and almost fell over a girl asleep on the floor in her bikini.

'Your horse is taking that.'

When he gaped at her in amazement, she tilted her blank face to one side and sighed. 'It was a joke. You really are very drunk, aren't you?'

She then forced him to knock back so much black coffee that he had to pee every twenty minutes.

On the plane, Dollar handed Dougie his new contract. It was almost thirty pages long.

'I'm not really into long, complicated airport reads,' he apologized, reaching into his pockets for a pen so that he could sign it.

Dollar plucked it from his hand and laid out the contract in front of her. 'We must run through the important points first,' she insisted.

Huffing irritably, Dougie signalled for an air stewardess to order a large bourbon, which Dollar immediately cancelled, asking for bottled water instead.

Dougie, who had hoped for first class, was disappointed to find himself crammed into business on a packed plane, small screens beaming out entertainment all around him. One of the films on offer was *High Noon*, he noticed wretchedly. A woman across the aisle was watching it and casting him discreet, excited looks. He closed his eyes and feigned sleep as Dollar started going through the contract and its many stipulations. Among them was a non-drinking clause.

Dougie's eyes flew open. 'No way!'

'All of Seth's staff refrain from alcohol. It is company policy.'

'Do you blood test that?'

'Occasionally.'

'Jesus!'

'We also prefer that employees' language is non-religious in the professional environment.'

'Does that apply to the hounds too? Because I warn you, most hunting dogs speak in tongues. That was a joke,' he added, when her eyes flashed dangerously. 'You really are very sober, aren't you?'

'No, Mr Everett, you are just not particularly funny.' Her voice dropped to a hiss. 'I am aware that you have had a very difficult week, and I am prepared to make allowances for your current state. But as soon as this plane lands, you are expected to respect Seth's values and principles.'

'Only if I sign the contract,' he reminded her, closing his

eyes belligerently. 'You only got as far as the no drinking and blaspheming clauses. Is my sex life also subject to employer-authorized bullet points?'

'I shall personally oversee that side as the need arises,' she said, without expression.

Dougie opened one eye, glanced across in surprised amusement, guessing her English had let her down. 'Oh, I'm sure it will arise, especially for you.'

'That is good to hear.' The steady, dark gaze met his with a half-smile before she returned to her notes, and he suddenly wasn't so sure her English had let her down at all.

Having donned a pair of dark glasses to avoid the furtive stares of all the passengers around him now watching *High Noon*, Dougie drifted into a restless sleep while that monotone voice outlined details of the hunt work at Eardisford. He dreamed that he was dressed in black tie, pursuing robot prey with high-tech laser guns, waking groggily to consume a meal that defied his body clock. With much-needed carbohydrates on board, he eyed Dollar again, feeling more like his old self. She really was incredibly pretty, her pink tongue savouring the plastic food – the vegetarian option – which she ate surprisingly fast.

'I must warn you, I'm now on the rebound,' he told her lazily, pushing the shades up on to his forehead.

She put down her teacup and swiped her tablet computer into life. 'This is to your advantage. I have information for you to read about Katherine Mason.'

'Who?'

'The girl who runs the sanctuary at Eardisford.'

'Ah, yes, the one you want me to marry.' He laughed, not believing for a moment that she seriously expected him to try.

But her big dark eyes were glowing from her blank face, as animated and sincere as he had seen them. 'That is correct.'

'And is this a part of the contract?' he humoured her.

'Indeed. We will cover that section now.'

'Does Seth know about it?'

She gave nothing away, her face as serene as the Madonna's, the tablet screen her newborn Saviour as she gazed into it, her finger stroking its cheek to reveal a blurred photograph of a girl with a huge smile. 'I am micro-managing your role. The details are down to me. Seth approves of arranged marriages. He will soon be entering into one himself.' Her voice tightened slightly. 'I have now met with Katherine Mason personally and I think she will be receptive to this approach. She is not very intelligent and is extremely juvenile, but she is attractive sexually. It will not be difficult for you to seduce her into marrying you. If you succeed in that task, you will be paid a one-million-pound bonus, tax free.'

He laughed, shaking his head. 'Make it a billion and I'll think about it.'

To his surprise, Dollar came close to a smile, the corners of her mouth definitely twitching. 'This girl could be a very good match for you. You have a great deal in common.'

'You just told me she's juvenile and not very intelligent.' He peered at the photograph again. 'I know your lot think marriage is best sorted out on a long distance Skype call to Aunt Jamila, but I prefer something a bit more intimate.'

'Given your track record, I'd suggest Aunt Jamila's judgement should definitely be taken into account,' she said starchily. 'I believe you have already had three marriage proposals accepted and you're only thirty.'

'That's nothing. My father's been married six times. Perhaps you should get him to do this for you. Admittedly he's not much use with a bow and arrow, especially Cupid's, but women adore him, he's always strapped for cash and he rules by absolute decree as well as decree absolute. I'll give him the heads-up if you like. Dad can follow the scent of fox and money better than any hound.'

She ignored the outburst. 'We'll cover your legal costs should you need to divorce swiftly. It's all in the contract.'

'A contract wooing. How quaintly old-fashioned. And what makes you think this woman will ever agree to marry me?'

'That problem is reflected in your pay scale,' she said smoothly. 'A million pounds is a great deal of money. And you are a very attractive man, a movie star and an English aristocrat. What impressionable girl would not want to marry you?'

'I can name three,' he said idly, but his ego was feeling slightly bolstered again. He moved closer and dropped his voice to an intimate purr, eager to test her sexy, humourless cool. 'Tell me, Dollar, are you Seth's lover as well as his PA?'

'I am neither. My Hindi job title is *Kali* – it is difficult to translate, but it is more of a personal protection role. And as for my lover, I'm still interviewing.' The half-smile twitched again and the dark eyes glowed as he remembered seeing them do in the ice hotel, a lightning fast intensity that was thrilling.

He beamed back, wondering how easy she would be to wind up. 'In that case, when are you available for dinner, or can I take you straight to bed for the oral interview?'

It was supposed to be a joke – and he knew it wasn't his best – but to his surprise she said, 'I will have to check my diary. I am not interested in dinner.' Then she turned back to her tablet. 'However, your attraction to me is irrelevant to this conversation. Your professional interest is in Katherine Mason.'

Dougie looked unenthusiastically at his million-pound bonus on screen, a small, scruffy redhead. On first impressions, she was absolutely not his type. In a few grainy photographs, courtesy of a *Mail on Sunday* feature about the contested will, she looked like a wannabe Anne of Green Gables. Definitely a gold-digger, he decided, cashing in on a frail and vulnerable old lady in her dying months. He'd be more inclined to accept the job of assassin than seducer.

Dollar started to scroll down and read: 'Miss Mason is thirty. Her father was in the army, her mother is a classroom assistant. They divorced when she was eight. She has younger brothers who are twins, now in the army. Both her parents remarried, although her mother's second marriage didn't last. Katherine went to school in Watford where she achieved good grades and subsequently trained to become a nurse. She was engaged at twenty-six to a firefighter, but the relationship ended two years later when she went to work for Constance Mytton-Gough. Nobody else appears to have been involved.

'She was the primary live-in nurse and carer at Eardisford for one year, although the job was not expected to last so long because Mrs Mytton-Gough was very ill when she started. But it seems she responded well to Miss Mason's care and enjoyed a happy and active final year of life. The two became very close and made an agreement in which Miss Mason would remain at Eardisford to run the "animal sanctuary" after her boss's death. This is why she resides at Lake Farm, where she is now living with a local man called Russell Hedges.'

'She has a partner?'

'It is a very recent relationship, we understand, and not serious.'

'Can't he marry her?'

'We do not believe he is in a position to do so. I have printed out all these files for you to read, along with your contract and purchasing brief.'

'Purchasing brief?'

'We have shopping to do, Mr Everett. Seth believes Eardisford needs horses as a matter of urgency. His advisers have drawn up a shortlist.' She swiped her screen a few more times. 'Appointments have been made to see them in the coming days. I will accompany you.'

'I can sort out my own horses, thanks. I'll make a few calls later.'

'Please do not waste your time. These are the animals we are seeing.'

'I thought the budget was mine to spend.' He peered at photographs of several classy-looking Thoroughbreds. 'And these are racehorses, not hunters.'

'Seth would like you to compete in a local race meeting next weekend. He feels it would be a good way for you to be introduced locally and raise your profile. These horses are all proven winners that have already been entered.'

'It might have escaped your attention, but I'm not a jockey. He should have hired Frankie Dettori.'

'This race is for amateurs. I believe you have competed many times in the past.' She was swiping her tablet again to bring up a photograph of a mud-splattered Dougie in brightly coloured silks receiving a bottle of champagne from an aged landowner in a wet field.

Recognizing himself in his father's racing colours, he laughed incredulously. 'I can't just swan in and try to take all the silverware at the local point-to-point. Do you realize how unpopular that would make me? Besides, one needs a certificate of eligibility and all sorts. Dad owned pointers for years and the paperwork drove him crackers.'

'All the paperwork is taken care of. Your popularity is not of concern. We want the people to see you as successful and audacious in the first instance.'

'I'm far from racing weight.'

'A week without drinking can make a great deal of difference, you will find.' She gave him that sideways half-smile again. 'And I assure you that you will be *very* well mounted. You have my word.' This time, he knew her English was entirely deliberate.

He smiled widely back. 'Where do I sign?'

By Heathrow, Dougie was having serious second thoughts about the job, which might kill his acting career stone dead as well as entombing him in contractual obligations he could never live up to. He had friends in London who'd help him out; he could go to see them. He'd been living away too long. He wanted to party with his old mate Mil in Soho; he wanted to take Harvey home to Cottesley; he wanted to see his father, who was an unmitigated bastard on most fronts but knew his horses and would understand his need to ride off demons. He was also feeling a sudden, unexpected drench of guilt for the way he'd treated Kiki. He hadn't even apologized or said goodbye. Talk about kneejerk. He longed to call her to explain but his phone battery had gone flat in flight mode. He was also desperate for a drink.

Dollar was a formidable warder, marching him through accelerated disembarkation, refusing to let him out of her sight until they had transferred by car to the Crowne Plaza hotel.

'Don't tell me, you've booked the penthouse suite for the afternoon to oversee my sex life.' He cheered up a little, even more so when he realized he was in close proximity to a long row of optics as the hotel bar beckoned.

'We are setting off from the helipad here,' she explained witheringly.

'In which case, excuse me.' He dived into the hotel to use the Gents. Creeping out after a lightning fast pee, he nipped into the bar. But Dollar was one step ahead of him and leaning against it, the corners of her mouth twitching again as she finished making a call on her mobile. 'Deepak's ready to take off.'

Dougie might have been disappointed by the standard transatlantic flight, but seeing the golden helicopter again cheered him enormously.

'Good afternoon, Mr Everett.' Deepak greeted him once the headphones were on. 'Did you have a pleasant flight, sir?'

James Bond fantasy back in place, a strangely uplifting comfort – albeit without the martini sun-downer – Dougie enjoyed the flight to Herefordshire, soaking in the familiar jewelled patchwork green and frothy white piping of an English spring beneath him. As soon as they swept down over Eardisford, his eyes widened. He turned to Dollar. 'This place is out of this world!'

She pointed out a huge curl of a lake in the midst of vast tracts of ancient parkland, its banks fringed with trees, among which was an exquisite farmhouse in a clearing. 'That's where you must shoot your arrow through a heart.'

'You do know that bow-hunting any animal has been illegal in Great Britain for years?'

She looked at him incredulously. 'I am talking about Cupid's arrow.'

Chapter 19

The brook that raced through the lower woods alongside Lake Farm was keeping Dougie awake at night in the mill house a quarter of a mile downstream. The waterwheel had long since stopped turning and was grandly displayed behind a glass wall in his basement kitchen – a great centrepiece design idea that was impossibly impractical because preparing anything to eat was deafening when the water levels were high.

Once rented out as a holiday let, the mill was relatively homely by estate standards, with a watertight roof, power showers and night-storage heaters. There was even a vast claw-footed bath in the master bedroom, which Dougie lay in for hours on his first evening, topping up the water and admiring the view across the river to the water meadows. Ideally, he would have preferred to live closer to the stables, but the two apartments there, which would be shared between the rest of the hunt staff, were damp ice boxes. His commute to the 'office' was a five-minute walk.

So far all he'd seen of Eardisford was the enormous, wrapped-up house, a glimpse of majestic parkland, his own noisy digs and – most importantly – the estate's stables, one imposing flagged courtyard for carriage horses and the other, cobbled and more modest, for hunters and hacks. The most recent incumbents had been the Brom and Lem Hunt servants, hounds and horses, based there from the 1940s when the army had handed Eardisford back to the Myttons after the war. The flats above the offices had been split into two for huntsman and whipper-in; the lower yard was divided with high walls and adapted to kennel hounds with raised fencing, chain-link barriers and pens; the stabling had been patched together over many decades to cope with decrepitude and excitable horses. Upon merging with the neighbouring Lemlow pack after the ban, the hunt had finally relocated to the dryer, more convenient purpose-built kennels of their new bedfellows. The magnificent buildings had been abandoned in recent years, but Dollar had been quick to point out the restoration work already taking place to bring them up to Versailles standard for visiting trigger-happy tycoons and globe-trotting oligarchs.

After twenty hours' travelling together, it was a relief to be rid of Dollar who, for all her calm beauty, was a tyrant. She was staying in a local spa hotel, from which she could keep in contact with the outside world and burn off enough energy in the gym to power a small generator.

Equipping the Eardisford Estate with the highest speed broadband and mobile reception was not proving as straightforward as anticipated, Dougie gathered, even with huge cash incentives available to expedite the process. Local residents, already locked in a painfully slow campaign to raise private capital to replace old cabling with fibre-optics and eager to get Seth onside, had not reacted well to his planning application to site a giant 4G mast on a much-loved hill.

The lack of any signal was a blessing for Dougie, who was grateful not to be able to make or take calls in the aftermath of his split from Kiki. In public, Kiki was serenity personified – the 'amicable' break-up was blamed on 'pressure of work' and the terrible fire. But the voice mail messages he'd heard before he lost the signal had made it clear she was tantrumming big-time. Finlay was obsessed with her, she said in one, practically *stalking* her. How could Dougie do this to her? She knew the girl in the restaurant meant nothing to him, she wept in another, that the fire had screwed with his head. He was her hero. He was a bastard, she screamed next. He'd never work in the film industry again if he spoke to the press about their relationship. 'We both know the truth, Dougie. You thought being with me would help your career, but I can't carry you. I'm worth more than that. You're dead weight. Go to your muddy little country and get a life.' In the next call, she begged him to come back.

Dougie threw his smart-phone into a drawer, aware that fifty per cent of his relationship had been conducted through a SIM card. His guilt for leaving was fading, and he was grateful to be spared more exposure. The confidentiality contract with Seth meant he had been deliberately vague about his whereabouts in England to his LA friends. No doubt the press would find him soon enough: the locals were hardly going to keep quiet once he was recognized.

He wasn't planning to dwell on his million-pound bonus. It was totally preposterous and impractical, and would get in the way of good sport. As his father was fond of saying, 'If one chases two scents in the field, one loses both.'

Yet Dougie found himself lying awake until the early hours, his body clock totally out of alignment, his mind whirring as he contemplated the challenge and imagined just what he could do with a million pounds. It would buy Harvey an awful lot of oats.

After a lightning breakfast meeting with Dollar, who had a packed schedule of appointments with architects and planners, Dougie spent his first day touring the jaw-dropping expanse of Eardisford's farms and forestry in a Range Rover alongside the po-faced, monosyllabic Scottish estate manager, Alasdair 'Dair' Armitage. Dair clearly disapproved of the new 'Hollywood huntsman'. Being generally off the Scots since meeting Finlay, Dougie made little small-talk and received almost nothing back, but he gleaned enough insight to appreciate that Seth was increasingly mistrusted locally: he shrouded himself in mystery, and his plans for Eardisford's sporting rights were being kept especially tightly under wraps. Both Dair and Dougie knew that private hunting was planned, but neither man made direct mention of it.

Dougie was blown away by the beauty of the estate, which was on a scale owned privately by only a handful of British aristocratic families. Having been run by a skeleton staff for decades, it was gloriously anachronistic and spectacularly run down, but the sheer unspoilt expanse of it was so magnificent it was hard to take in. Having complained to Dollar that it was very hard to hunt hounds on just one land holding, he was starting to see the possibilities.

The estate's tenanted farms were extensive, numbering at least twenty, mostly arable, accounting for more than half of the land. There were also huge tracts of rough pasture, including the hill where the mast was planned, mostly grazed by sheep, other areas forming artificial moorland where grouse-shooting traditionally took place. It was the sporting side of the estate that was the real show-stopper. It had been the only profit-making area for twenty years, Dair told him proudly. The shooting and fishing were second to none, and Dougie could see why, the river curling and twisting in a shoal of pebble-sided banks just perfect for coarse fishing, its tributaries and lakes positive orgies of carp and trout breeding. The woodlands were the size of small towns, rich and diverse, from the vast ancient chase, Duke's Wood, at the far end of the estate where medieval nobility had hunted boar and stag, to the swathes of pine plantations, new coppices and old coverts. The crowning glory was the parkland, almost five hundred acres of ravishing turf planted with spectacular specimen trees and fashioned with follies, bridges and lakes, including the majestic three-acre crescent that dominated the main park.

Dougie had fully expected Lake Farm to form part of his tour, but it seemed the subject of the sanctuary was off limits as far as the Scotsman was concerned. All he said on the subject, in a dour Highland whine, was 'No hunting dogs, guns or followers will be permitted on the land between the lake and the river under any circumstances.' From the reverent tone of his voice, Kat Mason was either a great deal more beautiful than her photograph made out, or she was some kind of witch. She certainly seemed to be adored by the tenant farmers they'd visited, almost all of whom had managed to drop her name into the conversation alongside that of Constance Mytton-Gough, always with chuckles and smiles. Seth's name made them sit up and clear their throats nervously.

Dougie was concerned by the high degree of local suspicion and mistrust about Seth and his plans, particularly from the neighbouring hunt, the Brom and Lem, who, Dair reported, were bristling that they were no longer welcome on Eardisford's fifteen thousand acres, which accounted for almost their entire Wednesday country. A furious letter was waiting for Dougie when he arrived back at the mill, addressed To Whom It May Concern and signed by almost every one of Eardisford's neighbouring landowners to support the hunt's long-standing service to the estate that had once been its home. As the new pack's master, one of Dougie's first responsibilities was to forge relationships with those whose land adjoined his country, and he'd not been given an easy start. He guessed swanning into the point-to-point would not improve local opinion of him.

Having plundered the fridge in the noisy kitchen at the mill – filled with green sludge health shakes, he discovered rather crabbily – Dougie planned to take a walk alongside the millstream to get a closer look at Lake Farm, but he was hit by a wall of jet-lag and crawled into bed. Within two hours, jet-lag had turned to fever and he sweated his way through an uncomfortable, aching night as twenty-four-hour flu took hold to welcome him back to England.

He awoke from nightmares of being chased by tigers as he galloped through burning forests to find Dollar looking down at him, arms crossed and eyebrows aloft.

'I was just dreaming about you.' He stretched out lazily, not caring too much where the bedding fell. The fever had passed, but he still ached, his head pounded and he was ravenous.

'You will get up. We have horses to see. I take it your quarters are comfortable?'

Propping himself up on one elbow, he rubbed sleep from his eyes with the other hand and raked back his hair to smile at her. 'Actually, they could do with a massage. This bed's seriously hard.'

Her beautiful face remained expressionless as she appraised his body. 'There is much work to do. You have a good physique, but you looked better in *High Noon*.'

He laughed, unbothered by the criticism, which he thought was probably fair. 'I worked out a lot for that role.'

'It was a very good movie.' She was still staring at him, the dark eyes glowing. But then she ruined it by saying, 'You smell bad. Take a shower.'

Wrapping the sheet around his hips, he wandered to the window where a sunny English spring morning cheered him, birds frantically flirting in the branches of the alders and willows alongside the millstream. 'I prefer baths.' He knew a shower was more practical, but the bath took for ever to run, which might buy him the time to wake up. Plus he needed to soak off the flu. He guessed he must have sweated off some weight.

'You have twenty minutes.'

He turned on the taps, looking up at her through the rising steam, giving her the biggest, sexiest Everett Effect smile in his armoury. 'Would you care to join me?'

Red spots in her cheeks, she thrust up her chin and stalked to the stairs. 'I have calls to make.'

'She blushes.' Dougie whistled to himself, clambering into

the steaming bubbles. 'How interesting.' He closed his eyes, wishing he didn't feel quite so rough. The muscle aches were punishing, a combination of detoxing, a long flight and flu.

Twenty minutes later, having failed to summon a signal on her phone anywhere in the vicinity, Dollar found Dougie still deep in the bath.

'Please dress and come downstairs. We will be late.'

'Thank God you're back!'

'Secular language only,' she reminded him.

'Thank fuck you're back. I'm stuck. Cramp. Need a hand.' He reached out, his face white with pain.

She hurried to help, but as soon as her hand closed round his, he let out a groan and rocked forwards, almost pulling her into the bath with him. His body was a slithery, muscular mass of sweet-smelling spasm as he rocked back again, the blue eyes filled with apology and amusement. 'Sorry. Bad idea. Be gone in a minute.'

Letting go and straightening up, she watched helplessly as he hissed through his teeth and braced his well-built arms against the sides, huge golden shoulders quilted with tension, handsome face paler than ever.

'This is a common problem?'

'Never had it before,' he said honestly. 'Not very manned up. Sorry, but it bloody hurts more than riding a battle scene with a broken arm, which I did, incidentally, just in case it helps convince you that I'm not a total girl's blouse.'

'I don't need convincing,' she said huskily.

Cramp subsiding, he looked up at her, the apologetic smile transforming into the big Everett come-on, as charmingly upfront and sexy as a four-poster made up with Egyptian cotton and scattered with rose petals. 'That's good to know.'

'You feel better?'

'Enormously. I'm sorry you got soaked.' The smile widened, blue eyes playful. 'Although that's a girl's blouse I'd be happy to look at all day.'

Glancing down, she saw that her shirt was dripping, her lacy red bra clearly visible through it.

'Would you mind passing me a towel?' He loomed out of the bath.

She made no move, red spots in her cheeks deepening, her eyes unable to tear themselves away from a glorious full-frontal erection. 'Bananas.'

'I beg your pardon?'

'For cramp.' She looked up at his face. 'Eat bananas. The potassium will help.' She took a towel from the rail to thrust to him. 'We leave in five minutes.' Poker-faced once more, she went to investigate the tumble-dryer.

Dollar had been busy, procuring Dougie a car and a small Indian groom, who spoke no English and appeared to be called Gut.

Dougie complained about both: the car was a flashy all-electric estate that would never take the workload around the estate's green lanes, and Gut, who had been working for a top flat-racing training yard, was built like a flea.

En route to see his first horse at a local point-to-point yard, he finally found he had mobile reception and called his father to ask if his old pick-up could come out of the tractor barn where it had been doubling as a chicken roost for several years.

'I heard you were back.' Vaughan Everett sounded delighted. 'Not getting married this year after all?'

'Watch this space, Dad. D'you know of any good kennel huntsmen still without a position for next season?' When his father learned that Dougie was going to be based at Eardisford, he let out a bark of recognition. 'I've been shooting there. Tremendous place. Old Ronnie Gough was a terrific card. Fought in El Alamein with your grandfather.'

'I assume your research team knew about my family connection?' he asked Dollar, when he came off the phone.

'It will be in the notes.' She sounded bored.

'Let me guess. It's as irrelevant as my interest in you.'

'I no longer consider your interest in me irrelevant.' She glanced across at him, the red spots in her cheeks glowing along with the determined eyes. 'Having reflected on the matter, I believe I may be able to help you with your rebound.'

Dougie found her formality a terrific turn-on. He would have liked to pull a James Bond move and drive the car off-road to a quiet spot to explore the rebounding options alongside the seat-reclining ones, but his ongoing flirtation was severely hampered by Gut sitting on the back seat looking car sick.

For all her cool, Dollar was not comfortable around horses, keeping her distance as she looked through the information on her tablet computer and used it to take photographs. Still pale and queasy, Gut made a silent and expert appraisal that impressed Dougie as he pointed out every conformation fault and blemish with a jerk of his head or flick of his fingers.

'Stringhalt.' Dougie nodded when the little man pointed out the way the horse snatched up one hind leg in walk. 'Shouldn't affect his action at full speed. Dad had a novice chaser moved like that, won the Foxhunter twice.'

The horse, a stringy bay called Kevin Spacey, was well raced and at the top of its game. Dougie was looking forward to some fast work on a Thoroughbred, as far detached from his beloved Friesians as Kiki was from Dollar, but as soon as the trainer legged him up into the saddle, he froze.

Dougie stared at the glossy black avenue of pulled mane in front of him and the questioning, black-tipped ears at its end, not understanding what was happening. He could barely hold the reins, cold sweat rising, his whole body clamping into a self-protective muscle lock. At first he assumed it was a throwback to the flu bug, but as the horse moved off and he was swamped by cold tremors, it occurred to him that this was the first time he'd ridden since the fire. As soon as he thought about it, he was fighting for breath, as though the smoke was still in his lungs. He'd never imagined it would affect him so strongly.

One short burst of canter along an all-weather track was enough to bring Dougie close to blacking out. The line of birch practice fences in the grass ridge at the top of the hill seemed to come in and out of focus.

The gelding was an honest one because they made it over eight full-sized steeplechase jumps without Dougie contributing a single thing to the ride.

'He's a great horse,' the trainer told Dollar, as they watched from his car. 'The owners want top price, but he's worth it. Could do a Grand National next year. Your jockey's a bit out of practice, I'd say.'

'Jet-lag.'

'Thought so.' He smiled charitably, although he secretly thought Dougie looked desperately outclassed and distinctly out of condition. 'Needs a few saunas to make the weight.'

'I have an exercise regime lined up.' Dollar smirked and watched Dougie trot back, pale face for once unsmiling.

'I think we should buy this one. He's a bloody saint. Even you could ride him.'

The next horse they tried was not so forgiving, unseating his rider over a simple hurdle, leaving Dougie with a bloody nose and two black eyes.

'We will have to disguise that on race day,' said Dollar, dispassionately. 'I suggest you do not introduce yourself to Katherine Mason until it fades. It is most unattractive.'

She had been coolly businesslike all day, barely reacting to his nasty smash, or apparently noticing that he was riding like a dork on a weekend pony trek. He guessed there were some advantages to her ignorance around horses.

'Miss Mason will be representing the sanctuary by riding in a race on Saturday,' she was saying. 'This will be your first encounter, so we need you to look very handsome and catch her eye.'

Dougie perked up slightly when he heard that Katherine Mason was an experienced horsewoman, capable of riding in a point-to-point. He'd had her down as a tree-hugging hippie. Getting to know her might be more fun than he'd anticipated.

'I'll be sure to use plenty of slap,' he muttered, mopping up blood, imagining himself course-side at the point-to-point in a movie-location makeup trailer, hitched up amid the burger vans and bookies' stands.

'Slapping will not be required,' she said, deep voice betraying an element of shock.

He eyed her with amusement. 'One can be banned for excessive use of the Pan Stik.'

When she stared at him blankly, not understanding, he mustered an Everett Effect smile. 'My father always used cayenne pepper and Vaseline on black eyes – he carried a pot ready-mixed in the pocket of his hunting coat.'

'Did he fall off as much as you do then?'

'He hardly ever fell, but he slept with a lot of married female followers. It was their husbands who gave him black eyes.'

212

Chapter 20

Like Dougie Everett, Kat was having a taxing day in the saddle, although her skills were far more basic.

'Kick on!' Tireless Tina called, from the opposite end of the sand arena, reading a text on her phone and not noticing that Kat was hanging on tightly while Sri cut the corners in a fast trot, curling ears flat against her head like a diving hawk's wings. Breaking into a loping canter, the mare then skewed away from the rails, let loose a fly buck and deposited Kat unceremoniously in the dirt before stopping and standing benignly over her. Watching from the arena rails, the Lake Farm lurchers – whom Kat had thought safely confined to the old kennels but had followed her to Tina's yard – narrowed their eyes against the blustery wind, which lent them a look of horrified disappointment.

Kat had been riding the skewbald Marwari mare for just over a week now and had fallen off every time. Spitting salty blood and sand from her mouth, she gathered up the reins and remounted. Constance had told her it took seven falls to make a rider, which, by Kat's calculation, made her a rider several times over. She had started to dread her lessons. Sri seriously objected to her retirement being interrupted. As critically steely, blue-eyed and domineering as the woman who had bred her, the mare lacked the sense of humour that had united Constance and Kat. She was a natural herd leader; a light touch, quick wit and instinctive talent gained her respect, and Kat had none of those skills in her riding repertoire yet.

She knew she wasn't anywhere near ready to take on Sri,

who had none of the tolerance and stoicism of Tina's old teaching horses, but her instructor seemed increasingly reluctant to lend her own, especially Donald, whom Kat was supposed to be riding in the charity race. 'Let's save him for the big day!' Tina had insisted cheerfully. Kat knew she was so bad that poor Tina couldn't bear to watch.

Sri knew it too. The mare might have accepted Kat as the main source of feed, comfort and occasionally fun, but she was a long way from believing that she had a clue what she was doing in the saddle, and Kat could understand why. The world's most uncoordinated rider on the world's most opinionated horse was not a good combination. It was like bringing a Ronaldo back out of retirement, pairing him with the local pub's worst five-a-side player for a kick-around and expecting him to be happy about it. Even Tina struggled to make Sri do as she was told, and she'd ridden and competed with horses all her life. 'I'll be frank,' she'd said, when she hurriedly dismounted after riding the mare for just a few minutes. 'I think she's very tricky. Okay, dangerous. Okay, psychotic.'

Yet Constance's challenge to ride the Bolt was all about the last of her Marwari herd, and Kat felt compelled to push herself harder, acutely aware that all eyes would be on her at the charity race that coming weekend, including Sri's. She might be riding another horse in it, but those blue eyes would be watching from the sanctuary stand where the rare Marwari horse was among several Lake Farm animals that would be on show while the volunteers rattled tins. Kat knew it was a bit batty, but she thought that if the mare saw her riding in a proper race on Donald, she might just accept that Kat wasn't entirely hopeless.

'Have I missed something?' Tina looked up from her phone. 'Why have you stopped trotting?'

'Just having a breather.'

Tina tucked the straggly blond curtains of her bob behind her ears. 'Frank says that Eardisford's new owner just bought Kevin Spacey for a small fortune.'

'He bought twelve trafficked teenage virgins from Albania yesterday, according to the earthmen,' she reminded her. 'But it turned out to be a geography trip from Brombury High School looking at the ridge and furrow pasture on Cuddy's Clump.'

'Kevin Spacey is a point-to-pointer.'

Rumours were flying around the village that Seth had moved in at last and was on a spending spree to populate his new manor, but Kat thought it unlikely, given that the huge house remained swathed in scaffolding and gift wrap just as it had been for the past ten weeks, builders' vans still lined the carriage sweep daily and JCBs were digging up great swathes of parkland to make way for a landing strip, helipad, polo field and a golf driving range. Lake Farm continued to be of particular interest to visiting engineers and surveyors, who had spent a lot of time eyeing it up from the other side of the water through April's thickening bulrushes and iris spears, taking photos with iPads. Kat was growing accustomed to looking across the lake to find a man in a grey suit and reflective waistcoat peering back through a theodolite.

Seth was no longer seen as quite such a Very Good Thing locally. When the Brom and Lem had been told that they could no longer hunt the estate, he was seen as a Less Good Thing. As soon as the planning permission application had gone in for a phone mast on Pick's Hill, he was seen as Quite A Bad Thing. If he didn't show his face soon, he would undoubtedly be upgraded to a Dangerous Thing. It was always the same in a small rural community, where knowing your neighbours dispelled the enemy.

In Watford, by contrast, Dawn was spellbound by the idea of

the dotcom billionaire moving in next door, demanding regular updates when calling to offload about the stresses of house selling. 'The agents now think we should do something about the garden,' she'd huffed the previous evening, 'so I have tons of topsoil, ten square metres of decking and a flat-pack gazebo on order. Dad and his mates are going to help me fix it up next weekend. It means I can't come to cheer you past the winning post, which I'm seriously down about, but I know you'll be amazing. I reckon Seth will whisk you away in his helicopter and woo you. I am *so* jealous.'

Kat wished she shared her friend's confidence in her riding skills and pulling power. Gazing at the curling skewbald ears in front of her now as she wobbled around the arena in an uncontrolled trot again, she felt nothing but relief that she would be riding Donald in the charity race, not dangerous, psychotic Sri.

But her instructor was delighted with their progress.

'We'll have your names engraved in the plinth for the Ladies' Race next year, eh?' Tina called out now. 'We might even swap your charity race entry to this girl on Saturday.'

Lifting her head abruptly, as though she had understood every word, Sri ground to such an abrupt halt that Kat flew on to her neck. Unlike kind Donald, who would lower his unbalanced rider gently, Sri dropped her head like a trebuchet arm ejecting a missile, leaving Kat indented in the dirt.

'I think the only engraving on plinths will be in memoriam,' she joked. '"Here lies flat Kat."'

Hacking back across the fields after their lessons was always Kat's favourite bit about riding Sri. The mare was completely in charge, curling ears pricked, eyes alert, knowing exactly where she was going as they marched along the headlands from Tina's little yard to Lake Farm, dropping through woods carpeted in a haze of bluebells now, and out into the Eardisford parkland, which had remained ungrazed so far this year. Meadow flowers jewelled the bottle green grass in pinks and yellows, polka-dotted with white dandelion clocks, like a gaudy hotel carpet.

Two yellow JCBs were do-si-doing around a large earth mound close to the walled haha, engines droning so loudly that Kat didn't hear the car approaching behind her as she crossed the main drive towards the woods, lurchers and terriers hugging the mare's heels. Then Daphne let out a warning yelp and the mare shot forwards down a sharp bank, throwing Kat backwards out of the saddle so that she dropped the reins and was almost sitting on her rump, arms windmilling in the air. The speeding silver car didn't even brake, its blond driver wearing such dark glasses that he didn't seem to see her, or the dogs, which escaped the tyres by inches as the unfamiliar car roared past, music blaring out of its windows. Scrabbling back into the saddle, Kat had just enough time to register that she'd met one of the passengers before when there was an indignant squeal beneath her and Sri took off across the park at breakneck speed.

'That's her!' Dollar called urgently, as the rider and horse sped into the woods, one's red hair matching the asymmetric red patches on the other's coat. 'Katherine Mason.'

'Unique riding style.' Dougie accelerated towards the house, ignoring Gut's nauseous groans behind him. 'Nice-looking horse. Strange ears.' He took the right fork to the stables and dropped off his groom.

Driving more steadily to navigate the bumpy back tracks that led to the mill house, he found Dollar's long fingers had moved from her tablet to his thigh. He looked across in surprise and found her radiating hot-skinned anticipation, dark eyes glowing in that immobile face. 'I will be spending this evening with you.'

Despite the pounding headache, Dougie felt a satisfying leap of anticipation in his groin.

'I will cook for you,' she said.

Dougie, who ate for fuel and had always found Mary Poppins domesticity a turn-off, felt his libido immediately drop to stand-by. He thought of the green sludge in the fridge. 'Really, you don't have to.'

'You must have a special diet between now and the race – low carbs, selected proteins, fat-burning super-foods. And you must taste my lobia.'

'That sounds delicious.' He cheered up. 'I'd like your lobia as a side dish with everything tonight.'

'It is a good source of the potassium you need and also fibre and protein. When I lived with a *kalari gurukkal* he often prepared it to his own recipe that I have kept.'

'Was he some sort of chef, then?'

'He is a grand master in the Indian martial art of *kalaripayat*. It is extremely skilled violence.'

'Is he still around?'

'He's in prison for killing a man.'

Dougie swallowed and flashed his big-screen smile. There was something about the way Dollar spoke that could be incredibly unsettling, particularly when she said things like that. 'I can't wait to taste your lobia.'

'Then it is fortunate your kitchen cupboards are filled with good spices. We will also need black eyes.'

'I already have those.'

'You do?'

He touched his fingers tentatively to his swollen nose, and the purple shiners on either side.

She flashed a rare smile. 'Dougie, lobia are black-eyed *peas*.'

'I gotta feeling,' he started to laugh, 'that tonight's gonna be a good night.'

Chapter 21

Still picking pieces of twig out of her hair from her unexpect-edly swift short-cut home, Kat found Russ and Mags in the Lake Farm sitting room designing flyers for the point-to-point on his laptop and listening to the Clash so loudly that even deaf Maddie was hiding at the opposite end of the house.

'We should call the press!' Russ leaped up excitedly when she told them about her near miss on the drive. 'They'll love it: *New landowner tries to runs down sanctuary owner after she refuses cash bribe to leave.*'

'I don't think it was deliberate.'

'Are *you* okay, love? Were you hurt?' Mags looked con-cerned, piercings clicking as she furled her brows and grabbed Kat in one of her bone-crushing hugs.

'Take more than a tit in a flash car to frighten Kat,' Russ insisted. 'I think we should tweet about it.'

'How do you know the tit was the new landowner?' Kat squeaked from the oxygen-starved confines of Mags's tattoos.

'She's right.' Mags let her go with a pat on the back that loos-ened Kat's fillings. 'The new squire probably does all his hit-and-runs by sedan chair.'

'Did you fall off?' asked Russ, noticing her dusty breeches.

'Not just now.' Kat went to the iPod dock to turn down the

music, unable to stop grinning as she remembered Sri flying through the woods at full pelt, the most incredible feeling of power and speed, however out of control. It made the Bolt much more than just a pipe dream: it was a taste on the tip of her tongue.

'How's the promo stuff going for the stand?' She looked at the flyer design on the computer screen. It said *Save Our Sanctuary* with a picture of a fallow deer fawn caught in a snare. 'I thought we agreed to have a photo of Usha and just general information.'

'This has more impact.' Russ turned back to the laptop and plugged it into the elderly printer, groaning when he noticed that the magenta cartridge was empty. 'Why didn't anybody order more?'

'Because we haven't got any money.'

'Let the trust pay for it.'

'Why should they when you were the one who used it up printing posters promoting your band?'

'The next gig is to raise money for the sanctuary.'

'That doesn't mean we have to pay to print *all* your flyers, Russ.'

'Enough!' Mags looked like she was about to knock their heads together. She had very straightforward relationship techniques, as witnessed by her recent reconciliation with Calum over cider, cigarettes and arm-wrestling after the Vin-the-drummer débâcle.

He set his bearded jaw, dark eyes brooding. 'I resent the insinuation that we're freeloading.'

'I said enough!' Mags growled at him. 'Kat's right. We'll buy some ink.'

Kat caught a look passing between them that she studiously ignored, uncomfortably aware that it was more like two parents playing good-cop-bad-cop with a whingeing child than star-crossed lovers.

Since Russ's revelation about his teenage fling with Mags and its possible long-term effect on his sexual performance, he had been at great lengths to prove that the old friendship was now purely platonic – which unfortunately seemed to involve him seeing a lot of Mags platonically at Lake Farm, accompanied by loud music. But Kat still couldn't entirely shake the worry that the hot air and volatile fights between the two indicated sparks from an old flame that hadn't been fully extinguished on either side.

This was all Dair's fault, she thought irritably. The duplicitous, interfering, flat-capped estate manager had been keeping a very low profile lately, no doubt trying to poison a few more relationships between liaising with Seth's glamorous assistant as they worked out how to eject her from Lake Farm for the right price; she wasn't holding her breath for her billion.

In the spirit of camaraderie, she now volunteered to cook supper, although the cupboards held little inspiration and her veggie patch had been raided by rabbits again, offering up nothing more than a few well-nibbled spinach leaves. All she had to supplement them with was a can of black-eyed beans, some ancient onions and whatever eggs she could collect, which vegan Russ wouldn't touch. She set about chopping onions for a bean fry-up to go with omelettes for her and Mags, listening to the laughter drifting through from the sitting room where they appeared to be making placards.

Mags had brought along some unwanted bottles from the Eardisford Arms, and Russ was already stuck into his third Cloudy Sickbay, a new scrumpy line that had unsurprisingly failed to be a hit. As usual when inebriated, he was talking about himself a great deal, now nostalgically recalling the liberation of his university's laboratory animals. 'The Cumbria ALF were the bravest band of brothers I knew. I kept a lab rat and called it Ken. He lived in my pocket throughout my third year, and came sabbing every weekend.'

'You're da boss, Russ!' Mags must have heard the story a dozen times, but ruffled his hair with motherly pride. 'Did you name him Ken after Livingstone?'

'Loach,' he said darkly. 'I watched *Kes* a lot as a student. I had a thing about falcons I needed to get out of my system.'

While Kat half listened, pulling herbs from the pots on the windowsill, Mags started to argue that it was Ken Russell, not Loach, who had directed the movie. '*Tommy* was a work of genius.' It soon turned into one of their trivia-trading arguments, which Kat found impenetrably boring.

Leaving them bickering over it while the onions sweated, she went out to check on Sri. She'd washed her off after her exertions but the horse had to be fed before she was turned out. All of Russ's residents on the wildlife wing needed feeding and watering too, and the chickens were hiding in the bushes in the back of their run, chuntering furiously, which she guessed meant Heythrop had been on the prowl again. The libertine fox was certainly alive and well, if recent evidence was anything to go by: they'd lost two chickens this week, and the lurchers were out on regular scouting missions following his scent runs. Kat worried for their safety now that the estate was so busy, dreading the thought of the Eardisford keepers taking pot shots if they got too close to the pheasant-rearing pens. But Constance had always said lurchers were forces of nature: *You will never confine them, Katherine. Simply distract them until danger passes, like the best type of man.*

The two Lake Farm lurchers were already out on walkabout again. She called in vain, but they were out of earshot.

The geese and ducks had left yet more eggs, all of which she gathered up, along with some dandelion leaves to reassure Russ she'd been foraging, making a mental note to take more eggs around to Bill and Babs the following morning.

The sun was setting so low over the lake that its red beams shone right through the house from front to back, turning it into a light-box. She could see the two figures in the sitting room silhouetted in it, apparently locked together in an embrace. Stepping back in surprise and dropping three eggs, Kat shielded her eyes to try to see better, but the sun was totally blinding her.

She hurried inside.

'. . . and then I told the jumped-up bastard to stick his hunting horn where the sun don't . . . ' Russ was cackling while Mags rummaged in her handbag for a cigarette. They were sitting a respectable three feet apart.

'You all right, love?' Mags caught her startled face in the door.

'Fine!' Kat relaxed, feeling silly. It must have been a trick of the light. This was definitely all Dair's fault for sowing the seed of doubt in her mind.

'Sure?' Russ blinked at her. Then his eyes slid to Mags.

'Sure! Bean, chervil and wild garlic fricassee coming up.'

'Great.' That look was exchanged again. Indulgent parents. Kat registered it with renewed surprise.

'I hope that's not the vegan dog eating these dropped eggs?' came a familiar nasal Scottish drone from the still-open door.

Kat flashed a big defensive smile at her small, tweedy Iago. 'Dair. How amazing – I was just thinking about you.' Behind her, Russ cranked up the Clash again.

Dair's cap peak was practically resting on his upper lip as he stood framed in the door, but his chin seemed terribly pleased. 'Good thoughts, I hope?'

'If you're into hard-core sado-masochism, maybe.' Moving away from 'I Fought The Law' booming behind her, she noticed Ché desperately wolfing up the broken yolks on the doorstep by Dair's feet.

The mention of sado-masochism had sent Dair hurrying back out to the yard. 'I brought your peacock back,' he called over his shoulder. 'He was pecking hell out of a Mercedes parked outside the mill house.'

'Thanks.' She followed him out. 'He thinks his own reflection's a love rival. He's longing for a mate.'

Dair let out a loaded sigh, clearly identifying with Trevor's plight. 'Is your lovely friend Dawn coming to the point-to-point?' he asked.

'She has a hot date with some decking at home, I'm afraid. Brawny landscape gardener. Huge biceps.'

Pursing his lips in silent disappointment, he headed towards his car to release the peacock, who was occupying the back seat like a *grande dame* heading for a ball and pompously ignoring Dair's gundogs in the boot on the other side of the metal grille, both barking at him furiously.

Watching Trevor eye up the gear stick, Kat remembered what Dair had said he'd just been pecking: the silver car that had almost run her off the drive had been a Merc.

'Who is the new tenant at the mill?' she asked.

Dair might be ridiculously cagey and two-faced at times, but at least she could rely on him for occasional gems of gossip. 'His name is Douglas, although he's about as Scottish as the Isle of Wight.' He opened his car's back door and a streak of turquoise feathery pique shot out. 'And he is to be referred to as "equerry" for reasons that seem to confuse him as much as they do me.' He turned back to her, eyes locking on her chest as usual. 'I met him yesterday. Bit of a lightweight, I thought.

He's some sort of stunt rider, I believe.' He cleared his throat awkwardly. 'You'll probably recognize him.'

'I don't know any stunt riders. Why would the estate need one?'

'I'm not at liberty to say.' He inclined his head towards the gales of laughter coming from an open window, overpowering even the Clash for volume. 'I'm just looking out for your interests, Kat. Nobody wants to see you hurt.'

'Something's burning in here!' Russ called.

'Been burning for bloody years,' Dair muttered under his breath, but Kat had already dashed back inside to rescue the blackened onions. She doused the pan with Cloudy Sickbay cider, but it was beyond help, plumes of noxious fumes billowing from the bubbling, charred mess.

'I'm on my way to the pub for a pot roast.' Dair peered inside before he left, waving a hand in front of his face. 'Perhaps I can offer you a lift.'

'No, you can't.' Russ appeared from the sitting room and marched to the door where he loomed over the little tweed-capped one. 'What are you doing here anyway?'

'Peacock.' Dair made it sound like an insult.

'Dair very kindly brought Trevor back.' Kat opened a window, eyes streaming. 'He says someone's moved into the mill, an actuary.'

'Equerry,' Dair corrected.

Russ's thick eyebrows shot up. '*Equerry?* I thought only the royal family had those.'

'The job title is indeed somewhat contrived.'

'Is he ex-military?' demanded Russ, suspicions alert.

'Mmm, I believe so. You probably know him.'

Kat could tell from Dair's chin that he was having a moral battle, clearly desperate to reveal more. 'He's a trick rider apparently.' She leaned over the kitchen counter towards them. 'Isn't that right, Dair?'

Dair cleared his throat, unable to resist baiting Russ. 'It would be more accurate to term him a professional huntsman.' He dropped the verbal match into the fireworks and stood back.

Russ exploded just as predicted. 'Hunting fucking *what*?'

Dair's mouth turned down thoughtfully. He was clearly pleased with the result. 'He will be responsible for all mounted sport within the estate. I can say no more than that.'

'But we're not talking gymkhanas I'll bet,' said Mags, coming through from the sitting room and reaching up to put a protective hand on one of Russ's big shoulders. 'That'll be why they've banned the Brom and Lem from Eardisford land. They're starting up a new hunt of their own. I'll get straight back and ask Calum what he's heard. There's bound to be talk. What's this guy's name?'

'Douglas,' Kat started to chop more onions, not quite knowing how to react to the news, which Constance would have celebrated with tears of joy, and to Russ was like a declaration of war.

'He calls himself Dougie,' Dair revealed, chest puffed out proudly as he pulled out his trump card, unable to keep the disparaging tone from his voice. 'Dougie Everett.'

'The same name as the actor?' Kat looked up in astonishment, wiping away the onion tears.

'See how you've upset her?' Russ raged at Dair. 'The idea of animals being slaughtered all around us for sport is too much for poor Kat to bear, you bastard.'

'I resent the impli—'

'Really, I'm not crying because of—'

'Russ, don't wind yourself—'

'Eighhaaarghhhhh!'

They all swung around to see Trevor the peacock at the door in full display, head on one side. He forced his way inside. Behind him, a mangy dog fox was sitting boldly in the centre of the farmyard, a bald cuff around his neck where a snare injury was scarring over.

Later, while Russ was plugged into the farm's dial-up internet connection – which was slower than communicating with semaphore but enabled him to email his hunt saboteur connections with the heads-up about Eardisford – Kat went in search of her dictionary to look up 'equerry' and read that it was an officer of honour, from the French '*écurie*' meaning stable, or '*écuyer*' meaning squire. As she pondered why Seth would need an officer of honour, the second batch of onions burned.

'Carbon footprint stew,' she joked, when she eventually presented Russ with food.

It was surprisingly tasty. Kat wolfed hers far too fast, along with an impossibly rich goose-egg omelette. By contrast, Russ ate slowly and deliberately as always, fixing her with the same dark, intense gaze he used during mutual massage sessions. There was no long lecture about blood sports as she'd anticipated after today's news. Instead, he was subdued and thoughtful, his eyes studying her face.

'Dair Armitage still fancies you,' he said eventually.

'Did you think he'd have gone off me by now?' She laughed. 'I think he's just pining for Dawn.'

'It's good you have his trust. It's going to be useful.'

'I don't think trust's quite the word you mean. Lust maybe.' She ran her finger around the plate to catch the last of the stew, sucking it appreciatively, thinking back to the last village hall movie night. 'Do you think this equerry could be the same

Dougie Everett who was in *High Noon*?' The memory of all those Wild West seductions remained a secret thrill.

'Unlikely. Mind you, I wouldn't be surprised if he needed a career change; I thought his accent was shit.' Russ reached across to the sideboard drawer that housed the joss sticks. 'The girl was quite good, though.'

Kat was almost deafened by Ravi Shankar's sitar starting up on the stereo. Russ was holding out his hand, dimples on show.

'Tonight,' he breathed, 'we will truly awaken your *kundalini*.'

Head still full of leather chaps, Stetsons and spinning spurs, she decided they should give it a go.

Dougie guessed Dollar's lobia was an acquired taste; it had the texture of lumpy wallpaper paste and one hell of an after-kick. He craved a huge glass of cold white wine to wash it down in place of the coconut water she claimed would help cleanse his system.

Her body, however, tasted exquisite, making for the perfect sweet dessert. She was extraordinarily well toned, almost too ripped for his taste, but the soft depth of her skin feminized the muscle and sinew, and she excited him enormously. He wanted to press her up against the cool glass of the internal window that looked over the waterwheel for a knee trembler, but she surprised him by saying, in a throaty purr, 'Let me massage you.'

Russ was humming a lot and moving his hands around a few inches above Kat's body as she lay back on two jewelled cushions spread on the floor, trying to identify which scent of joss stick he'd lit. It was the one that always reminded her of the cleaning fluid they'd used in hospital corridors. Ravi had got stuck on track eight again and was sampling away happily.

'You'll feel the heat of my hands,' Russ told her, in his softest Bristol burr. 'I am moving your *kundalini* up your body. Can you feel it?'

It was lovely to lie back at last – she hadn't appreciated how much she ached from falling off and then being bolted with – but it certainly wasn't very hot. She had a few goose-bumps, if she was honest, although there was no wall of frozen self-protection and fear, which she was certain was progress.

'Your *kundalini* is moving,' Russ breathed.

Something was moving as Kat's belly let out an almighty groan. 'I think it's the black-eyed beans,' she said, clenching her buttocks and hoping her *kundalini* hurried upwards.

'Je-*suuuuuuuus!*' Dougie warbled, like a Swiss yodeller, as Dollar hammered his long muscles with the sides of her hands.

'No religious words, remember? This sports massage will help prepare you for the week ahead. I am fully trained.'

There was a loud crunch as she bent his arm across his back and leaned on it as though preparing a chicken for deboning. Dougie howled in pain.

'Try to relax.'

'It bloody hurts.'

'We will have intercourse shortly, which will relax you.' She made it sound like an enema and, for the first time in his life, Dougie found himself doubting he could perform.

Kat woke herself up with a sharp snore, looked around in alarm and saw that Russ was sitting in the glow of his computer nearby, making changes to the flyer. *Save Our Sanctuary* had been replaced with *Stop The Eardisford Wildlife Slaughter* and abbreviated to *STEWS* in one hundred point red font that looked like splattered blood. 'Stew' was not a word she wanted to dwell on this evening as a low bubbling in her belly reminded her that her *kundalini* had stayed as firmly trapped as her wind. She must have drifted off to sleep, which was not unusual and Russ always graciously said was an important part of the healing process and sexual awakening, but she felt a stab of shame nonetheless.

'That was *sooo* relaxing,' she said warmly, to make him feel better, stretching out luxuriously, then regretting it: her body had stiffened from falling off Sri, but her trapped wind was determined to let loose.

Russ nobly pretended not to hear. 'I found a magenta printer cartridge in the desk after all – it was below all the unopened bills.'

Silently wishing he'd found her *kundalini* – and not mentioned the bills – Kat propped herself up on one elbow. 'Maybe we should tone down the slogan a bit. It's a hunt event, after all, and we really don't know what's happening on the estate. The equerry could be a lovely old horse-whispering hippie for all we know.'

'Fine,' he said tetchily, scrolling along the slogan *Stop the Eardisford Wildlife Slaughter* and adding *Man* to the end. 'Better?'

When Kat said that, no, it wasn't, Russ adopted one of his huffy expressions and grabbed his knapsack. 'I'm going to set up camp by the lower stream and see if the otters are back.'

Kat was quietly relieved that at least she could break wind at will.

'Jeeee—'

'Sssh!'

'Jeeeeshhhh!' Dougie had vastly underestimated his enthusiasm and performance power. He was on a gold run tonight.

The vigorous massage might have deboned the chicken, but there was one notable omission, and it was driving the Dollar higher and higher.

'Ooooh, my good Lord!' The deep voice rose to a girlish shriek.

'No religious language!' He laughed, then gasped and cried out a joyous, blaspheming stream of invectives as he exploded inside her. As infinite pleasure points found release through his pummelled body, like a shoal of arrows, he distinctly heard howling.

Turning his head, Dollar's breath now hot on his neck, Dougie ignored the fierce bass heartbeat pounding through his ears and listened hard. She'd heard it too, and she rolled out from under him with uncomfortable speed to reach for her handbag and run towards the windows. 'Wolves!'

'There are no – whoa!' Dougie spotted the glint of a gun barrel in the moonlight as she crouched into assassin stance at the open window, an ominous click indicating the trigger guard was off and she had something four-legged in her sights. He sucked his teeth, thinking fast. Explaining that wolves – and, indeed, firearms – were strictly licensed in England was going to be far too long-winded. He started to pull on his trousers. 'Put the bloody gun down and I'll chase them off.'

Outside, Dougie found two lurchers, one smoke grey, the other brindle, both howling at a peacock that was standing on top of the shiny silver Mercedes and looking argumentative. As Dougie stepped out of the shadows, the lurchers scarpered and the peacock's tail feathers went up in outrage.

'*Mayura!*' Dollar was laughing with relief at the window and lowering her gun.

Dougie admired the plumed display and said, in his best Bond drawl, 'A black-eyed peacock, how apt. Tastes delicious roasted with an olive stuffing.' He squinted up at her, his swollen eyes aching. 'How on earth did you get hold of that gun? Please don't tell me you managed to get it past Customs when we flew in.'

'Of course not, but Seth has contacts in this country that supply us with hand arms when we visit.'

'Why do you need a gun?'

'A rich man has many enemies, Dougie, as you will undoubtedly find out.'

'I'm pretty certain those dogs weren't after his loot.'

'I hate dogs.' She shuddered. 'In India, the pariah dogs carry rabies.'

'Well, here they're more likely to carry one's slippers. And if you're going to pull that thing out every time you see man's best friend, I wouldn't recommend a day at a point-to-point.'

Chapter 22

The Brom and Lem Hunt point-to-point was among the friendliest venues on the racing calendar. Held late in the season to give its flood-prone course the best chance of being dry, it was a big crowd puller with an end-of-term atmosphere, its attendance boosted by a country fair with gundog and falconry displays, a parade of the Brom and Lem hounds and a novelty charity race, this year in aid of the Constance Mytton-Gough Animal Sanctuary.

Kat, who had accompanied Constance to the event before her death, could never have imagined then that just two years later her own name would be on the race card. Muddy, gutsy point-to-pointing had been among Constance's favourite pursuits and she'd owned several winning horses, including the sanctuary's ancient, milky-eyed pensioner Sid in his hey-day. Highly competitive and disciplined, hunt race meetings were an opportunity for amateur jockeys to vie for honours 'between the flags', galloping super-fit Thoroughbreds twice around the mile-and-a-half course of nine hefty birch steeple-chase fences. The spectators were a far cry from the boozy urban punters who crowded the grandstands on licensed race-tracks. Here, on a windy Herefordshire hill overlooking the ancient course that ran alongside the river Lugg, local coun-trymen, landowners and farmers had already started to gather in human coppices of waxy green and tweedy brown as Tireless Tina's elderly horsebox swung in through the gates, its cab crammed with children, dogs and a nail-chewing ama-teur jockey. On board were several of Lake Farm's more placid retirees to draw visitors to the Constance Mytton-Gough Animal Sanctuary stand, along with Donald, the horse on which Kat would ride the charity race at the end of the day. Before that, she braced herself to endure a great deal of good-natured ribbing about the costume she reluctantly pulled on as soon as they parked.

'I lost a bet with Mags and Russ last night,' she told a star-tled Tina, explaining the Animal Magnetism home-made outfit, a pot-bellied deer suit of padded fake fur with a large sticking-out bottom, fluffy tail and dangling hind legs that made it impossible to sit down comfortably. 'I won't even ask if my bum looks fat in it.'

'As long as you're not planning to ride in it, that's fine. Very cute.' Tina smiled encouragingly, then ruined it by dissolving into giggles as she glanced at Kat flailing around in the cab, like an expectant mother in a furry onesie perching on a birthing ball.

At least the costume took Kat's mind off the charity race, which had kept her awake the entire previous night. She knew a five-furlong dash after the serious racing had finished was child's play compared to the terrifying leaps of faith involved in charging around the jumping course earlier in the day, but it was among the biggest dares she'd ever taken on.

It took her a long time to get from the lorry park to the sanctuary stand because she had so many people to say hello to, her antler head under one arm and a lead rope straining in each hand as the two Shetlands she was towing with her snatched at the grass underfoot. She deflected the teasing valiantly: 'I know, isn't it amazing? Mags made it.' 'Huge shoulders, yes – I'll have fun with the Portaloos!' 'Really looking forward to the charity race, yes.'

Wishing Russ and Mags would arrive to help – they'd still been face-painting one another in the Lake Farm kitchen when she'd set off with the animals – Kat delivered the ponies to their pen by the sanctuary stand while Tireless Tina hauled on her baby papoose backpack and gathered up her other children to take up her stewarding role amid loud promises of ice creams and an each-way bet if they behaved themselves. The point-to-point was run by an army of volunteers made up of the Brom and Lem's followers and supporters, regimenting the car park with military skill, charming all-comers to part with cash at the race-card stand, manning number boards, gates and enclosures, and keeping up a welcoming commentary. MFH Miriam, a hint of lace fluttering tantalizingly from the neckline of her tweeds, was supervising the horses and jockeys with a band of jolly ladies; Babs and Bill Hedges were manning the bar with red-faced cheer; the earthmen lurked excitedly by the fences ready to pack back parted birch as well as scooping up fallen riders and catching loose horses. Soon the hunt staff would be mounted in their red coats ready to steward horses on and off course, the huntsman blowing his horn at the start of each race to see them away.

High on the hill amid the burger vans, trade stalls and bookies, Cyn and Pru were already manning the sanctuary stand, which was decked with banners and posters, along with the collecting tins and boxes of STEWS flyers that Kat and Russ had delivered last night before unwisely heading to the Eardisford Arms.

'Why on earth are you dressed as a deer?' Pru demanded disapprovingly. 'We had T-shirts printed.' She'd matched hers with sensible moleskins and lace-up shoes, her German-helmet hair so shiny you could almost see the clouds reflected in it.

'I lost a bet in the pub last night.' Kat's head ached from too much Dutch-courage cider. She also had an unpleasant recollection of Russ betting at least a hundred pounds on her winning the charity race.

'We're both going to have a little flutter on you later,' Cyn announced cheerfully, making her feel even more anxious. 'And we're *definitely* fluttering on the film star in the Men's Open.'

'What film star?'

The sisters showed her the list of runners and riders in the race card, among which was listed a bay seven-year-old called Kevin Spacey.

'I think that's the horse's name,' Kat pointed out kindly.

'Below that.'

'*Property of the Eardisford Hunt.* Oh, God, don't let Russ see this.' The jockey was the Honourable D. J. H. Everett.

'Vaughan Everett's son,' Pru breathed reverently. 'He was born in the hunting field and his father's a master. The family rarely use their title, but he's an hon like Con. This young chap rode point-to-points many times before he was distracted by acting. We are in for a real treat.'

'It *is* the same man?' Kat was astonished, remembering the taut buttocks the entire village had enjoyed watching in action recently. The rumours had being doing the rounds for almost a week now, but nobody could substantiate them, and those who had met Dougie simply reported that he was very affable, knew his sport and had a brace of black eyes. Now they all had definitive proof that he bore the golden ticket of celebrity, the gathering crowds were agog to see the newcomer in action, and gossip blew around the course faster than the blossom and twigs being spirited along in the sharp wind.

In the flapping sponsors' tent, flirty Brom and Lem joint-master Frank Bingham-Ince was courting VIPs with largesse and champagne as he played down the loss of his best hunting country to the Indian billionaire and his celebrity huntsman. 'The English sporting estate is no longer just a playground for aristocrats and oligarchs – the rupee outclasses the rouble by a country mile these days. And Eardisford's modern maharaja clearly hires his staff to act the part. What are the odds he's got Rowan Atkinson as his manservant, Vinnie Jones as a hench-man, and Dame Maggie Smith will be installed in the Dower House before you know it?' He chuckled pompously. 'Mind you, if Dougie Everett's as corrupt as his father, we're in for trouble. Vaughan was notoriously bent in Westminster. He'd exchange anything for a peg at a good shoot.'

At the sanctuary stand, one of Russ's comely teenage cousins was touting Brom and Lem Hunt raffle tickets. 'Have you heard about Dougie Everett riding in the Men's Open? I am *beyond* excited!' She fanned herself with her ticket book. Dressed in the customary young-farmer-chic uniform of denim hot-pants matched with a nip-waisted tweed waistcoat, chunky knee-length tan leather country boots and a fur headband with her blond mane piled above, she was pink-cheeked with delight. 'Is it true he lives, like, practically next door to you, Kat?'

'So I believe.' Now sweating heavily in her butch Bambi outfit, Kat secretly regretted not wafting around to the water-mill with a basket of eggs earlier in the week.

'OhmyGod, that is, like, so cool,' the cousin gasped, fishing in her pockets for lip gloss. 'I read in *Heat* that his engagement with Kiki Nelson is off. I am so *in there*.'

When Kat headed back to the lorry to fetch the rest of the Lake Farm menagerie, an oversized fox was sitting on the ramp smoking a roll-up and texting. In her orange fake-fur hood, face paint and eye-mask, her figure corseted into a spectacular hour-glass, Mags was barely recognizable, although a few piercings and the quiff of her Morrissey tattoo still peeped from the Lycra.

'You look amazing!' Kat whistled.

'Heard there might be photographers here for this Hollywood star,' she rasped. 'Game of you to dress up too, Kat. We thought you'd wimp out, my love.'

'A bet's a bet.' She stomped up the ramp, wishing she'd stuck to her guns and refused gimmickry, but Mags could be very forceful and it had been a master-stroke to get the pub regulars to offer donations to the sanctuary if they all dressed up today. It had already raised a healthy cash injection to buy splints for broken-legged pheasants, although they appeared to be a badger down.

'Russ is shouting at one of the nastiest bastards in Shrop-shire.' Mags cackled, grinding out her cigarette and getting up to follow Kat into the lorry, then jumping aside as Kat flew straight out again with an over-eager alpaca, tugging a reluctant goat behind her.

Mags untied Sri, who barged down the ramp in their wake, blue eyes boggling as she looked from giant fox to deer with loud, suspicious snorts. 'I told him to stop, but he won't listen as usual, and I don't want to ruin my outfit by breaking up a fight.' She stepped away from the spinning mare now, eager to preserve her satin thigh boots.

'Should we rescue him? Here, let me take her.' Kat stepped forwards to take Sri, who gaped in horror at her deer bottom.

Mags gratefully claimed the goat. 'It's fine. The nasty bastard is my second cousin, so he won't hurt Russ.' She watched as Kat was towed off by whinnying Sri, an alpaca loping in their wake. 'Put your deer head on, my love! Photographers, remember?'

Standing patiently in the last partition of the horsebox, pulling lazily at a haynet, Tina's wise-eyed old eventer, Donald, watched as Mags hung back to check her reflection in a nearby wing mirror before following, fox brush swinging jauntily.

Chapter 23

Dougie Everett's name might have been on more spectators' lips at the point-to-point than Bill Hedges' increasingly potent cider cup, but his arrival was so low key that nobody noticed him. Dark glasses covering the still yellow bruising around his eyes, baseball cap crammed low over his nose, he was dressed in the buff country livery of caramel moleskins and checked shirt, with his official pass on his dashboard. Having parked his ancient and very muddy Land Rover in the shadow of his trainer's horsebox, the first sight to greet him was a wide-shouldered deer hurrying towards the course leading an alpaca and the weird-eared skewbald horse he recognised as the same one he'd seen Kat Mason riding, a distinctive Indian breed whose name he couldn't remember.

His phone rang. It was Dollar. 'Where are you? I'm in the public car park.'

'Just arrived.' He watched a curvaceous fox passing, trailed by a goat. 'Don't think much of the runners for the first. I'll come and find you.'

Jumping out of his car, Dougie spotted a man dressed as a badger waving his arms behind a nearby Hilux. His day was getting more surreal by the minute.

The badger was squaring up to a shaven-haired terrier-man, with British Defence League tattoos, who was selling Patterdale puppies out of the back of a pick-up. Only one was left, yapping furiously from the back of the box at the badger, who had claws fashioned from curls of brown plastic cider bottles and was loudly demanding to know the justification for removing the puppies' tails. 'Docking is cruel, unnecessary butchery!'

The dog breeder lit a cigarette and watched through a plume of smoke as Dougie approached with a polite nod to admire the remaining Patterdale puppy, trying to scrabble its way out of the box, tiny tail gyrating while Badger Man ranted about the cruelty of terrier work and tail docking. 'It's illegal and barbaric!'

Dougie had missed having a dog enormously while in LA. He liked Patterdales, the Jack Russell's lesser-known northern cousin, a friendly, black-coated exhibitionist. His uncle had once had one small enough to take anywhere in a poacher's pocket.

'Can I have ten per cent off for the missing tail?' Pulling out a wad of notes, he handed it to the Hilux owner, who winked and gave him the puppy, slammed his back box shut and headed off to lay a bet on the first race, leaving Badger Man shouting furiously at nobody.

Dougie found Dollar parked in her white Porsche at the front of the public car park, which afforded her a good view of the course. A group of young hoorays were admiring the car and its driver from the tailgate of a nearby Range Rover, drinking Peroni and comparing ski tans. With their casually unbuttoned checked shirts, bright trousers plunged into unzipped Chameaus – the luxury Range Rover of gumboots – and sun-streaked hair pegged down with flat caps, colourful laughing country dandies, they reminded Dougie of himself a decade earlier, and he had a sudden unpleasant sensation of having come full circle. He rapped on the Porsche window.

Dollar unlocked the door and recoiled as she spotted the puppy. 'I don't want that thing in my car.'

'Come and watch the first race.' He crouched, nuzzling the puppy. 'It's the members' cavalry charge so always good value. You look sensational in that suit. Wear no knickers for the rest of the day and I'll find an extra length for you.' He could never resist cheesy Bond lines with Dollar, which he delivered with ever-more twinkling panache and she studiously ignored.

'Kat Mason is here,' she said, in her most serious automaton voice. 'You will not flirt with me today. We are working.'

Dougie found Dollar impossible to read, but her body captivated him, and the more access she granted him to it, the more he wanted. In the past few days, it had been constantly available and delightfully insatiable, her detachment a terrific novelty and turn-on. She'd made it clear from the start that she wasn't interested in sleeping with him, and they hadn't once shared a bed, even in coitus. Nor could their activities possibly be described as making love. All they'd shared was pure sex, and it was sensationally athletic, with little or no affection, but a lot of mutual pleasure and carb-burning action. Dougie found her thrilling company when she was naked, less so when she was bossing him about fully dressed and when she was carrying a gun. The gun bothered him enormously. Disarming Dollar was a tough challenge in every sense.

'Here's the deal,' he suggested breezily. 'If I win my race, I want you to give me something. I can't think straight when I know you've still got them on you.'

'I am not removing my panties.'

'Not your knickers, your bullets.'

'You must introduce yourself to Kat Mason today,' she demanded, ignoring the challenge. 'She and her closest allies are here dressed as animals.'

'I think I've just met the boyfriend. Very hirsute.' He straightened up and looked across to the course, which he'd walked the night before and where three riders in red coats were now leading the field to post for the opening race, which was restricted to members of the hosting hunt. A rangy chestnut was being ridden by a girl with a deliciously round backside. He eyed it appreciatively, revelling in the loveliness of British hunting buttocks. 'Now that's one I wouldn't mind laying each way.'

Dollar snapped, 'Keep your mind on the job.'

'I'm just talking about a bet,' he said cheerfully, and wandered off to find a bookie.

Watching him go, Dollar snarled under her breath, knowing she'd have to keep very close tabs on him. She didn't entirely trust Dougie and found him difficult to control despite gaining rapid sexual leverage, an unexpectedly enjoyable tactic that more than rewarded all the fantasies she'd entertained while watching his movies. She still firmly believed he was the right man for the job: he was charming and cool-headed, a gifted lover, and he seemed totally unflappable. But his inability to take the bonus seriously made him dangerous. Nor was Seth reacting as jealously as she'd hoped to the heavy hints she'd been dropping that Dougie was her new plaything. Currently in Mumbai, increasingly agitated because he wanted her back there to run his life and protect him from the rest of his staff while he converted the Brides List data into bar charts, pie charts and flow charts, he remained frustratingly disengaged with Eardisford and her quest.

She sent him another message, telling him everything was going perfectly to plan. As always, the response was almost instant. *Kwl! U R gr8 $. IMY.* Dollar pressed the phone to her lips to shield a rare smile, knowing that only Seth's most trusted inner circle received his incomprehensible teen texts. To turn *IMY* into *ILY* would take nerves of steel and a watertight backup plan, but she had those covered.

Ignoring the calls from a nearby tailgate to join them for a drink, she donned her dark glasses and slipped after Dougie, wishing she'd worn something more practical than a white linen suit. Her research was normally impeccable, but this time she'd been let down by the vain misassumption that this muddy Herefordshire hillside would be akin to Ascot.

Chapter 24

At the sanctuary stand, the bizarre costumes were drawing almost as much interest as the real animals. Posing for a photo between the local farrier's young sons, Kat felt like Minnie

Mouse in Disneyland. 'Yes, it is quite hot, but all in a good cause!'

Overhead, the sun was staging scorching appearances between muggy, dark clouds, and the inside of Kat's deer head was pumping out stale nicotine and Brylcreem fumes, with a faint undertone of cheese and onion crisps.

Pru and Cyn, looking far more comfortable in their Constance Mytton-Gough Animal Sanctuary T-shirts, rattled collecting tins and offered passing families the opportunity to meet Sri and the Shetlands. Their progress was hampered, however, by Russ, who was prowling around in a wider orbit with his STEWS flyers, frightening off all but the bravest pony-mad child. 'Otters, deer and hares caught in snares suffer unbearable pain!'

'We must do something about him,' Pru muttered to Cyn. 'It's bad for business.'

'Along with the toxic fox,' Cyn agreed.

'Actually, she's our best money-raiser.' Pru watched Mags circulating amid the crowd in her sexy fox attire, roll-up smouldering between her lips, selling raffle tickets, crying 'Give us yer money, you bastards!' in such a threatening, piratical tone, she was outselling the official hunt raffle threefold.

On the public-address system, the commentator was doing sterling work encouraging race-goers to visit the stand and support the charity race later, although he'd long since tired of the sanctuary's full title and was referring to it as 'the Hon Con's Zoo' between plugging the local game fair and an upcoming Brom and Lem Hunt supporters' ball.

'We should have a ball to raise money,' Cyn said dreamily. 'Constance loved balls. She was always throwing them.'

'Comes from having lots of dogs,' laughed Kat, heading past with a group of children to introduce them to the animals.

As soon as she was out of earshot, Pru and Cyn moved in on Russ. 'We think you'd be better off targeting the bar,' Pru said firmly.

'Kat needs me here.' He pointed to the deer, who was trying to control a pygmy goat, two Shetlands, an alpaca and an overexcited Sri as they all posed for photographs beneath their flapping charity banner. The sisters closed in further.

'The charity committee can offer you expenses.' Cyn produced a twenty-pound note.

'If you don't go, I'll tell Kat exactly what I see going on in Mags's car when it's parked up by my silage clamps late at night,' Pru said darkly.

'Maybe you're right.' His attention was distracted by a call for final bets on the first race, in which one of his comely cousins was riding. 'Must place a small charity wager.'

In the roped-off animal enclosure, Mags had stepped in to help Kat control the marauding menagerie, not noticing the little goat helping itself to fivers from her raffle bucket. Kat let out wail of frustration as the smallest, greediest Shetland made a break for freedom and the refreshment tent. While she raced after him, antlers rattling, the goat prised the bucket from Mags's grip and upended it.

'Oi, give that back!'

'I've heard of drinking the profits, but eating them is a new one,' laughed a gorgeously husky voice, as a figure stooped down to remove several banknotes from the goat's mouth and drop them back into the bucket before pausing to admire Mags's thigh boots.

Dougie was struggling to admire much beyond the boots, but he knew that it was in his job description to make a flirtatious introduction. Straightening slowly, he smiled wolfishly as he handed the bucket back. 'Hello there.'

Behind his dark glasses, Dougie's blue eyes were assessing the crotch-length, white-bibbed orange velvet dress and fur-trimmed thigh-high boots amid increasing alarm. With the matching fur hood, she still seemed the obvious redhead, but she was a lot older and bulkier than he'd imagined. 'You must be the gorgeous ginger Kat everyone's been telling me about,' he battled on, with his biggest, sexiest smile in place.

Fishing through the cash bucket to check if it was all still there, Mags muttered distractedly, 'It's a bloody fox costume, mate. I'm a fox.'

'Aren't you just?' He held out his hand gamely. 'Dougie Everett. I hear we're neighbours?'

'That'll be Kat you're after.' She waved at a small stampede taking place near the tea tent.

'I am!' He beamed with relief, then balked at the sight of a huge, pot-bellied deer tripping over guy ropes as it chased an alpaca and two Shetlands.

'Fucking Nora.' The fox shot off in their direction, brush twirling.

About to follow and help, Dougie realized he'd been left in sole charge of a money-munching goat and the unusual skew-bald mare with the wall eyes and curled ears who was extremely agitated, desperate to follow the two runaway members of her herd and round them up. Circling, snorting and pawing the ground, she eyed the enclosure ropes, ready to take a run up.

Dougie grabbed her head collar, listening as the commentator announced that there now appeared to be a loose alpaca on the course. His phone was chiming with an urgent message. As he grappled for it, two elderly ladies strode in to take the horse and goat from him.

'Thank you, young man. So kind!' The taller one eyed him beadily. 'Are you the new Eardisford huntsman?'

Having introduced himself with a warm handshake, he listened with a stiff smile as the sisters skittishly described meeting his father as a young man at a house party where he'd behaved 'very naughtily indeed'. Dougie knew that there were few country houses in which Vaughan Everett had not behaved very naughtily indeed. He discreetly checked his phone screen. Dollar's name was attached to two words: *DEBRIEF NOW!*

Thinking excitedly of his no-knickers demand, he wished the ladies a polite farewell and hurried towards the car park.

Lurking behind a stall selling expensive shooting coats, Dollar huffed impatiently: she had seen Dougie target the wrong charity worker. They needed better tactical planning. She had yet to spot Kat Mason, and casing the point-to-point incognito was proving impossible: she was attracting far too much attention in her white linen suit, a rare exception to the ruddy-cheeked tweed masses. People all around were staring, and there were dogs everywhere. Her young admirers from the car park had now been replaced by a band of aged ones trying on hats, one of whom stepped forward in a Panama with the label dangling over his nose and proffered a hand. 'Frank Bingham-Ince.' He affected a deep, honeyed drawl. 'Are you connected with Eardisford?'

When she looked back at him coolly, one eyebrow aloft, he ventured 'Do ... you ... speak ... English?'

'Mr Bingham-Ince, I speak perfect English. I'm afraid I'm very busy right now, if you'll excuse me.' Eager for full camouflage, she grabbed a floor-length waxed coat and shooting cap and thrust a wad of fifties at the salesman before retreating to the Porsche to round up Dougie.

*

Having reclaimed the sanctuary's pony and alpaca deserters in time to catch the closing moments of the hunt members' race, Kat watched one of the Brom and Lem's young thrusters grasp victory on her chestnut by a neck. Witnessing the mud-splattered hands-and-heels final furlong, she felt even more apprehensive at the prospect of riding the same boggy turf later.

'Ground's bottomless,' the victor reported cheerfully, as she rode up to the winner's enclosure at the far end of the paddock.

Kat was grateful for the cup of steaming spiced cider that was thrust into her hand and Russ gave her a badgery hug. 'I just won a ton! I'm going to add it to my wager on you in the charity race.'

'Please don't.'

'Have faith. You're going to win, Kat. Trust me.' He high-fived her antler horns and loped heroically back to the beer tent.

She hurried back to the sanctuary stand to find Mags in a state of high agitation, fox hood dragged back to reveal pink hair on end, black mask thrust up into her fringe as she puffed on a roll-up. 'Dougie Everett was looking for you, Kat. Do not trust him, my love. I know his sort. Arrogant twat. Thank you for this.' She grabbed the spiced cider and downed it, then rattled her raffle collection bucket. 'Pay up!' she yelled at a passing gaggle of young farmers, who reached for their wallets in terror.

Kat tried to look insouciant beneath her deer mask, adopt a Mae West face and flick up an eyebrow, but it was wasted on the ponies, and on her elderly helpers, who reported that Dougie Everett was 'absolutely charming' and a 'hero of the hour' but 'not as dishy as he was on screen'.

'I gather he's quite the horseman,' Pru sighed.

'Puts the "neigh" into "neighbour" then,' Kat said brightly, wondering if it would be terribly vain to change back into her jeans.

Deciding that the ponies needed a break, she towed them back to the lorry to chill out with Donald, who had fallen asleep, snoring contentedly against his haynet. Bunking them all up together with more hay and mint bribes, she paused by a far glossier horsebox parked nearby and listened worriedly to the thumping and howling coming from inside.

Dollar had concluded that the best way to focus Dougie on the task in hand was more sexual leverage. Her Porsche was far too exposed and his Land Rover too grotty, but their trainer's horsebox proved a perfect debriefing retreat. Part stable, part Winnebago, it had a luxurious beechwood-and-leather living area with discreet blacked-out windows.

'You must concentrate on Kat Mason,' she panted, as they slammed against a cupboard, fittings rattling. She gripped an overhead shelf as her hips gyrated against his.

Dougie had been quite looking forward to watching a few more races and assessing the way the course was riding, but he could hardly complain about the distraction when it was so physically all-consuming. Added to which, he reminded himself, she was armed.

'My mind is definitely on Kat Mason,' he lied, vaguely aware that the puppy – which had been fast asleep – was now howling for attention. 'Kat Mason all the way!'

Astonished to hear her name, Kat crept towards the thumping, howling horsebox then started back in alarm as two distinctive crescents appeared against the darkened windows. Even with the thick privacy glass, she recognized the impression of male buttocks, followed by a fossil stripe of backbone. The horsebox was positively rocking. The shrill howling fell silent. Moments later, the crescents and fossil peeled away from the window and more thudding ensued deeper within the box.

Ducking down and tiptoeing away, her face burning, she pulled off her antler head, shook out her hair, then crammed it back on before rushing to the stand to rattle collecting tins and watch the racing.

Dollar was staring fixedly at the tinted window. 'I am telling you, a huge creature with horns was standing right there.'

'You're imagining it,' Dougie said easily, laying her back against a leather bench and angling her to perfection. 'England really isn't crawling with wolves, tigers and mythical beasts. I'm the only horny thing around here.'

She gazed up at him, the dark eyes glowing. 'That's why I hired you.'

Chapter 25

Tireless Tina was multi-tasking energetically as always, the dark smudges beneath her anxious whippet eyes accentuated by the Alice band drawing her unwashed blond bob back from her slim face. On full-time stewarding duty while rattling a sanctuary tin with her two small boys and a dog in tow, her baby in a backpack, she still found time to pep-talk Kat in preparation for the five-furlong dash later that afternoon: 'Think positive, Kat! You just have to stay on and point forwards!' By the end of the fourth race, with the track a skidpan of mud and casualties piling up in the blood wagons, she was sounding fractionally less positive.

Now, having gathered the number cloths as they came off the first three horses, she nipped across to the sanctuary stand where Kat was holding the long-suffering alpaca so that a group of giggling children could stroke her while their indulgent parents videoed them on iPhones. 'The course is still riding deeper than ever,' she said, as she panted up. 'Thankfully Donald is a total mud-lark – he's not named after a duck for nothing. He'll look after you.' She watched indulgently as her children joined the others while Kat crouched down and showed them how best to stroke the alpaca's long neck. 'You're such a natural with kids, Kat. Would you mind looking after mine for two ticks? They are *so* bored. I just have to get these cloths back for the Men's Open.' She started to shrug off her backpack.

To Kat's alarm, she found herself with two hyperactive boys at knee height and a baby on her back that was soon hitting her over the deer head with a set of teething rings.

Ten minutes later, there was still no sign of Tina and her boys were starting to pick fights with one another. The blustery wind was pushing rainclouds in overhead, droplets scudding into the stand. The baby, normally a stoic little soul, grew increasingly cold, bored and bad-tempered.

Kat looked around for help, but Russ was still drinking his winnings deep in the beer tent and Mags had sneaked off to put flyers under windscreen wipers advertising Animal Magnetism's 'wildlife benefit gig' in the pub later that evening. Cyn and Pru recoiled when she asked them to guard the boys while she found Tina.

'We'll look after the animals, dear, but we're not really equipped for lost children, and I don't think the health-and-safety officer would approve.'

Taking the boys with her, Kat hurried towards the stretch of officials' tents to look for Tina.

The jockeys were already coming out to mount the horses that had been parading for the Men's Open. One, resplendent in red and gold with a white silk on his skull-cap, was drawing a lot more attention than the others. Several members of the crowd were even calling him across for autographs.

Kat stopped in her tracks, baby weight lurching against her shoulders, deer head tipping forwards and blinding her as the eyeholes dropped level with her nose. She pushed it back. He was wearing dark goggles beneath the peak of his silk, but the sharp line of his jaw and the amused, sexy curl of his mouth were still unmistakable.

It was Dougie Everett, the actor from *High Noon*. He had been looking for her earlier. A blush raged beneath her deer mask.

Noticing Tina's boys had already burrowed through the crowd by the rails, she followed them to get a closer look.

The strutting bay favourite, Kevin Spacey, was napping badly, his little Indian groom barely hanging on as the gelding towed him around the ring while the jockey in red and gold was given a leg up. Hopping alongside with the trainer hanging on to his left leg, Dougie managed to make a well-calculated leap at precisely the same moment as Kat arrived at the rails beside him. Taking one look at the strange, Atlas-shouldered deer with the wailing baby on its back, Kevin shied and Dougie splatted to earth face first.

'Oh, God, I'm so sorry! Are you okay?' Kat tilted her huge stag head so that she could look down at him.

'No I'm not fucking okay!'

Kat was pushed aside by a shadowy figure in a long coat and a shooting hat. 'Leave this to me, Dougie,' she ordered, swinging round and snarling at Kat, 'That was a deliberate attempt at sabotage!'

Kat immediately recognized the beautiful Indian woman, who was squaring up to her and saying, 'I will report this. What is your name?'

'Kat,' she looked desperately around for Tina, 'and I promise you, it's not sabotage. Ow!' She ducked her head away as the baby jerked it back by the antlers, almost blinding her again. The little one was making a lot of noise in the backpack now.

'It's okay, sweetheart,' Kat soothed, jigging her up and down. 'We'll find Mummy soon, I promise.'

'You are Kat Mason?'

'Yes – ow!' The baby was wrenching one antler from side to side now.

'Here, let me help.' Suddenly all smiles, Dollar reached out to remove the deer head, but the baby had a firm hold of the antler and refused to let go, letting out an enraged squawk. Tugging harder, Dollar pulled off a fluffy brown ear, making the baby scream yet louder.

'Lay off our sister!' demanded one of the boys, hitting her with a collection jar.

'Yeah, leave her alone.' The other gave back-up with a rolled-up STEWS poster.

If there was one thing that frightened Dollar more than horses and dogs, it was children, and she backed rapidly away, smile fixed as she glared down at them. 'I must warn you to leave me alone before you regret it.'

'Whatever you do, don't get out the gun,' Dougie said, through gritted teeth, on the other side of the rails, picking himself up and discarding his broken goggles as he turned to mount, then realized his nose was bleeding.

'Oh, God, I'm sorry – I lost a number two somewhere!' gasped a breathless voice. Tireless Tina appeared at the rails and gathered her boys to her sides, beaming apologetically at Dollar. 'Have they been bothering you? Say sorry, boys.' But they were snorting too loudly at the idea that a number two had been lost to hear the order.

To Kat's surprise, Dollar was the one to apologize. 'Miss Mason, I would like to make up for my discourtesy just now,' she said stiffly, the forced smile still on her face. 'Perhaps you would like to join Mr Everett for a drink in the members' enclosure after the Men's Open by way of apology.'

'That's kind, but I'm riding in the charity race then,' Kat explained.

Dollar looked extremely put out. 'Of course. Another time.' She nodded formally and ducked under the rails to stalk across the paddock and talk to the trainer, still clutching a deer ear.

Tina turned to Kat in alarm. 'Is that the one who offered you money to leave?'

But she wasn't listening. She was staring at Kevin Spacey. The bay horse was taking another lap of the parade ring, Dougie stalking alongside ready to mount again, still stemming a nosebleed. The bay was practically hopping along on three legs. 'Is it me,' she said to Tina, 'or is he lame?'

Tina had eyes only for the jockey. 'Oh, boy.' She paused midway through hooking her baby off Kat's back to take in the wide shoulders, narrow hips and handsome face. 'Nothing lame about Dougie Everett. He's sublime. Look at the muscles on those thighs!'

Kat couldn't see a thing as her deer head twisted round, the baby still clinging to one antler. She could hear several girls calling, 'Good luck, Dougie!' as the runners and riders paraded past.

Tina was wrestling furiously with the backpack now. With the baby still attached to the antler, Kat's deer head came off with the child. As it did so, and her hair spilled around her hot, flushed face, she found herself looking straight into the most sensationally dark-lashed, bruised blue eyes imaginable as Dougie Everett rode past, feet feeling for his stirrups, horse skittering sideways, his handsome features surprisingly pale, dark smudges eclipsing the red scars beneath his eyes. To her surprise, he looked almost frightened.

'Good luck,' Tina called.

'Thank you,' he muttered, forcing a quick smile, his eyes sliding towards Kat's.

The big Mason smile beamed back and he turned to look at her as he rode away, his eyes locked on hers.

To her shock, it felt as though a bedspring suddenly gave way inside her, a jolting twang that shifted her vital organs up and sideways without warning. Just as surprising, the expression on his face had seemed to convey the same fleeting jolt before the horse bounded forwards. He was moving even more oddly, one leg snatching up as though in great pain.

'Wait! He's lame!' she called desperately, but Dougie was out of earshot, heading towards the track that led out on to the course.

Kat felt panic grip her, certain the horse couldn't race in that state. It was probably her fault. Kevin Spacey must have strained himself when he spooked at the sight of her in her deer mask. She owed it to him to raise the alert.

'Stop the race!' Battling her way around the ring and through the queue for the local pig farmer's hog roast, Kat marched into the officials' tent to find the veterinary officer, only to learn that he was still examining a horse that had fallen in the last race. In his absence, the paddock steward was summoned – a hunting-mad solicitor known as the Deckman because he fell off so often. As they went back out to identify the lame horse and recall it, Kat found herself being tailed by Dollar in her long coat and hat, looking curiously like Inspector Clouseau.

'You have a problem, Miss Mason?' She followed them into the parade ring, then jumped aside as a horse passed very close by.

'Kevin Spacey isn't fit to run.'

'You are mistaken,' Dollar said tightly, watching uncertainly as Dougie jumped off and an Indian groom led the horse into the centre of the paddock beneath the shadow of a big chestnut tree.

Now they could both see the weird way the leg moved. Beckoning to the groom, Dollar consulted urgently with him in a language Kat couldn't understand.

'What exactly d'you think is wrong with him?' asked the Deckman, who knew nothing about horses other than how to get on and off and open a saddle flask of sloe gin.

Resplendent in bright red and gold, now splattered with mud and blood, Dougie stepped in front of the official. 'What's the problem?'

The Deckman smiled apologetically. 'Just waiting on a course vet to check your horse, sir. Question mark over soundness.'

'He's perfectly sound,' Dougie snapped.

'He's lame!' Kat blurted, moving forward, which caused Kevin to start back and cannon into Dollar, who leaped away with a shriek and moved behind the tree.

Dougie registered Kat's presence with a groan. 'Put the antlers down. You're freaking him out again.'

As soon as she looked him in the eye, Kat's internal organs were jumping, her heartstrings twanging. Now was probably not the time to thrust out a hand and hot-headedly introduce herself, she realized, as he glared at her.

'I'm sure we can resolve this situation,' Dollar was saying from behind the tree. 'Perhaps we could talk somewhere more private. Shall we move away from the horses?'

'Before Miss Mason frightens any more of them,' muttered Dougie, a muscle ticking angrily in his cheek as he watched the rest of the field streaming down towards the course.

'Yes, let's go somewhere a bit quieter to wait, shall we?' suggested the paddock steward, aware that they were attracting quite a lot of attention – not least because the girl making the complaint appeared to be dressed as some sort of centaur – and the vet was still nowhere in sight. 'Walk the horse around a bit more,' he told Kevin's groom, ushering the others towards the officials' tent, lifting the walkie-talkie to his mouth and repeating his entreaty for the course vet to come urgently to the paddock.

Dollar hurried Kat on past the hog roast queue. 'I'm sure you have every right to be concerned, Miss Mason, but the horse has been passed fit to run.'

'Rubbish,' she said hotly.

'He's totally sound,' said Dougie, banging his whip impatiently against his boot top as they moved away from the noisy crowd to the relative quiet behind the pig roast spit. 'You have no idea what you're talking about.'

'You only have to look at that leg to see!' Kat stood up to the double assault, feeling the heat of the bonfire against her back.

They all looked across to the paddock where the bay horse appeared even more lop-sided as he jogged around, eager to be on course, snatching up one leg in a strange, unnatural fashion.

'The groom says it's just halter string,' Dollar said, with an authoritative air to her monotone.

'Stringhalt,' corrected Dougie, turning to look at Kat. 'Surely you've heard of it.'

'No, actually,' she said. 'But if this terrible lameness has anything to do with being tied up with string, that's downright cruel.'

'Stringhalt is a common conformation defect in racehorses,' Dougie said. 'The uneven flexion in the hind legs at walk causes him to snap one up higher than the other. In Kevin's case it's unnoticeable at racing pace, and certainly causes him no pain whatsoever in any gait. The horse is in terrific health and perfectly safe to run.'

Kat stepped back, feeling her face flame. She might have made a very stupid error.

Dougie was clearly livid. 'It's obvious you know fuck all.'

Dollar cleared her throat loudly. 'Dougie, I think that's enough.'

'Why? She should be shot for this – don't take that too literally.' He held up his hands quickly. 'Please don't tell me she's the one who runs the horse sanctuary. What demented idiot employed someone totally clueless?'

'You can say what you like about me, but don't you *dare* speak about Constance like that!' Kat flared. 'She knew more about horses than you ever will.'

'Shame she died before passing the basics on to you, then.'

Dollar hissed under her breath for him to keep quiet before stepping closer to Kat, her monotone suddenly infused with soft apology: 'Please believe me when I say that Dougie is not normally offensive. He is very tense about the race. You two have not been formally introduced, but as you will be neighbours, I insist you share that drink later.'

Kat snorted disparagingly, feeling like a squabbling child being told by a nursery teacher to make friends.

Closing his swollen, bruised eyes, Dougie muttered, 'Must I?' Then he ran his tongue over his teeth and a huge smile lit his handsome face as his eyes opened and locked on to Kat's, almost knocking her over backwards with warmth and charm. 'I must. We must! What a great idea, darling Dollar, you clever thing. It would be my pleasure.' His blue gaze drilled sexily into Kat's.

Kat felt the jolt inside again, but this time when her vital organs jumped, they landed on razor blades of anger. Perhaps he was justified in his rudeness, given that she had accused him of cruelty to horses, but his conceited attitude still made her blood boil, plus she was almost certain it was his buttocks she'd seen against the horsebox window earlier. Mags was right not to trust him. And Cyn was right that he wasn't as good-looking off screen – he seemed much shorter, his nose bigger, his eyes too close together and his manners despicable.

'I wouldn't take a drink from you if I was on fire!' she snarled.

As soon as she said it, she smelt burning.

Dougie smelt it too and his blue eyes widened in alarm, reaching out to grab her shoulders and turn her round. 'You fucking *are* on fire!'

Looking over her shoulder, she saw that the legs dangling from the padded deer bottom on her costume were ablaze, smouldering upwards like cartoon bomb fuses, ignited by the pig roast bonfire. And fake fur was highly flammable!

'I'm on fire!' she shouted with alarm, starting to pull at the Velcro.

'There's no time for that.' He lifted her up, carried her at speed to the big plastic water trough in the corner of the unsaddling enclosure and threw her in.

'You may know fuck all about horses,' he said kindly, 'but you have a seriously hot booty.' Grinning, he hurried back to the paddock, where Kevin Spacey was passed fully fit and was eager to catch up with the others already circling at the start.

Riding down to the course, Dougie pep-talked himself. He was determined not to freeze up or zone out as he had the first time he'd got back into the saddle after the fire at the stables. He'd ridden a lot in the past week, as well as sweating off weight in the sauna, screwing for recreation and toning up in the gym, and he trusted that he was utterly secure in the saddle, as familiar riding a horse as living in his own skin. But his mind kept wandering.

The bay was totally on its toes, head bobbing, crabbing this way and that as he tried to get his head. He was by far the most talented horse in the race, but also the most wound up, his neck and girth foaming with sweat. Dougie knew he had to give him confidence. They'd both been at far grander gigs than this, after all, and it was his job to persuade Kevin that today was a walk in the park: they were more than capable of winning this together. But the big occasion was getting to the little bay, and they'd not got off to the greatest of starts in the paddock.

He thought about Kat Mason, Bambi meets Emily Davison. If he lost this, it would be all her fault. On balance, he preferred the tattooed thug in thigh boots and too-tight fox outfit.

You are not going to lose, he reminded himself, lining up for the flag, furious with his heartbeat for spiking so soon. But the adrenalin had been charging through his blood since he mounted the horse for the second time. It had fast-tracked along a main artery from the moment he'd seen that cloud of red hair and felt something unpleasantly like an electric shock.

The flag came down and the field surged into a furious charge towards the first fence.

Dougie's mind, usually empty of everything but the track at this stage, was now racing, pushing together electrical connections that felt like two live wires touching. Chasing the fox had been a false trail. It should have been a stag hunt all along.

'Kat Mason,' he breathed, as he sized up the first fence in a hailstorm of flying mud. 'The girl in the paddock was Kat Mason.' He kicked for a long stride.

The little bay disagreed, putting down again so that his front legs dragged through the birch, making him paddle and peck on landing. Having committed to the flyer, Dougie was too far up his neck.

On the hill, the crowd gasped as the little horse that had started as short odds favourite stumbled and pecked at the first fence, its rider pitched forward over its neck, almost eating the dirt. And yet, as the little bay righted itself, nimble and athletic and determined not to be left behind, the jockey in the red and gold silks stayed put, a lion on his back, scrambling into the saddle to give chase to the rest of the field.

'Nobody I know could sit that!' Tina shrieked beside Kat. 'That's bloody amazing riding!'

Kat said nothing. She rarely wished ill on anybody, but she spent the next eight minutes clutching Tina's creased waxed coat around her sodden, charred deer costume, willing Dougie Everett to fall off. But the horse galloped and jumped like a stag after their first near miss. To her ongoing mortification, she could see Dougie had been totally right about the stringhalt not affecting his racing: the funny leg action he had in walk disappeared in faster work. The field was the biggest of the day and the soft ground, now churned and heavy after five races, made for a messy, false-paced race amid a lot of traffic with plenty of fallers. Choosing the best ground, Dougie tracked the field around the outside, picking the best take-offs and offering Kevin the dream run.

'The man can certainly ride,' breathed Tina, as she watched alongside Kat. Then, catching her indignant expression, added, 'Awfully rude, though.'

The combination beat their closest rivals by three lengths.

'Whose fucking arse is on fire now?' he called to Kat, as he rode back to the winner's enclosure.

Chapter 26

'Now is our moment,' Kat told wise Donald, as she tacked up for the charity race, trying to ignore Tina wiping away a tear and crossing herself nearby. 'We'll be superstars.'

'Just hunt him round the back,' Tina ordered, sounding unusually brusque.

'You said, "Lead from the front," yesterday.'

'I've changed my mind. Bring him home safely, Kat. And yourself, of course,' she added as an afterthought, blowing her nose.

Lauded for his skilful race riding, Dougie had charmed all who met him and been invited to watch the remaining three races from rival VIP tailgates. Observing him closely, aware that he was in his element and breaking down much-needed barriers – and secretly very impressed that he was sticking to mineral water – Dollar hung back, the forest of tweed and waxed cotton surrounding him tougher to penetrate than barbed wire and chain-link. His eyes sought her out often, playful and carnal, knowing that his reward was waiting for him. Dollar looked forward to bestowing it, and to making sure he was fully briefed before she left him alone at Eardisford to get on with the job, still not entirely convinced he would behave himself without her there. But, just as she decided the time was right for his charmed exit, she realized he was being spirited back towards the jockeys' tent to get ready for another race.

She consulted her race card. This wasn't in the plan.

When Kat walked into the paddock to mount laid-back Donald for the charity race, her teeth chattering, she was furious to discover that Dougie Everett was a last-minute entry and now firm favourite, having agreed to take a chance ride on a hunt horse offered to him by one of the Brom and Lem's amateur whippers-in, an old friend of his father. He was treating the race like a huge joke. To add to her indignation, the horse was called Cat Fight, a gift to the commentator who would now think up every suggestive connotation he could.

Riding out on course for the flag start, determined to beat him despite her rudimentary skills, Kat was vaguely aware that the rest of the field were all smiling and nodding at her as though she was a sick kid who had won a special outing, none more so than Dougie Everett.

'Not been riding long, then?' he asked, big blue eyes crinkling benignly.

She gritted her teeth, eyeing the flag. 'Years.' Two whole years, she thought anxiously, and she still couldn't canter without curling loops of mane through her fingers as she was doing now. Catching Dougie staring at her hands in amusement, she turned a circle. She wasn't even looking when the starter's flag came down.

Yet Donald was almost immediately out in the lead. As soon as the race got under way, it was obvious to all but Kat what was happening. Her blood was boiling too much to notice as she kicked for home, leading from the front.

On the hill, Tina groped for a tissue, weak with relief, not caring that Kat wasn't hunting around the back of the field as she'd asked. Instead, the field were the ones holding back.

'Aw, bless them all.' Her eyes filled with tears as she watched her very novice pupil and very experienced horse lolloping along ten lengths in front. 'They're letting Kat win.'

'Bloody good sportsmanship,' Frank Bingham-Ince said approvingly, lifting the flat cap from his salt-and-pepper hair to cheer her home. 'She's a gutsy girl, but Miriam was right – can't ride for toffee.'

'She's *much* improved,' Tina insisted, wincing as her baby hit her over the head with the plastic antler.

'Excellent result.' Frank admired the redhead clinging to the neck-strap as Donald sent up arcs of divots in his wake, tanking prick-eared to the finishing post. 'What a game girl.' Frank fished through his pockets for his winning betting slip. 'Could keep going all day. I'll have her out with the Brom and Lem, mark my words.'

For a moment, blinded by speed and deafened by the roar of blood in her ears, Kat was euphoric. 'I won! We won!' She hugged and patted Donald ecstatically. It took her almost a circuit to pull up, by which time the hunt staff were already parading the hounds along the course and the commentator was reminding the crowd to take their litter home with them. Then, hacking breathlessly back towards the main hill where a small, loyal crowd was cheering heartily, reality finally kicked in and she realized the race must have been fixed.

In the winner's enclosure Dougie, who had come second, was laughing his head off along with the third placed rider. Kat didn't catch the entire joke, but she was sure she heard 'toddlers' trotting race' and 'donkey derby'.

Jumping off Donald, she pulled her helmet off and marched up to him, red hair spilling across her shoulders, sweat stains under her arms. 'Was it you who told everybody to go slow so that I could win? Everybody knew it was a fix, didn't they? How *dare* you?'

To her surprise, he smiled at her with heart-stopping charm, head dipped, eyes locked on hers. 'Congratulations, Kat. You rode a blinder. It earned a lot of donations to a very worthy cause.'

Kat ignored the jolting heart and lungs as she snarled, 'I wanted to take part in a race, not lead a procession. I would have been happy to come last. I *deserved* to come last.'

'I've heard of a bad loser, but you're a seriously bad winner.' He was still smiling, but there was an edge to his voice. Then, as if remembering his manners, he stepped forward and said, in a seductive undertone so that only she could hear, 'I could give you some race-riding tips over that drink, if you like. If you don't mind me saying, you looked a bit random out there.'

Kat stepped back, her own big smile launched in self-defence. 'I said I didn't want a drink,' she reminded him tightly.

'Actually,' he looked at her through his long lashes, the tone unmistakably flirtatious, 'you said that you wouldn't take a drink from me if you were on fire, which you were. Surely I can buy you one now I've put the Kat out.'

'No, thanks,' she said determinedly, hurt pride burning the inside of her throat and chest. 'It takes a lot more than a water trough to put my fire out.'

*

Having watched the race with a satisfied smile from her white Porsche, Dollar sent Seth the video recording she'd made on her tablet camera, interpreted *U * $! x* as good, and then texted *Well done* to Dougie, adding, *You may now claim your prizes. D.*

He was sitting beside her within a minute.

'I said that dog cannot come in here.' She wrinkled her nose at the small, sleeping black ball in his arms.

'His name's Quiver and we won't be staying long.'

Tutting, Dollar fished in her handbag and pulled out the gun, slotting out the cartridge and emptying its contents into her hand to give to him.

'And the rest . . .'

With a long-suffering sigh, she opened the glove-box and pointed to the box of bullets there.

'Thank you.' He took them. 'I don't like arms around me. Of any kind. I blame my childhood. It was all guns and abandon-ment.'

'Remind me to ask for a bow and arrow next time,' Dollar said.

'A twelve-bore and a well-trained spaniel would be more acceptable round here.' He grinned, reaching for the door handle.

'You have forgotten something.' She held up a pair of frilly knickers.

'Thanks.' He pocketed them, eyeing her with amusement.

'You must be very stiff,' she said, in her deepest purr. 'I will give you a massage later.'

'For you, my gorgeous Dollar, I'm stiff on demand, but we'll have to make it an early one. I have a game of Kat and mouse to finish.'

Dollar's smile, so rare and hard-won, was triumphant.

*

Kat was trying to extract a very pissed man dressed as a badger from the beer tent.

The borrowed horsebox was already loaded and ready to roll with the hard-earning sanctuary oldies, along with heroic Donald, but she knew she had a responsibility to transport the wildlife too, especially since Russ had to be sobered up enough to perform on stage later. Mags was nowhere to be seen – Kat assumed she had left with Calum, who needed to get his falcons home after their display – but Russ was still crunching around on abandoned STEWS flyers.

'I have been working tirelessly all afternoon spreading the word,' he insisted, waving his plastic claws.

'I did wonder where you were,' she said tetchily, as she herded him outside.

'The poisonous old committee biddies sent me here on a secret mission. And they were right. I raised a mint for the sanctuary – look!' He held out a bucket positively brimming with coins and notes. 'So we've both been hard at it.' He lurched sideways and tripped over a guy rope, stumbling on to his knees in front of her. 'You're wearing breeches.'

'Well observed.' She helped him up.

'Oh, yeah. I heard you won the race. That's great.'

'You didn't even watch, Russ.' In a way, she was grateful that he hadn't witnessed the travesty, but she wasn't going to let him know that. She didn't care how much money he'd raised, his lack of support really hurt. 'It was all a total fix.'

'I was against that, but Bill thought it would be a big boost for you and the cause.'

'Your uncle fixed it?'

'Don't knock it. We doubled our money.' He rattled the cash bucket. 'Almost lost the lot when Dougie Everett refused to play ball, but the others talked him round on the way to the start apparently. He thought it wasn't fair sport, which is ripe coming from a bastard who chases innocent animals for entertainment. The man's a seriously nasty piece of work.'

'I'd gathered that,' she hissed, stomping towards the lorry.

'I'll see him off, never you fear,' Russ reassured her, as he lurched in her wake, ricocheting off a parked car before staggering into a dustbin and spilling the cash everywhere.

Chapter 27

Despite heavy leafleting at the point-to-point, the Animal Magnetism 'benefit' gig at the Eardisford Arms that evening drew no more than the usual suspects, a hardened core of fans largely made up of friends and family, plus the usual pub regulars and a couple of tourists staying in Miriam's holiday cottage. They had mistakenly thought it was a folk evening and were soon visibly wincing as they tried to bolt huge Herefordshire beef rib-eye steaks in order to pay up and leave. Relocated to a makeshift stage in the public bar due to a leaking pipe in the skittle alley, the band had failed to adjust their volume to suit the smaller space and were ear-splittingly loud.

Still in his badger outfit and far from sober, Russ was putting in an energetic performance as he pogoed around on stage, adding shrieking guitar riffs to the band's repertoire of Clash covers. The band members were all talented musicians, but the gimmicky costumes, authentic indie-punk playlist and deafening volume didn't work in their favour in the cramped confines.

Kat longed to be at home chatting to Dawn about her day,

but she knew that she would only have wound herself up more about the fixed race and Dougie Everett's smugness. Here she could smile and shrug it off, as well as wolfing down a portion of Jed's rabbit hotpot in exchange for offloading another glut of Lake Farm eggs on the pub kitchens.

Sitting with the Hedges sisters and the girl grooms from the local livery yard, she endured a lot of good-natured teasing about the slowest-run five-furlong race in history, along with the inevitable excited gossip about Eardisford's new huntsman. The consensus was that he was Hot, although the mysterious girl-friend was Not. Even when Kat indiscreetly described the buttocks in the horsebox window, it seemed only to add to his sex appeal.

'He is going to be *such* fun to have around,' sighed one of the grooms.

Just as Mags was murdering 'London Calling', another of the girls let out a shriek of excitement. '*OhmyGod*, DON'T look, but he's *just walked in*.'

They all immediately turned to look. Only Kat carried on munching her lemon meringue tart, watching Russ hip-thrust-ing his guitar neck suggestively towards Mags as the band moved from Clash to Cure and launched into 'The Lovecats'. Her eyes narrowed as Mags hip-thrust back, letting out a stream of feline yowls. The platonic friendship was always tested to the limit on stage, where Mags flirted outrageously with all her band members. Watching her practically mounting the key-board player from behind, Kat wondered how the notoriously hot-tempered Calum put up with it.

But when she looked, Calum was distracted at the bar, where Dougie Everett had parted the earthmen faster than a plough through soft loam, the object of intense fascination. Kat's excited tablemates kept up a running commentary as he ordered a drink – 'A pint ... cola by the look of it. Probably driving.' They then reported that the few-toothed ones had edged closer and were laughing raucously as he talked to them all, flashing that famous smile.

'He is *so* hot.'

'I can't believe I'm wearing no makeup!'

'I'm getting the next round in.'

'It's my turn!'

'No, I'll get these.'

'Wait, he's coming over!'

The girls licked their lips, all rising several inches like meerkats as they held in tummies and tightened their buttocks.

Kat licked her dessert spoon, still eyeing Russ and Mags, who appeared to be simulating sex with an amplifier and a mic stand respectively.

A throat was cleared overhead. 'If I promise not to put your fire out, Kat, can I buy you a drink as a peace offering – and your friends too, of course?' The clipped, husky voice was pure big-screen, feel-good Brit-pack idol, although he had to project it to be heard over the band, like a stage actor in a hearing-assisted Shakespeare matinée.

'I'm fine, thanks.' She didn't turn round, her words drowned by a flurry of requests for vodka Coke.

'Kat will have a pint of cider,' the girls insisted. 'She can drink five back to back without passing out. It's a ladies' pub record.'

'Another tremendous talent.' He headed to the bar.

'What did you say that for?' muttered Kat.

'Okay, so you passed out and were a tiny bit sick last time,' the groom gazed at the bar, 'but he is *so* ripped you have to let him buy us all a drink.'

When Dougie returned with a fully loaded tray, Kat noticed

that the regulars were now watching her table, not the stage, although the badger was riffing so loudly his plectrum broke. There was something about Dougie that drew the eye, like a fire flickering merrily in a grate: people couldn't resist inching closer to feel the warmth, but were nonetheless wary of being burned.

The girls all shuffled up to make space and a stream of introductions followed that Dougie couldn't have hoped to hear as he settled beside Kat on the long bench seat. But his smile was so charming and his expression so sexily intense that all the girls thought he'd committed their name to memory above the others. They raised their drinks in a toast and watched him eagerly, smiles fading as he turned to Kat, his intense blue gaze exclusively on her, and mouthed, 'Truce?'

For a puzzled moment she thought he was asking, 'Truth?' then grasped what he meant and shrugged a reluctant consent, annoyed at being cornered, grateful at least that the music was so loud there was no point in answering. When it was succeeded by Siouxsie and the Banshees' 'Dear Prudence', which was quieter, he tilted his head in front of hers again.

'It really was unforgivable to mob you up like that! Pre-race nerves!' He apologized with a lot of head-ducking and blue-eyed charm, albeit still shouting as loudly as a father from the touchline. 'I had no idea we're neighbours, and I really did mean it when I offered to help! I'm pretty hopeless at most things, but I know my horses and I gather you have a few at the sanctuary.' He looked at her through his thick lashes and, mistaking Kat's fixed expression for inability to hear him, shouted even louder directly into her ear, 'Can we get away from this God-awful racket?'

Kat tried hard to look offended. 'I'm enjoying it!' she insisted stubbornly. 'It's a vintage performance.'

The vintage performance paused as Mags, adopting a throatily intimate microphone rasp that was part Janis Joplin, part Hilary Devey, coaxed, 'Join me, ladies. Let's sing along! Here's one for Prudence . . . '

Pru and Cyn, sitting at their usual corner table with the most ancient earthmen, raised their glasses as the younger girls in the room started to serenade them, adding a quick 'and Cyn' to the refrain.

Deciding she'd been unfriendly enough – she hadn't even looked Dougie in the eye properly yet – Kat turned to him to explain what was going on. 'They always sing theme tunes for regulars with their names in – Mags started it with her last band. They offered to learn something with "Sin" in the title for Pru's sister Cyn, but she says that would be unChristian.'

His eyes didn't leave her face. 'What do they play for you?'

'"Lovecats",' she scoffed, 'although "Bitch" might be more fitting.' She waited for a reaction, but his smile was pasted on like a daytime television interviewer's. 'I'm more of a dog person.'

'Me too. Good point. Don't go away.' He leaped up, muttered an apologetic oath and abandoned his pint to dash outside.

'What did you say to him?' One of Russ's cousins sidled across the gap to reclaim a handbag from behind a cushion.

'That it's a vintage performance.' Kat shrugged.

'Pushing it a bit. He was *seriously* flirting with you.'

'Why would he do that?'

'Duh? He has a terrible reputation.' She looked thrilled. 'You can't deny he is Sex. On. Legs.'

Kat thought about the buttocks in the window. 'I prefer to keep my feet on the ground.'

'In that case, I'm going to redo my face, after which it's every woman for herself. Prepare to step aside, Kat Mason.' With a grin, she got up to hurry to the loo, followed by most of the girls at the table, the Eardisford Arms' ladies' lavatory being the local unofficial social-media hub in the absence of a phone signal.

Dougie's phone was still on the table, Kat noticed – not that it would do him any good around here. She picked it up and examined the custom case, a much-scuffed shell covered with Ds fashioned from bows and arrows.

'It has no reception,' Dougie told her, as he sat down, slightly out of breath.

She dropped it hurriedly. 'Nothing has round here.'

She wondered what he could have had time to do so urgently outside. He hadn't been gone long enough to smoke a fag or use the phone-box.

'I was wishing on a star.' He leaned closer, that husky, drawling voice intimate, but still clearly audible above the band's rollicking medley finale.

Caught off-guard, Kat gulped as the blue eyes drank her in and her vital organs did their lurching thing. Without thinking, she brought out the big self-defence smile, a thousand watts of unexpected light blinding him across the table. He looked delighted, smiling right back until Kat's heart, lungs, liver and kidneys threw themselves into action. Nobody fought back against the Mason smile that fast. She was up against a pro.

'What did you wish for?' She took the cue a split-second before seeing the trap she'd walked into, his eyes smouldering on hers, the word 'you' on his lips.

Kat watched his mouth form the letter Y as if in slow motion, and – like one of those movies where the woman watches a car crash and shouts, 'Noooooooo,' while bits of car and broken glass fly through the air in time delay – she recoiled. In real time, this reaction was the briefest of flinches, lasting barely a millisecond, then rewinding as Dougie hung on

Y, failed to add the car crash OU, and instead steered expertly out of the swerve.

'Usefulness,' he said. 'I want to be useful, Kat. Use me in any way you need.'

She regarded him cynically. 'And you just wished for this usefulness on a star?'

'Aries. The agrarian worker. My sign.' He pointed up, eyes not leaving hers, playful as a lion cub again now. 'What's—'

'*Don't* ask what my sign is,' she interrupted, really wishing he'd lay off the flirtation (and the eye-contact thing, which was pulverizing her innards). But she was quietly impressed he knew his astronomy. For all his star-gazing, Russ's constellation identification started and finished with the Great Bear.

'The sanctuary sounds an extraordinary venture,' Dougie was saying, edging closer all the time. 'Constance Mytton-Gough was clearly an amazing visionary and passionate about her horses – my father knew her and Ronnie. I would *love* to help you out. Looking after it all must be a hell of a burden for someone not used to animals. I gather you're a city girl. Watford, isn't it?'

'I live here now. And I'm very used to animals, thanks.'

'Stringhalt aside,' he teased, eyes now so flirtatious they were almost Eskimo-kissing hers.

Kat resented his glibness, the confident public-schoolboy charm that insinuated he could blaze in and rescue her with his superior knowledge, the smooth machismo that would make most men come across as smarmy gits, but somehow worked brilliantly for him, as sexy as it was charming. No wonder he was famous for seducing co-stars. The smile was growing wider now, the voice huskier, the eyes hypnotic through their veil of lashes. 'Tell me what I can help with. Anything. You name it.'

273

About to joke that he could lay off the Casanova charm, Kat realized that his offer had its practical uses. She certainly didn't need rescuing, but she was more than happy to delegate a few unwanted role.

'You can take over the pony ring at the village show, if you like.' She'd been trying to wriggle out of it for weeks. 'They've asked for rides and then a little gymkhana afterwards.'

'Happy to. I did the Prince Philip Cup as a kid.'

'Isn't that backpacking around Dartmoor?'

'That's the Duke of Edinburgh Award.' He laughed, giving her a see-how-much-you-need-me look. 'It's mounted games – racing around on ponies, basically.'

She felt foolish, sharpening her edge. 'You're a stuntman, aren't you? Maybe you can do a trick-riding display for the village at the show.'

Just for a moment the big smile wavered. 'I have no trick-trained horses here.'

'Could you jump off the church tower in a ball of flames instead? It'd be more exciting than the usual morris dancers.'

'I'll see what I can do.' He brought the flirty eyes into play again. 'I could shoot a few flaming arrows.'

'Isn't archery a bit dull?'

'Not the way I do it.' He moved closer to speak into her ear as the stage shook with Animal Magnetism's final riffs. 'Can I help with something more personal? Something closer to your heart?'

Kat saw Russ watching her from the stage, a huge lumbering badger hitting bum notes amid screeches of feedback, both protective and threatened. She knew she just had to raise a finger for the guitar to be cast aside and the vigilante to attack, her fierce bear of a free-range lover.

'Cricket,' she said, without really thinking, knowing it was

Russ's greatest passion after music and wildlife, and sometimes more important than both, especially one occasion each year. 'There's an annual match at the end of July, estate workers versus villagers. It's a hugely important event around here, but nobody knows what to do about it this year. The village pitch belongs to the estate, you see. If you can square it for the match to go ahead, and field an estate team, that would be great.'

'I'll do my best. Anything else I can help you with? Whist drive? Open garden? Climb a mountain? Slay a dragon?' He angled his face to look at hers, his charm guns blazing, his gaze disconcertingly on her mouth.

Kat engaged the smile again. He returned fire, but if she concentrated hard she could keep her vital organs in one place. 'Not unless you're a mechanic. My car's got a faulty starter.'

'Ha-ha,' he said, glancing at the clock above the bar and grimacing. 'Excuse me.' He stood up and hurried away.

Animal Magnetism was finishing its set with a victorious drum roll. The girls were returning from the ladies' loo, heads swivelling in horror as Dougie vanished through the main door again.

'What did you say to him this time?' Russ's cousin slid in beside Kat, her face now painted with huge, soulful, smudgy eyes and bee-stung lips.

'Asked him to fix my car.' Kat was clapping the band, rolling her fist in the air and whooping loyally.

He'd left his wallet alongside his phone this time. She was dying to have a peek, but the cat-calling had started for the Animal Magnetism encore, and she was duty-bound to join in, whistling and slow-clapping above her head to call them back. Russ gave her a personal power salute as he stomped back out of the loo corridor, where the band was obliged to wait for their

275

stage-storming finale. Kat realized she had no idea what star sign he was. Russ refused to celebrate birthdays, insisting it was a bourgeois affectation.

Dougie came back into the pub just as the band launched into the Undertones' 'Here Comes The Summer' as a deafening encore. The girl grooms had now relocated his drink, phone and wallet to the opposite end of the table so that they could win his attention. A pretty girl wearing too much makeup beamed up at him. 'We're both winners today! I won the members' race.'

'Good for you.' Sitting down, he tried to catch Kat's eye, but she was watching the action on stage. She hadn't touched the pint of cider he'd bought her. Following her gaze to the tall guitarist flailing at his fingerboard, he wondered exactly what the deal was with Badger Man.

The girl beside him was still talking about the point-to-point, shouting, 'Seriously hard going! Took a lot of stamina!'

Like flirting with Kat Mason, Dougie reflected. She was going to be a challenge, particularly after their bad start. He remained sceptical about his so-called bonus, but his ego wouldn't let him give up on Dollar's grand plan without some proof of his abilities, not least because he wanted to win her respect. He'd never met anyone capable of detaching sex from feelings, as Dollar could, or expressing so little outward emotion. By withholding so much, the slightest flicker felt like a breakthrough. By contrast, Kat Mason was an overload of smiles, anger, enthusiasm and passion that seemed messy and out of control. She also appeared to have a very big boyfriend.

'Is the guitarist local?' He nodded to the stage where the badger was doing a fret-climbing solo that was remarkably tuneful.

'My cousin Russ,' shouted the girl with too much makeup. 'He's an arboriculturalist. I'll introduce you.'

Dougie had no idea what an arboriculturalist was, but the fact it included 'culture' gave him hope that Russ might be an arty-farty type who rarely swung punches.

When Russ bounded off stage, he accepted a free pint from the bar, clanked it against the earthmen's, downed it in one, then followed his cousin's beckoning arm to meet Dougie Everett, squaring up to the newcomer, rock star to mere mortal. In this pub, Animal Magnetism was the legend that would live on. What he hadn't anticipated was that his badger outfit reeked so strongly of beer tent, cigarettes and stage sweat, it was impossible to stay downwind without feeling faint.

Standing up to shake his hand, Dougie took a sharp step back, knocking his chair over, spluttering a few platitudes about his musical talent, then dashed apologetically outside, his phone and wallet still on the table.

Swaggering away for a second pint, believing the smaller man was intimidated by his size and reputation, Russ left a trail of desolation as drinkers shrank away. Only the earthmen remained unbothered, sliding another drink across to him. 'Reckon that actor's after your bird,' one warned darkly. When Russ's eyes instinctively flew to Mags, canoodling with Calum by the dartboard, the earthman laughed. 'Not the missus, Russ. The other one.'

Coming out of the loo, mildly alarmed that wearing the deer's head all day appeared to have given her an itchy scalp and stained her forehead orange, Kat was disconcerted to find the earthmen doing their silent Greek chorus thing at the bar, staring at her. Behind them, Russ was discreetly sniffing inside his badger costume.

'There you are,' said a smooth voice, as Dougie Everett appeared at her side, pocketing his phone and wallet. Despite being shorter than he looked on screen, he was a good head above her, she saw, affording him a close-up of her itchy red parting. 'I'm going home, but I'll swing by and look at your car soon.'

She had an image of him yodelling into Lake Farm on a vine, like Tarzan on a vine. He had such a lazy, husky voice, it just had to be affected, in the same way those eyes were far too blue and flirtatious to be standard issue, staring so deeply into hers she half expected him to get out a watch on a chain and tell her she was feeling sleepy. Her vital organs were on the move again, huddling together nervously.

About to tell him there was really no need to swing anywhere, she thought about the starter motor she couldn't afford to get repaired, and said, 'We're usually around.'

'I look forward to it.' He flashed his devastating smile, did the look-through-the-lashes trick and ducked out of the pub to an audible chorus of female sighs from the large table by the stage, followed by a fluttering rush past Kat as the under-twenties headed back into the loos to gossip.

Kat went back to the table to gather her pint, which she suddenly found she wanted a good bolt of.

'Everything all right?' Russ joined her, sitting alongside.

She looked at him fondly, trying not to breathe in too deeply. His face paint had slipped so that he looked like Alice Cooper, but she was grateful for the kindness and concern in his dark eyes. 'I'm cool. You were great tonight.' She put an arm around him and snuggled tight, then regretted it as she found herself slithering against sweaty leather, her nostrils filled with acrid cider fumes despite the shallow breaths. Straightening up and gulping more of her pint, eyes watering, she asked, 'What's your star sign?'

Striking a rapper's pose, Russ held up his long fingers in a cat's cradle of geometry shaped like a five-pointed star.

Kat laughed: he probably had no idea. 'When were you born?'

'Early summer?' he guessed, counting through ten months on his fingers from the fruit-picking season when his parents had met. 'Anything else you want to know?' He pressed his palms together, fingertips on his nose, dark eyes mesmerizingly alive.

'What's my star sign?'

The palms went up.

'Sagittarius,' she told him. 'The Archer.'

Dollar's white Porsche was parked outside the mill, the kitchen table laid with goodies that played straight into Dougie's James Bond fantasies.

Settling the sleeping Patterdale puppy into his temporary cardboard box bed by the Aga, he picked up the small carbon-fibre composite bow with a sheath of lightweight arrows. The bow was custom-made, inlaid with wood set with his initials. 'A welcome gift from Seth,' Dollar explained. 'It is the very latest technology. He will look forward to a display of your skill when he visits with guests.'

Dougie tried to quash an image of himself in a Robin Hood hat skipping around the lime-tree avenue in front of suited businessmen, shooting flaming arrows into braziers of acceler-ant-doused wadding. 'When will that be?'

'Not for many weeks. By then you will have fully familiarized yourself with the estate and its hunting grounds. Your horses will be fit and the dogs in training.'

'I've made a start on the dogs, if not the hounds.' He looked

279

at Quiver stretching his small front legs rigidly in his sleep, then arching his back and settling into a tight curl.

'And of course you must gain Kat Mason's trust and affection as a priority. I take it tonight went well.'

'On target.' Turning back to the table, he selected an arrow and set it in the rest before drawing back his string hand and aiming at a particularly ugly oil painting above Dollar's head.

'Don't!' She ducked as he fired it. It sailed cleanly into the nose of an enraged-looking miller's daughter.

'That's better.' Dougie followed the arrow to its landing spot and narrowed his eyes as he pulled it out to examine it. He winced at the vicious angular ends, designed to inflict maximum damage, hopeless for target practice compared to the field points he normally used. 'I think Cupid might require a softer tip. These bastards are broadheads.'

'It is good that you have now connected with the girl.' Dollar picked up a chunky little mobile, which opened like a penknife to reveal an antenna. 'This is a satellite phone for you to carry at all times. You will report in to me regularly. It's pre-loaded with all the numbers you'll need. I will call you as soon as I arrive in Mumbai tomorrow. Please do not shoot any more furnishings while I am gone.'

'You're leaving?' He was momentarily nonplussed, accustomed to being closely policed.

'Seth wants me in India. His diary always falls apart when I am not around to organize it. I fly tonight.' To a bystander, her face would still be a beautiful, inscrutable mask, but Dougie knew her well enough now to read tremendous excitement in the eyebrow elevated to a high crescent, dark eyes glowing, lips trying hard not to curl into a smile. She couldn't wait to get home.

He looked around at his immaculate kitchen, at the snoring puppy and the polished floors, and suddenly realized he could be messy, loud and sociable again, a prospect that delighted him, along with ditching the vegetarian health food and punishing workouts.

'I have printed out details of your diet and exercise routine.' Dollar was hurriedly ticking off bullet points on her tablet.

Dougie was reminded of being dropped off at boarding school as a child, deposited there each term by a succession of over-controlling stepmothers and nannies. 'When will you be back?'

'Not for some time. I am no longer helpful here. The locals think we are lovers, and you must be seen as a single man.'

'We *are* lovers.' He moved towards her with a roguish smile, ready to run through a few highlights before she left.

'We both know that is no longer practicable.' She tapped her screen, turning away. 'I was very satisfied with your performance.'

Dougie imagined a tick-box beside his name being checked with a French manicured flick. The flare of anger he felt burned itself straight out. It was far too soon after Kiki for him to be shackled to a control freak, and he was relieved Dollar was leaving. Right now, he wanted to be surrounded by dogs, horses, woodland and tweed-coated cider drinkers who thought it normal for musicians to dress as wildlife. But he would miss the carb-burning, guilt-free sex.

Standing with her back to him, Dollar let out a long sigh, suggesting that she might just miss it too. Then she squared her shoulders and continued, in her bossiest monotone, 'You will report directly to me and nobody else regarding Kat Mason. The hound pack, horses and kennel staff are entirely your responsibility, but you will need to liaise with Alasdair Armitage on a regular basis so that his team can notify you of wild game sightings. Money should not be an issue. These have all been set up for you.' She fanned a selection of plastic cards on the table, like a croupier dealing a winning hand. 'There is no limit on the debit card, but our team will keep an eye on the activity on all your accounts, so don't go mad. There is also cash in the safe. Please put all gifts for Miss Mason on the separate charge card provided – flowers, chocolates and so forth.'

'I don't think she's the sort of girl who puts out for two dozen roses and her bodyweight in praline.' He turned over the AmEx. Then his eyes lit upon a bright yellow membership card among them guaranteeing him Home Start and he laughed. 'Then again, I might just be her dream man.'

Chapter 28

Having seen Lake Farm only from a distance, Dougie was shocked by the state it was in when he drove into the farmyard, his Land Rover axle groaning as it bumped over the potholes. The animals all seemed well cared-for and there were signs of new fencing and good pasture maintenance, but the old outbuildings and stables were leaning against one another at drunken angles and the house itself was a wreck.

Finding the door open and nobody inside – there was an ancient rheumy-eyed Labrador splayed on the cool flagstones of the kitchen and piles of half-folded clothes on the table, including some vast skull-and-crossbones boxers – he headed back out into the yard. Several rare-breed chickens watched him suspiciously from a pile of abandoned pallets while doves flew in and out of a loft through gaping holes in the roof. No wonder Seth wanted to buy the place back and overhaul it, Dougie reflected. It was falling apart.

The wind that had blown blossom around like a snowstorm at the point-to-point had now dropped and shower clouds clustered overhead, playing a coquettish fan dance with the warm sun. The bluebells were out in full force, a far more appealing sight than any red carpet Dougie knew as he headed along a track into the old arboretum, marvelling at the size of the oldest trees.

He finally tracked down Kat to a pig enclosure in the woods where she was trying to fetch a water bucket that had been knocked over and trampled on. A huge, affectionate sow rubbed her back vigorously against Kat's welly tops as a scratching post while she struggled for grip in the mud.

'Hello there!' He stepped into the enclosure, causing her to swing round in surprise and lose balance, feet planted in deep sludge. Leaping forwards, he grabbed her before she landed face down in it, noticing how soft and slight she was compared to Dollar's bodybuilder physique, and that she smelt pleasantly of soap and fresh hay amid the pong of pig. But this picture of fragrant, vulnerable femininity was shattered when she yelled at him, 'Get out! Quickly!'

He mustered his most heroic smile, refusing to be deflected, as he set her gently upright again. 'I've come to mend your car.'

'Seriously! Get out!' she wailed, as a series of outraged grunts started up. Moments later, he found himself being charged by a territorial pot-bellied pig.

'Jesus!' He winced as his legs were knocked out from under him by twenty stones of outraged swine, and instinctively hung on to Kat for balance. Still halfway out of her wellies, she was as unstable as a sapling and they went down together with a loud splat.

Squelching and slithering around like two mud wrestlers, fighting off the furious porker, they finally clambered out.

'Are you okay?' Kat checked breathlessly.

Dougie brushed the foul-smelling muck off his favourite red trousers. 'That boar is dangerous.'

'Pot-bellies are very defensive. They hate strangers coming into their space.' Kat turned back to the enclosure, making reassuring clicking and cooing noises to settle the agitated animal, which was still glaring at Dougie. 'And these are both sows. You might know a lot about horses, but you're talking out of your booty there.' She looked at him over her shoulder, green eyes amused. Behind her, the sow lumbered grumpily into her sty and flopped down next to her equally giant companion, who'd slept on throughout. 'She's very protective of me,' she told him, stretching over the fence for the stray bucket.

'Who can blame her?' Dougie admired her pert backside, determined to get the charm offensive back on track. 'I'd be exactly the same. Now, where's this car that won't start?'

'Would you like to wash that mud off before you look at it?'

'No need.' He cocked his head as a loud engine pulled up to the gateway on the wooded track leading in from the ford entrance and they spotted a flash of yellow truck through the trees.

'Excuse me!' called a cheery voice. 'Is this the right place for Mr Everett?'

'That's me.' Shooting Kat a smouldering action-hero look, Dougie went to open the gate. A moment later, an AA van drove past.

The AA mechanic diplomatically said nothing about the fact that his customers were dripping pig muck, although he politely declined a cup of tea as he looked into the faulty starter motor on Kat's coupé.

'Loose connection,' he diagnosed cheerily, putting it right.

'Nice sports cars, these. The little lady's, is it?' He nodded at the red-haired swamp monster trying to wash her legs off with a hosepipe. They both watched, transfixed, as she gave up on subtlety and hoisted the hose higher so that water ran across her shoulders and flooded down over her cotton shirt, which clung to her body.

Dougie perked up at her lack of inhibition, which came as a pleasant surprise. But Kat was no red-bra-wearing seductress with a high-grade body like Dollar. She had practical base layers and a sports bra of such reinforced enormity that no nipple bump would ever penetrate it. As she turned around, he could distinctly make out the lettering of the T-shirt she was wearing under the old cotton shirt, which read, I ♥ Dublin: Carly's Hen Weekend 2009. It clearly came from her previous life when hens had reeled between nightclubs wearing L-plates and suspenders, not pecked around underfoot. For the first time, he found himself wondering what had brought her here, the Watford party girl turned rural recluse.

The AA man was spellbound. He had seen nothing as exciting since his wife had forced him to watch celebrities in the jungle and one page-three model had repeatedly taken showers in nothing but her bikini.

Unaware that she was being watched, Kat started to hose out a big pile of feed buckets lined up beside the taps, attacking them with a scrubbing brush, red hair escaping from its topknot.

'Hard-working girl,' the AA man said admiringly. 'Lovely place you've both got here. Living the dream, eh? Or is it a hosepipe dream?' He laughed raucously at his own joke.

Dougie smiled stiffly – he had no choice, given that dried pig muck was now cracking across his face. Looking around the farmyard again, he could see there was an old-world charm about it. In fact, with the sun now dancing down through the tree-tops, and doves cooing on the sagging roof arches, it was almost Disney-esque.

'You're a very lucky man.' The mechanic sighed, gazing longingly at Kat again.

It was a seriously cute bottom, Dougie saw. He was still admiring the way it gyrated as she stretched forward to scrub a rubber poultry trough when Kat turned back and frowned at them.

'All sorted, sweetheart!' the mechanic told her.

The frown transformed into that amazing smile and suddenly the farmyard looked even more idyllic. Kat Mason's smile was seriously disconcerting.

Dougie reached for his wallet and flicked through his new plastic to find the familiar yellow membership card, far more helpful in his seduction plans right now than a Priority Pass.

When the AA van finally drove away, half-heartedly pursued by two elderly barking terriers, Kat offered Dougie the hosepipe.

'I'd prefer a hot shower and a back scrub.' He gave her the benefit of his best Bond smoulder, revving the flirt engine back into gear.

'We don't have a proper shower,' she apologized. 'There's a bath with a mixer attachment, but I haven't lit the range to heat any water and, anyway, the tub's full of ducklings. The mother's broken her leg,' she explained, smiling at his baffled expression. 'We found her in the lake last night desperately trying to look after them.'

He was genuinely shocked. 'Don't tell me you're taking showers with a hosepipe until she's fixed up?'

'It's not so bad. In fact, it's pretty refreshing after mucking out on a hot day like today. The sun dries you off in no time.'

Dougie remained unconvinced. 'It's no wonder your badger friend smells so high.' Seeing Kat's frown returning, he quickly flashed up his most disarming smile, voice dropping huskily:

'So you really do take in lame ducks. That is truly wonderful. Would you mind showing me round?'

'I'm afraid I'm totally flat-out today.' Kat regarded him suspiciously, arms crossed in front of her wet shirt. 'Another time, maybe. Let me give you some eggs to say thank you for ...' there was a tell-tale pause and one red brow lifted '... mending the car.'

Dougie was expecting far more gratitude than eggs, sarcasm and a brush-off. But, staying in role, he ducked his head, looking at her through his lashes, the playful smile so flirtatious and courteous it could have melted a chastity belt. This was the Everett Effect at full strength, perfect for medieval swashbuckling romances. 'I can offer you a personally run bath at the mill any time you need it. In fact, I insist.' He moved closer. 'It's even big enough for two.'

Kat was gazing back at him unblinking – incredible green eyes, he noticed – and he was certain he had her in his spell. But then she threw out that disarming smile and marched towards the chicken coop. 'You've been more than generous as it is.'

Dougie was certain she deliberately selected the pooiest eggs. He thanked her and headed to his Land Rover, where Quiver was sprawled asleep on the passenger seat. 'The offer's there if you need it,' he called back to her. 'My bath is all yours!'

'Thanks.'

He smiled suavely through the lowered window. 'Delighted to be of help. See you later!' As he drove away, Dougie realized his last few lines had sounded like a bad Brian Blessed impersonation, but he hoped she hadn't noticed.

'I know this sounds like I'm making it up, but Dougie Everett's just called round here and flirted really, really badly,' Kat told Dawn. 'He was like Pepé Le Pew with a dash of Brian Blessed on ecstasy towards the end. I think he might have a drug problem.'

'You're making it up,' Dawn said, blowing her nose at the other end of the phone line, her voice full of cold. 'It's sweet of you to try to cheer me up when I'm ill and my garden looks like a muddy medieval fortress, but you'll have to do better than that.'

'What happened to the garden?'

'Dad got the decking dimensions wrong.' She sneezed noisily. 'Instead of a little terrace for prospective buyers to visualize themselves enjoying a mojito and watching the sun go down, he's built Plank World. You can't see a blade of grass. Now I have to find a garden-hating hay-fever sufferer to buy it.' She blew her nose again. 'And it's made me realize I need grass. None of the flats I've looked at have gardens.'

'Come here! There's lots of green. It's lovely now the weather's better.'

'Don't tempt me. Will Dougie Everett come round and flirt with me if I do?'

'I really wasn't making it up.' She told Dawn about the point-to-point and then his strange dashes in and out of the pub later, followed by today's visit and the back-scrubbing bath offer. 'It's all so completely over the top, it's quite funny.'

Clearly jealous that she was stuck in Watford with flu while her friend had a heartthrob wooing her in the pig enclosure, Dawn's cynical explanation did little to boost Kat's confidence, but it made sense: 'Men like him flirt as default. And I wouldn't be surprised if he dabbles in a few substances – that would explain the sudden career change and all his swift exits the other night. He's really, really naughty from what I've read. You know he cheated on Iris Devonshire two days before they were due to get married?'

'Ew!'

'Every woman longs to be the one to tame him.' Dawn sighed. 'If you Google him, I think there might be a sex tape too.'

'Thankfully that's beyond my dial-up connection.'

'I'd still take him up on the bath offer.' Dawn giggled. 'He's seriously buff, and your plumbing's dire. You can fight him off with the loofah if he gets over-familiar.'

Kat had a sudden brainwave. 'I'll send Russ round in my place.'

'You can't!' Dawn's laughter turned into frenzied coughing.

But Kat thought it was genius. 'He can play detective while he's there. He'll love that and he's brilliantly observant. If the mill's a vice den of Class A and orgies, he'll figure out what's going on.'

'He'll probably move in and refuse to leave.' The voice on the other end of the line turned suspicious: 'He's not still crashing at Lake Farm and expecting you to wait on him, is he?'

'He comes and goes,' she said vaguely, reluctant to admit that Russ's washing was currently on her Pulleymaid overhead. He didn't stay over often, now the days were long and the nights mild, but when he did, she felt safe. And since Dougie Everett had moved into the mill, with his steamy reputation and immense charm, she needed to feel safe.

As Kat had predicted, Russ was more than happy to take a bottle of shampoo and a towel along the millstream path and stake out the huntsman's house, but despite some intensive snooping, he found nothing useful, reporting back that Dougie was the height of charm and had asked about the cricket match, promising to do his best to ensure the pitch would be available for the famous annual match between villagers and estate workers.

'We'll thrash their arses as usual, of course, but I'm not going to let on to that muppet,' Russ said, with satisfaction, as he roamed around the kitchen pulling down clean clothes because he'd forgotten to take anything with him to change into. 'I told Everett not to call in here uninvited again, by the way.'

'You did what?' Kat looked up from spooning baked beans into a pan.

'You said he was sniffing about earlier.'

'I said I don't trust his motives,' she admitted, wondering if she'd subconsciously sent Russ round to the mill to do exactly that, although no doubt hoping he might be a bit more subtle about it. She could imagine him towering like a bear in his towel, chest hair bristling and gargantuan shoulders squared as he told his host in his hardest Brizzle accent to keep his fucking distance.

'What did he say?'

'"Yah, like, sure, like, whatever."' He mimicked the husky drawl. 'Seemed a bit put out, but he's not used to our insular rural ways. He wears his collars turned up and says "totes",' he sneered. 'If you ask me, he's a puppet. There's somebody much bigger pulling his strings.'

'Or his stringhalt,' Kat muttered, quietly relieved the blue eyes wouldn't be catching her unawares in the pig muck again. She knew Dawn was probably right and Dougie Everett flirted with everybody on instinct, like debonair Brom Hunt master Frank Bingham-Ince, who would chat up an automated phone switchboard. But Kat found it disconcerting, and she was furious with her internal organs for doing their seismic-shift jigs every time Dougie looked at her.

By contrast, her *kundalini* seemed set to stay in the deep freeze that evening when Russ looked deep into her eyes, Ravi playing in the background, and suggested she needed to relax. He smelt sensational, having nicked a load of Dougie's bath oil.

Kat closed her eyes and focused on her chakras, eager to be spirited away to a higher plane where she could try to find her inner temptress again and not go weak-kneed over hell-raising actors with bad chat-up lines.

'Keep your eyes open,' Russ reminded her. 'Look into mine. Let's count.'

'Of course.' She did as she was told. But the clever dark gaze seemed to look straight into her head and find Dougie Everett there, collar turned up, blue eyes teasing, both hateful and charming as he said, in that sexily intimate undertone, 'Nine, eighteen, take your top off, twenty-seven, spread your leg, thirty-six, touch yourself . . .'

'Wow,' Russ breathed, noticing her pupils dilate and breath quicken. 'I think we're getting somewhere. This is the break-through moment.'

Appalled at herself, Kat wriggled back, holding up her hands apologetically. 'D'you know, Russ? I think we should leave it tonight.'

'Cool.' He nodded sagely. 'This is your journey. The bus stops whenever you ring the bell.'

Kat ruffled his hair gratefully as she headed past to extract Daphne from the cat flap where she was stuck as usual, but her face flamed.

Chapter 29

Kat arrived late to run her Pilates class in the village hall, finding her regulars already limbering up on their mats as she hurried in and slotted the CD into the stereo.

'Sorry – crisis with an escaped water buffalo . . . again!' she said brightly. 'Have we all done our warm-up stretches? Great. Let's get straight on and do the Hundred!'

As chill-out music started pumping from the speakers and a dozen local ladies in joggers and Lycra lay down obediently, she spotted a figure standing at the back, blue eyes devilish, big smile flashing. Dressed in black joggers that hung low on his lean hips and an Actors Studio T-shirt that clung to his broad shoulders and biceps, Dougie Everett seemed both amused and baffled as the ladies adopted the Tabletop position. A puppy was asleep on the rolled-up hoodie behind him.

Kat raised a hand in acknowledgement, furious with her body for staging an instant rearrangement of heart, stomach and lungs, all of which appeared to be palpitating like mad. She didn't want him hijacking her class for more flirting.

'And INHALE,' she instructed, grabbing a spare mat from her kit bag and hurrying to the back of the room.

'Hope it's okay to join in?' Dougie asked cheerfully, his voice already doing its husky seductive thing.

She didn't look him in the eye. 'Have you done Pilates before?'

'I work out.'

'It's the last class of the season so it's quite advanced. It can be very punishing, especially if you have ... ' she cleared her throat and lowered her voice to a whisper ' ... addictions.'

'Addictions?' His eyebrows shot up.

Kat had heard of young, fit stars dropping dead because they had abused their bodies so badly. She didn't want Dougie Everett pegging out during the Saw movement because his heart couldn't take it. '*Chemical* addictions,' she breathed, so that none of the ladies would hear.

He laughed incredulously. 'Since when did you need a drug test to take part in a village fitness class?' Then he leaned right into her ear so that she could smell the warm citrus of his skin as he murmured, 'I am totally, utterly clean.' He somehow made it sound thrillingly filthy.

Kat thrust the mat at him, her face flaming. 'I'm afraid most of the movements will be hard for you to understand at this stage in the course.'

'Oh, I'll pick it up as I go along.' He flapped out the mat like an eager Scout on a camping trip and plumped down on it, beaming up at her.

Kat turned back to her class. 'INHALE. Heads up, curl spines, see the scoop of your abs, hold the position . . . and EXHALE,' she instructed. She headed back to the front of the hall, determined to stay professional. 'That's right, Miriam. EXHALE . . . Legs and arms extended now, try to keep those legs low, hold the position and INHALE . . . Lovely, Tina! Fingertips reaching for that far wall.'

Tina, who was as fit as a marathon runner and only came along to get away from her kids – she had been known to fall asleep on her mat halfway through the class – was staring at Dougie open-mouthed, the creases on her sun-kissed twenty-something forehead in direct contrast to the lack of them on Miriam's fifty-something Botoxed one on the adjacent mat, although both women's eyes bore the same look of wonderment.

He was doing non-stop crunches at the back. He seemed to be able to pump away at will. Kat lay down to demonstrate the final part of the movement, trying hard not to think about her Tantric moment with Russ when *kundalini* had started moving for all the wrong reasons, mostly Dougie's torso.

'Now five short breaths – sniff, pant, sniff, pant, sniff, and move those feet and hands up and down. Make the abs do the work, remember. Relax your head and neck, Babs. Great!'

Still Dougie pumped, beaming at her every time he raised his head over his wide triangle of chest. No wonder he had such a sculpted six-pack on screen.

'Bring your knees up to your chests, roll your spines back along the floor and lower your heads.' She ended the movement in a rush.

As Kat ran through the mat exercises, Dougie became increasingly disruptive, gaining his own eager audience and doing his own thing. He found the notion of the Roll Up hilarious – 'If I'd known, I'd have bought Rizlas and a pouch of Golden Virginia' – and went on to pound through thirty sit-ups in the same time it took Kat's ladies to groan their way from lying to sitting with their fingers reaching for their toes, exhaling on command. He was similarly flippant about the Roll Over ('Reminds me, I must buy a EuroMillions ticket'), and took his puppy outside for a comfort break during the One Leg Circle ('Quiver needs a one leg lift'). His phone rang during Rolling Up Into Ball, cutting short an anecdote involving his father, the *Daily Telegraph* and his PPS's head in Westminster as he went outside again. Kat really hoped he wouldn't come back, particularly as her ladies had now lost concentration entirely, chattering in amazement about the fact Dougie had a phone signal and speculating on which Hollywood starlet he was talking to.

'It's such fun with him here. What a shame this is the last class. Do you think he'll come to boxercise when that starts up?'

'Let's do some leg stretches.' Kat clapped her hands to get their attention and started them off in the first sequence movement before going in search of a pen to write LADIES ONLY on her boxercise and self-defence poster.

'Pilates class,' Dougie told Dollar, standing outside the village hall, the line suffering from bad satellite delay.

'This is not wise,' she said, after a long, crackling pause.

'Why?' he demanded indignantly. 'You told me to get fit and seduce Kat Mason. I'm killing two birds with one stone.'

'You must maintain your enigmatic edge. This is impossible to achieve in a fitness class, trust me. You are not taking this job seriously. And please do not kill her. We are not considering that option yet.'

'It's a figure of speech.'

'And I was joking.'

'I forgot you do that sometimes.' He chuckled. 'Now who isn't taking the job seriously?'

'I take my job very seriously, and my neck is on the line over this, Dougie.' Her voice was steely. 'I knew it was too early to trust you on your own. There's a lot more at stake here than your summer bonus. Take a deep breath, then go in more slowly.'

'Sounds like a bloody Pilates move,' he muttered sulkily.

When Dougie came back into the class, his attitude had changed completely. Slumping despondently into his mat, he took instruction and performed the stretch movements, frowning darkly throughout. Kat longed to make him really sweat as punishment for being the class joker earlier, but he was suddenly a model student, pushing for the extra core strength with surprising polish and balance, totally in control of his body and far fitter than anybody else, including Kat. By the final few positions his blond mane was dark with sweat, his skin glistening and he was breathing hard, his body accustomed more to power than precision.

Kat found the sight highly distracting, especially when he looked at her. As she demonstrated the final side-kicks, she found his eyes on her again, no longer amused and playful, but hard, focused and determined. Instead of her heart feeling it was using her lungs as a punch-bag, the excited drumming was far lower now. Why did every position she adopt suddenly remind her of sex? The Inner Thigh Lift, the Seal, the Boomerang and the Teaser all took on hitherto unimagined sexual connotations. They became the *Kama Sutra* of body-toning mat movements as her brain slotted Dougie Everett into them. Finishing by demonstrating the Control Balance, a tricky shoulder-stand splits, she found her ninth chakra was truly staging a coup. She could think about nothing but oral sex. She had visions of Dougie's blond head between her legs, his arms wrapped round her thighs. Control and balance deserting her, she slammed back down on to the mat like a skittle, then leaped up and declared the class over.

Dougie was among the first to leave, pulling on his hoodie and gathering the tail-wagging puppy into his big front pocket before wandering across to thank her.

'How much do I owe you for the class?' His smile was guarded, no longer radiant with teasing naughtiness, the eyes still disturbingly hard and sexy.

'Have this one on me,' Kat said, acutely aware that her chakras had cashed in shamelessly. 'I still owe you one for the AA man and the bath.'

He was looking at the LADIES ONLY graffito she'd added to the boxercise poster on the wall above her head. 'I should have added that as a clause for free baths at the mill.' He gave her a wry look. 'Your boyfriend looks much better out of badger uniform.'

'He's not –' She stopped herself, reddening at the speed with which she wanted to explain away Russ's status, a man she had sent round specifically to back Dougie off and with whom she still occasionally hunted her elusive *kundalini*. '– conventional.' She finished lamely. 'He's not very conventional.'

'Neither are you.' He looked through his lashes, more like his flirty self as the smile caught an updraught of laughter. 'I like that a lot. Thanks for the workout.'

As he sauntered away, Miriam bustled up, flicking her pith helmet of blond highlights, still immaculate although she was sweating heavily in her reinforced body-shaping leotard and waving a poster about forthcoming village-hall movie nights, for which the ever-industrious Pru and Cyn had annexed the next slot as a sanctuary fund-raiser, the film written in as 'TBC'.

'Did you know about this, Kat? It hasn't had committee approval. I do hope *TBC* isn't another film in which everybody takes their clothes off in the first five minutes.'

Chapter 30

As May blossomed and bloomed between its bank holidays, choking the verges with cow parsley and jewelling Eardisford's walls and gardens with flowers, Dougie continued to charm the village. He became an increasingly popular face at the Eardisford Arms, where his affability and quick wit won him firm friends. His regular disappearing acts between pints of Coke were the subject of early speculation, until a few of the earthmen, lining up outside for a smoke, realized he was simply checking the puppy in his car. As soon as he'd had his jabs, Quiver joined the terrier regulars in the bar and was given an honorary cushion to lie on by the inglenook seat in the fireplace.

'I've never known a puppy so well behaved, or its owner.' Mags was enchanted. 'Dougie's a total gent. Do you think he's teetotal because he's got a problem?'

'Well, he's definitely AA,' Kat informed her confidently. She'd not been in the pub since the night of the point-to-point, partly because she was broke and partly to avoid her flirtatious neighbour, but it seemed she was the only one shunning it. Now Dougie took to stopping off in his local for a soft drink most evenings, and the hard-core regulars had trebled in numbers, rebalancing the sexual divide. Her boxercise and self-defence class had started up again, but was no longer fully subscribed as the village ladies swapped wrist-holds and right hooks for the wrist action of lifting pints.

'It's the long evenings and sunny weather,' the girl grooms insisted, eager to pounce on the newcomer and demand advice with a tricky equine problem. The Hedges sisters fought for his attention constantly, they complained. Miriam had turned into a positive cougar of biscuit-baking coquetry, and the mill-stream footpath – traditionally a boggy right of way most locals avoided – was suddenly awash with dog walkers in full makeup. But there were no rumours of drug-fuelled sex orgies at the mill. In fact, Dougie Everett seemed remarkably chaste.

While Kat thought this odd for a man who had already shown he was more flirtatious than a stallion hound, Dawn – who was celebrity mad and therefore fascinated by Eardisford's glamorous new bad boy – speculated that he was already conducting a secret affair. 'That's why he's stopped sniffing round you. She's got to be married. Men like Dougie don't hang about. And there are always more girls queuing up.' They joked that she should set up a beauty spa in Eardisford to cater for Dougie's many admirers.

Based on what she'd witnessed of his chat-up technique and heard about his philandering reputation, Kat couldn't understand why everybody was so enchanted by him. 'Even the men adore him,' she complained.

'Don't tell me Dair's forsaken me for a man?' Dawn wailed.

'Actually Dair's one of the only people who doesn't buy into the charm,' Kat revealed; the estate manager's nose still being firmly out of joint. Even Russ had promoted their closest neighbour from 'posh muppet' to 'the cunning stuntman', appreciating Dougie's superior knowledge of films and music, although they'd clashed more than once over hunting, especially as Dougie remained tight-lipped on plans for the estate's private foxhound pack. 'He won't say a bloody thing,' Russ grumbled. 'Just that it will all be completely within the law.'

Dougie was a regular figure on horseback and out running around the estate. He avoided the tracks around Lake Farm, his path never crossing Kat's as she walked the dogs or hacked to and from her lesson with Tina to do battle with Sri, whose latest ploy was to plant herself stock still and refuse to do anything. Galloping the full length of the estate between the quarter rings of the church clock seemed increasingly far off. More often than not Kat couldn't even get out of the yard.

Moving with far greater speed and ease around Eardisford's green lanes on a clutch of newly purchased hunters, Dougie's sublime horsemanship was much admired. He persuaded Brom and Lem joint-master Frank to ride out with him, a brilliant move that ensured far smoother relations with many of the estate's tenant farmers and neighbouring landowners than Dair had achieved with his starchy introductions. Frank and Dougie got on famously, and in this way the hunt supporters, all initially furious that their best Wednesday country was denied to them next season, were rapidly won round as they discovered that the handsome maverick knew his stuff.

The Brom and Lem's hunters were still all grassed off for summer, as tradition dictated, hound bitches whelping, the rest of the pack exercised on foot or by bicycle, so Dougie took advantage of the quiet time to forge links and gain local expertise. The estate kennels were soon resonating with the baying of several couple of hounds drafted from the Brom and Lem and from a friendly hill pack across the border, the brindled, broken Welsh coats mingling with the smooth, dapper English foxhounds like husks amid conkers.

'Old hunting parkland meets the Marches at Eardisford, so it's a fitting mix,' Pru reflected, at May's sanctuary committee meeting, which was dominated by talk of the reinvented sporting estate.

'He obviously cares passionately about his animals, just like we do,' Cyn sighed dreamily.

The sisters spent most of the meeting reminiscing about the good old days when the Brom and Lem's kennels had been based at Eardisford, hunting three times a week with Constance regularly field-mastering. Styling themselves on her as young women, the sisters had hunted with three packs along the Marches and partied with all their most eligible bachelors, and were now transported back to long days in breeches and woollen coats and evenings dancing and sparkling in formal dress. Dougie Everett's glamour brought with it just as much thrill as his sporting experience, and everybody wanted to be in on it. Having sent apologies for absence, it turned out Miriam was trying to sell Dougie a horse. Frank was also absent, having put his back out charging around with Dougie. The other grandees and stalwarts agreed that Constance would have approved wholeheartedly: 'Hunting's what this place is about.'

Kat, who was increasingly protective of the sanctuary and sensed a big conflict of interests, was grateful Russ was working in the orchards and not hijacking the meeting to climb on his soapbox as he so often did. She was already uncomfortable enough with the topic: she didn't like to think of Constance hunting – the joyful, compassionate old lady she had known close to the end of her life seemed such a far cry from a blood-thirsty Diana of the chase, thundering across her own land after fox, stag and hare before the ban. She knew Russ firmly believed Eardisford's new owner had a similar goal in mind and Kat was frightened he was right.

Gathered in the Lake Farm kitchen, the committee were far too buoyant to dwell on such uncertainties, cock-a-hoop that the sanctuary coffers had been boosted by a successful point-to-point fund-raiser, now eager to discuss how to make much more money as they laid into home-baked chocolate cake and almond thins.

Kat grasped the opportunity to suggest they seek permission to open to the public at last. 'I know it's a lot of red tape, but we all saw how successful the Open Day was last year. Visitors would bring in a lot of revenue. Then we can start to take in other old, unwanted animals – pets left behind when owners die, abandoned livestock, lame old horses.'

'Far too tricky to get local authority planning,' Pru, who was chairing in Miriam's absence, dismissed the idea with a sharp tap of pen against notepad, 'and the liability insurance would be totally prohibitive. We'll just have to raise more money privately. There's the village show coming up, of course, and movie night for which we must—'

'Balls!' trilled Cyn, making her sister drop pen and jaw. 'I told you! Constance loved balls! A masked summer ball would be marvellous. We'll ask Miriam to let us use her garden with a lovely big marquee. A peacock theme would be heaven. Let the young bloods boogie!' She gave an energetic jiggle, then winced as her neck cricked.

'We can't possibly afford to host a ball,' Pru said crushingly.

'Besides, we all know how twitchy Miriam gets about her RHS open days. I was thinking more along the lines of a pub quiz or a race night. And as I was saying before I was interrupted,' she glared at Cyn, 'we must now decide urgently upon a film to show at the village hall next month. People are already buying tickets.'

'I vote for something timeless and romantic.' Cyn sighed, shooting her sister a hurt look. '*Gone With the Wind* maybe. It has a ball in it.' She brightened as a thought occurred to her. 'We could all dress up.'

'How about a masked movie night?' someone chuckled.

'Genius!' Cyn clapped her hands together happily.

There were universal sounds of approval among the stalwarts: 'Jolly good idea. Sounds great fun,' before the vote was passed.

'Was the ball in *Gone With the Wind* really a masked one? I thought it was set in the American Civil War,' Kat queried, wishing they showed as much interest in the practical running of the sanctuary as the social jamborees. But the committee had already moved on to the need for volunteers for the village show where they had a host of displays and fund-raisers to co-ordinate.

'Kat will lead out the parade of the veteran horses on Sri,' Pru read from her list.

Kat swallowed uncomfortably at the prospect of persuading the irascible Marwari horse to go anywhere near the village.

'Before that, there will be pony rides followed by the mini gymkhana,' Pru read. 'How's that going?' she asked Kat.

'All in safe hands.' She thought guiltily back to her challenge to Dougie Everett to arrange it. She hoped he'd remembered.

Pru made an eager note when told that Eardisford's dashing

huntsman was now in charge of pony rides and races. 'Marvellous choice!'

'He said he might do some sort of stunt display too,' Kat remembered. 'Jumping off the church tower while shooting flaming arrows, I think.'

'We'll never get that past Health and Safety,' said one of the stalwarts.

'*I*'ll get it past,' Pru insisted. 'I think we should ask Mr Everett to open the show as well. There's bound to be press interest. Shall we liaise with him, Kat, or will you?'

She hurriedly said she'd much rather they did it.

'This will be our best village show ever,' Cyn predicted. 'That boy's *such* an asset.'

'We could call it the Dougie Everett and Eardisford Show,' Kat muttered, realising she was now responsible for having turned him into even more of a local hero.

'I think that's a bit of a mouthful.' Pru had written it down and was looking at it.

'That's what happens when you bite off more than you can chew.'

Chapter 31

The Eardisford village show traditionally took place on a stretch of paddock land between the church and the Hedges' orchards. It was known locally as God's Plot because a succession of cash-strapped vicars had tried and failed to persuade the diocese to sell it off for development. Despite being lovingly tended and mown by parishioners, it was a notorious mole playground and this year was no exception, the marquees, stalls and rings set up on turf so pockmarked with red mounds it seemed even the moles had been popping their heads up all week in hope of encountering the village's new star resident.

When Dougie Everett officially opened the proceedings to a small crowd in bright sunshine, his Hollywood glamour attracted a host of local press, including a television camera from the regional BBC news programme. Dressed in leg-hugging faded red trousers and a bright blue shirt that brought out the colour of his eyes, collar turned up as always, he was utterly charming, giving nothing away about his new role while enthusing about Eardisford.

'Smarmy show-off.' Russ was unimpressed, wasting no time in earmarking the reporter from the *Brombury Gazette* to make sure he included a mention of Animal Magnetism, who were playing a special version of 'Here Comes The Summer' while the local jazz band took their lunch break before the maypole dancing.

With Miriam and Frank on the gate, flirting with everyone, most especially each other, and jolly Bill Hedges on the PA, visitors were welcomed to a riot of double-entendres and bonhomie, enjoying a rare day of unbroken bank-holiday sunshine. Pale flesh and new flip-flops were out in force as the village raided its summer wardrobes and towed freshly bathed family faithfuls along for the novelty dog show. Alongside the tombola, bric-à-brac, refreshment tent, bookstall and plate smashing, a long stretch of God's Plot had been roped off for the children's pony show, starting with paid rides.

Incredibly grumpy at being shampooed and wheeled out in the heat, manes and tails threaded with ribbons, the Lake Farm

Shetlands were dragging their feet around one small circle, led by the Hedges girls in the tightest hot-pants imaginable. Meanwhile Gut, the Indian groom, and the girls from the livery yard were putting out bending poles and taking ringside entries for the races, which had attracted a host of smalls on Thelwellian ponies. There were more glamorous high-heeled ring stewards, rosette-holders and judges than there were at the Horse of the Year Show. Having casually mentioned in the pub that he might need some volunteers to help with the pony show, Dougie had been so overwhelmed with offers that he didn't need to do anything, apart from take the credit.

On the PA, Bill Hedges was profuse in his praise: 'We're very lucky, ladies and gentlemen, to have a Hollywood actor and stuntman with us here today. The multi-talented Dougie Everett has been working tirelessly backstage as well as front, a true ambassador for the Eardisford Estate's new team. I hope you'll all extend a warm welcome to him.' There was a smattering of applause around the field, and a riotous cheer from the pony ring where Dougie's female fans were lovingly running events. 'The novelty dog show is about to take place in the main ring, so please have your four-legged friends ready for our expert judge Miss Katherine Mason from the Constance Mytton-Gough Animal Sanctuary, one of the many good causes for which we are raising funds here today. Class One is the Dog with the Waggiest Tail.'

Kat braced herself before entering the ring. Having agreed to judge the contest because she'd been assured it was a doddle compared to the political hotbed that was the children's mounted fancy dress, she found herself facing a far bigger quandary.

Dougie Everett was first in line for the judge to admire. Quiver's tail might be small, but it rotated as fast as a strimmer wire when she approached. She didn't look Dougie in the eye, eager to protect her vital organs from sudden movement, and to remain impartial.

'What a handsome chap,' she said, wondering why she suddenly sounded like the Queen.

'So everyone says.' His voice, by contrast, was honeyed with warmth. 'The dog's rather cute too.'

Quiver wagged his tail even faster, whole body wobbling in his determination to win his master a few rosettes as reward for all his efforts. Beside him, equally determined but rather less suited to the task, Dair Armitage's German pointers cowered at heel, tails firmly rammed between their legs while he glowered sideways at Dougie from under his flat cap. Miriam, meanwhile, had abandoned the gate and was on Dougie's other side, makeup freshly reapplied and tummy held in as she showed off her overweight retriever, whose plumed tail wafted around like a punkah-wallah's fan. Further adrift, Babs Hedges held a snarling terrier, two earthmen had even more snarly terriers, and Mags escorted Ché, who only wagged his tail if he smelt sausages.

Eager to avoid any accusations of favouritism, Kat awarded the prize to a small child she didn't recognize with a flag-waving beagle, only to discover the boy was one of show chairman Frank's grandchildren and the whole thing looked like a fix. She was similarly blighted by the Prettiest Bitch, Most Handsome Dog and Best Veteran, all of which she tried to award to people she didn't know, only to discover they were closely related to those she did. By the final class Dougie, who was clearly a very bad loser, was looking increasingly peeved. It was the Dog the Judge Would Most Like to Take Home, and as Kat stooped to the Patterdale puppy again, he whispered, 'If Quiver wins, will you take me home too?'

'Depends if you're house-trained.' She smiled as the little

dog tipped straight over and offered her a very pink stomach to tickle.

'We won't steal food, but we'll both lie on your sofas and try to get into your bed.'

She looked up and instantly regretted it. She was no match for those teasing blue eyes, determined to persuade her that she did want to take him home very much indeed. His bewitching smile hadn't diminished while he'd been galloping around the estate and charming every local. Neither had Kat's involuntary reaction to it. Her organs were circuit-training down there. She retaliated with the big guns, smiling him down.

Kat had been going to make Quiver the winner because he was by far the sweetest dog in the class, but she didn't want to give Dougie anything that could be construed as encouragement, so instead she awarded the prize to Miriam's ever-smiling retriever. As she guiltily clipped the second-place rosette on Quiver's collar with a royal 'Jolly well done!' she didn't look at Dougie, hurrying to distribute the other rosettes before belting out of the ring.

'Well, what a superb show of top-class bitches and underdogs that was!' Bill Hedges was on his third cider punch as he resumed his commentary on the PA system. 'Please all give a huge round of applause to the contestants and to our lovely judge, Kat Mason, who works so tirelessly for them poor old animals. I've just been told that there will be a special masked movie night showing of *Gone With the Wind* in the village hall in aid of the sanctuary next month, with a prize for the best Scarlett and Rhett fancy dress, and a mint julep bar running all evening. There's an early-bird ticket offer today, so hurry before they get all the worms.'

'Who sanctioned this?' Miriam squawked, still in the ring with the retriever. 'It sounds perfectly dreadful. What's wrong with the film *TBC*?' She looked accusingly at Kat, who held out her arms helplessly. It was impossible to control Cyn and Pru's enthusiasm now they'd fixed upon the idea.

'We knew you'd love it as much as us,' Pru said staunchly, when Miriam rounded on her. 'Constance would definitely approve.'

'She'd be horrified. She refused to watch anything Vivien Leigh was ever in. Said the daughter of a British cavalry officer in India should be less flighty.'

But the sisters would not be deflected. Not only was Cyn sporting an ancient ball dress to promote the fund-raising movie masquerade, but they also intended to hijack the veteran horse procession to add to the publicity. 'Pru's brought her old side-saddle and we thought we'd pop Kat up on that with a mask and a frock,' she told Miriam eagerly. 'She'll look ravishing. Dougie's jolly handsome, isn't he?'

'Looks just as sinful and swashbuckling as his father.' Miriam's mascara-heavy eyelashes narrowed together, not fooled by the charm – she'd had her fingers burned with Vaughan. But she couldn't help admiring Dougie's beauty as he sauntered past now to put his little Patterdale in the back of a muddy Land Rover and fetch out a longbow.

Gathering up her skirts, Cyn hopped after him, eager to find out whether he'd got the estate's go-ahead for the cricket match. 'I always do the roster of ladies volunteering to help with lunches and teas, you see, and today is such a good opportunity to find out who's available. Bill's been mowing the field in his own time and tending the wickets. Nobody plays on it now, so he says it's a bit green-top but should be perfect for fast bowling by late summer.'

'Just how I like it.' He was pulling more archery equipment from his boot. He turned back to her and smiled easily. 'Faster the better, don't you agree?'

Such was the impact of Dougie Everett's smile – those white teeth, the dirty blond mane tickling the long dark lashes that laced together around bluer-than-the-Indian-Ocean eyes – that Cyn quite lost her thread, which happened rather a lot these days. She looked down, screwing up her forehead in concentration. What was it? Something to do with fast balls and Scarlett O'Hara?

'I hope you're coming to the masked movie night!' She remembered at last. 'There's a fancy-dress prize. Perhaps you can judge it for us. I'm going to make Kat take part. She's such a pretty girl, but really has no idea, and she works so hard with so little thanks. It would be lovely for her to get something back.' She gave him a conspiratorial wink, not realizing she was trying to rig a competition to favour the woman who had just over-looked Dougie's adorable puppy in the dog show.

He smiled wider than ever, making Cyn feel positively faint. 'Of course I'll do it.'

'Oh, how wonderful!' She gathered her skirts and skipped away.

Bill was coughing importantly into the PA again. 'Starting in the main ring now we have an archery display by the world-famous Hollywood actor and stuntman Dougie Everett.'

'If your uncle says "the Hollywood actor and stuntman" one more time I'll strangle him with his microphone flex,' muttered Kat, who had joined Russ at the ringside. She wished he wasn't wearing his badger outfit again. It smelt seriously bad.

'I don't think "Hollywood twat and equerry" means a lot to folk round here.' Russ put a big badger arm around her shoulders, almost gassing her.

They watched as Dougie sauntered into the ring with a bow under his arm and that devastating smile on his lips. Over the speakers, the music was a thundering, fast-moving bass beat that got the crowd clapping.

Archery, unless mounted, was a pretty static pursuit. Having been banned from using incendiaries of any sort by the committee on health-and-safety grounds, Dougie didn't even have his show-stopping flaming arrows to fall back on, but he was a born performer. Joking and interacting with the crowd all the while, he fired off arrows into the row of targets set up with ever-smaller balloons, each exploding with clouds of glitter and streamers. The kids loved it. He shot a huge dragon made from green and red balloons, which his army of volunteers had spent hours lovingly blowing up. He went on to shoot a watermelon, an egg, water bombs and a row of plates blagged from the white-elephant stall. Dougie then did a comedy version of shooting one arrow through another, the first arrow being as fat as a cigar, but no less highly skilled for the slapstick entertainment that left the crowd in stitches, roaring their approval.

Russ, secretly enthralled, pretended to be unimpressed as Dougie swapped the longbow for a lightweight horseman's bow and threw apples up in the air, shooting them before they came down.

'What if he misses? I calculate the trajectory of those arrows would take them straight into the tombola.'

'Somehow I don't think he misses.' Kat was astonished at the skill on display. 'And the arrows are tiny – look.'

When Dougie called for a volunteer to take the apple on their head for his grand finale, he ignored the eager hands shooting up among his many female fans and homed in on Kat, the Everett Effect smile on speed ten. She smiled straight back, engaging in combat, knowing this was revenge for the dog show.

'Don't do it, Kat,' hissed Russ, arm tightening around her.

'I'm not about to let him point a lethal weapon at me.' She spoke through the smile.

Dougie was walking towards her now, charm on his lips, retribution in his eyes. 'Will you join me, Kat?'

Russ pulled her towards him. 'You'll notice her arm isn't up.'

'That's because she has a six-foot badger holding it down,' he pointed out. 'Shall we let Kat decide?' Leaning over the ropes he breathed so only she could hear, 'Dare you.'

Kat started. Those two words were her red rag.

Before she could reply, a figure leaped into the ring nearby. 'I'll do it!'

It was Mags, in her sexy fox ensemble. Having battled to get Dougie to notice her since his arrival, she had spotted the perfect opportunity.

Letting Kat go so fast she spun round like a top, Russ ran to her. 'I won't let you, Mags! Besides, Kat's doing it now.'

Kat wasn't listening. She was looking at Dougie and he was looking at her. The smile-off had dropped away. Her vital organs were staging a serious punch-up.

Bill, who had been keeping up an overexcited, cider-fuelled commentary throughout, was beside himself: 'Kat Mason, ladies and gentlemen!' He forgot to switch off his mic as he asked someone nearby, 'Are we insured for this?'

Chapter 32

Standing two feet in front of the straw target boss with an apple on her head, Kat stared unblinking at Dougie as he eyed her along the arrow, one blue eye closed, the other utterly focused.

311

Her mind whirred. *You're letting him shoot at you. Are you mad?*

He dared me, the voice in her head reminded her, a familiar voice that had been silent for years. It was joined by Constance's laughter-laced encouragement: *Atta girl. You show him!*

The blue eye winked.

The bow released.

Thwwwwaaaa—

The apple flew from Kat's head before she realized it was gone.

Steeling herself – because she thought she might faint, and she didn't want Dougie Everett to guess how frightened she'd been – Kat winked back.

'Ladies and gentlemen, I give you the *legendary* Hollywood actor and stuntman, *Dougie* Everett!' Bill cheered over the PA.

The crowd shrieked and clapped.

Smile back in place, brighter than ever, Dougie strode forwards and clapped Kat, calling for more applause as he took her hand and raised it. Matching his smile and acknowledging the crowd, Kat bowed before pulling her hand away and indicating for them to clap Dougie instead. Then, looking down, she saw that the arrow he'd used had a foam head.

'They're used in archery tag – it's like paintball.' He gave the crowd a bow, glancing across at her. 'At worst it's like being hit by a softball, but I knew I wouldn't miss. Don't knock it. You look good. They all think it was a real arrow.'

'You don't have to make me look good.' She smarted, her bravery undermined.

'Nobody can make someone as beautiful as you look any better,' he said, straightening so that his face was inches away from hers, the eyes back to their default, full-frontal flirt, as instinctively appealing as Quiver offering his belly. But there was a spark of something new in them that Kat recognized with delight: respect.

In the crowd, simmering with resentment because the archery display had bumped his falconry show off the bill, Calum the Talon was not impressed: 'Do that again with a galloping horse and I'll buy you a drink!'

The earthmen and some of the other Brom and Lem faithfuls hear-heared around him.

Dougie's face was very still, and Kat saw pain move across it like a cloud before the sun came out with his entertainer's smile. 'I haven't got any trained horses any more.'

'A Shetland can take an adult!' Calum goaded, pointing towards the pony rides where the sanctuary's Thelwellian duo were short on customers, the entire crowd focused on the archer.

'Okay! Bring one over here!' Dougie laughed, then whispered to Kat, 'Don't go away.'

Kat was pretty gutsy if given a challenge, but the thought of Dougie shooting arrows at her – even foam-tipped ones – while careering around on one of the sanctuary's ancient, evil Shetlands was alarming.

'I really should be getting changed for the procession soon,' she said wimpily.

The larger of the pair was brought to the main ring, radiating ill temper after a long morning trawling around with small children on his back.

Bill was having a terrific time: 'Ladies and gentlemen, the Hollywood actor and stuntman Dougie Everett is giving us a fine display of bowmanship, I think you'll agree, and he is now going to show off his horsemanship with the aid of our own lovely Kat Mason!'

To amuse the crowd, Dougie put Kat on the Shetland first and insisted they trot around him while she held an apple on

313

her head. Much to Kat's humiliation, the pony had to stay on the lead rein and one of Dougie's eager volunteers towed him along. Her toes trailed the ground as she bumped along, apple bobbing. It was like sitting on a moving washing-machine during a badly loaded spin cycle.

'Hold it still!' he ordered.

Thwwwwaaaa—

The apple was gone.

Kat burst out laughing, climbing off and hugging the little pony, which got the apple as a reward. She looked up as Dougie put his bow under his arm and clapped her again, the flirtation in those blue eyes now even more diluted by respect.

'Put your hands together, ladies and gentlemen!' called Bill, now so pissed and enthralled he forgot to switch his mic off again as he added, 'Fuck me sideways, this is good.'

The crowd roared for more, stoked by Calum, knowing that the best trick was yet to come.

Dougie flexed the wooden curve of his horseman's bow across his knee and hooked the string tighter in the one grooved end to increase the tension. Then, indicating for Kat to stand in the centre of the ring with another apple, he swung a leg over the Shetland, nodded for the lead rope to be unclipped, and was off.

The sight of him careering around with no steering, the pony's ears now pricked as he was given his head and bucked for fun, had the crowd hooting and clapping long before the apple flew from Kat's head. In truth, none of the arrows he shot got close. Realizing that Dougie was far too out of control to take aim and was deliberately shooting wide, Kat waited for an arrow to fly past and flicked her head back, sending another apple on its way.

Taking Kat's hand to share a final bow, Dougie squeezed it tight. 'I owe you one.'

'I made us both look good.'

'We make a good-looking couple then.' His fingers laced through hers as he held up her hand, bowing again. Kat felt that hand buzz with sparks, which threaded into her arm and the rest of her body in a carnival conga.

On the PA, Bill was now fighting hard not to slur his words: '. . . proshession of veteran horses in five minutes and then the gymkhana will begin in the pony ring with the maypole dancing shtarting in the main ring at exactly two.'

'Oh, Christ, I have to get Sri ready.' Kat pulled her hand away from his and rushed off to the horsebox, grateful for the escape as the conga threatened to spiral out of control.

Cyn's ball dress, which Kat had been crammed into in a tearing hurry, was a hideous coral pink 1960s number and far too tight. Sri certainly looked horrified when Kat rustled towards her, bright red in the face from all the corset-string-heaving, her breathing shallow and painful.

'I had a hand-span waist as a gel,' Cyn said wistfully, as she and Pru helped her up into the unfamiliar saddle, guiding her right leg around the leaping horn before arranging her skirt so that it covered her legs and feet. 'Sri knows all about side-saddles – she was trained to take one so that Constance could be mounted at the Brom and Lem Hunt's bicentennial meet; must have been eighty-eight or -nine by then. Such an amazing horsewoman. You'd make her very proud today.'

'Shouldn't I be wearing a hard hat?' Kat asked nervously, as Sri skittered sideways.

'Nonsense.' Pru reached down to haul up the girth. 'Impossible to fall out of a side-saddle. I hunted in a bowler. Never took a tumble.'

'Besides, I brought you a mask and Mummy's tiara to wear,'

said Cyn, groping in a plastic bag for them. 'It goes so beauti-fully with the dress. I wore it when I came out, as did Pru. We were quite the talk of the town.'

Hanging on tightly to the reins as Sri snatched at the bit, Kat wondered if the elderly spinsters were Eardisford's incestuous Sapphic secret, but then Cyn added, 'Of course, we were both debutantes in the days one was presented to the Queen. Nowadays one's presented on *Made in Chelsea*. Lean down.'

Doing as she was told, Kat found herself wearing a Venetian mask with a huge nose and a remarkably heavy jewelled tiara.

Before she could straighten up, Sri shot off, crabbing side-ways again, determined to show that she barely qualified as veteran: she was, after all, in her early teens. By comparison, the other Lake Farm oldies shuffled along in the sun like Chelsea pensioners at Trooping the Colour, led in hand by Cyn, Pru and a small clutch of pony-mad teenage volunteers, and fol-lowed by a host of local equine pensioners brought along for the occasion by their owners.

Wrapping the reins twice around her hands before bracing them together and grabbing a hunk of mane, Kat clung on with all her strength to stop the mare tanking off. As she tried to accustom herself to sitting with one leg wrapped around a fixed head pommel, she found the tiara slipping over her eyes, like a pair of dark glasses, pushing the mask over her nose and mouth, but her hands were full so she couldn't reach up to shift it back. She shook her head, but that just dropped the tiara even lower on to her nose, and now she couldn't see a thing.

Watching from the sidelines, Quiver furiously attacking his boot toes, Dougie snorted in amusement at Kat's ridiculous sparkly spectacles – she looked like Dame Edna. Then he realized they were blinding her.

Further back in the procession and equally blind, the sanctuary's ex racehorse Sid was happily following the familiar big, grey rump of his ancient field-mate as he was led along by Pru. When she stopped to chat to a WI friend, ignoring the old horse's desperate attempts to drag her along in his wake, she had no idea that she was effectively taking away Sid's white stick. Losing sense of his friend's whereabouts entirely, he panicked and plunged into the bric-à-brac. Meanwhile, the smaller Shetland had towed his teenage handler to the cake stall, where he was laying claim to a Victoria sponge. Not to be outdone, and maddened by flies, his bigger sidekick led a stampede to the Pimms tent. Oblivious to it all, tiara over her eyes, Kat sat out a few skittish bucks from Sri as she led the march across God's Plot, those curling ears so tightly pricked that the tips were overlapping.

In the wide tented pagoda where a sound stage had been set up for the bands, a smoky, screeching wail came through the speakers, so loud that two nearby toddlers burst into tears and Quiver dived behind Dougie's legs.

Sri shot forwards, then went rapidly into reverse and up on her hind legs as instinct had taught her, tall and fierce against the predators doing a soundcheck, front hoofs paddling. Unaccustomed to the extra weight of the old side-saddle on her back and the rider tipping badly to one side, the mare reared up beyond her balance point.

'Oh, shit, she's going over backwards!'

Dougie leaped into action. Taking a running jump, he launched himself across the mare's withers, tipping her back to the ground. She jinked sideways in a messy stagger then found her feet in a splay-legged landing, just as another feedback screech echoed from the pagoda speakers and Mags rasped into the microphone, 'You all right, Kat love?'

That was too much for Sri. With Dougie still lying across her neck, she spun around and headed fast for the nearest exit, almost wrenching Kat's arms from their sockets.

A chorus of alarm went up as yet more veteran horses charged off in all directions, apart from the lame old Lake Farm hunter: he dropped his head to eat the grass beneath him.

'Whoa, Sri!' Kat screeched. Wherever they were headed, it couldn't be good.

Dougie had a better view, but agreed it wasn't good. They were fast approaching the gateway that led from God's Plot to the church graveyard, a small kissing gate facing straight on to the Mytton mausoleum and private plot.

'Try pulling the reins,' he suggested, assessing the narrow gateway and realizing he wouldn't fit through it in his current dead-stag position.

'You're lying across my hands,' she pointed out, surprisingly calmly. 'So either hop off the bus or take over the steering wheel.'

Dougie steered, rather too quickly. He was accustomed to riding horses in every conceivable daredevil stance, so scrambling into the driving seat, leaning down to grab the reins and apply the brakes was no great challenge, but it took both Sri and Kat by surprise. One stopped dead. The other kept going, taking Dougie with her.

Kat landed front down in a bank of long, spongy grass, grateful for the soft cushion. She lifted her head and saw Sri standing to her left – the mare was looking down at her with a benign what-are-you-doing-down-there? expression – and Dougie lying to her right, his blue eyes less benign because in the long grass he'd landed on there was a hard mound of mole-hill.

'I thought it was virtually impossible to fall off a side-saddle?' she said breathlessly.

'Depends whose side you're on.'

Chapter 33

'I wish I'd bloody been there!' Dawn sounded awestruck by the report Kat had given her of the show.

Phone propped against her shoulder, Kat raced around the kitchen feeding the dogs, kissing the cats' noses and awaiting the Lake Farm horses' return in the lorry with Tireless Tina. She was still wearing Cyn's ball dress.

'It was the best *craic* I've had all year,' she said honestly. 'I felt *alive*, Dawn!'

'Adrenalin junkie,' Dawn scolded. 'You'll be riding that Wingnut thing before we know it.'

'The Bolt. And you know, after today, I think I can.'

'Then you can come home.'

'It's not quite as simple as that,' Kat laughed, leaning out of the kitchen door into the yard as she heard an engine in the distance.

Dawn's voice dropped to a conspiratorial whisper, as though aged parents and jealous husbands were listening in. 'I seriously think Dougie Everett has you in his sights.'

'Well, he *was* shooting at me,' Kat pointed out, moving further into the yard as the lorry pulled into the gateway, the dogs surging out to greet it.

The elderly Lake Farm horses were exhausted after their group outing at the show. When Kat turned them out in the evening sun, they each rolled ecstatically before retiring beneath the shadow of the biggest chestnut to stand nose to tail, swatting flies – all apart from Sri who, at her most aloof and Greta Garbo, wandered away from her herd to the edge of the lake while Usha wallowed in the shallows nearby.

Trailed by the dogs, Kat went to find the hosepipe, which had to be hauled out to fill the field trough. As she dragged it to the nearest tap and started to unravel its kinks, cursing Russ for not rolling it up properly, she realised there was another horse in the field. At first she thought it was the old grey hunter, but he was still head to tail with best friend Sid, his coat white as bone. This grey was covered with tiny chestnut flecks, like her own freckles. As tall as Sri, the horse had appeared from between the gorse bushes behind the beech tree and joined the tail-flicking herd to make polite conversation.

Kat made her way towards them, marvelling that his speckled coat looked the most sensational shade of oyster pink in the sunlight. She had no idea where he had come from, but he seemed very affable, enduring a pompous display of alpha one-upmanship from Sri's deputy, the larger Shetland, before turning to nuzzle Kat when she approached. From the deep hollows above his wise limpid eyes and the low sag of his belly, she guessed he was close to twenty, an elderly ambassador in horse years.

'You poor old boy.' She rubbed his withers and glanced towards the lake, amazed Sri hadn't smelt the newbie and thundered back, teeth bared, to see him off. But she was turning a blind eye, gazing towards the house, as she often did, as though Constance was giving her a pep talk: *Stop being so disagreeable with poor Katherine and take her on the Bolt.*

The old horse had rested his drooping chin on Kat's shoulder now, heavy as a sandbag, and let out an indulgent sigh.

Somebody must have brought him here while she was away at the show, she thought, turning to head back to the yard to fetch a head collar, anger flaring at the selfishness of whoever it was for abandoning him. He couldn't stay in the field with the others: not only would Sri and her evil Shetland henchman try to kill him sooner or later, but he might have worms or, worse, a virus he could pass on.

But when she came back, the flea-bitten horse had no intention of being caught, trotting calmly away every time she approached. She tried rattling a bucket of feed, but one of the Shetlands immediately charged her from one direction while his sidekick took her legs out from the other. The grey gave her a sympathetic look before trotting off to chat to the hunter and Sid. After a frustrating half-hour of trying to corner him, watching him trot away whenever she got close, Kat was at her wits' end.

'He'll come straight away if you offer him a mint,' called a familiar, huskily clipped voice from the gate. 'Berwick Cockles are his favourite.'

Shielding her eyes from the lowering sun, Kat saw a glint of blond hair and looked quickly away before the blue eyes could trap her.

This was stooping too low, she decided angrily. Planting a poor old horse deliberately as an excuse to come here on his disturbing charm offensive was too much. 'You have to take him back,' she shouted across the field. 'You can't just dump him with me.'

'I thought you were dedicated to looking after old animals.'

'We can't afford to look after everyone's rejects.' It came out far harsher than she had intended. 'Sorry,' she told the grey.

'Harvey came here of his own volition today.' Dougie was crossing the field towards them. 'He's always been a bit of a wanderer. He no doubt thinks the sanctuary would be the perfect spot for him after all he's been through in the past year.' He smiled, looking across at the lake. 'I know how he feels.'

'You need a sanctuary?' she asked, remembering the Hedges girls saying something about a broken engagement.

He kicked at a clump of dock with his toe. 'I neglected poor Harv horribly when I was in LA. When things went wrong there, he was good enough to forgive me. He even came to the States to find me. I didn't deserve it.'

She was surprised by his honesty. She was equally surprised that he wasn't looking at her – no flirty eyes, no high-grade smile.

'In the past when I've fucked up, I've always jumped on Harv and galloped off into the sunset like a good lonesome cowboy should.'

'Isn't that what you're doing?'

'The sunset's certainly here,' he turned to squint across the lake at the red glow, 'but old Harv doesn't do galloping any more. Turns out he has a severe heart murmur. Only found out a couple of weeks ago. Hard for him to understand why he can't come out and play, poor chap. It's why he keeps going walkabout. It'll break his heart when the hounds set off without him.'

Without the smile in place, Dougie's face was quite different. It was an open book, the glitzy cover that had promised racy, sexy fun briefly cast aside to reveal a far more complicated sub-text.

Looking at him, Kat registered a sharp edge of sadness behind the charm. His frustration was as belligerently, high-spiritedly hidden as Harvey's. 'So instead of galloping off into the sunset to join the French Foreign Legion, you came here to be a billionaire's personal huntsman?'

'I'm his equerry,' he corrected.

'Yeah, and I'm his lady-in-waiting.'

He looked at her, eyes hardening. '"They also serve who only stand and wait." What are you waiting for?'

'I'm here for the animals.'

He looked at Harvey. '*Touché.*'

'I thought you'd been hired to chase and kill animals.'

Dougie let out a weary sigh and turned to look at Lake Farm's ramshackle buildings in the near distance. 'This place was a hunting lodge long before the formal stableyard was built,' he told her. 'Centuries before the Brom and Lem was formed, the Mytton family kept a private pack. Lots of old grand families had them, a mixture of sight hounds for coursing, and running hounds to follow scent. They were kennelled behind the stables, and looked after by a veneur and his page.'

'If that's what Seth's trying to re-create now, somebody should tell him this is the twenty-first century.'

'The history of this place is amazing – there are archives dating back to the fifteen hundreds. Not many houses stay in the same family's hands so long. Mytton men were always obsessed with hunting.'

'As well as racing, card-playing, cock-fighting, shooting, drinking, whoring, religion, politics and warfare.'

He laughed. 'Sounds like my father's entry in *Debrett's*.'

'Constance warned me about Mytton men.'

He turned to look at her again, voice adopting a teasing chill. 'Are any still hanging around we should know about?'

'She said their ghosts gallop alongside when one rides the Bolt.'

'What's the Bolt?'

Kat crossed her arms and lifted her chin, trying to remember the adrenalin surge of the first arrow coming at her earlier, before she'd known it had a sponge tip. She needed that daring. If she told Dougie Everett about Constance's challenge, it would be another step towards doing it.

She chewed her lip, glancing across the fields at the infuriating mare standing on the banks of the lake. 'Promise not to laugh?'

'Depends how funny you are.' He raised an eyebrow.

Dougie laughed uproariously when Kat confided her goal to ride from Duke's Wood to the Hereford road between the church clock quarter bells on a Marwari horse, swimming the lake, jumping the haha and galloping into the grand vaulted hall.

'Why would you want to do that?'

'Constance dared me to.'

Dougie stopped laughing when he saw that she was serious, and gutsy enough to take it on. 'You'd do it for a dare?'

'Yes.' The green eyes brightened.

'That's why you let me shoot the apple from your head. It was because I dared you.'

She nodded. 'It's a bit of an Achilles heel, really.'

He smiled, whistling for Harvey, who threw up his head before ambling over, a Shetland snapping at his rump. 'I'm sure Tina's a fine teacher, but you'll never crack the Mytton Bolt in rising trot. I could have you galloping flat out with no reins like a Cossack in a couple of weeks.'

'No thanks.' Kat snorted disbelievingly, remembering him making her ride a pony on the lead rein, followed by that day's disastrous side-saddle dash.

His big, charming smile wrapped its way around the handsome face. 'What if I *dare* you?'

Kat growled as her Achilles heel throbbed and she looked away before his eyes could trap hers in their merry dance. 'Don't you dare dare me.'

'There's nothing else for it, Harv.' Dougie gave a barely perceptible clicking sound and the old horse looked up. 'You'll have to get down on one knee, mate.'

With a long-suffering groan, Harvey folded one flea-bitten leg under him, touched his muzzle on the ground and bowed on one knee in front of Kat.

She laughed in amazement. 'How do you train a horse to do something like that?'

'Told you he'll do anything for a Berwick Cockle.' Whistling for Harvey to stand up again, he reached in his pocket for a sweet as reward. The horse rubbed his long, freckled face against his master's side before resting his chin on Dougie's shoulder, still crunching his mint, eyes contentedly half closed.

'How could any woman resist a proposal like that?' Kat patted Harvey, who lifted his head to give her a whiskery, sweet-smelling nudge.

She knew there was a lot more to it than bribery. The bond between man and horse was so absolute. She longed to have even a tiny bit of that total trust relationship with Sri, but the mare was always leader, and Tina was clearly running out of ideas. Her instructor had urged her to get more help and Kat badly needed more control to have any chance of riding the Bolt. Training with a top stunt rider would be a huge advantage, she realized, even if he was an incorrigible flirt. If she was clever, she could even do some detective work about the mysterious Seth and the estate's future plans. She just had to remember not to look him in the eye. Being shot at was far easier than being seduced, and she had no intention of letting either happen when she had her goal in her sights.

'You really think you can teach me to gallop in a fortnight?'

'We guarantee it, don't we, Harv?' He rubbed a knuckle on the freckled neck and the horse nodded. 'He'd shake your hand farewell and kiss your cheek, but he always saves that for a second date.'

Harvey's ears pricked as a spluttering car engine came roaring over the potholes towards the yard.

'That's Mags's car.' Kat started towards the yard. Behind her, the old grey horse followed Dougie out of the field with no need for a head collar and rope.

'Are you still surviving with no bath?' Dougie asked, as he closed the gate behind them.

'Tina lent us her kids' paddling pool.'

'You bath in that?'

'It's for the ducklings.'

Unloading his guitar and amp boxes from the old Citroën, Russ was at his most bristling, highly irritated to find Dougie there ('Thanks to you, every child in Eardisford now wants a lethal weapon – eyes will be lost, mark my words!'). He was clearly itching for a fight, but Mags hustled him inside, bossily telling him to get out of his badger suit.

'Do they live here?' Dougie watched them go.

'Not really. Mags shares a cottage with Calum and his warring kids in the village and Russ shares a leaky caravan with a lot of mice in the orchards.'

'And you give them sanctuary?'

Kat knew he was gazing at her again. 'They help me a lot.' She saw him out of the back gate on to the estate track that led alongside the mill chase, patting Harvey farewell. 'When do we start galloping?'

'Tomorrow evening.' Dougie's voice was refreshingly businesslike. 'Come to the yard about six. But please don't bring the badger – they frighten horses.'

'Is the target engaged?' Dollar demanded, in her characteristic, deep-voiced monotone, when she called Dougie for an update later that evening.

'If you mean Kat, I think she's just cohabiting, although I've found out it could be a threesome, which is thrilling.'

'Do not attempt to be funny, Dougie. And naturally I am not referring to her marital status. Do you have her interest?'

'She has been targeted, and we have interest.' He matched her tone.

'This is good. Seth will be pleased.'

'I need to talk to him.'

'What about?

'Cricket.'

'He is a very busy man. He does not have time for sporting small-talk. But for cricket, he may spare a few moments.'

Dougie explained about the annual village versus estate match on Eardisford's private pitch. 'It would be very good for PR.'

'I will inform him.' She rang off.

Ten minutes later, Seth called, his voice raised over a roaring engine. 'Dougie, *yaar*, how's it hanging? This cricket thing – love it. House should be done by then, so I might bring some mates, have a party. Do we need to get a team together?'

'That's the idea.'

'I'll make some calls. The Indian international coach is an old mate, so we're cooking, man.'

'I don't think you need to –'

But Seth had already rung off.

'– field professionals.'

Dougie whistled for Quiver and set out for the pub to break the good news in the Eardisford Arms, calling Dollar back on the way to insist that no Indian fast bowlers needed to be flown in for the occasion, although a new set of scoring numbers for the pavilion board would be great because somebody had stolen the 4s and 0s a few years earlier to use as a birthday greeting on local roundabouts.

'It will be arranged.'

'I take it Seth's a big cricket fan?' he asked, realizing he had a useful card up his sleeve.

'It is his second mistress,' she said heavily.

'What's his first?'

But she had rung off.

Chapter 34

Already complaining bad-temperedly that Dougie Everett had turned the village show into a farce, Russ was furious to learn that Kat had agreed to take up his offer of help with her riding: 'It was probably that idiot shooting arrows all over the place that frightened the mare in the first place.'

'She bolted when you started your sound check,' she pointed out, equally riled that he wouldn't accept any of the blame.

'It was *not* the music. You were transferring your fear to her after Dougie Everett frightened you witless.'

'Thanks for your support on that one,' she snapped. 'You were more than happy to let me stand there once you realized Mags was the alternative.'

'I knew she'd never hold her nerve like you can,' he tried to placate her, 'and she'd probably have punched him. But I wasn't happy – that bastard could have caused a serious injury.'

'The arrows had foam tips. Riding Sri past an amp turned up to eleven was much more dangerous, especially in a wonky tiara.'

'Why did you let those old witches talk you into riding side-saddle? It's a symbol of female repression.'

'That's not why she ran off. It was you acting like Eardisford's answer to Brian May.'

'Rubbish. She respects me. She sees the guitar as an extension of me.'

Later that evening, Russ dragged an amp and guitar outside on an extension lead to set up just inside the gateway to the horses' field.

'What are you doing?' Kat rushed out from the mesh run where she'd been putting the chickens to bed.

'Proving my point.' He plugged in the leads. 'It's all about animal communication. They trust me as herd leader.'

The herd, dozing nose to tail in the evening sun, ignored him. Grazing nearby, Sri pricked her curly ears.

'I really don't think this is a good idea.' Kat panted up to the gate.

He was already looping the guitar strap over his head and striking a pose as he hit the strings with his plectrum and ran through a few arpeggios.

The horses under the tree started in alarm. Closer to, Sri flattened her ears and swung her head towards the noise, blue eyes hardening.

'An alpha mare will only truly co-operate with a handler or rider she trusts and respects,' Russ shouted over the reverb. 'In the wild, that would be a stallion with which she co-dominates the herd. In captivity, it's the alpha human.'

Greedy as ever, the bigger Shetland had already trotted across to investigate what was going on, his smaller sidekick trundling up behind him.

'Russ, I don't think she wants them near you,' Kat said

worriedly, as Sri swung her head again, then launched into her floating trot towards them, teeth bared at the little ponies – they ducked their heads and skidded away.

'She will chase them away from me, but I am perfectly safe,' he insisted, riffing his way into a few bars of 'Teenage Kicks'. It was an unfortunate choice as Sri arrived in a cloud of dust, spun promptly around and gave him both barrels of her hind legs.

The guitar took the brunt. Flattened into the rutted, dry mud by the gateway, Russ tried to maintain his dignity as Kat hauled him out to safety.

'The village show must have upset her more than I thought,' he muttered, as he limped back to the house with his broken guitar.

Following behind, coiling up the extension flex, Kat stopped herself disagreeing, aware that his ego was as bruised as his ribs. She dumped the amp in the kitchen and found the arnica before going back outside to finish shutting away the hens and geese.

Far from looking traumatized, Sri was back at the edge of the lake and leaning over the rails, nose to nose with Usha, alpha mare to buffalo.

Kat was so enchanted that she forgot to check the coop door was closed properly.

The following morning, the scene of carnage that greeted Kat in the chicken run made her fall to her knees in horror. Every one of the chickens and bantams had been killed, from the fat-bellied proud Buff Orpingtons that laid the best eggs to the small, strutting Pekin bantam and the silkies, which looked like animated white powder puffs. They were all dead, piled up like abandoned feather dusters.

'Fox,' Russ quickly concluded. 'It's like laying on a big food bowl when they can get into a run like this.'

Kat was distraught. 'It's all my fault. I can't have turned the hen-house latch.'

Clearing up took them all morning, particularly as Russ insisted on burying the bodies in a communal feathery grave he styled to look like an ancient burial mound, complete with standing stones hauled from the banks of the stream. Complaining that his ribs were still agony from the kicking he'd taken, he made Kat do most of the digging and lifting, which she felt was a fitting punishment for her fatal neglect, although she was grateful that he laid no blame at her feet, insisting that Nature's cruelty was 'ecological karma'. But Kat could tell that he was as upset and shaken as she was, particularly as they both secretly knew the killer had probably been Heythrop.

When Kat tacked up Sri to hack to the main Eardisford stableyard that evening, she wasn't in the best frame of mind to be told how to ride by an arrogant show-off. For once, Sri didn't plant herself in the gateway and refuse to leave Lake Farm. In fact, she jogged along far faster than Kat was comfortable with, but when she tried to slow her down, the mare let out two huge bucks that propelled her into orbit.

'I give –' she wailed, as she watched the ground coming up to meet her '– up!'

Sitting dazed on the track, Kat heard Constance's merry laughter in her head for the first time in weeks.

You'll never ride the Bolt if you keep falling off. This Dougie chap rides fast and loose, but he knows his stuff. Pick yourself up.

Sri was looking down at her with customary concern. Mood blackening, Kat got back on and they jogged and crabbed the rest of the way to the grand Eardisford stableyard, heeled by the Lake Farm terriers who Kat had brought along for moral support.

Chapter 35

It was the first time Kat had seen the historic old yard since the estate had changed hands and she hardly recognized the main courtyard of coach houses, stalls, stables and offices. It was so immaculate it could have been a film set, its brickwork now re-pointed, the woodwork repainted, the jet-washed cobbles gleaming like mussel shells and not a stray hay stalk in sight. Equally well turned out, Dougie sauntered from the tack room, blond hair swept back, long leather boots shining, handsome face wreathed in smiles. Kat half expected a cameraman to follow him out for his close-up.

'I always start my lessons with a question-and-answer session.' He smiled up at her, eyelashes clustering so darkly around those blue eyes that she wondered if he had them dyed. 'Hop off. You won't be riding her this time anyway.'

'But it's Sri I have a problem with.'

'My lesson, my rules.'

He insisted the mare was untacked and put in a stable with a fat net of hay before he led Kat to a tack room lined with loaded saddle racks; the Indian groom, Gut, was quietly cleaning a bridle hanging from a hook in the central beam. There was a bottle of wine chilling in a cooler on a table in one corner, and he poured her a glass.

'I'm fine, thanks.' She held up her hand. 'I'll just fall off even more if I drink.'

'This is a mandatory part of the lesson.' He stepped closer to hand her the glass, and she noticed his aftershave, a heady infusion of pepper and citrus. 'Tell me, how long have you been riding?'

'Almost two years.'

'Ever ride as a child?'

'No.'

'Why not?'

'I think you've mistaken me for someone middle class.' She tried the wine, which was so delicious she shivered with pleasure. It was a million miles from reject pub ciders and Bill Hedges' home-made grog. It was the taste of special nights with friends and romantic dates. The last time she'd tasted anything so good was on Constance's ninety-fourth birthday.

She heard her laugh again in her head now, egging her on to bait Dougie, but shook it away.

Dougie was still all smiles. If he'd noticed the dust on her breeches from falling off, he chose not to mention it. He was looking at her encouragingly, the handsome, flirtatious face intent.

'So you think you can make me a better rider?' she asked bullishly.

'I can't make you any worse.' Those predatory blue eyes were positively burning holes in her this evening, she noticed.

She swigged more wine. 'I want to ride the Bolt.'

'We can do that.'

Remembering her secret plan to do some detective work, she crossed her fingers behind her back and launched the big Mason smile in his direction. 'And hunt.'

His eyebrows shot up. 'Hunt?'

'Frank says I could have a lot of fun out with the Brom and Lem.'

'You will! Good for you.' He was clearly delighted.

'And now there's going to be an Eardisford pack, perhaps I'll come out with you next season too.'

'It's a private hunt.' He took her empty glass to prop in a nearby wall alcove. 'Invitation only.'

'How do I get invited?'

'Do I really need to tell you that?' He smouldered, the rakish smile pure theatre. For the first time, Kat realized he hadn't had any wine.

He really was laying it on far too thick, she reflected. The way he flirted was all too slick and off-pat, and absolutely not her bag. But the wine had gone straight to her head, making her skin flush and her body feel pleasantly languid, and she was no longer spoiling for a fight with man or horse.

'Let's get you mounted.' Dougie led the way back into the yard, where Gut had brought out one of the gleaming new Eardisford hunters, a mountain of a horse whose outrageously feathered legs reminded Kat of the little dead bantams, a jolt of reality sobering her fast.

'Meet Worcester, the best of all shires with a dash of sauce,' he said. 'We bought him for Rack, the kennel huntsman, who couldn't sit on a king-size bed across country if you tied him to it, but this chap looks after him, and he'll look after you. Don't worry about his size. He's totally trustworthy. And he's got a measure of Thoroughbred in him, so he's faster than he looks. I'll give you a leg up.'

While she tried to get used to the thin air so high up, Dougie got on to an eagerly dancing grey.

'Harvey looks well,' she said, battling a wave of adrenalin.

'This is Rose,' he corrected, and she saw now that this horse was younger, its coat lightly dappled, not flea-bitten, grey. 'I don't ride the old boy any more.'

'Don't you miss riding the stunts?'

'I miss the training side more. I have an amazing young Friesian stallion.' He reached down to tighten his girth, grinning up at her from beneath his hat brim. 'You'll love him when he gets here, but his lungs are still too damaged for him to travel.'

'How come they're damaged?'

Just for a moment the big smile faltered. Saying nothing, he led the way out of the yard through the big coach-house clock-tower arch. But instead of turning left towards the old sand school, as Kat had anticipated, he rode back in the direction of Lake Farm. There was an edge to his voice now, a trace of irritation cut in with the husky flirtation. 'What's your boyfriend doing this evening?'

'If you mean Russ, he's seeing a man about a guitar in the pub.' She told him about Russ's disastrous gateway serenade to Sri, feeling disloyal as he hooted with laughter. Then she found herself telling him about the chicken massacre.

'Natural horsemanship and foxes – two of my pet hates.' They rode on for a full minute before he added, 'And fire.'

'Was the fire in LA?'

'Two months ago.' When he described the barn in which he'd stabled his Friesian burning down, he spoke with the tight control Constance had always adopted to remember the most agonizing moments in her life, which she inevitably glossed over quickly to stop the pain penetrating.

'That must have been so terrifying.'

'I was too angry to be frightened. They were going to leave the horses to burn to death in there.'

'You saved them.'

'Zephyr's special. He was set to become the best bowman's horse I've ever trained.'

'Do some people still hunt that way?' she asked, then cursed herself for prying as he clammed up and adopted a shining suit of fake-charm armour, his voice deepening huskily.

'Bow-hunting is illegal, but shooting apples from the heads of beautiful girls is a favourite hobby of mine.' He was quick to power up the seductive big-screen smile, so charismatic it almost knocked her out of the saddle. 'I'm training Worcester to do a few tricks.'

She smiled back at full beam, more comfortable engaging in battle from horseback. He might be the better rider, but their big charm weaponry was evenly weighted. And she was determined to gallop.

They rode around the wooded curve of the lake that skirted Lake Farm land beyond the millstream, taking a little-used track to a big swathe of emerald pasture nicknamed Lush Bottom that lay in the dell between two banks of woodland. Along one side of this hidden meadow, a stream led from the mill race to a nursery lake in which Dair and his team raised young carp.

'This is truly great turf,' Dougie told her, as he kicked his grey into a canter and waved an arm behind him for her to follow suit.

Kat braced herself. Normally at this point when she gave Sri a canter aid, it was like pressing the accelerator on a Corvette in a skidpan. But Worcester surged into a powerful, lolloping canter that was pure Range Rover on Roman road. She couldn't resist a whoop of laughter as the horse speeded up in Dougie's fast-flying wake, leaving the dogs far behind as they sliced through the springboard turf to the nursery lake, pulling up twenty yards short of its edge where an army of new hazel whips had recently been planted, protected by plastic tubes.

'You don't need me.' He turned to her, laughing. 'You're fine.' He seemed genuinely impressed.

'I couldn't hope to do that on the mare.'

'That's where you're wrong. You're a perfectly capable rider and you have pretty much all the skills you need to ride the Bolt, apart from confidence, and that's a breeze.' He made it sound as simple as blowing a dandelion clock. 'Now shorten your stirrups five holes and we'll go again.'

She found herself practically kneeling on the saddle like a jump jockey. 'This is way too short.'

'To go as fast as you'll need to, you have to get your weight right off his back. Hold on to the neck-strap while you're getting used to it. Ready?' Not waiting for an answer, he turned his grey around and kicked back towards Lake Farm.

Standing up in her stirrups, her weight now pivoted through her knees – it felt weird, but balancing was surprisingly easy with the neck-strap to grip on to – Kat whooped in his slipstream again, wind on her face, ducking the divots flying behind him. It was the best fun she'd had in a long time.

Gut had already tacked up Sri when they returned to the main yard, leading her out like a second horse at a hunt as Dougie and Kat clattered back in on Rose and Worcester.

'Am I galloping Sri now?' she asked, eager to go fast again.

'You're not ready for that,' he said crushingly, jumping off and handing the grey mare to Gut before bringing Sri across. 'We'll see how you do tomorrow.'

'I'll have to check my diary,' she said loftily, furious that he thought she wasn't even up to riding her own horse. She tried to dismount with aplomb, but because Worcester was so tall, the ground was a lot further down than usual and she landed crookedly, lurching off to one side and grabbing Dougie for balance in an unintentional clinch. His body was hard as rock. She backed quickly away and tried to regain her dignity by mounting Sri with super-slick speed, but she overdid her enthusiasm

337

and Dougie was forced to grab her leg to stop her falling straight off the other side.

'Thanks.' She tried not to catch his eye as she struggled back into the saddle.

He helped her find her stirrup, hand still warm on her leg as he looked up at her with the philanderer's smile, voice as playfully soft as his blue eyes were sexily hard.

'Until tomorrow.' He fed Sri one of Harvey's pink striped mints, which made her curl her lip.

Hacking home, Kat diverted back to Lush Bottom, determined to gallop Sri. She pulled her stirrups up a few holes, eyed the horizon and urged the mare into action.

Sri planted, refusing to budge. As Kat grew increasingly redfaced and frustrated, legs and elbows working furiously, the mare let out a long sigh and put her head down to graze.

In the tack room, Dougie dialled one of the pre-sets on his satellite phone.

'How is it going?' Dollar demanded. 'Is she keen?'

'Eating out of my hand,' he assured her, throwing the cellophane sweet wrapper into the bin, 'but I'm not sure the redhead will be quite so easily won.'

'Is there no chemistry?' Dollar sounded almost pleased.

'I couldn't tell you. I failed all my science exams. I was good at woodwork, and that side won't be a problem. She's a lot of fun. I just don't think she's the marrying sort. You know the saying: there are two types of girl, those you want to marry and those you –'

'Don't let personal desires get in the way of this, Dougie!'

'– don't,' he finished, hanging up.

Chapter 36

'Nothing pressing in your diary, then?' Dougie asked Kat, when she hacked across to the stables the following evening.

'Nothing I couldn't cancel,' she said coolly, wary of sharing personal information with Dougie. Russ was currently playing with his new guitar, much as he had all day, shaking Lake Farm to its foundations as he ran through his entire repertoire at maximum volume. She was grateful for the escape.

Grinning, Dougie offered Kat a drink – chilled white port this time, which was delectable – and put her on Worcester again. She didn't object. She just wanted to gallop.

They raced the length of the hidden meadow, chasing scudding rain showers, her whoops and laughter streaming behind her like a knight's pennant. The Everett charm weapons were out in force once more – Kat was amazed he didn't get flies on his teeth like a car's radiator grille as he smiled at her throughout each cavalry charge – although he was more critical of her position this time, complaining that Tireless Tina had tried to turn her into a dressage rider ('and a bad one at that, like a novice eventer. You've got a natural forward seat . . . Just stand up and enjoy the ride! I want to admire that hot arse of yours!').

Kat tried to ignore the flirtation and concentrate on her riding, rejoicing in the confidence Worcester gave her, amazed that a horse so big could feel so fast and smooth. Constance's laughter was ringing in her mind: *Atta girl! Kick on! Show him what you're made of!*

'If you want to ride through the estate for the Bolt, you'll have to learn to duck!' he shouted, veering into the woods.

Following him, Kat found a low branch flying towards her head and dived down on to Worcester's solid neck, the branches and leaves flapping around them, smacking against her helmet and shoulders.

'You bastard!' she shouted, as they burst back out into the light of the meadow, deep golden sunshine gleaming between the clouds now. 'My horse is taller than yours.'

'You'll have to duck lower.' They reined to a halt and Dougie reached across to remove a leafy twig from her helmet and admire the tiny yellow flowers on it. 'Lime – smell.' He pressed it under her nose. 'Far prettier than a bunch of roses. There.' He tucked it into Worcester's brow-band. 'Now he's sublime, which is what you need to be to stay under those branches at full speed. And you will be sublime.'

'Ha-ha.' Kat groaned. 'I'm all over yew like a rash.' She pulled more twigs from her hair and clothes.

'I only wish you were.' He tried to catch her eye, the predatory smile waiting, but she was quicker at ducking away from that than passing branches. Navigating the woods at full pelt had seemed the least of the problems she had to overcome to ride the Bolt, but the sheer scale of the challenge daunted her: it was impossible to cross the estate without going through acres of forestry. Duke's Wood, where the contest started, was far darker and more closely planted than this one, the tree branches embracing low over all the paths and tracks. Even walking through it on foot was tricky.

'So "duck lower" is your only tip?' she said.

He climbed off Rose. 'Hop off and hold this one a minute.'

Jumping on to Worcester, he started to canter around Kat in a big circle. 'I'd normally have a trick saddle to do this,' he explained, his feet out of the stirrups as he shortened the outside stirrup leather and pulled the inside one off its hook, throwing it aside. 'But this boy's a pretty accommodating chap. We've been having quite a lot of fun with this.'

Suddenly he was upside down, hanging off the saddle by one leg threaded through the far stirrup leather, still smiling as he held out his arms. 'This is called the "death drag" – the Cossacks would use it in battle to fool the enemy into thinking they were dead. Comes in handy against the antis out hunting. Useful for riding under low-hanging branches, too.'

'That's amazing.'

'Want to try?'

'Not just yet.' She laughed despite herself.

He pulled himself back on to the saddle, riding into the circle to jump off and reclaim the dropped stirrup, looking up at her through his lashes as he straightened, Casanova smile in place. 'Then you need to duck lower.'

Acknowledging his point, Kat took back Worcester's reins and let him leg her back up. 'Where d'you learn stuff like that?'

'I started as a small kid doing mounted games and picked more up as I went along – tent pegging in the army, hanging out of the saddle to score in polo. It's mostly self-taught, although I learned some of the more advanced tricks like this from other riders. And, of course, the hunting field really is the best place to learn to ride through the trickiest situations.' He remounted and rode into her sightline where he caught her unawares, with no smile and no witty one-liner. Instead he looked into her eyes with such scorching intensity that, for an embarrassingly long, stopped-clock moment, she could do nothing but look back. 'You are extraordinarily pretty, Kat.'

She gripped Worcester's neck-strap and kicked him into action.

341

'What are you doing?' he laughed as she flew into the woods.

'Ducking!'

When they got back to the Eardisford stableyard, Gut was once again waiting with Sri fully tacked up and ready for Kat to ride home. Dougie's tactics had been planned in advance: he knew that the formality of a prompt farewell worked in his favour. He needed to leave Kat wanting more and force himself to demand less. Impatient, horny and impulsive, Dougie didn't trust himself not to overcook it.

As the little Indian groom led the two hunt horses away, Dougie watched Kat mount, admiring the shapely backside swinging into the saddle, wishing he could throw caution to the wind and offer her another drink. But he wasn't allowed alcohol, he reminded himself. Nor must he seduce her too soon. His charm offensive might not have cut a lot of ice, but he sensed a chemistry that could melt a polar cap, and he didn't want to let the momentum slip. He walked with her to the entrance arch. 'I'll see you tomorrow, then.'

'I'll be at the pub quiz. Russ is MC-ing. Thanks for this evening.'

'Tell him you have a headache and come riding instead.'

'I can't do that! Next week, perhaps.'

Left-footed, Dougie flashed his most wolfish smile. 'Maybe I'll come along to the quiz.'

'Why not? You need to be on a team to take part, but there are usually wild cards.'

Knowing he'd only show up his ignorance on most subjects – and he could hardly flirt with her in front of Badger Man – he hedged: 'I'll check my diary.'

As Kat hacked away, Dougie headed into the tack room to

342

track down his satellite phone and make the call to Mumbai he knew was eagerly anticipated.

'All going well.'

'Is she falling for you?'

'By her own admission, she's all over me like a rash.'

'This is good.' Dollar's deep voice purred across the continents. 'What is your next move?'

Dougie thought about the quiz again. He liked hanging out in the pub, and he knew from the gossip he'd heard there in recent weeks that Kat's co-habitation was a far from conventional relationship and that Russ liked to call himself 'free range'. And he was always suspiciously close to pink-haired Mags. It would do no harm to monitor the situation, and he had twenty-four hours to mug up on his general knowledge and work out if he could cheat.

'A master huntsman needs to use his mind,' he told Dollar. 'That's my next move – a mastermind triumph. Tell me, can I Google things on this satellite phone?'

'He's a total show-off and a pain in the arse,' Kat told Dawn as she padded around Lake Farm after her ache-soaking bath, adjusting buckets under leaks that were dripping through from a summer-night downpour, a towel on her head, 'but I've learned more in two days than in two years with Tina. I'm galloping – really galloping.'

'Does he want you to hang upside down from the saddle too?'

'Only if I'm under attack from Bolsheviks and need to play dead.'

'Better warn the wall-Russ,' Dawn said drily. 'What does he think?'

'Don't call him that. He's cool about it.'

'So he's definitely not lighting joss sticks at your place any more?' She was clearly listening to the background noise, which was three parts guitar to one part rasping alto.

'Mm. He comes here for band practice, and he's been using the dial-up. There's a pub quiz in aid of the sanctuary so he's researching questions.'

'Such as, which Hollywood stuntman turned actor is currently trying to get into Kat's pants?'

'He is not going to get into my pants. We both know flirting is his default setting.'

'Mine is disgruntlement.' Dawn let out a resentful sigh. 'I'm freaked out stuck in this chain with the perv from Ruislip.'

'What perv chain? Is this another dodgy internet date?'

'House-selling chain, Kat. The Ruislip perv is the decking-fetish man who thought Plank World was fantastic, then locked himself in my bathroom for an hour on his second viewing and came out all sweaty. Dad thought he was inspecting the hot-water tank, but after he'd gone I found he'd been through the laundry basket and all my dirty knickers were missing. It didn't stop us accepting his offer, only now his sale has fallen through. The agent wants us to hang tough. My life revolves around shouting at conveyancing solicitors, pricing up storage and waxing bikini lines. I want to move to the countryside and gallop around with the most shaggable man in Herefordshire like you.'

'I'm in training to ride the Bolt,' Kat said defensively. 'I promised Constance.'

But Dawn was hyped by house-selling stress and in need of a vent. 'What is it with British aristos and their what-ho challenges and silly stunts? Face it, Kat, the old bird's dead – she can hardly sue you for not doing a dare. I've just seen a lovely flat in Rickmansworth we could rent together.'

'I have a life here.'

'Donning your mob cap and bobbing at the nobility between mucking out the pigs?'

'I don't bob at anybody! And I like the pigs – they're highly intelligent. They charged at Dougie when he came here, remember? They know he's after something.'

'It's not him I'm worried about. He sounds good fun, and God knows you need some of that. It's the vi-Russ you need to get out of your system.' Dawn fell silent to listen again, then huffed. 'I take it that flipping awful racket is him?'

'It's "Eloise".' Kat cocked her head away from the phone to check. 'Damned song.'

Suddenly Dawn started to laugh. '"Damned song". You're even starting to talk posh.'

'"Eloise" is a song by the Damned.' Kat sighed.

Russ's reaction to the ongoing galloping tutorials was now disconcertingly enthusiastic as he saw the advantage of a spy in the enemy camp.

'Excellent work, Kat,' he congratulated her, between guitar riffs, only just stopping short of adding a 'comrade'. 'What have you found out?'

'That I have a natural forward seat, but tense up too much to stay balanced through the spooks, and Sri takes advantage of that by playing up.'

He gave her a long-suffering look. 'All the sanctuary animals' futures are at stake, and that man holds the key. Has he let anything slip?'

'Not even his saddle.' She told him about the 'death drag'.

Russ looked pensive. 'If he's practising Cossack war moves, this could be even more serious than we fear.'

'I don't think he's planning to storm the sanctuary on horseback.'

'He's a Trojan horse one way or another. Keep a close eye on him, Kat.'

Kat was finding it hard to do anything else when she was near Dougie Everett, but she wasn't about to tell Russ that. As he abandoned his guitar to return to his quiz notes, she headed outside to fetch the hosepipe and haul it across to fill the bowser that was towed with the quad bike to all the fields without automatic drinking troughs.

The horses were standing in a different spot from usual, she noticed, not fly-flicking under the shade of the big oak but out in the open. The old hunter was whinnying constantly. For once, Sri was with her herd, one of which was lying down. Kat squinted across to try to work out who it was, making out the familiar big-bellied, bony-bottomed shape of Sid. Something wasn't right. As she crossed the field to investigate, she felt her throat tighten.

His milky blind eyes were still open, but they were no longer struggling to see. Kat knelt down beside him and cradled his big head in her arms, grateful for the bliss in his dead face and the staunch support of his friends. He had slipped away peacefully among companions he had known for years, just as Constance had wanted, she knew, but it didn't make it any less painful for Kat to say goodbye.

She felt a warm pressure on her shoulder and turned hopefully, desperate for Russ's calm practicality right now, but it was Sri's blue eyes that were watching her.

When she finally went back to the house, tears pouring down her face, Russ had left a note to say that he'd gone to the pub and planned to sleep in the orchard that night where he'd set up a hammock for summer star-gazing.

Kat called Miriam, trying desperately not to cry but ending up blubbering so much as she broke the news that it was several minutes before she made herself understood.

When the Brom and Lem huntsman and one of his kennel men came round to fetch Sid's body at dusk, she was grateful for Russ's absence, knowing he'd have kicked up a fuss and tried to bury the old horse on the farm, digging the grave himself if necessary. But Constance had wanted death to be handled in this way for her small remaining herd, sending them to the kennels after they'd met their end. That was where every Eardisford horse had gone over many centuries. Kat's own feelings were ambivalent, but she respected Constance's wishes. When the old grey pony had died soon after she'd moved into Lake Farm, the hunt staff had been wonderful. But the new huntsman, hired for the coming season as a replacement for his carousing predecessor, was small, weasel-eyed and wet-lipped, dropping heavy hints about a drink, eager to gossip about Dougie and the Eardisford pack. Kat was too choked to say much, struggling to hold back Sid's old grey companion who was bellowing at the sight of his friend's body being taken away. She was grateful when Miriam trundled up in her car, as reassuringly crisp-shirted, scented and buxom as ever, smiling retriever hanging out of the window. She had brought wine and tissues with her.

'You poor, dear girl. Always feels like a gunshot down the windpipe when they go.'

But even Miriam had an ulterior motive, it seemed. No sooner had she mopped Kat's tears and poured her a huge glass of white than she was quizzing her about Dougie. 'I hear you two are hacking buddies!'

'He's teaching me how to gallop.' Kat was too wrung out for more than bare truths.

'How exciting! You must find out as much as you can about his plans for the pack and let us know – the Brom and Lems are all dying to know what'll happen to our old Wednesday country and whether we can win it back.'

347

'I really don't think I'm the best person to find that out.'

Miriam gave her a steely look. 'The sanctuary relies upon the goodwill of the Brom and Lem to survive, Kat. You know that. You owe it to us – and them.'

It seemed Kat was now a double agent.

Chapter 37

Dougie couldn't stop yawning. Having stayed up very late the previous night with the copy of *Pears Cyclopaedia* that he'd found on the mill house's bookshelf, then exercised horses and hounds from dawn, and spent the afternoon forging relations with several tenant farmers over buckets of tea and long reminiscences, he was struggling to remember his own name as he hurried to the Eardisford Arms quiz, let alone the capital of Venezuela.

'Douglas, young man!' Ageing glamour-puss Miriam hailed him to her table on the Constance Mytton-Gough Animal Sanctuary team, where Pru and Cyn were flanking Frank Bingham-Ince, a square-jawed fount of cricketing knowledge and political facts. 'You must join in, we're a head short, and we need a young un to help with popular music and television. I've called the troops for support – my son Johnny was on *University Challenge*, unbeatable on politics and pop – but he can't get here till eight. Get him a drink, Frank.'

'A Coke would be great.' Joining them, Dougie scoured the room, delighted that he'd secured his wildcard slot on the sanctuary team. He only hoped his cribbing didn't let him down. 'Where's Kat?'

'I told her not to come, poor thing.' Miriam sighed, beautifully plucked eyebrows straining together across the artificially smooth forehead. 'She had a horse drop dead last night and was terribly upset.'

Dougie swung back to look at her. 'Not the coloured mare?'

'No, the blind bay. He was positively ancient, but we all know what it's like. She's terrified she'll lose another.' Miriam's voice dropped to a whisper as Russ stepped up to the mic to issue a long list of rules. 'I hope you know your onions. Russ takes no prisoners, but Frank's hidden a cricketing miscellany in the gents, so we're playing sport as our joker.'

Dougie managed to stick out three rounds featuring incomprehensible questions about left-wing politics, cult movies and indie music from the eighties and nineties, none of which he got right, before Miriam's son joined the team to fire out answers about the miners' strike and Joy Division B sides. Resigning his slot with relief and apologizing that he must check his horses, Dougie drove home in the setting evening sun via Lake Farm, where neither Kat nor Sri was in evidence.

When he got to Lush Bottom, the sun was still blazing low along the meadow from the nursery-pond end, like a flame-thrower, and he could clearly make out the silhouette of a horse and rider in it, apparently spinning around furiously then stopping, head-shaking and reversing. As he approached, he admired Kat Mason's fabulous backside again, the buttocks tight with tension as they bounced on and off the saddle.

'You're positively callipygian!' he called. It was one of the few things he remembered mugging up for the quiz with the *Pears Cyclopaedia*. Unfortunately, his voice made the mare jump and Kat fell off.

'Is that Latin for a crap rider?' she muttered.

'Are you okay?'

'No I'm not okay!' she snapped. 'I told you I'm hopeless and she knows it.'

'She knows you're upset.'

Kat glowered at him from under her helmet peak.

'I heard you lost a horse yesterday.' He helped her up. 'I'm sorry. It always hurts like hell.' He kept hold of her hand, squeezing it reassuringly.

She nodded, clearly trying not to cry.

Stepping closer to offer a comforting shoulder, practised husky platitudes and a hint of expensive aftershave, Dougie found himself hugging thin air as she slipped her hand hurriedly from his and went to catch Sri, grazing nearby.

'He was over thirty,' she said, in a no-nonsense nurse's tone. 'He had a great innings and a dignified end. It's his field-mate I feel sorry for, the old hunter. He's so lost and just keeps calling.' There was a catch in her voice, but she controlled it, throwing Sri's reins over her head. 'The ponies are all right, they have each other – and Sri doesn't need anyone.'

'That's where you're wrong. She needs you.'

'I can't ride her for toffee.' She straightened the stirrup and stared at it, girding herself to step back up to the altar on which she continually sacrificed her pride.

'Let me have a sit on her,' Dougie offered, before thinking it through.

'Would you?' She looked at him over her shoulder. 'That might really help. Tina's too scared of her to do it now.'

Having gone to considerable lengths to scrub up to dashing country casual in thigh-hugging burnt-orange trousers and Timothy Foxx polo shirt with the collar up, Dougie wasn't dressed for riding, and balked at Kat's insistence that he must borrow her hard hat, a modern plastic one that looked part bicycle helmet, part Alessi fruit bowl. 'It won't fit.'

'I have a surprisingly big head.' She thrust it at him.

'And I have an *un*surprisingly big one.' He gave her a playful look, trying it on to prove his point, only to find it fitted perfectly. The pink headgear was deeply undignified, as was the fact that his trousers were so tight he couldn't get his foot in the stirrup and needed a leg up, but he gamely jumped on the mare, eager to wow Kat with a few moves. Instead, he immediately found himself spinning and reversing with no perceptible control.

'Okay, she might take a while to crack,' he conceded, at which point Sri's long curling ears twitched and she took off like a rocket, carting him into the sunset.

Kat watched them race away across the meadow with some satisfaction, her morose mood lifting briefly as Sri took charge, a small patchwork missile.

'Atta girl,' she said, echoing Constance. After such a wretched twenty-four hours, it was a shamefully enjoyable sight.

He really is a very *handsome boy, Katherine. Lovely relaxed hands. And quite fearless.*

'Eardisford's own cavalier,' she said out loud, as she watched him charge past in the opposite direction.

When Dougie finally pulled up, his smile was so wide it almost touched his ears. 'This mare has some spirit!' he called, as he rode back to her. 'They say you tell a gelding and ask a mare, but this one needs a peace force. She was born for a challenge like the Bolt. How soon do you plan to attempt it?'

Kat could still hear Constance's voice, forthright and passionate: *It will set you free*.

'This summer.'

'Then we'll have to put in a lot of work.' He looked excited, the big smile no longer remotely wolfish. 'She needs to be fitter and you need to be the one in control.' Pulling at the mare's curly ears, which were flicking back and forth on high alert, he dismounted so that he was standing beside Kat, his eyes catching hers and holding them, flirtation creeping back. Only Dougie Everett could look absurdly sexy in a pink plastic helmet. 'I want you here every evening.'

When Kat looked up 'callipygian' in the dictionary later, she found it meant having well-shaped buttocks.

Chapter 38

'I can't believe you let his body go to the hunt kennels!'

Russ had come back to Lake Farm to wash, collect some clean clothes and use the computer before setting off for a mid-summer-solstice music festival. An evening that had started with a much-needed Russ bear-hug to console Kat over the loss of Sid had quickly degenerated into a debate about the morality of Constance's wishes.

'The old bat belonged to another era, we know that – and asking you to ride the Bolt! She was bloody barking.'

'I am going to ride it!'

'You don't stand a chance, everyone knows that.' He was pulling T-shirts out of the laundry basket while he waited for his bath to run.

'Constance had faith in me even if you don't. She said it would set me free.'

'Bollocks it will. It'll just land you in hospital. The Hon Con was a decrepit old imperialist who got her kicks out of ordering her minions about – even after her death.' He threw a pair of mismatched socks with holes at both heels on to his pile.

'Daring you to ride the Bolt was a sick old masters-and-servants joke, unlike condemning her animals' cadavers to be ripped apart by foxhounds after their death, which is just sick.' He picked up the socks again and laid them on top of the dresser where the sewing kit lived.

Watching him, Kat realized she couldn't let it drift any longer. The list in her head kept being added to by the day: no more dirty laundry, no more Tantric sex, no more of Mags's pheasant casualties, no continued abuse of the Lake Farm printer, no lectures about Constance – on it went, and it was her responsibility to re-lay boundaries and claim back the sanctuary and her home.

'Russ, we have to talk.'

'What – now? I'm running a bath.'

'After your bath. And please don't use my Body Shop mitt this time.' It was another item on the list: remove scum-line and pubic hair from bath and toiletries.

Kat decided to write a few bullet points to help her explain herself, but by the time Russ joined her at the kitchen table and started opening two Sui-Ciders – which the Eardisford Arms had been trialling through June without success – the piece of paper in front of her still had just one line. *This is my home.* As she tried to explain the new ground rules, she saw in horror that there were tears in his eyes, his Shakespeare-hero face at its most misunderstood and tragic.

'Do you want me to move out permanently?'

'I think it's best you don't sleep here any more.'

He nodded, chewing at a thumbnail. 'And the injured wildlife?'

'They can stay. You can come and go as much as you like – if you need to leave some stuff here, that's fine. You're a huge help to me and a great friend, and I love hanging out with you and all that you do to help here, but I need my space back all to myself.'

'It's the sex, isn't it?' He put his head into his hands.

Kat doubted it would make him feel better if she pointed out that, no, it wasn't just the sex. It was the mean-spirited, bad-tempered, selfish freeloading and the totally obvious undying love for Mags, which was undoubtedly the reason he couldn't get aroused. His compassion for animals was inspiring and his intelligence was breathtaking, but he was the broodiest sod she knew and appallingly undomesticated.

All this raged in her mind as she took his hands and forced herself to stay calm. 'You'll overcome this problem, Russ, I know you will. Just not with me.'

'That's exactly what Mags says. She says two wrongs don't make a right, and the fact you have such big hang-ups about sex just makes me worse.'

'There you go,' she said tightly, appalled that he'd told Mags.

'It's hard for her to understand my problem. It never happens when I'm with her, you see.'

'Really?' She let go of his hands, her voice climbing scales. 'You found this out recently, did you? Was that before or after you offered me your "fidelity"?'

'You can't stop a grand passion like this, Kat. It's like a tsunami.' The tortured bear eyes lowered. 'I have only ever loved one woman. I'm sorry, Kat. I tried so hard not to go there again. She'll never leave Calum and his kids for me, I know that, but he can't give her what she needs either.' He cleared his throat. 'He's only into C and B sex these days.'

'What's that?' she asked in alarm, imagining a torture chamber beneath the falconer's cottage.

'Christmas and birthdays. Even that makes me want to kill him. I can't share her. He doesn't deserve her. He's a jealous sod

354

too. I half suspect Mags wants it out in the open so we can fight for her.'

'Well, it's bound to be harder to keep secret now you can't use me as cover,' she muttered, horrified that she had been so naïve as to believe all the lines about a teenage love affair that had petered out.

'It wasn't like that, Kat! I care deeply about you.'

She rubbed her forehead. 'What are you going to do?'

'If she really won't leave him for me, I'll move on after the apple harvest's in, I reckon. Go travelling, find a volunteer project overseas where I can do some good. The orchards are in great nick now. It'll be a record-breaking year if the sun stays. Guess we got one thing right as a couple. The Wassail King and Queen brought a bumper harvest.'

She smiled sadly, thinking back to the wassail ceremony on Twelfth Night and their first kiss, fuelled by Bill's spiked cider, followed by the first of many disastrous attempts at seduction.

Sitting up straight again, Russ launched into one of his rallying cries: 'Rest assured, Kat, I'm not leaving this village until I know that you and the animals will be safe here, and the estate wildlife is protected.'

'I'll be fine.' She smiled.

But he shook his head, dark eyes flashing a warning. 'It's not safe here. This farm's too important to the estate for them to leave you in peace, especially if they're hunting outside the law. Dair's wearing his flat cap lower than ever and Meat and Two Veg are patrolling the footpaths like never before. There's definitely something dodgy going down. I bet Everett knows the truth. What's he said?'

'That he's hunting with stunts. "Shtunting," I guess.'

He didn't smile. 'You are 'mazing to put up with all his crap, Kat. I know how hard it must be riding out with the bastard, but you've got to keep digging for the truth. I'm still here to look out for you, you know that. Me and Mags. We both love you to bits.' The bear-hug offered itself again.

Kat forced a smile and accepted the gesture, deciding that, as break-ups went, it was a very comforting one.

Chapter 39

In the hidden meadow the following evening, Dougie buckled an old stirrup leather around Sri's neck and ordered Kat to leave the mare's mouth totally alone. 'Keep the loosest rein contact and hold on to the neck-strap if you need to balance.'

As soon as they tried to pick up canter, the mare gave a huge buck and Kat fell off within three strides.

'Try again,' Dougie said cheerfully. 'That's just exuberance.'

She did, and fell off again.

He was unapologetic. 'Once more. You've got to learn to sit a buck. It's easy with practice.'

The next fall was starting to hurt. Fed up and humiliated, Kat picked herself up from her grassy crash mat and straightened her helmet. 'You show me how to sit a buck if it's so easy.'

'I knew I should have brought Worcester.' He kicked out his stirrups and ran a reassuring hand along the neat peppery mane in front of him before jumping off. 'You'd better hop on Rose. She'll never stand still if you try to hold on to her from the ground, but she usually has better manners when ridden.'

Kat looked doubtfully at the enormous mare: she was far taller than Sri – at least seventeen hands – and had white-rimmed eyes that rolled a lot. With her long back and a stride that could cross a field faster than a bird's shadow, she reminded Kat of Tina's Donald, on which she'd ridden the charity race. She had to be easier than Sri, she decided, not noticing the worried expression on Dougie's face as she grabbed the stirrup.

Refusing his offer of a leg up, Kat spent a long time hopping on the ground in order to mount, the saddle being a lot further up than she'd realized. When she finally made it, she could feel the heat of Dougie's backside still on the leather, which was curiously reassuring as the big, rangy horse started to dance beneath her.

'Just sit very quietly and she'll be fine,' Dougie told her, glancing briefly up to the skies in prayer, which she was too busy shortening her stirrup leathers to see.

Sri's curling ears twitched like hot butterfly wings as soon as she felt him on her back, primed for another race where she dictated the pace. When asked to canter in a circle instead, she gave Dougie her full repertoire of bronco gymnastics.

'Are you okay there?' he called across to Kat whose big mare was jogging on the spot, like a runner waiting at a pedestrian crossing. 'Want to swap back?'

'Fine! I'll stick to this one, thanks.' She watched anxiously as Sri almost turned herself inside out in her determination to get her head and gallop, but Dougie sat on her easily, chatting as though he was lounging on a sofa with a mug of tea.

'The secret is to avoid tipping forwards,' he explained, as Sri rodeoed around. 'Try to imagine your legs are Velcroed to her sides, your back a strong spring and your bottom is plugged into the saddle.' Realizing that bucking was getting her nowhere, Sri now dropped into a light, bouncy canter. He gave her a pat. 'Good girl.'

Kat was incredibly impressed, but had no time to say so as

Rose decided the lights had changed on the pedestrian crossing and started to march forwards.

'Good idea – lovely evening for a hack.' Dougie rode upsides. He was doing the all-smiles thing as usual, but his blue eyes watched Kat closely. 'Relax your hands a little. We'll stick to walk for now. Happy?'

'Very,' she insisted, struck by how far away the grey's ears seemed compared to Sri's little curling archway at the end of the narrowest skewbald neck. The grey mare, by contrast, had a huge long stretch of runway to the pricked, black-tipped peaks. Kat was particularly taken by being so much higher up than Dougie. 'She's gorgeous.'

They moved into the long shadows of the trees alongside the woods, sending a small group of muntjac scattering for cover ahead as they were chased by the terriers, who had accompanied Kat to the meadow as usual.

'I used to think muntjac got the nickname "barking deer" because they stripped bark off trees.' Dougie watched them go. 'Then I heard the racket they make.'

'It gets pretty loud here after dark,' Kat agreed. 'I couldn't sleep when I first moved in.'

'Heard one of your horses calling last night.'

Kat thought about the old hunter charging lamely up and down his field hedges. 'He still thinks his friend's going to come back.' She'd spent a lot of the previous night trailing out to comfort him, wishing there was something more she could do to ease his grief.

Going slowly meant talking, which Kat wasn't entirely comfortable with given how overtly flirtatious Dougie was, but she was loving the feeling aboard the long-striding grey mare, and he seemed happy to chat about everything from horses to movies, the estate's farms to the forthcoming cricket match, occasionally breaking off to remind her to bend her elbows and relax her hands. She could fulfil her promise to Russ and Miriam, she thought, and asked about the role of an 'equerry'. 'I mean, what is it really? You're a huntsman, right?'

'Seth hired me to help entertain important house guests.'

'A court jester?'

'That's probably closer to the truth, yeah. I'm a trick rider, after all. Keep your lower leg still.'

'So how does the horseback archery fit into it?'

'I'll slay dragons.' He dropped his reins and mimed drawing an arrow, causing Sri to bolt forwards. Glancing over his shoulder as he pulled her up, he saw Kat still idling along beneath the sweet-chestnut branches twenty metres behind him. 'Well held!'

Kat, who hadn't needed to hold on to the mare because she hadn't broken out of her loafing walk, looked at him curiously.

He waited for her to catch up, still watching her closely. 'Sit up, you're slouching. Heels back. We'll take it up a notch.'

'When is Seth moving in?' she asked, as they broke into a trot. 'We've all been waiting so long.'

'I don't think he's planning to live here.' He was sitting out more bucks as Sri fought to go faster. 'It's more of a corporate hospitality thing,' he added, momentarily vanishing as the mare spooked at a rabbit shooting out of the undergrowth nearby, reappearing on Kat's other side. 'He's due to visit for the cricket match next month and there's talk of him hosting some sort of party, but the new landing strip's not long enough for his plane so he won't be dropping by until that's changed.'

'That'll explain why the bulldozers were out again this morning,' she said, grateful that her mare was lolloping along so charmingly while Sri crabbed into a sideways canter, bucking again.

'The work on the house is pretty much complete, I believe.' Dougie was bobbing up and down like a kid on a trampoline. 'I've not been inside, but it's got to be amazing. The palm house is now full of mango and banyan trees. There's a man called Sanquat especially employed to look after them. It's all he does. He even sleeps in there. Like you and your animals.'

'It's so beautiful here.' She looked across at the woods to their left, above which peeped the main clock-tower, its face pink in the sunset, telling them it was almost nine. 'I love this time of year.'

'Longest day tomorrow.' He pogoed alongside again, their stirrups ringing out as their legs brushed together. 'The mid-summer solstice.' His voice dropped to purring seduction. 'Sacred to lovers.'

Kat fell silent as they turned to trot alongside the small lake at the far end of the water meadow, sending a pair of wild ducks quacking off into the sunset. She hoped Sri would bolt again so that he couldn't ruin the moment with his Pepé Le Pew moves, but he had her well anchored.

'Will Badger Man be serenading you with his nose flute at dawn?'

'If you're referring to Russ, he's playing at a vegan-awareness festival near Ludlow.' She wasn't about to explain to Dougie about Russ's free-range life or last night's new house rules. Letting him believe that Russ was her live-in boyfriend might be somewhat dishonest, but if it meant she got in the riding practice she needed without Eardisford's disreputable new bad boy trying to add her to his bedpost notches, she was happy to keep the myth spinning. It wasn't as though anybody would tell him differently. Russ's walkabout season had truly begun, a nomadic round of music festivals while the apples ripened, his sleeping quarters constantly shifting, the caravan and hammock in the orchards backed up by a hide tent in the woods and an earth shelter by the river.

'Can we gallop?' she asked, eager to get some more in. The big grey mare's trot was revving up as she turned for home.

Beside them, Sri pricked her curly ears at the word 'gallop', almost pulling Dougie's arms out.

'Are you sure?' He glanced at the grey colossus powering past him. 'That girl is seriously fast.'

Kat stood up in her stirrups as they broke into a canter. 'If I'm going to gallop Sri into the end of the longest day tomorrow, I'd like a dress rehearsal.'

'Don't tell me you're missing the vegan festival!'

'Some things are more important than tofu.'

'In that case, hang on very tight.' He nodded at her, clicked Sri into action, and they flew past in an arc of divots.

Sitting on the grey mare as she accelerated behind them was like perching on a bobsleigh along an Olympic run. Kat had never felt anything so exhilarating. This was by far the most powerful horse she had ever ridden. Catching up effortlessly to streak across the meadow alongside Sri, she turned to Dougie and gave a thumbs-up.

'That's just her cruising speed. Amazing, isn't she?' he shouted.

It was only when they'd turned a big loop in the meadow's basin and pulled up to walk, taking the horses back towards Lake Farm, that Dougie admitted the big grey had a terrible reputation. 'I got her for a song from a friend of Dad's because nobody there could ride her. My staff can't hold her at all. She's monumentally bloody-minded and strong.'

'I think she's lovely.'

'Because you had confidence in her, you trust her. You should trust Sri. She has a very big heart.' He patted the curved skewbald neck in front of him. 'I normally don't work with mares as trick horses, but I think she'd be incredible. There's a third part to the saying "tell a gelding, ask a mare" which is "discuss it with a stallion". This little Marwari reminds me of my Friesian stallion.'

'Are you accusing my horse of being gender confused?'

'I'm saying she's got balls. And tackling the Bolt will take plenty of those. The same goes for you.'

She let out a cynical snort, remembering Nick and his fire-fighting cronies' similar obsession with 'cojones', as though courage could only be weighed in a scrotal sack. Dougie clearly came from the same male chauvinist mould.

The horses had pricked up their ears as they spotted an old flea-bitten grey shambling towards them, led by the little Indian groom Gut, who was very out of breath.

'Of course, Harvey has no balls whatsoever but he's still the bravest bugger I've ever known.' Dougie laughed as the horse let out a bellow of recognition and towed Gut towards them.

The little groom talked animatedly in Hindi, waving his arms around and huffing a lot before nodding farewell to Kat and walking Harvey on towards the main Eardisford yard.

'He got in with your horses again,' Dougie said apologetically. 'Gut says he was a sod to catch.'

'I didn't know you could speak Hindi.' She was impressed.

'I don't understand a word he says,' he admitted, eyes smiling up at her through the long lashes. 'But I know Harvey. He's like me. Once he finds a kindred spirit, he can't keep away. And I just can't keep away from you, Kat.'

Battling hard to quash the tell-tale tangle of heart, stomach and lungs that squirmed inside her when he laid on the Everett Effect, Kat braced herself for another smooth invitation to share his bath. But before he could speak again, his phone began ringing in his pocket and he was forced to sit out a massive fawn-leap from Sri, who rocketed into the woods.

'How come you have a signal here?' Kat asked, when he finally got control and made his way back to the track.

'Satellite,' he explained. 'Your boyfriend listens in to the walkie-talkies.'

'So you've got something to hide?' she asked suspiciously.

'Only my desire for you.' His handsome face wore the most devastating example of his smile repertoire – as sexy as it was self-mocking. 'If Badger Man's away, you can invite me in for a drink.'

They had arrived at the Lake Farm gates. The phone was ringing in his pocket again. He ignored it. 'You shouldn't be all alone somewhere as isolated as this.'

The tangle in Kat's chest tightened uncomfortably at the memory of banishing her growling bear. There was no reason she couldn't invite Dougie in for a Sui-Cider, which would be only polite, given she'd already taken several drinks off him and he was helping her so much, but self-protection had to come first.

'I'm not alone,' she reminded him, as the dogs that had stayed napping in the yard surged out to greet those who had accompanied Kat out riding. 'And I'm not inviting you in.'

'How is it progressing?' Dollar cross-examined Dougie as he rode back to the main stableyard, the line lagging badly with a satellite delay, making her deliberate monotone sound more computer-generated than ever. 'Have you seduced her yet?'

'We're saving ourselves for our wedding night.'

'This is excellent news. You must keep the pressure on. Your time will soon be taken up providing sport for Seth's guests, so make the most of this opportunity. We would ideally like her gone within a month.'

'I don't think I'm quite ready to book tickets to Las Vegas,' he said, shocked.

'Then you must increase the pressure.'

'I'm intending to,' he assured her, already looking forward to galloping into the sunset. He found the riding challenge far more interesting than the seduction one, which he strongly suspected was still going nowhere. Kat's company was a lot more fun when he laid off the Casanova stuff, although she certainly wasn't immune to his charms. She had a curious way of looking at him, which was one part desire to one part fear, the rest amusement, which put him off his stroke. She was far too defensive to risk going in fast and hard. In any case, Dougie had discovered a curious anomaly in the past two days. The less he flirted, the more attractive he found Kat Mason. When they were having a riot, like this evening's gallop, he forgot his motivation for being there.

'The flat in Rickmansworth's still available,' Dawn told Kat when she called her for another after-bath debrief. 'And Pervy Buyer's had a cash offer, so we're back in business. I definitely think we should live together again. We had such a laugh as students.'

'I'm going nowhere. This is the best fun I've had in ages.'

'Just don't forget how truly terrible Dougie Everett's reputation is.'

'Like the grey mare's,' said Kat, still reliving the feeling of pure power beneath her. 'She just gave me the ride of my life.'

'As soon as the house sale completes, I'm coming up to Herefordshire to see you,' Dawn insisted. 'Don't do anything silly before then.'

'Don't worry, I'm not nearly ready to ride the Bolt.'

'I wasn't talking about the Bolt.'

Chapter 40

On the morning of the summer solstice, Kat found speckled grey Harvey in with her herd again. He was standing quietly beside the old hunter, nose to tail like two commuters on a tube train.

As she crossed the field to catch him, Harvey bobbed his freckled face as though nodding in welcome, his eyes incredibly wise. Kat knew he was just shaking off flies, but there was something almost human about him – she half expected him to bow courteously again. When she led him back along the lime avenue and up the parkland ride to the estate stables, she heard him grunt as he walked, like an old man humming under his breath.

At the Eardisford yard, Gut managed an energetic mime to thank her for bringing the horse back and explain that Dougie and his kennel man were out with the hounds. But by lunchtime Harvey had broken back in with the retired herd again and was nibbling the old hunter's withers.

This time when Kat took him back, Gut mimed that Dougie was at the feed merchants, although it could have been that he was at lunch or possibly even committing hara-kiri.

An hour later, Kat heard excited whinnies from the horse field and groaned. She went to the gate to find Harvey and the hunter racing around like a pair of youngsters.

The klaxon was ringing to alert her to a land-line call, and she found Dougie on the line, profuse with apologies. 'He's with you again, isn't he?' His voice was fabulous on the phone – that husky, clipped timbre like warm oil in an aching ear. 'The old grey bugger can get out of any field or stable if he sets his mind to it.'

'Perhaps he should stay with me for a bit,' Kat suggested, quashing a ridiculous suspicion that she was being set up, especially when Dougie said he'd personally bring him Berwick Cockles as well as paying for his keep. But Harvey's presence seemed to soothe the old grey hunter, which had now stopped charging lamely alongside the rails and hedges in search of poor Sid. Exhausted after his grief-stricken week, he was happy to nod off under the big chestnut tree with his new chum, ears flopping, one hind hoof rested on its toe.

'He can stay as long as he likes.' She was glad that her herd was happy again.

Feeling guilty that she'd refused to offer Dougie a drink the previous evening, Kat brought cake and home-brewed cider in a backpack, which she and Sri reduced to fizz and crumbs as they jogged all the way to the hidden meadow, anticipating a full-throttle gallop. It was only when she was almost there that she realized Harvey had jumped out of his newly adopted field and followed them.

Dougie was on foot for once, standing knee-deep in grass that was as golden-blond as his hair in the evening sun, and from which Quiver the puppy bounded to catch the old tennis ball he was throwing for him. He laughed as Harvey loped up and nuzzled his jeans pockets for mints. 'Let him watch if he wants to,' he told Kat, who was shrugging off her backpack while Sri danced sideways. 'Give her five minutes' warm-up then take her for a gallop and see how you do.'

'On my own?'

'I think it's having another horse with her that winds her up so much. You'll be riding the Bolt on your own, so it makes sense to find out now. Would you like me to take her for a pipe-opener first?'

'No, I'm fine,' she insisted, too proud to admit how wimpy she suddenly felt. 'What about Harvey?'

'Harv'll stay where the cake is.' He settled back in the grass to share some of the sweet crumb rubble with the grey horse. 'This is seriously good. Did you make it?'

Kat was too anxious to discuss her baking prowess as she let Sri trot round, half listening to Dougie chat easily about his hounds. 'People see the pack as a whole entity, but they're wildly differing characters, all such amazing individuals. Humbug is the joker, Horace the old pedant, Hawthorn the flirt. There's one called Honour reminds me of you. Her coat's unbroken chestnut, which is unusual for a hound. She's always getting into scrapes, setting off on her own course.'

Kat found being compared to a wayward hound strangely cheering compared to his usual heavy-handed flattery, although as he watched her, she was aware that her hair, which hadn't been washed for three days, was a matted tangle in a lumpy plait secured with a post-office elastic band.

'We need to take this a lot faster.' His tone changed and he stood up. 'Move her into canter and get up off the saddle so I can admire that gorgeous arse of yours, which remains my primary motivation for coming here, although the cake is a revelation. You'd be a very easy woman to fall in love with, Kat. I'm halfway there already.'

Kat was too flustered by the charm attack to notice that Sri didn't buck once. 'Do you flirt with everybody?'

The big smile revolved as she circled round him. 'Do you ever flirt with anybody?'

'I can flirt.'

'I dare you.'

She glanced at him, wishing her body didn't leap each time he issued a challenge. 'Why would I want to encourage you?'

'Because we're attracted to each other,' he said simply, turning faster now as he watched her careering around him. 'You can't deny it.'

Kat said nothing, aware that she was blushing furiously. She could feel her nipples hard as bullets against the hefty strapping of her sports bra, grateful that it was thick enough to hide the obvious double thumbs-up of agreement.

'I think you've warmed up enough.' He grinned. 'Off you go.'

Delighted to escape the flirtatious interrogation, Kat laced her hands through the chestnut and white mane as she turned the mare to face the open arc of the meadow, closing her eyes tight and urging Sri onwards. Only too happy to oblige, she surged into action and this time stayed on a straight line. As they pounded across the turf, Kat opened her eyes, looked through those curved ears and whooped. The sunset was in her sights, warm air rushing past her face. It was heaven.

Leaving Dougie far behind, Quiver's excited barking fading away, they thundered along the springiest stripe of turf, sending up skylarks in front of them and great divots in their wake as they ate up the ground between the millstream track and the nursery lake.

Then the water came closer, a sheet of gleaming gold guarded by the rows of newly planted maple whips, like spears. Kat tugged ineffectually at the reins, but nothing happened. They slalomed through the little trees, plastic wraps rattling against the mare's legs.

'Whoa!' she bellowed, heaving all her weight against the slipping reins, but that just made Sri plunge her head around and increase her pace.

Dougie had taught her how to go fast, Kat realized, but not how to stop. The mare seemed blinded by the sun, not knowing what lay ahead.

On the brink of the lake, Sri suddenly saw the water and swerved dramatically right. Kat flew from the saddle and saw the water come towards her like the sky turned upside down.

The cold, whooshing suffocation that engulfed her stopped all thought. Eyes closed, ears muffled, breath halted, she let herself sink, let the heavy cage start to form round her stultified body.

Then, like a harpoon flying in her wake and spearing her consciousness to register pain, the fight came bursting out of her, legs and arms thrashing, water roaring in her ears, eyes blinking through the weed-choked gloom for the light.

As she fought her way back to the surface and erupted through it, she saw Sri's wall eyes gazing down at her worriedly, joined seconds later by a far brighter, long-lashed blue pair as Dougie rushed to the edge of the lake.

Her first, illogical, thought was, how on earth had he got there so fast? Then she felt a tremendous tug from below as the reeds dragged her down again.

She thrashed away from them, resurfacing with a desperate gasp for air as Dougie was hauling off his sweater and tearing off his shoes to dive in, sending a great bow wave over her so that they both disappeared beneath the surface. She saw his arm flail past in the gloom, his legs kicking away the reeds that entwined themselves around him too as he swam towards her.

But Kat was already at the bank, the water turning opaque with mud as she scrabbled out, coughing up great lungfuls of water.

Dougie dragged himself up alongside her, pulling her to his

side, rubbing her cold arms. 'It's okay. You're fine. Ssh. What the fuck happened?'

Kat looked up into his eyes, so blue and intense. His lashes were all wet, she noticed. She tried to say, 'I couldn't stop,' but it came out as gobbledygook because her teeth were chattering. To her embarrassment, she started crying.

It took Dougie a while to piece together what she was saying, all the time trying to warm her, the sweater he'd abandoned on the bank now swamping her narrow shoulders, her water-filled boots and sodden breeches pulled off and baking in the evening sun. He'd never known anyone shake as much.

It hadn't quite been the heroic rescue he'd envisaged during those last lung-burning, mind-racing yards of sprinting to the lake. Kat had saved herself long before he could be of use. But the incident had taught Dougie two things: first, that Harvey still relished being ridden and was remarkably healthy – the two had galloped the length of Lush Bottom faster than Pegasus, both burping cake all the way – and, second, that he cared enough about Kat Mason to risk life and limb for her. His own safety was something he gambled on a regular basis, but risking Harvey meant that Kat had now got beneath his skin.

'You can't swim?'

She shook her head. 'I'm a strong swimmer. Something happened when I was a kid that meant I took every life-saving and swimming award I could. I thought it would make it better.'

Kat's parents hadn't allowed her pets: the restrictions of army life in her early childhood had meant too many moves and unsuitable accommodation, and then, after the divorce, her mother blamed lack of money and time. But when they had settled in Watford, she'd been allowed to walk the neighbours' small, cat-hating elderly Heinz 57 dog after school.

'My friend and me used to take him along the canal towpath in Cassiobury Park.' She drew her knees up to her chest, pulling the jumper over them and down to her ankles. 'One day there was a barge going down in the lock that had a cat sun-bathing on the roof. I was busy talking and didn't even see what happened, but he must have lunged at it because the next thing he was between the boat and the side of the lock, with all the water coming in through the lock gates, six feet below me. I jumped in after him, but he'd gone under the barge in the water swell and I couldn't reach him, couldn't stay under long enough. Then the boat moved against the side wall and trapped him down there. The people on board didn't know what was going on until my friend raised the alarm, but it was too late by then. The dog had already drowned. It was my fault.'

'Of course it wasn't! You risked your life trying to save him. You were just a child.'

'I started taking extra swimming classes afterwards. I even competed for my local club in open-water races and triathlon. I used to have a bit of a reputation at school for being fearless.' She looked at the lake with a sad smile at the irony of it. 'Give me an extreme sport and I'd try it. Dare me, and I'd do it. Adrenalin was my addiction, but water remained my enemy, however many times I took it on.'

'And you're still afraid of it now?'

She pressed her white-knuckled fists to her mouth. 'It's one of the reasons I came here.'

'Funny place to escape from water.' He followed her gaze across the lake. 'You practically live on an island.'

'I hadn't realized Constance would set me up quite so royally with aversion therapy, once she found out why I'd left Nick and how screwed up I still was about it. She insisted I just needed to jump straight in,' she remembered with a wry smile.

'She was probably right. I'm still here, still trying. I swear Sri's her ghost sometimes.' She glanced across at the mare standing companionably with Harvey. 'That move just now was pure Mytton.'

'Nick was a boyfriend?' he asked, already feeling illogically jealous.

She nodded. 'We were engaged.'

'What made you break it off?'

She shook her head. 'It's the past. I've buried it.'

'Not if it makes you terrified of water.'

'I'll be better next time.' She stared at the lake. 'It was the shock, that's all.'

But Dougie wouldn't let it go. If whatever had happened had made her run here from Watford, it had to have been serious, and the bastard who was responsible deserved to suffer. 'Did your fiancé hurt you?'

She didn't answer.

'My guess is he tried to drown you. Where was it? In a lake like this? Out at sea? At home in the bath?'

'It was an accident,' she said quickly.

'Now you have to tell me.'

She turned to look at him, green eyes unblinking, realizing she'd fallen into a trap. She didn't have to tell him, of course, but Dougie knew she would. She possessed that brand of honourable honesty in common with his closest allies.

'We'd been at a boozy Sunday lunch in the pub with some friends.' Her voice was flat and hurried, dispensing with any preamble. 'They'd been badgering us to name the day, and Nick was all for it, joking that we were planning an extreme sports wedding. I'd known it wasn't working out for months, but Nick was in total denial and just refused to listen. He'd become really overbearing and aggressive. I was frightened of him. That day he'd talked all over me yet again and I'd had enough. We'd had a lot to drink and it gave me the courage I needed. When we went to Cassiobury Park to walk off the wine, I told him I wanted to call off the engagement.

'He tried to make out it was all a big joke, but I just kept repeating myself until it went in. It was only when I gave him the ring back that he knew I was completely serious. Then he got really mad, and accused me of trying to humiliate him. He was apoplectic. He made a big gesture of throwing the ring into the river before remembering it had cost almost as much as his car, so he waded in after it. We were by the reed beds, not far from the point where the river and canal merge near the lock where I'd jumped in after the dog as a child. Nick knew all about that, of course, and started shouting at me because I wasn't helping him, goading me that I'd tried to save a drowning dog but not our relationship. He kept diving down to look for the ring. Then he disappeared right under and didn't come up. When I swam out to save him, he pulled me under and held me there.'

'That's no accident.'

'He was still very drunk. He wanted to frighten me but it went horribly wrong. I got caught up in the weeds, like here, and couldn't get back up to the surface.' Looking out across the little lake, she started to shiver again. 'It's not a deep river, but there are hidden hollows where the reeds can wrap round your legs in seconds. Nick tried to drag me back up, but I was completely trapped.

'Two runners came to the rescue when he started yelling. I could see their legs and air bubbles everywhere. I had no breath or fight left. I must have blacked out under water. I thought I was going to die. The last thing I remember was spotting the bloody ring on the riverbed.'

'Surely the police were involved.'

She shook her head. 'Just medics. I needed CPR when they got me out. Nick was terrified I'd shout "attempted murder". He was contrite afterwards. My lungs had taken a real battering. I had headaches and blackouts for weeks as well as a vicious cough. But the worst was the panic attacks. Nick refused to talk about what had happened, but it was all I could think about. I knew I had to get away from him, but I was frightened what he might try to do if I did. That was why I planned it so carefully. I came here, where I knew he couldn't trace me. I can't believe I'm telling you all this.' She put her head into her hands. 'I haven't told my best friends.'

'You told Constance,' he reminded her, then his mouth fell open. 'That's why she left you Lake Farm, isn't it? To keep you safe?'

She looked up at him through her fingers, a touch of a smile showing to either side. 'She was amazing. She had a way of finding out one's darkest secrets. There was other stuff Nick did, things that left far deeper scars and she—'

'He *hit* you?'

'Emotional scars.' She took her fingers from her face, the smile fixed and defensive. 'I'd rather not talk about it, but you're right. Constance gave me a safe haven.'

'What "other stuff"?'

'It's really not relevant to riding the Bolt.'

'Everything's relevant, Kat.'

When she still didn't answer, he murmured, 'Truth or dare?'

She snorted disparagingly. 'Do I look sixteen and caned on vodka Red Bulls?'

Dougie could have kicked himself for his tactlessness. As soon as he'd said it, he knew it was wrong, however well intended. He'd wanted to wrap a comforting arm around her and hold her to his side while she confided more about what had led her here, but instead he'd back-slapped her with a juvenile challenge. And it was too late to retract now.

'Forgive me. I'm not a particularly evolved life form, as you yourself have pointed out,' he said easily. He'd slipped totally out of role again, but he found he had no desire to thrust a rose between his lips and try to tango his way back on course for his bonus. He just wanted to cheer her up.

'That makes two of us.' She rested her chin on her knees and squinted at him through the sun, her red hair almost dry now and tightly spiralled like bracken fronds. 'Dare.'

He looked at her in surprise. Then he laughed, not giving her a chance to change her mind as he saw a chance for redemption. 'Gallop again?'

'Now?'

He nodded. 'Haven't you heard you must get straight back on after a fall?'

'My breeches are still sopping wet.'

'Ride without them.'

She looked at him suspiciously, but he kept the wolf's smile from his face. 'You'll have to go bareback.' He stood up to unsaddle the mare. 'I'll co-pilot.'

'Your jeans are wringing wet too.'

Dougie unbuckled his belt and peeled them off. 'If Red Indians can ride in loin cloths, we can do it in pants.'

'You'd seriously do this?' She looked astonished, particularly at the sight of his cockerel-patterned 'Crown Joules' jockey shorts, which he was grateful his polo shirt almost covered.

'Christmas present from my father.' He followed her gaze. 'The ferret ones are worse.'

Moments later, the green eyes were wet with tears as she clutched her chest and went into rapturous giggles, laughing so much that it took him a while to grasp she was accepting the dare.

375

Aware that his move that hadn't done much for his masterly, heartthrob status – although it had certainly cheered her up – Dougie jumped on to Sri's patchwork back, then reached down to help Kat up behind him. 'This will be seriously good for your core stability.'

Setting off at a steady canter to let her gain her balance, he knew that this was selfishly as much for his pleasure as her stability, but the laughter in his ear as they speeded up to full tilt was a magical reminder that it had a healing purpose, just as the warm, lean heat clinging to the length of his back connected him to the woman he had started to see in an entirely new light. Evenings with Kat were a misleading Happy Hour cocktail that had promised high kicks and a huge cash bonus, but delivered conflict, chemistry and increasing respect. Today had made that mix a lot more potent, adding something Dougie's emotional palate rarely tasted: the throat-burning, heart-speeding warmth of affection.

When he pulled up by the woods, the mare was barely blowing and Kat, still laughing, insisted, 'I'm going round again!'

'Sure.' He got ready to urge the mare forward.

'Wait!' She reached forwards to stop him, chin on his shoulder as she took hold of the reins, her warm breath making his skin dance. Turning his face towards hers, seeing her eyes as bright as spearmint amid the smile-widened freckles, his mouth started moving instinctively towards hers long before his brain registered how badly he wanted to kiss her.

She turned her head away to look across the meadow. 'Will you get off?'

'Of course. Sorry,' he said awkwardly, as he gathered the reins. 'Let's go.'

'I meant get off the horse, Dougie.' She laughed. 'I'm going round again.'

Realising she wanted to gallop solo, he had to resist an even greater urge to kiss her.

He jumped off and watched her streak around the field, laughter and pride fusing together in his chest and forcing an unfamiliar lump into his throat. It might have taken a dare that went wrong and a truth still only half told, but she'd gone from barely trusting the mare to galloping bareback in the space of an evening.

Kat Mason was a revelation. She had incredible guts and faith, and her curious beauty grew on Dougie every day: the big smile that revealed her furnace-like warmth but hid her vulnerability, those watchful green eyes and that extraordinary mane of hair he couldn't wait to see spilling across naked freckled skin and white Egyptian-cotton pillows. Somewhere along the line a keystone of her self-belief had been stolen from her. He wanted to be the one to restore it, and to find out the truth. Next time he tried to kiss her, he vowed she'd want it just as much. And he wouldn't be sitting on horseback wearing cockerel pants.

As midsummer's evening finally set into dusk, Kat rode back towards the woodland track with Dougie walking alongside, dogs at their heels and Harvey at his side. A hare power-sprinted along the avenue of trees ahead of them, silhouette coming and going as it crossed the stained-glass arches of sunset light between the black trunks.

Dougie turned to watch Kat ride, those luscious freckled legs demure in breeches once again, although her still-damp boots hung on her saddle rings from their garter straps and her bare feet dangled out of the stirrups. She was the only female Dougie knew, apart from his young nieces, who hadn't had a painted pedicure, yet she had the neatest, pinkest nails he'd ever seen, like little shells. He had a sudden image of lifting them to his lips in the big claw-footed bath in his bedroom and watching the laughter and lust on her face.

'Tell me the truth about you and Russ Hedges,' he asked suddenly.

She didn't look at him. 'If I remember the truth or dare game right, it's my call now.'

'I always cheat.'

She was staring at the mare's ears, one as red as the other was white. Looking at them, they reminded Dougie of the flags to either side of the point-to-point jumps he'd kicked towards when he was first trying to impress a girl in a ridiculous deer costume whom he'd thought was a pain in the arse, especially when hers was on fire.

She pulled up Sri to turn and look down at him, the last red sun streaks stabbing through the trees behind her like an approaching lynch mob with torch batteries running low. Her voice was so rushed and quiet, he could hardly hear. 'He helped me through a very tough time.'

'Has he healed the emotional scars?'

She missed a beat, glancing away. 'Not quite.'

'So you're not about to take the plunge with Badger Man?'

'Unfortunate turn of phrase.' Kat smiled that big, crazy, heart-lifting smile that Dougie had yet to learn to read. It was a smile that short-circuited his thoughts every time, putting his foot, heart and bravado straight into his mouth.

'I'm sorry,' he said honestly. 'But I want to push the hairy bastard straight into the lake and take you to bed for a week. Trust me, you wouldn't be able to walk afterwards.'

As she looked down at him, green gaze blistered with pain, he saw to his horror that the smile went nowhere near her eyes. She kicked Sri on and rode home without another word.

*

'Still going well?' Dollar asked Dougie when she called later.

'Swimmingly,' he said flatly.

'Good. You have one month before Seth will be entertaining an important guest at Eardisford. I will remind you that we would like the Lake Farm situation resolved by then. The estate must provide total privacy for the best sport.'

'I need more time.' He thought uncomfortably of his most recent conversation with Kat.

Dollar clearly thought he was referring to the sport. 'You will be required to ensure all traditional means of game hunting are available.'

'It's hardly the right season,' Dougie pointed out reluctantly, surprised by how jumpy he felt at the prospect of his idyll being invaded by marauding businessmen eager to follow hounds. When it came to field sports, he was a purist who followed rules, and his team weren't ready, the time of year unsuitable. The only Eardisford tradition he was really interested in right now was the Bolt and his desire to watch Kat do it, preferably followed by watching her climb into his bath to have her toes thoroughly washed and sucked.

'We're aware that this is precipitant,' Dollar's voice droned on, 'but this man is a *very* important guest and his entertainment is of paramount importance. Dair Armitage will make sure there is fishing and shooting available, and you will provide good quarry. And take care of the girl or we'll need to use other means.'

Dougie had an unpleasant flashback to Dollar telling him that Kat could stay at Lake Farm until marriage or death.

'What other means?'

But she had rung off.

'I might as well quit,' Kat told Dawn. 'I'll never get across that lake. Does your new landlord accept pets?'

'I had to pay a whopping deposit to get my kitten past the letting agents, and he's neutered and house-trained,' Dawn said apologetically. 'I can call the rescue centre near Watford bypass, if you like?'

Kat knew nobody would want an assortment of elderly pets, horses and livestock, especially as she would demand to be rehomed with them. She could never leave the Lake Farm animals. But Dougie Everett had unsettled her so much that her urge to protect herself and get away from the estate was now searing her skin, like the sunburn she'd got in recent days, despite slathering herself in factor fifty. It wasn't just his insensitivity, his overt flirtation, or the way her organs rearranged themselves when he looked at her in that hard, sexy way, or even those glimpses of extraordinary kindness, trust and good humour that were all too rare and made her lift up on her toes with involuntary joy as she tried to catch them. She just didn't trust her body around him, and she didn't trust him around her body. There had been a moment earlier, pulling up after the bareback gallop, when she had wanted to kiss him very badly. The jolt of animal attraction and terror had been so violent she'd leaped back as though touched with a cattle prod.

'Did you say you have to swim the lake for the Bolt?' Dawn was saying, in disbelief, at the other end of the line.

'I'll be on a horse.' Kat tried to make it seem achievable, but she knew it sounded as convincing as 'I'll have lead knickers, concrete boots and a leaky rubber ring.'

'I keep telling you that you don't have to do this thing.'

'I won't let it beat me.' Kat rallied, hearing Constance's voice taking over hers. It was what she'd said about death when Kat had first cared for her, a pronouncement of such determination it had worked against all odds for more than a year.

Dawn heard it too and laughed nervously. 'Good to know

you're still possessed by an aristocrat who wants to drown you from beyond the grave. At least stick to dry ground until I'm with you.'

'You're really coming to visit?' Kat was cheered.

'We exchanged contracts this morning. So in four weeks' time I will no longer be a woman in chains, property or ball-related, and you and I will celebrate with champagne.'

'That's so brilliant.'

'Isn't it? House sold to Pervy Man, check. First husband divorced, check. Second husband identified, check. When will the elusive Seth be in residence? A dotcom-billionaire playboy ticks most of the boxes. The only question is, how do I get close enough to catch his eye?'

'Go to Mumbai. He's never here.'

'Damn.'

'I've heard he might be coming for the village versus estate cricket match in July – there's talk of him fielding half the Indian second eleven – but don't hold your breath. Most players' batting average is lower than their shoe size and the teas are famously awful.'

'What's the date? I'll put it in my diary,' Dawn said. 'If not, I'll take a square man with a third leg as compensation. How's Dair?'

'It's third man and square leg. And I've not seen him lately.'

'I see him in a recurring dream a lot right now.'

'That must be a nightmare and a half.'

'Don't laugh. He captains a yacht in full *Officer and a Gentleman* kit. I still don't really remember what he looks like – Hopflask should be prescription-only – but he's lovely in my dreams.'

'You're in for a bit of a disappointment,' Kat said kindly.

'Please tell me there's at least one gorgeous eligible bachelor playing.'

'Dougie Everett.'

'He's yours.'

'He is not! He flirts with everyone in the village. I only put up with him to improve my riding. Today was awful. I told him a bit about Nick and he was a completely insensitive shit.'

'You told him about Nick?' Dawn breathed in amazement, and Kat realized she had already given herself away. But she was unwilling to admit to the confusion that had been stirred up along with the mud as she scrambled from deep water.

'I won't let it beat me,' she said again.

Later, Kat lay awake beneath her hot blanket of elderly snoring dogs, grateful that it was the shortest night as she tried not to relive the one day that had changed her life's direction totally. Flashbacks of today's total submersion kept haunting her, and she longed for a reassuring body to cling to.

She got up to go outside and watch the dawn stealing across the lake, sitting cross-legged beneath the black willow, a magnificent broad-trunked relic from the Edwardian arboretum.

'I won't let it beat me,' she whispered.

A warm breath on her neck made her jump out of her skin, and she turned to see two blue eyes looking at her worriedly. 'Sri.' She scratched the mare's forehead, running her hand along her neck still looking across the lake. 'Tell me we can do it.'

The mare rubbed her face vigorously against Kat's arm before looking up suddenly with a deep, wary snort.

Then Kat saw the stag on the far bank of the lake, cast in the first silver cloak of dawn, his antlers like winter trees, head lifted high as he registered her presence with a gleam of a dark eye before loping off, tail flicking.

She stayed to watch the steely fingers of a new day's light

stretching across the water and tried to imagine herself on Sri, sending ripples in their wake as they raced towards the house. She could do it easily if Dougie rode with her as he had today. Riding pillion to a stuntman was a confidence shot like no other.

She had an image of them swimming on horseback together now as she gazed across the water, seeing his blond head turning to look at her over his shoulder, the big smile full of encouragement, and those dark-lashed eyes full of pride. But then he ruined it by shouting instructions at her through a megaphone like a boat cox. 'Stroke! Stroke! Stroke! Don't catch crabs! It's sink or swim!' She sat up with a start, realizing she'd drifted off to sleep. Heaving herself up, she headed back to the house to get dressed in her yard clothes. She envied Dawn her recurring dreams of yachts with a man dressed in officer uniform, even if he was Dair Armitage. Her own dreams still revolved around water, drowning and – increasingly – Dougie Everett turning on her.

Chapter 41

Posters for the masked movie night had been pinned all over the village hall notice-board. As Kat warmed up her ladies for their Bums and Tums class, she found her eyes drawn to Vivien Leigh swooning in the arms of Clark Gable, flames leaping in the background.

Babs Hedges edged closer as they did shoulder shrugs, red-faced and eager in ancient cycling shorts and a faded

Countryside Alliance T-shirt. 'You must be missing Russ while he's away touring with the band.' She made her husband's nephew sound like Eardisford's answer to Jimmy Page.

Kat gave a vague hum and a noncommittal smile as she moved into side stretches.

'He's always been a bit of a wandering minstrel, but he comes back eventually,' Babs reassured her kindly, arms crisscrossing now as though she was directing traffic around Hyde Park Corner. Rumours of a rift between the reigning wassail monarchs were clearly doing the rounds and she wanted the low-down. 'I hear you've been riding out with the young hunt master every evening,' she said leadingly. 'The ladies were worried you'd cancel Bums and Tums. Viv has her daughter's wedding coming up and still can't get into that Jaeger dress.' She nodded towards a figure silhouetted by the tall windows, waving her bingo wings enthusiastically. 'We need you, Kat love.'

'I wouldn't let you down,' she said, flustered to be the subject of such intense gossip. 'Dougie's just been teaching me race riding.' She hadn't told him she would be here this evening instead of riding, but he'd been horribly flippant yesterday and she didn't want him joining her class again.

'Dair mentioned you two have been thundering about Lush Bottom like a pair of hares every evening,' Babs was saying, a frown bearing down on her button eyes. 'You're not still seriously thinking of riding the Bolt, are you, Kat love?'

'Why not?'

'You do know Constance wasn't the last Mytton to ride it? One of the daughters tried it in the seventies. Back then, the hunt kennels were still on the estate and a few Brom thrusters egged her on to do it. The horse drowned. Terrible business.'

Kat stood still, shocked. 'Constance didn't mention it.'

'She never knew. She and Ronnie were away – Italy, I think, pearl wedding anniversary. It was all hushed up, and the huntsman behind it left soon afterwards.'

'I wouldn't do anything to put Sri at risk.'

'Of course not. That young Dougie Everett will see you right.' Babs gave her engine-tick laugh. 'My girls are totally smitten and – what is it they say? – "well jell" of all the rumours about him setting his cap at you.' Seeing Kat's horrified face, she chuckled. 'Oh, you know what pub talk's like. Don't worry, Russ told them there's nothing going on and never would be.'

'Russ told them?'

'The night of the quiz, it was. A few of the earthmen got a-chuntering when you weren't there and young Dougie left early, but Russ said you knew what you were doing.'

Kat realized the entire Bums and Tums class was listening in fascination to the conversation now. 'Oh, yes, I do,' she said brightly, glancing up at the *Gone With the Wind* poster as she reached for the stereo to flip to a high-energy track. 'Time for the thirty-minute burn, ladies. *Are you ready?*'

Dougie dealt with the news that a VIP might be arriving at short notice in the same way he dealt with anything he didn't want to dwell upon: by ignoring it. It was out of season, and no fool would want to follow hounds in midsummer. In any case Dair was set to rustle up some shooting.

By contrast, he found it impossible to ignore the nagging doubt that he'd pushed Kat too far and misjudged the situation. Whenever he tested her riding nerve, he found the hardest steel, yet her emotional temperature shot up and down, like the mercury in a thermometer. She seemed so fearless, but her past clearly chased her, no matter how fast he rode. Her failure to turn up at the meadow that evening bothered him deeply, and his impatience was no longer about deadlines or dares. He wanted to see her to apologize for coming on too strong and to try to make the smile reach her eyes again.

He rode to Lake Farm, but found nobody at home, a dachshund barking at him furiously through the cat flap.

Several miserable-looking pheasants were lined up in makeshift runs and coops in the open-fronted barn. He remembered Kat saying they drove her mad and were always dying for no good reason – it was one of the only negative things she'd said about Russ and his obsession with rescuing wildlife. Double-checking that nobody was around, he liberated a few of the healthier ones. Dougie found Kat's loyalty to Russ Hedges baffling and infuriating. He could only imagine that she saw the big, hairy militant as one of the many animals she cared for in the sanctuary, plus occasional guard dog, and he thought it was high time for a badger cull.

Sri was turned out in the field along with her small herd, he noticed, and Harvey charged up to say hello as Dougie approached, pushing at his pockets for mints, barely recognizable because he'd been rolling in the red Herefordshire soil so that his grey coat was patched with chestnut, like a poor impersonation of the Marwari mare.

Dipping his hand into the water trough, Dougie wrote his phone number and DOUGIE on Harvey's red side, followed by a handprint on his still-white quarters like a Hindu sacred cow. He was about to add a smiley face when he stopped himself, appalled at his sentimentality. Harvey shambled off to roll again, then shook himself and trotted away to his rejoin his new best friend, at which point Dougie saw he had smudged off the number.

*

Having popped in to see Miriam after her class and stayed on for supper and too much Pinot Grigio – only to find herself grilled about Dougie's hunting plans and her own Bolt-riding ones – it was dusk by the time Kat came home. When she checked the horses in the fading light, she briefly mistook Dougie's old stunt horse for Sri and thought she was seeing things at first, a message from Constance beyond the grave appearing on one dark patch. Then, realizing it was Harvey, she felt the wine kick in and addressed the horse as though he was his master whose name was written on his side.

'You are a gorgeous, arrogant bastard, you know that? I don't trust you at all. And I wish it was as simple as tumbling into bed with you for a week until I can't walk, but for me that's more terrifying than riding through any lake you could show me. And, God help me, I fancy the arse off you.'

As Harvey pricked up his ears and turned his heard sharply towards the woods, Kat heard crashing through the under-growth and groaned, imagining her Catherine the Great speech doing the rounds in the pub. But then, to her relief, she saw the unmistakable shape of the big stag's antlers moving away through the trees.

When Kat took Sri to the hidden meadow the following evening, Dougie was already riding there, cantering Rose along the row of willows. A storm was gathering overhead as they caught up alongside.

'I'm so glad you came.' He laughed, the blue eyes earnest, pupils huge.

'I can't stop,' she confessed breathlessly.

'Me neither,' he said, riding closer. 'I've never felt like this.'

'I mean I have no brakes,' she shouted, demonstrating her

problem by pulling on the reins, which Sri cheerfully deflected with a flurry of fly-bucks, then speeded up more. 'I literally can't stop!'

Dougie's smile widened and he accelerated to match. 'The secret is not to try too hard. Race me to the first horse chestnut.' He nodded at it.

Flying along in his slip-stream, Kat knew she was really galloping now, that flat-line, breakneck speed that was a feeling like no other. It was why she was here, she reminded herself. The adrenalin kick was astonishing, and the thought of racing from one end of the estate to the other at such speed, with a stretch of water to cross, was beyond daunting.

'You'll need to cover ground at this pace through the main stretches of old parkland and the best headlands to buy yourself time through the woods and the lake,' Dougie told her, as he pounded alongside on the grey mare. 'But you'll need much better brakes, you're right. That's what went wrong the other day. Take more contact, apply pressure with your legs and start to sit up – great. Now kick on again, fast as you can to the big oak over there, where we'll slow up enough to turn and gallop back.'

Turning wasn't something Sri was eager to co-operate with. Nose in the air, ear tips practically criss-crossing, she managed to keep up a rapid sideways pelt without knowing where she was going until they both went their separate ways under a low branch.

'What did you say about trusting her?' Kat grumbled, picking herself up from a mercifully soft landing in a mossy dell.

'She has to trust you too. You were totally unbalanced and tugging at the bit like a gym-freak on a rowing machine. Now do it again.'

After half an hour, sweat pouring from her face, she was

flying around the oak like a rodeo barrel-racing champion. 'Better?'

He nodded, his eyes darker than ever. 'I think we're almost ready to name the day.'

She looked at him curiously.

'The day you ride the Bolt.'

Chapter 42

'Thing is, Harv mate,' Dougie glanced across the paddocks to the sagging roof of Lake Farm, his knobbly bicycle tyres bouncing slowly through the ruts as he let his hounds jog ahead, 'much as I admire your taste in accommodation – and, indeed, hostess – this is not a long-term option. We can't get attached. She has to relocate, and it's our duty to help her. It's either that or come clean.'

Shambling along on the opposite side of the fenced rail that divided the millstream track from sanctuary land, Harvey regarded him wisely and very muddily, his grey coat its customary dusty chestnut from rolling.

'In your case, coming clean will take some time.' Dougie conceded and pedalled on as Harvey stopped to touch noses with an eager, smiling hound.

Dougie had been out since six thirty that morning, covering almost ten miles of roads and tracks, and was ravenous. He briefly contemplated calling in on Kat, imagining scrambled goose eggs on thick doorsteps of toast, steaming mugs of tea and her dressing-gown falling open as she passed the salt. But he knew she wouldn't play the game. Neither would she thank him for bringing eight couple of hound into her farmyard. Theirs was an evening acquaintance that existed separately from their normal working and social lives, despite his best efforts to lure her off a horse, flirt her towards his bed and guard her like a sentry. The trouble was, he was also flirting with a million pounds, and that had started to feel like a curse rather than a bonus.

He saw the summer as his own time, a long stretch of hazy days and naked nights before the hunting season began, a time in which he'd get his horses fit, his hounds disciplined, his local knowledge up to speed, and in which he'd do whatever it took to help Kat Mason ride for her life across water.

He called back Honour, the bitch with the unbroken chestnut coat: she was snuffling down a rabbit hole, detached from the pack as usual.

One summer school holiday, aged about fourteen, Dougie had developed such a fierce crush on one of his father's girl grooms that he'd got up obscenely early to walk his terrier past her shared cottage in the hope of seeing her open her curtains. He had gone out again at dusk to watch her shut them. This was quite separate from the obscene amount of showing off he'd done, in and out of the saddle, while hanging around the stables all day trying – and failing – to impress her. Nor was it an attempt to glimpse a thrilling flash of underwear or nipple. He had simply been so besotted that he wanted to see her from the very start of the day to its finish. To his increasing disquiet, he was now starting to feel the same way about Kat.

This was, he was certain, largely down to the summer-holiday boredom of being in rural confinement. His bonus felt like the homework he was putting off – the Bolt was far more fun.

That surely had to be why he counted the hours down until seven o'clock each evening, like an avid *Archers* fan.

That evening when he met Kat to hack side by side through the estate, he started to plan the route for the historic Mytton challenge, searching out the best galloping stretches and short cuts through the trappy wooded sections.

'So you've been getting to know all these coverts and gullies ready to hunt them with hounds?' she asked, swatting midges away as they ambled alongside the river.

He knew she was digging. She'd done it several times before – a flurry of intensive questions followed by a quick change of subject. She was so gloriously transparent and he found her pink-cheeked shiftiness adorable to watch. In turn, his tactic was to flirt with increasingly outrageous suggestions, which usually backed her off.

'That's right, to entertain estate guests, although I'd far rather entertain you covertly, naked and with champagne bubbles popping on every freckle as I drink it from your gullies.'

She shot him a withering look, although her eyes couldn't quite meet his and the mare started to jog, picking up on her rider's tension. 'Won't all those international magnates and tycoons find trail-hunting a bit tame?'

'I'll show them some very good sport.' He rode closer, his eyes not leaving her face, watching the bloom of a blush stealing across it to match the pink sunset.

But she refused to back down. 'Hard to explain the Hunting Act to a bloodthirsty banking baron, or can you bend the rules for a private foxhound pack?'

'Totally different laws apply,' he teased in an earnest voice.

'What are they?'

'Man-hunting laws,' he said coolly. 'Seth's got a regular supply from the Mumbai slums.'

'That's so unfunny.'

'It's all perfectly legal under the Seasonal Agricultural Workers Scheme.'

His flirtation was gaining less purchase, he realized impatiently, sliding off her as she built her defences higher. Yet the dares they shared had lost no edge as they raced through the deepest dry streambeds and along high ridges, pounding down the estate's steep parkland slopes with G-force pushing their hearts into their throats, then crossing the vast, weed-choked water meadows, like settlers chasing the best land flags in the Wild West. Dougie was amazed by her nerve. She could be pretty hairy in the saddle, but she never stopped driving and whooping. She and the mare were starting to trust one another and really have fun at last.

He led her back through the woods along the gravel-bottomed stream, wading through its shallows. She barely batted an eyelid, he noticed. But when he suggested cutting across an edge of the lake where he knew it to be boggy but no deeper than a garden pond, Kat froze, her whole body ramrod tense. Picking up on her fear, the mare started to nap, shaking her head and backing away from the water.

They rode the long way round. Increasingly curious to know more about the scars her ex-fiancé had left, Dougie decided to draw her out by switching the game to truth.

'I've been engaged three times,' he started conversationally, hoping to get a thread going. 'They all ended in a bit of a bloodbath.'

'You attacked them?'

'I was talking emotionally.' He was aware that he was wielding a broadsword conversationally when he needed a scalpel. 'Got as far as the altar once.'

'Did she jilt you?'

'More an act of God, who pretty much struck us down with a trident. Good move on His part really. We weren't ready to settle down. Besides, Iris was far too good for me.'

She snorted disparagingly. 'All men say that.'

'Kiki was bad for me.' Dougie – for whom this sort of conversation was akin to haemorrhaging blood from a main artery – cleared his throat uncomfortably. 'I rushed into it. Don't get me wrong, she's a great girl, but we made a lousy couple. Hence I ran away here.' He felt a physical pull of relief, like a thorn from his side, as he got to the point of the conversation at last. 'So we're both runaways, you and I. We have so much in common.' He brought out the big smile, riding closer, theirs leg brushing and stirrup irons clanging.

'Did she try to drown you too?'

'Fire was my demon.' He found the smile impossible to sustain as he dropped out of role. Flirting was tough when you suddenly wanted to bare your soul to somebody, and when touching them – even the clunk of two leather-booted ankles – made a tidal rapid of energy roll up your whole body.

'Are you frightened of it now?' she asked.

'I don't light a lot of bonfires.'

Kat looked across the lake as they approached it. 'That must be such a hard thing to get over.'

'No more awful than almost drowning.'

They watched as a pair of Canada geese drifted past on the glittering black surface of the water, honking tetchily at the riders. 'Constance always insisted that if I swam the lake my fear would go,' she said. 'She dived in and out of it every summer as a girl. She said it was like a hug to her. Her parents were living in India. They left her here from the age of two – it's unimaginable now. She had a nursemaid, a nanny and later a governess too. Apparently the entire household swam in the lake one drought-stricken summer in the forties, including the kennel hounds and horses.'

'Sounds bliss.' He looked across at the evening sun, eyes creasing. 'Shall we try it?'

'Right now, I'd rather walk over burning coals.'

This time, Dougie wasn't fooled by Kat's big smile, the apparently open invitation to make light of life that covered scars she'd kept hidden from everybody except Constance.

'I might hold you to that,' he said carefully. 'Then we can ride through a lake to cool off. Take the plunge together.'

'Ha-ha.'

'Constance was right. You need to jump right in. Like getting back on a horse or falling in love.'

'I don't rush into things like you, Dougie, especially not that.'

They were riding along two parallel tractor ruts, the overhead branches so low that they continually had to duck to avoid them. Dipping their heads and turning their faces as an arch of brambles loomed, they found their eyes inches apart.

'Did what happened with your fiancé make you frightened of marriage proposals too?' he asked, irritated that all his soul-baring had backfired, and now she saw him as even shallower.

She looked at him curiously. 'Not particularly. Why? Are you thinking of asking?'

'I might.' He put on his suavest Rhett Butler voice: 'Did you ever think of marrying, just for fun?'

'If that's a dare, it's not funny.'

'Actually the line is something like "Fiddle-de-dee, marriage is only fun for men."' Dougie's Vivien Leigh impersonation was, to his chagrin, far better than his Clark Gable. Seeing her blank face he explained, 'It's a scene from *Gone With the Wind*.'

'I've never actually seen it,' she confessed, a smile playing on her lips again. 'I didn't have you down as a fan of epic romances.'

'I have eclectic taste.' He adopted a deep, thoughtful look. In fact, the only reason he knew it so well was because he'd been in the running for the key role in that network television series now tipped to be the biggest hit of the decade. Nagged by Abe and Kiki, he'd dutifully read the book and watched the film four times before the first casting session so that he could practically smell the rifle fire amid the cedars and swamps. He had no desire to see it again in his life, but he wasn't about to admit that.

'Are you dressing up tomorrow evening?' he said.

She rolled her eyes. 'I have no choice. It's a sanctuary fund-raiser. Cyn is lending me a dress. The skirt's so wide I'll take up most of a row.'

'In that case, I insist on giving you a lift. You'll never fit it into your little car.'

'I'd rather walk,' she said, too quickly for his liking. She was avoiding his gaze again, he noticed.

'Then we'll walk together. No burning coals. Never a good idea with a long skirt.'

'You must have her entirely in your hold by now?' Dollar checked later.

'She's certainly hot for more,' he assured her.

'And marriage?'

'We've talked about it.'

'Already? I am impressed. Keep the heat on. A million pounds is a very good dowry.' Her deep voice was as modulated and emotion-free as usual.

As soon as they rang off, Dougie called an old friend from the *Ptolemy Finch* crew who now worked in the BBC's wardrobe department. 'Micha darling, how soon can you get hold of a Confederate uniform and courier it to me?'

Chapter 43

The *Gone With the Wind* dress was a lot more flattering than the one that Cyn had persuaded Kat to wear at the village show, although almost as tight. The formal blue velvet off-the-shoulder ballgown was just the sort that the Princess of Wales would have worn to whirl around in the arms of world leaders in the eighties. It reeked of damp cupboard, its vast full-length skirt was dotted with cigarette burns from hunt balls thirty years ago, and it had a dubious brown stain on the neckline, but the bodice gave Kat a sensationally narrow waist and it certainly looked authentically war-torn. Insisting that it resembled a portrait in the movie, Cyn had matched it with a cream lace piano shawl and had even bought Kat tinted hair mousse in Boots: 'Scarlett has raven black hair and green eyes.' If Kat hadn't already possessed the latter, she was certain Cyn would have demanded that she borrow Dawn's turquoise contact lenses.

She had no doubt that had Dawn been there she would have gone for the full Vivien Leigh movie look, incorporating several costume changes and lots of 'fiddle-de-dee's. In their most recent conversation she'd sighed jealously at the idea of the fancy-dress screening. 'I just *love* that film. The costumes! The romance! Eardisford is so much fun compared to here. I can't believe I'm stuck doing mani-pedis for a hen party while you're going to a masked movie night.'

Kat desperately needed Dawn's expertise that evening, and was aware of looking more than a little Calamity Jane when she stomped out of the house to meet Dougie, the blue velvet skirts lifted to reveal her sensible yard clogs, the end of the lace shawl gripped between her teeth to stop it slipping off her shoulders.

By contrast he looked sublime in a long grey military jacket with crocus yellow braiding, a high collar and gold epaulettes that shimmered as he gallantly offered her his arm.

'I'm fine, thanks.' She hurried past him, wishing she'd been quicker at thinking up an excuse not to walk to the village with him. Riding made for a conveniently quick getaway if he dropped his voice to the predatory purr that made her pulse go bananas or looked at her in the way that sent her internal organs spinning like dancers in a ballroom.

'Amazing hair.' He strode alongside her as she set off in a spirited jog.

The dark tinted mousse, which had proved wholly inadequate for Kat's acres of mane, had only covered the top half before it ran out, leaving her two-tone. It was more Lady Gaga than Scarlett, but Dougie seemed enchanted. She sensed his eyes all over her as she raced along as fast as her skirts allowed. Her *décolletage* was embarrassingly low, and she had no strapless bra so was relying upon the boned bodice to keep her in. She crammed her scarf ends down there and shooed away Trevor the peacock, who was intent on following them. Soon they were pounding along the track through Herne Covert like a pair of unlikely Victorian power joggers. Talking was next to impossible, although Dougie made a few valiant attempts, mostly to compliment her Mo Farah speed in a ballgown and ask how exactly the 'masked' bit fitted.

'A local printing company that supports the sanctuary is

donating party face-masks of Scarlett and Rhett,' Kat panted, tugging up the front of her dress. 'It was Miriam's idea.'

'Just when I thought this evening couldn't get any worse,' he muttered. 'You must promise to sit next to me, Kat. You're the only reason I'm here.'

By the time they arrived at the village hall, Kat was breathless and flustered, and incredibly relieved to see the familiar voluptuous figure of Miriam, who was dressed in an extraordinary frilly white meringue matched with a vast straw bonnet clamped to her head with a green pashmina. Her face was unrecognizable, disguised by the pouting prettiness of Vivien Leigh printed on cardboard with cut-out eyes.

'That's quite scary,' muttered Dougie, then glanced around to see lots more big frocks and Scarlett masks, his blue eyes widening. 'In fact, this is all quite freaky. You might need to hold my hand, Kat.'

Miriam had spirited a tray of bright green iced drinks towards them sprigged with foliage.

'What a beautiful pair you make!' She shot Kat a very obvious wink of her painted, spike-lashed eye through one eyehole. 'Have a mint julep – weaker than Pimm's, so perfectly safe. Can you believe the bloody *Herefordshire Life* photographer hasn't turned up? Doesn't everyone look amazing?'

'Amazing,' Kat agreed, noticing a few Rhetts with black gambler hats and beer bellies trying to navigate their way around their masks with drinking straws to get at their mint juleps.

'Jesus.' Dougie grimaced, as he sniffed it then held it at arm's length. 'What's in that?'

Kat took a cautious sip. 'Hopflask.' She identified the familiar throat-burning, nose-numbing sensation. 'Mixed with cheap Scotch, mint and lemonade, at a guess.'

They were quickly parted as Dougie's huge female fan club fluttered up like butterflies to a buddleia, all wearing Scarlett masks, demanding his attention and grumbling that he rarely came to the pub any more. Meanwhile Kat was cornered by Mags and Russ, both defiantly dressed in their Animal Magnetism costumes, and eager for insider information.

She hadn't seen Russ since their big talk, although she knew he'd been to Lake Farm several times to check on his charges, deliberately coming and going when she was out. A broken-winged buzzard and another of Mags's RTA pheasant victims had appeared in the sanctuary's 'aviary wing'. He now gave an over-loud spiel about how busy he was, running between gigs, orchard-tending and badger-watching, which seemed to be more for the benefit of everyone else in the hall – most specifically Calum, who was glowering nearby with a mint julep and two young daughters – than for Kat.

'I'm only here for the free drink – I'm not staying for the film,' he explained in an undertone, relieving her of her barely touched mint julep. 'Everett looks a total prat in that outfit. It's fantastic he trusts you so much now. What more have you found out?'

She looked across at him, still cornered by Scarletts, holding up his hands politely to refuse a moustached Clark Gable face mask, explaining with a charming smile that he was the far more British and heroic Leslie Howard. 'Wasn't she in *Birds of a Feather*?' asked one of his female admirers loudly. Catching Kat's eye, he burst out laughing, his face so unspeakably handsome it deserved to stay unmasked, she decided. She now knew when his smile was sincere and his laughter genuine, and when his regret was real too. For a moment, Kat could think of nothing but Dougie's confessions of failed engagements.

Feeling horribly duplicitous, she mumbled to Russ about the Mumbai-slum manhunt joke and his comment that different laws applied. 'I think he's very strait-laced when it comes to fox-hunting, though,' she added quickly. 'He knows it's an old field sport with new goal posts, and it has to work with the law. He talks about the Act, and laying scent trails.'

'It's all an act and a false trail, trust me,' Russ sneered, thick bear brows lowering. 'The hounds are a side-show, a little bit of old England for the spectacle, as is Everett with his pretty face and old-school manners. Most likely they'll hunt rare game with guns. You can fast-track shotgun licences to shoot pretty much anything around here, apart from each other.

'I found out today that Seth's used his IT business base – and all that gaming development expertise – to move into flight simulators, most specifically military ones.' He drew Kat to one side. 'Now it makes sense why a vegetarian Sikh philanthropist – a self-confessed petrol-head and city boy who gives millions to educate slum kids – has bought a very private sporting estate.' He lowered his voice to little more than a breath, glancing over his shoulder to ensure Dougie was still under siege by girls in bonnets. '*Arms deals*. Yanks and Russkies chasing military franchises like killing things for fun before signing deals.'

Kat felt clammy-faced with shock and fear. 'Are you saying they'll be trading arms here?'

'We're not going to see crates of Kalashnikovs and ground-to-air missiles heading along the lime avenues.' He polished off the last of her julep with a shudder. 'The principle's the same as business deals made on a golf course or squash court. Seth brings his associates here to hunt, shows them the best sport, and they give him the business. It's Dougie's job to provide that sport, and it's a pretty safe bet that no redneck magnate is going to want to come here and gallop around after a few hounds on a false scent trail. You must keep probing him for details while he's still so hot on you.' He glanced across at Dougie, whose cool blue eyes tracked Kat wherever she went.

'He's hot on all women,' she scoffed.

'That's very true.' His dimples deepened. 'It's good you've figured him out, Kat. All those animal-behaviour lessons are sinking in, which is useful because that man *is* an animal.'

A small, round Scarlett O'Hara in an outrageously vampish, corseted red dress with red feather plumes in her hair handed Kat her mask as everybody found their seats, her own exquisite mask lifting briefly to bestow a warm kiss on her cheeks.

'You look delightful.' Cyn squeezed her hand, watery eyes admiring the ballgown with an indulgent sigh. 'Such a pretty dress, and a perfect length now we've unpicked the hem. I received my last proposal wearing it. This is *so much* fun that we're going to make it a regular event. Pru wants us to show *Lawrence of Arabia* next.' She nodded towards a tall, waspish figure in a long-tailed suit and waistcoat selling raffle tickets, dark grey hair slicked back, by far the best Rhett of the evening. 'No doubt that means we'll be the camel, but I'm planning my revenge with *Dr Zhivago*.' She replaced her mask, rejoining the cloned faces all around them. 'It's about to begin!'

The capacity audience meant that Kat's skirts had to be confined to just one plastic-backed chair in her row. She was crammed next to Tireless Tina, who was still wearing her yard clothes and whose husband was babysitting for once so that she could enjoy a 'girly night out' and who complained that Cyn had refused to give her a mask because she hadn't dressed up.

'Here, have mine.' Kat handed it across gratefully.

As soon as the lights dimmed and the opening titles came on,

Tina fell asleep with her head tipped back and Vivien Leigh's black-eyed face staring at the ceiling.

On Kat's other side Dougie was watching her as much as he was watching the action on screen. It was impossibly stuffy in the hall, the scent of damp wardrobe overwhelming as her dress warmed up. Sweat was soon trickling between her breasts and beading on her forehead. She was paranoid her hair tint might start dripping out with it, like Dirk Bogarde's in *Death in Venice*. She was equally worried that her hand was undergoing an almost out-of-body urge to creep towards Dougie's, lying relaxed and long-fingered on his thigh.

Kat was acutely aware of him beside her, his every tiny movement, his breathing, the delicious scent of his aftershave that occasionally drifted across and over her mildewy dress. She almost jumped through the roof when she felt a firm pressure on her shoulder, thinking he was putting his arm around her, but it was just Tireless Tina's head lolling sideways as she snuggled against one puffy velvet-capped sleeve.

Kat tried to concentrate on what was happening on screen, but it was impossible to take in much. How could Scarlett's crushes and tantrums and Rhett's amused, passionate despair compare to Dougie reaching up to rake back his mop of hair, or to his long, muscular thigh shifting closer to hers, or his deep sighs and occasional fidgets, or to his gaze, warm and exploring, constantly moving around her face and body? Her own eyes stayed facing front, but she saw almost nothing, acutely aware of him at all times.

Rhett and Scarlett were on screen together, tension simmering. 'No, I don't think I will kiss you,' Rhett drawled, 'although you need kissing badly. That's what's wrong with you. You should be kissed often and by someone who knows how ...'

Kat closed her eyes briefly and imagined being kissed by Dougie, those wise-cracking, curling lips so sensual and expert against hers. He certainly knew how: she'd seen the evidence on screen in this very hall. The way he kissed was the stuff of blogs and fan sites, those strong fingers so gentle on her neck, drawing her up and into his mouth, tasting it like it was the sweetest delicacy on earth. But within moments of her fantasy starting, the warm, explorative mouth in her imagination was drawn away as the ritual began: the thick-breathed excitement of selecting the viewing. And it definitely wasn't *Gone With the Wind* or even *High Noon*. Her eyes snapped open and she glanced sideways in a panic to reassure herself that he wasn't Nick. But he was definitely Dougie, blond hair swept back off his forehead, a familiar half-smile on his face, which dropped away as he saw the frightened expression on Kat's.

In the half-dark those dark-lashed blue eyes gazed back at her and she felt the jolt right through her, the unmistakable quickening of breath, heart and hope that seemed to flip her solar plexus over, desire kicking in. Now she couldn't look at the screen at all. She was staring straight into Dougie Everett's eyes in the half-dark and thinking about kissing him.

When the lights went up, she looked away, her face flaming.

'That was shorter than I remember,' Dougie murmured, gazing around as though the walls of their private tent had just been ripped from around them.

'It's only halfway through,' yawned Tina, stretching indulgently and pushing her Scarlett mask on top of her head like a coolie hat. 'There's an old-fashioned intermission now for refreshments, the raffle draw and the fancy-dress prize. How's Sri going, Kat? Have you tried that new bit I lent you?'

While Kat talked to Tina about horses, she was aware of Dougie being besieged again, called away to judge the fancy dress. His eyes kept finding hers. Now they'd started looking at one another so much, it seemed they couldn't stop.

'The heat coming off you two could raze Twelve Oaks,' whispered Tina, pulling off her mask and fanning herself with it.

'There's really nothing going on,' Kat insisted.

'Oh, come on, you're clearly crackers about one another,' Tina giggled, 'and I can't say anyone was surprised to hear that you and Russ have split.'

The gossip at the julep bar was clearly in full flow tonight. 'We're still friends,' Kat said carefully. 'We just came off benefits.'

They both watched Miriam sweep up the aisle as she carried her raffle-ticket box to the front in a gale of flapping crinoline, cornering Dougie to get his fancy-dress winner. His eyes were on Kat again. She hoped he didn't fix it so that she won: there were far better Scarletts in the room. And even though he was dressed as Ashley Wilkes, there was only one man who came close to Rhett in her mind.

'He's Ever-Rhett,' she breathed, in Scarlett's petulant drawl.

'Fiddle-de-dee,' came an equally arrogant drawl as a mint julep was thrust at her and Dougie landed back in his seat, maintaining the Yankee accent as he handed a second glass to Tina. 'Your good health, ladies. May I see you home tonight, Miss Mason?' He looked at her in a way that left her in no doubt what that meant.

If you walk home with him, you'll kiss, Kat thought, the delicious flip turning in her stomach again. But already she was planning a way to avoid it. If they kissed, she'd be lost, the old wounds ready to open. They could end up in bed and her demons would be waiting there to spoil everything. This time it would be far, far worse than with Russ, to whom she had never been as attracted as she was to Dougie and who had later so nobly tried and failed to help her. She couldn't go through it again, and certainly not with Dougie.

'I have a lift,' she said quickly. 'Tina's taking me back.'

'I am? I am!' Stifling another yawn, Tina looked mildly confused, but good-naturedly assumed she must have agreed to it somewhere along the line. 'I'll take you both back. My pleasure.'

Miriam had clambered on stage now, removing her mask, which hampered her ability to project her voice above the crowd's hubbub. 'Ladies and gentlemen, the winners of the fancy dress – kindly chosen by our local acting star Dougie Everett – are Babs and Bill Hedges!'

There was a unanimous cheer as the portly, chortling duo who had raided the am-dram costume store swept up to collect a brace of claret bottles, Babs resplendent in Maid Marion's green velvet gown from last year's panto embellished with curtain ties, and Bill in a white tux, ribbon tie and Panama.

'Good choice,' congratulated Kat.

'I was supposed to fix it for you to win,' he admitted in an undertone, checking that Tina couldn't hear. 'Cyn asked me at the fete; she thought it would cheer you up.'

Kat burned with indignation. 'I don't need favouritism like that!'

'That's what I said. Besides, I couldn't possibly award a fancy-dress prize to someone I'd far rather see naked.'

The raffle draw was now in full swing, but Kat didn't take in a word because she'd fallen into Dougie's eyes again and they were both treading water, a blue oasis that made the room disappear.

'For the last time, yellow THREE SIX TWO!' Miriam shrieked, so loudly that the oasis was momentarily as crowded as a Club Med swimming-pool. Still holding Kat's gaze, Dougie groped in his pocket and found a wad of tickets, handing them to Tina.

'It's yours!' Tina announced cheerfully then, realizing that nobody was listening, leaped up to claim the prize.

Watching the second half of the film, Kat barely followed a thing. The mint julep she'd drunk in the intermission had made her light-headed. She tried and failed not to look at Dougie through the darkness, but his eyes were always waiting there, watchful, amused, reassuring and dangerously carnal. She only realized that her hand had slipped into his when his thumb drew a line on her palm from the soft dip of her wrist to the valley between middle and ring fingers. Back and forth it danced, then drew spirals in and out of the centre of her heart line. Kat was getting ever hotter, ridiculously aroused. Any minute now, she'd be throwing her head back and easing her thighs apart. Still his eyes stayed on hers.

'Get a room,' somebody behind them muttered, and Kat dragged herself back to reality, remembering this was the village hall where she taught the women to power-punch, Pilates stretch and pump the burn, where they held flower and produce shows, harvest suppers and parish council meetings. Here was not the place to fall in lust and love with Dougie Everett.

She forced herself to look at the screen and realized that the voice behind her had been referring to Babs and Bill canoodling noisily in the row in front, already well into the claret. Beyond them, Scarlett and Rhett were taking a tour of their Atlanta mansion. The warm hand was still in hers. It tightened its grip. She tightened hers back but then, worried that she was misleading him, snatched it away. No touching was safe, she remembered. With Nick, the merest passing stroke of his hair could lead to the hand flying up to clamp her wrist. He'd taken possession from affection and cauterized desire.

Tugging up her dress front, which had plunged again, she determinedly didn't look at Dougie as she watched the figures moving about on screen, the sumptuous sets, the dresses, the passions and tragedies that made up the death throes of a truly epic love story. She was determined not to think back to her little Hertfordshire new build with its Next Interiors finish, its immaculate tidiness, the mini gym in the spare bedroom, the trashy novel her side of the bed, spy thriller his, and the smart TV on which they could have watched big, beautiful films like this while holding hands, but never had. It had served a very different purpose. Their relationship's death throes had been so small and suburban compared to this, yet she'd found her way to a Tara eventually. Tomorrow she would ride faster and further than she ever had before. If Rhett frankly didn't give a damn then she wasn't about to hold his hand.

Tina's car smelt strongly of horse, crisps and Sudocrem. Kat found herself sitting on a grooming kit, an empty Red Bull can and several rosettes, but at least she could justifiably commandeer the whole of the back seat for her skirt, and Tina put the radio on so loudly that there was no need to talk. Better still, they dropped off Dougie first, the driveway to the mill being far easier to navigate from the estate's newly tarmacked parkland drive than the wooded Lake Farm track.

Engine still running, Tina thrust a big fake-fur kitten at Dougie. 'Don't forget your raffle prize. It's a bed buddy. You heat it up in the microwave.'

'Keep it as a thank-you for the lift,' said Dougie, stepping out to open the back door. The radio was so loud that Tina didn't

hear him add, 'There's only one cat I want in my bed tonight.'
He offered his hand. 'Let me walk you home from here.'

Kat gripped the seat. 'I really need to get straight back to the
dogs. It's just two minutes further in the car. And I promised to
give Tina back some tack she lent me.'

'No worries,' Tina shouted, over the radio, putting the
stuffed kitten on the seat beside her and patting it. 'The kids'll
love this. Thanks.'

Illuminated by the car light as he held open the door,
epaulettes gleaming, Dougie gave a formal bow. 'I'll see you
tomorrow, then,' he said.

'Indeed!' she said brightly, just stopping herself from adding
'Great balls of fire' which was exactly what it felt as though she
had burning in her chest right now.

Chapter 44

Beside the big chestnut tree in the meadow, Dougie had lit a
campfire that was smoking merrily, a billy-can bubbling on a
hook. Worcester grazed nearby, bit jangling, and Quiver dived
in and out of the long grass trying to catch bees. He knew it was
a cliché cowboy pose, and that such showmanship could easily
backfire, but he needed to hide his quandary behind self-mock-
ery. Setting the scene for seduction had cheered him up
enormously, although the dark mood he'd been carrying around
all day still lingered. The simmering resentment he'd built at
being side-stepped by Kat the previous night sat heavily alongside the fact that he was deceiving her. He half expected her not

to come, but at seven o'clock on the dot, he heard hoof-falls. His heart was stampeding.

She rode up cautiously, colour spotting her cheeks, clearly reluctant to dismount.

'This evening, we're both facing our demons.' He held up some inflatable armbands and a snorkel, which, to his relief, made her laugh.

'Are you planning to walk over hot coals?' She indicated the fire.

'No – I just want a cup of tea and a chat. Hop off.'

Her green eyes flashed and for a moment he thought she would turn around and gallop away. Dougie could hardly blame her: he usually reacted to people saying they wanted to talk with exactly the same urge, but telling her he wanted to press her up against the chestnut trunk and pull her legs up around him would send her off even faster.

Jumping down, she watched him unhook the billy-can and pour hot water into two enamel cups. 'Wouldn't it have been easier to bring a Thermos?' She pulled Sri's reins over her head and perched on one of the logs Dougie had set up around the fire.

'Where's your sense of outdoor adventure?' He couldn't get her to look at him at all. Last night's connection felt like another lifetime. He wanted to bring dusk forward, dim the sun and put on an epic movie.

She was looking into the fire. 'I'm not sure I can swim the lake on one cup of tea. I'll probably need vodka.'

'We've got to get you and the mare into the drink somehow, but I'd rather you weren't drunk.' He handed her a steaming mug before settling on a log on the opposite side of the flames. 'I have a trainer mate who has a horse swimming-pool. We could start there?' He found the idea of her ducking and diving around racehorses in a bikini highly appealing.

'It's only open water that frightens me. Or anywhere I can't see the bottom.' She grimaced at the effort of explaining, tin cup clutched in her hands. Behind her the two terriers that had come with her joined Quiver diving for insects in the undergrowth, all yapping eagerly. 'I know it's just a mental block, but however many times I tell myself it's different this time and it's safe, I literally can't breathe for fear. I can feel myself go through all the motions, but it's all too frantic, too desperate, and I don't have time to think or relax, yet at the same time I'm shutting down like a crocodile, sinking to the bottom of a river, imagining I can fill my lungs with air, slow my heartbeat and survive until it's over.'

Watching her, Dougie wasn't entirely sure that she was just talking about swimming. It was impossible to read the expression on her face as the air danced and twisted in the heat above the fire. 'Think you could get into the lake here on horseback this evening? Face your demon?'

'Unlikely,' she admitted, looking down at her cup. 'This tea tastes weird.'

'It's Earl Grey, and don't change the subject. If you want me to help you, we need to talk about that demon. What could possibly go wrong for a strong swimmer who is as clever and brave as you?' When she didn't reply, he said, 'Your ex left you frightened of more than just open water, didn't he?'

Again, she didn't answer. Then Dougie realized she was looking straight at him and he almost couldn't speak for the blood rushing through him. She looked haunted. She had looked at him in the same way last night. He wanted to wrap his arms tightly around her and make the demon go away, but she was already standing up, using the log as a mounting block. 'Thanks for the tea, but I'd rather do a dare.'

He emptied his enamel cup and threw it down by the

knapsack at the fire's edge, casting a regretful look at the chestnut tree. 'Okay, let's ride.'

As soon as Kat was back in the saddle, she visibly relaxed, the big smile flooded with warmth, the thrill of a dare coursing through her. Sri quickly fell into step alongside Dougie on Worcester, and they rode beneath the long shadows of the woods, watched by two roe deer tail-twitching behind the first tree line. Dougie watched her profile, willing her to look at him, but she kept her eyes fixed between the mare's curled ears.

'See that sheep feeder there?' He pointed far ahead.

'Yup.'

'I dare you to tell the truth before we reach it.'

'That's cheating.'

'I've told you, I always cheat at games.'

'Is this a game to you?'

'No.' It was Dougie's turn to look away, aware of the hypocrisy in demanding the truth. And yet it didn't feel anything like a lie when he said, 'I enjoy spending time with you.'

'Will Seth's corporate-hospitality clients get to enjoy this level of personal service while they're on the manhunts?' she asked.

Dougie registered the renewed scrutiny with irritation. 'As long as they call me Master and wish me good night before they leave.'

'I shouldn't think oligarchs are too keen on calling anyone Master.'

He looked across at her sharply. 'What makes you think they're oligarchs?'

Kat was threading her fingers through the mare's mane, pulling out tangles, her brow creased. 'I heard that's who Arjan

411

Singh does most of his business with these days. Big arms deals between Russia and India.'

'Who's Arjan Singh?'

'Surely you know Seth's real name? He's your boss.'

'None of my business as long as I get paid,' he muttered, feeling foolish for not knowing.

'So how does huntsman work compare with Hollywood rates?'

'I was on a pretty low pay scale there,' he admitted, trying not to think about the debts he'd left behind and the vet's bills still racking up. 'I was never going to have the dedication to make acting a long-term career. The fire made me wake up to reality. I love making movies and I liked my taste of stardom, but I found the film industry seriously dull.' He hadn't told anybody this, and found it surprisingly liberating. 'Seth had been chasing me to do this job for a while. When I realized how much I'd screwed up with Kiki, I came here to sort my head out. Finding you was an added bonus,' he said, wincing at the accidental choice of word. They were almost at the sheep feeder already and he was the only one baring his tarnished soul.

She was looking at him now. He tried for a big, flirty smile but it wouldn't come. Her eyes hypnotized him.

She didn't smile either, the big defensive show-stopper held in check, lower lip pressed beneath her teeth. He adored the way it emphasized her upper lip, curving up at its centre like a Scythian bow.

'I want to help you, Kat.' He tried the big smile again, but again it failed him as his eyes got caught up in hers, amazed at their greenness. 'I want to see you ride the Bolt. And to do that, I need to understand what happened to you. I know exactly what it's like to get such almighty flashbacks you can't function. The first time I got on a horse after the fire, I froze, and it wasn't just flames in my head. You almost drowned, but I don't think that's what made you run away from Nick to come here.'

Dougie had now seen a photograph of Nick in the research files that Dollar had left him – a smug, handsome no-necked rectangle of over-pumped testosterone. He disliked him instinctively.

'How long were you together?'

'Three years, and engaged for one,' she said eventually. 'Some mutual friends set us up – he's a firefighter into free-running. I was a fitness-fanatic nurse who'd do anything for a dare. We both loved spicy food, adventure holidays, action movies and clubbing. We seemed the perfect match. It was fun and physical.' She looked down at her hands, fingers slipping into the mare's mane.

In the minute of silence that followed, Dougie became aware of her change in breathing over the hoof-falls, the clank and creak of tack. However hard Kat tried to hide it, the breath was punching in and out of her lungs, the oxygen diminishing. He wanted to breathe for her, a kiss of life that he knew was far more complicated than resuscitation. The realization shook him.

Then she started talking, a rushed account of her first big relationship and her sexual awakening. How Nick had been amazing to begin with. How she'd had boyfriends before and it was fun, but what she'd had with him had blown them all out of the water. How he could be very assertive, but she'd liked that, and he had seemed so self-assured and experienced. It just kept getting better.

Dougie glared at the horizon as he listened, seriously regretting his determination to know this. She was probably still hooked on him, he decided furiously, cut down by his own jealousy, wondering how fast he could ride to drum heroic Nick from his head. He knew he had asked for this, demanded it even, but now he wanted it to go away. Yet something in her voice kept him listening, the tight pinch of fear in her larynx, endearingly gruff and heart-breakingly honest.

'He never made a secret of the fact he liked porn,' she was saying. 'All his mates watched it too. They'd download it at the fire station while they waited for shouts. He introduced me to it, and at first I thought it was amazing. We watched it together, got off on it, and it was a real kick. But as time went on, he always wanted to watch it when we had sex and do the things in the movie. I played along, but he got more demanding, less loving. He seemed to need more extremes all the time. I grew to hate it, but if I complained he got really angry and aggressive. He frightened me.' She dropped one rein and rubbed her face, blinking hard. 'God, what was in that tea? It's like a truth drug.'

'Don't change the subject,' he said softly. The relationship had been a long way off Aphrodite and Adonis. 'Was he violent?'

'Not violent exactly – overbearing sometimes, especially in bed, but that had been part of the attraction at first so he thought I was playing a part when I begged him to stop.' She bit her lip. 'My girlfriends all thought I was so lucky, with my own firefighting Christian Grey – but he took it way too far once or twice and it was hard to trust him after that.'

'How do you mean "too far"?' Dougie had become so familiar with her face now that he knew when it was about to put on its impenetrable defensive mask. 'Please don't smile.'

She chewed her lip harder with the effort of holding back the big smile.

He knew she must have smiled at Nick, the confused signal with which she charmed the world, both reassuring and defensive. It could make her appear ever-complicit when in fact she was protecting herself and even when she was terrified. She'd learned to use that smile in an abusive relationship as a pacifier. If Nick didn't figure out the smile in three years, he couldn't have worked Kat out at all, Dougie thought furiously.

'Sex became a performance,' she told him quietly, eyes clenching shut. 'There was no affection. He insisted on the porn every time and it grew more degrading. He said it was normal, that all couples did it, a communal dirty secret. After a while, I just went cold at the thought of having sex. I had to drink half a bottle of wine to go there. I did anything to avoid it. It affected our entire relationship. Nick said he worshipped me, but he pushed me around like meat and talked over me. He wouldn't ever admit there was a problem. He said it was in my head. He accused me of being frigid.' She screwed up her face, opened her eyes apologetically and glanced at him, embarrassed. 'I'm only telling you all this for one reason, Dougie. I want the flirting to stop. You have to understand that I am not going to sleep with you. I am *not* an easy lay.'

'I never thought you were,' Dougie said quietly. All he wanted was to reassure her, but everything he said seemed glib and cavalier. 'You don't get rid of me that easily.'

He resisted an urge to crash his forehead on to Worcester's hogged neck, certain she knew the fire and the tea had been accessories to a fantasy cowboy seduction, just as she'd always seen through his full-on charm offensive, which had started out as tongue-in-cheek but had intensified into a very real and overwhelming desire to take her to bed and savour every inch of her. His Don Juan approach must have horrified her after what she'd been through.

Dougie's own hypocrisy was yet again battering at his temples. He'd screwed with triple-X movies playing in the background more than once. He was a big-ego horny show-off who thoroughly enjoyed performance-fucking occasionally. Yet right now, unable to take his eyes from Kat's and unable to smile, he felt like a puritanical redneck determined to scorch hard-core filth from every hard drive on the planet, and to string Nick up by the part of him that had ruled his brain and messed with Kat's head. He wanted to teach her to enjoy again what her body could do and feel with another's. He wanted to look after her, to roar at anyone who threatened her. But he also knew that everything he instinctively wanted to do for her would make her feel more threatened – apart from riding like a maniac across a Herefordshire estate.

'What *was* in that tea?'

'Magic mushrooms.'

She dropped her reins, fingertips raking her forehead. 'You *drugged* me?'

'Actually, it was just Earl Grey.'

To his relief, she laughed. 'Does getting pushed off a horse at speed give someone amnesia? I'd quite like you to forget what you just heard.'

'There's no point in running away from the past. You don't learn from it,' he said, surprising himself with his wisdom. 'You had to be held under water to see what really lay at the other end of that aisle.'

'Perhaps you're right. Nobody saw me as an individual any more, least of all me. We were Nick-and-Kat, problems and all.'

'How hard was it to cut loose?'

'Very. Nobody knew how unhappy I'd become – I hid it too well. Our friends thought we were Ken and Barbie. We owned a house together – we still do on paper – his parents insisted I called them Mum and Dad and my mum worshipped him. Nick was the golden boy, the local hero. After I came out of hospital, he promised to change, but it was never going to work. He was just as controlling, couldn't give up the porn or admit it was a problem. I found amphetamines in the bathroom cabinet, flushed them down the loo and he hit the roof when he found out. I was frightened of him by then, of what he might do if I tried to leave.'

'So you ran away here without saying anything?'

'I handed in my notice at the hospital in strict confidence and joined an agency to look for a job with accommodation where I knew he couldn't find me. I never intended to come this far west, but Eardisford was so perfect. There's no phone reception here, so ignoring his calls and emails was easy. Constance paid cash. I wrote Nick a long letter explaining why I was doing it, and I trusted a couple of very close friends with my contact details, but apart from that, I cut all ties.'

They'd ridden the full circuit of the meadow and were almost back at the fire, weary dogs gravitating towards it.

'And you've not seen him since?'

She shook her head. 'From what I've heard, he basked in sympathy and self-pity for a few months, after which he took up marathon running and never looked back. When Constance died and the news story about Lake Farm made a couple of nationals, he contacted me through solicitors to ask me to sign over my part of the house, but I didn't reply – I'm a bit rubbish about things like that. I think they'll go away if I put them in a drawer. The last I heard, he was living with a sports masseuse.'

'Meanwhile you were shacked up with Badger Man.' As soon as he'd said it, he regretted the dismissive kneejerk comment that placed his foot firmly in his mouth, especially after what she had just confided. 'Sorry. That was crass.'

'Russ was good to me, but it was never going to work.'

'Did he try to help you beat your demons?' he asked jealously.

'He has too many of his own.' She looked at him and this time she didn't look away.

The explosion of fierce emotion in his chest could have brought down a cooling tower. 'I'll take on all your demons.' He leaned out of the saddle to reach for her hand. 'I'll help you beat them. You and I are going to be sensational together. That's a promise.'

To Dougie, it was among the most romantic declarations of his life. He was carrying her through battlefields as shells rained down, holding her on the prow of the *Titanic*, wrestling Red Indians from horses to rescue her from a burning tepee.

Kat looked put out, gathering up her reins and urging Sri forwards. 'I asked you not to flirt.'

'I'm not flirting!' he protested. 'I'm—' But Sri had already broken into a canter and put five lengths between them, flying into top gear now, hoofs thundering across the turf. 'I'm baring my soul.' He set off in pursuit.

The big heavyweight Worcester took longer than Sri to reach maximum speed, but his big stride was soon eating the ground between them as he caught up.

'Are you always so arrogant?' Kat shouted across.

'You do seriously scary truths as well as dares,' he shouted back.

'Your turn, then.' She crouched low as they flew beneath the heavy overhanging branches from the wood. 'Truth or dare?'

'Truth.' Kicking the horse faster, ignoring her shouts behind him, he streaked the full length of the Lush Bottom meadow, straight towards the nursery lake where its shallowest corner was shadowed by the woods. Flat-bottomed and reed-ringed, he'd ridden through it several times that week and trusted that there were no hidden hazards.

Worcester pounded in, big legs sending up great arcs of water in front and bow waves in his wake. As Dougie reined back and turned to look for Kat, he saw she'd pulled up on the bank.

'Come back out! I want a truth. It's only fair!' She glared across at him and he realized again just how extraordinary her eyes were, like iridescent opals.

'Come *in* here and ask.' He looked down, the water foaming and eddying around him as Worcester pawed at it. 'It's barely past this boy's hocks. A bath is deeper.'

Not taking her eyes from his, she rode in. Her knuckles were as white as marble, sinews leaping in her neck. He knew just how much guts it had taken.

'Well done!' he breathed, the unfamiliar lump back in his throat as more detonations took place in his chest.

'I think I've earned a truth, don't you?'

He nodded. He couldn't deny it.

Her eyes were totally bewitching, the deep green reflecting through that opal luminosity. He nudged Worcester closer so that their knees brushed, close enough to reach out and touch her face if he wanted to, to kiss it even. He wanted to do both very badly, but he managed to stop himself, just as he stopped himself smiling or his eyelashes lowering seductively. Instead, he stared at her with wide-eyed honesty, struggling to hear himself speak above the artillery tattoo taking place in his chest.

'I wasn't just hired as a huntsman,' he told her. 'I was hired to target somebody.'

She went very still, the big green eyes watchful. 'You mean there's really truth in the manhunt story?'

'I'm here to make you marry me, Kat.'

Chapter 45

Kat's hearing wasn't serving her too well. Her own heartbeat was thundering in her ears, much as it had been on and off since she'd ridden into the meadow to see Dougie waiting there, now more amplified than ever from plunging into a lake with a horse. Riding into the water had given her the mother of all adrenalin spikes, but that had been nothing to the moment she'd thought Dougie was going to reach across and touch her, kiss her even, the kick of desire almost knocking her out of the saddle. Her skin still burned from the anticipation of it, a half-breath caught between throat and heart, like a stitch.

Her ears were consequently struggling to take in much beyond a hundred and twenty frenzied beats per minute and her own breathing, embarrassingly loud, rapid-fire wheezing pants. And there was a lot of splashing going on beneath them.

Yet she was certain that Dougie had just said he'd been hired to marry her.

She felt as though she'd galloped bravely over a cliff only to find herself as the end-of-pier amusement. She'd just told him her most painful, personal truth and he'd come back at her with a joke about being a marriage assassin. At least it served to remind her that he was a flippant bastard. And, more surprisingly, it made her laugh, a shocked reflex that helped shake off the fear. Dougie's dry, deadpan delivery drew a delicious ripple of laughter up through her, as unexpected as it was joyful.

Laughter was such a relief after the intensity of talking about Nick, confessing the truths she'd never intended to spill again, certainly never to Dougie Everett. She should be furious with him for rewarding her with this childish joke, but it was too gloriously surreal – especially given they were both sitting on horses in a lake – and she was overwhelmed to have ridden Sri into water up to her belly. Laughter helped enormously: it stopped her thinking about the water. Wiping tears of mirth from her eyes and hanging on to Sri's mane, she laughed until it hurt.

'I told you I was lousy at truths.' Dougie was looking at her curiously. Beneath him, Worcester was pawing at the water, trying to get his head down.

Dropping the reins, she reached across and cuffed his arm. 'But you've really cheered me up. Thank you.' Her eyes caught his and he held her gaze so intently that the last of the laughter melted away. 'Dougie, please don't—'

'I am *not* flirting,' he second-guessed her with an impatient huff.

'I was going to say "propose".'

Amusement creased in the corners of his blue eyes. Then his expression changed to one of alarm as the Marwari mare, who had put her head down to drink, started to crumple.

Kat let out a scream as Sri dropped towards the water beneath her. 'What's happening?'

'She's trying to roll. Grab the reins and pull her head up!'

Preparing to cool off in the water with an ecstatic sigh, the mare was already down on her knees and hocks. Leaping from his saddle, Dougie threw himself across ten feet of water to rescue her and almost got mown down as Kat kicked and cajoled so energetically that Sri stood up and spun towards the bank. A moment later they were streaking across the meadow.

'Not even Sri's allowed to go down on one knee!' she shouted over her shoulder.

Galloping helped clear Kat's head. Eventually, she pulled up at the edge of the woods, lungs bursting.

'Never, ever do that to me again,' she told Sri, whose curly ears were revolving like radar dishes at something she'd sensed in the woods. 'If we're going to get across the big lake, there'll be no seal rolls. And Dougie Everett needs keeping under tight control. Don't give him any more excuses to be heroic.' She rubbed her sweaty face on the back of her sleeve, resting her arm against her eyes for a moment to blot out the sun setting through the trees. She groaned. Telling Dougie about Nick had been a huge mistake, she was certain. Her best survival tactic would be to laugh it off. And at least he'd been generous enough to supply the running gag.

At that moment, Sri went sharply into reverse as she took exception to whatever she'd sensed in the woods, almost tipping Kat out of the saddle. Swinging around, she let out a shrill whinny and set off at full tilt towards the reassuring bulky shape of Worcester: Dougie was jockeying him across the meadow towards them at his gambolling canter.

'Oh, shit.' Kat pulled hopelessly at the reins as she found herself inadvertently riding towards Dougie through Lush Bottom's jewelled carpet of flowers, like a swooning romantic heroine about to embrace her manly hero. Judging from the width of his smile, he was enjoying the show.

Determined not to lose face, she shouted, 'So how are you going to make me marry you?'

Dougie was sopping wet and frustrated that his honesty had backfired, but the sight of her galloping towards him had cheered him up a lot, and he was equally determined not to lose

422

face. Swinging Worcester around so that they were riding alongside one another, he played along with the joke she clearly found so funny. 'I'll propose.'

'Go on then!'

'Is that a dare?'

'If you like.'

'Will you marry me?' Worcester was blowing hard, accompanying the question with snorts, groans and clanking metal. Dougie brought the horse back to a trot, letting him stretch out his neck and relax.

'If I say no, will you lose your job?' Kat called, struggling to apply the brakes, her long red ponytail twirling.

'I might get a formal warning.' He wished that he had kept quiet about the bonus. She was right to dismiss it as a joke.

'And if I say yes and we rush off to a register office, I lose Lake Farm under the terms of my lease.' She reined to a halt, eyebrows shooting up. The big, defensive smile was back in place, he noticed, with a sinking heart.

'Clever girl.' He rode level before pulling up too. 'You spotted the evil master-plan.'

Just for a moment he saw her eyes flicker behind the smile and knew she was questioning her laughter. Yet she couldn't bring herself to push that door and find a big HAHAHA waiting after all.

He mustered a self-deprecating smile. 'I take it the answer is no?'

To his surprise, she didn't immediately answer. She was looking at the stables clock-tower, only just visible beyond the woods. It was eight fifteen. From the opposite direction, they could hear the village church bell ring the quarter chime.

'I'll give you my answer after I ride the Bolt. As long as you promise not to flirt with me until then. Not once.'

Chapter 46

Dougie honoured the flirting ban. For three weeks, he and Kat met almost every evening as the birds roosted and the hay was cut in the meadows around the estate, trading truths and dares, riding ever faster, tracking the course of the Bolt from Duke's Wood right up to the house. By day, he ran his hounds and exercised horses while Kat juggled aged animals, budget nightmares, dippy volunteers and endless maintenance. But each evening, for an hour or two, they stood in their stirrups and rode the loveliest turf in Herefordshire, intent on a joint mission. The marriage proposal remained a running joke, but the historic Mytton challenge was something they both took increasingly seriously, a dare that must be met.

Dougie had plotted two routes, one of which avoided the lake but would require Kat to ride a great deal faster and more accurately. He broke it down into sections and they tackled each in turn, perfecting every change of direction and pace, like rehearsing a stunt sequence. Kat was a tireless if occasionally stubborn pupil, fearless yet precise, listening to every instruction, determined to get better. She was also surprisingly easy to talk to.

By not flirting, Dougie found himself laughing more than he remembered doing in years, as well as shouting, coaching and trading satisfyingly furious insults. Their conversations were fast, furious and laughter-laced, breathlessly gasped between bursts of speed, covering childhood, careers and engagements, of which they'd broken five between them if you counted Dean Stoppard, who had proposed to Kat at the age of eight.

'His dad was being posted to Germany, so we exchanged rings and had an engagement party, promising to stay true to other until we were sixteen and could legally marry. He wrote to me every day until I replied six weeks later breaking it off because his ring had given me a green finger.'

'With our track record, we'd better skip engagement and heard straight for Vegas after you ride the Bolt. Race you to the haha.'

They embraced their common ground, trading memories of childhoods with divorced parents and a succession of evil step-parents, romantic disasters, favourite films and music, sharing their unswerving love of animals and a fierce loyalty to their friends, whom they saw rarely because, after all, they had both run away here. Most of all they made each other laugh, trading insults with increasing joy.

'You're almost human for a posh boy.'

'You're pretty cool for a common cow.'

Not flirting turned them into two children playing through long, balmy, midge-hazed summer evenings, lost in a world of chivalric challenges, silly jokes and breakneck races. Much later each night, it transformed them into two sleepless, sheet-twisting teenagers, hollow with longing, stomachs churning with anticipation. With friends and acquaintances, it turned them into two self-satisfied puritans who could very honestly report, 'We just ride together.' They blithely rose above the village gossip, which had cast them as the Lancelot and Guinevere of Eardisford, and determinedly ignored the approaching storm of Seth's first VIP visit.

Dougie counted the minutes to those snatched hours each evening, although he dreaded the call that inevitably came afterwards. Dollar's questions were increasingly personal, the monotone voice calm as always but her mistrust clear. 'I think it is unrealistic to expect this of you. You are clearly becoming too attached.'

At first, he was evasive and glib, insisting it was all in hand, anything to buy himself more time. Then, in a masterstroke of unwitting impatience, he told Dollar that he had proposed but that Kat would only answer after undertaking an historic challenge. 'Constance Mytton-Gough did much the same thing. It's a local tradition. She's very old-fashioned like that.'

To his surprise, Dollar thought this perfectly reasonable. 'This is excellent. You will keep me informed of her progress. She must undertake this challenge before Seth's visit.' After that, their conversations became much easier, and thankfully Dollar was soon too distracted by Seth's ambitious weekend plans to delve into too many details and discover the no-flirting clause.

'He will be hosting a Bollywood party on the Saturday. His weekend guests will enjoy a banquet in the house, but there will also be a marquee in the grounds to which he would like to invite the estate staff and villagers. Invitations will be circulated shortly.'

'A servants' ball.' Dougie laughed, guessing his tactics. 'How very archaic. Let me guess, we get the village cricket team so pie-eyed at the ball they can't bowl straight the next day. Meanwhile, estate staff are contractually obliged to stay sober.'

'Everybody will be encouraged to have a good time, although Sunday's cricket match is of great importance. For Seth, cricket is second only to religion,' Dollar said, adding briskly, 'and his mother.'

'Is Kat going to be invited to the ball?'

'That would not be appropriate. In the event that she has not vacated Lake Farm, contingencies are in place for the weekend. However, I strongly recommend you pursue your objective.'

'Leave it with me.' He promised nothing, increasingly aware that he was on borrowed time and that his objective had changed. He knew that the open proposal was just a joke to Kat, and he wasn't focusing on that any more. As far as Dougie was concerned, all that mattered was that she had a chance to ride the Bolt before Seth's visit, yet he knew she was far from ready. Nor was he ready to let go of their shared evenings. Every minute was precious as he charged along the rides and headlands with Kat, timing each section, adoring her determined expression as she sought to improve, the way laughter burst from her when her time was shorter, the hugs and kisses raining down on Sri's neck.

When she heard about the servants and masters ball and learned that she would not be invited, Kat simply laughed and joked that she should ride the Bolt that night. 'It's just the sort of thing Constance would have done.'

She talked about Constance often, relating conversations about Marwari horses, the history of the house and estate, and the many legendary runnings of the Bolt, so many steeped in failure and a few in tragedy.

'The Myttons who accepted the challenge would ride up the steps and through the grand hall, out on to the front carriage sweep and along the drive to the Hereford road,' she explained, when they examined the final leg, eyed suspiciously by a battalion of cameras now discreetly positioned in amongst the Jacobean architecture.

'Not easy to make sure the house is open.' He sucked in his lips thoughtfully. 'We could try bribing someone on the staff, but they're a pretty tightly briefed team. The security is seriously high grade now.' He knew he could speak to Dollar, but it seemed like cheating, and compared to crossing the lake, it was a minor worry. They'd now clocked enough section times to know that there was no way Kat would make the time if she went around the water: she had to ride through it.

Kat had stared at the lake almost every evening that summer, trying to imagine herself swimming across it, but the first time Dougie assessed it with her close-up, on foot after they had ridden out one evening, he let out a low groan. 'Fuck, it's huge.'

This hardly gave her great encouragement. 'You've seen it loads of times.'

'I always forget how big it is. It looks quite small from the top of the parkland.'

'That's an optical illusion from the oxbow.' Kat stood at the shallowest curve of bank alongside the ornate stone-plinthed causeway, knowing it would be the obvious place from which to gallop a horse through the lake, but just looking at the black, weed-choked water left her breathless with panic. Two football pitches separated her from the far side.

'The water is only deep for about ten metres in the centre,' Dougie shouted over his shoulder, wading in to his thighs. 'Horses swim incredibly slowly, so this is the shortest crossing point and it has great visibility. She'll hesitate at first, so you'll need lots of leg. Come on.' He reversed up to her standing on the bank, holding his arms out.

'What are you doing?'

'Giving you a ride. I'm the horse.'

'I can't.'

'Come on, get on. We'll just go in a few feet and come out.

428

You won't even get your feet wet. I dare you, you bloody wimp. We're getting you across this lake by the end of the week, I swear. I'll even tell you another truth. Anything.'

It was the first time Kat sensed real anger in his cajoling and frustration. She hesitated, already clammy-handed and breathing shallowly, but her blood was up and she wasn't going to be accused of wimpery. Having banked on going round her nemesis, she now knew she had no choice but to face it.

Cursing under her breath, she put her hands on his shoulders and jumped on to his back, wrapping her arms around him for balance. As soon as she did it, she realized her mistake: the sense was knocked out of her with a white-out of sensory overload, feeling the hard breadth of him, smelling his sweetness, feeling his hair against her cheek. His lips touched her arm, whether by accident or design she had no idea, but they rested there, his breath soft on her skin, and she was certain he knew how attracted she was, how her body cleaved to his no matter what her mind was telling it to do, drawing his skin against hers, absorbing its warmth. For a moment they remained still, a lakeside piggy-back of strange, heavenly connection.

Then she screeched with laughter as he turned away from the lake and cavorted along the bank towards the lime avenue, carrying her at a reckless bouncing, jigging pelt, slaloming through a few trees before kinking right into the arboretum.

'You should have kicked on. I'm now running away with you!'

He finally let her down in the farmyard, where the last rays of sun were slicing right through the house, as they so often did, turning it into a light-box. He stepped away swiftly and decorously as soon as she was on the ground, upright and eyes-front as a guardsman.

'This is a beautiful place.' He admired Lake Farm's ugly artisan face, the Pompidou Centre drainpipes and loose wires transformed by its magic-lantern windows. 'It deserves to be lived in and loved.'

'I love it very much.' Kat admired it too.

He wandered inside, surrounded by dogs – they now thought of him as a great mate and ushered him excitedly into their lair along with Quiver, eager to help him explore.

'You have nothing whatsoever to drink.' He looked in the fridge. 'Or eat.'

'I wasn't expecting a guest.' Kat edged after him cautiously.

'I'm not thinking of me – I have a fridge full of goodies – I'm thinking of you. You're feeding the mare extra rations for all this work she's doing. What about you?'

'I get by.'

'Come to dinner.'

'No thanks.' She didn't trust herself for a minute with wine, good food and Dougie, worried she'd be a total pushover, the easiest notch ever grooved on his much-striped bedpost. 'You've already proposed – it's a bit late to start the courtship.'

'Have I flirted?'

'No.'

'There you go. Dinner between non-flirting suitors is an entirely nutritional event. You need to eat.'

He wandered deeper into the house, framed in the sunset, looking around the tatty sitting room. The Tantric corner had been cleared away behind the sofa again. There would be no more Ravi Shankar in Lake Farm this summer. Russ still came and went occasionally to tend his rescue cases, leaving big piles of foraged food, occasionally releasing one of his wildlife victims or adding another, but he was free-ranging so widely now, he was almost feral.

Seeing no evidence of co-habiting, Dougie cheered up. Feeling the sexual energy crackling in the room, Kat started to panic in much the same way she did when faced with the lake.

'Truth or dare?' he said, as he so often did, admiring the photograph on the windowsill of Kat and Dawn in their graduation outfits.

'Truth,' she said quickly, unable to face another piggy-back ride.

He stood silhouetted against a red-stained window. 'I want to kiss you right now.'

Kat couldn't speak, her belly so full of marauding electric butterflies she almost expected to lift up in the air.

But instead of making a move, he stooped to say farewell to the dogs and headed for the door. 'We'll do a timed run at the end of the week.'

'I don't think I can swim the lake yet.'

'I can. I'm riding it first. I'm the stuntman, remember. Start eating properly.'

Early the next morning, a Waitrose delivery van rattled into the Lake Farm yard, its driver shaking from the trauma of battling through the woods, gates and ford, but grateful for the detailed directions that had been supplied with the order, without which there would have been no hope of supplying Kat with fresh ready-meals, fruit, veg and an array of deli products that made her want to kneel down and worship the fridge all day.

'Thank you!' She greeted Dougie ecstatically in the lime avenue that evening, indigestion raging from bingeing on artichoke hearts, sun-blush tomatoes and stuffed vine leaves.

'All vegan,' he pointed out proudly.

'I'm not a vegan, Russ is, only he's not living with me any

more. I eat anything. I just tend to forget to buy anything to eat. But I've eaten all your food so fast I can hardly breathe.'

At that moment, Dougie felt something painful in his chest, a small harpoon blade. The first deep cut of love.

Kat had such raging indigestion, she posted her slowest times so far and was furious with herself. It was only much later that night, as the heartburn failed to shift, that she realized it was something else. Something far longer-lasting and harder to deal with.

'Bugger, bugger, bugger.' She tipped the dogs off the bed as she trailed downstairs to eat the luxury dark vegan chocolate currently in the fridge.

Soon coasting on a huge chocolate fix, she lay wide awake for hours, contemplating Dougie and his quest to make her ride the Bolt, his joke proposal, his love of hunting hounds and his sheer, unadulterated enthusiasm for life, open air and thrills. None of it added up to her idea of a dream man, yet it had triggered an ever more volatile chemical reaction inside her, bubbling effervescently around her dancing organs and raging heart. She was falling wildly in lust and love, and all without the aid of a single dinner date, Tantric chant, dirty movie or kiss.

She sat up in bed in the early hours, heartburn still raging, knowing she had to kiss him.

Chapter 47

Kat thought about kissing Dougie a ridiculous amount the following day, her lips seeking out her fingers, knuckles, wrists, pen

432

lids, cup rims and the tops of the dogs' heads at regular intervals, like a live wire needing an earth.

She rode straight to the Eardisford yard that evening, far too early, but to her frustration Dougie was already sitting on Worcester, who let out a rumbling whicker of recognition when Sri bounded in.

As they trotted out through the arch, their stirrups clattered together, knees bumping. Kat looked across and saw it mirrored in his eyes, the deep blue come-on between the dark lashes, the kiss in waiting, just needing its signal.

'We already have a wager on you riding the Bolt,' he reminded her, as they cantered along the tracks to Duke's Wood. 'What shall we lay on *me* doing it?'

'Each other?' She said it without thinking, then blushed crimson.

'Are you flirting?' His smile was a country mile wide.

'Of course not,' she said, uncomfortably aware that even her ears were puce.

Reining back to a walk as they reached the edge of the woods, he looked remarkably florid-cheeked too, eyes bluer than ever.

Kiss, kiss, kiss, Kat's brain screamed, as they moved closer together through the forestry gate. She turned as he did, hat peaks clashing, mouths a breath apart, just as Sri let out a furious squeal and kicked out at Worcester before napping away.

'She's rampantly in season,' she apologized breathlessly, knowing Sri wasn't the only one.

'Better keep her behind.'

He was issuing instructions over his shoulder, which she hardly took in, outlining the plan that he would set off on a timed run of the whole route and she would follow but drop out at the lake. Kat listened to his voice, loving its clipped huskiness, remembering the catch when he'd told her a truth and said, 'I want to kiss you right now.'

Even redder-faced, she followed Dougie up to the far corner of Duke's Wood, the derelict folly that traditionally marked the start of the Bolt, where Sri ruined Kat's attempts to get close enough for a good luck peck on Dougie's cheek by squealing, cocking her tail and squirting at a mortified Worcester.

'You ready?' Dougie checked.

No, Kat wanted to yell. I need to kiss you! But for the first time it struck her that he was genuinely uptight at what he was about to do. He checked his girth, a muscle slamming in his cheek, eyeing his watch. The last time she'd seen him look so tense was in the parade ring at the point-to-point. It's a big deal, she thought. The Bolt is scary stuff. Even Dougie Everett is daunted.

'If you fall back, don't worry,' he told her, cheek muscle still drumming, his eyes serious. 'The gates are all open and there's no livestock, but watch out for hay baling.' He unclipped his helmet harness and pulled it from his head to rake his hair back from his eyes. 'At the lake, if your blood's up and you're close behind, follow us through, but for God's sake shout and let me know so I look out for you, and if you're more than a few lengths behind or feeling uncertain, wait for me there. Take your helmet off a moment – there's something under it.'

'What?' She pulled it off, shaking her head.

Bareheaded too, Dougie kicked Worcester alongside, braving Sri's hormones, and reached out and drew her towards him. 'This.'

As the lips landed on hers, Kat was aware of shifting beneath her, but whether it was the horse or the earth moving,

434

she couldn't say. There were more squeals and a grunt, the jangling of bits and clashing stirrup irons, and she felt Dougie's arms tighten around her, his kiss harden, his weight supporting her as she was lifted out of one saddle and on to another, laughing as she kissed and scrabbled herself into place. And then she was sitting astride Worcester in front of Dougie, facing the wrong way, kissing her heart out. Her mouth, her eyes and her soul so full of Dougie that she thought she might burst with happiness.

'This isn't flirting,' he breathed, as they finally broke apart, his mouth brushing against her upper lip, her cheeks and then her ears, which made her shriek with a shiver of delight. 'This is kissing. It's entirely different.'

She laughed, as their foreheads pressed together, eyelashes tangling, and she remembered the night she'd stared out to the lake and imagined them swimming it together. This was like her vision, she decided, only she was floating on air, not water.

Their mouths drew together, hungrier now, this time unable to break apart as their kisses deepened, fingers through hair, hearts and groins roaring for more.

Oh, God, I'll be making love on a horse in a minute, Kat panicked, as Dougie's fingertips traced her throat, her chest-bone, the curve of her breasts where her nipples were as hard as pea-shooter ammo. His lips chased his fingers down while she arched back, ecstatic under his touch.

'I'll hold you to your wager if I ride this.' He kissed the shelf of her breastbone. Then his mouth found hers again and Kat knew she'd never been kissed so exquisitely in her life, or wanted to drag someone into a derelict folly so badly.

The village quarter bell had rung twice. They were losing

the light. Eventually they pulled apart again and he reluctantly helped her down to go and catch Sri, who had thrust her head through one of the folly's glassless windows.

Clipping her helmet back on, Kat mounted and awaited the signal. She felt totally fearless. Bring on the lake, she wanted to shout. I can walk on you now.

Blowing her a kiss, unable to stop smiling, Dougie pressed the stopwatch button on his clunky wristwatch and charged into action, Kat flying in his wake. He was riding Worcester because he knew that he wasn't the fastest conveyance and would be closer to Kat's speed when she took the challenge, making it easier to gauge how realistic the time was to achieve.

It was a warm, muggy evening without a hint of a breeze and Worcester was already puffing hard as they reached open country beyond the woods, his sides drenched in sweat. As always, the sound of Kat laughing cheered horse and rider on, hard on their heels, shouting for him to go faster before she mowed them down.

Riding the hormone-fuelled Sri, Kat was in danger of being totally run away with as she sat out some back-flipping bucks that would have propelled her into orbit just a few weeks ago. Worcester was positively ponderous in front as Sri jigged all over the track behind, pinging up her back legs. They careered along field margins and through freshly cut hayfields, Dougie navigating the route he'd plotted so carefully in recent weeks.

'Let's see how good you're getting at ducking.' He turned to the woods.

Having totally forgotten the route, Kat only realized he'd disappeared into the trees when Sri swerved dramatically to plunge after him. Worcester was groaning and snorting with every stride now, the evening heat hard to bear.

'He's exhausted!' she yelled after him, crouching low on Sri's neck as they gave chase into the shadows.

'Ride the Bolt to the end and you'll really feel an exhausted horse beneath you,' he shouted back over his shoulder. 'Trust me, this chap is fresh compared to that, and he's not hunting fit yet.'

'Hunting for what exactly?' demanded a furious voice, as a balaclava-clad figure stepped out in Worcester's path. 'The wild Kat?'

Worcester stopped dead, eyes boggling at the unlikely sight of a camouflaged vigilante with white-tipped hair wielding a camcorder.

Cannoning into the ample brown bottom blocking their path, Kat and Sri parted company. As she flew towards a tangle of tree roots, Kat realized it was Russ in front of them. She also realized that she hadn't done up the chin strap of her helmet properly and it was whizzing in the opposite direction.

At the time of her fall, Kat thought she was taking everything in. Landing was a bit of a blur, as were the ensuing few hours, but she distinctly remembered telling everybody her name, date of birth, the current prime minister and the nine times table to prove her alertness. Not that anybody seemed impressed, just telling her to lie still because there was blood coming out of her head. There was talk of air ambulances and a lot of shouting.

She saw Dougie's lovely blue eyes coming in and out of her vision, saying reassuring things that she later couldn't remember. And there had been more shouting. Quite a lot of shouting, mostly Russ's distinctive deep deer bark with its Bristol accent. Not that she remembered a word he'd said. That was the funny thing about concussion. You thought you had a memory of what had happened and then – *poof*. Gone.

437

Chapter 48

Dougie had his satellite phone pressed to his ear, cursing the signal cutting out.

'I've got my eye on you, Everett!' Russ raged, videoing him with a camcorder. 'I know your game!'

Ignoring him, Dougie crouched beside Kat. 'Are you still okay?'

'Eight times nine is seventy-two.' She nodded, smiling up at him lovingly.

'Leave this to me, Kat.' Russ loomed over them. 'He knows what game I'm talking about.'

'Is this about the cricket?' Dougie suggested, trying to dial out on the phone again.

For a moment Russ was nonplussed – the mention of cricket always acted like a stun-dart on him – but then he squared himself up and snarled, 'This is definitely *not* fucking cricket.'

'Soccer, rugby, ping-pong, Pictionary?' Dougie muttered distractedly, holding up the phone and wondering whether the trees were blocking the signal. He didn't want to leave Kat. She was repeating David Cameron's name in a worryingly rapturous fashion now.

Bear-like Russ growled under his breath, 'Little boys play with bows and arrows.'

'Archery's a sport, not a game.' Dougie pulled off his waistcoat to put under Kat's head.

'It's July the twentieth,' she said gratefully.

'It is a *blood* sport when the super-rich get to play Robin

Hood in the woods,' the Bristol accent shouted. A camcorder zoom closed in on Dougie's face with an electronic whirr. 'Except in the Eardisford Estate they won't be stealing from the rich to give to the poor. They'll just shoot anything that moves, won't they, Dougie Everett?'

'You don't know what you're talking about,' Dougie muttered, patience snapping as he looked over his shoulder to find a lens inches away.

Russ was doing a strident voice-over now. 'Seth – a.k.a. Arjan Singh, an IT dotcom billionaire – has bought the Eardisford Estate specifically to entertain some of his most powerful global contacts, of whom many are shooting-mad Anglophiles, and a select few take their hunting a lot more seriously than that. Seth has no personal interest in field sports, but he knows how to provide the best game platforms in the world. It's what made him rich in the first place. Only this one is real, and the "game" is protected wildlife being hunted illegally.'

'All hunting on the Eardisford Estate will be done strictly within the law,' Dougie said authoritatively, turning back to brush Kat's hair gently from her face and check her pupils, which were still worryingly dilated.

'George Osborne,' she said seductively.

'Is that the law that's different for private packs?' Russ was raging. 'The law that says you can shoot your prey with arrows? Chase Mumbai's slum kids around with dogs?'

'I think he was joking about that bit,' Kat muttered groggily, adding, 'Nine times nine is eighty-one.'

Dougie looked down at her in disbelief. 'Did you tell him all this?'

But Kat, deathly pale with blood trickling from her nose, only managed the home secretary and nine times three.

'Kat's been reporting back on all your conversations,

Dougie,' Russ moved to her other side and checked her pulse, still videoing, 'but I think the time's right to pull her out from undercover work. Anything else just wouldn't be cricket.'

'Undercover work?' Dougie repeated carefully.

Russ put a protective hand on Kat's limp arm. 'We both have the sanctuary's best interests at heart. Safeguarding our animals and the wildlife here is paramount. Nobody trusts you, Dougie.'

'Clearly not,' Dougie said tightly, looking down at Kat again.

'Twentieth of July,' she murmured again, green eyes glazing. She was paler than ever, incredibly fragile and beautiful. Just a few minutes ago, Dougie had tasted those lips. Now he wasn't sure he believed a word that had come out of them. He looked at her as though through thick sheets of glass, trust sliding away. She was Snow White in a casket. Another prince could kiss her to wake her up.

'Nick Clegg,' she said, in a bright voice. 'Dodgy.'

Anger evaporating, Dougie slid his hands beneath her and picked her up, carrying her back out of the woods so that he could call for help. He buried his face in her hair as he walked, breathing in her sweetness.

'I told you the truth about my job, Kat,' he said quietly. 'Double-cross my heart and hope to die.'

'What truth is that exactly?' demanded Russ, videoing in hot pursuit.

When Dougie didn't answer, he started a breathless voice-over again, interspersed with curses as he fell over tree roots. 'The Animal Liberation Posse has heard on the nod that the Eardisford gamekeepers are briefed to expect a VIP guest any day. The estate will be on a major security clamp-down. We think it's wild-boar hunting. They've been tracking the sounders all week.'

'I know nothing about this,' Dougie snapped, setting Kat

440

down on a grassy bank and gratefully dialling out from his phone.

'Of course you bloody know!' Russ was pointing the camera at him accusingly, relishing his undercover exposé. 'You're part of the team organizing it. You're the bowman.'

'Fuck off,' Dougie muttered, then, hearing the outraged voice at the other end of the line, quickly apologized. 'Not you, Dair. I need your help.'

Russ was watching him closely, his voice dropping to David Attenborough gorilla-observation whisper as he told the camera, 'Everett is on the phone to the estate manager, Alasdair Armitage, who is in control of all illegal hunting at Eardisford. He will no doubt bring heavies to force me off the estate at gunpoint.'

'Can you or one of the keepers get transport down here?' Dougie spoke into the phone. 'Kat needs to go to A and E.'

'Kat has been injured in the line of duty, possibly deliberately,' Russ told the camera in his breathy undertone.

Kat was complaining groggily that she didn't want to go to hospital. 'I am perfectly okay, see?' She sat up, gripping the ground to either side. 'I'm Katherine Mason. It's July the twentieth, I'm holding up two fingers, or it could be four – six even.' Her eyes crossed as she focused on them and then, blinking hard, she groaned and clutched her head.

'For God's sake, lie down again,' Dougie ordered, worried she was about to pass out. 'You're going to hospital whether you like it or not.'

'I'm definitely not marrying you if you're going to boss me about like that,' she grumbled. 'Or is the proposal off now you know I'm a spy?'

The camera zoom whirred frantically.

'Shut up, Kat,' Dougie breathed.

'Don't worry, I didn't tell them the bit about you coming to Eardisford to trick me into marrying you so I have to leave the farm.' She looked at him blearily, totally disoriented, one pupil noticeably bigger than the other. 'Russ is right. I have been injured in the line of duty. My heart's been broken. That was the most amazing kiss of my *life* but it's just all an act for you, isn't it?' She looked away tearfully and spotted the camera at last. 'Shit.' She gave it her big smile, her green eyes glazed. Then she groaned and lay down in the grass.

'I think you should go.' Russ gave Dougie his bear growl, towering over him.

'I'm not leaving her like this.'

'You come near her again and there'll be a village lynch mob out.'

Dougie looked at him furiously. 'I'm going nowhere.'

'You want this on YouTube?' Russ switched the little camera to play, flapping out its touch-screen and jabbing his finger on the thumbnails. Images of Dougie round the estate on horse-back, cycling with his hounds, riding with Kat and letting loose a few arrows from Worcester, who he was training for stunt tricks to entertain guests.

'Do what you like with it,' Dougie muttered, checking Kat again. She'd closed her eyes and was muttering her way through times tables again.

'And this one?'

'They're otters.' Dougie identified the creatures on screen impatiently. Then the picture swung around to show the mill house through the trees, its windows illuminated at dusk. The footage had been taken back in late spring when bluebells had surrounded it. The camera zoomed in on one window where Dollar, lithe and naked, was riding up and down on what at first appeared to be large dildo poking from an ornamental clock, but Dougie recognized was in fact himself shot from a strange angle. The picture swung around again with a lot of rustling and then resumed from a higher angle so that Dougie's blond hair and laughing face could be seen.

'You fucking pervert,' he hissed at Russ, glancing anxiously at Kat, but her eyes were still closed.

'It gets better.' Russ fast-forwarded to Dollar pointing a handgun out of the window at the two Lake Farm lurchers and Trevor the peacock. Moments later Dougie appeared outside, shouting his head off about roasted peacocks with apricot stuffing and how to get hold of illegal handguns.

Dougie felt a sickening lurch of *déjà vu*. His reputation had been severely rattled by some very compromising CCTV footage once before. 'This proves nothing,' he muttered.

'Leave. Kat. Alone,' Russ hissed.

Chapter 49

'I'm no longer interested in the bonus option,' Dougie told Dollar, with tight-lipped restraint.

'What is wrong?' Her voice purred with reassuring cool.

'I've changed my mind.' He let himself into the mill house, the puppy wriggling in ahead.

'That is very inconvenient. Removing Kat Mason and her sanctuary is now a number-one priority. We would like Lake Farm made vacant and repatriated to the estate as a matter of urgency.'

Dougie snorted at the use of 'repatriated', as though Lake

Farm was a refugee in a war zone. 'That's not my problem any more.'

She gave an exasperated huff, tapping on her tablet in the background. 'We will need to deal with this before Seth and his guests arrive next weekend. Igor will hunt and shoot both days.'

'Who's Igor?'

'You should be aware of this. Dair has been given the security briefing to distribute. Igor is a *very* important guest. Read up on him.'

Dougie looked at the pile of unopened post on the table, one of which was a hand-delivered A4 envelope addressed to The Hon. D. W. J. Everett, MFH. Only Dair was that formal and evasive.

'I'll look through it again tonight.' He threw his keys down on the table and headed to the fridge for a Coke. 'There aren't a lot of sporting options right now, but I can set something up with a scent trail.'

'That is not what we want, Dougie.'

He felt his scalp tighten. 'What precisely do you want?'

'We have promised Igor English medieval hunting. This is entirely within your brief. We have assured him of your full co-operation. He expects to be entertained.'

'You want me to dress up in doublet and hose?' He played it dumb, but he knew that he couldn't play it any dumber than he inadvertently, stupidly and blindly already had.

'He is an experienced bowman. He will bring his own equipment. Your job is to provide the horses and to track the game.'

'You know I can't do that. It's completely illegal.'

There was a long pause. 'Dougie, have you read your contract?'

'I obviously have a lot of reading to do tonight.'

'You have half an hour.' She rang off.

Dougie knew he couldn't hope to find his contract in half an hour. Instead, he called his father's mobile. 'What do you know about Arjan "Seth" Singh?'

'Are you in trouble?'

'Should I be worried if I am?'

'Not unduly. He's very well liked.' Vaughan Everett didn't hesitate, the name as familiar to him as Bill Gates or Mark Zuckerberg. 'I was working for the Treasury when Seth's first company was floated on the stock exchange for a cool eight figures. That must have been fifteen years ago or more. He was a computer genius from Bradford who made a mint through developing online gaming sites. He was known as Britain's richest teenager by the tabloids, but he hated the publicity and quickly disappeared behind a privacy wall. I think he's based in India now. His enterprise is absolutely huge, one of the global IT heavyweights.'

'Would global include Russian arms deals?'

Vaughan promised to do some detective work and call back within the hour.

Dougie went to throw open a window, cursing himself repeatedly under his breath, his forehead pressed against the frame. Quiver leaned supportively against his legs as Dougie scrunched his eyes closed and breathed in the air outside so long, low and mournfully it seemed to pull every muscle in his chest.

He thought of Kat Mason and the irony that they'd both been trying to dupe the other, he flirting for a million-pound bonus and she playing detective for the sanctuary. He knew he should be darkly amused by such bittersweet double deceit – an ability to laugh at himself was his strongest armour these days – but jealous anger twisted inside him: his own allegiance had shifted while she had clearly stayed loyal to Badger Man and the village.

Now he knew what Seth expected him to lay on for his VIP visitors, Dougie could hardly blame Kat for spying on him, judging him, hating him. How he could be so naïve and walk straight into this situation appalled him. He'd ignored its obvious traps, too blown away by the escape Eardisford had offered and the easy money to question the details.

He needed a drink, but all he had was Coke and coffee, and he was jittery enough as it was, heart lurching when his phone rang.

It was Dollar, her stonewall voice as inexpressive as ever. 'I have discussed the forthcoming visit with Seth and your services will not be needed. Shooting will be the focus.'

'Sensible choice,' he muttered. Let Dair worry about what the Russian could track in the off season.

'We will need the horses to be available at all times. Igor is a very keen horseman. And you must keep the girl away. Drug her if you need to.'

'I'm the huntsman, not a henchman,' he reminded her. He was feeling jumpy as he thought back to his conversations with Kat, which had revealed how little he knew about Seth's real identity, let alone his connection with oligarchs and arms deals. And then the idiot Badger Man had started spouting on about rich tycoons slaughtering wildlife. Suddenly the James Bond fantasy he'd harboured at the start felt less silly and far too close for comfort. 'Who exactly is Igor?'

'That is none of your concern. As well as mounting our guest on a very well-behaved animal, you will be required to work as part of the team ensuring we have discretion and security. His visit requires total privacy. Sunday afternoon is the estate versus the village cricket match. The pitch is on the far side of the church, and so it is an excellent distraction. Everybody will be out of the way. The day before will be harder because so many villagers walk their dogs through the estate. We have surveyed the public rights of way and Dair Armitage has it all in hand.'

'Is he organizing a rough shoot?'

'On the contrary, we need it to go smoothly.' Her voice softened. 'I would like to see you alone.'

'I'll be playing cricket and distracting girls, remember?'

'We will see each other.' With this, she rang off, leaving Dougie feeling oddly as if he'd been threatened.

Unable to sit still for more than a minute at a time – certainly not long enough to read Dair's impossibly long and boring security briefing – Dougie took Quiver for a walk past Lake Farm to visit Harvey. There were several cars parked in the farmyard. The voices coming from the kitchen sounded positively party-like.

He found Harvey lying on his side in his field and sat down beside him, using his rump as a back rest so that he was facing the lake, looking across to Eardisford's illuminated windows as he called Dair, who had also been equipped with a satellite phone but was hopeless at using it. Dougie had been calling and texting all evening to find out how Kat was and had heard nothing, but this time he was in luck as the phone was picked up. The delay, however, was terrible.

'Hello? . . . Can you hear me, Dair? . . . How's Kat?'

'Dougie? It's Kat . . . Dair left his phone in the cubicle.'

'Kat! . . . Where are you?'

'Concussion and a nosebleed . . . They're letting me out in a minute.'

'Are they keeping you in overnight? . . . I am so bloody sorry.'

'Hospital.'

'How do you feel?'

There was a long pause and he thought at first they'd been cut off. Then she said, 'It hurts, Dougie. It really, really hurts.'

Despite the confused cross-purposes of the phone delay, he knew she wasn't talking about her head. A moment later, Dair's brusque Scottish tones were on the line and he told Dougie that Kat was fine and he would be informed of any change.

'It goes without saying that today represents a very serious security breach,' he said darkly. 'I want you to reread the brief about next weekend's hunting party very carefully, Dougie, and it is probably advisable to have no association with Miss Mason in the immediate future. I warn you, there are some pretty incendiary rumours going around, but thankfully nothing has spread yet. You *must* keep your nose clean. This is much, much bigger than you.'

When Vaughan rang his son back, he said, 'Seth's company is currently pitching to be a part of a Russian bid to produce flight simulators for the Indian Army. The Russians would rather keep it all at home, but they know that if the licence to develop the simulator software is granted in India, it will make it a more tempting contract for the army. And it would make a huge difference to Seth's net wealth.'

'How much is it worth to him?'

'Seven or eight billion at a guess.'

Dougie whistled. 'Which makes buying an English country estate in which to entertain the main players a fairly wise investment.'

'Most definitely. They love their hunting, these Russkies.'

'Even if it's outside the law?'

'That's part of the thrill. They want to ride over Queen and country like ancient conquerors. They can legally bow-hunt boar in Hungary or go pig-sticking in Spain, even shoot big game in Africa for enough dollars, but hunting deer in the parks of jolly old England on horseback like Henry the Eighth is a real culture kick for a post-Communist self-made man.'

Dougie knew he could trust his father for the heads-up. He only wished it didn't make him want to hang his own head in shame, particularly when he asked his father if he knew of any Russian arms dealers called Igor who were fond of slaughtering British wildlife.

'Could be Igor Talitov – known popularly as "I-gotta-lot-of". Met him on Hay Meredith's grouse moor last year. Total dipso and a terrible shot, but rather jolly for an oligarch. Lock up your daughters, mind you. Man's a total lady-killer.'

'I hope you don't mean that literally,' Dougie said weakly.

Dougie lay awake that night, feeling like an unwitting pawn in a game of chess or, more accurately, an animated character in a computer game.

Much as he loathed to admit it, Badger Man was right about one thing. The estate had been bought by an expert in virtual gaming action, and it was the platform on which Seth was designing a very real and ludicrously expensive diversion to entertain his guests. The English Hunting Game, a jolly jape through the woodlands with a spear and a trusty guide providing the walk-through and weaponry. Dougie had battled his way through plenty of virtual worlds drunkenly with friends, but it had never been a big addiction. This time, he couldn't drop the console and turn away while the characters met grisly ends. He already cared too deeply about those involved, most especially the redhead who was only ever destined to star in Level One of the game, the training level where nobody had big weapons and where techniques and strategies were honed and enemies identified.

Dougie had failed Level One. He wanted to retake it, but it was too late, and he was locked out of Level Two.

He spent most of the night searching the house, but finally located his contract in the sports bag he must have carried as hand luggage from LA. It seemed a lifetime ago. His jagged signature spoke of DTs, fast exits and flirtation, the happy-go-lucky scrawl of a chancer who never read the small print. The contents of the contract were heavily embedded in legalese he didn't understand. He read it so many times his eyes started to cross, fathoming out just a few basic facts, mostly that he owed back a hell of a lot of money, much of which he'd already used to pay off the worst of his debts in the States. The legal wording was too hard-core to understand more.

He picked up his phone, aware that it was the early hours now, scrolling through the numbers, lingering on Lake Farm, then flicking on to his old friend Milligan, who ran a club in Soho and would be barely warming up for the night: 'Might need somewhere to hide out, Mil.'

'Not a problem.' Mil, who was extremely well connected and largely moral-free, had helped his friend out of several troublesome situations, usually when Dougie's love life blew up in his face. 'When do you arrive?'

He looked up at the oil painting of the miller's daughter, now with no nose. It was another reminder of his naïvety. He had shot an arrow into it to show off to Dollar, unaware that he had already shot himself squarely in the foot by signing an unread contract, just as he'd always taken film parts without reading the scripts. The old Dougie might have stayed on for the hell of it, chancing his luck and playing at being a medieval huntsman. Equally, the old Dougie would have thought nothing of taking the opposite path and telling Seth to stick his job, packing up and leaving that night. Dougie figured he could pay back the money eventually, and his inbuilt bravura told him that the dotcom billionaire was hardly going to sue his arse in public, given that what he'd hired him to do was illegal. But that wasn't what was making him hesitate about leaving Eardisford. It was Kat. He needed to keep his head down and carry on working until he figured out what to do. He couldn't walk away knowing she thought so badly of him or abandon her before she'd attempted the Bolt, a feat he still worried was close to impossible. And he couldn't leave Harvey, his hounds and the hunt horses without knowing they were in safe hands. He also wanted to bowl out Badger Man.

'It might be a day or two,' he told Mil vaguely. 'Got a game of cricket to play.'

'You always had your priorities right, Everett.'

Chapter 50

The first concrete memory Kat had after falling off was bouncing around on the back seat of Dair Armitage's Range Rover with her head resting on a cartridge bag and the guns rattling on the rack above her. Later, at the County Hospital, there had been nurses and a nice female doctor who said she had a horse too and talked about dressage. Dair had appeared occasionally, asking how much longer it would take because he'd had a call to deal with some poachers.

Then Mags had arrived to take her home to Lake Farm, pink hair on end, driving far too fast as usual, although Kat recalled that no pheasants had been mown down on the way. She asked about Dougie several times and got no reply, although that might have been another memory blank. There had been a lot of loud music.

Officially declared mildly concussed, Kat went straight to bed while Mags raided the last of the Waitrose goodies in the fridge. Later, Cyn appeared for a night shift – an over-enthusiastic Florence Nightingale in winceyette pyjamas who woke Kat constantly with wet flannels and pulse-checks. It was only when tall, dour Pru took over in the morning that Kat learned the truth about her reputation.

'I hear you've been spying on Dougie Everett for the antis *and* the Brom and Lem.' Pru delivered a breakfast of doorstep toast and brick red tea on a tray at a quarter to six, turning on the radio for *Farming Today*. 'Frightfully impressive subterfuge, my dear. To think we all just assumed you and Dougie Everett were shagging like stoats. You're Eardisford's own Mata Hari!'

The sanctuary committee and volunteers all rallied to provide cover for Kat, insisting that she must rest for at least forty-eight hours after a head injury, but Kat wasn't good at resting, especially with such a heavy heart. She seemed to have a constant stream of visitors and 'carers', plonking down a cup of tea, asking if she was suffering blurred vision or dizziness and then asking if it was true that Dougie Everett had been hired to marry her.

'We're treating it as strictly confidential information for committee and activists only, Kat love,' Mags reported kindly. She and Russ seemed to have elected themselves primary carers, playing a lot of loud music and arguing. 'Russ thinks the more

452

cards we keep up our sleeves the better. For now, he says direct action is the way forward. And we all think you need protecting.'

'I can look after myself,' Kat insisted, wishing she could see Dougie. She still couldn't remember anything of her fall or its immediate aftermath, although Russ had it all on camera and said it was damning stuff. He had also told Dougie she never wanted to see him again, which infuriated her.

'You have no right to interfere with my life!'

'Irritability is a classic post-concussion side-effect,' Russ said calmly.

'I'm not irritable. I'm fucking annoyed at being treated like a psychiatric patient. I want to make some phone calls. In private.'

Waiting until Mags and Russ were out in the yard with the animals, Kat phoned Dawn.

'Promise me you're definitely coming next weekend? I need you to help me evict Russ.'

'I thought he'd moved out months ago.'

'He's found a reason to move back in.' She dropped her voice: 'I'll explain when I see you, but I'm practically being held *prisoner* here.'

'I'll bring the wire-cutters baked in a cake,' Dawn reassured her cheerfully.

Taking a deep breath, Kat phoned Dougie. He answered from one of the kennel pens, hounds baying all around him. She waited while he moved somewhere he could hear better, his voice husky and breathless: 'How are you?'

'Much better.'

'Thank God.'

'Can I see you?'

He hesitated. 'I'm not sure that's such a good idea.'

'Please, Dougie.'

There was an even longer pause. 'No, Kat. Trust me, it's for the best.'

'Trusting you is something I'm finding hard to do right now,' she breathed, but he had already rung off. She still held the phone tightly to her ear, as though some part of him was still inside it and she could keep it close. 'Loving is another matter.'

Chapter 51

Eardisford might have no mobile-phone signal or reliable internet coverage, but news that a pink car with eyelash decals stuck around its headlights was heading towards Lake Farm reached Kat almost half an hour before Dawn located the potholed track that was being patrolled by an aggressive peacock.

Setting out to meet her on Sri had seemed like a great idea, but it was Kat's first ride since the fall and she hadn't realized how nervous she'd feel. The mare was popping from several days off and raring to go, trying to tow Kat to the hidden meadow while her rider tried to persuade her to head through the woods towards the village instead. Then Kat met Meat and Two Veg in high humour because they'd just redirected the pink convertible several times from private estate roads where its driver was lost, each time sending her an even more roundabout way.

'Reckon she'll be halfway to Abergavenny by now!' Spud cackled.

Sensing a heroic chase might be in order, Kat decided to canter home at a good pelt, but Sri thought otherwise, particularly when she spied a box of pheasant poults on the back of Turnip's quad bike and went into sharp reverse before planting herself indignantly between two elder bushes, as though imagining she could no longer be seen.

The gamekeepers watched impassively as Kat flailed her legs in an attempt to get the mare moving again.

'You not riding out with the new master today?' asked Turnip, sounding like something out of *Black Beauty*.

'If you mean Dougie Everett, then no,' Kat mumbled, well aware that the entire village was gossiping about them now. Amazingly, the arranged-marriage story remained confined to a very few, sparing her at least some humiliation, although the rumour that somebody had put out as a smokescreen was not much better. The latest gossip – she strongly suspected Russ and Mags of spreading it – was that Kat had discovered Dougie *in flagrante* in the Eardisford tack room with a male groom.

She kicked some more, but Sri thrust her nose in the air and refused to budge.

Shrugging off his shooting waistcoat, Meathead strode forwards and waved it around his head like a football rattle. 'Get going, you old bag!'

At this Sri shot out from the bushes, dancing in the direction of home in a crab-like sideways trot, straight into the path of a bicycle freewheeling down the park drive, hounds teeming around its back wheel. As it slid to a halt at an angle in a shriek of brakes, she heard the familiar voice calling the hounds back urgently and turned to find Dougie looking up at her.

It was the first time she'd seen him since the confrontation in the woods. To her shame, as soon as she caught the glint of tousled blond hair in the sun, she felt the breath snatched straight out of her lungs and her tongue stuck to the roof of her mouth as though she'd just chewed on Pritt Stick. As Sri crabbed, she noticed that Dougie had fierce red streaks in his tanned cheeks, eyes intense as blue blowtorch flames.

Just for a moment the mare stood still and Kat knew that her own face was colouring too as her eyes fixed on his and couldn't look away.

'How are you?' he asked, in an undertone.

'Fine.'

'I hear Russ has moved back in.' There was an arrogant, urgent snap to his voice.

'He doesn't think I should be on my own so soon after a head injury, but I have a friend staying this weekend,' she said, flustered and aware that the keepers were watching, the smiling, kind-eyed hounds bounding around, four-legged reminders of everything old-world-colonial and wrong about Eardisford.

'It's good to see you back in the saddle.' He moved closer, dropping his voice so that only she could hear. 'You still have to ride the Bolt, Kat. It's so important to you.'

It seemed feeble to explain that she couldn't do it without him, but it was how she felt. His fierce positivity, encouragement and bravery had fuelled her in recent weeks. She'd felt true daring pumping back into her veins and it had been glorious, just as his loud, occasionally lusty affection had triggered a sea change within her. The cold glacier in which her libido had been trapped had melted, hot springs bubbling around her body, geysers of lust fountaining through her. They still did, just looking down at him now, holding his gaze, remembering the way he had pulled her right on to his saddle to kiss her.

'You've got the guts and the ability,' he urged, the husky voice so persuasively sexy that she knew she would be tempted to jump the moon if it asked her to.

'Will you help me?' she asked, lost in his eyes.

He looked away, watching his hounds milling around him, hands raking through his hair. 'I can't.'

Hurt, she glared at the wind socks that had appeared alongside the landing strip in front of the lake. 'Of course, Seth's arriving this afternoon, isn't he? Don't you all have to line up on the steps to doff caps?'

Dougie looked furious. On cue, the mare started spinning and backing up again. 'You need a stronger right leg and a better contact,' he told her brusquely, then put a hunting horn to his lips and called the hounds back with a series of long, shrill blows, to which they came leaping up, tongues lolling and tails spinning.

At this Sri pricked her curled ears and shot into the woods.

Kat was still plunging around in the undergrowth when Dawn rolled gently along the Lake Farm track in her new pink car, satnav loudly insisting she must take the first available U-turn and proceed to the public highway. She was being pursued by a furious Trevor, pecking at the shiny rear bumper.

'There you bloody are!' Dawn yelled, with relief, through the window, sending Sri into another hissy fit as she practically sat down in shock at the sight of the pink convertible, then doubled back when Trevor fanned his tail for a celebratory strut.

Dawn's tan was from a bottle, her blond hair sporting new extensions and streaked with on-trend blue to match the colour the air turned once she finally spilled from the car into Lake Farm, proffering two bottles of sparkling wine and two fat steaks. Beneath the gloss, she was clearly frazzled, turquoise contact lenses positively spinning with stress.

'You look amazing!' She hugged Kat with the relief of one who felt she had just crossed time- and war-zones by camel caravan, tank and microlite to reach her destination. She held her at arm's length to admire her. 'You are ripped! There's not an ounce on you. But, Kee-rist, do you need me to sort out that hair and the Scouse brows!' She kissed her nose and thrust the wine at her.

'You look fantastic too.' Kat laughed. Dawn arriving was like a rainbow coming out in a force-ten gale.

'Why can't you live somewhere normal?' Dawn marched into the house. 'Tonight, we're eating meat and decrying men, girl. Please tell me the vegan nursemaid's sleeping in his tepee in the woods this week.' She spotted Russ, sitting at his computer in a gloomy corner trying to upload video files. He didn't take this in good spirits.

'I'm here to look after Kat now,' Dawn said brightly, 'so you can push off and free-range, -lance or -load or whatever it is you do.'

Standing up, he adopted a heroic Heathcliff stance, somewhat marred by the fact his earphones were still plugged into the computer. The two squared up to one another, enmity exactly where they'd left it in February.

'Kat needs protecting right now,' he said darkly.

'Especially on the days you run out of clean pants,' Dawn muttered, under her breath, as Russ pulled out the earplugs and stalked towards the door, muttering about cricket practice and whistling for Ché, who was drooling beneath the table where Dawn had dumped the steaks.

Seeing Kat's open-mouthed shock at her rudeness, Dawn winked unapologetically. 'You did ask me to get rid of him, and for a man who doesn't live here any more, he still looks very much at home.'

'I think he's worried Seth's team will try to abduct me and force me into an arranged marriage,' she admitted. Russ had become very controlling in the days since the showdown in the woods, populating the few remaining spare runs, hutches and cages at the sanctuary with dull-eyed Death Row wildlife 'for their own protection', disappearing for hours on end with his video camera to 'monitor' Dougie exercising hounds and horses, and holding forth in the pub, where the talk was all of Bollywood balls, cricket balls and Dougie's tack-room lover, commonly believed to possess balls.

'We are going to discuss this at length later.' Dawn already had a bottle of wine open and her own emotional baggage to unload. 'Man, is it good to see you! *What* a month. I could kill Dave . . .'

Kat, who hadn't touched alcohol since her concussion, hoped it was safe to start again. She'd never been very good at daytime drinking, but it would be rude not to join Dawn, who was already pouring her heart out.

Selling the house had opened a lot of old wounds, and the exes' amicable parting of ways had broken down into vicious spats more than once over possession of the Dualit toaster or plasma TV as the tension of dividing their belongings coincided with pedantic solicitors, a bad survey, delayed completion, rented accommodation falling through and Dave's new girlfriend interfering.

'Dave has a girlfriend?' said Kat, watching Dawn's face pinch with pique.

'Brace yourself – they've been seen out double-dating with Nick and the sports masseuse.' In turn, Dawn watched Kat for a reaction, but there was no flinch of pain at the mention of Nick's name. 'The new squeezes are best friends. Just like old times.'

Kat's green eyes filled with compassion. 'How do you feel about that?'

'A lot more miserable than I should,' she muttered, pouring more wine and unloading her anger as one only can with the closest friends. 'I know we all move on – and I never want to be with Dave again – but nobody told me it would hurt this much. Getting divorced was like breaking out of Colditz for both of us, so why do I feel jealous every time I hear his new girlfriend's name?'

'Maybe you're not ready for him to be happy just yet.'

'I'm certainly pissed off he's got a sex life while I'm at home in a onesie with a *Downton* box set.'

'What happened to internet dating?'

'It's exhausting, Kat. I needed a break. It's like interviewing for a job every day of the week. All those questionnaires and top fives, then the emails and phone calls – not to mention Google detective work – and that's before you even meet. Then you do and it takes all of ten seconds to realize there's no chemistry at all.'

Kat gave her a sympathetic smile. 'I suppose there's also no friendship group to fall back on to give you time to let that chemistry develop naturally.'

'Maybe,' Dawn murmured doubtfully. 'I just hate it when they say "successful businessman" and it turns out they sell stuff on eBay. There are *so* many losers out there. And there's you living next door to a *bona fide* Hollywood heartthrob.'

'He hated Hollywood.' Kat drank more wine. 'His reviews always contained more about his love life, his background and his crooked teeth than his acting.'

Dawn watched her face closely again, noticing how luminous her eyes grew, a smile crossing her mouth like the sun bursting out briefly between clouds before she bit it away.

'So, tell me, if this crooked-toothed Hollywood failure living next door floats your boat, what went wrong?'

'The boat sank. He's employed by the estate to resurrect cruel, antediluvian pastimes for a few rich men's pleasure.'

'Stop talking like Russ and tell me how you really feel.'

'I happen to agree with Russ on this one. Private landowners have no right to think that, just because they have thousands of acres, they can put up *No Trespassers* signs and slaughter anything that crosses their land. This isn't medieval England, no matter how good Dougie looks in tights. He's totally out of date. He should have been born a Regency rake.'

'Reminds me of all the erotica books we swapped around on the cruises. I loved the historical ones. Rakes were always fantastic in bed, keeping their mistresses' quivering quims in a constant state of readiness.'

Kat reached for her glass again and, seeing it was empty, helped herself to more while Dawn still watched her closely, noticing the fierce red blush.

'You fancy the arse off him, don't you?'

Kat was increasingly uncomfortable with the direction her friend's line of questioning was taking. 'Everybody fancies the arse off him, Dawn.'

'Look me in the eye and tell me Dougie Everett doesn't turn you on more just by looking at you than hours of Tantric sex with the love wal-Russ?'

'I can't.' Kat drained half her glass. 'But I'm pretty sure I'm not frigid, whatever Nick said.' She blushed, just thinking about Dougie making muscles she'd forgotten about twitch and quiver.

'Hallelujah! Bollocks were you ever frigid!' Dawn flashed. 'Nick was a shit to make you think that. Trust me, Dave fiddled a lot in the final months and I thought there was something wrong with me, but there was simply no magic left in the wand. I'm as randy as a hot bunny in a spring meadow when the big bucks are in play. It's no wonder you freeze when Thumper gets out the organic joss sticks. We like our men to spoil us. Russ just brought you flea-infested wildlife to nurse in a cage.'

'You are so shallow.' Kat snorted with laughter. 'Russ really cared about this place and me – he still does. Some of us aren't turned on by money, Dawn.'

'Were you really turned on by Russ?'

She looked down at her glass, surprised to find it empty again. 'I'm not sure I ever truly was. I just hoped he might have the answer. He was like one of the feral cats here, coming and going as he pleased.' She smiled ruefully. 'I respect feral cats. They look after themselves.'

'They rely on you for food and shelter,' Dawn reminded her.

'They don't live in the house. If I wasn't here, they'd cope. Nothing else would last a day.' She looked across at the ancient, weak-hipped Labrador, who was flat out on the doormat where he slept for approximately twenty-three hours a day. Every time she passed him she checked that he was still breathing. 'I lost the old racehorse since you've been here, and I think the llama's on the way out. And a fox killed all the chickens.'

Dawn looked incredibly pleased with herself. 'That's why you're going to leave the committee and volunteers in charge here for a week and come on holiday with me. I knew I was right to plan something! Here,' she fished in her bag for a brochure, 'I still get a hefty discount from the cruise company so it's going to be my treat.'

'I can't abandon the animals.' Kat took it and then started to laugh as she read *The Love Boat Experience*. 'Dawn, this is a matchmaking cruise!'

'It's the solution to all your problems,' Dawn insisted. 'We're *both* going to find rich husbands. Yours will buy you a beautiful farm to run the sanctuary, preferably a lot nearer Rickmansworth.'

462

'I hope this is your idea of a joke.' Kat read the brochure, giggling at the photos of elderly couples on deck in sunset clinches.

'You have to marry to fulfil your promise to Constance,' Dawn reminded her, hurt by her lack of enthusiasm. 'And, trust me, there's no way you'll find a husband buried away in the middle of nowhere.'

'That's where you're wrong.' Kat was still laughing, reaching for her glass and tipping it up to her lips, not even noticing that it was empty. The wine had gone straight to her head and her freckled cheeks were very red. 'I received a marriage proposal only recently.'

Dawn's eyes widened in amazement. 'Not Russ?'

'God, no.' She fought to calm the giggles.

'Who then?' Dawn was agog.

Kat was shaking her head, the laughter dying now. 'It meant nothing. It was just a dare thing.'

'Dair?'

'That's right. A very stupid dare.'

Misunderstanding, Dawn thought the Dair in question was the bald, butch estate manager vying for her friend's hand. Having secretly been very excited at the idea of finally reacquainting herself with him and finding out whether the Vin-Diesel-meets-Sean-Connery man of her dreams matched the man she'd spent a drunken night with in Eardisford, she felt the wind dropping out of her sails.

'He must be smitten,' she said in a frozen voice.

'It was just a wind-up.' Kat glared at her empty glass. 'I was tempted to call his bluff and say yes, but some dares aren't worth the humiliation.'

'You were *tempted*?'

'Only to see the look on his face.' She shrugged, trying and failing to play it cool. 'The trouble is, he thinks he can get anything he wants by snapping his fingers. I know he's the hottest thing round here for miles – half the village ladies have burning crushes, and he's going to inherit a small fortune, according to Russ's cousins who are front of the queue – but I'm not playing truth or dare with him any more. They can all fight over him.'

'I had no idea he was so popular.'

'They'll all be after him at the Bollywood party.'

'What Bollywood party?' Dawn perked up.

'We're not invited,' she waved a hand drunkenly, 'although I've been dabbling with the idea of gate-crashing.'

'I'm game for that,' said Dawn, who had once sneaked into Jonathan Ross's Hallowe'en fancy-dress party, thanks to three pumpkins, a bin bag and a lot of chutzpah.

'Have you brought your riding kit?' Kat snorted.

'Eh?'

The giggles were ripping through her again, and Dawn regretted doling out the wine quite so fast. In the old days, they'd be on their fifth vodka Red Bull before Kat reached the weeping-with-laughter stage. She was already wired, and not warming to Dawn's millionaire-cruise suggestion. Dawn was struck by how much happened in Eardisford compared to Watford. Suitors seemed to be as abundant here as hops, apples and cattle.

'You need a real man,' she said, 'not some jumped-up Dairdevil, or that hippie drop-out you've adopted like one of the animals.'

The giggles had abated and Kat's green eyes glittered. 'I do *not* need a man, Dawn, even less a husband. Constance didn't order me to get married from her deathbed like some ancient Mrs Bennet on a bender, trying to palm me off on the first bloke with enough money to keep the dogs in Bonios. To her generation of women, marriage was a social requirement, and to ours it's a choice, but she passionately believed in it. She told me to marry for love, remember.'

'Because she didn't?'

'She married for the love of Eardisford.'

'Lighten up, Kat.' Dawn reached for the brochure. 'It's just a fun holiday. I'm not really about to dash back up the aisle.'

'I *am* light. I'm very light. Mine is the unbearable lightness of being single. I see the light!'

'Would you like a coffee?' Dawn asked. Kat was on inebriation fast-forward. She'd moved swiftly through the strident-debate to the surreal-statement stage without drawing breath. Soon she would adopt the excited look she always wore when she was about to do something dangerous, but first came the burst of fury.

'Who the fuck says love's such a great thing anyway? It just hurts you. That's why they call it falling in love. I've fallen a bit too hard lately, and it's bloody painful.'

'You're *in love*?' Dawn gasped.

'Of course not! Infatuated, maybe. Stupidly infatuated. Oh, shit, Dawn. All the time I've played truth or dare, I've been lying to myself.' Leaping up, she hauled a saddle from a rack in the kitchen and reeled outside towards the yard.

'What are you doing?'

'Playing the forfeit. Bolting before the stable door's closed.'

Dawn hurried after her friend, who was lurching into a stable with an alarmed-looking horse that Dawn recognized as the evil two-tone one with the funny ears.

'Kat, are you going riding?'

'Yup.'

'I hate to criticize your hosting skills, but I've only just arrived.'

'I promise I won't be long.' Kat tacked the mare up clumsily, Sri now blinking in blue-eyed astonishment, curly ears flicking back and forth. 'In about twenty minutes, you need to be standing by with the rubber ring, Dawn.'

Dawn stood back as she led the mare out into the yard. 'Is that a bit of stable equipment?'

'It's a life-saving device.' Kat grabbed her hat from a gatepost and crammed it on. 'There's one hanging up by the lake. I am *so* grateful for this, and I promise I'll make it up to you. Wish me luck and make sure the dogs don't follow me.' Kat mounted drunkenly and trotted away, almost falling off before she even got through the gate.

'Er ... how?' asked Dawn, as several four-legged friends shot in Kat's wake. Only the fat, milky-eyed Labrador stayed behind, waddling back into the cool of the house to try to work out how to get at the steaks.

Realizing she'd forgotten to say it – although she had no idea what Kat was trying to do – Dawn raced after the fast-disappearing horse. 'Good luck!' she yelled, sprinting through the gate and turning to look down the track. 'Good—Fuck!'

A huge shiny Range Rover grille was coming straight at her.

Seconds later, she found herself lying across a car bonnet. Through the tinted windscreen, she could see two worried eyes peering at her from between the rims of dark glasses and the peak of a flat cap. A song she recognized was booming out of the stereo.

'"Beautiful Dawn",' she gasped.

Chapter 52

Kat felt as if her veins were filled with pure liquid courage. Suddenly she understood why all those mounted hunt followers swigged vast quantities of alcohol in order to gallop across country. Why hadn't she thought of this before? Riding the Bolt would be easy. Sri was super fit; she was ready. All Kat had needed was Dutch courage. Dougie had told her she had the talent and ability to do it and he was right.

They jogged through the coppices and along the headlands to Duke's Wood at the far end of the estate and on to the folly. She tried not to think about the kiss they'd shared here, a kiss that had, for a brief moment, made falling in love the most exciting and delicious freefall of her life – until minutes later when she had fallen off and landed back in reality with a bump.

As soon as she heard the clock ring out the quarter-hour, Kat urged the mare into a gallop. 'We'll do it, Sri. We'll show them!'

She'd already ridden this part of the route at breakneck speed, but as soon as Kat set off at full tilt, she knew she'd made several fundamental errors in deciding to ride it drunkenly on spec. One was her inability to see straight or steer; the other was that most of the gates were still shut. She was in serious danger of literally gate-crashing.

'Whoa!' She hauled Sri up at the first, clambered off to open it and lead her through, dragged it shut again, then hopped around for what felt like minutes trying to get on again before pounding back into a belting canter, determined not to regret this, however dizzy she was feeling.

'Are you all right?' Dair had leaped out and now reached across Dawn sprawled on his bonnet to check for signs of life. 'Are you hurt?'

'I'm okay,' Dawn assured the rugged, tweedy man, whom she didn't recognize, although she immediately clocked a vintage Rolex on his wrist that was probably worth more than she'd just sold her house for, along with a signet ring on his little finger that had an enticing crest on it. She definitely recalled them from her drunken night in the Eardisford Arms.

'It's Dawn, isn't it?' he was saying, tilting his head down to line up with hers. 'Remember me? Alasdair Armitage?'

'Dair! Fancy bumping into you like this.' She beamed at him, and found herself looking at her own reflection in his mirrored dark glasses. Not bad for a crash victim, she decided, as she took in the casually tousled mane, wide eyes and car-show-model stance. He looked pretty impressive too – at least, the chin, which was all she could see, was fabulously square and manly.

'I am *so* sorry,' he was apologizing, offering his hand to help. 'I was swerving to avoid the peacock, then thought I spotted a horse heading off the public bridleway. I simply didn't see you running out.'

'Honestly, I'm cool.' She took the hand – lovely strong grip – but found she couldn't get herself off the bonnet.

'You *are* hurt.' He reached up to pull off the dark glasses. His eyes were the most amazing shade of caramel hazel and really rather kind. What was it Kat had called him? The hottest thing round here for miles?

'Really, I'm fine. You were only doing about five miles an

hour – I was probably the faster-moving object.' She admired the leather interior through the windscreen at close range. It was immaculately tidy, she noted approvingly. Dave's van had always been a tip, which she hated.

He tugged a bit harder, but still she stayed put.

'I think my bra straps have got caught up in the wipers,' she explained, flapping her arms to demonstrate. 'I'm trapped.'

Out of sight, Trevor let out a sympathetic cry as he strutted towards a wheel to give hell to a hubcap, pecking at Dair's calf as he passed.

Dair jumped sideways. A nervous smile flashed on and off. 'I'm afraid I'm somewhat averse to large birds.'

'I'm only a bloody size ten.'

'I was referring to the peacock.'

'Whoa!' Kat dragged Sri to a halt again and jumped off to open another gate leading into the conifer woods. As she did so, she realized the wine had not only made her fearless and light-headed but had also gone straight through her. She needed a wee urgently.

Hanging on to the reins with one hand and fumbling with her breeches with the other, she squatted between a mound of pine needles and a fringe of bracken. Sri regarded her with blue-eyed impatience, eager to get on, tugging back just as Kat got her knickers to her ankles so she keeled over into a patch of nettles. 'Ouch!'

Alarmed by the shriek, Sri pulled away further, and this time Kat was forced to let go of the reins. The mare stood a few feet away, watching disapprovingly as Kat hurriedly emptied her bladder.

At first, she thought the stinging around her knees and thighs was from the nettles, but then she saw her legs were crawling with wood ants, furious that she was weeing on their nest and determined to march across her bare bits to enact revenge.

'Ouch! Get off!' Still mid-flow, she moved away in a crab-like walk, brushing them off frantically. As she did so, Sri threw her head up and whickered, ears pricking.

'Oh, heck.' Kat stumbled backwards as she heard hoofs approaching, catching her heel on a root and crashing back into the nettles once more. The ants were still everywhere. 'Ouch!'

'Kat?' It was Dougie's voice, dropping to click and coo as he caught Sri. 'Are you okay? Did you fall off?'

'Fine! Stay back!' She fumbled frantically with her breeches, tipping off to one side and into a bank of ferns, the ants still clinging on and nipping angrily.

'What are you doing?'

'Just dropped my whip. Won't be a sec.'

She burst out from the undergrowth to find him looking down from an unfamiliar chestnut horse that backed away in alarm. The little Indian groom Gut was further back on a wiry Thoroughbred, alongside kennel man Rack on Worcester.

'You're not supposed to be here. This isn't a bridle path.'

'I was bolting but I'm too slow.' She could hear the church clock ring out the next quarter, mocking her failure. The wine was still coursing through her veins and the ants stinging, making her feel tetchy and belligerent as she glared up at him, all the more furious because he was so heart-turningly, stomach-kickingly good-looking, posing about in her life with those perfect cheekbones, jaw-line and straight nose, as though he was fresh from his trailer and a film camera was about to swing past on a wire at any moment.

'What the fuck possessed you to try now?' His face hardened. 'It's way too dangerous.'

'You told me to!'

'Not like this. Not today.'

'Well, I didn't get too far as you can see.' She clenched her buttocks tightly together as she felt an ant stinging its way beneath her pants.

'Have you been drinking?' he asked, watching in confusion as she shook one leg and did a few small jumps.

'Just a stirrup cup – you taught me the benefits of that,' she bluffed as the ants grew increasingly aggressive and she had to jump up and down harder, throwing in a few leg stretches to make it look as though she was warming up. 'I'll ride on if that's okay. I might not have made the time, but I'll carry on with this run as far as the farm, unless you're going to arrest me for trespass?'

'Of course not.' Dougie cleared his throat and glanced back at Gut and Rack, who were watching the encounter with interest. Turning to face her again, he eyed her warily before peering into the undergrowth behind her as though suspecting she'd been wiring up a hidden camera. 'You mustn't be seen here. There's a lot of extra security this weekend.'

'For Seth and his guests.' With a final few bunny hops, she took Sri's reins back and remounted. 'I know. It's all right. I'm going. Gotta keep galloping.'

He looked anxiously at his companions. 'I'll ride with you.'

'I'd rather you didn't,' she muttered. She was desperate to get out of sight somewhere private, then remove her breeches and pants to shake the ants out. They were eating her alive now.

For a moment Dougie's horse barred her way, along with the intense blue eyes that chased hers for contact.

'Your flies are undone.'

'Thanks.' She did them up and cantered off with as much

471

dignity as she could muster, given she was still carrying a small colony of stinging insects in her underwear.

'"Beautiful Dawn".'

The two words rendered Dawn momentarily speechless. Being wrestled manfully from the bonnet of a Range Rover by 'the hottest man in Eardisford' was alarming enough, but she couldn't be entirely sure that he hadn't just sung to her. It could be his accent, she reasoned, as she admired the cleft in his chin. He was taller than she remembered, and broader. And there was just one of him while there had been ten or twenty all spinning around last time she'd looked.

'It's great to see you again.' A shy smile appeared below the flat cap. 'You've changed your hair colour.'

'Do you like it?'

'"Beautiful Dawn".'

Oh, God, he *was* singing. Dawn had never admitted to music-snob friends like Kat that she'd played the James Blunt song on a loop on her iPlayer at the gym for months.

The man's only just proposed to your friend, the swine, Dawn reminded herself sternly. 'Are you here to see Kat?'

'I came to remind her about the ash dieback.'

'Sounds like a colour treatment.'

'It's a tree disease. Need to check she knows about the felling this weekend. Dangerous to go near Duke's Wood. Lots of big trees coming down.'

'Timber!' She beamed, admiring his neatly ironed checked shirt, its contents pleasingly flat-stomached and lean-hipped. Surely if Kat had turned him down, it would do no harm to flirt. 'I've always wanted to know more about lumber-jacking. Perhaps I can come and watch.'

'Definitely not. It's not something for ladies' eyes.'

'I've seen plenty of wood in my time.'

'I'm sure you have.'

'But of course there's leather against willow this weekend, which will be a sore sight for ladies' eyes. I love cricket. I bet you're a demon at the crease, aren't you, Dair?'

Dair smiled stiffly. 'I'm working all that day. Simulated game shooting.' He cleared his throat. 'Clay pigeons.'

'What a shame. I love a man in whites. Would you like a drink? There's a bottle of Prosecco open and I'm sure Kat won't be long.'

He glanced at his beautiful watch and grimaced. 'I have to meet a plane. Will you and Kat be in the pub later?'

'You can bet on it.' She gave him the umpire signal for 'six', both hands in the air, fingers pointing up.

Bottom on fire with ant bites and nettle stings, head throbbing, Kat trotted back to Lake Farm and found Dawn in a state of squiffy agitation as she rushed outside to meet her, wine glass in hand, having cracked into the second bottle. She was carrying the rubber ring.

'I'm here!'

But Kat had already jumped off, landing on the ground and bouncing up and down as though the concrete yard was a trampoline, desperately trying to loosen the invaders from her knickers.

'Aren't you swimming?' Dawn asked, as Kat quickly untacked Sri and pulled out the hosepipe to wash her off.

'What's the point? I thought I could rise to the challenge with a bit of fire in my belly, but I might as well face the fact I've got no backbone left.'

'Bollocks!'

'I'm sorry, Dawn. I'm a shit friend. You know the stupid

things I do when I'm drunk. It was selfish to leave you here.'

'I always love the stupid things you do when you're drunk, Kat. And I'm *so* grateful you left me here. Really. It's one of the best things you've ever done, buggering off like that. Hooray for doing stupid things when drunk. I will follow your lead.'

'Sorry?' Kat didn't hear as the water jetted out of the end of the hose in loud splurting hiccups and she ran it across Sri's patchwork body, bringing out strange blue freckles in her white sections.

Watching it pouring down on to the cobbles, Dawn remembered cheering Kat as she emerged pale, freckled and dripping from lakes and rivers to don a helmet and shoes ready to leap on a bike and pedal away furiously. The friends had swum together at the leisure centre two or three times a week when they were both nursing. She now turned to look out across the lake.

'What if *I* cross it first?' she asked, seeing a way to help, and to feel less guilty about chatting up Dair.

'You are kidding, right?'

'Why not?' She turned back. 'What are you doing?'

Kat had the hose end in her breeches now, shuddering with cold and relief as she doused the ant stings in a soothing flow of water. She didn't think Dawn was serious for a moment, knowing her tendency to talk things up, then back out. But she hadn't accounted for just how much wine Dawn had poured into an empty stomach.

'If you see me doing it, you'll know there's nothing to be afraid of.' Dawn pulled off her top to reveal a frilly red bra. 'I still swim every week. I'll leave the horse out of it for now, and I could do without that buffalo being around, but I don't mind. I'll be across it in two minutes. Then we'll do it together.'

She threw her T-shirt over a stable half-door, then took off her skirt.

Kat started to laugh. 'You really are going to swim, aren't you?'

'Follow my lead!' she shrieked, running towards the bank and diving in.

She resurfaced amid pond weed and alarmed duck calls. 'Jesus! It's cold!'

Kat switched off the hose and raced towards the bank. 'You're mad! Come out at once!'

'You'll have to come in and get me.' Dawn was already swimming out into the deeper water. 'Fuck, my contact lenses have gone funny! I can't see where I'm going!' She started swimming in a loop, heading blindly towards the causeway and the weirs that took water down towards the millstream.

'Turn left!' Kat yelled, pulling off her wet breeches and cursing as she tripped towards the rowing boat, the dogs running after her.

There was a frantic honking from the lake as one of the regular pairs of Canada geese started to warn Dawn not to get closer to his clutch of goslings.

'My eyes!' Dawn wailed, thrashing around as she tried to tread water.

Panic rising, Kat untied the rowing boat and hauled it to the end of the jetty, posting the dogs in before stepping in herself, the familiar terror already gripping her throat so tightly she could barely breathe.

As she began to row towards Dawn, who was now splashing blindly within inches of the angry goose, Kat heard another noise above the screeching, whooshing and honking: a plane engine.

Looking up, she saw an aircraft circling overhead, coming

down towards the landing strip. Maddie started to bark
furiously.

Chapter 53

Seth was not having an easy time piloting his VIP guest to his
country retreat. He'd planned to fly Igor personally from
Moscow to England, but Igor had protested that he had his own
Boeing on constant standby with a full complement of staff, so
why would he want to cram them all into the Indian's
Bombardier? Eventually, he'd ungraciously accepted a lift from
the London airport where his big private jet was now parked,
sending his entourage ahead in a fleet of glossy black people-
carriers. Seth, who would normally use a helicopter for such a
short transfer, was eager to show off the plane he'd just had
refitted with state-of-the-art technology, but Igor seemed far
more interested in Dollar. He had been trying to persuade her
to become the fifth Mrs Talitov for the entire flight. She loathed
the portly little Muscovite, with his bloodshot bullet grey eyes
and Miniature Schnauzer beard, and was playing it with
admirable professionalism as always, passing him Stoli Elit shots
and brushing off his lascivious advances. But Seth knew Dollar
was volatile at the moment. She had been very touchy since he'd
caved in to parental pressure and chosen his top three from the
Brides List – a choice he would consolidate on this UK visit –
and he was concerned that the Russian might just tip her over
the edge.

Unusually for Igor – who generally travelled with at least a brace of glamorous girlfriends – he'd brought nothing more feminine with him this weekend than cotton buds to clean his guns.

'I am here for sport,' he told Dollar, in his deep growl, hands creeping towards her rear end. 'My expectations are high.' His tarnished little bullet eyes targeted her buttocks.

'You will find this an exceptional sporting venue,' Dollar assured him coolly, her dark eyes deadly. 'Please return to your seat.'

As he did so, news came through that Igor's support team was stuck in a convoy behind an overturned livestock lorry on the M50. He was still snarling furiously into a mobile phone when they came in to land at Eardisford. Seth and Dollar, who both spoke Russian and recognized a lot of '*dolbo yeb!*' profanities, knew that it was more than his team's lives were worth not to find the quickest way around the three hundred chickens currently roaming the central reservation between junctions one and two, even if it meant driving straight over them.

Flying down over the estate, Seth hoped to distract his guest with the incredible beauty of the place – it was certainly making his own jaw drop: he had never seen it in its high summer glory or actually landed to inspect his investment in person until now – but Igor was still shouting into his phone, apparently firing at least one driver: '*Chush' sobach'ya, dobloed!*'

At last he threw his phone aside and peered angrily out of the windows as they roared low over the lake.

'*Ohooiet!*' His face lit up. 'That is a beautiful welcome, my friend.'

Seth relaxed. He'd always known Igor would love it. Eardisford was the sweetener guaranteed to win him the deal.

But the Russian wasn't looking at the house and parkland: he was gazing at a girl climbing out of the lake in nothing but a lacy red bra and panties, her hourglass body shimmering between the bulrushes.

'You gave me Ursula Andress! This is good start!'

Closer to, Dawn wasn't looking so hot. She had pond weed and algae in her hair, insect bites all over her goose-bumped skin and goose feathers stuck to her arms. And she was almost blind as she scrabbled through the bulrushes.

'Kat! Where are you? Did we make it to the other side?'

'Right behind you, and, yes, you did it!'

'Yay! *We* did it!' Unable to hear the rhythmic stroke of the oars or a small dog barking over the engine roar, which she took to be one of the JCBs, Dawn assumed her friend had swum in her wake.

'I rowed.'

'You rode the horse across!'

'No, I rowed a boat.' Kat clung to the sides of the little dinghy as the plane roared lower, its dark shadow crossing overhead as it lined up with the landing strip alongside the lake.

'You got across. That's what counts. What's that noise?'

'The new neighbour's just arrived. We have to get you out of here.' Kat was still almost paralysed with fear, wobbling her way towards the marshy banks. The dogs raced around on board, thinking they were about to get off, unbalancing the boat as she tried to angle it alongside the rushes so her friend could get in. 'Hang on, I'll –'

'I'll drive you both,' insisted a sharp Scottish voice, as a figure in a flat cap loomed amid the reeds and irises to swathe Dawn in a checked blanket and whisk her away before the plane landed. 'Get out of the boat, Kat.'

But Kat was floating rapidly back out to open water on a conveyor belt of ripples.

The plane was on the grass now, engines screaming as it braked.

'I'll see you back at the farm,' she called. Rowing across the lake as fast as she could, catching crabs all the way, she was behind the cover of one of the islands when the steps were lowered on the newly arrived plane.

She let the boat drift for a moment, exhausted. There were still twenty yards of lake to cross before she reached the jetty. Now she saw a figure standing on the rickety wooden planking, the sun behind him, his hair a halo of gold.

'Swim it! I dare you!' called a persuasively husky voice.

In the boat, Maddie went into a frenzy of barking as she spotted her chum Quiver admiring his reflection in the water.

Kat stared at Dougie's square-shouldered silhouette, butterflies rising through her so fast she was surprised they didn't jet propel the little boat straight across the lake and on to the jetty. Her heart was going crazy, like a guitar tremolo. She could hear it strumming, ringing, pounding in her ears.

Equally excited, Maddie bounced around at the prow of the boat, claws skittering against the wood as Quiver yipped in greeting. With a loud plop, she threw herself in to swim to him, quickly followed by a less elegant splash as ever-faithful Daphne flew in her wake with a Dachshund belly-flop.

'Shit!' Kat stood up in a panic and the boat gave an almighty lurch, making her sit down again. The ringing in her ears was coming and going and she was terrified she was about to pass out.

The dogs were already halfway to dry land, pursued by an irate Canada goose.

'They're fine and so will you be!' Dougie laughed, scooping Quiver up and stooping down to fish the elderly terriers out as they paddled up, grateful for the cool dip in the evening heat. He gazed across at her. 'Just trust yourself.'

Kat gripped the sides of the boat, wobbling to her feet, telling herself that that she could not be outdone by a pair of deaf and incontinent dogs. *I am going to do it.*

The ringing in her ears was back. Then, as she looked across to the jetty to gauge the distance, she realized Dougie's high-tech mobile satellite phone was ringing, stopping and ringing once more.

She sat down again gratefully.

'You can do it, Kat!'

'Answer your phone!'

'It'll go to voice mail. I want to see you swim.'

'It could be an emergency.'

Wearily, he plucked it from his pocket and looked at the screen. Then he held it out and let it fall into the lake.

'What did you do that for?'

'It's a dropped call.'

'You idiot!'

'Idiotic indeed,' carped a dry Scottish voice.

Kat squinted across the lake as another silhouette joined Dougie on the jetty, shorter and squatter with a shadowed cowpat of a flat cap on his head.

'That phone is not your property, Dougie,' Dair berated him. 'Your friend's in the house, Kat!' he called, across the lake. 'I've lit the range.' He turned back to Dougie, eager to gather his stray team member. 'We're needed, Everett.'

'I'm not interested. I'm watching Kat swim.'

'This is not the time to enjoy bathing diversions. Come with me.'

'Fuck off.'

'Your job depends on it.'

'Tell them to stuff the job.'

'*My* job depends on it.'

480

'Ha!'

'I've heard the rumours. We all know what you're doing to Kat. Leave her alone.'

'What's he doing to Kat?' Kat yelled from the boat.

'Yes, what am I doing to Kat?' Dougie growled at Dair.

'The whole village is talking about it. How you took a bribe to try to make her marry you.'

As both men squared up to one another on the narrow jetty, eclipsing the sun, an aggrieved moan came from the lake and Usha bobbed towards them, horns full of pond weed, defending her territory. Such was her bulk, the rip tide curved back to Kat's little boat, causing it to sway back into the island, ricocheting off a fallen tree. She flattened down in the jolting hollow, her head swamped with flashbacks. The blackout, ear-ringing fear was overwhelming now. All she could see was cold, breathless darkness, although she could clearly hear two men shouting above the lowing of a distressed water buffalo.

'Kat knows exactly what I was asked to do!' Dougie yelled.

'Leave her alone.'

'That's up to her to decide, not a bunch of interfering locals.'

'You have been warned of the consequences, Dougie.'

'I'm just here to get her to swim, nothing more.'

Right now Kat did not want to swim anywhere, and Dougie making her heart explode for no better reason than his desire to see her do a Rebecca Adlington across the lake was no help when she was in the middle of a panic attack. She just wanted silence and a chance to regroup.

'Don't be so fucking selfish, Dougie!' Dair bellowed. 'Think of your colleagues.'

'I am not tipping my cap to a fucking Russian hood.'

'That's enough!' Kat wailed, boat rocking. 'Both of you

go! You're not on estate land. You are trespassing. GO AWAY!'

Dougie and Dair stopped glaring at each other and turned to the mass of red hair and white knuckles in the little boat.

'I'm not going anywhere.' Dougie was already kicking off his shoes and turning to dive in past Usha. 'I'm coming to get you.'

'I do *not* want to be rescued!' Kat held up her hand. 'I'm very happy right here where I am. And stop stressing Usha out!'

'You heard the girl,' Dair said, with satisfaction, stepping forward to block Dougie's path. 'Let's go. We were due at the security briefing five minutes ago. You'll get a formal warning for this, Everett.'

'Get lost,' Dougie snarled, but he stepped back and called across to Kat. 'You're really okay?'

'I'm fine, Dougie! Jolly boating weather. It's all part of the therapy. Please just leave me to it. I mean it.'

Usha was bellowing her head off now.

Casting a final worried glance over his shoulder, Dougie turned to leave.

Dair raised his arm to Kat in farewell as he hopped after Dougie, protesting furiously that he was insufferable and probably working with Russ's undercover vigilantes, his voice trailing away.

Kat wasn't listening. She was just relieved to be able to cling to her boat and find breath eking back into her lungs.

'Wimp, wimp, wimp,' she berated herself, pressing her face to the sun-warmed wood of the plank seat, breathing creosote and sun-cream. Knowing they were gone, she slumped down with relief, harvesting all her will-power to make it to the safety of the wooden jetty.

*

It took Kat half an hour of loin-girding and prayers to get back into Lake Farm, by which time she was astonished to find the house sweltering from the roaring range and Dawn ensconced in the bath.

'Dair lit it,' she called, through the bathroom door, when Kat tracked her down. 'He's incredibly practical, isn't he? He had to dash off for a meeting with Seth – man, it sounds so glamorous in that house. He's hired a clutch of supermodels just to drift around looking pretty this weekend, like rented floristry. I can't wait to hear all the gossip. I said I'd buy Dair a drink in the pub later as a thank-you. I'm hoping I might get us tickets to the Bollywood bash. Do you have any eye drops?'

She had taken the last glass of wine up to the bath with her and the lurchers had stolen the steaks, leaving Kat with little choice but to take her friend to the pub if they wanted to eat more than beans on toast and goose eggs, yet she felt jumpy at the prospect of village scrutiny. She needed a long heart-to-heart with Dawn: she wanted to unravel her confused feelings and figure out what to do. But Dawn was on a mission.

'Dair couldn't have been kinder. I think you've got him all wrong,' she insisted, as she wriggled into a strappy dress, covering her reddened eyes with dark glasses. 'You don't mind him being there tonight, do you? I know you two have recent history, but I always think it's best to move swiftly on from these things, don't you? It's only a quick drink.'

'I'd hardly call it history.' Kat pulled on a pair of jeans and trailed into the bathroom to clean her teeth. 'Constance used to call him the Highland Bull, which she pretended was to do with his flat cap looking like a forelock, but you can guess the real reason.'

'He's hung like one?' Dawn asked hopefully, shivering with anticipation.

'I think it's more to do with the crap that comes out of his mouth.'

Chapter 54

Dougie was furiously bowling a tennis ball against a wall in one of the old carriage houses, making Quiver spin and yap as he leaped in the air trying to catch it. He was aiming at one dis-coloured brick at wicket height, the angry repetition the only thing that was stopping the coiled spring in his mind over-wind-ing to breaking point. He was sparring for a fight – the desire to knock Dair's block off earlier had been almost overwhelming – but he could hardly march into the main house and start swing-ing punches at Seth and his VIP guest, which would only make him look more of a prize idiot and probably get him killed by a bodyguard before he'd rescued the girl and driven off into the sunset. In his head, he had a legion of heroic feats he would enact to prove to Kat that he wasn't a total numskull moron, but in his heart he couldn't shake the belief that he was never going to slay a dragon so well armed and connected. It would take a cleverer head than his. All he had was forty hours, then forty overs of cricket.

He struck the discoloured brick square, imaginary wicket flying, before bad light stopped play, the last rays of red sunset flooding through the arched doors.

Dougie guessed his armour was pretty tarnished, and Kat clearly had no truck with heroic stunts, which rather limited his repertoire. He probably wouldn't impress her by bowling out the entire village for ducks, but he was still determined to acquit himself with honour and help his team to victory.

Having been handed the task of captaining a cricket team for the Gough Memorial Trophy match, Dougie had enlisted the help of one of the estate groundsmen, Vic, who had once tried out for Gloucestershire and was among the few remaining Eardisford staff from Constance's era. Vic knew everybody and was such a friendly, chatty soul that he had no difficulty in hoodwinking some of the newer employees into the first eleven, which both men were convinced was a crack team. Guest and entourage, it was assumed, would have nothing to do with the lowly village match, but Dougie hadn't forgotten Seth's passion for the game.

As he bowled again, he heard a step behind him. 'Cricket is the only reason you are still here.'

The ball was wide, ricocheting off the mortar and disappearing overhead towards the open doors where Dollar caught it. She continued reading an email on the tablet she was holding with the other hand.

'You will have to do better than that on Sunday. It is a very good thing that we have brought professionals, I believe.'

He turned to look at her, magnificently out of place in a tailored red linen dress and high heels that emphasized her aggressively toned slenderness, chital eyes kohl-rimmed and huge. Rack the kennel man was hanging over a half-door nearby, open-mouthed. Equally entranced, little Gut was pressure-hosing the cobbles a few feet behind her, not noticing that the nozzle was pointing at his own feet. The water spray catching in the evening sun cast a rainbow over her head.

'Are you talking about hunting or cricket?' Dougie asked, wandering across the dusty flagstones to collect his ball.

'Cricket, of course. Seth has no interest in hunting, luckily for you.' To Dougie's surprise, her eyes glowed with warmth when they finally looked up. She tucked the tablet under one arm and pressed her hands together in a *namaste* greeting. 'Where is your phone? I've been calling, but there is no answer.'

'It fell in the lake.'

'No matter. We will replace it.' She pulled out her tablet again and tapped a note into the screen. 'This stableyard is looking most impressive. The horses are very fit, I take it?'

'They're getting there. They'll be hard-core by the start of the season.' Dougie stepped out into the courtyard. He was nonplussed by her upbeat attitude, having fully expected her to be in Kali warrior-goddess mode, ready to read the Riot Act and pull out her gun, demanding that he show respect and gallop after muntjac, bowstring drawn.

'Seth is very much looking forward to the cricket match,' she told him, a hint of a smile touching her wide, scarlet-painted lips.

He groaned when she broke the news that two professional Indian international cricketers had been invited to guest in the team – to be passed off as members of Seth's staff – and were staying at the local spa hotel, awaiting Dougie's instructions.

'Please tell me this is a joke.'

'Why would I joke? Seth takes cricket and business very seriously,' she informed him, smile vanishing, dark eyes studying his physique and noting the changes with approval: his body had hardened with physical work and tanned deep butterscotch in the sun, which had bleached near-white streaks in his tousled hair. 'You are in better shape, although your personal grooming still lacks finesse. We must get your hair cut before Seth sees you.'

Dougie resented being assessed like a show horse, but that

was nothing in comparison to having his cricket team hijacked, and he refused to be side-tracked. 'We can't put hired ringers in the estate side. The village is mutinous enough as it is. I need to speak with Seth about this.'

'That isn't possible. He is fully occupied with his guest tonight. There is a very precise schedule of entertainment.'

'Don't tell me he's flying in Elton John and Rihanna, or is he saving them for tomorrow?'

Dollar cleared her throat, not looking at him, and he realized he was far closer to the mark than he'd imagined. 'Tonight is just a select gathering. Tomorrow evening, as you know, we have a Bollywood theme and three hundred guests have been invited. Sunday will be devoted to cricket. We hope that the estate will be preparing for victory.' She studied her screen again. 'Seth himself will bat third.'

Dougie's team line-up was now in disarray. 'Why didn't you say he wanted to play too?'

'Of course he will play. It is good PR. Igor and the rest of the party will be kept fully entertained by Dair's team throughout the weekend so Seth can be available to play on Sunday after-noon. He would like to keep his identity very low key until the end of the match, when he intends to make a small speech to introduce himself before the trophy presentation.'

'Won't the villagers recognize him from the party?'

'He will be anonymous there too. Seth is a very modest person. He feels it is important to make a positive impression on the local community before he reveals who he really is.'

Dougie looked up at the sky. 'He won't do that by buying his way to victory, no matter how many mango cocktails he hits the locals with the night before, especially as they'll be at the "servants' party".' He looked at Dollar, blue eyes imploring. 'Didn't he learn anything from the point-to-point fiasco? This isn't a computer game you can beat with a cheat code, demoting everyone else to drones.' He ran his hands through his hair despairingly. 'I suggest we offer the village team one of the pros and call them "international guest stars", and we can probably rescue this with full honours.'

'Seth will not be prepared to do that,' Dollar said matter-of-factly. 'He wants to win the match.'

'In that case, tell him I quit. Cricket was a reason for staying here, and this definitely isn't cricket.'

For once her face betrayed her, dark eyes widening to saucers. 'This is most unwise. Your contract cannot be verbally terminated, Dougie. I have already had to work *very* hard to gloss over your reluctance to honour it in recent days. There will be very severe consequences if you insist on leaving us completely, on this weekend especially.'

'You hired the wrong man.'

Glancing over her shoulder to see Rack still gazing at her in mute wonder and Gut pressure-hosing the same few inches of cobbles, Dollar stepped closer to him, lowering her voice to an undertone: 'I would s*trongly* advise against this. You have a lot of ground to make up, it is true. Your start has been unsatisfactory, and the business with the girl is very disappointing, but we can still turn this around.'

'I can only hunt within the law,' he hissed. 'And I'm not some fucking gigolo.'

'You should have thought of that before you signed the contract.'

'I was in no state to sign that thing, as well you know.'

'Indeed.' She stared at her screen again, her deep voice little more than a whisper. 'You are not alone there. I should have warned you, but my curiosity and attraction were too great.'

'What are you talking about?'

'I will come to the mill later. We can only talk about killing contracts in complete privacy.'

Put like that, it sounded worryingly lethal.

Chapter 55

If the biblical silence that fell when Kat walked into the Eardisford Arms told her instantly that she was at the centre of a village scandal, the fact that Dawn and Dair didn't appear to register it told her they were in the centre of an equally big and unexpected village romance.

Mags frantically beckoned her to the bar. 'Is it true?' she stage-whispered, already pouring her a free pint. 'Did he really propose?'

'Give him a chance, they're only just sitting down.' Kat watched Dair holding back a chair for Dawn at the table by the unlit fire, where his obedient pointers were already *in situ* amid the resident terriers, watching their master jealously. Was it her imagination or was Dair bowing now?

'I'm talking about Dougie Everett,' Mags pursued. 'I mean, we know he was paid to marry you, but I hear he actually *popped the question*?'

'What'd you say?'

'She said, no, o' course.'

Kat pulled out her biggest smile. She had an audience several earthmen deep. 'This has been blown out of all proportion,' she assured them. 'Really. It was just a joke.'

'Not what we heard.'

489

'Trying to get you out of the farm, he is.'

'The Hon Con would be tossing in her grave.'

'We'll get the bastard for this.'

'Leading a poor young girl astray, and him a Hollywood star.'

'Did he give you one?'

Kat deflected the attention as best she could, smile to the fore, wishing she had her own bubble to climb into as Dawn and Dair clearly had. There was a chair for her at their table, but she hung back, preferring to take her chances with the Greek chorus, however gladiatorial, than to muddy the waters between Orpheus and Eurydice.

She'd thought the drunken tête-à-tête between them on her friend's first visit had been a one-off, but within minutes of Dawn buying Dair a pint, the two were going heart to heart as well as nose to nose, comparing house-selling horror stories, box-set viewing tastes, quiz-show favourites and some alarmingly right-wing views about immigration. Seeing them together again, it was blatantly obvious they got on famously, Dawn providing the bubbles to Dair's dry sophistication. And they looked good together too, Kat was surprised to note. Suddenly Dair looked more Bruce Willis than William Hague, manning up alongside such feminine glamour; and cast against his tweedy splendour, Dawn was less a gaudy urban bird of paradise than a kingfisher.

'There's chemistry there.' Mags sighed and the earthmen united in agreement as they watched Dair and Dawn laughing, body-mirroring, self-grooming, touching fingers and drinking like fish.

'Make a nice couple.'

'Needs a wife, does Dair.'

'He's a good catch.'

'Lovely man.'

'Backbone of Eardisford.'

'How can you *say* that?' Kat lamented. 'He's a terrible shit-stirrer.'

'Can't avoid shit if you work with beasts and earth.'

'Oh, stop being so bloody rural. This is my lovely mate. With *Dair*.'

Kat had a suspicion that Dawn saw trips to Herefordshire like the stress-busting all-night benders they'd once enjoyed as students, then later on package holidays and hen nights where different rules had applied. When Dawn let her hair down, her common sense went with it. Her dodgy male conquests had once been legendary, along with her table-dancing, gate-crashing high spirits. From what Kat could gather, she had adopted much the same philosophy while on board the cruise ships, but with less bed-hopping and more tabletop tangoing. The last few weeks had clearly stressed her out enormously, and tonight she was letting her hair down with old-style binge-drinking bravado.

She was skipping towards the Ladies now, dark glasses on top of her head, and, to Kat's horror, blowing a kiss to Dair over her shoulder as she went. Just as alarmingly, he blew one back. Kat stalked hurriedly after her for a private loo consultation.

'Kat, is that you? Dair's offered to buy us dinner,' Dawn said happily, through the cubicle door. 'So kind.'

While Kat knew her friend could certainly do with something to soak up the booze, she wasn't keen on sitting between the two if they were blowing kisses after the garlic mushrooms and talking about claw-back agreements and *Game of Thrones*. 'We can't leave the dogs much longer, and Jed's already putting us together a take-out.'

'Don't be a spoilsport.' Dawn burst out to wash her hands before rearranging her breasts inside her balcony bra, her dark glasses falling back on to her nose.

'Dair's got a big day tomorrow.' Kat tried another tack. 'Best not keep him out late.'

'Ah, yes, the Russian shooting guest. Apparently he's a *really* big player. Dair says Dougie Everett's in deep shit because he refused to take him hunting out of season or something.'

'He did?' She levered up her friend's dark glasses to stare into her eyes. 'He refused to hunt?'

'Dair thinks he'll be out of a job soon.'

They turned as two girl grooms bustled in for a confab, eager to claim the Eardisford Arms ladies' sanctuary for themselves.

Dawn quickly applied more lip gloss, betraying how drunk she was when the sponge applicator shot up her nose. '*Please* say it's cool with you to stay and eat here, Kat.'

'It's cool to stay and eat here.' She sighed, smiling at the way Dawn's face lit up. 'But I do have to go and check the animals, so I'll bring the car back to pick you up.'

'Are you sure?' Dawn hugged her.

'Please have a big pudding and lots of coffee.'

'I promise I'll behave. No boffing while you're gone. Shit Friend of the Year Award transfers to me.' Her voice dropped from a whisper to a breath in Kat's ear. 'I *really* fancy him. That's the one thing you forgot to tell me when I woke up with Hopflask amnesia.'

Kat was taken aback. 'Are you talking shag, marry or die, or really fancy?'

'I'm talking shag him, marry him, die for him. He's just my type. You *know* he's just my type.'

'I genuinely didn't.' She laughed, bewildered but pleased. 'And you have every right to call this one. You have maximum respect. You swam the lake.'

'You'll do it. Follow my lead, remember?' Dawn rushed for the door.

'Nose!' Kat called her back, fetching a hunk of loo roll to remove the lip gloss.

'I haven't felt so attracted to a man since before I was married.' Dawn blotted it gratefully, pulling off the dark glasses, eyes no longer sore and red but glittering like smoky quartz. 'I don't even care if he sees it. It's like being drunk on lust.'

'That's just because you're drunk, Dawn.'

When Kat headed back to the bar to fetch her bag, talk had moved on to Seth's arrival at Eardisford.

'You should have seen all the blacked-out cars arriving earlier – it was like one of those earth summits.' Mags was holding court. 'And there've been helicopters this evening. I thought Russ would be casing the joint, but he's still at nets.'

'We all know how obsessive Russ is about cricket.' One earthman cleared his throat.

Another chortled, 'The only thing guaranteed to distract young Hedges from wild animals is cricket.'

Kat's suspicions were alerted. 'Is he really at nets?' she asked Mags, realizing most of the village cricket team were drinking around her. It was unlike Russ to keep such a low profile.

'You know Russ.' Mags wiped the bar with a cloth. 'If he says he's at nets, he's at nets. He's as honest as the day's long, that boy. And days are long this time of year.' She looked up, her wide face at its most cheerily blank, a round apple of life-is-rosy reassurance. 'What are you wearing to the Bollywood party, Kat? Think I can get away with my fox costume and a turban?'

'I'm not invited.'

'Course you are. Everyone is. Check your post-box, you daft cow. More cider?'

'No, thanks. I've got to get back to the farm. Whatever you

do, don't let Dair buy Dawn any Hopflasks, Jägermeisters or flaming sambucas.'

Taking a deep breath, she headed to the table to penetrate the flirtation force-field. 'I'll be back in an hour or so.'

'I'll see this lady home later, Kat,' Dair insisted, eyes not leaving the smoky quartz come-ons.

'That's *so* kind.' Dawn smiled widely, gazing straight back. 'It would save poor Kat a journey.'

Kat knew she could never hope to police this amount of mutual attraction. 'I'll leave the door open. Try not to startle the dogs when you come in. Or me.'

Chapter 56

Having paced around the mill house all evening, furious with himself that he'd junked his phone and cut off his means of contacting the outside world, including Kat, his father for legal advice and a legion of friends and contacts to launch himself back into London life – or possibly wish farewell to it if Dollar's 'contract termination' was as sinister as it sounded – Dougie was about to give up on waiting and set out to the pub when she finally appeared, glittering luminously in a dress that appeared to be made of huge pink sequins sewn together with fishing line and feathers.

'Forgive me. I was trapped at the party. Igor is hard to get away from.'

He was almost floored by a kiss that seemed to come from nowhere, accompanied by a full body slam.

'I . . . have . . . been . . . eaten alive . . . waiting for this,' Dollar gasped.

She had him pinned up against the back wall of his hallway already.

'Whoa – whoa!' He prised her off as best he could, whistling Quiver away as he growled underfoot. 'We need to get some facts straight.'

'We will have intercourse first, talk afterwards.' She was ripping at his belt now.

'Let's take this a bit slower.' He ducked away, big charming smile coming out in self-defence. 'I think we both deserve a quick debriefing before any briefs come off.'

'It is admirable that you refuse to marry the Mason girl.' Her mouth chased his. 'I think you and I will make a great team.'

'Slower than that.' He gulped. He had totally misread the obsessive technical interest she'd always shown in her calls, the deep, modulated voice so good at covering emotion. Even now, she sounded as though she was reading a quick news bulletin, as she insisted, 'I cannot stay long. The party is proving difficult. Igor is an evil man. He has already hinted that he wants to buy the house, and Seth would sell him anything to get this deal, but it is too early to play our best negotiating card. You and I need an exit strategy, Dougie, and I have the answer. We must kill our contracts with a suicide pact.'

Dougie cleared his throat, mind reeling. 'That sounds drastic.'

'It is not so difficult. We can escape together.' She wrapped herself around him again, lips closing in.

Caught in an uncomfortably amorous half-nelson, Dougie leaned away. 'If Seth sells Eardisford, my job would cease to exist.'

'All Eardisford-based staff contracts automatically transfer to the new owner in the event of its sale, like any business acquisition. You'd simply be sold along with it, Dougie.'

'Will Seth really sell it? The paint's still drying.'

'Seth is very impulsive. He buys many investments that he doesn't keep, and some of them become a part of business deals. He has a personal connection to the estate here, but he has no great attachment to it. It was purchased to impress Igor, and Igor is already entranced by its history, its beauty and the *rusalka* he believes lives in the lake.'

'What is a *rusalka*?'

'It is a Russian river mermaid.' She started to undo his shirt buttons. 'It is a fantasy figure of great seductive quality. Igor swears that he saw one as we landed.'

Remembering that Kat had been in the lake at the time, Dougie felt his veins harden with anger. Shirt hanging open now, he retreated to the coffee-maker – which he had never used, preferring instant shaken straight from jar to mug – and busied himself with it to keep Dollar at a distance.

'I do not want a beverage, Dougie.'

'I do.' He unhooked a filter. 'Is Igor a serious threat?'

'If this weekend is a success,' Dollar leaned against the millwheel window to watch him, 'Eardisford will almost certainly become a part of the deal.'

'What about Lake Farm?' He looked at her over his shoulder.

'That is not yet Seth's to offer,' she said softly.

He let out a sharp breath of relief. 'And this deal Seth wants to be a part of is a bid to build simulators for the Indian Army?'

Dollar's eyes widened almost imperceptibly. 'How do you know about it?'

'Everybody knows about it,' he bluffed, turning back and scooping up fresh coffee grounds. 'Like everybody knows I was offered a mint to marry Kat. You can't keep a secret round here. My name is poison right now and Seth's will be too, once the jungle drums spread the word that he's letting Igor Talitov take pot shots at Eardisford's protected species to broker arms deals.'

'Is this a blackmail threat, Dougie?'

He shook his head, tamping down the coffee and slotting the filter back in. 'It's just what happens round here.'

'It is incredibly important to Seth to secure this deal. His charitable foundations in India make education possible for the poor. His colleges for engineering and technology are already producing some of the brightest graduates in the country. But there is much prejudice to battle, and a contract like this will provide work opportunities for a great many.'

'And put Seth among the world's richest entrepreneurs.' Dougie was unmoved, pressing buttons randomly on the coffee-maker.

'That is true. He could buy ten more Eardisfords if it succeeds.'

'And if it doesn't?' He pressed a few more buttons and the machine started to hiss.

'He does not see failure as an option. There's something about Seth you have to understand. He seems childlike, laid back and generous, like everything's a great joke, but he is the worst loser in the world and he cannot let failure go.'

Dougie noticed how her eyes changed when she talked about him. For a woman who had just body-slammed him lustily, demanding they run away together, she spoke with extraordinary tenderness and her face, usually so expressionless, had lit up.

'Like you, I would very much like my freedom,' she was saying, 'but my contract is a lot more complicated than yours and my debt a good deal larger. I owe Seth my life. He saved me. I am called Dollar because he bought me for that amount.'

Dougie's mouth dropped open.

'My real name is Dulari,' she explained, without sentiment. 'It is not so different. I was born in Bengal, the fifth daughter in my family and of little value to them. Ours was a very poor rural village and we all dreamed of getting out. I was barely educated when I left at thirteen with a group of young girls. We were told we would be chambermaids in big hotels in Delhi. Instead we were sold to a brothel. It was owned by an industrialist and I was offered to rich clients to sweeten their deals.

'The other girls survived by day-dreaming that these men would rescue them, or by prayer and drugs, but I was not like that. I fought the men and I was beaten regularly. When they could not make me work, I was due to be "disposed of". That was when a young British businessman came to the house, a guest of the owner, who thought his girls would seal the deal. The man was very angry with what he saw, but I think he hid it well. He asked for me. They tried to make him take another girl, but he was adamant. As soon as we were alone, he talked very quickly, as I am talking now, asking me questions in fluent Bengali with the craziest accent. It was the first time I had laughed in months because his voice was so silly, but he talked very seriously and I had to listen. He wanted to save all the girls, and he guessed I was in the biggest danger so he wanted to buy me that night. He promised I would be safe, and I trusted him. The owner let him buy me for a dollar. It became my name. He always said it was the best deal he ever made.'

'That was how you met Seth.' Dougie moved closer, amazed by what he was hearing.

She nodded. 'He could not save the other girls. The brothel owner guessed his game, and it was all closed down and re-located within hours of our leaving, but that just made Seth even more determined to help the young girls traded from rural villages. He has always had such a kind heart, but he was very idealistic and naïve. He thought it was simply a matter of taking me back to my family. He believed they would welcome me with open arms. He had no idea then how things worked. When he tried to return me to my parents, they refused to accept me because of the shame my circumstances brought on them.

'He was stuck with me – a thirteen-year-old foster child with a hapless new parent whose mother still did his washing when he returned to Bradford. He took me to America to be educated. I was an A-grade student, but academic studies bored me. I was angry. I wanted to fight. I was a serious pain in the ass, and after I graduated he agreed to send me to be combat-trained in Russia instead of hot-housed for another year at Harvard as he had planned. Now I am his bodyguard as well as his personal assistant. It is a very effective role. I am a trained killer, but people do not see me as a threat.'

Dougie was seeing her as quite threatening right now, but kept that quiet. 'You protect Seth from his business enemies by brainpower and force?'

'Indeed.' She lifted her chin with obvious pride. 'He has been a father figure to me and – briefly – a lover, but now I have outgrown him.' Her eyes flashed angrily. 'I do not like the line he treads. His foundations in India create education and work for the poor, but in order to help the untouchables, he makes deals with unspeakable men. The Russian is a spoilt child like Seth, but he is also a bad man and a bully. They are like boys playing Top Trumps. To win his patronage, Seth is willing to pimp me, this beautiful park, his faith, your career.

'We have both been bought by Seth, Dougie. We have to get away.' She wove towards him seductively. 'You are the sterling to my dollar.'

'He paid more than a quid for me.' He backed off, alarmed to find himself cast as half of a fugitive double-act. He was struggling to take it all in, his James Bond fantasy in his wooded English hideaway shattered by a bigger world picture. Would Seth really sacrifice so much just to broker a deal? He looked at Dollar now, utterly composed and controlling, yet entirely dependent upon one man, her loyalty at breaking point. 'Surely he knows that the girl who risked death rather than allow herself to be used by a brothel would never allow herself to be traded.'

'Seth is a good man, but he has been distracted choosing a virgin bride.' Her eyes darkened furiously. 'This deal would pay for many thousands of Dollars to be saved, and for that to happen, maybe he thinks one can be sacrificed.' She swallowed hard, the steely composure as close to cracking as Dougie had ever seen it. 'I must get away. You will come with me.'

Dougie retreated behind his butcher's block uneasily. 'Given that Seth liberated and educated you, why will he not let you leave if you want to?'

'I left once before. I was to be married. It went wrong and I came back.' Her beautiful face was masked again, giving nothing away.

'The man who taught you how to cook lobia,' Dougie remembered.

'He was devoted to me.'

'You said he killed a man.'

'Yes, that was unfortunate,' she said coolly. 'Seth helped me out of a very difficult situation once more, and now he doesn't trust me not to leave again, but he knows he cannot stop me. If I demand to go, he will let me. He has always been very generous to me. It is you he will not release so easily, Dougie.'

'Come on, I'm hardly his best recruitment choice,' Dougie scoffed. 'Our mutual boss may be a big kid and a fantasist with enough money to buy the whole of Scotland as a fishing retreat, but he'll be grateful to see the back of me. I love my field sports, but I'm not prepared to hunt illegally, and certainly not slaughter wildlife with arrows, however many impoverished slum kids it will ultimately employ in his factories. Trying to marry Kat to get her off his land is a Bollywood twist I can't hope to make stick, however romantic a notion.'

'That was my idea,' she reminded him.

'It was a bad one.' He leaned back against the slate surface behind him.

'Seth is fascinated by aristocrats. There are not many of those who can hunt with a bow and arrow, fewer still who look good and can be bought.'

'I'm not one of them.'

'Hock Mytton could.'

'Who?'

'Lieutenant General Henry "Hock" Mytton,' she spoke the name in her newsreader monotone, 'an arrogant bastard by all accounts, even official ones. He was a notorious misogynist and philanderer.'

'Sounds like my father.'

'There are parallels,' she agreed sardonically. 'He had a great passion for hunting, especially big game. He was a renowned shot, but he was also a skilled archer. Seth's great-grandfather Ram was his adjutant. He was in the 16th Infantry in British-occupied India, a fearless sower – so-called because he was a cavalryman who carried a sword – and also a brilliant horseman. With Ram's help, Hock Mytton led legendary tiger hunts in Simla. He was the only British officer who could ever boast that he had killed a Himalayan tiger with a bow and arrow. I believe that tiger's skin served as a rug in the main house until Constance's death.

501

'Ram was a loyal and discreet adjutant, which cannot have been easy with a man like Hock Mytton as his commanding officer. Hock had many mistresses and relied upon Ram to cover his tracks. One of those mistresses, who was very highly strung and equally highly married, became pregnant with Hock's child. The affair seemed destined to ruin his military career. Then she shot herself. The circumstances are very suspicious – the note she left was clearly fabricated – but her death was officially recorded as suicide. It was rumoured that her child's birth would have revealed the father. That she had been having an affair was common knowledge, although her lover was known only to a very few among the highest British élite. That élite closed ranks, refocusing the blame on Hock Mytton's adjutant.

'Ram took the blame for her pregnancy more or less as a military order. He accepted full responsibility, dutifully and without protest. He had no choice. He was naturally court-martialled and expelled from the army for gross misconduct and his family were dishonoured. They lost their position in Indian society, expelled from the Kshatriya caste and becoming untouchable. Ram died in poverty, but not before he had sold his medals to pay for his oldest son's passage to England.

'That was Seth's grandfather, who arrived in this country with nothing, and built a business from scratch. Seth adored him. He loved to listen to his memories of India in change and revolution. He learned of the injustice Ram had suffered at the hands of a man named Hock Mytton.'

'Seth bought the Eardisford Estate to avenge his great-grandfather,' Dougie realized.

'It narrowed down the choice, shall we say?' Dollar's eyebrows lifted. 'There is a certain *Schadenfreude* in taking something that was of such value to an enemy and treating it as no more than

502

a business asset. Seth bought Hock Mytton's ancestral home as easily as you or I would buy an antique vase. He loved that.' She moved towards him again. 'And you are the bunch of flowers he bought to make that vase smell so much sweeter.'

Furious that he had allowed himself to be bought, Dougie was even more put out to be described as a bunch of flowers.

'Of course you have turned out to be more thorny than we anticipated,' she went on, the dark eyes glowing. 'I take responsibility for that. As you know, I had more than field sports in mind when I head-hunted you.' Her gaze lingered on his bare chest where his shirt was still open. 'I loved *Dark Knight* and I told Seth he must see it. Like many women, I found you most attractive in the part, and also later in *High Noon*. I knew that you would not only make the perfect huntsman, but also a sublime suitor.'

Dougie thought about Kat and felt an ache of regret so strong he had to turn away, anger flaring. 'I should never have agreed to come here.'

'We left you with little choice.'

'You can't stop me leaving.'

'Not if you take me with you.' She was standing just a few feet away now and the tension in her voice was almost palpable, a wellspring of emotion threatening to burst through the carefully modulated calm. 'I have to get away.'

Dougie felt his anger evaporate as he understood how vulnerable she really was beneath the rigid self-control. 'Dollar, are you frightened by Igor? Are you in danger?'

'Of course not,' she said indignantly. 'I could kill him with my bare hands if he tried to force himself on me.'

'Would that be wise?'

'I could kill *you* with my bare hands if you do *not* force yourself on me.' She smouldered up at him. 'Now, we will make love.' She exploded against him again, a whip of tension. 'Hold me!'

Dougie could feel the heat of her body against his but otherwise nothing, except a cold, clammy fear that he was in a lot deeper trouble than he'd imagined.

Chapter 57

Eardisford's grand façade was lit up as Kat headed home from the pub, a luxury cruise liner out in its dark sea of parkland, glittering at her between the masts of the trees as she took the track through Herne Covert. She was strangely cheered to think of it occupied and vibrant once more, no longer a *Mary Celeste* dry-docked amid its skeletal gardens, although she wasn't certain Constance would approve of the house guests, or indeed the new master.

That rather depends which master you are referring to. She heard Constance's throaty laugh in her head. *Eardisford needs an old-fashioned rake like Dougie Everett, Katherine. Guts, good manners and a passion for country sports are prerequisites.*

Constance would have adored Dougie. Kat rarely heard her voice in her head when they were alone together. In fact, she'd hardly heard it at all in recent weeks. Now, however, she was in full flow.

He is so like the legendary Mytton men, with that quick charm and even quicker temper. Impossible to control a man like that. Equally impossible to resist. Whatever possessed you to try to do so, Katherine?

He was fooling me all along.

You were fooling yourself. Look at your friend and Dair. I always said he was a jolly good man. Your friend saw it straight away. You can see it in Dougie Everett, but will you admit it?

The chemistry between Dawn and Dair had come as a surprise to Kat, and made her acutely aware that her physical attraction to Dougie was still top-shelved in a glass jar marked Handle With Care. An overturned periodic table of combustion and synthesis occurred each time she found herself beneath his Bunsen burner gaze. She could no longer deny her desire, her total loop-the-loop belly-lurch whenever he was near, the fierce burn in her heart. His voice was a perpetual, obsessive echo in her head. Now she knew that he had refused to hunt with Seth's guest, she was desperate to see him, to ask him to reconsider helping her with the Bolt. She wanted him to look her in the eyes and dare her to do it again.

Stopping to gather her post from the box at the first gate – it was crammed full – she listened to the millstream roaring and looked across towards the deeper woods where Dougie lived. His recent rebellion meant he might not be partying at the big house as she'd imagined. He might even be at home.

A twig cracked behind her and she swung around, terriers growling at her ankles, but there was no movement among the twilit trees. Kat was accustomed to the noises of the Eardisford Estate, and its animals both wild and domesticated on the loose. Nevertheless, she turned and hurried along the track, post clutched to her chest. Then, adrenalin making her heart leap, like a salmon swimming upstream, she cut right across the narrow wooden bridge that spanned the roaring chase and raced towards the mill house, approaching with the huge wheel ahead of her, shadowed in the glow from glass wall behind it like a giant hoopla ring.

Through it, silhouetted on the opposite side of the full-length windows, a couple were kissing as though their lives depended upon it. The woman was climbing up around the man in a way Kat hadn't seen since Nick had propped his smart-phone on the pillow with a porn movie streaming. The woman was dark, exotic and appeared to be a trained contortionist from where Kat was standing. The man with his back pressed to the glass was unmistakably Dougie.

Kat slid to a halt, her heart feeling as though it was rupturing into her throat.

As she turned to flee back towards Lake Farm, she crashed straight into a huge figure dressed in black. Before she could scream, he hushed her with one big gloved hand to her mouth, the other gripping her shoulders to pull her into the shadows.

'Will you – please – get – off me!' Dougie wrestled away again, barely able to breathe after Dollar had suctioned him to the glass with urgent kisses. 'I really don't think this is a good idea. You are beautiful and clever and hugely desirable, Dollar, and it was fun while it lasted, but this is seriously bad timing. I am not having sex with you right now, or running away with you for that matter.'

'We must go together. I have it all worked out.'

'I've made other plans.'

'You are in love with somebody else!' she snarled jealously.

Dougie looked at the black, ferocious anger in her face. Unmasked, she was terrifying. He hurriedly tried to deflect her with a few clichés. 'I hardly know you, Dollar.'

'We will get to know one another.'

'I'm a shit to be around for more than five minutes.'

'So am I.'

'I love horses and dogs.'

'I love Indian thrash metal and kick-boxing. We both need me-time.' Her deep voice was staccato and ferociously determined. 'As soon as the deal with Igor has been secured, we will fly to LA. I will be your manager. You will be a very big star. You just need discipline.'

He closed his eyes, appalled at the thought, aware that the truth was probably his best ally right now. 'You're right, Dollar, there is somebody else.'

'Is it still Kiki?'

The name broadsided him. He hadn't thought about Kiki for weeks. He must be a better actor than he'd thought if Dollar hadn't twigged who it really was, and that the huntsman had become totally enraptured by his own quarry. All that nonchalant deflection he'd given out in their many progress calls had laid a false trail. However much he longed to be honest – saying it out loud would feel so good – he didn't want to get Kat into any more danger and it seemed imperative to protect her. So he pulled his mouth into the inverted smile his father had used when lying to parliamentary committees and gave a ghost of a nod. 'I'm not ready for another relationship.'

The response was extraordinary and immediate.

'You should have said.' She let him go, straightening her dress and gathering her computer tablet from the table. 'I would not have wasted our time tonight had I known that both our affections already lie elsewhere. That is a very poor statistical start for a relationship.'

'*Both* our affections?'

'My plan relied entirely upon your narcissism. It is too much of a risk if you love another woman. I will have to turn to my contingency plan.' She tapped her tablet to life and flicked through its carousel of files to a spreadsheet. 'You will need a new job, Dougie.'

'"Brides List",' Dougie read over her shoulder, his heart plummeting. 'I am not about to marry somebody—'

'These are not *your* brides, Dougie. They are intended for somebody else.'

Reading the list of Indian girls' names, Dougie remembered Dollar telling him that Seth would be entering into an arranged marriage. These, it appeared, were his choice of matches. And Dollar – who, he was quite certain, was very much in love with her boss – was scrolling down them like a hit list, selecting and deleting the majority with relish.

'There are now only three left to get rid of,' she murmured darkly, almost to herself.

'What have you done to the others?'

She looked up at him, eyes glowing. 'This may take *all* of your considerable charm, Dougie.'

'The answer is no!' He held up his hands. 'Absolutely not. Whatever it is.'

'You don't have to marry them,' she reassured him. 'Just seduce them.'

'Absolutely not.'

'But I will pay you—'

'No,' he repeated firmly.

She turned off the tablet with a huff. 'Then I must rethink. I am very disappointed in you, Dougie.' She glanced up at the wall clock. 'Seth will have noticed I am missing. I must get back to the party. Do not leave Eardisford this weekend. Igor's visit must go smoothly. You remain cricket captain. The professionals will play. Seth will bat third. Tell him *nothing* of this conversation. If you break your word or your contract there will be very serious consequences. And, you will remember, I

508

always carry a gun.' She reached down and drew a tiny hand-gun from her stocking top in a move so fabulously Bond, Dougie had to smile, albeit very nervously, especially when there was a loud cry outside, agonized and guttural. She instinctively flicked the safety catch and flattened back against the wall.

'It's just a muntjac deer barking,' he told her. 'Probably heard Igor's here.'

Kat looked down guiltily to where Russ was reeling on the ground, clutching his crotch and groaning, his eyes watering.

'You know you should never grab me from behind,' she hissed. 'What are you doing prowling around here? I thought you were at nets.'

He didn't have a chance to answer as the mill house's outdoor lights suddenly came on, like search lamps through the trees, a door slammed and they heard raised voices. Then a car engine started up and headlights swung away through the woods.

'I have been at nets,' he whispered, sitting up cautiously. 'Got some old sab friends from Bristol to come and help me. We've been setting up miles of that old stock-netting from the barn to stop dogs flushing anything bigger than birds from cover and to slow the hunting party right down.'

Kat was impressed by his initiative, but wished he'd been a bit more guileful. 'They'll trace the stock nets straight back to Lake Farm!'

'Of course they won't – it's just old sheep fencing. Even if they do, it's not criminal damage.' He smirked, carefully straightening up with his hands over his groin. 'We're all sleeping out here tonight. The Bristol lads are having a barbecue in the orchard and we want to keep the game away from Duke's Wood. There's boar weanlings and fawns everywhere, only just leaving their mothers' sides.'

'They won't hunt those, surely?'

His eyes gleamed in the half-dark. 'Don't be naïve, Kat. For God's sake, keep all the dogs in tomorrow. Now you tell me what *you're* doing here.'

Kat glanced at the mill house, thinking about Dougie and Dollar against the window, and found she couldn't speak.

Imagining she was stricken at the thought of all the animals that might get massacred at dawn, Russ folded her in his tight bear-hug. 'We won't let the bastards kill innocent wildlife, Kat,' he promised.

Feeling horribly shallow – and appalled at the thought of the shooting frenzy that might be in store – Kat hugged him back.

Hurrying from the mill house to his Land Rover, determined to drive to Lake Farm and talk to Kat, Dougie saw movement in a clearing just beyond the garden and stepped quickly behind the shadow of his car, picking up Quiver before he sensed the other dogs. A couple were embracing in the last steely rays of twilight. He would have recognized that spill of red hair anywhere, along with the enormous hirsute man-mountain folded lovingly around her.

Reality hit him like a wrecking ball. Kat was obviously still hooked on Badger Man. She had always stayed loyal to him. She'd played detective for him, reported back to him on their conversations, cared for his rescued wildlife. Russ had been the one to look after her when she fell from Sri. Dougie had no right to burden her with his own overloaded heart.

Pulling the car door open so violently that the handle came off in his hand, he leaped in to drive to the high ground on the

510

main road where there was mobile-phone reception and call his father.

When she heard another car engine, Kat pulled gratefully away from Russ – who smelt distinctly feral – and turned to see red tail-lights speeding away along the parkland track.

'They'll be heading for the main house,' Russ pointed out. 'Dougie's bound to be a guest of honour, given he's the estate's resident Hollywood actor and stuntman.' He impersonated his uncle's drunken commentary at the village show. 'I wonder if Seth knows that jammer's been shagging his pretty PA from the day he got here.'

His intense dark eyes watched Kat's face. She was struggling not to crumple, desperate not to give herself away.

'I'm sorry.' He put a big, warm hand on her shoulder. 'That was harsh. But I don't want you getting any more hurt than you already have, Kat. Toffs like that have the same morals as their bloody hounds, and I know you're mad about him. I've known all along. Animal behaviour, see?'

She hung her head, her heart feeling as though it was burning to a crisp.

He held his arms wide. 'We were always free-range, remember? I hope you meet someone who'll look after that 'mazing heart of yours.'

'Like you chose Mags?'

'You don't choose love, Kat. It shoots you down, and sometimes its aim's so true you can't ever get up for anybody else.' She saw his eyes glint through the gloom. For the first time she could remember he was making a joke at his own expense. 'That's forever love.'

'I think I've just taken a fatal shot,' she said, in a small voice.

He engulfed her in another earthy hug. 'I was afraid of that.'

When Dougie drove back to the mill house in a hurry, having forgotten the car charger for his flat-batteried old mobile phone, he saw Kat and Badger Man still canoodling beyond the woods and was quite tempted to put his foot down and drive over them. Instead he executed a bad three-point turn and shot off towards the village call box instead. On the passenger seat beside him, Quiver threw up.

Russ let go of Kat and peered at the retreating tail-lights suspiciously. 'There's something very odd going on. I need to liaise with the Bristol lads. If Everett's on to us, we'll need to change tactics and move into deeper cover.'

'Dougie's refused to hunt,' Kat said proudly.

He shook his head. 'That's just a pile of crap they're putting out to wrong-foot us, like the rumour about professional cricketers on the estate team. Have you ever heard the like? Illegal hunting's one thing, but nobody in their right mind would try to pull that stunt at a village match. It's all propaganda, see. We must rise above dirty tricks like that.'

'What about the rumour that Dougie was being paid to get me to marry him?' Kat eyed him warily through the dark. 'Who spread that, Russ? They're baying for his blood in the village.'

'Where there's smoke there's fire, Kat.' He stooped down to pick up the pile of post she'd dropped. 'He said he came here to slay dragons. Dragons breathe fire, and so does this village.'

Fire is Dougie's biggest demon, thought Kat, unhappily.

Chapter 58

'We went to spy on the party at the main house!' Dawn burst into the Lake Farm kitchen. 'It's so funny, Kat, full of hired guests. You okay? Have you been crying?'

Curled up on the sofa with two loudly snoring lurchers and unopened post scattered around her, Kat was about to sob that, yes, she had been crying her heart out because she knew she was hopelessly hooked on Dougie Everett, who was too busy shagging glamorous Porsche-driving women against windows to give a stuff, when she saw Dair standing behind her friend, flat cap at an unusually jaunty angle.

'I invited Al back for a coffee.'

'Al?' Kat pressed her palms quickly to her puffy eyes and wandered into the kitchen, where Dawn was fetching mugs down from a shelf and Dair was lounging against a worktop.

'I like Al,' he insisted, in a lusty, infatuated way that hinted he'd agree to be called Catkin Bunnywinkle if he thought he might be invited to stay the night.

'I like Al a lot too,' Dawn cooed.

Kat felt another lurch of panic-stricken regret that she had failed to acknowledge her own thunderbolts until they had started to hurt too much to ignore, by which time Zeus had moved on. Now she was cornered in a kitchen with Mr and Ms Pheromone.

Dair glanced at his watch and grimaced. 'I'll have a half-cup. I must be away soon. I'm up at the crack of dawn tomorrow.'

'Is that a promise?' Dawn giggled.

Listening to their flirty laughter, Kat thought of Russ's nets and chewed her lip anxiously, busying herself by fetching cat food to put out for the yowling masses in the yard, then went out to check the animals one last time.

Vaughan Everett was blisteringly unsympathetic when his son told him the full truth of what was going on. Feeding pound coins into the slot in the old-style red call box in Eardisford that was photographed by tourists more than it was used, Dougie tried to ignore the smokers outside the pub peering at him as his father gave him short shrift.

'Frankly, it's nothing I hadn't guessed,' Vaughan barked. 'Seth's probably justified in wanting the Myttons hung out to dry.' He chuckled at the inadvertent joke. 'The Everetts weren't much better behaved in British India, I fear. They still aren't, judging from your recent behaviour. What the fuck did you think you were doing taking on a job as a gigolo?'

'I am not a bloody gigolo!' Dougie shouted, noticing too late that one of the pub smokers had shuffled up, pretending to read the parish notice-board so he could listen in.

'You were prepared to marry for money, Dougie, which, one assumes, includes consummating the union. There are very few degrees of separation between that and tapping on a car windscreen asking for business.'

'I'd never stoop as low as that!' raged Dougie, then hung his head as he remembered that, in a previous life, he'd stooped very low indeed, fully prepared to sleep his way to the Hollywood A-list a honeymoon suite at a time. Now it seemed it was payback time.

'I suggest you get out as quickly as you can,' Vaughan

advised, in his clipped voice. 'I'll get a legal adviser to look at your contract as a matter of urgency. Just keep the family name out of it, whatever you do. In fact, keep your trap shut about everything. This isn't an anecdote for a chat show.'

'I can't leave her here.'

'I'm sure she can look after herself. Didn't you say she was Russian combat-trained? The woman sounds frankly danger-ous.'

'I'm not talking about Dollar. I'm talking about Kat, the girl who runs the sanctuary.'

'The one you're supposed to marry? Well, there's a very obvious solution to that, assuming your contract is as watertight as you say.'

'What solution?' he asked desperately, noticing that a small crowd was looking at the parish notice-board now, feigning fas-cination with the church cleaning rota.

'Offer to split the million if she marries you. You can buy yourself out of the contract and she can set up somewhere new. At least you both get something out of it.'

Dougie knew that Kat was unlikely ever to forgive him, let alone play along and split the profits – she was far too straight and stubborn – but his father's advice made him see that she deserved his total honesty. If Badger Man still had her heart, he could at least earn her respect.

Watched closely by the crowd, Dougie rang off and flew out-side to his car, no longer thinking straight, his head full of apologies, escape plans and blind fury.

He drove straight to Lake Farm, the Land Rover boun-cing crazily over ruts and potholes, Quiver taking refuge in his lap.

When he swung through the gates into the farmyard, he almost drove straight into the back of Dair Armitage's Range

Rover, which was parked outside. Dougie didn't need to get out of his own car to see the shadow cast from the kitchen window, the silhouette of a couple kissing passionately.

'Christ, she has a bloody stable of us on the go,' he muttered to Quiver, under his breath.

Fury and jealousy burned in his veins as he threw the car straight into reverse.

Hearing a car driving away at speed as she came back from checking the horses in the field, Kat assumed it was Dair leaving, but when she walked around the side of the barn into the farmyard, she saw the Range Rover still parked there. Dawn and Dair were framed in a curiously old-fashioned Bogart and Bacall clinch in the kitchen window.

She wanted to hang back to give them a little more time together, but the dogs had already rushed inside so there didn't seem much point in pretending she wasn't back. She followed them in, grateful that conservative Dair – hugely flustered to be caught kissing – made lots of throat-clearing I'm-leaving-now noises and put his flat cap back on.

Having waved him off, Dawn bounded inside, sobered up by copious coffees and a breathtaking clinch, eager to dissect the whole whirlwind romance with Kat and to broach an urgent new dilemma. 'Apparently Seth is hosting two Bollywood parties tomorrow night – the commoners in the tent and a full-on maharaja's banquet in the main house with *actual royalty* invited. Oh, Kat, Dair's asked me to be his guest. Please say if you'd rather I didn't go. I promise I won't mind. My loyalty is to you. Oh, God, you're crying. Really, I won't go. We'll have a girls' night in. Please don't cry. I'll stay with you.'

'It's not that.' Kat mopped a stray tear as she moved through the sitting room to the windows overlooking the lake and stared out at the house, its windows glowing. She was trying very hard not to break down. 'I went to the mill house earlier tonight. I saw Dougie through the big windows there. He was ...' She screwed up her face with the effort of saying it out loud. 'He was having sex with Dollar.'

'The eighties pop duo?' Dawn was too astonished to stop and think.

'Dollar is Seth's personal assistant.' Kat swiped away another tear, lower lip trembling. 'Apparently they've been an item all along.'

'And that's how big a problem?' Dawn asked carefully, already guessing the answer. She'd predicted Dougie Everett would be a romantic dilemma long before Kat had.

Kat stared at the lake. 'If a drip of water is a normal problem, my Dougie problem is that lake. He's partying with her up in the big house now.'

'Gate-crash!' Dawn urged the old daredevil Kat. 'Give me ten minutes and I'll transform you. You'll never get in looking like that. We are going to make you look like a million Dollars.'

'Thanks, but I'm not in a party mood.' She mustered a brave smile.

'Of course you are. Fight for him, Kat! Dawn knows best. I swam the lake, remember, so I'm allowed tell you what to do. Let's get to my magic makeup kit.' She headed for the stairs. 'Follow my lead.'

Kat headed rapidly for the door. 'You're right!'

'What are you doing?' Dawn squawked. 'You can't do this in old jeans.'

'You're right again.' She stripped down to her bra and knickers and ran outside.

517

'Oh, fuck, she's truly lost it now.' Dawn hurtled after her, yelling, 'Kat, do *not* gate-crash that party in your pants!'

Kat ran along the jetty, not allowing herself to think. She was going to conquer the lake. It was as simple as that. This time, she would take on her nemesis and win.

Checking Usha was well out of range, she set her focus on the far bank and imagined Dougie was there, laughing, daring her to do it. She would swim straight to him, beating her own triathlon personal best, skimming across the lake's black surface as lightly as a water boatman. When she got there, she would climb out and push the deceitful bastard straight in. He might have her heart on a pike, but she was going to prove she could do this without him.

Taking a deep breath, she dived in with a loud belly-flop.

Igor was enjoying a quiet cigarette on his balcony, staring across the parkland to the magnificent silver crescent of lake and the wooded, moonlit hills beyond, excited by the sport that their dark bulk held in store for the following morning. He spotted a figure moving in the water. Another *rusalka*! He hurried to fetch his binoculars for a better look. This one was a redhead, but no less glorious than the first. It was an omen, he was certain, an omen that became even more propitious when he turned to listen to a rattling sound coming from beneath one of the huge trees in the park and spotted a stag of near-mythical beauty stepping out into the moonlight and raising his head to display antlers like petrified oak.

He had started to like this estate very much indeed. If tomorrow's sport lived up to expectations, he would stop at nothing to add it – and its *rusalki* – to his private collection.

*

518

Kat felt empowered with every stroke, the fear pushed ever-further behind her, her anger helping her power through the water. She could hear Dawn whooping behind her as she crossed the lake in less than a minute, her feet finding the solid gravelly base before she waded out to the grassy bank to do a victory dance and punch the air, so ecstatic she threw in a cartwheel, which pitched off sideways into an ungainly forward roll that left her sitting on the grass, staring across the perfection of the moonlit park.

She gasped in delight as she saw the stag silhouetted against the rising full moon, its magnificent antlers now full-branched.

Super-charged, Kat swam back, not feeling the ache in her muscles or the burning in her lungs. All she was aware of, with every stroke, was the shedding of the fear she'd bolted around herself for so long.

Dawn helped her on to the jetty and hugged her tightly, tearful with pride and relief.

'Mind your dress – I'm dripping wet.' Kat warned, her teeth chattering, although she was laughing too much to notice or care. She pushed her wet hair back from her face. 'That was the best *craic* ever. Why didn't you tell me how much fun it was?'

'I was terrified when I did it,' Dawn admitted. 'But you were always the daredevil, Kat. That was bloody fantastic to watch. If the Dougie Everett problem is that lake, you just swam straight through it.'

'Dougie who?' Kat shook back her hair in an arc of drips and headed towards the house.

Dawn could tell she was putting on a brave face, but she loved her spirit. The old Kat she knew and loved was definitely back in business.

Chapter 59

'Dougie, *yaar*! So glad you showed, man!'

It was an unexpectedly warm welcome, given that Dougie had arrived at the party as most of the guests' cars were streaming away along the parkland drive towards the Hereford road.

Wearing a skinny T-shirt and jeans, his raven hair slicked back and a doe-eyed beauty hanging off his arm, Seth beckoned him through his cathedral arch of a front door, calling off the security guards who had been trying to bar Dougie's way. 'I tell you, people have no staying power round here. In Mumbai, we party all night. Come and talk me through the cricket strategy. What's this I hear about you disapproving of the guys I brought over?' Waving the girl away, he thrust out an arm to give his shoulder-dislocating handshake before steering Dougie towards his inner sanctum. They crossed a huge panelled and galleried hall as big as a tennis court, newly restored marble floors gleaming beneath a baronial chandelier, the shipped-in celebrities and society beauties drifting around like birds of paradise in an aviary. There was, Dougie noted gratefully, no sign of Dollar.

'Igor has gone to bed,' Seth told Dougie, with obvious relief, as he led the way along a dark-wood corridor. 'He takes his hunting seriously. I'm the same about cricket, *yaar*.' He mimed a few strokes, then swept his hand in front of his chest like an umpire calling a boundary four.

'You're in to bat third on Sunday,' Dougie said stiffly, finding his bouncy familiarity disconcerting.

'Great! I'm well out of practice, man, but I was a shit-hot attacking batsman in my day so I hope the old magic's still there. You heard about my internationals?'

'I'm well aware of them,' he said, feeling like Blackadder accompanying an enthusiastic Prince Regent. 'Are you taking part in the hunt tomorrow?'

'No way. I hate early starts, *yaar*. I'll join them for lunch. I'm sending Doll out with them at dawn. She only needs four hours' sleep and likes guns, so I've packed her off to bed early to mug up on her Russian hunting slang. Man, was she sulky about it. At least I get my morning run this way. Always do ten miles.'

'You'll have a beautiful day for it.' Dougie was alarmed by his own voice, so obsequiously sardonic-manservant. He'd be whipping out a handkerchief and twirling it with a rakish bow any minute.

'Can't stand fresh air. I use a machine. We've had part of the cellars converted for a gym. It's all climate-controlled so I can match it to my optimum atmospheric temperature, humidity and oxygenation.'

'The fresh air here's pretty high grade,' Dougie assured him. 'Probably best in small doses, if you're not used to it. Would you prefer us to move the cricket match indoors?'

Seth shot him a speculative look, aware that he was being teased but enjoying the dry English-butler delivery too much to be annoyed. Then his face split into a wide smile. 'Yeah, maybe you're right. I'll try running outside tomorrow. Gotta acclimatize before the match. What do you think of the old place? Looks like a film set, doesn't it? It's not really my thing, but it's a great weekend party crib for now.' He looked at the panelling, its edges notched from centuries of servants' trays bumping against it. 'Tomorrow night, this place will be full of Indian dancers. I know Dollar put you on the VIP list.'

Relaxed and chatty, he seemed a million miles from the private and enigmatic power figure Dollar protected so fiercely. He guided Dougie through secret passages of the house – a vision of no-expenses-spared glossy restoration and carefully concealed gadgetry – talking him through the fibre-optic cables, fingerprint recognition and deeply buried eco-heating.

'It's stunning.' Dougie admired discreet control panels disguised as artwork.

'Takes ten cleaners to keep it mint. Ridiculous, man. I prefer minimalism. You should see the Mumbai crib – looks like a tower block outside, but inside it's all straight lines to infinity. Beautiful, *yaar*.'

They swung through a door concealed in the panelling and Dougie found himself in a vast armour-lined dining room dressed with more Civil War heraldry than a lavish costume drama set, an untouched midnight breakfast laid out along its heavily carved oak sideboards. There were trays of kedgeree, sausages and scrambled egg, croissants and Danish pastries.

'Help yourself to anything.' Seth poured himself a coffee.

Dougie's stomach was churning too much for food, although he couldn't remember the last time he'd eaten. Sounding disappointingly like his father leaving his cabinet post after the cash-for-questions scandal, he said, 'I regret to inform you that I wish to tender my resignation.'

Seth ignored the statement, picking up a spoon to study the crest on its handle. 'The family sold off the Mytton silver just before I got the place – crying shame. I've been trying to buy it back, but it's been divided up and is all over the place. The same goes for the art and furniture collection. No respect for the past, those kids.' He looked up at the restored strapwork ceiling with an avuncular sigh, even though the Mytton beneficiaries had been considerably older than his own parents.

'I wish to terminate my contract,' Dougie said more forcefully.

Seth turned to him and Dougie was reminded of just how deadly sharp his eyes were, for all the Bradford-lad camaraderie. 'Y'know, Constance Mytton-Gough was a bonkers old bird by all accounts but a good custodian of this place. And, man, they loved her round here, didn't they?'

Dougie nodded. 'The land and farms would be in as many different hands as the family silver by now if it weren't for her.' He cleared his throat. 'I want to terminate my ... contract.' He omitted 'fucking' with great self-control.

'Is that because Dollar wants you to marry the girl from Lake Farm?'

'You know about that?'

Seth rolled his dark eyes up to the ornate plaster ceiling again. 'Of course I bloody know about it. It's total genius, *yaar*, as so many of Doll's ideas are. I'd make her my company vice president if ninety-nine per cent of the stuff she came up with wasn't illegal or unethical. Plus she's too violent to risk among my board members. Has she hit you yet?' He grinned across at Dougie.

'No.'

'Good girl. She's really chilled out, these days. She might even cope with my wedding.'

Dougie thought uncomfortably about that ruby-nailed finger violently stabbing at names on the Brides List.

'You know, Constance M-G married to save this place.' Seth wandered over to admire a suit of armour. 'I had the history of the house researched when I bought it. There's a book in the library here full of pictures of her handing out sandwiches to

Land Girls during the war.' He tipped up the helmet visor and peered inside.

'Her father promised to sign across Eardisford if she rode a famous challenge called the Bolt.' Dougie related the story as Kat had told it to him. 'Constance took it on believing her future was riding on it, but her father broke his word and made her marry.'

'Hock Mytton was a bastard.' Seth let the visor drop with a clank.

'I agree, but his daughter was nothing like him. She had a backbone of iron. That's why this place still existed in its entirety when you bought it for your "movie set", apart from the contents her children flogged to cover death duties. It's easier to buy silver spoons than to be born with them, these days.'

'We all have an opportunity to redeem the past, Dougie. My great-grandfather Ram would have been very proud of me. Three generations after his honour was sacrificed for the Mytton name, his descendant has the title deed to their land holdings.'

Dougie was about to snap that adding it to a goody-bag in an arms deal was hardly an historic redemption, but he bit back the sarcasm. 'What if the Bolt was ridden again?'

'You want to try it?' Seth was admiring the Jacobite weaponry hanging on his lime-washed walls now.

'Will you terminate my contract if I do?'

'I'll let you off marrying the girl.' He grinned over his shoulder.

'If I marry her, do I still get a million?'

'Doll offered you that?' Seth whistled, picking a claymore sword off the wall. 'That's way too much. Then again, she fancies the pants off you, and she always overvalues the things she wants most.' He swung round with the sword and Dougie ducked just in time to avoid partial decapitation.

'Sorry, mate.' Seth laughed, setting the sword down on the gnarled, wicket-long table. 'It's seriously heavy, *yaar*. Give me small arms any day. What d'you think of Dollar's arms? Beautiful.'

Dougie had good jealous-husband instinct. He'd been the clandestine lover enough times to identify a cuckold on the scent. Dollar might not be Seth's wife, but he definitely wanted ownership, and the arms he was talking about had been wrapped around both men more than once.

He mustered a charming smile. 'Call me old-fashioned, but I prefer a bow and arrow any day.'

'Except when it comes to entertaining my weekend guests.' Seth raised one eyebrow to a forty-five-degree black stripe of sarcasm. 'You're lucky Dollar likes you so much. You've let me down big-time, Dougie.'

Dougie was on high alert now, smelling danger. No wonder he had been welcomed in so genially. The leopard had come padding into the tracker's house.

Seth was refuelling his coffee. 'I don't want to talk hunting, man. All that tweedy shit is seriously beat. Let's talk cricket.' He turned and looked at Dougie, unsmiling, the hey-dude demeanour hiding a cobra. 'We play it my way.'

If he'd been handed any other topic, Dougie might have backed down. But this was cricket. 'I won't field professionals,' he said firmly. 'If you want that, someone else can captain the estate side.'

'You're the village hero, Dougie. We need that goodwill.'

He laughed. 'Not any more, I'm not. Word's got out I'm your hired groom as well as private huntsman. Some don't take kindly to that around here.'

'They can be won round.' Seth regarded him over his coffee

cup. 'Bowl the maiden over and cover yourself in glory. You can still earn that million.'

'You'll pay out if Kat Mason marries?'

'Everything has a price, Dougie. Even you.'

'Kat doesn't.'

'More fool her.' Seth looked at him irritably. 'The deals I do impact directly on the charities I run. This place is playing its part in something that will change many thousands of lives in India. It's worth paying top dollar if it's something that close to your heart.' The scimitar brows lifted meaningfully as he sucked espresso froth off his upper lip. 'You come from a long line of political marriages, don't you, Dougie?'

'My lot all married up,' Dougie said distractedly, thinking about his father's advice to split the money with Kat for honour and liberty. 'We're only a few generations away from merchants and serfs.'

'I come from a long line of high-caste cavalrymen, but my father was a carpet-fitter.' Seth's fingers were drumming on the sideboard behind him. 'My mother wants me to marry next year. She has a short list drawn up of well-born Sikh girls. I've narrowed it down to three. I have to choose one this weekend.'

Dougie remembered the red nails clawing angrily at the screen, the desperate plan to turn virgin brides into deflowered castoffs. 'Can you not marry any woman you choose?'

Brows lowering fast, Seth looked set to tell him to sod off and stop prying, but then his eyes fixed on the sword on the table and he pouted thoughtfully. 'This way has always worked for my family.' His fingers drummed again, one eye closing as he played something over in his mind. 'How did the village find out that you were a "hired groom"?'

'I told Kat and she told ...' he winced at the memory of

526

Badger Man wrapped around her, worse still big-bore Dair bending her backwards over the kitchen sink '. . . others.'

'Why the fuck did you tell her, man?'

Dougie looked at his hands, turning the signet ring around on his little finger, trying not to dwell upon Kat's tempestuous love life. 'I thought she deserved the truth.'

'Are you in love with her or something?'

'You can lose the "something",' Dougie said quietly.

Seth gave a whoop, slapping his palm on the table victoriously. 'I bloody *knew* you'd suit one another, man! That's why I let this thing roll on when I found out. To be honest, I reckon Doll figured you'd break the girl's heart and that way she'd bugger off and leave Lake Farm of her own accord. She's very taken with you, is Dollar. She made me watch the movies you were in so many times it did my head in. Forgive me, but you're pretty shit in *Dark Knight* after the tenth time – it's no Oscar winner, is it? Dollar watched it every night for a month.' Seth's nails rattled on the sideboard in an ever-faster bhangra beat. 'Did she come to see you this evening?'

Dougie remembered her warning not to breathe a word of their conversation. He thought uncomfortably of the brush-off he'd just given her, and wondered if Seth knew they'd been lovers. 'She's pretty formidable.'

He laughed. 'Yeah, that's an understatement. She used to be so aggressive I had to give her a rubber stick to bite on in meetings, but she's calmed down a lot. She's my beautiful, caged tiger and I throw her more toys to play with, these days.' He gave Dougie a slow smile, revealing front teeth as white and upright as a cricket eleven in a team shot. 'She likes playing with you.'

He knows, Dougie realized, as he flashed his most charming,

diffident smile in return, his own cricket eleven drunkenly lop-sided but Persil white.

Seth's eyes belied his fury. 'If she asks you to run away with her, take my advice and don't. The last time she did, somebody got killed. Caged tigers aren't easy to release from captivity. Believe me, I've tried. Did she tell you how she got her name?'

'Yes.' He realized his mistake as soon as he said it. Seth's eyes darkened further. He was now aware that she was intimate enough with Dougie to share such close truths.

'I've told her loads of times she should change it back, but she says it's a reminder that she still owes me. She's ferociously intelligent.' Despite his anger, Seth's eyes glowed in the same way Dollar's did when she talked about him. 'She's too clever to be my PA.'

'And bodyguard.'

'That too,' he acknowledged, with a sideways nod. 'I want to set her up in business of her own, but she claims she wants to be a wife and mother. I just can't see it, man. She did get engaged once,' his eyes blackened to boiling tar, 'but she broke it off when the bridegroom killed my bodyguard. He died saving me. Dollar said protecting me was her job, so she came back.'

'Her fiancé tried to kill you?' Dougie stared at him, things starting to add up in his head.

'The press reported that it was a bungled contract killing, but it was a straightforward crime of passion. Dollar's fiancé found out she was in love with another man and he wanted to kill that man. It happens.' He picked up the claymore sword from the table and lifted it to his shoulder, fixing Dougie with a death stare. 'If I see dollar signs in somebody's eyes, I want to ter-minate the acquaintance too.'

Dougie knew exactly what was going on. Slotting the lobia-cooking murderer into the picture had been the final decisive clue. This was not just about avenging the distant past: it was about a love affair that was still being played out, and he had stumbled into the middle of it to be used as a weapon. Seth had played Pygmalion to Dollar and given her extraordinary opportunities, but however great his success and riches, he could never marry her without incurring the wrath of his family. Dougie knew that his father would strongly advise him to refrain from comment at this point, but he heard Kat's voice in his ear, forthright and generous.

'She's in love with you.'

'Everyone loves me, man!' Seth looked away, his bravado acting as covering fire. But the need to stand up in the open and defend his territory was too great. 'Dollar is beautiful and fearless and much cleverer than me. I'll destroy anyone who hurts her again.' He slotted the sword back on the wall, running his fingers along its shaft, his voice quiet and earnest. 'I could never have achieved what I have without her. We've travelled the world together. We even lost our virginity together. She's more than a wife to me. She knows I'll give her anything she wants except marriage. I've tried to explain to her that business deals and marriages are much the same thing. You must look beyond them to see a bigger picture.'

'She sees a bigger picture. She thinks you're offering her to Igor, along with Eardisford.'

'She should know me better than that.' Seth swung round furiously. 'I'd never trade Dollar. You're the one risking the girl by backing out on a deal, mate. If Igor takes on this place, they'll be digging little Kat's grave alongside all those other pets the Mytton family loved so much. He'll have no scruples getting rid of her. She won't stand a chance.' His voice dropped to a hiss. 'If you won't marry her for the money, do it for her safety. Call it a rearranged marriage.'

529

Chapter 60

The biggest Eardisford stag was far too wise and wary to be tracked easily, but the man with the radio mic who had him in his sights was among the best in the world. Small, stealthy and hugely experienced, he had been called out by his boss many hours earlier, enabling him to track the beast into woodland close to a small farmstead, clearly a favourite spot where it munched tree bark and shoots, helping itself to the contents of a pheasant feeder before locating a well-shaped tree to rub its forehead and antlers.

The tracker checked his GPS to whisper his co-ordinates back to base.

When Kat woke up to feel steam billowing across her face, she imagined she'd been brought a mug of tea in bed – a very rare treat – but then she opened one eye and spotted a bowl of piping hot water into which Dawn was dropping essential oils before soaking a flannel.

'What time is it?'

'Just after six. I haven't been able to sleep for thinking about Dair, so I thought I might as well get up and give you a steam facial. I know you're always up early, and those pores have to be mucked out before the pigs.'

Kat groaned and rolled over to bury herself into the cool side of the pillow. 'Much as I admire your dedication to your work, I'd rather sleep for another half-hour.'

'I'm here to make you look a million Dollars.' Dawn swept

aside the curtains in Kat's room and came back to scrutinize her sleep-creased face. 'Either you've been crying again or you have hay-fever. I can deal with puffy eyes, and your brows are crying out for my finest threading, plus those lashes need a tint. Then I'm on the case with that fluffy upper lip.'

'What fluffy upper lip? They're freckles. I'm a redhead.'

'Yeah, you and Yosemite Sam. You are getting the full Beautiful Dawn treatment this morning. Beautifu—'

'Whatever you do, *don't* sing it.'

'Thinking about it, I might have enough facial hair bleach to strip off that horrible tint.' She peered at the top of Kat's head where the temporary dye had left it dull brown. 'There's henna in your bathroom cupboard. It'll be tricky to get right, but it's worth a go.'

'There I must draw the line. Last time you bleached my hair, it took four hours and ended up white.'

'Looking a million dollars can't be rushed, and white is very on trend. All the top models have it this year. Dougie Everett has pretty classy taste – Kiki Nelson is platinum blonde. Sorry, I made you cry again.'

'It's hay-fever. Why would I cry over a man I've only kissed once?'

'One kiss is sometimes all it takes, trust me. Dair is *such* a good kisser. I love the little gap between his front teeth.'

'Too much information.' Kat groaned again, closing her eyes. 'I am not bleaching my—' Her protests were cut short as a hot wet flannel landed on her face.

In Duke's Wood, Russ and his vigilante team had taken up their positions just before first light, hiding out around the day nests of a big sounder of female wild boar and their weanlings, which would make easy pickings for the hunt party. The nets they had strung across the paths and tracks were already spun with spiders' webs jewelled with dew. They grew stiff and uncomfortable as they crouched behind the curtained canopy of an old hazel thicket, trying to keep up their spirits with a Thermos of rooibos tea and a packet of vegan biscuits, but inevitably arguments broke out over tactics – a common theme between them – and the activists divided over the decision not to drive all the game from the woods before the guns arrived.

'This isn't a little forestry shoot in the Cotswolds,' Russ hissed. 'This is the Eardisford Estate. It's bigger than Cheltenham. Imagine chasing a drift of pigs round that.' They shut up.

Dair's Range Rover was first to arrive, pulling the canvas-sided shooting trailer in which dogs and guns were being transported. Having spotted some of the activists' nets, a furious Dair sent off his keepers to remove them while barking into a small piece of technology that appeared to have broken. He got increasingly frustrated with it until one of the guns pointed out that he hadn't turned it on.

'Which is the Russian?' breathed one of Russ's companions.

'I don't think he's joined them yet.' Russ scanned the assorted faces.

It seemed they were all waiting for their guest of honour. While his comrades bickered about who would get the last biscuit, Russ edged closer to try to listen in.

'What have you done, Dawn?' Kat wailed, looking at her reflection. One eyebrow had recently been an expressive little arch but was now a thin ginger line surrounded by inflamed, reddened skin.

'It'll settle down in a bit. You always had sensitive skin. I need to do a patch test before I do your lashes and upper lip.'

'I really don't have time. I have about a million things to get on with. Everything needs feeding, Usha's fence needs mending again and I haven't let the geese out. I can't waste all day lying around having beauty treatments.'

'I'm just trying to help.'

'I know, Dawn, and I'm incredibly grateful, but I don't think I'm going to sort my love life out with reshaped eyebrows alone.'

'Where are you going? I've only done one!'

'I'll be back after I've fed the animals.'

The stag was on the move again, squeezing his way through some broken stock fencing and into more sparse woodland skirted by pasture that was being cropped by a raggle-taggle of mixed livestock, all clearly used to their visitor. Watching over a further fence, a horse bobbed its head and whinnied a welcome.

The tracker followed, guessing the stag was looking for somewhere to lie up for the day before the sun rose too high. As soon as it did, his boss could spring a surprise.

'Looks like it's going to be a walk-up shoot,' whispered one of the Bristol sabs, as they watched the guns hanging around the trailer drinking tea and glancing at their watches, excited dogs milling underfoot. 'Can't do much about that. Boar and muntjac are legal game even at this time of year.'

'These are all estate staff,' Russ noted, as one of Dair's gundogs came perilously close to the saboteurs' hide-out and pointed helpfully for his master, only to be called back with a sharp reprimand. 'There are no invited guns here. I still smell trouble.' He turned to watch as an incongruously glossy black Land Rover Defender with blacked-out windows appeared along the track. 'Here we go.'

A glamorous Indian girl leaped out, whom Russ recognized as Dollar, although he had only ever seen her through the mill-house windows with most of her clothes off. She was immaculately dressed in lightweight tweeds and country boots but looked totally out of place and extremely disgruntled as she picked her way through the dogs to have a word with Dair.

'You bloody *what*?' the estate manager exploded, pulling off his flat cap.

Eager to find out what was going on, Russ edged his way further along behind the cover of a bank of bracken. As he did so, there was a furious squeal behind him. With lightning response, he grabbed an overhanging tree branch and pulled himself up so his legs were out of the way as the boar charged past. But the hefty female wasn't interested in him, he realized, as she charged out of cover, teeth and tusks bared, to warn off Dair's dog, which gave a terrified yowl and ran behind his master's legs.

Dollar was directly in the boar's path. With even faster reactions than Russ, she pulled out a handgun and aimed it between the sow's eyes. But Dair was already making a heroic lunge to pull her out of the way, grabbing her as her fingers closed over the trigger and causing her to misfire across the clearing.

'Ouch!' came a furious wail, as a figure in a balaclava dropped out of a nearby tree. 'You just bloody well shot me. Oh, Christ, there's blood everywhere.'

As the sow screeched off into the undergrowth, Dollar holstered her gun and ran with Dair to check on Russ who was now wailing, 'Somebody call an ambulance!'

'No need.' Dollar pulled aside the backpack, which was strapped to him and gushing hot tea everywhere, the Thermos inside it having taken a clean shot. 'He is not hurt.'

*

After a sleepless night spent trying jealously to come to terms with the fact that Kat was in a tempestuous love triangle that he was honour-bound to square off, his father and Seth having urged him to push his seven-figure suit for her sake – the facts of which would no doubt convince her once and for all of his tarnished morality – Dougie blazed a path to Lake Farm just before seven. He could see no way of offering Kat a clearer signal of his love than offering this to her. It was all he had to sacrifice; his pride was already surrendered. This would secure her future even if he couldn't be part of it.

As he drove into the yard, Kat emerged from the feed room, scoop in hand, wearing her pyjamas, plastic clogs and a surprised expression, one brow lifted curiously. He'd never known her more beautiful. No wonder she had all the men on the estate wooing her.

'We have to get married, Kat,' he said.

'Hi, Dougie. Good to see you too. Would you mind running that past me again?'

'You *must* marry me, Kat. You'll get a million pounds and you'll be safe.'

'Again.' The eyebrow was still riding high.

'When I took this job, I was offered a million pounds if I could persuade you to marry me. Seth will still honour that. I checked. You can have it all.'

'One more time would be great.' She was shaking her head, eyebrow higher than ever.

'I'll give you the lot. My father suggested splitting it, but I'd rather do it this way. We'll divorce straight afterwards, of course – or go for an annulment. By then you'll have the pay-out, so you and the sanctuary will have a secure future.'

'I think I'm up to speed now.' She nodded slowly. 'Thanks.

I'll think about it.' Turning away, she stomped back into the feed room.

Dougie waited a moment, then dashed after her.

Kat was deep-breathing into the pig-nuts bag, trying to regroup her grand plan. In her many fantasies about Dougie striding up to sweep her off her feet – and last night there had been many, all revolving around a Cinderella moment gate-crashing the Bollywood ball – she hadn't ever imagined a dodgy deal brokered in a farmyard. She'd envisaged passion, contrition, laughter, forgiving mistakes and retrieving hope – possibly involving a death fight with Dollar on the Eardisford ramparts – and instead she'd just got the cash offer. Anger was knitting her ribs together, stealing her breath and twisting her vocal cords.

His shadow loomed in the door and he cleared his throat. 'I appreciate this is probably coming as a bit of a shock, Kat.'

'Telling me.' She tried to breathe, but she was almost suffocating with indignation now.

'I told you the truth in the meadow. I said I was asked to target you. I tried to warn you.'

'Thanks for that,' she said tightly, scooping out enough pig feed to make the Vietnamese pot-bellies explode. 'It always makes for a romantic proposal.'

In the half-light, Dougie couldn't read her face clearly, although her skin was flushed a becoming pink, he noticed, and that raised eyebrow was still doing its ironic thing above eyes showing a lot of white.

'Actually, you haven't given me an answer yet,' he reminded her. 'You said you'd give it to me when you'd ridden the Bolt.'

'That's not going to happen today.' Her voice was strange, all breathless and tight. He hoped that meant she was overcome with emotion. She turned to look at him over her shoulder. She still had one eyebrow raised, he noticed. And her bottom in those pyjamas was ravishing. 'I'm sure it hadn't escaped your notice that Duke's Wood is full of Russians swigging Bloody Marys and taking pot shots at wildlife – which we're all supposed to believe is tree felling.' She cupped a hand over her ear, listening for bangs.

'So you'll definitely think about it?' He peered into the gloom.

'I think we can safely say it'll be on my mind. Is that all you came to see me about? Only I have a lot to do.'

'Will you come to the Bollywood ball as my guest? Not the fancy-dress servants' bash in the marquee, the big black-tie masters' do in the house. Free upgrade. That way you can meet Seth. He's a sly bugger, but it might help to talk to him face to face about this place. You might not even have to marry me.' He gave an ironic laugh that was met with stony silence.

Kat's first, hopelessly shallow, reaction to the ball invitation was to wonder what on earth she'd wear, but then the red mist descended once more.

'I'll come back for an answer later, shall I?' He showed no sign of leaving.

'Probably best.' She was blind with anger now, as inarticulate and blood-boiling as a punch. She kept seeing him with Dollar, pressed against the window. My heart is worth more than money, she wanted to scream, but the sanctuary's future held her anger tightly in check.

His silhouette hadn't moved from the doorway. She could almost swear he was breathing as crazily as she was.

'Is it true you refused to hunt this weekend?' she asked.

With the light behind him, she couldn't see his eyes. His

answer was clipped and defensive, covering all emotion: 'I won't hunt out of season. Almost as bad form as marrying for money or cheating at cricket.'

Another hot blade of anger entered her side as she remembered Russ saying that Dougie's refusal was just a smokescreen to cover the illegal goings-on. She couldn't shake the image of him in the mill last night, Dollar wrapped around him, as urgent and carnal as one of Nick's porn movies. 'I don't want to go to the ball, Dougie. I don't want a free upgrade. I don't want a million-pound upgrade. In fact, I don't want ever to see you again. I just want to be left alone here to get on with my life.'

'You can't stay here, Kat. That's the point. You have to—'

'I'm not a servant or a master,' she interrupted hotly. 'And I won't honour and obey a hypocrite who thinks he can double-cross both, not even for five minutes. You represent everything I've always hated, Dougie. I could never trust you. If you have any respect for me at all, please just go away.'

His silhouette dipped for a moment, head lowered, then vanished from sight, leaving early-morning sunlight flooding in.

When Dawn brought out a cup of tea five minutes later, she found Kat still standing in the feed room holding the scoop of pig nuts. Loud, angry complaints were coming from the fields and pens as the sanctuary animals awaited breakfast.

'Dougie was just here,' Kat said, in a strangled voice.

'I can't believe I missed meeting him again! What happened?'

'He offered me a million pounds to marry him, then invited me to the ball tonight.'

'Bloody hell.'

'I told him I could never trust him.'

'I'd better do your other eyebrow.'

*

538

Unsettled by the Lake Farm livestock's complaints, the stag moved deeper into the wooded enclosure, but his way was barred by the stock fencing. He had cornered himself.

The tracker watched him closely through the trees, certain the moment was approaching. When the red-headed girl appeared on a quad bike to throw feed out into troughs, the stag watched her warily from his wooded couch, but he didn't make a move to break cover. He seemed content to hide there for now.

The tracker gave the signal to move in.

Dougie was still monstrously uptight when he arrived at the kennel yard just before seven. He needed the horses to soothe him, especially Worcester, the genial comedian, who liked to rest his moustached muzzle on his master's shoulder and let out a sigh of such deep content it was guaranteed to lull even the most fevered heart.

'Why the hell have you turned so many out?' he snapped at Gut, when he saw empty stables. 'The horses have to be available at a moment's notice today.'

Gut, whose English still extended only to a few words, babbled incomprehensibly in Hindi, miming finger-snapping and muscle flexing, then pointing to the sky and tapping his watch with a surprised shrug and some eye-rubbing.

Dougie was getting a lot better at interpreting his head groom's mimes. 'Oh, fuck, they're already out riding, aren't they? I bet they left at bloody dawn. What weapons did they take?' he demanded. '*Wea-pon?*' He mimed a gun, then bows and arrows.

Gut mimed back something that was part light sabre, part *Saturday Night Fever*.

'Spear?' Dougie suggested, imitating a spiking motion.

'No, no, no, sir.' Gut moved on to John Travolta dancing in *Reservoir Dogs* before striking a Rambo pose.

'Machine-gun?'

As the two men mimed weaponry, like small boys enacting an imaginary battle, a member of the security team, who'd been posted beneath the arch in the entrance to the carriage court-yard, muttered at intervals into his lapel, then waited for a response in his earpiece. The Russian party might have been out since dawn, but the house and its gardens remained under close surveillance from both Igor and Seth's private squads. Head cocked in suspicion, the guard eyed Dougie and Gut's strange dance through very dark glasses.

Dougie quickly gave up on his guessing game and stalked into the tack room to use the land-line to try to summon Dair. A man who preferred to communicate with memos and letters, only using the estate's walkie-talkies if the situation was life-threatening, the Scot had battled to get to grips with the satellite phone he'd been equipped with since Seth's reign, but this time he picked up within two rings. 'I knew you would be behind this, Everett.'

'What the fuck is going on?'

'I could ask you the same thing. I've tracked these woods for days preparing to flush the best ground game. Instead, I now have guns, dogs and picker-uppers sitting in the back of a trailer wasting time while a fucking Russian is apparently galloping around Herne Covert with a cross-bow. He wants a stag.'

Dougie let out a groan of horror. 'But Herne Covert's right by the lake. The sanctuary's beside it.'

'I'm on my way there now. Whatever you do, don't let him near the farm and *don't* alert Kat to what's going on. It's all under control.'

*

True to his word, Seth had set out on his daily run around the estate's parkland instead of in his state-of-the-art gym. He found the early-morning air a revelation, his lungs filled with cool, dewy sweetness as he hammered along the landscaped avenues. The contours of the park were far steeper than the settings on his machines and he soon regretted wearing such heavy ankle weights. The bodyguard accompanying him was already struggling to keep up, Seth noticed, as his ears pounded with MIDIval Punditz from his iPod. Dollar would have had no trouble keeping pace, he reflected, but she had always fallen into step with his life perfectly, until she'd kicked him squarely in the balls because he wouldn't marry her, then enacted her revenge by announcing she was leaving to marry someone else. That had not worked out – Seth had kept quiet his involvement in her lover's murder conviction and the length of his sentence – but she had been far less compliant since her return, the controlled anger bubbling ever closer to the surface, along with the rebellion. Seth knew she would not accept any wife he took, and had now grasped that he had to deal with it head on rather than tossing her playthings like Dougie to distract her.

He regretted sending her out with the Russian on his early-morning hunting trip. It was another thing she'd find hard to forgive. Igor was thoroughly unpleasant.

Mounted on Worcester, whose normally kind eyes were already edged with white from the spurs assaulting his sides, Igor splashed through the ford, leading his three outriders, all of whom were trusted friends of long standing and always travelled in his coterie. They had hunted with him and his tracker across six continents. Breaking into a canter as he rode up the slope, he saluted the little man in Russian military camouflage, barely visible among the trees, then jumped the horse through the gap where the fencing was broken. He posted one of his outriders there to stand point while the others crossed the field to open the gates on to the lakeside, where he intended to drive the stag so that he could pursue him through the parkland.

What Igor hadn't accounted for was the panic-stricken reaction of Lake Farm's elderly grazing herd.

As the stag broke cover with textbook grace, he quickly drew unexpected outriders of his own – a llama and two alpacas, several sheep and goats flew alongside the big red deer as he belted into the sanctuary's horse field, where a wall-eyed mare flattened her ears and gave chase too.

'*Mat! Kon govno!*' A stream of obscenities came out of Igor's mouth as he spurred Worcester in hot pursuit. To his alarm, he found two evil-looking Shetlands closing in on him in a pincer movement.

Chapter 61

Dougie had borrowed Gut's scramble bike to rattle to Lake Farm – taking his car would mean a huge diversion and going on foot was just as time-consuming. The tinny rattle shrieked at top velocity as he snaked through the parkland and on to the causeway. One of the few structures in the Eardisford grounds that hadn't been touched in Seth's lavish restoration, the narrow wooden-planked promenade that stretched across the lake remained a decaying, slime-caked death trap of potholes and crumbling stone spine that he skidded across far too fast, almost pitching into the lake.

When he slithered into the farmyard behind the house, the dogs surged out to greet him and Kat followed, still in her pyjamas. She had both eyebrows raised now, and was frantically wiping something off her upper lip. She looked furious and utterly beautiful. 'When you said you'd come back later, I thought you meant *much* later.'

'Igor's galloping around here with a cross-bow.' He ignored Dair's advice to keep her in the dark, knowing Kat needed to protect her livestock. 'He's after a stag.'

She gasped, eyes wide with horror. 'We must stop him. That's totally barbaric.'

Momentarily lost in those eyes – why had he never noticed the little silver flecks in the green? – Dougie took a split-second to catch up. 'He'll only hit trees – and us, if we get in the way. Dair think he's after the big chap from Herne Covert, but there's not a chance of him finding him. The Lord Lucan of stags, that one.'

Hearing a thunder of approaching hoofs, they turned towards the open yard gateway. At the same time, Dawn leaned out of an upstairs window wearing a face-pack and a towel on her head, her high vantage-point meaning she was able to see beyond the farm buildings to the approaching stampede. 'Ambush!'

The yard was filled with a clatter of hoofs as a stag led a charge of three horses, two alpacas, a llama, three goats and several sheep, closely pursued by four riders whooping with war-like shrieks, trailed by two fat Shetlands who ground to a grateful halt as soon as they saw the open feed-room door and headed inside.

'That's half my livestock!' Kat ran to her quad bike and fired the ignition, then opened the throttle so fast, it stalled.

'And Harvey!' Dougie retrieved the scramble bike and kick-started it, accelerating into the dust-cloud left by the stampede.

Dawn ran outside breathlessly as Kat frantically tried to get the quad started again. 'What can I do to help?'

'Get the Shetlands out.' Kat started the engine again with a whoop.

'To do what?' Dawn shouted over it. 'Roman riding?'

'No. Just stop them stuffing themselves.' She sped off.

Having run in a big arc along the parkland's open rides and around the beech woods, Seth found himself at the far side of the lake. His legs were really pumped now, lactic acid building, the punishment of uneven terrain and sharp cambers making him truly feel the burn. Music playing in his ears, he ran along the lime avenue towards the lake, admiring its golden surface in the early-morning sun with the huge Jacobean house perched beyond it where a shower and massage were waiting. The bodyguard had fallen far behind, totally outpaced by his marathon-running boss. Again, Seth felt a pang for Dollar's company. She would probably start competing with him on a run about now, putting in a burst of speed, goading him to stay with her.

Imagining her racing ahead of him, he ran on to the causeway, not realizing how dilapidated it was until he was part of the way across and the uneven footing forced him to steady himself and look down. That was when he saw the crumbling stonework and the broken wooden boards, increasingly sparse underfoot. Making a mental note to instruct his team to renovate it, he slowed to a careful walk, puffing hard. As he did so, he heard crashing through the beeches that ran alongside the lake.

Seth watched transfixed as a huge stag leaped out of the woods skirting the far bank, antlers tipped back, its eyes bright with alarm. Swerving left in a spray of earth divots, it headed straight towards him along the rickety causeway. As soon as it saw him, it leaped neatly off the open side, landing with a great splash in the lake, and began swimming to the far bank.

More crashing was coming from the direction of the woods now, along with hollering voices. Three more terrified animals burst from the undergrowth, swerving left in the stag's wake, and at first Seth thought they were more red deer. Then he took a nervous step back as he was joined on the bridge by a llama and two alpacas, all boggle-eyed with fear and lolloping towards him at such speed that the metal struts supporting the planked walkway were shaking. When Seth turned to run back the way he had come, there was an ominous groan beneath his feet. He had just enough time to look down and register that he could see quite a lot of black, weed-filled water when the rusted metal truss and rotten planks gave way and he dropped into the lake's darkest, reediest depths.

The llama and alpacas cannoned to a halt to avoid falling through the hole too, sliding to a stop in a gaggle and snorting fearfully, heads shooting up and twirling like periscopes, well aware that danger was right behind.

A mountain of a horse was crashing out of the woods now, its rider bellowing in Russian as he lifted his cross-bow to his shoulder, still galloping flat out, and took aim at the biggest of the long-necked hairy camelids trapped on the gap-toothed bridge. 'I have the stag cornered!' he yelled in Russian. Then he peered closer and swore under his breath as he realized it had no antlers. Instead of being a great trophy for his wall, it was a very peeved llama.

Igor reined to such a sharp halt, Worcester almost sat down.

Standing up in his stirrups to survey the terrain around him, Igor spotted his target in the water twenty yards from the bank, its antlers like magnificent, skeletal sails on a well-battled flag-ship. Shooting an animal in water was never ideal, but he would let his assistants worry about recovering the trophy. He had a clear shot. He let out a victorious bellow.

'No!' Kat screamed, as she hurtled on the quad bike along the bank of the lake, her eyes swinging wildly from the swimming stag to Igor taking aim on the far bank. There was no way to get close to the Russian without crossing the causeway or swimming the lake. Dougie was far ahead of her on the scramble bike and already accelerating towards the frail old walkway. Abandoning the quad bike, she knew what she had to do. Shouting to get the Russian's attention, she sprinted towards the lake, diving in over the rushes.

In the blackest water beneath the bridge, Seth was flailing madly, unable to swim to safety. Gripped by searing cramp, held down by his running weights, his cries for help inaudible over the shouts and engines, he let out a sob of relief as he saw someone dive in, certain rescue was coming. It turned into a wail of anguish as he saw that she was swimming away from him.

Above Seth's head, an increasingly infuriated llama was stumbling and crashing around on the broken planks, his panic-stricken alpaca friends herding around him, braying in terror.

Roaring along the bank towards the walkway on the scramble bike, unaware that Kat was in the water behind him, Dougie eyed the crumbling ornate stone supports that sloped up from the lakeside to the elderly structure like flying buttresses. They made a perfect motorcycle ramp. He accelerated towards one, engine screaming.

*

Still a strong, fast swimmer, despite the long break from competition, Kat was between Igor's bow and the stag in just a few strokes.

'*Bliad'! Wed'ma! Ty troop! Cuchka derganaya! Unbju!*' Igor yelled, as the redhead blocked his shot. The stag was moving out of easy range.

He pointed the cross-bow at her threateningly. 'Get out of the way, *rusalka*!'

'No!' She gave him the finger – which was probably ill-advised, given her situation – and trod water.

As she did so, she heard a familiar bellow coming from the spinney beside the farmhouse and groaned in horror. 'Please don't do it, darling. Just this once, stay away from the water.'

But she knew it was hopeless as Usha came shambling companionably out of the bulrushes.

Eyes lighting at the sight of a pair of horns as wide as a sea eagle's wingspan, the Russian aimed at the water buffalo.

Realizing he was about to take a pot shot at Eardisford's oldest and most eccentric bovine resident, Kat plunged towards Usha instead.

With a victorious engine roar, Dougie's bike landed on the far end of the rickety causeway in true stuntman style, back wheel spinning as he swerved it to face Igor on the opposite bank of the lake. That was when he saw that the causeway was already quite crowded. Feeling it tilt and shake, he also suspected it was about to collapse.

Masked from view beneath it, Seth was coming up for the fifth or sixth time. The cramp in his legs had solidified to splints of pure pain that refused to move, the weights on his ankles felt like concrete and were now entangled with the weeds that kept dragging him under. He tried to shout again, but there was so much noise nobody could hear him.

Glaring along the causeway at Igor – who was swinging his cross-bow sight between Usha, Kat and the stag, spoilt for choice – Dougie revved the engine, ready to hurtle across to him and pull him from his horse. 'Out of the way!' he shouted at the two alpacas and the llama. Instead of doing as they were told, the alpacas finally jumped over a huge gap that had appeared in the planked walkway and came cantering towards him, eyes popping. Behind them, the big llama let out a furious spit of disapproval. Still at the far end of the long bridge, he hung back, weighing up his options. More aggressive than his companions, less keen on swimming than the stag, averse to motorbikes and not trusting the rickety, swaying structure he was standing on, the llama spun round and sprang towards the Russian's big horse, taking Worcester completely by surprise.

The llama was in a very bad mood now. Despite being less than a quarter of the horse's great size, he threw back his head, puffed up his chest and reared against Worcester's side, which was blocking his way.

'Stop it, you fucking rug on legs!' Igor's bolt swung back towards the llama again.

Seth's bodyguard-cum-running-companion had finally panted around the edge of the beech wood. Taking in the scene, he fumbled for his radio mic to call for back-up. As he did so, two grey horses, a patchwork one with blue eyes, and several goats burst out of the woods immediately behind him, jinking past him and out into open parkland.

'We have a situation,' he told his team nervously. Like most trained fighters, armed men held no fear for him, but large animals were another matter.

With an almighty scream of its engine, Dougie's bike was still waiting to power its way along the planked platform, but the traffic was a nightmare. The alpacas were blocking his way as they loped towards him and then stopped, heads shooting up. Exploding with impatience, Dougie knew he had to let them get across. He cut the engine and they shuffled cautiously towards him while he waited, feeling like an elderly motorist letting pony riders hack past.

Beneath the shadow of the bridge, Seth was weakening. He'd swallowed so much water he could barely breathe when he gulped and gasped to the surface each time, struggling to stay there for more than a split-second before the pains in his legs corkscrewed him round and down, the weeds and weights holding him there. The muffled silence under water was far outlasting the brief, bewildering cacophony above it. This was, he realized with horror, probably the last sound he would ever hear. He would never see his parents again, his sister and nieces, aunties and uncles, his friends and Dollar. He would never be able to tell Dollar just how much he loved her. He *had* to live. As he made one final desperate bid to surface, he felt something grab his hair. He reached up a hand to embrace his rescuer, only to find his fingers full of feathers.

Across the lake, Kat was treading water between Usha and the stag, still marking Igor's cross-bow, which was swinging around wildly now he was under llama attack. Her eye was caught by one of the Canada geese flapping and pecking furiously beneath the bridge. A part of it had collapsed, she saw, and broken planks bobbed on the surface. Then she did a double take. A hand was poking from the water. She let out a horrified gasp and started swimming towards it.

As the alpacas finally sprang past Dougie, he kick-started the scramble bike again and let off the clutch. The bike roared into action towards Igor, who was trying to aim his cross-bow at the llama chest-butting his legs. Edging the bike's wheels on to the narrow stone kerb at the causeway's edge to bypass the gaping hole in the planking, Dougie glanced down and saw a shot of red hair in the churning black water below. As soon as he reached a more solid footing, he slid to a halt and threw down the bike, running back to see Kat in the water below, swimming in frantic circles as she looked down into the black water.

'Someone's trapped down there,' she cried.

'Leave it to me.' Diving in, Dougie almost landed on top of her.

'I can handle this!' She disappeared beneath the surface.

He dived down too.

Usha was bellowing mournfully in her bulrushes. Now unguarded, the stag had almost reached the far bank and Igor was once again trying to get a clear shot, ignoring the body-slamming llama, which Worcester was stoically enduring beneath him.

'*Ty troop!*' he muttered, as the llama spat on his boot.

Just as he lined up his cross-bow, there was a commotion behind him as a lynch mob of balaclava-wearing saboteurs flew out of the woods.

Before Igor could take in what was happening, the masked men had pulled him from the saddle, swiftly disarming him before disappearing back into the trees.

Apoplectic, Igor shouted for his men, realizing for the first time that they were nowhere in sight. He'd kill them for letting him down like this.

'Do something!' he yelled in Russian at Seth's bodyguard, who was trying to fend off several goats tugging greedily at his baggy jogging bottoms.

In the woods, Dair greeted his keepers. Meat and Two Veg gave triumphant salutes as they ripped off their headwear, the celebration shared somewhat starchily with the real animal activists whose headwear they had commandeered, and who had been left holding the horses rather than sharing the action.

Russ, who had wanted to be the hero of the hour, was most put out that the estate manager had taken over his operation to put a stop to the shooting party, but he couldn't deny the positive result. As soon as Dair had realized the Russian was conducting his own private stag hunt, he had proved refreshingly militant, confiscating the activists' disguises and ordering his own men to take action.

'It is for the greater good,' he insisted wisely, hurrying through a thicket to check on Igor's sidekicks, who were now being held out of sight at gunpoint by Dollar. Telling Seth's ferocious PA that he believed Igor's men were Russian Mafia and posed a serious threat to her boss's life had perhaps been a mean trick, Dair reflected, but it had paid dividends. She was magnificently fierce – he'd have had no hesitation in hiring her as a gamekeeper. The estate was not a playground for redneck hunting, any more than it would ever host television costume dramas, corporate bonding weekends or celebrity weddings. He was upholding Constance's honour.

The lake beneath the bridge was a torrent of rip tides and ripples now. Kat and Dougie burst up through the surface again, gasping for air. They had been down twice, fingers tangling and arms entwined in the least romantic way possible as they struggled to pull Seth to the surface, battling against the weight of the weeds that had twisted like a shroud around his legs. They knew they had just one more chance. Seth was breathing only water now, no longer clawing at them in his panic.

Kat looked across at Dougie as they gulped air to go back down, his dark lashes star-fished around the blue eyes, his face white. He looked back at her and his expression made her heart inflate like a life-vest in her chest, dragging in oxygen and hope.

'I love you,' he said, diving back down.

Kat's mouth opened in shock. Following him down, she realized too late that she hadn't taken a breath.

Under the water, sound muffled, she saw Seth through the gloom and kicked hard to the lake floor, grasping the reed-choked weight around his legs and gripping with all her might, while Dougie wrapped his arms around Seth's chest and pulled upwards. With an almighty whoosh of water, his feet were released from trainers and weight rings and Dougie could carry him up.

Kat was now so desperately short of oxygen and had swallowed so much water that she feared she'd pass out, but as she broke the surface she managed to gulp enough air to control the blurred dizziness and used the reflection of the causeway to swim in a straight line until she found solid ground beneath her feet. Lungs raw and legs weak, she followed Dougie as he hauled a worryingly lifeless-looking Seth on to the bank and put him into the recovery position.

'What do we do next? Mouth-to-mouth or the chest-punching thing or both?' he asked urgently, as Kat scrambled up the bank beside him.

'I'll do it.' As she stepped forward to apply CPR, she was knocked sideways by a lithe, tearful figure body-slamming past them both to crouch by Seth's head, cupping his face.

'If you die, my darling, I will kill them all, then commit sati upon your pyre,' Dollar sobbed. Then she applied such vigorous CPR that they could all hear the ribs creak, but Seth spluttered back into the world with a gratifying series of belches and coughs. Soon he was sitting up and complaining that his chest hurt.

Thrusting her phone at Dougie and telling him to call an ambulance, Dollar wrapped her arms around Seth, cradling him and soothing him in Hindi and English.

'You saved my life,' he gasped in wonder.

Dollar hugged him tighter. 'I told you this was a bad place to buy. *Glar ka bhedi lanka dhayey.* Your enemies are insiders. They tried to kill you.' She glared up at Igor, who was trying to hide his extreme bad temper behind contrition that Seth had got caught up in the hunt.

'Of course none of this would have happened if the *rusalka* had not interfered. It is all her fault.' He glared at Kat, who was still too busy trying to catch her breath to notice or care. She felt dizzy and increasingly nauseous; the last dive had wiped her out.

Having called for an ambulance, Dougie sat close beside her, arm sliding round her shoulders. 'That was bloody brave,' he said quietly. 'Must have brought it all back.'

'It probably helped lay the ghost.' She was reluctant to admit how close she'd come to blacking out. Yet she hadn't for a moment doubted her own survival, her determination to save a life too overwhelming to let in fear. She reached up and found his hand, sliding hers into it without thinking, the squeeze of reassurance like a heart massage. Looking across at him, she was mesmerized by the concern in his eyes. 'You were bloody brave too. He'd have died if it wasn't for you.'

'You were the one who saved his life. You're amazing.'

She was about to protest that they'd done it together when he reached up and wiped something from her cheek. His fingers stayed there, his eyes unblinking, and she found she couldn't speak. They might have been the only two people in the world, back in the secret meadow, trading secrets and dares.

'I meant what I said in the water just now,' he breathed, his fingers sliding up into her hair, drawing her face towards his. 'I fell in love with you the moment you set your arse on fire.'

Kat didn't trust herself to speak, seeing such honesty in his face yet unable to shake his great betrayal from her consciousness. He'd been paid to target her. She'd had a price on her head all along. He'd just offered to pay it over to her, but surely the fact he'd accepted it in the first place was beneath reproach. Her trust was too fragile to test her weight on it, especially not here amid such chaos.

She was suddenly aware of Dollar's deep voice soothing the still-spluttering Seth behind them, that same voice that had, no doubt, been whispering sweet nothings into Dougie's ear the night before. Anger bubbled up in a familiar spurt of lava.

'I know about you and Dollar,' Kat whispered.

Dougie closed his eyes and groaned. 'That badger bastard told you, didn't he?'

'I saw it for myself last night.' She wriggled away and rubbed her wet hair back off her face. She could feel the first symptoms of shock kicking in. She was starting to shake, her breath shallow, pulse jumping.

'That really wasn't what it looked like,' he muttered.

Kat had turned to glance at Dollar, who was rocking Seth in her arms, covering his head with kisses, tears on her cheeks, telling him she loved him. What was more, he was kissing her tearfully back, saying much the same thing and coughing a lot.

Kat rubbed her face in confusion. The shock was making her feel faint, her skin ice cold and clammy.

'We must talk,' Dougie said urgently.

From the bank above them, Dair was shouting for Dougie to come and look after the hunt horses. People were running down towards them, voices talking across each other, walkie-talkies burbling. Someone had driven one of the big black cars down from the house to take Seth back and await the paramedics. Several voices were yelling in Russian, Igor's sidekicks and security guards furious about the ambush in the wood.

Dougie's eyes didn't leave Kat's face. 'I have to see my beasts home and change into dry clothes. I'm sure there'll be hell to pay over this. I'll come and see you later. Will you be all right?' He looked at her worriedly.

She nodded. 'I have my friend at the house.'

'Dougie!' Dair shouted. 'We need you here NOW.'

Dougie stood up reluctantly, taking Kat's hand to help her up. 'Tell your friend you need sugary tea, a hot bath and a rest. Meet me later.'

Russ was bounding down the bank towards Kat, a bearded bear-hug in a hoodie. 'That was bloody 'mazing! D'you hear what happened, Kat?'

Dougie stepped away. 'Usual time and place.'

Enveloped in eau-de-twenty-four-hour-camp-out – with a top note of rooibos tea – Kat was nevertheless grateful for the six-foot-four prop holding her up.

'Think this Bollywood thing will still go ahead?' Russ was saying excitedly. 'I asked the animal-liberation lads to stay on and celebrate.'

*

Now reunited with his loyal hunting coterie, Igor was ranting furiously at them in Russian for shaming him and ruining the day. Stepping in to calm the situation, Dair made a diplomatic apology on behalf of the Eardisford Estate. 'There were saboteurs lying in wait for us unfortunately. It's a damned inconvenience with British field sports. They'll be long gone now.' He cleared his throat guiltily and peered across the parkland to where Meat and Two Veg were trying to round up loose horses cavorting around the ancient trees with several sheep and goats in tow. The llama had turned his attention to Seth's bodyguard now and appeared to be chasing him the length of the lime avenue.

Dougie climbed aboard Worcester, taking the reins of the three other hunt horses to lead them back to the stables. He gave one loud wolf whistle, which brought Harvey trotting over to follow him, like a dog. The sanctuary horses were far less compliant, cavorting rebelliously around the park rides enjoying snatches of lush grass between bursts of speed, the red faced game-keeping team panting in their wake.

Dair barred Kat's path as she squelched up from the lake, deathly pale. 'Leave them to my boys to bring back,' he told her, noticing that her teeth were chattering uncontrollably and that Igor was still eyeing her murderously, his heavies gathered around him. 'You go and dry off. Where's Dawn?'

'Holding the fort,' Kat assured him.

'Sterling girl.' He hid his besotted smile beneath his flat cap.

Back at the Lake Farm yard, Dawn greeted Kat with a wail of relief from the feed room, where she had been trapped for the past twenty minutes defending herself from the Shetlands with a broom and a scoop. She was still wearing her towelling turban, her face-pack cracked, like a dry riverbed. 'Where have you been? I've been in *total peril* here!'

As Kat grabbed a thick forelock in each hand and backed the little ponies out, ready to herd them back to their field, Dawn saw she was soaked. 'Have I missed something?'

Chapter 62

The Russian party left within an hour of returning to the house. There was no farewell or apology.

Having been checked over by medics and found to have nothing worse than badly bruised ribs and a racking cough, Seth disappeared in a small private plane, while Dollar summoned Dair and Dougie to an incredibly high-tech office in the old library that neither man had been into before. Both had to resist gazing around like small boys.

'Well, that was a total cock-up,' Dollar said coolly. Once again power-dressed and blank-faced, she fixed the two men with her death stare. 'Seth is very tempted to dismiss you both.'

'On what grounds?' Dair demanded.

Dougie said nothing, glancing at his watch, longing to get away. He was desperate to see Kat.

'You are both very lucky,' Dollar went on. 'We have a cricket match to win, and cricket is more important to Seth than anything – almost anything,' she corrected, two spots of colour appearing in her cheeks, the chital eyes softening uncharacteristically. Even more unexpectedly, she flashed a ravishing smile to herself. 'Personally, I am very glad that

Igor Talitov has gone and I think you are both to be congratulated.'

Dougie looked up: he was amazed that rigid, controlling Dollar would share such a personal opinion, let alone one that threatened her boss's business deals.

She tucked the smile away and tapped a flat computer screen to one side of her, which burst into life with a list of files. 'Seth wants morale to be high here at Eardisford,' she said. 'He insists the Bollywood party will go ahead as planned tonight.'

'Are you sure that's wise?' Dair looked appalled, having been against the party for the villagers from the start, more so now that rumour would run rife about today. 'The locals are a bloody rowdy lot.'

'Near-death experiences can sometimes have a euphoric and strange after-effect, I gather,' Dollar explained, the secret smile back again.

'Where is he?' asked Dougie.

'Bradford.' Her smile fell away and she swallowed uncomfortably. 'The doctors advised rest, but he is in a very bullish mood. He has promised to be back here in time for the party, although he still prefers that his identity is not revealed to guests. I believe his costume will prove a very effective disguise.'

'Is he coming dressed as a waiter?' muttered Dougie.

Dollar's impassive mask was firmly back in place, monotone strident: 'The marquee for locals and villagers is arriving at any moment. The extra security staff will be staying on for the full weekend, so they will be tasked to keep things in order and make sure that the VIP guests are safe.'

'Masters and servants kept well apart,' Dougie murmured, remembering Kat accusing him of double-crossing both. He glanced at his watch again, hoping she was okay. She'd been so pale when he'd left her. It was hard to take in that it was barely lunchtime. Today had been such an unholy mess so far. His timing had always been lousy. Offering to give her the bonus money had backfired; telling her he loved her hadn't gone down too well either. He couldn't wait to complete the hat trick and tell her the entire, unabridged truth. If she still said she never wanted to see him again after that, he would have no choice but to honour her wish.

Dollar was droning on. 'Dair, you will brief the security team about all the outside areas which must be out of bounds, then speak with the fireworks people. Dougie, you will come with me.' She stood up and headed for a bookshelf. Following her, Dougie fully expected the shelves to slide aside and reveal a hidden passageway, but instead he almost cannoned into Dollar's back as she pulled out a foxed hardback.

Beckoning him with a nod, she led the way out into the main hall and on through the spectacular armour-decked dining room where a catering team were arranging banqueting tables for that night, a rainbow of coloured linen and glittering gold tableware lined up ready to decorate them. Dougie was tempted to grab a pikestaff from the wall as he passed in case he had to defend himself. He'd never known Dollar as random as this, her usual rigid cool breaking out into weird smiles and nervous tics. Given the extreme volatility that he knew simmered just beneath the surface, he wouldn't have put it past her to throw in a sudden violent turn.

She went out on to the terrace, which was being tented and decorated with maharaja luxury. Picking her way through acres of flapping silk, she walked to the steps and perched on the top one, flicking through the book to find a black and white picture plate featuring a pretty, elfin-faced girl sitting on a pony, surrounded by hounds, with Eardisford's lake framed behind her.

'Constance Mytton-Gough.' She held it up for him to examine. 'A very English lady. Seth would like to ask Kat more about her tonight. He is looking forward to meeting her.'

'They already have met. She pulled him out of the lake, remember?'

'He is very grateful to you for your help.'

'Does he actually know that it was Kat who saved his life? She deserves the credit.'

'Trust me, Dougie, you and I will both gain far more advantage by taking the credit, and that includes advantages for Kat Mason.' She pulled a ticket from her pocket. 'This is your reward. First class to LA, leaving on Monday. Abe Schultz will meet you at LAX. We will organize accommodation and a generous living allowance. There's a small part for you in a very significant movie that Seth is co-funding. It starts shooting next month, after which you should have found your feet again. Somebody out there cannot wait to see you.' She pulled out her tablet and tapped the screen. 'We now have lightning fast WiFi here. It is about the only thing to recommend the place.'

On screen, Kiki's face appeared, her lips huge and scarlet. 'Hello, stranger!'

Dougie gaped at it in horror, trying to find the off button.

'I feel so bad about what happened. I knew that fire screwed with your head. I missed you, baby. We gotta get together when you're back. I can't believe you've got a part in *the* biggest movie of the decade. I'd kill to be in that – they say the budget's record breaking and I've always wanted to work with Spiel—'

Finally, Dougie hammered enough buttons to cut the video feed, clenching his eyes tightly shut.

'You turned it off by mistake.' Dollar took the tablet back, trying to resurrect the link.

'Please don't!'

'I thought this would make you happy.' She stared at him in confusion. 'You told me just last night that you are still in love with Kiki.'

'You brought up her name, not me. I just said there was somebody else,' he said, staring at the ticket. 'What about the hunt mastership? The kennel staff and the hounds?' He swallowed the ashes in his throat. 'The bonus?'

'The contract is cancelled, Dougie. This movie will earn you more than any arranged marriage and be *much* better for your image.'

'I thought you said it was just a small part.'

'It's a very big movie.'

Dougie chewed his lip, staring at her in mounting horror. 'I know you're superhuman, Dollar, but you can't tell me that you arranged all this between Seth getting fished out of the lake and now?'

She looked down at the pad, smirking. 'It was already arranged, apart from making contact with Kiki, which I did last night after you told me you still loved her and I realized I would prefer not to be a part of this.'

'You were going to come too?'

'Los Angeles was my getaway plan for us both. You can be a very big star, but you need a strong woman behind you. You are so easy to fall in love with on screen. That is a very magical quality. I see you as the next James Bond – that was my goal as your manager. I asked Seth to release you from your contractual obligations here last week, when you called to say that you would not marry the girl. It was easy to persuade him that you were wrong for the job when you refused to hunt.'

So Seth had known about this last night, had been complicit in it. Yet when Dougie had repeatedly asked about terminating his contract, he'd been given the brush-off. 'Did he know you were planning to come with me?'

'He knew I would not stick around once he got married.' She looked up anxiously, pressing her fingers together beneath her chin. Her hands were shaking and the secret smile back. 'I must tell you something, Dougie. For if this does not go right, I will take down every sword in this house and throw it from the ramparts tonight like the goddess Kali attacking Raktabija.'

Dougie knew he'd been right to be wary.

'Seth has flown to Bradford to ask his parents' blessing to marry the woman he loves, a woman who is not of high birth or unimpeachable innocence, and who met their son when he bought her from a brothel for a dollar.'

'That's wonderful!'

She looked away, those shaking hands wringing together now. 'If they say no, he will not disobey them and he will not marry me. He will take their choice of wife. I have simply been added to the Brides List and put at the top.'

'You love him very much, don't you?'

'I would die for him – and kill for him,' she smiled down at her hands, 'but he wants me to live long and be happy, so I try to give him what he needs. In turn, if I want something, Seth gives it. That is why he gave you to me in the first place.'

'Was I the compensation prize?' Dougie looked at the ticket in his hands.

'We could have been a good team, I believe. Seth thought I would grow bored of you and perhaps he was right. Cerebrally I find you very limited, but sexually you are extremely impressive.'

'Thanks.' He wished he hadn't asked.

'It is unfortunate you were a terrible gigolo. The girl clearly cannot stand you. But you are a very exciting movie star. The screen loves you. That's what you should be doing. Seth totally agrees with me. He thinks you are a very good investment.'

Dougie snorted, remembering the comment about *Dark Knight* being shit after the tenth viewing. He had a feeling that Seth was so devoted to Dollar that he trusted her judgement on high risk ventures, even marriage, it now seemed.

'The one thing Seth was always very uncomfortable about was stopping you getting the part in the big network series,' she was saying. 'He thinks it would have made you a huge star.'

'Maybe he did me a favour.' Dougie gazed across the estate, thinking about the sheer pleasure he drew from its changing landscape, the delight of working with his hounds and horses. The only reason he would want to use the ticket in his hands right now, he realized, with a jolt, was to visit Zephyr, still on stable rest in a veterinary recuperation barn, having his oxygen treatment. 'Was the fire deliberate as well?'

'No! Seth would never harm any animal.' Looking out across the estate, a five-hundred-year-old hunting ground for the super-rich, she hurried on. 'You are free to go back to LA, Dougie. Seth just asks that you don't leave before the cricket because you are captain of the team.'

He laughed in amazement. 'I'm forgiven for fucking up his multi-billion, poverty-ending deal to build flight simulators, but woe betide me if I let him down over the village cricket match?'

'He's in a forgiving mood.' She tilted her head. 'You just saved his life.'

'What if I say I want to stay?' Dougie muttered, looking across to Lake Farm, briefly imagining himself taking on Badger Man and tweedy Dair in jousting duels and tournaments, fighting for her favour.

'There is no job for you here.'

'What happens to the sanctuary?'

'It is safe for now. The estate will even pay for its repair, starting with the bridge. Seth was most insistent about that. He would like it designed like this one.' She held up the book again and Dougie realized that she hadn't been showing him Constance but the lake behind her, across which stretched a beautifully ornate wrought-iron bridge. 'When this photograph was taken, there was a far more substantial bridge. It was dismantled during the war so that the metal could be used in munitions. Only the stone pillars remain, upon which the plank causeway was built. It will significantly improve the look of the parkland for the next – incumbent.'

'Will the estate be sold?'

'That is not decided. Nothing is decided.' She gripped the book so hard the picture plate snagged from its spine stitching and he saw how terrified she was, her knuckles white.

'You guarantee Kat's going to be safe? You won't try to get her out?'

'Maybe we will find her another husband.' Dollar chuckled, not noticing his frozen face. 'She may be able to stay here as long as she likes whether she marries or not.' She flicked the page. 'The Bolt is the challenge to which she aspires, is it not? It says here that the prize for its completion is the Eardisford Purse.'

'What is it?' Dougie had never heard Kat mention it.

She read aloud, '"For the generations of Mytton men who undertook this legendary challenge, the honour of joining the ranks of the very few to achieve the near-impossible feat was far greater than receiving the Eardisford Purse, although that prize was notable in its eccentricity. The Purse contained a signed apple wager between the participant and the estate's owner."'

'What's an apple wager?' Dougie took the book to look at the page. 'Are you saying they went through all that for a bag of Bramleys?'

'It's a local term. It's a simplistic reward and forfeit system basically. Seth's researchers think it is as straightforward as "Climb that tree and I'll give you a pound – fall off and you can give me a pound." Constance Mytton entered an apple wager with her father over the estate, but he failed to honour it. Perhaps marrying Ronnie Gough was really her forfeit.'

He wondered what Kat would be willing to risk losing. Certainly not the farm.

'Is Seth going to challenge her to an apple wager?' he asked, feeling sick at the prospect.

'Kat's wager was agreed with the previous owner,' Dollar explained. 'It was signed before Constance Mytton's death. I do not believe Kat understood the significance of it, and it's not legally binding in itself, but the Mytton solicitors looked into it in great detail, as have Seth's. It could possibly hold up in court. The old lady clearly thought it would be honoured.'

'Kat gets the farm if she succeeds?' It made glorious sense to Dougie. Constance had been denied her own wager; she would redeem the past through Kat.

'I have not seen the document, but I believe that is the gist of it.'

He couldn't wait to tell her. Constance hadn't let her down. Kat had a very real chance of taking control and making the sanctuary into the veteran-animal haven he knew she longed to create there.

'Of course, if she fails,' Dollar said quietly, 'she must leave.'

He stood up, horrified. 'The cantankerous old bat! How could she?'

'She knew her own mind. She was obviously a strong

woman. She saw herself in Kat. She had not failed in this and saw no reason why Kat should. She was an uncompromising egotist with great charm. I think she sounds wonderful.' Dollar was clearly enraptured, reclaiming the book. 'I gather Kat was very fond of her.'

'She loved her. She wants to ride the Bolt in her memory, purely because Constance asked her to. I'm sure she knows nothing about this apple wager.'

'I'm certain you are right. It took a great deal of detective work for Seth to find out the details.'

Dougie went very still. 'He knew about it all along?'

'His legal team saw a reference to it when the purchase took place. His researchers took a while to find out the details, but he got the picture. Then he learned that you were training Kat to ride the Bolt and he was most delighted.'

Dougie closed his eyes, the truth dawning on him. 'I was the only one who encouraged Kat to do it, who helped her and believed in her. Everyone else is convinced she'll fail. That was why Seth was happy for me to stay. I've double-crossed her again.'

'So you think she'll fail?' Dollar's impassive face was trying to hide her loyalty, but she was clearly hoping for a yes.

He thought about Kat's glacial white face today. Riding the course in a quarter of an hour required almost suicidal speed, even without that fear of water. Kat had the speed, the guts and the determination; she was as light as a professional jockey and as tough as one, always bouncing back, always thinking her way around the next bend. But she had yet to swim the lake on the mare. His head was spinning like a weather vane in a typhoon. He remembered her small voice saying she couldn't do it without him. If he made her try, it might cost her the thing she loved most.

'I'm not going to give her the opportunity to fail,' he said determinedly. 'She won't ever try it. It's far too dangerous. She won't get married, at least not to me – that's way too dangerous too. I'll fly to LA on Monday. At least I can't hurt her any more there. She wants me out of her life and she's right. I just bring hurt.'

Chapter 63

Kat saw Harvey first, a white ghost horse among the meadow flowers, muzzle down. He threw up his head and whinnied when he recognized the Lake Farm dogs. Having brought all five of the pensioner pack out together for once, Kat's attempt at a dignified arrival was marred by a bitch fight between the terriers, the lurchers coursing off after a rabbit and the Labrador flopping down to rest with a flatulent fanfare as they came through the gate. Dougie turned, still wearing his yard clothes, hands in his pockets, kicking at the ground. He looked up as she approached, blue eyes gleaming. She felt as though her heart had stopped.

'I thought you'd be dressed for the Bollywood party.' He took in her shorts and faded T-shirt.

'Can't get a date. What's your excuse?'

'My dinner suit's already packed.'

Having spent a lot of the day working around Dawn's frantic pre-party pampering, Kat was exhausted. Her life-saving moment earlier had barely had a chance to sink in. She felt as though she was wading through ball bearings connected to the mains, jumpy and desperate to keep moving. Dawn had been sweet, trying to talk to her about what had happened, to draw her out about Dougie, but Kat was too busy jogging everywhere on overdrive to stop and think, ignoring all advice to rest. She'd disinfected the animal pens, stock-checked and decobwebbed the feed room, given the returning Lake Farm fugitives baths, cold-hosed puffy legs, kept a vigilant check for colic and soothed an apoplectic llama. Anything to stop herself thinking about Dougie. It had succeeded about 0.5 per cent of the time.

'Why is your suit packed?' she asked, standing a respectable three feet away, watching the dogs.

'I'm flying to LA.'

Kat swallowed what felt like a fireball. 'Moving on to another acting role so soon?'

There was a pause. 'That's right. Turned out I was miscast for this one. I'm getting out of your life as requested.'

'So the million-pound proposal is off?' She tried to match his deliberately clipped, glib delivery, but she lacked his acting skill and sounded like a Munchkin with blocked sinuses.

He stepped sideways as Harvey barged into the conversation, checking out pockets. 'Seth withdrew my funding. There is no million. I have nothing worth offering any more. Worthless, that's me.' The big charm smile came out, so unfamiliar and defensive.

'What about the Bolt?' she asked, her chest in flames now.

He cleared his throat, smile fading. 'Don't be a fool. You're not good enough.'

Kat felt as though he'd just punched her. She stepped back.

He was looking down, the dark lashes veiling his eyes as he watched Quiver play-fighting with the two old terriers. His voice was uncharacteristically hard, with none of its customary lazy huskiness softening the blow. 'I'm telling you this for your own good.'

Kat guessed he was trying to spare her the humiliation after he'd left. She still wasn't fast enough. She couldn't cross water. Their one dry run had been a disaster. But her anger flared, like a box of matches dropped in a bonfire. She was devastated that he thought her incapable, decimated that he was leaving.

'I don't care. I will do it one day,' she said angrily, remembering Constance's fierce belief that she was capable of it. 'I'll do it without you. You never belonged here anyway. It's a place for stayers, for loyalty and for dares.'

'And badger men.'

She stared at his set profile. 'What are you talking about?'

He looked up, eyes like lasers. 'The thing with Dollar lasted only a few days when I first got here. What you saw last night was nothing – she wanted a quick buck, but I wasn't playing. What *I* saw last night was you wrapped around Badger Man, then Dair Armitage.'

Kat registered the rage of jealousy, a collision of lowered brows, flared nostrils, slamming cheek muscles and pouting lips on that handsome face. And despite her infuriation, the hurt and the indignation that made her want to thump him, her heart rose into her throat.

'Dollar's in love with Seth,' he was saying. 'Turns out he's in love with her too. You think people would tell each other these things rather than involve other people all the time, wouldn't you?'

'It makes sense.' Kat remembered him saying, 'I love you,' in the water before vanishing beneath the surface to save Seth. Her lungs still burned from diving down when he had literally taken her breath away. She was almost on tiptoe now, her heart in her mouth.

He was still staring at her, blue eyes defensive, blinking at one-second intervals, voice controlled. 'It's better I go. The marriage thing. Sorry. I've never regretted anything so much in my life as agreeing to it. I hope you can forgive me.'

It burst out of her like a round of gunshot: 'I love you too.'

'Give it time, we'll both see the funny side,' he was saying tight-lipped, and then looked up in surprise, no longer blinking. 'What?'

'I love you.'

Dusk hadn't come early, nobody had dimmed the lights and *Gone With the Wind* wasn't playing on the big-screen horizon over Duke's Wood, but Kat and Dougie couldn't stop staring at one another. They stared for a ridiculous amount of time.

Practically *en pointe* now, heart on her lips, Kat watched Dougie's eyes start blinking again, as though he had been given an adrenalin shot. 'I am a no-good,' he said very quickly, voice heart-breaking and husky. 'Kat. I am unreliable and selfish and so screwed up in love with you that I can't think—'

Harvey swung his long freckled face around and knocked Dougie squarely into Kat.

Lust and love made for lightning reflexes. Their arms were around one another in an instant, fingers threading through hair, bodies drawn urgently together, lips colliding. Kat had never been kissed the way Dougie kissed her. His eyes drank her in, his hands warm on her face, guiding her mouth into his, thumbs sliding into the soft hollows beneath her ears and stroking them with exquisite tenderness.

'I thought you hated my guts.' He laughed as they pulled breathlessly apart for the fourth or fifth time.

'Having guts is a good thing,' she insisted, no longer sure if she was *en pointe* because she appeared to have lost the feeling in her lower legs, her knees jelly. 'You use yours so freely – showing off, riding too fast, shooting things, seducing things, saving drowning things and runaway things.' Her eyes sparkled at the memory. 'I'd love your guts.'

'You have my guts, Kat – and some. And you have my heart, every worthless beat it makes.' His eyes danced between hers. 'Here's my plan. I go to LA. I work my arse off acting for a year or two. I get a bit of money, some horses, breed a few foals – Zephyr the Friesian is going to be a daddy. You come out and visit. I come here and visit. I get secure and I get trustworthy. I *will* earn your trust, Kat, and my living. I'll do it the hard way and I'll do it for you.'

She wanted to scream in protest that he mustn't leave, but he looked so earnest she hesitated. 'I thought you hated LA.'

'I do, but I need a job, and a chance to prove I can stick with something at some point in my wasted bloody life.'

Kat knew Dougie could act. He might not be able to emote his way through *Hamlet* in the round six nights a week live, but on screen he was something else. She'd witnessed the Everett Effect before meeting him and could vouch for its power. Yet his face here and now didn't smack of ambition or a desire to do it for anything beyond duty and accountability. 'What do you *really* want to do in life?'

'Truthfully?'

'Would you rather take a dare?'

'I don't need anybody to dare me to want this.' His laughter warmed her skin on its way to her mouth and besieged it with more kisses. 'I want to work my hounds, to train another team of trick horses, to fly Zephyr here. I want to earn your trust, Kat, to ride with you, sleep with you, and for your voice to be the first and last thing I hear every day. I want to swim in the lake with you, work with you, play with you. I want to marry you one day, but not for money – we'll probably be stony broke for life, frankly. But it'll be for keeps. For ever. For us.'

Kat's voice was a squeak of emotional overload. 'Your proposal technique needs brushing up, but the package sounds good.'

'I'll remember that next time I go down on one knee.'

'As you pointed out this morning, I haven't actually given you my answer yet. I haven't ridden the Bolt.' Suddenly gripped by fervour, she looked towards the clock tower beyond the woods. There was at least an hour of daylight left.

'No, Kat.' Dougie was shaking his head violently as he read her thoughts, gripping her shoulders tightly.

But her blood was up, Constance's voice in her head and her mouth. 'I can do it.'

'I know you can do it, Kat, but there's so much more at stake.'

Kat knew what was as stake. And she wanted to give him her answer so badly that she would ride faster than she ever had before. Not staying to listen to his protests, she sprinted back towards the millstream track. 'Unpack your dinner jacket. I'll see you at the farm in twenty minutes. There's nothing you can say that will stop me, Dougie.'

Dougie had never put on a dinner suit so fast, tied a bow-tie so lop-sidedly, or fallen over a dog so much. Quiver trembled with anticipation underfoot, sensing something life-changing about to happen. As he dressed, Dougie thought about all the things he could say to stop Kat, played them through in his head incessantly, rehearsed them and dismissed them. If he doubted her now, he would destroy her self-belief. Constance had not wanted her to know about the wager in the Eardisford Purse. She'd believed in Kat. He must too.

As he gathered Quiver up to leave the house, he pressed his lips to the small black head and said his first prayer in years. 'Please keep her safe.'

*

Kat had pulled out the Tantric accessories from behind the Lake Farm sofa. Now she dragged a fat floor cushion from its jewelled cover, attacked its seams with scissors to create a neck opening and arm holes, then pulled it over her head. She turned another into a pair of shapeless knickerbockers that she dragged over her breeches and secured with a belt before admiring her reflection in the microwave door – the closest thing Lake Farm had to a mirror. It was a quirky but no less dramatic look, she told herself encouragingly.

Dougie arrived as she was wrapping a sari over her helmet to create a huge turban headdress that was unlikely to survive twenty yards into Duke's Wood. Arms full of fabric, she stopped when she saw him step through the kitchen door. In black tie, Dougie Everett was suaver than Brosnan, sexier than Connery and more ripped than Craig. His eyes were bluer and hotter than a Mauritian ocean bay.

He took the ends of the sari from her and slowly unravelled it. Then he pulled the cushion cover back over her head and pressed his mouth to her shoulder. 'Fancy dress optional. Nerves of steel compulsory.' He took her face in his hands and tilted it so that she was looking straight into his eyes. 'Are you sure about this?'

'You know I have to do it.'

His lips landed hard against hers, then softened to draw her in, long fingers threading through her hair as she found her body curling into his, the perfect fit.

'Do this for yourself, Kat. Forget about the marriage proposal. Forget about Constance. Forget about this place. Let this be for you.'

'You don't get out if it that easily. You're still getting your answer. You dared me, remember?'

573

Chapter 64

Bollywood had come to Herefordshire. Staged to impress Igor, the Eardisford party was on an epic scale with no expense spared, no cliché left out and no chance of a moment's boredom for the hundreds of guests. It was a sensory overload of colour, rhythm and entertainment. Big screens had been erected throughout the old house to show the dance sequences from the iconic movies, the catchy music piped into every room. Pretty Indian waitresses in traditional costumes whisked around with trays of champagne or bite-sized bhajis and samosas. There were snake charmers and illusionists, puppeteers and acrobats. The central run of reception rooms had been tented in peacock blue, scarlet and saffron, the draped ceilings backlit to glow like a sunset, hand-pulled fans sweeping back and forth. Vast gold-sprayed prop-store statues of Hindu gods lined the walls, and dancers glittered and jingled between the rooms, matching the movements on the screens.

The carnival atmosphere carried on outside in the balmy, midge-speckled dusk of a high summer evening, where the water in the floodlit fountains had been dyed orange, pink and purple, jewel-coloured streamers and banners glowed like neon in the setting sun and a huge, domed marquee sat like a mini Taj Mahal on the lawns, booming out the music that was playing in the house. In every corner of the gardens, more entertainers drew the eye, fire-eating and juggling, sword-swallowing and balancing, and most of all dancing.

'I hope this has been health-and-safety-checked,' said

Miriam, eyeing a troupe of acrobats balancing on a camel. Her cerise sari had corsetry and a platform bra built in and she'd added a high-grade pedicure to her spa treatments that day – her jewelled flip-flops were set off by the softest fish-nibbled skin and sparkling nails.

Vivacious in an emerald body tube, Dawn wasted no time in introducing herself, Dair loyally at her side in a tweedy-coloured turban that was tipping ever-lower over his forehead. 'We met through Kat Mason in February,' Dawn reminded Miriam. 'I'm interested to know if you think there's any call for a mobile beautician in this part of Herefordshire.'

Miriam replied eagerly that she thought there was indeed a tremendous call – she would love to be pampered at home, as would most of her girlfriends. And many local women would embrace a higher standard of personal care if it were on offer in a convenient venue one day a month – 'At the village hall, say.' She nodded pointedly at two elderly sisters hip-jigging by a coloured fountain.

Cyn and Pru were clearly entranced by the music. They clapped repeatedly, wrists and bodies jangling like sleigh bells from the beads and sequins covering their home-made costumes. Tall Pru was sporting a makeshift *salwar kameez* consisting of a brightly coloured seventies kaftan and clashing eighties harem pants dug out of her jumble-sale box, while little Cyn had a brightly jewelled gypsy *ghaghra* skirt and ill-advised pink crop-top, a matching beaded chiffon scarf draped loosely on her head. Both were sporting sparkly bindis on their foreheads – sticky-backed jewels prised from a great-niece's birthday card – and matching expressions of unalloyed rapture.

'There's a snake charmer!'

'There's an elephant!'

'You wouldn't think we were in a global recession, would

you?' chuckled Frank Bingham-Ince. His eyes were nearly popping out at the sight of so many exotic maidens baring their midriffs. Unfortunately he was being policed by his wife for once, sixteen stones of moral disapproval in a Thatcher blue sari wound tightly around her bulk. 'I thought he was a philanthropist.'

'No doubt it's all offset against tax,' observed Dair, tweedy turban lowering towards his nose now as he rolled up to introduce Dawn to Frank and his wife, who quickly admitted that, yes, a mobile spa would be a terrific boon, especially for one's 'garden topiary'.

'Doesn't Boyle do that with the secateurs?' barked Frank, listening in.

'I love people round here,' Dawn told Dair, as they moved up the terrace steps towards the main house. 'They're just so . . . chilled. It's all so chilled this far out of Watford.'

'Would you like to borrow my coat?' Dair offered gallantly.

'God, you're lovely.' She threaded her arm through his.

Dawn tried not to think about Kat, whom she'd been forced to leave behind, despite much cajoling all day and a great many beauty treatments, mostly performed in an ambush while she was mucking out an animal enclosure. Kat insisted she was fine and that she was meeting Dougie before coming. Dawn respected that dynamic far too much to interfere any more, but she knew when she was being shut out. It made her want to move in all the more.

'Do you think there's much call for male treatments round here?' she asked Dair now, as they moved smoothly through security into the main house. 'Back, sack and crack type thing?'

'Absolutely not,' he said firmly.

Dawn loved the fact Dair was so masterful. She was thrilled

that being with him tonight meant having access to both the servants' party in the gardens and marquee, and the masters' in the house.

Up here amid the tented sunsets and big screens, guests had been shipped in from every cosmopolitan corner of the globe, including several Bollywood stars and another pouting clutch of rented Baltic models. There were local landowners, London bankers, American financiers, Chinese capitalists, Euro royals and hordes of hired celebrities trading air kisses and posing endlessly against a backdrop of swagged silk for the society photographer. Seth's most trusted team players had been tasked with ensuring the guests mingled, introductions were made, the biggest business allies felt the centre of attention and the crowd formed a constant happy drift of high spirits.

Overseeing them all, Dollar was playing hostess in turquoise and gold silk, as ravishing as any Bollywood heroine. Traditional costume transformed her. Dawn, who had never seen her before, decided she was by far the most beautiful woman in the room when Dair pointed her out in a whisper. She had an almost ethereal femininity, the glittering gold of her necklace and headdress softening her face in which the dark eyes seemed far too large, the thoughts incredibly deep.

Dollar was close to meltdown. Outwardly cool and controlled beneath the jaunty, happy soundtrack, the tremor of her jewellery resounded like a hive of bees. Seth was still not back from Bradford, his phone switched off. In his absence, the mantle fell on her to ensure the event was a great success. It was a constant round of overseeing the big picture and micro-managing smaller problems, which normally used a fraction of her active brain, but tonight her ever-churning heart was demanding a majority share, and the mutinous villagers were trying to claim

577

more ground by the minute. As she suspected, the 'servants' were causing problems with a combination of raucous, drunken rubber-necking and mutinous rabble-rousing. They had been trying to infiltrate the masters' party all night. The hired security staff – mostly Eastern European man-mountains brought in for Igor's benefit – were in danger of being too heavy-handed. Several earthmen were already sporting fresh black eyes and more lost teeth.

'I knew this was a bad idea.' She had cornered Dair, who was looking extraordinary in an open-necked satin shirt, turban like a tweed mushroom, a curvaceous and sweet-smiling blonde in a glittery green dress beaming at his side. 'You must calm them down, Dair. We have to avoid negative PR at all costs.'

'I warned you this was a bad idea. Russ has been whipping them up all day.'

The estate team were trying to play down the events of that morning by the lake, hoping the party would take everybody's mind off them, although rumours of Igor's archaic stag chase – wildly exaggerated through much retelling at the Eardisford Arms at lunchtime – now featured an army of bow-wielding Russians shooting arrows at baby fawns, elderly llamas and terrified sheep.

It wasn't the hunting news that was causing the most ongoing outrage in the servants' tent however. It was still Dougie Everett's indecent proposal. The story, which had been doing the rounds all week, had got no less salacious. The scandal was all the more shocking because everyone had liked Dougie so much. But they adored Kat.

'Just like his bastard father,' Bill Hedges was ranting at a trainee *Herefordshire Life* reporter, who was supposed to be taking down names for the social-pages photographer. Having raided the am-dram costume store again, Bill was in a full-length gold *sherwani* coat with a turban as wide as his shoulders. 'Vaughan Everett took cash for questions, and Everett junior takes cash for marriage vows. Poor little Kat stood up to all the Mytton beneficiaries bullying her – now this. Old Constance will be coming back to haunt this place if it doesn't stop, mark my words.'

Chapter 65

Arriving at the Bollywood party, Dougie was deathly pale and unsmiling. Having just thundered the length of the estate on the sanctuary's quad bike, opening gates, pushing back brambles and checking for new livestock, his dinner suit was covered with burrs and dust, and his blond hair full of twigs. He hadn't shaved, had forgotten his invitation and had a dog with him, but such was his beauty and class, he was granted instant access to both servants' and masters' revels, turbaned and veiled heads turning to stare at him as he marched through the main house. Navigating his way past acres of festooned silk that made him feel as though he was trapped inside a tumble-dryer, he made a bee-line for Dollar, who was lying low in a panelled corridor shouting into her mobile phone.

'What do you mean I can't speak to him, Deepak? You are piloting a plane and you answered your phone. Put him on the line! . . . Oh, I see.' She looked up at Dougie, her face unmasked, her eyes huge. 'Very well. Tell him I will be waiting beside the landing strip . . . *What* delicate situation?'

Dougie paced urgently up and down the corridor until she

came off the call, when he told her in an undertone that he was going to need her help. 'In about fifteen minutes, we'll have to get people away from the terrace steps and the main hall.'

'Is it a bomb?' she breathed, reaching for her phone again to call her head of security.

He covered her hand to stop her. 'Only if you classify my heart as a life-threatening incendiary device. Kat's taking on the Bolt.'

'What a stupid thing to do tonight of all nights.' She checked her wrist watch. 'In a quarter of an hour, Seth's plane will be landing.'

'Can you get him to circle out of the way for a few extra minutes?'

'Absolutely not. His elderly parents are on board.'

'I don't care who is on board, they can't land yet. She's about to ride a horse through the lake.'

To Dougie's dismay, he heard a familiar metallic click as a gun's trigger catch came off and he saw something glint under Dollar's sari. 'I will let *nothing* risk upsetting Seth's parents, do you understand? Nothing. You must go and stop her.'

'Frankly, I don't think anybody could stop her right now,' he admitted, 'not even a plane.'

Standing at the brow of Duke's Wood, listening out for the church clock, Kat knew her route, so carefully planned and practised, galloped a thousand times in her head. Dusk was falling, red fingers pushing through the tree line behind her.

Sri was on maximum alert, keyed up and desperate to get going. Kat looked at those familiar curling ears twitching, feeling the mare growing ever-taller beneath her as the spring coiled, lifting her ribs and putting her on her toes.

You can do this, Katherine, came a familiar rallying call, as

Constance's gravelly, laughter-infused voice urged her on. *It is the best feeling in the world. Do this and you can do anything.*

In the valley below, the hour bell rang out at last. She loosened her grip on the reins, barely needing to touch the mare's sides before they were streaking into a gallop like a Derby contender exploding from the start gates.

I want you to do it because it will set you free. You will understand what I am talking about when it happens.

It was happening.

At the servants' party, Russ was sporting flip-flops and a Gandhi cap along with a *dhoti* made from a hop sack. Knocking back Kingfisher beer faster than a bad lad in a curry house, he was holding forth about his heroics to the Eardisford Arms regulars, who had regrouped to line the bar in the marquee. 'If the bullet had been a centimetre to the left, it would have gone straight through me. Always knew there was illegal hunting planned. You can't get away with it these days.'

The earthmen exchanged glances and shuffled off for more free beer. Mags remained loyally gazing up at him above her jewelled veil, marked by Calum the Talon who was dressed in a shiny dinner suit that still had raffle tickets in its pockets from the last five hunt balls. Looking more belly-dancer than Bollywood in a costume that revealed the full glory of her tattoo collection, Mags had been so impressed by Russ's daring near miss that she'd placed the Thermos with the bullet hole on the 'trophy shelf' behind the bar in the pub.

'Do you think he'll try again?' she asked.

'If he does, I'll be waiting. I don't care how many bullets I have to dodge.' Russ clasped his beer bottle to his chest staunchly. 'Shouldn't think he'll stay now he knows he can't make up his own rules.'

'We all miss the Hon Con,' said Calum the Talon, eyeing a pink-watered fountain with distaste. 'She was a gutsy old bird. Galloped to save this place, she did.'

'Her lot were just as bad,' Russ pointed out hotly. 'I took a bullet for its future.'

'Will you shut up about the bloody bullet?' snapped Calum. 'It weren't much more than a ball-bearing. Besides, it missed you.'

'Calm down.' Mags arm-locked them both in an affectionate cuddle. Over her head, Russ shot a swaggering smile at Calum, who glowered back and drew a finger line above his hawk-themed bow-tie to mime a throat being cut. The two men had been squaring up for a fight for several weeks, which Mags found thrilling.

'Shall we try and get upstairs again?' Russ suggested, the beer making him militant. 'I refuse to be segregated.'

'Better entertainment down here,' said Mags, as their little group was joined by Dair, proud as a peacock with Dawn on his arm. She was still conducting eager market research as she quizzed Calum about his grooming preferences.

The villagers and estate staff mostly stuck together in their usual social groups in the marquee, intimidated by the glamour and ostentatious wealth on show in the house. Their home-made costumes were a colourful hotchpotch of scarves, curtains and throws with lots of turbans at jaunty angles, along with a few dusty dinner suits and ballgowns.

'I can't wait to see what Seth looks like,' Dawn said eagerly, pulling Dair closer. 'Apparently he's been delayed on family business in Yorkshire.'

'Probably getting last-minute cricket coaching with Rashid,' Russ muttered, stalking off to ask a waitress which of the canapés on her tray were vegan.

'Has Russ come as Jesus?' Dawn giggled, admiring how dapper and manicured Dair looked after his pre-party Beautiful Dawn session, although he did admittedly whiff rather badly of fake tan. She saw herself as Victoria Beckham to his Golden Balls.

She checked her watch. 'I'm sure Kat should be here by now. I'm worried about her. She was meeting Dougie over an hour ago. What did he say to you again?'

Before Dair could answer, there was a collective hush as the man himself hurried into the marquee. Hair dishevelled, collar open and bow-tie undone, he was the epitome of a bad-boy bounder who'd just spilled out of a mistress's bed. The villagers eyed him suspiciously, some with open contempt.

'He's got a nerve coming tonight,' growled Mags.

Dawn, who had almost given up hope of ever meeting Dougie Everett, was blown away by how handsome he was in the flesh, the bone structure as beautiful as anything constructed by a Disney animator conjuring a fairytale prince, his eyes cliché blue, the sun-bleached hair like tousled spun gold and the triangle from broad shoulder to narrow hip in perfect proportion. He was built to wear a dinner suit. She'd happily buff his fingernails and admire his fabulous skin all day. Lucky, lucky Kat.

He didn't seem to notice the frosty stares around him as he hurried to Dair's side and muttered urgently in his ear.

'What? Right *now*?' Dair stepped back in shock as Dawn leaped forward to introduce herself as Kat's best friend, noticing as she did so the deeply troubled expression on his face, the black smudges beneath those blue eyes.

'Where is she?' she asked anxiously. 'What's happening?'

'She's riding the Bolt,' Dair told her, in an undertone.

Dawn let out a shriek. 'She's—'

Dair clamped his hand over her mouth. 'We mustn't let word get out yet – they'll all get overexcited. First, we have to figure out how to stop a plane landing. Sorry.' He removed his hand from her mouth.

'I love you being demonstrative.' She shuddered happily. 'What plane?'

Dougie was looking around urgently, running his hand through his hair so that it stood on end. 'If we don't delay it, it'll roar down in front of the lake just as she's crossing it.'

'I'll get Dollar to radio Deepak.' Dair reached for his phone.

'I've tried that. She refused. Apparently Seth's parents are on board.' He lowered his voice. 'She's pretty wound up about them visiting. She even pulled a gun on me. It seems that there's some sort of emergency and they can't delay landing.'

'What emergency?' Dawn was thrilled by the turn of events, which was better than a *Die Hard* movie.

Dougie cleared his throat and dropped his voice even lower. Dawn strained to hear anything he was saying over the party hubbub, although Dair plainly could.

'Surely they can cross their bloody legs for five minutes,' he fumed, marching off, intent on finding Dollar. He stopped and hurried back, swallowing nervously. 'Did you say a gun?'

'Yes. I got her to put it away by promising I'd try to stop Kat. But I won't. She deserves this moment. She doesn't need that fucking plane coming down in her path.' His eyes flashed and he looked at his watch again, the red streaks deepening in his hollow cheeks, the muscles there hammering. 'Oh, Christ, she'll be on her way.'

Watching his face, Dawn realized that he really was deeply, hopelessly and fiercely in love with Kat.

Dougie looked at her in despair. 'If the mare panics – oh,

Christ. This is entirely my fault. I'm going to have to go out there and stop her, aren't I?'

'No!' Dawn looked around at the crowd in the tent, their makeshift saris and turbans. 'I have an idea.'

Kat and Sri had come flying out of Duke's Wood into the setting sun bang on target, racing across two cut hayfields and alongside a rapeseed crop before dropping through the steep spinney to thunder along the bank of the nursery lake and into Lush Bottom, where she passed her next time marker at the oak and checked her watch again. She'd lost ground.

Faster, girl. You have to make the quarter bell. You can do it! Give him your answer!

She kicked on, feeling the surge of speed beneath her as they streaked across the familiar stretch of soft turf before taking a tug so they could turn back into the woods again.

Ducking low, feeling the heat of the mare's neck against her cheek, she laughed at the sheer energy rocketing through her. 'You are sublime!' she told Sri. 'We are sublime!'

Seth was seriously regretting his decision to allow the party to go ahead and to visit his parents so soon after coughing up two lungfuls of lake water. The euphoria that had hit him after his near-death experience had been replaced by total exhaustion and a racking cough. He'd run out of arguments to stop his mother insisting she and his father must come back with him. He should have taken Dollar with him to Bradford, he thought, not left her to cope with everything while he dashed off to see his parents like a guilty teenager.

Now his mother was glaring at him from the seat opposite, handbag clamped to her knee, clearly regretting that final cup of tea before they'd set out. Unlike his luxurious jet, the super-fast little Cessna was the Porsche of the air and had no on-board lavatory. His father was staring excitedly out of the window, commenting on the engineering behind the lines of pylons they were flying over. They were crossing some of the most stunning countryside in Herefordshire, but Japinder Seth Singh was more interested in his bird's eye view of the National Grid than admiring the Malverns, marvelling at the engineering and the superstructure. Seth smiled to himself, knowing that he was exactly the same. The countryside was largely wasted on him. He was more excited by Eardisford's new 4G communications mast than the tens of thousands of acres in which it was hidden. Although it was disguised as a tree, its arrival had caused a lot of local consternation, and tonight's party was an important part of winning villagers around.

With a jolt, Seth realized he had forgotten his fancy dress. He looked around the small plane interior for inspiration, but there were just a few sleep masks and a BCCI cricket hat.

At the controls, Deepak lifted one of his earphones and called back. 'There will be a delay before we can land, I'm afraid.'

'What delay?' demanded Mrs Singh, clearly horrified.

'There appears to be a lot of debris on the landing strip.'

Seeing his mother's frozen face, Seth closed his eyes and groaned.

'Thank you, guys!' Dawn clapped her hands above her head, spinning around and beaming with gratitude at the half-dressed villagers she'd rallied into urgent action.

The small semi-naked crowd that was now standing on the grass around her stared at a small plane circling high in the sky.

Only Dair was looking in the opposite direction, tilting his head and peering along the broad grass landing strip that was criss-crossed with hundreds of metres of unravelled sari and turban spelling out two words.

'I'll get fired for this for sure,' he muttered, as he read it. 'Isn't that advertising?'

In ten-foot lettering, the turbans read, Go Kat!

'We didn't have enough time for "Beautiful Dawn".' Dawn kissed him tenderly on the mouth.

Dair was bursting with pride for his clever and gutsy new girlfriend. She was a sensation. It was all he could do to stop himself getting down on one knee right there.

Dollar was running towards them across the parkland now, turquoise sari flapping. 'What are you *doing*? I will call security and have you all thrown out. This mess must be removed *immediately*.'

Dawn glanced at her watch, then across the lake to the last sunset-stained fields and woods beside the farm. 'We'll have it all cleared away again in five minutes.'

Dollar stepped closer and growled: 'If Mrs Singh has been forced to avail herself of a plastic cup, that five minutes may have cost you your life.' She stalked off.

'Is she always like that?' Dawn asked Dair, amazed.

'More or less.'

Lined up on the terrace, Bollywood dancers gyrating around them, guests peered out across the dusk-flooded park. Unable to stand still, Dougie paced up and down the stone balustrade by the dining room, then bounded down the stairs to the lower terrace where some of the villagers were gathered, puffing cigarettes and demanding to know what they were supposed to be looking out for.

'Fireworks?' suggested Cyn, now very tipsy on champagne, sequins raining down as she leaned over the balustrade, kicking up her skirts.

Pru hauled her sister back before she fell right over. 'Shouldn't they wait until it's dark?'

And then they all held their collective breath as they saw a horse galloping along the lime avenue on the far side of the lake, its coat an unmistakable patchwork of chestnut and white.

'Kat's riding the Bolt!' Miriam gasped. 'She's bloody well doing it!'

Kat had expected Sri to hesitate on going into the lake and was ready to give her lots of leg-kicking encouragement as Dougie had taught her. But instead she took a huge running leap, belly-flopping in and almost losing Kat in the process. She clung on tightly as the mare splashed in a paddling, plunging canter through the shallows, sending up arcs of water, her knees high. Then she felt her drop lower beneath her, her neck stretching out and the rhythm changing as she lost her footing and began to swim.

For a moment blind panic engulfed Kat, black water swirling around her. She wondered why she was doing this, what possible good it could do to re-enact an archaic dare just so she could give Dougie Everett his answer. Then she remembered Constance's eyes, bright as full moons whenever she spoke of doing it, her utter faith that it had given her the extraordinary fortitude and confidence that had spirited her through life. She saw the beautiful house in front of her and felt the amazing power of the horse beneath her, bred from a forefather that had completed the same challenge, and suddenly she knew for certain why she was doing this. She was riding a ghost home to rest: she was taking Constance home one last time.

Atta girl! Feels amazing, doesn't it? Bloody marvellous. What a horse.

Sri snorted loudly as she swam, a strange bellow-like rhythm that comforted Kat as they powered along, passing a puzzled moorhen and then looming up above the waterline again as the horse's feet found the bottom and she started plunging in her water-splashing canter towards dry land.

'You beauty!' Kat hugged her neck, breathless with exhilaration and relief.

As they scrambled up the bank, she checked her watch. She had just over a minute and a half to get to the Hereford road. There was only the climb up through the parkland to do now, but Sri was tired. They had never timed this section because it was impossible to rehearse, but Dougie had guessed two minutes. Urging Sri to go faster, Kat could see the house glowing in the gathering dusk like the mother ship, the vast marquee and the jewel-covered awning on the terrace its sails. She could hear a strange sound, a roaring cacophony. Then she realized it was cheering.

Kicking back into a gallop, she reached into her pocket for the red scarf she'd tucked in there and pulled it out to hold up so that it trailed behind her in the wind as she charged out of the lime avenue and up to the haha. Rallying her last reserves of energy, Sri jumped in to it in one tiger-like bound and they thundered into the gardens.

Low in the sky behind her a plane engine was roaring as it came down to land, causing the tired mare to put on a burst of panic speed so that she charged through the Italian garden rather faster than Kat had intended, sending box leaves flying and almost flattening a couple canoodling behind a high bank of lavender – was that Russ and Mags looking up at her in shock? – and before she knew it, she was at the base of the terrace steps.

Unable to stop smiling now, she rode up them exactly as Constance had done almost eighty years previously, in through the double doors, clattering across the marble floor where guests and jingling Indian dancers had parted to form a wide path for her to trot through, some astonished, others clapping and whooping.

The crowd began following now, running to keep up as horse and rider trotted out through the double front doors to the long chestnut-lined front drive that led to the Hereford road. Kicking back into hunt-chase pace, Kat's ears strained for the clock's quarter chime.

Not that she'd have a hope of hearing it once she spotted Dougie waiting between the tall stone posts supporting the ornate cast-iron gates, each topped with a lion rampant. Kat's heart was now crashing far too loudly to hear bells, or even Sri's hoofs. Overwhelming pride and relief lit his face as she galloped towards him and he held out his arms, shouting something she couldn't hear. She didn't need to hear it to know how he felt. Kicking to go faster, fifty yards between them, she finally understood what looking love straight in the eye really meant.

Behind her, the music boomed, the aeroplane roaring down beyond the house, but Kat barely heard more than a distant rhythm and a tinny buzz. The wave of party guests following her along the drive were cheering, a rowdy, shrieking babble, familiar village voices whooping her name, but Kat heard only her own rasping, exhausted breaths and drumming heartbeat as she came to a halt at last, reaching up to touch one of the lions rampant and looking down to see Dougie clapping and whooping, his handsome face wreathed in smiles – was that a tear? – telling her she'd done it, she'd really bloody well done it, and she was amazing and he really bloody loved her with all his heart.

Still hardly able to take it in, Kat slid from Sri on jelly legs and covered the mare with pats and kisses, while Dougie loosened her girth and noseband. Kat thanked her over and over again. Then she thanked Constance, out loud, for challenging her to do it, for telling her that it would be the most amazing feeling, that she would understand once she had done it, that it would set her free. 'Thank you,' she shouted gleefully at the house, the lions, the sky. 'You were right. Thank you!'

But Constance's voice had fallen silent in her head now. She'd found her way home in style.

Dougie stepped behind her, wrapping his arms around her. 'Hear that?'

The quarter chime was ringing out, and she let out a cry of euphoria, pressing her face against Sri's hot neck. 'You are beautiful. You are more than sublime.' She turned to Dougie, her heart so overwhelmed with emotion it felt as though it was bungee-jumping between the moon and the earth. She suddenly found she couldn't speak.

He had no words either. Instead he kissed her, a kiss that turned her tired legs into air, her aching muscles into pure energy, her over-pumped, exhausted heart into a furnace.

When they pulled apart, his eyes didn't leave hers, arms tight and protective around her, foreheads pressed together and lashes tangling.

The party guests had started to catch up. One of the girl grooms from the village took Sri to walk her around to cool off. Congratulations were coming thick and fast. Mobile phones were out taking photographs, voices chattering that this was the last time the Bolt would ever be run, that Constance would have been proud, and a few less charitable, that Dougie Everett should sling his hook right now and leave Kat alone.

Neither Kat nor Dougie heard a word.

'I have my answer for you,' she told him.

He blinked, his thick lashes soft against her cheek, then carried on looking so deeply into her eyes she thought he'd probably seen exactly what she was saying before it passed her lips.

'My answer is not yet.'

Somebody in the crowd shushed the others, the noise spreading like a hiss before it fell quiet.

His eyes danced between hers. 'That's a good answer.'

Kat's voice cracked with emotion. 'Now I have a question for you.'

'Anything.'

'Will you stay?'

He didn't hesitate. 'Yes.'

On the landing strip, Mrs Singh was the first on to the steps, lifting her sari as she stepped hurriedly down. Waiting at the bottom, an attractive girl was holding open the door of a glossy black car. She pressed her hands together reverently. '*Namaste*.'

Mrs Singh threw herself inside. 'Don't wait for the others,' she hissed. 'Drive!'

Dollar rushed round to the driver's side and leaped in, flipping the shift. They reached a bathroom within thirty seconds, a luxurious haven out of bounds to party guests, into which Mrs Singh hurried. Two minutes later, she reappeared, smiling, acknowledging the girl with a grateful nod. 'Please now take me back to my son.'

It was a start, Dollar told herself. A small, bonding start. She could do the life-saving heroics later.

When she delivered Mrs Singh back to Seth, both women were startled to find him wearing a black sleep mask with holes cut into it like Zorro, topped with a cricket Panama. Even half covered, Seth's worried face told Dollar that he'd momentarily believed she'd abducted his mother. But then his mouth split into its big-kid smile, and he said, 'Mum, Dad – I'd like you to meet Dollar. The girl I want to marry.'

Dollar flew to his side, fighting tears of joy: Seth introducing her like that meant his parents must have given their approval. 'You've told them all about me?' she whispered happily.

He swallowed hard, looking from one parent to the other. 'This is the first they know.'

Mrs Singh cast her eye up and down Dollar. 'I hope you are not planning to start family life here in this house. It is far too large for small children and it will be impossible to heat.'

'I wouldn't want to carpet it,' Japinder agreed, looking at the acres of marble floor.

'We'll buy somewhere smaller,' Seth said. 'Closer to Bradford. Mostly we'll live in Mumbai. Until the kids arrive, at least.' He gave Dollar an encouraging smile.

Mrs Singh's dark eyes bored into her future daughter-in-law's, disapproving yet resigned. 'Japinder and I were hoping he would introduce you eventually. He has clearly been in love with somebody for many years. I threatened him many times that I would choose him a wife and found him many suitable girls in the hope that it would force his hand, but nothing worked. What has changed your mind, Arjan?'

'She saved my life today,' Seth took Dollar's hand and kissed it, 'and I realized that life is not worth living without her.'

'Ah.' Mrs Singh seemed unimpressed. 'Is that why you are dressed as the Lone Ranger? He was quite obsessed with the TV show as a boy,' she told Dollar, rolling her eyes at Seth's *ad hoc* disguise. 'And who are all these people, Arjan? Do you know them?'

'A few,' he admitted.

'Then ask them to go home. I would like to go to bed and they are very noisy. What is your real name?' she asked Dollar.

'Dulari.'

'That will be what I will call you. It is pretty. Japinder, wish your son and Dulari good night. Where is our room?'

'You have sixteen bedroom suites to choose from,' Seth told her proudly, beckoning for one of his staff to take his parents' luggage and show them to the best guest suite.

'Why did you not tell me this is a hotel? Now it makes sense. I would have preferred it if you had booked one that is a little quieter, Arjan, but it has a very attractive lake.'

Seth's father gave him a long-suffering smile. 'Cricket match tomorrow, you say?'

Seth nodded. 'I don't think it's exactly Headingley, but it's the first time I've owned my own pitch.'

'Now you know you've made it.' Japinder grinned, gripping his shoulders. 'Your mother's mighty relieved, lad. She was starting to think she might be a fella.' He nodded at Dollar.

Seth hugged him. 'Dollar's everything to me.'

His father gave him a toothy smile. 'Happen you'll be a good husband. Your mother's right about this house, though. It's far too damned big.'

Kat and Dougie leaned over the gate, watching Sri roll in the moonlight.

'When I bring Zephyr home, we'll put her in foal to him,' he promised.

'Who says she wants a foal?'

'You don't ask horses, Kat. You put them together and see what happens.'

'Offering them a million doesn't work, then?'

His eyes gleamed in the half-light. 'Are you ever going to forgive me for that?'

'In a year's time when the estate's been sold as a country club and we're totally broke with lawyers on our arses and geriatric goats on the loose round the golf course, I probably won't forgive you for not doing your job properly.'

'If I'd done my job properly I'd have been galloping around with a bow and arrow.'

'That may also feature in the next-year scenario if we can't afford to eat, although I would prefer it if you stick to hunting fish.'

'God, I can't wait to live this year.' His mouth found hers, moreish and greedy, tasting of night air and naughtiness.

'Midsummer's Day,' she breathed between kisses. 'Next year.'

'What about it?'

Their kisses grew more urgent, the gate clanking.

'Ask me again then.'

'It's a promise.'

Laughing with such overwhelming happiness that she could no longer keep her feet on the ground, Kat wrapped her arms around his shoulders and jumped up into his waiting grip, her mouth landing joyfully against his.

'There is ... one thing ... I should ... probably tell you,' Dougie said, between kisses. 'Have you ever heard ... of an apple wager?'

Chapter 66

The Eardisford cricket pitch was no longer green. A month of sun had baked the wicket to crackle glaze and the outfield was a crisp bisque.

Having breakfasted on food she thought far too rich and been driven around the estate, which she'd declared very big and rather boring, Mrs Singh settled uncomfortably in a designer deckchair and prepared to snooze in front of a cricket match, grateful for something familiar to criticize at last. Sitting eagerly beside her, Japinder was as excited as he had been when he'd watched his son bat for the first eleven at school. Perched on the opposite side of Mrs Singh, already exhausted from a morning with them, Dollar discreetly pulled out her tablet to surf property sites, then discovered there was no signal. The sooner they got away from Eardisford the better, as long as they moved no closer to Bradford.

The village won the toss and elected to field, then selected their fearsome spinner, Calum the Talon, to bowl. His middle finger was shaped like the bird's claw after which he'd been nicknamed. He dismissed the handsome opening batsman with his first ball. The crowd cheered the wicket with partisan delight, and a few crueller cat calls.

Dougie took his duck with a heroic bow and good humour, then loped off with a shrug and a smile to Kat, who had been cornered by Frank Bingham-Ince and Miriam, both looking secretive and eager.

'I think I have a bit of work to do on my cricket *and* my public image,' he said to them.

'Can't help you with either of those, I'm afraid.' Frank flashed his debonair smile and lowered his voice. 'But I hear you might be looking for a job.'

They were both distracted as the crowd let out an admiring sigh and a ball whistled far overhead into God's Plot.

*

596

At the crease, batting third, was a handsome Indian man that the villagers took to be one of the several who were now part of the Eardisford workforce. He prepared to take the next delivery, eyes narrowed behind a high-tech face cage. In whistled a short ball, which he struck easily to the boundary again, this shot lightning quick and low.

'What's his name?' checked a few in the crowd.

'Singh.'

The delivery that followed was even shorter. This time it cracked away at shoulder height, fast as a bullet.

'Mine!' shouted Russ at point, diving for it, his hands cupping a fraction too late. The ball hit his forehead with a crack louder than a wicket splitting. He dropped to the grass like a felled oak.

The bloodthirsty, primeval scream from the refreshment tent woke Mrs Singh in a clatter of fast-folding deckchair as Mags rushed out, tea-towel still in hand, throwing herself down at Russ's side to check for a pulse. First aid not being one of her strong points, she let out a groan of anguish and turned towards the batsman. 'You've killed him, you bastard! You've killed the man I love!'

'Oh, hell.' Kat watched in alarm. 'I think Mags is going to punch the batsman.'

'Is Russ okay?' Dougie peered hopefully at his lifeless form.

'I can see his legs moving, but it looks like Calum's going to finish him off. Quick!'

While the rest of the village watched agog, Kat raced across the pitch. She brought down Mags just before she tried to smash a fist into the batsman's face mask.

*

'She's definitely back,' Dawn said proudly, as she watched Kat walking Mags to Russ, now sitting up and cross-eyed, while Dougie hauled Calum off the pitch and entrusted him to the more strapping earthmen. 'That's the old Kat I knew and loved. I hope she's here to stay.'

'Are you going to stick around and find out?' Dair asked hopefully.

'I think there's quite a demand locally for Beautiful Dawn treatments.' She nodded happily, eyes sparkling into his. 'The village needs me.'

'I could use a few more. And I heard the new Eardisford tenants are very glamorous. Might bring a few new faces along. Journalists, mostly.'

'Tenants?'

'In the big house. It's being leased. Seth's a canny operator, always has a contingency plan. They've been waiting on his call, apparently.'

'Who are they?'

'Young couple with a toddler. Can you do a hair weave?'

'I like bald men, Dair.'

'I wasn't talking about me.' He whispered a name in her ear.

'You're kidding! I'm definitely staying. Kat needs me. God knows, those eyebrows won't stay in shape on their own.'

Behind the peeling white screens shielding the village pitch from God's Plot and the graveyard, Kat's eyebrows were riding high as Dougie's mouth delved ever lower, her giggles muffled in his sweet-smelling hair, her heart thundering close to his soft, exploring mouth.

'Can you cope with a year of Eardisford's love triangles and vicious circles?'

'Geometry was never my strong subject. And who says it's just a year?'

'Talk to Frank.' She drew his face up to hers, pulling him into a kiss that lasted three overs.

'Remind me, where exactly are your professional players?' Dollar asked Seth as he came off the field after the twentieth over, his half-century contributing to a healthy but beatable declaration from the estate team of 105 for 8 before tea.

'I'm sure they're enjoying their guided tour of Hereford Cathedral.' He pulled off his gloves, casting a rueful smile over his shoulder at his village opposition coming off the field, all back-slapping cheerfully as they contemplated the victory march ahead. 'Dougie is right. You simply can't cheat at cricket.'

'Rubbish!' Japinder argued enthusiastically from his deckchair. 'Every nation cheats at cricket. It's how honourably you cheat that counts.'

'I did take out their best batsman – at some considerable personal risk,' Seth reminded his father, who laughed with ribald approval, waking his wife with such a jolt that her deckchair folded up again.

'I had the woman with pink hair who tried to attack you in my gun sights throughout; you were perfectly safe,' Dollar assured Seth in an undertone before turning to extract her future mother-in-law with as much dignity as possible from her snapped mouse-trap of striped canvas.

Watching them, Seth wondered how he could have ever contemplated marrying anybody else.

After a cricket tea of cakes worthy of a televised bake-off, guaranteed to thicken arteries and waists – as well as thicken a few heads thanks to Babs Hedges' minted cider cup – the rival teams embarked on twenty more overs in which Dougie Everett almost clinched the estate's victory with bowling so accurate that it seemed he could have taken out the wasps hovering over the pavilion wheelie-bin a wing at a time, only for the assault to be foiled by a hook from Jed the pub chef that sent the ball so high it sailed through the church tower arches out of play and had to be replaced. The new ball had a bounce all of its own making, never going the same way twice.

'Full of lead shot one side,' one of the estate's oldest retainers told Seth wisely as they fielded gully and point. 'They always do this if we bat first.'

The match came down to the last ball of the twentieth over, fast bowled by diminutive Gut, whose long run up involved a facial expression of such fierceness and a Quasimodo stoop of such impossible angularity that the batsman was still watching open-mouthed when the ball whistled past his gloved fingers and struck the wicket.

'Howzat!' Gut threw up his arms.

'NO BALL!' shouted Dair, who was umpiring, the low tilt of his Panama making all who watched wonder how he could see.

'Out!' yelled the second umpire.

Soon a cacophony of protests and counter protests had broken out.

'DRAW!' called Dollar, her deep voice so authoritative it silenced all.

Seth turned at her in horror, thinking that she had pulled out her gun. But she was simply appealing for a truce, her slender arms held wide, calling for Eardisford village and estate to shake hands and declare the match too close to call.

The village ladies were the first to join in with her rally, 'Draw!'

Soon the earthmen were a bass part of the chorus. 'DRAW.'

'Draw!' The estate gamekeepers and gardeners added their baritone bellows.

'Draw!' shouted Mr and Mrs Singh in descant.

'Draw,' Seth mouthed at Dougie who was eyeing him from mid-wicket and nodded almost imperceptibly.

Meanwhile the umpires had consulted and were nodding too, Panama dipped to Panama, hands raised, eliciting a great cheer as they led a cavalcade to the pavilion bar.

Dougie admired the bubbling amber trunk of the first pint of beer he had lifted all summer and turned to the man who had just offered him the chance to sample many more such draughts by drafting him into a local institution.

'You want me to be the Brom and Lem huntsman?' he asked Frank Bingham-Ince in amazement.

'New chap we hired broke his leg unloading a horse from a lorry first day out on mounted hound exercise. You'd be helping us out of a spot. Wage isn't anything to write home about, but there's accommodation and the best hedge country in Herefordshire.'

'Can I bring my own horses?'

'Bring as many as you like.'

Starting to laugh, Dougie took his plane ticket to Dollar. 'Do you think I could possibly swap this one for an aisle seat for a Friesian stallion?'